THE BUTTERFLY CREST

EVA VANRELL

Book I of the Protogenoi Series

PUBLISHED BY THE OJIME GROUP

SECOND OJIME GROUP TRADE PAPERBACK EDITION, SEPTEMBER 2016

THE BUTTERFLY CREST

Originally published in paperback in the United States by
The Ojime Group in 2014.

Edited by Oskar M. Pérez

Second Ojime Group trade paperback edition © September 2016

ISBN-13: 978-0-9977047-0-9
ISBN-10: 0-9977047-0-5

LCCN: 2016910842

Library of Congress Cataloguing-in-Publication Data is available.

Printed in the United States of America

*To O. and V., without whom these words would
mean absolutely nothing.*

PROLOGUE

AS THE FRACTURED LIGHT of dawn breached the threshold, two voices spoke in whispers in the fading dark.

"Are you going to coddle her the entire time?" hissed the female voice, the quality of her tone brittle and wispy, like the rustle of desiccated leaves. She was the Keres, the goddess of violent death, believed by humans to be three spirits but in truth was only one.

Death, her brother, sat across the room from her, holding a mortal woman in his arms. The woman writhed and twisted, struggling with the demons in her sleep. With careful hands, Death brushed the hair out of the woman's face and then lifted his crimson gaze to his sister's.

"Why do you care?" he asked.

"Because I do not want you to end up like Dionysus. She's going to die just like the rest of them," the Keres said.

"Up until a few decades ago, you were all certain the bloodline had died out. And yet here she is, the Heir of the House of Thebes." The sarcasm was lost in the apathetic tone of his voice. Death brushed his fingers against the back of the mortal woman's neck before continuing. "If I was a betting man, Keres, I would bet you were wrong again."

"I am seldom wrong, Thanatos."

"It is of no use to me when you are wrong at the most important times."

The Keres hissed, and the shadows trembled in the dark. "I grow weary of this side of you. I have been asked to inquire as to your intent."

"Isn't it obvious, sister? I intend to bring her to Tartarus."

The Keres laughed, the sound hollow like the rattle of bones. "Are you mad? It is forbidden."

"It is the will of her father, and I intend to see it through. Tell my mother, we should not be long."

With a baleful cry, the Keres was gone.

CHAPTER ONE

ELENA ALWAYS HAD the same dream. She could not remember a time when she didn't have this dream. Abstract. Darkness at first, then suddenly the feel of ice-cold arms wrapping around her, pulling her to the surface.

To the surface of what, she didn't know. She wasn't drowning. There was no water around her, and yet she was being pulled upward. She was struggling to breathe. Someone was holding her, helping her, but she couldn't see the person. She couldn't hear a thing.

Her perception shifted. She saw shards of colors—brilliant icy blues, bright vibrant reds, and through them a deadly silence.

Then she woke up.

Her moods were always unpredictable when she started her day waking up from this particular dream. Some days she was melancholic, others anxious, sometimes happy, but never, ever calm. And today, of all days, Elena needed to be calm. Today, she needed to have her head in the game and not on some stupid dream.

"Stay awake," Elena told her reflection in the mirror.

She had just stepped out of the shower and was applying her makeup. The same reflection she saw every day stared back at her; a raven-haired girl with an oval face, straight narrow nose, green almond-shaped eyes, and full lips—the upper lip faintly downward-turning. She was pretty, but not what Elena would call beautiful.

Elena peeked out of the bathroom door to check the clock on her nightstand. It was 7:17 a.m. She was running a little late, but she could make up the time. She pulled the damp towel tighter around her and finished applying her eyeliner. She didn't rummage through her closet like she usually did, trying to find the right pieces to pair. Instead, she went with the easy, no thought needed whatsoever choice—a dress suit. It was a somewhat plain ensemble, so she slipped on her favorite pair of red-soled heels to make a subtle statement. Then she brushed out her long black hair, put on her mother's opal ring, ate a quick bowl of cereal and headed out the door.

Elena didn't realize she had forgotten the file until she was half-way to work.

She was twenty-three minutes late by the time she drove back home to retrieve it and walked into the office. The receptionist gave her a stern look but Elena ignored her, as well as the group of people she could half-see inside of the conference room. She walked straight past the receptionist and down the various halls to her office, praying no one noticed her. When she finally reached her door, her secretary was waiting for her with a cup of hot green tea in her hand.

"You are a godsend, Amelia. Has she asked for me yet?" Elena's tone was hushed and she quickly stepped into her office, motioning for her secretary to follow.

"No, but Ms. Marjorie's been calling and asking for you every five minutes," Amelia said, and took a seat in front of Elena's desk, giving her a knowing look before sitting down. "She wants the expert's report and the spreadsheets you finalized last night." After a brief pause, she added, "they started sniffing around about twenty minutes ago."

"Did you kindly remind Marjorie that there are PDF copies of the expert report in the computer?" Elena was finding it very difficult to keep the annoyance out of her voice, and she would have to get that in check before walking into the conference room for the morning's scheduled deposition.

Elena was a second year junior associate at the firm of Callas, Moraitis and Galanis. Ms. Marjorie was Ms. Callas's secretary; a position she apparently thought made Elena her personal lackey. This morning's deposition would be a document intensive affair, and Ms. Callas would be taking the lead. It had fallen on Elena to prepare the spreadsheet summarizing the documents for Ms. Callas to refer to during the depo-sition. The spreadsheet had been complete for weeks, but as usual Ms. Callas insisted on a myriad of last minute changes—at 5 p.m. yesterday afternoon. To make the changes on time, Elena had taken home a file full of documents to work with through the night. It was *that* file of docu-ments she had left at home earlier in the morning.

With a resigned sigh, Elena set the file down on her desk and took the cup of hot tea Amelia offered. Tea for Elena was a religion; it reminded her of the most vivid memory she had of her mother, who had died when Elena was just seven years old. Born in Japan, Elena had lived there until both of her parents died in an accident. Her father had been an urban planner working for an American firm in Tokyo, and her mother an artist and sculptor. After her parents' death, her mother's childhood friend, Cataline, took Elena in. Elena's earliest memory was of her mother preparing tea in a room overlooking their garden.

"I reminded her about the PDF copies on the computer," Amelia's voice interrupted Elena's thoughts, "but Marjorie insisted that she couldn't find them, so I had to print them out myself and walk them over. Ms. Callas knows you were late, although she didn't technically ask for you. They're waiting for the spreadsheets. The deposition is set to begin in less than thirty minutes."

As always, Ms. Marjorie couldn't be counted on knowing anything other than the latest office gossip, and god forbid Ms. Callas go onto the computer herself to find the file. That was Elena's job—secretary, personal assistant, courier, and lawyer last. It wasn't unheard of for Ms. Callas to call Elena to request retrieval of a file that happened to be located immediately outside of Ms. Callas's office. It was too logical for her to ask Ms. Marjorie, whose desk was less than twenty feet away from the file cabinet, and so it somehow became Elena's job to walk halfway across the firm to Ms. Callas's office and pull the file herself.

That was only one of the many reasons Elena hated her job.

"Thanks for holding down the fort, Amelia. I guess I better head down there." Elena took several sips of her tea before she began to rummage through the file, as if she would somehow find a solution to her problem there. Of all days to be late, today was not the day to do it. It didn't matter that she had never been late before; Ms. Callas wouldn't care. With a heavy sigh, Elena grabbed the file from her desk and began the dreaded walk to the conference room.

At least she had on a nice pair of heels; the day's only silver lining.

Elena wasn't paying attention when she opened the door to the conference room, and she slammed right into someone. At least it felt like a slam; she didn't have a running start and she definitely wasn't that strong so it shouldn't have hurt, but Elena felt as if she'd ran into a wall. For a minute, there was dead silence in the room. Elena could almost hear the collective breath, and then everyone was moving and talking all at once. The person Elena ran into, however, hadn't moved an inch. He just stood there, unnaturally still.

Over his shoulder, Elena could see people moving towards them; Ms. Callas and a few others couldn't be bothered. Ms. Marjorie appeared out of nowhere to Elena's left, demanding the finished spreadsheets. Elena wanted to scream. This place was like high school, but with a more lethal variety of bullies. Standing up to these bullies was like cutting your nose to spite your face; Elena couldn't afford to get fired, not with bills and the exorbitant amount of school loans she needed to pay.

The file was on the floor, a casualty of the collision, and papers were sprawled everywhere—and with Elena's luck entirely out of place now. She needed to start picking up the mess, but she couldn't because the man she ran into was blocking her way; for what reason Elena didn't know, because the man remained completely silent. There were no apologies, feigned or otherwise, and no attempts to help Elena retrieve the file, not even an "*Are you ok?*" The man just stood there. Silent.

"Excuse me," Elena managed to whisper, anxiously tucking a strand of hair behind her ear as she looked up to meet his gaze.

Elena was surprised to see he was so young. He looked around her age, in his mid twenties, and didn't look like any lawyer she had ever seen. He was dressed impeccably, in a slim-cut suit and tie. He even wore a pocket square. He was tall and very slender, which added to the intensity of his overall presence, but it was his face that floored Elena. He was fair skinned, so much so it reminded Elena of snow, so pale, you could almost see a shimmer of blue beneath the surface. His features were fine and sharp. He had a Greek nose—perfectly straight and narrowly defined—and his cheekbones were pronounced. His lips were beautifully proportioned, something she rarely associated with a man, and his eyes were a pale icy blue. His hair, worn short, was a pale blonde.

His eyes met Elena's only briefly, and he regarded her with a stoic indifference that left her reeling. Then he turned away from her, stepped around her and was gone, not a single word passing between them; only silence.

CHAPTER TWO

THE REST OF Elena's week was just as disastrous. Ms. Callas made Elena miserable at work, the few hours of peace Elena normally had at home were slowly being swallowed up by extra work Ms. Callas was having her do, and, it didn't matter how hard Elena tried, Ms. Callas was never satisfied. The way she expressed her dissatisfaction, in this cold and deceptively passive way, left Elena feeling inadequate, an emotion she was not comfortable with.

To be fair, even without Ms. Callas's special brand of torment, Elena wasn't happy. Somehow, between the demands of her career and 'living the dream,' discontent had slowly taken root. Elena loved the practice of law. She had wanted to be a lawyer for as long as she could remember—every pet she had during her childhood she had named Cicero—but the reality of law, the business of it, was not something Elena had anticipated or been prepared for. She had been so idealistic about her career that it had left little to no room for the pragmatic aspects of its practice, where quantity was more important than quality; a truth Elena couldn't reconcile.

This had been her frame of mind for months. Even so, Elena continued to get up every morning to go to a job she didn't enjoy. She wanted to believe she did so out of a sense of duty or honor, but it had more to do with pride. She refused to be defeated, and so she struggled not to let the discontent consume her. Fortunate for her, she was temperate by nature.

Living in Japan during the first years of her life, and the devastating loss of her parents, had left an indelible mark. Ritual, privacy, modesty, honor and decorum; these things were incredibly important to Elena. Most of all, she was not the kind of woman to wear her emotions on her sleeve. With her, the adage was true—still waters ran deep. And so Elena continued on her path, trying to find the right balance in her life, and hoping she would soon find it.

Thinking it might lessen her unhappiness Elena focused the few work-free hours of her week on doing things that made her happy. On Wednesday, for instance, she visited the New Orleans Museum of Art during her lunch hour, and ran in City Park after work. There was something sacred about walking through the stone halls of the museum, a profound sense of calm, and finding peace beneath the shade of a giant oak tree at the end of her run. On Thursday evening, Elena dined with Cataline.

It was spring, Elena's favorite time of year in New Orleans, and one that traditionally brought with it evenings spent outside. Since her earliest memories, April was a time for eating in Cataline's garden, surrounded by blooming hydrangea bushes, the gurgle of a fountain and a continuous stream of birdsong from the trees. Thursday evening was no exception.

"So, tell me about your love life."

Cataline made her request without any preamble, a teasing smile brightening her face as she set down a plate of roasted brussels sprouts on the table. It was a surprise she hadn't asked the question before; questions about Elena's love life were usually the first thing out of Cataline's mouth, and Elena had arrived an hour and a half before to help with dinner.

"Nothing to tell, really." Elena made a face and then took a sip from her drink. The food was spread out between them on the patio table, and each held a cocktail in her hand. Elena speared a brussels sprout and chewed on it quietly, while Cataline stared at her across the table.

Cataline was the opposite of Elena. Where Elena was reserved, Cataline was loud and full of life. The daughter of a French pianist and a Spanish cook, Cataline grew up in New Orleans and was childhood friends with Elena's mother, and, like her, was also an artist. Elena liked to think of her as hippie chic. She had long, curly chestnut brown hair with deep amber highlights, light olive skin, deep-set hazel eyes, and cheekbones to die for.

"Nothing to tell? Is that your story, *really*?" Cataline stared at Elena with a perfectly arched brow, and downed half of her cocktail in one swallow. "A girl as beautiful as you and no love story to tell. Elena, you're too serious for your own good. You need to put yourself out there. Every girl needs a good love story, and the love affair with your shoes doesn't count. Although I can see how red-soled shoes could get any girl's heart fluttering."

Cataline's smile was warm, and as comforting as the summer sun. Elena wished she could smile with that kind of confidence. When she was younger, all Elena wanted to be was like Cataline. Tall, lithe, almost ethereal looking, Cataline was uninhibited and vibrant, something all together different than Elena and the more reserved culture she had grown up in as a child. When Elena had first arrived in New Orleans after her parents' death, she was floored by the contrast. Cataline wore every emotion on her sleeve, and never kept anything to herself. She was full of joy and she lived every second to the fullest, without reservations.

"You know I splurge on very little," Elena replied to Cataline's earlier remark. "I can at least have one weakness," and red-soled heels were it.

Although Elena's parents had left her a trust fund with enough money to see her through her childhood and a decent part of her adult life, she did not spend it frivolously. She lived as modestly as her profession allowed, and it was important for her to have savings just in case the worst were to happen to her or Cataline. Cataline didn't have anyone taking care of her—she was a divorcée—and raising a child had not exactly been economical. Cataline had inherited a house in the Garden District from her parents—an old Greek Revival that was as much a part of Cataline as Cataline's buoyant personality—and she and Elena had lived in it since Elena's parents died, but the house was beginning to show its years and if something were to happen to them, they would only have a deteriorating house, and Elena's dwindling trust, to fall back on.

"I did run into a handsome guy the other day at work, *literally*," Elena added, and then recounted for Cataline the story of her encounter with the blonde-haired man. Elena told her story quietly, as they ate, the crisp spring air growing cooler around them as night settled over the small garden. Halfway through, Cataline ran inside to grab a cardigan but the cooler air didn't bother Elena, although she had to admit it felt colder than it should have.

"And you didn't even get his name?" Cataline chided her in the end, resting her chin on her hand and giving Elena a half smile; she had topped off her drink only moments before. "That's what I'm talking about, Elena. You need to take a few risks. Live a little. You should have ran after him and asked for his number or his Facebook name. Isn't that what you kids do today?"

"I don't have a Facebook account, Cataline." Elena tried not to roll her eyes. Instead, she took another sip from her cocktail. "And what was I supposed to do? He was really rude about it. He didn't offer to help me pick up the papers, and he sure as hell didn't apologize; not that it was his fault, but it would have been the gentleman-like thing to do. He didn't even speak. He stared at me like I was a fly in his drink and then walked away." Now that she thought about it, the incident made Elena angry. The man hadn't been civil at all.

"He sounds handsome, though."

Cataline's voice took on a dreamy lightness when she said it, and Elena couldn't help but laugh. As Cataline reached for her drink something moved in the air above her shoulder.

Elena leaned forward to see a small, pale blue butterfly fluttering in the air, which she somehow hadn't noticed before. "Of course, in your school of thinking good looks cures everything," Elena replied, then shook her head and continued to eat her dinner. By the time she looked up from her plate, the butterfly had gone.

Before Cataline could pick up on the conversation, Elena decided to change the subject to something less annoying; she didn't want to think about that man or her work. Cataline was obsessed with art, and so for the rest of the meal Elena distracted her with a discussion on the latest art exhibit at the New Orleans Museum of Art, an exhibit on Zen art from Japan. After dinner, Elena helped Cataline clean, agreed to meet her Saturday for lunch at Café Degas—their favorite restaurant—and left before Cataline recalled their prior topic of conversation.

THROUGHOUT THE WEEK, every time Elena closed her eyes, she found herself unwittingly thinking of the man she had run into. His pale blue eyes would bleed through the emptiness in her mind, followed by the fine lines of his nose and the shape of his mouth. Sometimes, she would see him in her dreams. Even so, she never found the courage to ask Ms. Callas who he was. A few times during the week Elena found herself walking through the halls to Ms. Callas's office, but the moment she stepped inside her resolve left her. The look on Ms. Callas's face stopped Elena cold, and she would stumble through some weak law-related excuse to explain why she had interrupted her.

Livia Callas was icy; it was the only way to describe her. She was a hard woman and, from what Elena could tell, as cruel as she was beautiful—and Ms. Callas was strikingly beautiful, with hair as dark as midnight and eyes an ashen gray-green. She had an oval face, strong jawline, perfectly full lips, and almond-shaped feline-like eyes. She always dressed in designer clothes, and there was nothing *laissez faire* about her. She had a husband Elena had never met and rarely heard of, and a twin brother, Mr. Moraitis, who was also a partner at the firm. Elena had never met him, but heard he was even more imposing and unapproachable than Ms. Callas. He spent most of his time traveling for work, and in New York at the original firm offices. Elena had looked at his photograph once, on the firm website, and he had the same black hair and gray-green eyes as his sister.

Ms. Callas and Mr. Moraitis were originally from New York. The success of their firm in New York City led them to open an office in New Orleans fifteen years before. Elena tried to do the math all the time, but she could never manage to reconcile their age with the way they looked. They must have been close to fifty years old, but they didn't look a day past thirty-five. In the past fifteen years, the twins had made a name for themselves in New Orleans, and were very active in the community. On Saturday, for instance, Ms. Callas would be hosting a benefit at the New Orleans Museum of Art and Elena was expected to attend.

Friday, of course, turned out to be a busy day at work. Not only did Elena have her daily work to complete, she also had to assist Ms. Callas with certain details for the benefit. It was well past dusk by the time Elena stepped onto the elevator to the parking garage. If it hadn't been for Holden, another associate at the firm, Elena would have had to stay even later to finish everything. She was texting him a *"thank you"* when the elevator doors opened onto an unlit floor.

The sight took Elena by surprise. She stepped forward out of habit, startled when the elevator doors closed shut behind her, cutting off the only source of light and plunging everything into darkness.

"Shit."

Elena's voice echoed through the dark and empty space, the hollow sound sending a chill down her spine. Nervous, she fumbled with her phone. It took her a second, but she managed to put in her security code to unlock it. The first thing she did was check that her text to Holden had gone through. Relieved once she saw that it had, Elena wrote him another quick text.

This time, it didn't go through.

Elena looked to the top of the screen. There were three bars. The text should have gone through. Annoyed, she decided to call. Why she hadn't done that in the first place was beyond her. Elena brought the phone to her ear and waited, but nothing happened. The call hung in the air, silent.

Flustered, she almost threw the phone. None of it made sense. If there were repairs to be done or the lights were malfunctioning, she would have received an email; she had not. The reception on her phone was fine and she had half the battery left, but for some reason the confounded thing didn't want to work.

At this point, she had two choices: get back in the elevator and risk more work from Ms. Callas once she made it upstairs, or suck it up and walk to her car. If she didn't want to ruin the rest of her evening, the second choice was her only option.

At least she had a flashlight app on her phone, she thought to herself, but was quickly disappointed; even with the flashlight, it was difficult to get her bearings. It was so dark the app could only illuminate a few feet in front of her, not enough to help her locate her car. She parked in the same spot every day so she had a general idea of where she needed to go from the elevators, but she was completely disoriented in the dark. All she could do was hope she was moving in the right direction.

A few minutes in and her phone buzzed.

It was a text from Holden.

"Did you leave? The lights are out in the garage. Didn't you get the email?"

Obviously not, Elena thought to herself.

With a resigned sigh, she closed the flashlight app to answer the text.

"No email. Halfway to my car in the dark. I'm not going back up there." Elena hit send, and again the text hung without sending. She tried every way she knew to force it through but got nothing.

She was about to reboot the phone when a sound echoed in the darkness to her left, a distance away from her. Was it a door? Elena couldn't tell; the sound was so distorted by the time it reached her. Determined to make it to her car, she opened the flashlight app again and started walking.

And again, her phone buzzed.

"Ele, not funny. Ms. Callas and I are headed down. Let me know where you are."

Elena could already imagine the look on Holden's face; half worried, half crossed. Again, she tried to reply to his text, to no avail.

Elena decided to walk back to the elevator when she heard another sound. This time, she couldn't tell the direction. For the first time since she stepped out of the elevator, she felt afraid. The sound could have been Holden or Ms. Callas, but they would have called out for her.

Quickly, she pocketed her phone; if someone were out there, they'd be able to locate her easily if she was using a light.

She gave her eyes a chance to adjust, and after a minute the darkness was not as pitch-black as before. Elena needed to get back to the elevator, and all she had to do was walk back the way she'd come. Slowly, she began to move, her arms outstretched so she could feel for anything in her way.

Several seconds later, she heard the sound of shoes.

It was a warm sound, compared to the metal-like ones she'd heard before. It sounded like someone walking slowly, the sole of their shoes scraping lightly against the cement ground. Panicked, Elena began to move faster; she would have started running if she could. Even so, the man behind her—and it had to be a man because of the quality of the sound—did not increase his pace. He continued on with a slow and steady stride, the sound strangely menacing.

Elena was so alarmed she didn't notice a parking space bumper less than a foot ahead of her and tripped, breaking her fall with her left elbow. A sharp, hot pain seared all the way up her arm to her shoulder, making her cry out in pain. For a few seconds, she forgot all about the approaching footsteps, until she heard someone laugh.

The sound was pleasant, almost amiable. For a fraction of a second, Elena was no longer afraid. There was no cruelty in it or menace. But then just as quickly it changed. Elena heard, almost palpably, the moment the laughter faded into a sneer. The footsteps then quickly resumed.

Elena rushed to her feet without thinking.

As she lunged forward, the sound of a metal chime stopped her in her tracks. A vertical sliver of light appeared in the darkness immediately in front of her, seconds before the elevator doors slid open. Elena had to shield her eyes from the light.

She had made it to the elevator and was standing less than three feet from its doors. Inside stood Ms. Callas, Holden and a security guard who was cradling a large portable spotlight in his arms.

"Elena?" Ms. Callas questioned, her gaze devoid of all patience. It was amazing how the woman could turn something as innocent as a name into a scathing reproach. "Playing in the dark, are we?"

Elena didn't respond immediately. She straightened up and dusted off her clothes, as the three stepped out of the elevator. The security guard turned on his spotlight and illuminated the area around them. "I was trying to get to my car," Elena finally replied to Ms. Callas, exchanging a look with Holden, who was mouthing indecipherable things from behind Ms. Callas's shoulder.

"Did you not get the email?" Ms. Callas asked, the annoyance now clear in her voice.

"No, ma'am, I'm sorry. The second I stepped off the elevator, my phone started acting up."

Ms. Callas shook her head, displeased. "It was sent over an hour ago. If you didn't have your head in the clouds all the time perhaps you would have noticed it."

It took all of Elena's willpower to bite back a sharp reply. In the mean time, Ms. Callas watched her, waiting. Holden shook his head discretely behind Ms. Callas; able to read the turn their conversation was about to take. Holden's silent plea gave Elena time to consider what she had wanted to say, and him the necessary opening.

"Is everything ok, Ele? You look like you may have hurt yourself in the dark," Holden asked in his characteristically friendly tone.

Of all the people she worked with, Holden was someone Elena considered a friend. Warm, good-natured and naturally funny, Holden was that rare breed of person one could only describe as 'good people'.

"Yeah, I'm fine," Elena lied, trying not to look too suspicious as she glanced around.

Ms. Callas continued to watch her, eyes narrowed, but didn't say a word. The woman was obviously irritated; the sound of her heel tapping the floor repeatedly made her sentiment clear, but Elena tried not to let it bother her. Instead, she concentrated on the fact that the foot-steps had stopped. Her fear was also completely gone. Had she imaged it all?

"Head in the clouds again?" Ms. Callas asked, her tone now verging on acerbic.

Elena tensed, not surprised to see a scowl on Ms. Callas's face when she finally looked up. Recognizing it for the warning it was, Elena decided to ignore the quip and steer the conversation in the direction Ms. Callas wanted; if not, she'd pay for it tomorrow. "If you don't mind," Elena said to the security guard, forcing a smile, "could you shine the way to my car?"

ON SATURDAY MORNING, Elena woke up early with her cat Cicero curled up next to her in bed, laying on top of an open book. Elena had gotten home around 9:15 the night before, ate a light dinner, took a long warm bath, and then curled up in bed with a good book. She must have fallen asleep reading. Thanks to Holden, who had called to check in on her an hour after getting home, she didn't dream of the footsteps or the laughter.

Holden had a way of making light of everything, without ever sounding condescending or cruel, and after confiding in him about what she'd heard in the darkness, his response made Elena feel completely at ease; he insisted, in a very grave and serious tone, that it had been the *Rougarou*, the werewolf of Cajun legend that hunts down Catholics for failing to follow the rules of Lent. The laughter, of course, had been the werewolf's reaction when he got up close and saw for himself that his prey was nothing but a rule-breaking, petite-sized heathen who wasn't even Catholic to begin with; the *Rougarou*, naturally, has a very discerning palate.

"After such an absurd explanation, how would anyone be afraid?" Elena mused aloud to Cicero, recalling the conversation. The cat, who was now contentedly purring on her lap, imperiously lifted her head and stared at Elena with an expectant expression. The petting had ceased. With a clipped cry, she demanded it continue, and with that, Elena forgot all about the matter. She loyally performed her duties as 'feline personal assistant', then got out of bed, took a quick shower, slipped on some comfortable clothes and had breakfast, before leaving the house to complete the slew of things she needed to get done before lunch with Cataline and Ms. Callas's party.

First, Elena visited a few boutiques on Magazine Street, in search of a particular undergarment that would work with her dress for the evening. After that she stopped for coffee, went to the ATM, picked up her dry cleaning, and finished with grocery shopping at Whole Foods. She got back home just in time to change for lunch with Cataline.

Elena and Cataline had agreed to meet at Café Degas, a restaurant in Bayou St. John, a tree-lined neighborhood across the canal from City Park. The restaurant was one of Elena's favorites. The food was always fresh and the atmosphere unique—a covered patio turned into a sidewalk restaurant. It was only a mile away from her apartment, and Elena could walk there easily. She got to the restaurant a little earlier than Cataline, so she sat at the bar, ordered a Kir Royale and chatted up the bar tender. Once Cataline arrived—fifteen minutes late, as usual—they were led through the wooden deck dining room, which was built around a large tree, and into the open-aired section closest to the sidewalk.

For starters, they shared a paté and cheese plate, and a French Onion soup—the best in town; and for lunch Elena had the rabbit and Cataline the duck. Sitting so close to the sidewalk on such a beautiful spring day, it was easy to get lost in the atmosphere and let the time pass. Elena could almost imagine she was in Paris. Cataline was going on about a man she just met, and Elena was happy just listening. Plus, their table allowed them the perfect vantage point to people watch. They had champagne, great food, excellent desert, and wonderful conversation. Elena was about to put a fork full of chocolate cake in her mouth when she looked up and saw a glimpse of pale blonde hair, perfectly groomed, coming toward them on the sidewalk.

The person was walking behind a group of people, so Elena couldn't see his face. Instantly, she felt a knot in her stomach. She must have looked sick, because Cataline was asking her what was wrong, and Elena just sat there, staring at the sidewalk. Their table was flush with the patio rail, her right side to the sidewalk, and she was facing the direction the man was approaching from. Elena met Cataline's eyes and breathed deep; trying to ignore the blonde hair she could see past Cataline's shoulder.

"I think that guy I told you about the other day... the one I ran into... I think he's walking down the sidewalk, coming towards us."

Elena had whispered the words so softly that not even the person sitting at the table behind her, less than three feet away, could hear, and yet the blonde-haired man stopped mid stride. He stopped for a long enough time to let space grow between him and the group of people walking in front of him. He moved his head to the left, toward the street, and then to the right, toward the restaurant. His pale blue eyes met hers and Elena quickly looked away.

"Fuck."

"Elena! Language," Cataline called out in a half-giggle, never one to appreciate the importance of being earnest.

Cataline moved to turn around, to get a better look at the guy, but Elena reached across the table quickly and grabbed her hands, sending the espresso cup sprawling across the table, espresso spilling everywhere.

Two for two. If Elena had a chance to make an idiot of herself, history seemed to establish she would take it; at least where this guy was concerned.

Elena hissed for Cataline not to turn around, wishing the waiter wouldn't come right at this moment to clean up her mess. Elena reluctantly let go of Cataline's hands, and inadvertently caught the man's gaze. He had started walking again and was less than a foot behind Cataline's shoulder. Again, he was dressed impeccably, this time in a gray, fine wool sports coat and dark charcoal wool pants. As he came closer, Elena could see there was a texture to the material. He wore a darker gray button down cotton shirt with a continuous leaf print in three tones of white, a black velvet tie and a graphite colored silk pocket square with some kind of design on it that looked like fern leaves.

Everyone in the restaurant grew quiet as he walked past. He stared at Elena with the same detached look as he had before, but Elena could have sworn she saw him smirk right before he went out of view.

For a moment Cataline just stared at the empty space where the man had been only seconds before, and then lifted her gaze to Elena, a stunned look across her features. "By the gods, Elena, you said he was cute. You failed to mention the man is gorgeous!" Cataline interrupted her own train of thought as she waved over the waiter. "I'll need something stronger than this," Cataline purred to the man, motioning to her glass of champagne, "a glass of your best Cognac." She offered the waiter a warm smile, always the eternal flirt, and then picked up the conversation without skipping a beat. "Granted, I only got half a look when he walked past, since you went into Cataline-containment-mode, but wow. Men like that are rare, Elena. And the suit! He is definitely not from here."

"I wouldn't know, Cataline. For all I know, he's mute. He doesn't say a word." Elena downed what was left of her champagne, shaking her head. Her heart was still in her throat. She wasn't sure why this guy affected her the way he did, but she certainly felt something. Right now, she was feeling pretty foolish. "Let's just forget about it, okay? We need to finish lunch so I can get back and start getting ready for the benefit. I have half a mind to ask Ms. Callas tonight who the hell he is. She has to know. I mean, he was there, in her conference room."

At this point, Elena was rambling and Cataline just watched her with a knowing smile, kind enough not to bring the man up again.

The walk back home was exactly what Elena needed to settle down. Her mail was waiting for her on the floor of her entryway when she stepped into the apartment. She thumbed through it as she walked up the stairs and into her living room. There was junk mail, a credit card statement and a letter from a bank in Japan.

That was odd.

Elena dropped her purse on the dining room table and opened the letter. It was short and to the point. The National Bank of Japan was requesting she contact them as soon as possible regarding the contents of her mother's safety deposit box. Elena didn't know a thing about a safety deposit box, and she couldn't call now because it was the weekend. She would ask Cataline about it, and call on Monday morning from the office. Elena put the letter back inside the envelope, dropped the envelope in a small basket on the marble mantelshelf—where she kept important mail—and went to get ready for the benefit.

<u>CHAPTER THREE</u>

ELENA ARRIVED AT the benefit on time, choosing to walk the block and a half to the museum rather than use the car. It was a spectacular night and Elena enjoyed the brief walk through her neighborhood, and then the oak-lined pathways that wove their way around one of the lagoons in City Park. She could get lost in the scenery for hours. There was something calming about sitting on a stone bench and looking out onto the lagoon, watching egret wade through the banks looking for food. Elena would have given anything to continue her evening enjoying the quiet solitude the grounds could provide, but duty called.

She reluctantly made her way through the mall to the entrance of the museum. For the occasion she had chosen a light champagne colored dress Cataline had given her for Christmas. It reminded Elena of a prima ballerina. The dress was made of silk chiffon draped across the front and ruched into various lines to form a tight bodice, the folds of chiffon continuing in layers to her ankles, forming a gossamer skirt of hand-pleated fabric. It had spaghetti straps and a modest neckline. A champagne silk ribbon tied around her waist made an elegant belt. Elena was certain it was a designer dress, but she didn't pay much attention to that detail. She finished off the look with a pair of red ballet slippers. She wore her mother's opal ring, an antique gold locket and a metallic clutch. Her long black hair cascaded down her back in loose waves, a sharp contrast to her pale color palette.

The main portion of the benefit was being held in the museum's Great Hall, a large rectangular room at the entrance of the museum made entirely of white marble. It was flanked by a colonnade of Ionic columns on three sides that created an open-aired peristyle framing an atrium in the center of the room. The colonnade held up a second story balcony that lined the peristyle below, allowing guests to look down onto the main floor. In the back of the hall was a grand staircase that led to the second story. The first story floor was paved mostly in white mosaic stones with dark blue tiles framing the colonnade in a Greek meander design, physically separating the corridor from the central atrium. The high ceiling was made entirely of glass. The museum's various galleries were accessible on all sides of the Great Hall.

For this particular event, the Great Hall was decorated exquisitely in saturated hues—deep aubergines and bright emerald greens set against delicate ivory and blush. Two lavish floral arrangements made of black calla lilies, ivory magnolia blossoms, light pink spider chrysanthemums and green hypericum flanked the grand staircase. Smaller versions of the large arrangements decorated the center of several round tables placed around the room.

Entry to the benefit was exclusive to two hundred guests. Tickets were a minimum of $1,000, and the proceeds would all go to charity. Guests could choose, at their own discretion, to donate more per ticket. The ticket purchased them a gourmet meal catered by one of the city's best Chefs accompanied by a local Jazz band, and access to the museum's many galleries. The Besthoff Sculpture Garden would also be available to guests during the event, a treat since the garden was usually closed during the evenings.

Elena decided it would be best to get her work duties over with early. She surveyed the room, quietly searching for Ms. Callas, whom she found standing in front of the grand staircase surrounded by several affluent-looking people. As expected, Ms. Callas was a showstopper. She was dressed in a magnificent vermilion gown, the red so bright it made her pale skin radiant. It was a strapless gown with a neckline that cut into a shallow 'V' at her chest, the fabric molding perfectly to her torso and flowing effortlessly against her tall and slender form. She looked like a goddess. Elena felt incredibly plain as she approached.

Ms. Callas was speaking with an older couple. Elena recognized the man as an equity partner in one of the largest firms in town. He was of medium height and build, had salt and pepper hair, and a pompous demeanor. The woman, presumably his wife, looked a little older and was quite beautiful. She had a quiet elegance that made her seem too good for the man standing at her side.

"Good evening, Ms. Callas. I'm sorry to interrupt. I just wanted to say hello." Elena had to make an effort to appear comfortable. These kinds of events were not her forte.

"Ah, Elena. I'm glad you made it. It seems you're one of the first associates to arrive. I can always count on you to be prompt." In public, Ms. Callas always went out of her way to seem overly polite. It was like watching Maleficent feign goodness and grace. Ms. Callas smiled a perfect smile, subtly looking Elena over. "You look... pretty tonight," a tactful way of saying *plain*. "Please allow me to introduce Mr. and Mrs. Ellis. Tom, Victoria—this is Elena Vicens, one of our Associates."

"Pleased to make your acquaintance." Elena shook their hands and exchanged kisses, a common custom in Louisiana. Mr. Ellis was running through the list of his credentials, when Elena noticed another gentleman and lady standing in their group.

The woman was a brunette dressed as eclectically as Cataline would have been, in a peacock blue silk jumpsuit that hugged tightly at her waist. The top looked like a blouse with long billowing sleeves that cuffed at her wrist, and the pants were cut perfectly to her form. She wore tall bronze heels, a large chunky necklace, and a plethora of bracelets at her wrist.

The man was just as interesting. He was dressed in a perfectly appropriate dark suit, but it was his look that set him apart. He looked like a rockstar forced into a designer suit. He had thick black shoulder-length hair, a goatee, and lined dark eyes. His face was long, with a square jawline, and a straight but prominent nose. Elena could see ink peeking through the man's shirt collar.

Ms. Callas tactfully interrupted Mr. Ellis to introduce her other guests. "This is Angela Lewis, the Director of our charity this evening, and my husband, Lucian."

Elena was shaking the man's hand and she stilled, the shock plain on her face. "Pleasure."

Lucian smiled, the gesture bright and full of mischief. He found her shock amusing, something he was obviously used to. He leaned forward to exchange a kiss, and Elena couldn't help noticing his hands were extremely warm.

"Trust me, she's a deviant on the inside," Lucian whispered the words in Elena's ear.

His tone was so intimate that it made the heat rush to Elena's cheeks, and every red flag she had went off. She needed to duck out, and quick. Elena pulled away gracefully, not daring to look at Ms. Callas. To

Elena's dismay, Lucian held her hand a little longer, and continued to watch her once he let go.

"Nice to meet all of you. I'll leave you to your previous conversations." Elena bowed out quickly, all too aware of Ms. Callas's watchful gaze. Elena didn't miss the hardly contained laugh from Ms. Lewis.

Well, that was pleasant.

Elena moved away from the grand staircase, snatching up a glass of champagne from a server's tray. She looked around; the sea of unknown faces making her feel really uncomfortable. Elena hated being at a party where she hardly knew anyone at all. It made her anxious, and it was best to avoid it if she could. She weaved her way through the crowd toward McDermott Lobby, just past the Great Hall, but the lobby was full of decorated tables and more guests. Elena visited the museum often enough to know the elevators in the lobby would take her to the collections on the floors above, but before she could reach the elevators a group of firm associates called for her attention.

The associates were all clustered by one of the tables, drinks in hand. A group of them had arrived while Elena was talking to Ms. Callas, and overheard the introductions. Most of them were younger associates, and had converged on a group of senior associates to ask about Lucian. The senior associates—one of them being Holden—had confirmed Lucian's identity, but no more.

"Hi guys. If you don't mind, I'd like to see some of the exhibits before dinner starts and I only have a few minutes." Elena was judiciously trying to pull away from one of the girls who had latched on to her arm. Her name was Melissa, and Elena could count in one hand the times Melissa had spoken to her before. Two other girls watched them both, expectantly. The senior associates, Louis, Ana and Holden, just watched, amused.

"Oh, come on Elena. The others won't give any details. You're our only hope." Melissa's manner was as fake as her feigned friendship.

"Melissa, there's nothing to tell. He's her husband." Elena shrugged out of Melissa's arm, and exchanged a quiet look with Holden.

"But what's his name? What does he do? God, he's hot." Melissa was as easy as she was fake; there was a rumor around the office that she was having an affair with one of the partners.

"If you want to know details, go introduce yourself." Elena's response was short, and the tone of her voice left no room for further discussion. She turned around and walked away.

"God, she's such a stuck up bitch."

Elena heard Melissa call out behind her, but she didn't respond. She just continued walking toward the elevators. She pressed the button and waited. The elevator couldn't come fast enough. She heard laughter behind her and she pressed the elevator button again, like that would do something. It was like high school all over again; another one of the reasons Elena did not enjoy her job. The sense of relief once she was inside the elevator was profound. The doors closed and she just stood there for a moment, trying to clear her head. Elena's favorite collection was on the third floor. She pressed the number three and hummed quietly to herself as the elevator slowly began to move.

Elena stepped out of the elevator onto the third floor and turned left, into the gallery housing the Japanese section of the museum's Asian Art collection. Elena could stare at this collection for hours; at its hand painted screens, porcelain vases, Bizen earthenware, suits of armor, and woodblock prints and paintings from the Edo period depicting the Floating World—the transient culture of beauty and pleasure-seeking entertainments of Edo-period Japan. One of Elena's favorite pieces was a beautiful wooden screen depicting a winterscape on a gilded background, with snowcapped cherry blossoms, tranquil waterfalls, mountains and various types of birds.

Elena took her time walking through the exhibit, finally stopping at one of the two samurai suits of armor on display. It was an intricate work of indigo lacquer, dark iron, brass and leather. An unexpected voice broke the silence from behind her.

"He's a music producer."

Elena jumped, startled by the sudden company. She turned around to face the person, shocked to see the familiar face.

"You."

"Yes."

The blonde-haired man watched her quietly and Elena took a step back, finding herself against the glass of the exhibit.

"You're the guy I bumped into in the conference room."

"Yes."

Was that all he knew how to say? God, he was infuriating. Elena felt the heat rise to her cheeks and she quickly inched away, annoyed when he pressed closer.

"What do you want?" Elena's voice shook, and she chided herself silently. Why was she always making an idiot of herself in front of this guy?

"They asked you what Lucian did. He's a music producer." There was no emotion in the man's voice. He said it as matter-of-fact as he would tell you the weather.

Again, Elena caught the slight curl of a smirk on the corner of his lips.

"You were listening?" she asked him.

"I pay attention."

"You mean you stalk?"

"I mean I happened to be walking by and overheard the conversation."

Every time, his tone was flat. Elena couldn't tell if he was bored or amused. Was he trying to make fun of her? "So you know Lucian?" Elena tried desperately to keep her tone neutral.

"You can say that."

"What the hell is that supposed to mean?" So much for neutral. This guy was getting under Elena's skin. She prided herself in her level of self-control; she was seldom emotional, and never irrational. Yet here she was, fractionally raising her voice.

The man inched closer and Elena froze, not able to tear her eyes away from his gaze. Cataline was right. He was gorgeous. The pale blue of his eyes appeared to deepen, and the effect sent a shiver down Elena's spine.

"Lucian is my father." He whispered the words so softly that Elena heard her breath catch.

"What?" The question came strangled from Elena's throat.

He repeated himself again, this time pulling himself away, giving Elena a chance to breathe. "Lucian is my father."

"Your father? You're joking, right?" Elena couldn't help but look him over; rude, but necessary. There was no way this man was Lucian's son. This man was every shade of pale. Lucian was dark-featured, like Ms. Callas. "Oh fuck, Ms. Callas. Does that mean Ms. Callas is your mother?" Elena's voice sounded close to a shriek.

"Well, not necessarily. In today's society it could mean many things. Lucian could have had me illegitimately before he got married to Ms. Callas. He could have also been married before, and I could be the issue of that marriage. Another possibility is that he had an illicit affair, and had me on the side. Those are all viable options."

Elena was speechless. She inched further to the side until she could clear the glass and then stepped around the exhibit, putting the glass-encased armor between them.

"However, your first guess was correct. Ms. Callas is my mother." The smirk reached the full set of his lips, and Elena quickly recognized it. It was identical to Lucian's.

"Please don't take offense, but you look nothing like them."

"I get that a lot." He pressed his hand to the glass as he spoke, his smirk slowly settling into an almost imperceptible smile. "Do you like Japanese art?" He watched her through the glass as he said it.

The question took Elena by surprise. She looked around at their surroundings, the exhibit coming back to life in sharp relief. It was as if the exhibit had faded completely when he walked into the room, the only palpable part of it the glass exhibit she had been touching. The effect was completely disorienting. What the hell was wrong with her?

"Yes." Now she was the one with monosyllabic responses.

"Would you like to take a walk with me through the Sculpture Garden?" He stepped away from the exhibit, and ran a hand through his hair.

Elena noticed for the first time that he was dressed in the same suit she saw him wearing earlier that day, when she was having lunch with Cataline.

"You want me to go with you to the Sculpture Garden?"

He took two long strides toward her and his faint smile deepened, to staggering effect. "You shouldn't answer a question with another question."

He came to stand a foot away from her, and Elena found herself rooted to the spot. "Sorry. I'm just surprised."

"Why?" His voice grew heavier, richer. Before it had been cool and crisp.

"Well, you were kind of rude before."

"I was?" For a fraction of a second, shame bled into his features. Then it was gone. "I get that a lot."

She was about to respond, when he caught her hand. It was icy cold and she flinched, but she didn't pull away. He must have read the surprise on her features, because he stopped and looked down at his hand.

"My extremities are always cold. Bad circulation."

Elena laughed. It was such an unexpected explanation, and so incredibly awkward.

"Well, will you take a walk with me in the garden or not? Seems to me you have a choice between stuffy people and those insufferable co-workers of yours downstairs or a quiet stroll with me. I promise I'll let my mother know it was my fault."

Elena nodded and suddenly he was pulling her along to the elevator. He pushed the button, a tiny bell-like sound indicated the elevator was there, and the doors opened. He stepped inside and pulled her with him, silent all over again. When the doors closed, Elena felt like the world closed in around her. The space was too small or maybe his presence was too big? She dropped her gaze to the floor, and tried to ease her breathing. Well, at least she would have something to tell Cataline in the morning.

He didn't speak another word until they were outside. When the elevator doors opened, he led her through the McDermott Lobby toward a side exit, conveniently avoiding the entire crowd. They crossed a small street to the garden. Since dinner was being served, most of the guests were inside. The garden was quiet and peaceful, just the way Elena preferred it. It was beautifully illuminated at night, and they both stopped to admire the sight.

"Do you have a favorite sculpture or spot in the garden?"

He was first to break the silence. He was moving ahead of her, on the path to their right, and stopped to look at her over his shoulder. Elena couldn't read him at all.

"Well, there's a bridge made of stepping-stones along the water. I enjoy that very much." As for the sculptures, Elena enjoyed all of them; she had inherited that from her mother.

Thoughts of her mother consumed Elena as she followed him through the garden. She was beginning to appreciate the fact that he was quiet; that he didn't need to fill the silence with empty words. Elena seldom met people like that. Once she caught up with him, he had led her through the small footpath that wound around the garden, stopping briefly at every sculpture. If Elena showed interest, he would stay as long as she desired. If she did not, he would continue to lead them along, their pace unhurried. Soon, she felt more relaxed than she had in weeks. The lack of words made the experience more intense, at least for Elena.

"So, tell me what you like about Japanese art." His voice was a whisper.

When Elena looked up, they had reached the path of concrete stepping-stones. A man-made lagoon opened up to their left, and a small modernist pond with a bronze central sculpture to their right. The water moved from the pond through the stepping-stones and into the lagoon.

Ms. Callas's son stepped onto the first stone and offered his hand. "If you fall, you might ruin your beautiful dress and then I would feel awful."

Elena studied his hand and then looked up into his face. It was illuminated by the dim lighting and Elena could see specs of icy blue in his eyes, peeking out from behind the shadows. The light carved out the lines of his cheek and jaw, highlighting the pale column of his neck. She followed the light to the edge of his shirt, finally noting the details of his appearance. Every article of clothing was tailored to his form. The tie was in its proper place, his pocket square level and centered. When she looked up again, he was watching her with an arched brow. Elena blushed.

"Thank you... for the compliment about the dress." Elena hoped that she hadn't been staring for too long. She took his offered hand and stepped onto the first stone. "And I just have an affinity to Japan, that's all. It calls to me, for some reason." There was no need to divulge too much.

He didn't respond. He simply nodded and helped her across a few more steps, until they were in the middle of the stepping-stone bridge. Because of the silence, the sound of trickling water seemed uncommonly loud. It was very soothing.

"I feel the same way about Greek art," he said and looked out onto the man-made lagoon, pulling Elena's attention back to him.

"Really? I have a degree in Classics." Ancient Greek and Roman literature, philosophy and history had been an obsession during Elena's early adult life, but the pressures of law school had dimmed almost every outside interest and her career made them difficult to delve back into after that.

"That's a peculiar background for a lawyer, isn't it?"

"I guess it is, yes, but I hated political science, and it hated me back."

His laughter filled the silence, a rich and yet easy sound, as he led them across the rest of the stepping-stones to the footpath on the other side; somewhere in the middle of things, his voice had become animated and his manner warm. Elena followed him through the path, the trees and shrubs around them breaking the moonlight into uneven patches of shadow and light. He stopped at a metal bench and motioned to the empty space beside him. Elena sat down, and looked straight ahead; she didn't want to chance staring again.

"I know a Japanese story," he said, his gaze shifting to a distant willow tree, and then dove right into it. Elena knew the story well. It was the story of Aoyagi. A distinguished samurai was sent by his *daimyo*—his lord—to render assistance to the service of another lord. The journey was long, and before the samurai reached his destination he had to travel through a mountain path. He got caught in a winter storm and was forced to find shelter. He found a cabin with three willow trees in the front and a couple with a daughter living inside. He humbly asked for lodgings for the night, and they kindly agreed. Their daughter was so beautiful that the samurai fell madly in love.

After learning that the daughter returned his favor, the samurai asked for her hand in marriage. The parents, though honored, could not presume to allow him to marry their daughter, a commoner, but the samurai insisted and her parents finally acquiesced. The samurai was desperate to marry her but could not return home to ask for the permission of his *daimyo*, which all samurai required to marry, because he was expected in the other lord's court. The samurai resolved to marry her without anyone's knowledge, and brought her with him to his new post. They were careful that the wife not be seen in public but were ultimately found out, and the lord sent for the woman as his concubine.

Because the samurai could not disobey or question the lord, on penalty of death, he had no choice but to allow his wife to be taken. His loss was so much that he sent her a secret letter proposing their escape. The lord found out about the letter and called the samurai before his court. The samurai was certain he would be asked to commit *seppuku*—ritual suicide—but when he arrived before the court the lord announced that he was so moved by the expression of love written in the letter, which had been conveyed in the form of a poem, that he would give his consent to the marriage on behalf of the samurai's *daimyo*, and married them on the spot.

As Ms. Callas's son told the story, Elena lost herself in the sound of his voice. It was so soothing that she began to drift, images of the story weaving in and out of her consciousness. She shifted her position on the bench and leaned her arm against the backrest, holding her head in the crook of her arm as he continued to speak. Soon, Elena was fast asleep. She missed the ending of the story, the sad recitation of how after five years of blissful marriage, while the samurai and his wife enjoyed each other's quiet company, the wife suddenly experienced a sharp, debilitating pain. The pain was so strong that she could hardly find the strength to warn her husband; she was going to die. The samurai, trying to console his wife, assured her that the pain was nothing and would quickly pass, but the wife, knowing the truth, revealed to her husband the certainty of her death.

At that very moment, in the mountains where the samurai and his wife had first met, a willow tree in front of her home was being cut down, and that she, rather than being human, was the tree itself. Once the job was done, she would die. As another sharp pain consumed her, she assured her husband of her devotion and love, and collapsed on the ground. The samurai dropped to the floor to assist his beloved, but all that remained of her were the empty folds of the clothing she had worn. Several months later, on his return to his home, the samurai stopped by the mountain cabin that had been his wife's home. There he found three stumps; all that remained of the three willow trees outside of her home.

When Elena woke up, she was disoriented.

"Good morning," came the voice.

Elena followed the voice until the world came into focus. Quiet eyes watched her and she straightened up, suddenly hyper-aware of her surroundings.

"I must have bored you to death," said Ms. Callas's son, a thoughtful look on his face.

"No, no. That's not it at all. I knew the story. My mother—" Elena was about to tell him that her mother used to read her the stories as a child but she stopped herself, and he didn't push.

"It's pretty late. The benefit was over about half an hour ago. You looked so peaceful, I didn't want to disturb you." He saw the shock in her eyes, and just smiled. The gesture seemed more natural this time. "Don't worry about missing the dinner. I'll handle my mother. Can I walk you to your car?"

Elena was speechless. She couldn't believe she had fallen asleep on him. Worst of all, he had sat beside her the entire time. Suddenly, Elena felt extremely self-conscious and vulnerable.

"I... I didn't drive," she answered.

"Can I offer you a ride home?"

"Th-that's not necessary. I live less than two blocks away. I can walk back."

"Granted, perhaps I was a little rude before and didn't give you any reason to expect better of me, but do you really think I'm just going to let you walk home alone, in the dark?"

Elena didn't get the opening to protest. He quickly got to his feet and helped her off of the bench. They walked together out of the garden and through the winding paths of the park. Along the way, they discussed his story. He told her his brothers worked frequently in Japan, and had told him the story after coming home from one of their trips. Elena was surprised to learn Ms. Callas had more children. The revelation peaked her curiosity. She wanted to ask how many siblings he had, but she didn't pry. She also never shared the fact about her mother. She told him her favorite part of the story was the revelation that the wife was the spirit of a willow tree. He confessed his favorite part was the recitation of the samurai's poem. The conversation made the walk home go by very quickly, and Elena was surprised to suddenly find herself in front of her house.

She wasn't surprised when he insisted on walking her to the door.

"Well, thanks again for everything." Elena thanked him, rummaging through her clutch to find her keys. This shouldn't have been difficult, since the purse itself was small, but it felt like it took a lifetime. The entire time, she could feel him standing behind her, so close her heart began to race. She brought the key to the door.

"My pleasure. Good night." He lingered for a moment longer and then briskly stepped away. He waited for Elena to step inside and didn't walk away until she closed the door.

Elena listened to the sound of his fading footsteps. When everything was silent, she stepped back from the door. She locked it and made her way up the stairs to her living room. She still needed to take a shower before going to sleep. After reaching her room, she lazily slipped out of her clothes and stepped into the shower. A thought flitted across her mind.

All that time, and she never asked him his name.

CHAPTER FOUR

"**Y**OU'RE KIDDING, RIGHT?"

Cataline sat across the table from Elena, a Bloody Mary in her hand. Her scarlet lips were pursed and her hazel eyes narrowed. Elena knew the look well—it was the same look Cataline gave her when as a teenager Elena would come home late and give Cataline a carefully crafted excuse.

"About which part, Cataline?"

"Elena! You know this isn't good for my nerves." Cataline breathed the words with an exaggerated air of drama.

"No, Cataline. What isn't good for your nerves is that Bloody Mary you're drinking so early in the morning." Elena narrowed her eyes as she said it, looking around for a menu. She was certain this establishment did not serve alcohol.

"Oh, for crying out loud, Ele. We live in New Orleans. There's nothing wrong with having a little pick me up in the morning. Especially with a breakfast as rich as this." Cataline made a gesture toward the plate of shrimp and grits in front of her, a smug and satisfied look on her delicate face. She watched Elena for a little while longer and then took another sip from her plastic cup.

The first thing Elena had done when she woke up that morning, after convincing herself that the evening before had actually taken place, was call Cataline. They agreed to meet for breakfast at a cafe and juice bar that arguably offered the best breakfast in town. The atmosphere was right up Cataline's alley—small, eclectic, and full of that New Orleans charm. Elena ordered freshly squeezed satsuma juice and biscuits in gravy, while Cataline ordered the shrimp and grits. Elena looked over a menu she snatched from the table next to theirs and confirmed Cataline had smuggled the Bloody Mary in. She must have picked it up at the nearest bar on her walk to the cafe.

If there was something Elena could always count on, it was Cataline's fervor for the art of living. To Cataline, life was meant to be experienced with all the senses, at full throttle, all the time. Cataline wouldn't know mundane if it bit her in the ass, and Elena had always envied her for it. It had been the best part about growing up with Cataline—like being raised by a very melodramatic, tortured-artist type older sibling. On paper, the formula shouldn't have worked. In actuality, though, it had played a major role in healing Elena's fractured life. They were partners in crime in a world that had left them broken. As Elena grew, their relationship blossomed into that of intimate friends. Every now and again, when Cataline had a little too much to drink, she would confess to Elena that having Elena was like the gods had given her a part of Isabella back. Isabella was Elena's mother.

"Earth to Elena." Cataline snapped her fingers an inch away from Elena's nose.

As she did quite often, Elena had gotten lost in her thoughts. She tried to think back to what they were talking about, but she'd lost her train of thought.

"Were you kidding or not?"

"What?" Elena was dazed, Cataline annoyed. Then suddenly, Elena remembered the night before and the thread of their conversation came rushing back. "Well, yes, I was kidding about him being the child of an illicit affair. Everything else was true."

"You expect me to believe that after all that time together, alone in a garden, you didn't have the sense to ask the man his name? I know I raised you better than that."

"How I was raised, Cataline, has nothing to do with it. I got swept up in the moment and just forgot to ask."

"Well, what do you plan on doing about it?" Cataline asked, taking another bite of her breakfast.

"I have no clue."

"Are you pouting?"

Cataline leaned toward Elena when she asked the question, completely amused. Elena was not.

"I am not pouting, Cataline." But she was. She really had no idea what to do about the situation, and it was bothering her. How on earth had she forgotten to ask his name?

"You should ask Livia."

"Are you insane?" There was no way in hell Elena was going to ask Ms. Callas a thing about her son. In fact, she planned on avoiding Ms. Callas all together, as much as Elena's work would allow.

Cataline grinned and dismissed Elena's shocked expression with a graceful wave of her hand. "I don't know why Livia concerns you so much. She's not the devil, Elena. Take a risk. You should ask her about her son."

Because of Cataline's family name, she and Ms. Callas were social acquaintances. Elena suspected there might be more to the story, but she never pushed. If Cataline wanted her to know the details, she would have confided in Elena long ago. Truth be told, after last night, Elena was grateful she didn't know a thing. With a husband like Lucian—dark, edgy, physical and luridly sexy—Elena was certain there was plenty of room for scandal.

"I'm not asking Ms. Callas anything. She may not be the devil, but she could put him to shame." Elena dropped her gaze to her plate. She took another bite of her breakfast, and tried to ignore the look Cataline was giving her. This whole conversation had Elena riled up.

"Give me that." Elena took the drink from Cataline's hand and downed the rest of it. She could see Cataline's knowing smile from above the rim of the plastic cup, but conveniently ignored it. When she gave Cataline the empty cup back, Elena cut her off before she could get started again. "Can we *not* talk about him anymore? There's something else I need to talk to you about."

That definitely peaked Cataline's interest.

Elena leaned over to pick up her purse from the floor. She took out an envelope and handed it to Cataline. "I received it on Saturday in the mail. I have no clue what to make of it."

Cataline read the letter carefully. At first, she seemed as curious as Elena would expect her to be, but then something changed in her eyes. Elena couldn't place it exactly, but something about Cataline's demeanor completely changed. When she was done reading the letter, Cataline set it down on the table.

"Your mother had a safety deposit box?" Cataline's surprise seemed genuine enough, and her demeanor was now back to normal.

"I don't know. I was hoping you might know something about it. I've never heard of any safety deposit box. When you handled her succession, was there anything mentioned about a safety deposit box?" Elena's hands were shaking. She set her fork down and brought her hands to her lap beneath the table.

"No. Not that I can recall. We would have had to empty its contents if that were the case. I don't recall it listed in any of her documents. You know your mother was very meticulous. Everything was perfectly set out before she died."

What Cataline didn't say was that it had been as if Isabella knew she was going to die and prepared her affairs accordingly; at least that's how it had always sounded to Elena.

Cataline arrived in Japan on the third day after the death of Elena's parents. It had been Cataline who handled everything, and then returned with Elena to the States. When Elena was younger, Cataline confessed to her that she was thankful Isabella had always been such a stickler for details, because it had made a terribly difficult situation a lot easier for Cataline to handle, in practical terms. There had been a will and a detailed accounting of their property. Isabella had left specific instructions for how things were to be handled in the event of her death. Everything had been written with the assumption that her husband would survive her, and in the event he did not then Cataline was to assume the tasks. Neither Isabella nor Elena's father had any family other than their child. The responsibilities fell on Cataline, and Isabella's forethought made it easier for Cataline to focus on mourning the loss of her best friend and taking in her orphaned child.

"I'm going to have to call this Mr. Inoue tomorrow and figure out what to do." Mr. Inoue was the gentleman who had signed the letter. Elena took the letter from the table and placed it back in her purse. "Do you remember dealing with anyone by that name when you were in Japan?"

"No, Ele, not at all. It looks like his branch is in Kyoto. I didn't have any dealings in Kyoto after your parents' death. I can't imagine why your mother would have a safety deposit box there. You lived in Tokyo. That doesn't make any sense."

Cataline seemed troubled, so Elena decided to change the subject. "Do you want to go to Canal Place after this?" Canal Place always made Cataline happy. It was the upscale mall in town. "We can walk around the Quarter afterward, if you like. Maybe have some coffee and beignets?"

Of course, Cataline agreed. Why wouldn't she? Shopping followed by a stroll through Jackson Square to get their favorite pastries was a perfect way to spend the day, in Cataline's mind. It was a time-honored tradition. Even when they traveled, Cataline always found a way to combine great shopping with a stroll through a plaza to find coffee and pastries. Granted, it was easy, since Cataline always chose Europe or

South America to visit—she hadn't visited Asia again since the death of Elena's parents.

THE NEXT DAY, Elena's legs were killing her. Even so, she woke up early and went for a run in the park. A new scenic walk had been constructed in the last year, beside the Museum of Art and around a large lagoon, where people could run, walk, bike and skate. Elena loved running on the path in the early hours of the morning, when the mists clung to the ground, creating a sea of translucent white beneath the giant oaks. When she was younger, she and Cataline would walk in Audubon Park, and on mornings when the mists crept across the ground Cataline would tell her stories about the Fae—the faerie folk—and the mists of their kind, what the Irish called the Ceo Sídhe. If a human were lost among the mists they could inadvertently find themselves in the Other-world and never find their way back.

It was because of that, on mornings like today when the ground was covered in a white wispy haze, Elena spent most of her run lost in bittersweet memories of her childhood. Today, however, her mind was on Saturday night, on pale blonde hair and light blue eyes, and the smile on his face when she woke up on the bench beside him. No matter how hard Elena tried, her mind wouldn't stop thinking of Ms. Callas's son. The fact that she didn't know his name just made the obsession even stronger.

Elena felt vexed by the time she got back home. She fed Cicero and spent a few minutes smoothing her hand over her cat's silvery fur, hoping the gesture would calm her. It helped, a little. She wasn't surprised to find Cicero sitting on her bathmat when she stepped out of the shower, looking up at her expectantly with her large coppery eyes. Elena put on her robe and fixed herself some oatmeal. After breakfast, she did her makeup and got dressed. She still had fifteen minutes before she had to leave. She grabbed a book, Marcus Aurelius' *Meditations*, and sat on the sofa to read, Cicero curling up beside her. Reading kept Elena's mind preoccupied, away from the blonde hair and blue eyes.

Elena wasn't so lucky on the drive to work, but at least it was short, and by the time she got to the office there was too much work for her to think about a boy who's name she didn't know. Mondays were always difficult. At least Ms. Callas was at a hearing in court and wouldn't be back until the afternoon. Elena spent the morning finishing a draft of a motion that needed to be filed in court next week, and completely forgot about the letter from Mr. Inoue.

It wasn't until Elena was searching through her purse for money to go get a snack downstairs that she realized she had forgotten about it. She took the letter out and read it again. She took out her cell phone and pressed on the clock icon. It had a world clock feature, and Elena went about adding Tokyo so she could figure out the time difference. It was now a little after 3 p.m. in New Orleans. The Tokyo clock popped up, showing a little after 5 a.m. tomorrow morning. Elena wouldn't be able to call Mr. Inoue until later tonight. She set an alarm for 8 p.m., so she wouldn't forget to make the call, figuring 10 a.m. would be a good time for someone working at a bank.

It turned out to be a lucky day for Elena. She didn't bump into Ms. Callas once, which meant she didn't have to ask about her son or explain why she missed dinner during the benefit on Saturday. Elena and her secretary had coffee in the coffee shop of their building after work, and then Elena drove home. On the way home, she stopped at the supermarket to pick up a few things for dinner that she hadn't bought on Saturday—wheat pasta, ground turkey, and Arrabiata sauce—and some kitty snacks for Cicero. Once she got home, Elena took her time preparing dinner, trying to shorten any downtime between now and the call. She ate quietly on her dining room table and then did the dishes by hand, washing and rinsing them twice.

When Elena looked at the clock, she still had thirty minutes to go before she could make her call. She decided to call Cataline and they talked for a few minutes, since Cataline was on her way out for a date. Elena promised to call her later that night with details about the letter, and then hung up. A text message came in from one of her law school friends; someone was in from out of town and they were having drinks, and planned on going to dinner at a restaurant afterward. Whether Elena would go depended on the call to Japan. Elena had already eaten, but she wouldn't mind sitting at the table for conversation. The person from out of town was a law school friend Elena hadn't seen in years. Elena texted back that she'd let them know within the hour.

Finally, it was 8 p.m. Elena grabbed the letter from her purse, found the phone number, and began to dial. Her hand was shaking. Elena took a deep breath. The line began to ring. A man answered in Japanese, identifying himself as Mr. Inoue. It had been years since Elena practiced the language. The closest to practice she got was a healthy dosage of Japanese animation with subtitles.

"*Ohayō gozaimasu, Inoue-san,*" Good morning, Mr. Inoue; "*Watashi no namae wa Elena Vicens desu,*" My name is Elena Vicens; and that was as far as Elena's conversational Japanese could go. She continued in English. "I received a letter from you about a safety deposit box in my mother's name, Isabella Vicens. I am contacting you, as you requested."

There was silence for a moment on the other end of the call. Then in very beautifully enunciated English, Mr. Inoue responded. The rhythm of his voice took Elena back to the early part of her childhood—to quiet afternoons at a temple with her mother and governess, to the sound of her father's footsteps on the worn wooden floor as he came home from work late at night.

"Thank you for calling, Ms. Vicens. It was very important that we speak."

Mr. Inoue paused for a moment and Elena felt her heart begin to race. Then he continued.

"Twenty one years ago, your mother opened a safety deposit box in our bank, here in Kyoto. Her instructions in the event of her death were very specific, regarding the contents she placed inside. The box was to remain sealed until the time her daughter, Elena Vicens, reached the age of twenty-three. It is my understanding you have recently turned twenty-six, is that correct?"

"Yes," Elena managed to confirm. She cleared her throat, and took a seat at her dining room table. "I turned twenty-six two months ago, on February 3rd. I'm having a little trouble understanding, Inoue-san. If I was to be informed of this when I turned twenty-three, why am I just hearing about this now, three years later?"

"Forgive me, Ms. Vicens, but it has taken us this long to find you."

There was silence again, and Elena didn't press him.

"At the time your mother opened the deposit box with us," Mr. Inoue continued, "she funded a bank account that would pay the monthly rental fee through the time you turned twenty-three. She named a local firm as her agents and placed the key to the box in their possession, to be delivered to you on your twenty-third birthday. Does this make sense so far, Ms. Vicens? Forgive me, but at times I have trouble with the translation."

"Yes, Inoue-san, it makes perfect sense. Please continue." Elena tried to keep her voice from shaking, but too many emotions were surfacing, things she had buried inside of herself long ago. It was like opening an old wound, hearing of her mother in the present tense.

Mr. Inoue continued. "When your twenty-third birthday came, we contacted your mother's agents here in Japan. For various reasons that I cannot understand, the agents claimed they could not locate you.

This posed a significant problem in light of the stipulations in the rental agreement.

"According to the agreement your mother signed, if the rental fee were to become past due for three months the bank must commence the requisite procedures to either have the fees paid or the box seized. The rent for your mother's box went unpaid the three months following your twenty-third birthday. We mailed the necessary letters to your mother's agents, but they were unable to locate you and the rent went unpaid another month.

"At that time, the box was opened, and the contents inventoried and stored. The agents now had three years to locate you in order to recover the property. After three years, if there were no response from the property owner, you, the contents would be sold at auction, as per the rental agreement.

"The agents finally contacted me last week with an address they believed was accurate. I then contacted you in accordance with your mother's wishes. As I am sure you can surmise, it is imperative that you claim the contents of the box immediately, as it is scheduled to be sold at auction in two weeks."

Elena didn't know what to say. This was too much. It sounded like something out of a movie—a safety deposit box, unknown contents, a rapidly approaching deadline of doom. This had to be a joke, but Elena knew deep inside that wasn't the case. There was no way this man went through all of this trouble for a joke. If the bank had been a local one, Elena might have questioned it, but this was coming from Japan. She had made the call herself. There was hardly room for deception.

"Inoue-san, what is in the box?" That was all Elena could think of asking.

"That I cannot divulge over the phone, Ms. Vicens. I can, however, tell you that your mother insured the property at the time she opened the box, and provided the bank with a copy of the proof of insurance. The document we have indicates that the property was insured for over $5 million dollars."

Elena choked. She also dropped the phone. She scrambled under the dining table to grab it, feeling completely dazed. Elena made her apologies as she crawled back out from under the table, sitting back on her heels on the floor beside it. She brought the phone back to her ear.

"Forgive me, Inoue-san, but are you telling me that I need to fly out to Japan within the next two weeks to claim this property, which is allegedly worth, at a minimum, $5 million dollars, or it will be auctioned off?" Elena hardly recognized her own voice. This couldn't be happening.

"Yes, Ms. Vicens, that is precisely the nature of this discussion. I recognize that this must come as a surprise, and I apologize for any stress and inconvenience it may be causing you, but it would have been a shame if something so dear to your mother fell into a stranger's hands when I was fortunate enough to find you before the deadline."

"Inoue-san, this is a lot for me to process. I am, quite honestly, speechless." Elena was white-knuckling the phone. She pushed herself up from the floor and began to pace. "I am sure you can appreciate that it might be extremely difficult for me to drop everything so suddenly and fund a trip to Japan."

Elena wasn't sure why she was saying that. She knew that regardless of the consequences, she would be flying out to Japan this week. She would take the money out of her trust fund, and find a way to pay it back. If what the man was saying was true, she could sell whatever was in the box and live comfortably for a very long time, although Elena knew she would never do that. Whatever the property was, it was something her mother left specifically for her.

"Again, Ms. Vicens, I recognize the impracticalities involved and the almost absurd nature of the situation, but I assure you it would be in your best interest to claim your mother's inheritance."

And there was the rub. This was her mother's inheritance; something so precious she didn't even list it in her carefully plotted-out contingency plans. "I will make the necessary arrangements and will let you know the details as soon as I can. *Arigatō gozaimasu. Sayōnara, Inoue-san,*" Thank you very much and goodbye, Mr. Inoue.

After she set the phone down, Elena sat quietly on her sofa, staring out at the screen of her TV. She forgot about texting back her friend; her mind was on her mother and the deposit box that had appeared out of the ether, calling up ghosts that had been buried for almost twenty years. Cicero came to sit beside her, and for the longest time Elena just sat completely still.

She was having issues processing everything Mr. Inoue had told her. For twenty years, all Elena had left of her parents were a few trinkets and memories she refused to let wither over time. Now, quite suddenly, something tangible had emerged, something that made the memory of her parents corporeal. In a matter of days, Elena would set foot back in Japan, a world that did not exist in Elena's mind without them. That single fact was mindboggling.

After about a half an hour of pondering the situation, Elena found herself with a massive headache. She got up from the couch and took some migraine medication. She was drawing a bath when her phone rang. She was too dazed to even notice who was calling.

"Elena?"

It was Cataline. Elena would have recognized her voice anywhere.

"Yeah."

Elena was having trouble saying much more than that. Cataline knew something was wrong the moment she heard Elena's tone. When she couldn't get the answers she wanted over the phone, Cataline told Elena she was coming over. Elena turned off the water to her bath and put on a robe. She waited for Cataline on her sofa. Cataline had keys, so Elena didn't have to get up and open the door when she recognized the sound of Cataline's car outside. When Cataline walked through the door into the living room, Elena just stared at her, not even sure where to start.

"Was it that bad, Ele? You look like you've seen a ghost."

Cataline sat down next to Elena, and dropped her purse down on the coffee table. Cicero jumped up on the sofa and carved out her spot between Elena and Cataline. The sounds of her purring filled the silence between them. The touch of Cataline's hand brought Elena back to the moment.

"I don't know where to start, Cataline. It's insane." Elena shook her head, feeling the sting of tears in her eyes. She hated crying, and yet there was too much inside of her right now. She needed some kind of release. It wasn't long before she felt Cataline's arms wrap around her and pull Elena gently toward her. Cicero made a sharp cry and hopped off the sofa. Like those first few months after her parents' death, Elena wept quietly in Cataline's arms.

For all of Cataline's exuberant and impatient nature, Elena always found it interesting that in moments like these she never pushed. She waited quietly until the moment passed, allowing Elena to begin her story on her own terms. Cataline listened patiently as Elena told her of the unbelievable nature of Elena's conversation with Mr. Inoue. It took Elena a little while to get it all out, and in the mean time Cataline just ran her fingers through Elena's long hair, smoothing the length of it down her back. It made Elena feel safe, and not alone.

"You're certain this isn't some kind of prank?" Cataline asked the question once Elena was done with her story, her tone gentle. She was trying to avoid Elena getting upset.

"I'm certain. It's too elaborate to be a prank. I called that man in Japan. Why on earth would anyone go through this trouble?" Elena pulled back just enough to look up into Cataline's face.

"I don't know, baby. It just all seems a little suspect to me. I mean, nineteen years later and some insane timeline for some multi-million dollar mysterious item. I was Isabella's best friend, and she never said a word to me about something like this. She would have said something to me, Elena."

Cataline's voice was strained, and Elena swore she saw a hint of defiance in Cataline's eyes. After a few seconds, it was gone. Cataline brushed Elena's hair away from her cheek, her face filled with concern.

"Please don't be upset with me for saying it, but is there a chance she might just not have told you about it? Is it possible she wanted to keep this between us?" Elena straightened up and pressed her lips together so that they wouldn't tremble. She was grasping at anything to believe this was true—something of her mother's, now, in the present.

"I guess anything is possible, Ele. I just don't want you to get hurt. This all seems so unlikely. What if it's a trick, and you get to Japan and something happens to you?"

"Like what, Cataline? I'm not the daughter of some world-renown billionaire or important politician. No one's out to get me. There's no one to even get a ransom from." Elena tried to smile when she said it, but failed miserably. "I already made the decision to go, Cataline."

"Then I'm going with you, Ele. There's no way I'm letting you do this alone."

It was in moments like these that Elena felt extremely thankful. She had lost everything as a child, but fate had left her one good thing. Elena watched as Cataline stood and moved into Elena's study. She came back with Elena's laptop in her hands.

"We might as well buy the tickets now," Cataline announced, a bittersweet smile on her face.

Her patience only lasted so long, and Elena knew not to argue. It was best to let Cataline do what she wanted to do, since it was Cataline's way of making things as okay as she possibly could. By the time Cataline was done, she had booked two first class round-trip tickets to Osaka, the closest airport to Kyoto. She also made reservations at a *ryokan*, a traditional Japanese inn.

"Cataline, you didn't have to do that. I mean, first class and a *ryokan*? Don't you think that might be a bit much?" Elena nodded quietly as Cataline excitedly showed her images of the *ryokan* on the computer. It was absolutely beautiful.

"If we're going on some fool's errand, we're going to do it comfortably, Elena. You deserve some good R & R."

Elena didn't know what to say. She did know there was no point in arguing, and Cataline was making a valid point. "Let me know how much my end of it is, and I'll write you a check."

"You're insane if you think I'm letting you pay for this. I decided to go posh, so the treat is on me." Cataline smiled, but then her features smoothed. She assumed a semi-serious demeanor. "Let me do this for you. If this is for real, it is going to be a very emotional journey."

Elena couldn't help the foreboding feeling she suddenly felt. Cicero crawled onto her lap and meowed. "Okay, I promise not to secretly deposit the money in your account." Elena tried to smile. She pet Cicero, her eyes dropping to the cat's silvery coat. "Thanks. I'm happy you're coming with me, Cataline."

And the conversation ended at that. There was only so much emotion Elena could handle. Cataline stayed for another hour, watching TV with Elena and Cicero. Once Cataline was gone, Elena took a quick shower. Then she drew her bath again and soaked until she couldn't take it anymore; when her temples throbbed from the heat and she started to feel a little dizzy. She drained the tub and turned on the shower to rinse herself off with cold water. Then she went to sleep.

ELENA HAD TROUBLED DREAMS. She had nightmares about telling Ms. Callas that she had to leave for a week. In one of her dreams, it was the Ark of the Covenant in the deposit box; never mind that it was far too big to fit in a drawer. But it was her last dream, the one that consumed the early hours of the morning, which terrified Elena the most. It was the same silent dream Elena always had—darkness, the feel of ice-cold arms around her, and not being able to breathe. Again, she saw fragments of color, polar blue and crimson, like Aurora Borealis but strange, as if seen through the looking glass. There was still no sound, but this time the darkness began to fade. The fragments of color began to take shape and Elena saw the contours of a face. She woke up before the darkness vanished completely.

The image haunted her even after she woke, bleeding through the quiet panic in her mind. So much had happened in an instant. During breakfast, Elena couldn't help but wonder if she had somehow brought this on herself. She had been so discontent, praying silently for something, anything, to happen, and now, change had come in a matter of minutes. One simple telephone conversation and the story of Isabella's life, and thereby Elena's, was altered. It was unnerving to consider, and weighed heavily on Elena as she went through the motions to begin her day.

While in the shower, Elena daydreamed of different scenarios, playing out the myriad of reasons her mother might have had to go about things in this way. She imagined her mother walking through the streets of Kyoto to the bank. Had she been alone? Had Elena's father gone with her? Where had Elena been at the time? Elena remembered going to Kyoto several times as a child. Had it been during one of those visits? Elena tried to recall the name of her mother's friend, with whom they stayed when visiting Kyoto, but for the life of her Elena could not remember. Only images came out of the ether—beautiful temples, tranquil gardens, cherry blossom petals floating in the air. Her mother had taken her to a castle, and several shrines. A woman had always accompanied them, a Japanese woman with long black hair and eyes the color of honey. Elena thought the woman must have been some kind of princess because she always wore a *kimono*. It was the kind of *kimono* the women of Kyoto often wore about town, but to Elena's childlike eyes, limited mostly to the views of a modernized Tokyo, it was an unforgettable sight.

While putting on her makeup and dressing, Elena's mind was consumed with the fractured recollection of her dreams and the slowly rising fear of having to discuss the situation with Ms. Callas. The latter made the drive to work seem eternal, and by the time Elena reached the office she was a ball of frayed nerves.

Of course, her secretary noticed, and all Elena could do was give a reserved accounting of the fact that she had received some important family news the night before and would need to go speak with Ms. Callas immediately. Before going to Ms. Callas's office, Elena checked her email and prepared some tea. She called Ms. Marjorie to make sure Ms. Callas was available, and then began the uneasy walk across the firm to Ms. Callas's office. Along the way, Elena walked by Melissa and didn't say a word. They exchanged looks, Melissa offered a tentative smile, and Elena remained stone-faced. It was only a matter of seconds before Melissa would find her way into another associate's office, most likely a female associate, to complain about it.

Elena lost her resolve when she reached Ms. Callas's door. She hesitated, acutely aware that Ms. Marjorie was staring at her. Elena closed her eyes, called up the memory of her mother's face, and knocked on the door.

"Yes, come in," a voice called out from inside.

Elena opened the door and stepped inside. Ms. Callas's office was beautifully put together. Elena had only been inside it a handful of times, and every time she had the same reaction—a pleasant sense of surprise. It was very modern, with mid-century teak pieces and bright, vivid works of art. Bookcases filled with books lined a far wall, and the opposite half of the office was wall-to-wall windows.

Carefully chosen decorative pieces in vibrant colors and abstract designs were strategically placed around the room. Two beautifully upholstered wing-back chairs, the fabric designed with an off-white background and foliage motif in brown, bright green, yellow, orange and red, were placed in front of her desk. A chocolate brown leather chaise stood to the left of her desk with a tall, round side-table beside it. If Elena looked carefully, some of the decorations were items from different places around the world—a small Minoan statuette, an Etruscan urn, a Mesopotamian cylinder seal, a Gaelic torc necklace, and woodblock prints and Zen art from Japan on various walls.

Ms. Callas was sitting behind her desk, watching Elena quietly. Elena couldn't tell if she was amused or affected by the way Elena admired the room. She waited for Elena to speak.

"Good morning, Ms. Callas," Elena whispered, taking a seat once it was offered. "I'm sorry to disturb you this morning, but there is something I need to speak to you about."

"Have you finally come to tell me why you missed the dinner at the benefit?" Again, that perfect smile.

Elena blanched. "I'm sorry, I thought your son had already discussed that with you. He was kind enough to keep me company and we lost track of time. He's a very good storyteller."

"Indeed, he is." Ms. Callas reached for her cup of coffee. The phone rang, but she didn't answer it. Instead, she called out loud for Ms. Marjorie, who quickly made her way into the room. "Marjorie, please hold my calls." Ms. Marjorie nodded and left the room. Ms. Callas brought the cup of coffee to her lips in a graceful, fluid motion and then set it down when she was done. "Well, Elena, you have my undivided attention."

No pressure, Elena thought. She lowered her gaze, and remembered to breathe.

"Well, go on child, spit it out. If you've come to tender your resignation don't waste your time. I won't accept it." Ms. Callas's tone was clipped.

Elena looked up into Ms. Callas's face, unable to keep the surprise off of her own.

"Oh good, we got that out of the way. Now, Elena, what can I do for you?" Ms. Callas rapped her fingers on her desk blotter, her nails making a hollow sound against it.

Elena held her hands together on her lap; the only way she could keep them from shaking. Why this woman affected Elena so much was a mystery, but it seemed to be a Callas family trait. "Ms. Callas, I'm not sure if you know, since I do not believe we have ever discussed it, that my parents died when I was very young. I was living in Japan at the time, where I was born and raised until I was seven years old. Last night I was informed of a situation involving my parents' will that I must attend to immediately, and will, regrettably, require me to leave for Japan as soon as possible. I have been assured the matter should take no longer than a week to resolve."

There, it was finally out, and, to Elena's dismay, she said it all in one breath. Ms. Callas narrowed her eyes and studied Elena quietly. Like her son, she was completely unreadable. Her husband, however, didn't seem to have the same trait.

"Well, that was a mouthful." Ms. Callas leaned back in her chair and called to Ms. Marjorie for her calendar. When it was finally in her hands, Ms. Callas opened it to the particular week at issue and began to look through it. Elena watched as Ms. Callas guided her pen along the pages, stopping at various entries. After two or three minutes, she finally looked up at Elena. "There is a bit of a problem, Elena, because as I am sure you are aware, we have a court hearing and two very important depositions taking place within the week." *We* was the operative word.

"Ms. Callas, I do realize that there are several things on the calendar, but this is a situation I cannot ignore. The gravity of it is unique, I assure you." Elena knew immediately it was the wrong choice of word.

"What exactly is unique about it, if you don't mind me asking?"

Ms. Callas leaned forward on her desk, a look of interest on her face that Elena had never seen before. Elena could tell Ms. Callas was treading lightly, and that was out of character for her. This was the second time in less than a week that red flags went off in Elena's head; first with Lucian, and now with Ms. Callas. Why this was happening, Elena couldn't venture to say.

Elena chose her words carefully. "I'm sorry, Ms. Callas, but I am not at liberty to say. It is a very private matter, and I hoped it would suffice to say it involved my parents' will."

Ms. Callas looked irritated with Elena's response. She ran a frustrated hand through her hair, looked over her calendar again and poked at the pages several times with a long, plum-colored painted nail. "Regrettably, Elena, it does not suffice. I hope you realize this places you in a very difficult position. As associates, we groom you to develop and grow into attorneys who excel in their profession and who understand the importance of being part of a team. To be part of this team, I, the partner, must be able to rely on you, the associate, to my benefit and the benefit of my client. Do you understand?"

Elena responded with a nod, wary about where the conversation was going.

Ms. Callas continued. "Perhaps an example will illustrate my point. When must you leave for Japan, Elena?"

Elena tensed. "First thing tomorrow."

"And so you are only giving me 24-hour notice. You were to take one of the depositions next week, and assist me with the other and the court hearing, which, as you know, is very convoluted. Your role, which you might think is minimal, is actually important to me because of the scope of this particular case. Now, I will have to find someone to cover for you on an extremely complicated matter and in a very small window of time. It's a recipe for disaster. Worst of all, this will cause me to rely on you less in the future, which is directly detrimental to your growth within this firm." Ms. Callas said it all in a very amiable tone, as if she were doing Elena a favor.

Elena was at a loss. How on earth was she supposed to argue with that kind of logic? "Ms. Callas, this is a family emergency. It is completely out of my control, and I am sure you and the partnership can appreciate that kind of situation."

Of course, Ms. Callas was already prepared for that. "While I recognize this is of an urgent nature, it seems shocking to me, Elena, that a matter involving a nineteen-year-old will would require you to leave so quickly. What's more, when I question you about it, you decline to explain why."

Elena had a lot of issues with Ms. Callas, but she would have expected even a woman as difficult as her to understand the nature of this kind of situation. This was a family emergency. The nature of emergencies required them to be unforeseen, and the family context should have made the situation an exception to the rule. Ms. Callas, however, was making this about business. The more Elena thought about it, the more upset she became. "Ms. Callas, what exactly are you saying? Are you trying to insinuate that if I leave I may not have a job when I get back?"

Ms. Callas shook her head, a shocked expression on her face. "Of course not, Elena. I'm just trying to mentor you, to advise you. Life is difficult. There are choices we must all make, choices, which may or may not be detrimental to you in the long run. I'm telling you what I wish someone would tell me if I were in your shoes. No, you will not be fired, but you must understand the inconvenience this causes and how it will affect you in the future. I would be remiss not to tell you the possible unforeseen consequences of your choices before you make them. In the end, the choice is yours. Your job will be waiting for you when you get back."

Elena was beside herself. She stood, not sure exactly what to say. Finally, she decided the best thing to do was simply to excuse herself and walk away. "Thank you, Ms. Callas. I appreciate your advice, and I hope you understand these are extenuating circumstances. Please relay my reasons to the partnership. I will be back no later than next Wednesday. I'll make sure to have email capabilities and a cell phone, in the event you need to reach me." With that, Elena nodded and walked out of the office.

Elena spent the rest of her day tying up loose ends at work and finding someone to cover for her. If Ms. Callas didn't have to do that herself, it might appease her a little. At this point, Elena didn't even really care if she lost her job. This place had been making her miserable, and there wasn't a paycheck big enough to make it worth her while. Elena avoided Ms. Callas, and the rest of her co-workers, the remainder of her day. She left early, around 3:00 p.m., to pick up some things at the mall.

Elena got home around five, and spent the rest of the evening preparing for the trip. She located her passport, did laundry, watered the plants, made dinner, made arrangements with her downstairs neighbor to come feed Cicero and handle the litter for the week, and left the packing until the end. By the time she was done packing and took a shower, Elena was exhausted and ready for bed. It was half past nine. Elena set the alarm clock to 3:00 a.m., since Cataline would be picking her up at 4:30 to be at the airport by 5:00 for the 7 o'clock flight. Five hours of sleep was better than nothing.

Elena's last lingering thought before sleep was a silent plea, that if she dreamed her silent dream she wouldn't wake up before the darkness vanished completely.

<u>CHAPTER FIVE</u>

Eᴸᴱᴺᴬ ᴰᴵᴰᴺ'ᵀ ᴰᴿᴱᴬᴹ that night. She woke up feeling strange-ly bereft, as if the lack of dream had left her hollow. She couldn't remember the last time she hadn't dreamed. She might not always remember her dreams, but that didn't mean she wasn't dreaming. Dreams left an imprint, like a footstep in a blanket of snow. When Elena woke up the next morning, there was no imprint—only a vast expanse of unblemished snow, cold and empty.

Suffice to say, she wasn't in the best of moods. Her mind should have been on the trip, on making sure everything was properly taken care of before she left, but instead she was obsessing over a face half hidden in shadow. The one time in her life she begged for that dream, and she got nothing. Elena called up the image in her mind, but no matter how many times she did it, she couldn't get the darkness to vanish completely. When she wasn't obsessing over the face, she was berating herself for obsessing in the first place.

"Sorry, Cicero."

Elena's cat stared up at her from the kitchen floor, eyeing her spilled food with an air of disappointment only a cat could express. In her distraction, Elena had poured half of the dry cat food into the water bowl. With a heavy sigh, she dropped to the floor. She sat cross-legged and let Cicero curl up on her lap. The cat closed her eyes and began purring loudly. "I'll miss you too, kitty. Make sure to be nice to Mrs. LeBlanc." Mrs. LeBlanc was Elena's downstairs neighbor. After a few more minutes of petting Cicero, Elena slowly crawled to her feet and grabbed the water bowl. She dumped the contents in the sink, washed out the bowl and dried it, filled it with fresh water, and then returned it to its proper place. All the while, Cicero followed her movements with an expectant gaze. "There you go. Enjoy." Elena put the cat food in its proper bowl this time, and gave Cicero one last rub behind her ears.

Since Elena wasn't very hungry, breakfast was simple—toast and coffee with milk. Of course, the milk overflowed in the microwave, leaving a nice little mess of milk and instant coffee. At least her toast didn't burn. Elena treated herself to lingonberry jam along with some butter, and fresh grapefruit juice. Louisiana grapefruits were just coming into season, and they were sweet enough that Elena didn't have to put any sugar in her juice. It was perfect.

By the time she was done with breakfast, Elena only had forty-five minutes to shower and get ready before Cataline arrived. She was packing her final toiletries and makeup bag when Cataline walked into the apartment, calling out her name.

"Is that it?" Cataline asked with a raised brow as she walked into Elena's room, looking at the suitcase and carryall at the foot of the bed.

"What do you mean? Of course that's it." Elena looked her luggage over and finished zipping her carryall bag. Cataline didn't say a word; she just stared at the luggage and shook her head. "What are you talking about, Cataline? Everything I need is in here." Elena grabbed the notepad from the floor next to her suitcase and started going over the things she packed. Yes, she was that kind of packer. Elena left things to the last minute, but that never stopped her from being thorough. The list looked fine. She couldn't think of a thing that was missing.

"Nothing, Ele. I was just surprised, that's all. I could hardly fit my things in three suitcases."

"Three suitcases? You're not serious, Cataline." Elena just stared at her, trying to focus on calming down. Cataline always did this sort of thing—the over packing—and it drove Elena nuts. After Elena graduated from college, Cataline insisted on taking a trip through Western Europe via train. Cataline, in her infinite travel wisdom, packed enough luggage for a six month trip. It was the worst trip of Elena's life. Between the narrow corridors of the train, the small luggage accommodations, the constant need to switch trains, and the infinite amount of stairs in most European train stations—it was a miracle Elena hadn't killed Cataline. "We'll only be there a week. We'll be going into a bank and coming right out. That's pretty much it. Hardly a need for three suitcases."

"Oh, come on, Elena. Don't be upset," Cataline pleaded, "we'll be in the old imperial capital. It's the epicenter of traditional Japan. Don't even pretend like we'll just be stuck in a bank all day. Plus, you never know. I could meet a future husband there." It was an olive branch.

The second Cataline said it, with that bright, warm smile on her face, Elena's ire melted. She sighed, feeling oddly deflated—cold and empty like before. "Sorry, Cataline. I'm just in a horrible mood. I didn't sleep very well last night."

"It's okay. Don't worry about it. It's only natural for you to be worried. I told you, if this deposit box thing turns out to be true, it's going to be pretty emotional. Let's try to take it one step at a time, okay?" Cataline grabbed Elena's carryall and motioned toward the bedroom door. "Come on. Let's go. Your chariot awaits!"

Elena smiled and followed Cataline out of the room, dragging her suitcase along with her. She made sure all of the lights were turned off, the windows properly closed, Cicero had water and food, and that her passport and phone were in her purse. She realized she forgot her cell phone charger and ran into the room to grab it. The travel adapters were already packed. Cataline helped Elena with the suitcase down the stairs. Her Land Rover was parked up front, so they didn't have to drag the luggage very far. Elena did, however, have to employ some creative arranging to fit her suitcase in the back along with all of Cataline's luggage and the usual mountain of things she kept back there.

Cataline lit a cigarette the second they were off. "Sorry, love. I'm not looking forward to those long flights without a cigarette." Cataline mumbled the words with a cigarette dangling from her scarlet lips. She winked and reached for the car lighter. With a well-practiced motion, she had the cigarette lit.

"It's alright. Better you get your fix now. Plus, at this point I should be used to it, right?" Elena shrugged. Cataline nodded and focused on the road ahead. Elena took the opportunity to watch her. It was a very familiar sight—Cataline with a cigarette in hand, lost in her own thoughts. Because of Elena's asthma, Cataline didn't smoke in the house, but you could always find her with a cigarette out in the garden, her movements so graceful it was almost a dance. Elena always remembered the aesthetics of it—the brightly painted nails standing out against the white wrapper, Cataline's unruly hair, her eternally scarlet lips, the lipstick stain on the cigarette filter, the curl of pale smoke dancing in front of her, and the floating fabric of whatever vintage robe she had chosen for the occasion. That was Cataline's imprint in Elena's mind; how Elena would always remember her.

The rest of the ride to the airport was quiet. Elena's mind was once again on her lack of dreaming and on the face she couldn't see.

Traffic was nonexistent, since it was an ungodly hour, and they made good time. They parked the car in the long-term garage. The trek across it, and the adjacent short-term garage, to the departures counter wasn't so easy. The pathways and walkthroughs set up for easier access didn't exactly help the cause, since they struggled to manage the four suitcases, their carryalls and purses. Elena had flashbacks to the train trip, but she didn't mention it.

The ticket counter had a long line, but Elena was happy to be reminded that they were traveling First Class. That particular line was empty and check-in was painless. The security line took a little longer, but it wasn't too tedious. Cataline was talking about the new guy she was dating and Elena listened attentively, hoping the conversation would distract her from her own thoughts. The flight to San Francisco was pretty full, but uneventful. The layover went quickly, and soon enough they were sitting in their assigned seats on the international flight to Kansai International Airport in Osaka.

Overall, the trip from New Orleans to Osaka took a little more than nineteen hours. About three hours into the flight from San Francisco to Osaka, Elena found herself mentally thanking Cataline for the First Class accommodations. There were plenty of movies to watch, better food selection, free-flowing alcohol, warm towels, fantastic little snacks, excellent legroom, and a nifty seat that could recline completely into your own personal cot. Elena slept a good quarter of the flight, and again she didn't dream.

They arrived at Kansai International Airport in the afternoon, close to half past three. Elena was exhausted and jet lagged. Immediately after de-boarding, Cataline found a smoking area and Elena waited patiently as she had her fix. They went through customs and then Cataline declared she was hungry, so they stopped at a restaurant and ordered a rice bowl and some *soba* noodles. The food was delicious. By the time they went through customs, ate, grabbed their luggage and got on the train to Kyoto, it was a little after five. They took the Haruka Express to Kyoto, and Elena slept through the entire hour-and-fifteen-minute train ride. Again, she did not dream. It made her extremely irritated, and Elena almost snapped when Cataline asked her to help with one of her suitcases. From the train station, they took a taxi to the *ryokan* Cataline had booked. The ride was very short, no more than twenty minutes, but Elena fell into a deep sleep. Cataline had to shake her awake when they arrived at the inn.

It took Elena a second to start moving. She looked at her watch, which she had adjusted at Kansai Airport. It was almost 6:45 in the evening. It was dusk, and the street outside was bathed in twilight. As she stepped out of the taxi, Elena found herself standing at a wooden gate. There were Japanese characters, written in white, on the threshold above her and to her right. Beautiful tiles lined the eaves and gabled roof above the entrance, and along the walls surrounding the inn. An open-faced, worn wooden fence ran along the sidewalk at both sides of the gate, following the length of the street. The street itself was quiet and charming, a side street that cut the inn off from the present and enveloped the area in the shades of the past.

A sound from behind the gate pulled Elena to the present. The wooden doors were pulled aside from the inside, and a kind-looking older woman dressed in a *kimono* bowed and welcomed them inside. She was the *nakai-san*, the hostess who would care for them during their stay. Elena and Cataline bowed to her in return. Elena looked over the woman's shoulder and noticed that the stone walkway leading from the gate to the front doorstep was splashed with water, a symbol of welcome in Japan. Elena was immediately reminded of her mother, who had followed the custom during Elena's early childhood any time they received guests. Elena waited for Cataline before she stepped into the stone walkway.

Behind her, the taxi driver removed their luggage from the trunk of his car, and Cataline instructed him where to place it. Elena couldn't help but notice the luggage was slowly taking up the entire space on the stone sidewalk in front of the entrance. If the *nakai-san* was bothered by the ridiculous amount of luggage, she did not give herself away. Instead, she waited patiently for them to finish and then led them both inside. At the entrance to the main building, the *nakai-san* gestured to two sets of corridor slippers, which were to be used at all times while inside the inn. Elena and Cataline removed their shoes, which they left at the entrance, put on the slippers and stepped inside.

The buildings that made up the inn were built around an internal garden. The frame of these buildings was made of sand and clay walls. Inside, the buildings were divided by the use of sliding doors made of wood and heavy paper, called *fusuma*. Most of the walls facing the direction of the inner garden, however, were lined with shōji, windows and doors made of Japanese paper that allowed light to filter through. The *shōji* screens opened onto the *engawa*, an outside wooden veranda with a sloping roof that provided access to the garden. The inn itself felt small and intimate, but in fact comprised of various buildings cloistered around the inner garden and connected by garden pathways housing a total of almost thirty rooms.

As they stepped inside, Elena was immediately transported back in time. The inn was an ode to old Japan. Everywhere she looked, she was greeted by warm, lustrous woods and elegant *tatami*—woven straw mats used as flooring. As they were led through the entrance of the inn, she observed the *fusuma* that divided the various rooms of the main house, each one with gilded backgrounds depicting nature in various forms, the color scheme made up of rich tawny tones of yellow, orange and brown. The wooden lintels above the *fusuma*, called *ramma*, were either left bare to showcase the beauty of the natural wood or accented with stenciled paulownia flowers in a dark stain.

Elena recalled with an almost sweet regret the *engawa* in the home she had been raised, which could be closed with heavy wooden doors or left open to the elements. In this particular inn, the *engawa's* sliding doors were made of glass framed in wood. When closed, the sliding doors formed a beautiful hall of large glass panels framed in dark wood that opened out into the garden, allowing the tranquil beauty of the garden within. The sides and top of the wooden frame were no more than a few inches wide, and the bottom was made of a wooden panel two feet in height. Bamboo blinds outside the glass sliding doors could be lowered or raised, as shade was required.

The inner garden could be seen from almost every room in the main building, the central focus a stone lantern and bamboo fountain. These features were accented with beautifully sculpted bushes, clipped moss, stone pathways and graveled areas that made Elena think of the sea. In the Zen tradition, rock gardens were designed to represent natural landscapes. The gravel or sand represented water elements, the larger stones symbolized mountains or islands, and the moss forested masses of land. These traditions found their way into the modern Japanese garden, and Elena could see them reflected here in the way the moss, stone and gravel were arranged.

As they were led through the main building to their room, the *nakai-san*, speaking in a soft voice, explained the inner workings of the inn—how and where breakfast and dinner were served, time preferences, the use of slippers and robes, the custom of a spa bath before dinner, the number of baths available for use, both private and communal, and the need to make reservations to use the baths. They came to a stop at a set of *fusuma* sliding doors decorated in gold leaf with a scene depicting two lacquered carts, one large and one small, each carrying a carefully arranged assortment of branches and blossoms. This was the main door to their room, a large corner room in the main building that faced the inner garden. Here, they were instructed to remove the corridor slippers before stepping inside onto the delicate *tatami* mats.

Before stepping into their room, Elena took a second to study the *fusuma* door. In the larger of the two carts, she recognized a branch of maple with leaves the color of red clay, pale chrysanthemums, a hanging flower that looked like lily of the valley but wasn't, and cuts of green branches with leaves that softened the sharper lines of the arrangement. The smaller cart held an arrangement with a sparse branch of some type of blossom, plum or cherry Elena couldn't tell, and another type of flower she didn't recognize.

Through the open *fusuma* door, Elena could see their room was made up of a central space with two alcoves to the right, and a recess at the end adjacent to the *engawa*. The left and far sides of the room faced the inner garden. In the central space were arranged a low table with two chairs. The chairs had no legs and sat directly on the *tatami* mats, lined with a cushion to sit on. The backrest was left bare with only the wood, and there was a single cushioned armrest on the left-hand side. A large, round paper lantern hung over the table and provided warm light. This was the main part of the room, and the dining table and chairs would be removed after supper and replaced with the thick cushioned *futon* bedding of traditional Japan.

Immediately to the right of the central room, as they entered, was the first alcove. The floors were made of polished wood, and it was in this alcove where they could place their luggage. Beside it, toward the end of the central room, also to the right, was the second alcove. This was the *tokonoma*, a traditional wooden-floored alcove used for displaying scrolls, flowers or ceramics. This particular one displayed a hanging scroll of a large white heron framed by bamboo, an arrangement of fresh flowers and a stone incense burner. The *nakai-san* kindly reminded them that the *tokonoma* was a place of honor, and should not be used to place any of their belongings.

On the opposite side of the room, *shōji* sliding doors lined the left and far walls that opened out onto the *engawa* and garden. The far wall, however, was *shōji* only up to the center, where the room then cut back into a large recess made of sand and clay walls, and lined in *tatami*. Large glass windows lined the right and far walls of the recess, facing the garden, and a writing desk stood below them against the far wall. *Shōji* screens could be closed over the windows to provide privacy. On the desk was a lacquer box with paper and writing utensils. A tall floor paper lantern at the entrance to the recess provided light.

As Elena and Cataline admired the room, the *nakai-san* offered them tea and inquired if they would like to have their dinner. Elena and Cataline gladly accepted. Since it was already so late, they would not be able to enjoy a spa before supper, as was the custom. The *nakai-san* then helped them fill out the inn's register and showed them where they could find the robes they were to wear while within the inn—an informal cotton *kimono* known as a *yukata*, and a shorter robe to be worn over it called a *haori*. Then she bowed and quietly left the room.

For the first few minutes they were alone, Elena and Cataline just stood in silence, partly from exhaustion but mostly from a desire to enjoy the scene. To Elena, it all felt surreal, as though she might be dreaming. She was lightheaded, and her body was sore from the flight. She turned her gaze toward the *engawa* and the inner garden beyond. The stone lantern had been lit, and it glowed with a warm and ghostly kind of light. Elena exhaled sharply, as if she had been holding her breath until now.

Cataline broke the silence first. "We should change." She motioned toward the *shōji* and they quickly slid them shut. They undressed and put on their *yukata*.

"Make sure to wrap the left side over the right," Elena reminded Cataline.

"Why is that again?" Cataline was having trouble with the ties.

Elena moved toward her to help. "Right over left is for the dead."

"Well shit, that would be embarrassing, wouldn't it? They sure have a lot of protocol to follow—shoes off, slippers on, slippers off to walk on the mats, special slippers for the baths and for the garden. How on earth am I going to keep track of all of this?" Cataline asked with a dazed expression on her face.

"You look really tired," Elena teased, smoothing out the robe at Cataline's shoulders once it was tied right. She made sure to pull the tie on the sash toward the back. "I'll keep reminding you, so don't worry about it. Just think that every time you switch places in the house there's probably a slipper to go along with it, and on *tatami* no slippers or shoes at all."

There was a soft knock at the door. Elena walked across the room and slid the *fusuma* open. The *nakai-san* bowed her head, perfectly balancing the tray of green tea in her hands. Elena returned the bow— always a good rule to follow—and, after whispering a polite greeting, the *nakai-san* stepped inside. Elena followed her toward the low table in the center of the room, and then she and Cataline took their seats. As the *nakai-san* served them tea, she informed them that supper would be served shortly and asked if they would like to reserve one of the private baths for after their meal. Of course, they agreed. The *nakai-san* re-opened the *shōji* doors facing the garden and then took her leave.

"So what do you think?" Cataline asked.

"I think it's perfect." Elena took a sip of her tea and looked out toward the garden. One of the *engawa's* sliding doors was open, and they could hear the soft sound of water coming from outside. "It reminds me of mom."

"I know what you mean." Cataline's voice broke just a little and she cleared her throat, offering Elena a faint smile.

Then they both fell into a comfortable silence, enjoying the tranquility in the room.

Supper was the traditional multi-course Japanese dinner known as *kaiseki*. They were served an appetizer, squid and tuna sashimi, a simmered dish of vegetables and tofu, grilled white fish, miso soup, pickled vegetables, a steamed course, and a dessert of seasonal fruit and rice cake. The courses were all served individually, in artistic arrangements laid out on beautiful lacquerware and ceramic pieces, decorated with fern leaves and flowers. There wasn't much conversation during the meal, since they were famished. After dinner, Elena and Cataline spent a few more minutes looking out onto the garden and then they each took their turn in the bath.

The bathroom was narrow and long. The walls, up to three feet, and floor were lined in stone. The rest, including the ceiling, was dark polished wood. The bathtub was at the far end of the narrow bathroom, against a wall decorated with stained glass. The tub was made of cedar, and was meant only for soaking. Before stepping inside, Elena had to sit on a small wooden stool and wash herself with soap. She rinsed with water from a wooden bucket. There was a faucet nearby, in case she needed more water. Once she was completely rinsed off, she stepped into the bathtub to soak. The water was warm and reached up to her neck. It took Elena a moment to get used to it. Then she leaned back and closed her eyes. The silence was deafening. She concentrated on emptying her mind, and little by little she felt herself relax.

The first few thoughts to enter her mind were of her childhood. Those images floated away until there was nothing at all, only darkness. That's when the image of her dreams rose up from the shadows, shards of color slowly fusing together to form the outline of a face. This time, she wasn't dreaming. Elena was fully awake. The memory surfaced from the depths of her mind, trying to piece together what she had not been able to see, but it was useless—she still couldn't piece together the face. There were no discerning features, only lines and slivers of color. Then the image was gone.

Elena opened her eyes. She was still in the bathtub. Some time must have passed, because the water wasn't as hot. Slowly, she pulled herself up and stepped out of the tub. She dried herself off and quickly gathered her toiletries. She blotted her hair with a towel, and then put on her robe. She threw the used towels in their proper basket, wrapped on the *haori*, put on her corridor slippers and walked quietly back to the room. She had to remind herself to remove the slippers before stepping inside.

The dining table and chairs had already been removed, thick *futons* put in their place. Cataline was asleep. A small paper lantern by the *futons* lit Elena's way. Elena removed her robes, put on her pajamas, turned off the lantern and crawled into bed. The room was cold, and the thick, downy comforter came in handy. In a matter of moments, she was fast asleep.

ELENA WOKE UP the next morning before Cataline. She was a little disoriented, but only because she didn't have a grasp of what day of the week it was. The purpose of their trip hovered in the back of her mind. Her meeting with Mr. Inoue was scheduled for mid-morning on Monday, and Elena didn't know what day of the week it was. She had to think back to what had happened during the week. She remembered she initially spoke with Mr. Inoue on Monday night, and gave her notice at work the very next day. That meant they had flown out on Wednesday morning and must have arrived here in Kyoto Thursday night. That made today Friday. Immediately, Elena relaxed. She had three full days before she had to deal with the deposit box situation. The thought alone made Elena smile.

She sat up in bed and looked around. Morning light filtered into the room through the *shōji*, soft and welcoming. She quietly crawled out of bed, careful not to disturb Cataline. She wanted breakfast, and also to confirm the day of the week, just in case. Elena put on her robes and slippers, and stepped out of the room. She found the *nakai-san* making a flower arrangement for the *tokonoma* in the building's main room. Elena took off her slippers and stepped into the room. She bowed to her host and asked her the day of the week. It was Friday. The confirmation was a huge relief. This entire situation was outside of Elena's control, so to know she had three days to simply enjoy herself was immensely satisfying.

After a few quiet moments, the *nakai-san* interrupted Elena's thoughts. "Would you like to have your breakfast now, Vicens-san?" Her tone was as calm and even as the night before, her smile warm. In the daylight, she seemed a little younger.

"Yes, please. If you don't mind, could it be served here on the veranda? My friend is still asleep in the room and I would prefer not to disturb her."

Like most rooms in the inn, the main room had access to the veranda facing the garden. It was a large open room set with various low tables. It was decorated with beautiful Edo period paintings, ink scrolls, a large gilded screen depicting the different seasons and several wooden chests. The room was available to guests throughout their stay, and served as both sitting room and dining room. The veranda around the room was also set with tables and chairs, so that guests could sit closer to the garden.

With a polite nod, the *nakai-san* invited Elena to take a stroll through the garden while her breakfast was prepared. Elena thanked her, bowed and silently made her way across the room toward the garden. Before stepping onto the gravel from the veranda, she put on the wooden *geta* provided for her on the stone step. They felt odd at first, since she hadn't walked on wooden sandals since she was a child, but Elena got used to them pretty quickly.

The morning was cool and crisp. Elena pulled the *haori* tighter around her and began to walk across a pathway made of flat stones. It was peaceful at this hour, silent except for the chirping of birds and hollow clap of the bamboo fountain. The garden was completely enclosed by the inn, shutting out any signs of the modern city. The scene was as perfect as it could get.

Elena walked quietly through the stone pathway, inadvertently reminded of her walk with Ms. Callas's son. She was certain he would have enjoyed the scenery, although she didn't have much of a basis on which to substantiate the thought. She walked a few steps further and came across a stone bench, so she sat down and spent the next several minutes just enjoying the solitude. Soon, guests would be getting up and Elena suspected the inn wouldn't be as peaceful as it was now. She watched quietly as shadows played across the glassy surface of a small pond just a few feet away, fallen maple leaves and flower petals dotting the surface. A few minutes later, the *nakai-san* called her back to the main room. Her breakfast was ready.

Elena was led back to the main room through the inside of the building. This time, she was not alone. Another guest was seated at one of the tables inside the room. They walked past him as the *nakai-san* led Elena to her table on the veranda. He was seated alone, with a newspaper in his hand. It was the *New York Times.* Elena tried not to stare. Seeing someone from the States halfway across the world was always an interesting experience. That person was a total stranger, but the common background gave the misguided feeling that you just ran into an old friend.

Elena's breakfast was laid out for her on the table, course by course. It consisted of miso soup and a bowl of rice accompanied with grilled mackerel, tofu and a variety of pickled foods—eggplant, plum, and daikon radish. She took her seat and began to eat. She made eye contact with the stranger once, and he offered her a smile. He had sky-blue eyes, made brighter by the blue pattern on his *yukata*, long blonde hair and a warm smile. He looked very Central European, and Elena began to consider that perhaps her initial assessment had been shortsighted.

Most tourists here would speak English, even if it were not their first language. It would make sense then that the only English newspaper available at the inn would be an American one. It would either be that or a British one. Her theory was confirmed when the *nakai-san* returned and offered Elena a *New York Times.* Behind the *nakai-san*'s shoulder, the other guest nodded to Elena, almost as if he knew what she had been thinking, and then continued to read his paper.

Halfway through breakfast, Cataline walked into the room. She wasn't as tactful as Elena. She openly stared at the other guest as she was led to the table. "He's kind of cute," Cataline whispered, but her voice carried loudly in the silence of the room. Of course, Cataline didn't care.

"I guess," Elena responded, trying not to look up. She could tell the man was looking in their direction.

Elena and Cataline ate quietly, discussing what they might do for the day in whispers. There was a lot to pick from. Cataline had brought the travel guide with them, and they both leafed through the pages in between bites.

The inn was located in the Gion District, the famous *geisha* quarter in the heart of the ancient capital. Close to the inn, within walking distance, were various sites. There was Nijo Castle, famous for its nightingale floors. Near Nijo Castle was the Imperial Park with several imperial palaces. Across the Kamo River from there, in the Higashiyama area, was Maruyama Park, Kyoto's most famous cherry-blossom viewing site, and Kiyomizu-dera Temple. On the northern edge of Higashiyama was the Philosopher's Walk, a path lined in cherry trees along a canal made famous by a philosophy professor who walked along it for daily meditation, and which ended at the Silver Pavilion. Three other possible sites were outside of walking distance—the Golden Pavilion covered in pure gold leaf, Ryoan-ji Temple with its famous rock garden, and Fushimi Shrine with its avenue of red *torii* gates.

Elena and Cataline decided they would visit the Higashiyama area first, to see Maruyama Park, Kiyomizu-dera Temple, the Philosopher's Walk and the Silver Pavilion. Tomorrow they would go to Nijo Castle and the Imperial Park. On Sunday they would see Ryoan-ji and the Golden Pavilion. They would leave Fushimi Shrine and its avenue of *torii* gates for Monday afternoon, after their meeting at the bank.

After breakfast, they walked east across the Kamo River to Higashiyama. The streets were busy, but not uncomfortable, and the weather was perfect for walking—a fresh spring morning with a light breeze that energized every muscle in Elena's body. She and Cataline spoke sparingly as they enjoyed their walk to Maruyama Park, too absorbed in their strange yet familiar surroundings.

The gardens of Maruyama Park were stunning in spring, their beauty enhanced by the season and crowned by the full bloom of its famous cherry trees. It was the Hanami Matsuri, the *sakura*-viewing festival held every spring—*sakura* meaning "cherry blossom"—and the park was full to the brim with people enjoying the scenery. Tables were set up for picnics beneath the blossom-covered boughs, lanterns strung carefully among the ephemeral blooms. Elena and Cataline had a small snack beneath the trees, and agreed to return that night to see the festival lanterns lit up among the trees. As they continued their walk through the park, they saw the famous weeping cherry tree—the park's centerpiece—and several *maiko*, *geisha* apprentice, posing for photographs. Then they made their way to Kiyomizu-dera Temple.

Kiyomizu-dera—or "Pure Water Temple"—was a sprawling temple complex built on a forested ravine, on the site of the Otowa waterfall. Its most celebrated feature was a large veranda supported by a matrix of wooden pillars, which protruded from the main hall over the treetops. Not a single nail was used in it's, or the main hall's, construction—a feat that was almost impossible to reconcile considering the hall's size and precarious location. Elena and Cataline enjoyed the incredible view of Kyoto from the veranda for almost an hour, before making their way through the temple grounds to drink from the Otowa waterfall, located at the base of the hall.

Otowa-no-taki, or "Sound of Feathers", as the waterfall was called, was divided into three streams that passed through stone channels set within the roof of a portico supported by a stone gate. Visitors passed beneath the roof of the portico with ladles to catch the water, which spilled from the stone channels positioned above their heads into a pond. Drinking from two of the three streams was said to grant health, wisdom and longevity; drinking from all three was considered greedy, and would cause misfortune. While Cataline would normally champion the cause of being daring, they both quietly agreed on taking the safest route.

After drinking from the falls, Elena and Cataline visited the Jishu Shrine, dedicated to Ōkuninushi, a god of love and good matches. On Cataline's insistence, they both attempted to walk between a pair of 'love stones' with their eyes closed; whoever reached the other stone with their eyes closed was said to find true love. Cataline was successful. Elena was not, and ended up with a bruise on her shin for the effort.

On their way out of the temple complex, they stopped at a stall for *dango*, a type of Japanese dumpling made of rice flour. This particular kind was called Hanami Dango, and was traditionally made during the *sakura*-viewing season. It consisted of three skewered dumplings of different colors—pink, white and green. Elena and Cataline washed the *dango* down with green tea before continuing on their way to the Philosopher's Walk.

A little over a mile long, they walked the stone path at a leisurely pace, south to north along the canal, enjoying the view. The path was lined with blooming cherry trees, and it reminded Elena a little of St. Charles Avenue in New Orleans. Of course, this was a walking path and not a street, and the boughs of cherry trees provided a gossamer shade instead of the sprawling branches of towering oak trees. *Sakura* petals floated through the air like pink snow.

They were close to reaching the Silver Pavilion, Ginkaku-ji, at the north end of the walk when Elena noticed a familiar face sitting on a stone bench along their side of the path. It was the other guest they had seen at the inn during breakfast that morning, except now he was dressed in dark jeans and a light colored sweater instead of a *yukata*. His long blonde hair he wore in a ponytail, and he was reading a travel guide. As Elena and Cataline walked past him, he looked up and met Elena's gaze. He was very handsome. She smiled and continued walking.

"Excuse me," the man called out behind them.

Elena and Cataline stopped on the stone path and turned around, just as he closed his travel book and stuffed it into a backpack he was carrying.

"You're the guy from the *ryokan*, aren't you?" Cataline asked, bold as always.

The man looked relieved. "Yes, I'm Alexander. Nice to see friendly faces."

That was simple, Elena thought; two seconds with this guy and she already knew his name, and it was a very nice name. He looked like an Alexander. He was tall and lean, but not what she would call skinny or slender. She could see the lines of well-defined muscle through the light fabric of his sweater. This close up, he wasn't just handsome, he was gorgeous. His features were sharp but still masculine. He had long golden hair and bright cerulean eyes. His smile was warm, and his manner very relaxed. He made Elena feel comfortable instantly, which was not something that happened often, particularly with someone this attractive. He looked older than Elena, but not by much.

"I'm Elena and this is Cataline," Elena answered, motioning to Cataline beside her, who was staring at Alexander unabashedly.

Alexander didn't seem to mind. He offered them both a bright smile and tucked a loose strand of hair behind his ear. "Nice to meet you. What part of the States are you guys from?"

"New Orleans," Cataline answered. She took a cigarette out of her purse and offered him one. Alexander accepted. She lit her cigarette and then handed him the lighter.

"I'm from New York City," he said, lighting his cigarette.

He didn't have a typical New York accent, or feel for that matter, so Elena assumed he wasn't originally from New York. Even so, he had a slight accent and she couldn't place it. His speech was crisp and perfectly enunciated, with a faint staccato rhythm.

Since they were standing in the middle of the path, the three of them moved to the bench Alexander had been sitting on.

"What are you doing in Japan, if you don't mind me asking?" Cataline asked, accepting the lighter in return. She was flirting like crazy, with her beautiful doe eyes and scarlet smile.

Alexander, obviously very used to being admired, was flirting right back. "I'm teaching English for a year, in Okinawa. I'm on break right now, so I decided to finally visit Kyoto. I only have a few months left to teach."

"That sounds like a lot of fun. Have you enjoyed teaching?" Elena had considered doing the same after college, but had decided to go straight to law school instead.

"Yeah, it's been a really nice experience. A good break from what I had been doing before. What about you?"

"We're here on some family business." Cataline responded, and Elena gave her a look.

Cataline didn't understand the concept of privacy, at all, and Elena decided it would be best to change the subject before Alexander could ask any questions. It would only be natural to wonder what family business they could possibly have in Japan. "We were on our way to see the Silver Pavilion," Elena quickly interjected, "would you like to join us, Alexander?" And to her satisfaction, he readily accepted; successfully steering their outing and prior conversations in a completely different direction.

The Silver Pavilion was located amidst moss and sand gardens, nestled between ponds trimmed with elegant bridges, murmuring streams and beautifully pruned trees. Its sand garden was known as the Sea of Silver Sand, said to resemble a silver sea by moonlight. Elena, Cataline and Alexander walked along the meandering paths enjoying the views of the temple, which wasn't actually covered in silver. Even so, it was beautiful. After looking in his travel guide, Alexander explained that the *shogun* who built the structure, originally meant to be a retreat, intended to cover it in silver leaf, in tribute to the golden pavilion built by his grandfather, but the work was never completed because of the Onin War, a civil war in 15th century Japan.

As the three of them walked through the grounds, Elena and Cataline learned a little more about Alexander. He had arrived in Japan almost eight months before through a government-sponsored program. He had applied for the program through the Japanese Embassy in New York, and worked assisting Japanese language teachers in public high school. He really enjoyed his work, and was considering applying for another year. He didn't really go into what he had been doing in New York prior to Japan. Most of the conversation was between him and Cataline; they had a very similar style of interacting with the world, and Elena simply enjoyed watching them.

After the Silver Pavilion, the three of them took a bus back to Maruyama Park to view the cherry-blossoms at night. It was dusk and the park was beautifully lit up, garlanded with white lights and paper lanterns. The centerpiece was the giant illuminated weeping cherry tree, with its enormous branches propped up by giant stilts. They found a grove of *sakura* trees with picnic tables set up beneath their flowered boughs. The small tables were set on top of low wooden platforms covered in red cloth. Sitting cushions were provided along with each table. Elena and Cataline sat down while Alexander went to get food and drinks at one of the food stalls.

"Well he's a nice guy, isn't he?" Cataline observed. She had a contented smile on her face. Beneath the glow of the lights and the pink-white haze of the blossoms, she looked ethereal—like a modern version of a faerie queen.

"Yes, he's very nice. You two seem to be getting along," Elena responded. Her feet hurt from walking, and she was happy to finally be sitting down. For the first time in months, she was relaxed. Being here in Kyoto, especially during Hanami Matsuri, was magical.

"You're being too quiet," Cataline added.

"Cata, please don't start on that again." Elena only used the diminutive when she was really desperate.

"Come on, Ele. He's obviously into you."

"Is that all you think about? And he's not into me." Elena sighed, turning her attention to the table behind Cataline. The area around them was packed with groups of people, friends and families, celebrating the beauty of the blooming trees. Laughter and lively conversation filled the air all around them. "He's just happy to find some people from the States. Traveling alone has to get lonely, I'm sure."

"I'm glad you said it, because I invited him to come sightseeing with us the rest of the weekend."

"You did what?" Elena had to whisper the words because she could see Alexander making his way back toward them with *sake* and some snacks.

Cataline only smiled in response. Alexander set down the *sake*, some *edamame* and dumplings on the table. "Do you guys want anything else? Tea? *Udon* noodles?" he asked, and quickly added, "I saw a *dango* stand."

"Ooooh, Elena loves *dango*," Cataline purred.

Elena wanted to kick her under the table, but it was too low and they were sitting on cushions.

"Would you like some, Elena?" Alexander turned his sky-blue gaze toward hers. He wore his usual easy smile.

Truth be told, Elena was hungry. They hadn't really eaten much all day. "You don't mind, do you?"

"Not at all." In a few seconds, Alexander was up and walking back toward the food stalls.

From the corner of her eye, Elena could see Cataline's knowing smile as she poured herself some *sake*. Elena just shook her head. "Will you please stop playing matchmaker? He's a really nice guy. That's it. Not everyone who travels is looking for love, Cataline."

"That's a load of crap, and you know it. You need to loosen up, Ele. I'm not talking love. I'm talking fun. He's nice, gorgeous, and your age. He's staying at the same inn with us and he's unattached, I checked."

Cataline winked, and then reached into her purse for her cigarettes. "I wonder if smoking is allowed here. Anyway, if you don't jump on it, I certainly will."

"Be my guest." It was all Elena could think of saying to shut her up. It was always lovers with Cataline, and Elena just wasn't the type. She was too busy with her career to worry about that kind of thing. The closest to a romance she'd had in years was a couple of hours in a garden with a man who's name she didn't know, and she'd fallen asleep on him. That wasn't to say Elena wasn't tempted. Alexander was gorgeous and, best of all, she wouldn't see him again after the end of the week, but a fling just wasn't something she had the energy for; not now, not with the reason she was in Japan to begin with. "And please don't smoke here, Cataline. Whether they allow it or not, no one is smoking. They're all enjoying the natural beauty of the scene. Smoke is kind of the opposite of that."

Cataline gave Elena a look and then returned the pack of cigarettes to her purse.

Alexander came back with a large serving of *udon*, three *dango* skewers and a cup of green tea. He handed everyone a set of chopsticks and they all quickly dug in. The food was delicious, and the atmosphere as perfect as it could get. They ate and drank in earnest, enjoying each other's conversation beneath the blossoms.

They didn't get back to the inn until after nine. The three of them had some tea out on the veranda overlooking the garden, then retired to the baths and bed.

THE NEXT MORNING after breakfast, Elena, Cataline and Alexander set out together to Nijo Castle. The castle was a masterpiece of ornate interiors, and famous for its nightingale floors. It consisted of a network of staggered buildings connected by covered wooden walkways. These walkways were constructed in a way that they would squeak, similar to the sound of a bird, when stepped on, warning the palace of intruders. According to Alexander's travel guide, the castle was built by the first *shogun* of the Edo Period, Tokugawa Ieyasu. It was within its elaborate halls that he received the *daimyo*, feudal lords, who came to pay their respects. The reception rooms, all lined in *tatami* mats, were elaborately decorated with embellished ceilings and gilded *fusuma* doors depicting natural landscapes and animal scenes. Elena's favorite was a painting of a heron in a winter landscape, followed closely by that of a flowering cherry tree located in the Kuroshoin chamber of the castle.

After almost three hours of touring the grounds, Elena, Cataline and Alexander ended their tour by walking through the castle's gardens.

On their way to the Imperial Park from Nijo Castle, the three of them stopped at a small restaurant for lunch. They shared a large plate of *sukiyaki*—beef simmered with vegetables, noodles and tofu in a mixture of soy sauce, sugar and *mirin* rice wine—enjoyed a little *sake* with their lunch, and then spent the afternoon strolling through Imperial Park, where the residences of the Imperial family and court had once stood. They returned to the inn in time for the customary spa and an early dinner. That evening, Alexander invited Elena and Cataline to a *Kabuki* play at the Minamiza Theatre in the heart of Gion. The play was *Kanadehon Chūshingura*, the famous tale of the revenge of the Forty-Seven Rōnin who track down their lord's killer, a court official, and exact revenge. The *rōnin*, lordless samurai, then carry the killer's head to their lord's grave, where they all commit ritual suicide, acknowledging that the act of revenge itself was also an offense.

On Sunday, the three of them set out to Ryoan-ji Temple and the Golden Pavilion in northwest Kyoto. They reached Ryoan-ji by bus a little after 11:00 a.m. Elena had wanted to get an earlier start, but Cataline and Alexander had stayed up much later than her the night before, sampling some *sake* Cataline had picked up on the way back from the theatre. Elena had been too tired to keep up, and after about a half an hour she had excused herself and gone to bed. She didn't feel the *fusuma* door open again until several hours later.

"Come on you guys. I've been wanting to come back here for years," Elena called out to the two of them, as she made her way along the path beside Kyoyochi Pond.

Kyoyochi, meaning "mirror-shaped", was a man-made pond at the entrance of the complex constructed more than eight hundred years ago. The complex was much more crowded than Elena had expected. There were tourists everywhere. She began to walk up a set of stairs that led to the main building, and then turned around. She was much further ahead than Alexander and Cataline were, so she waited impatiently until they caught up.

"Cut us a break, Ele," Cataline begged, a little out of breath. She wore her hair up, in a loose knot, and thick shades that hid the evidence of her hangover. The usual bounce in her step was completely gone.

Elena almost felt sorry for her, but not enough to let her off the hook. "It's not my fault you two decided to drink *sake* on the veranda until dawn."

"If you would have stayed like I begged you to," Alexander countered, "you would be just as slow as the rest of us and much more relaxed." He softened his sarcasm with a smile. Unlike Cataline, there wasn't a hint in his appearance that he had been drinking the night before. It was in the gravelly tone of his voice, but otherwise he looked as right as rain; not a shadow around his eyes or hair out of place.

"Come on you two. We just need to get up the stairs to the main building. Then you can sit down in the temple while I look around." Elena continued up the stairs. "Who knows? Maybe you'll find enlightenment staring at the garden."

Ryoan-ji was a Buddhist temple famous for its Zen rock garden. The garden was rectangular in shape and made of white gravel, with moss and fifteen large stones. It was bordered by a frame of river stones in shades of blue and gray, and was surrounded by low clay walls. The meaning of the garden itself was unknown and was up to the interpretation of each visitor. Some saw islands within a sea, others a tigress carrying her cubs across a stream, and then there were those who believed it was an exercise to reach enlightenment. The latter ascribed to the belief that the stones were placed strategically so that when viewed from any angle only fourteen stones could be seen at one time, and only through attaining enlightenment did the fifteenth stone then become visible.

Elena, Cataline and Alexander passed through the entrance into the main building. They made their way to Hojo Abbot's Chamber, the head priest's former residence. It was from there that the garden could be seen. The second it came into view, everything around Elena fell away. The last time she had visited the temple had been with her mother. She could remember in perfect detail how she held her mother's hand as she was led through the chamber toward the garden. Elena could still recall the lilting tone of their hostess' voice, her mother's friend, as she began to tell them the history of the temple. She could still see the detail of the woman's *kimono* in relief against the background of the rock garden. Elena remembered thinking the pink tones in her robe matched the blossoms on the weeping cherry that spilled over the garden's back wall.

Elena sat down on the wooden veranda facing the rock garden, faintly aware that Cataline and Alexander did the same. The area was full of visitors, but Elena was able to zone them out. She lost herself in the lines of the gravel, and the gentle rise of the various stones. The weeping cherry tree she remembered from her childhood was still there, it's blooming branches spilling over the wall in a graceful bow. It softened the garden's otherwise stark aesthetic. Beneath the weeping branches of the cherry tree, a patch of moss rose up from the sea of white gravel with two of the fifteen stones, one jutting out vertically like a mountain peak and another horizontally, reminiscent of a mountain range. Elena stared at this particular island, losing herself in the space between the stones and the branches of the cherry tree.

Out of nowhere, a flutter of butterflies converged in the space. There were at least seven of them in myriad shades of gray and blue, from the palest ash to bright azure. How she could see them with such detail, at this distance, was a mystery to her, but the scene itself felt so profound that she didn't dare question it. Time seemed to stop. As the butterflies danced within the space, their movements slow and deliberate, Elena could see one of them had rich midnight blue wings outlined in brilliant white, its hindwings changing tone in gradient shades from deep to lighter blue with bright orange markings etched out at the bottom corners. Another had a body of glacial blue that bled out to white through its wings, ending in black eyelets along the edges. They danced gracefully in the space between the stones and branches, some alighting between the blossoms and others on the edges of the stones, until only the two remained.

"Cataline, are you seeing that?" Elena whispered, turning to look at Cataline. She and Alexander were looking out at the garden, as lost in the scene as everyone else.

Cataline seemed to pull herself out of the moment, blinking once as she turned her attention toward Elena. "Seeing what, sweetheart?"

"The butterflies between the rocks and the cherry blossoms."

Cataline leaned forward, squinted and shook her head. "I don't see anything, Ele."

"I don't either," murmured Alexander.

"Look closer," Elena insisted and gestured toward the space. The butterflies were gone. "I swear there were at least seven of them, all of them with different shades of blue. I've never seen anything like it."

"Maybe you were daydreaming," suggested Cataline.

"Or maybe you saw between the veil," Alexander added. "Butterflies have very spiritual connotations in Japan—transformation, death and rebirth. Some believe they carry recently departed souls to the other side, others that they represent the deceased themselves. I've even heard stories about them as messenger spirits."

Elena looked between the two, a pout forming on her lips.

"Just take it for what it is," Alexander suggested, and Elena decided to take his advice.

Regardless of it's meaning, it was something she wouldn't soon forget.

They remained at Ryoan-ji for about two hours, walking the grounds after they were finished meditating by the rock garden. They saw the tearoom, which was closed to visitors, and its famous stone water-basin, used for rinsing one's hands and mouth before entering. They viewed the moss garden, the temple bell and the exterior of Buddha Hall. The grounds were filled with beautiful greenery and blossoming trees, from azalea bushes to Japanese magnolia. Along their walk they even spotted a few small stone statues scattered along the grounds.

By the time they walked to Kinkaku-ji, the Golden Pavilion, the three of them were perfectly content. They approached the temple along a tree-lined path, which led them into a garden with a beautiful central pond. The Golden Pavilion stood, resplendent, at the opposite end of the pond. The structure was a three-story building, the top two stories covered in pure gold leaf. It was a magnificent sight. The Zen garden they had just visited was its polar opposite, but no less magnificent. According to Alexander's travel guide, the grounds were built in accordance with descriptions of the Western Paradise of the Buddha Amida, and were meant to illustrate a harmony between heaven and earth.

The three of them walked along the path, which took them by the head priest's former living quarters with its ornate set of *fusuma* doors, and then behind the building through its gardens where they saw several statues with coins strewn across their base, thrown by visitors for luck. The tour ended at the temple's teahouse. Outside of the grounds, they stopped at the tea garden for some *matcha* and sweets. In the souvenir shop, Elena saw the most incredible postcard of the Golden Pavilion after a snowfall, and was surprised to find *it*, and its surrounding garden, was more beautiful in winter than spring. She made a mental note to try to visit again during winter.

Afterward, Elena, Cataline and Alexander took a bus back to Gion. They decided to visit Hanami-koji, a street lined with traditional wooden townhouses now mostly serving as restaurants and *ochaya*, the famous teahouses where Kyoto's *geisha* entertained. They walked along the street, talking and enjoying the scenery. Then they walked a few blocks north to the Shirakawa area, where there was another stone-paved scenic walk along the Shirakawa Canal. The canal, cordoned off by a picturesque bamboo fence, was lined with willow trees and weeping *sakura*, with a row of traditional houses on each side. It was much quieter than Hanami-koji, and Elena found she enjoyed it much more.

They returned to the inn through Pontocho Alley, one of the few *geisha* enclaves in Kyoto. It was a narrow street with a really great atmosphere at night, which reminded Elena of a wood-block painting. It was lit up with traditional lanterns and lined with restaurants, bars, *geisha* houses and *ochaya*. Alexander pointed out a few brothels, and they even caught a glimpse of a *maiko* ducking out of the alley into an *ochaya*.

It was late evening by the time they got back to the inn. The three of them had dinner in the main room, attended by a different *nakai-san* than before. Afterward, they ordered more *sake*, green tea and sweets to have out on the veranda overlooking the garden. As the *nakai-san* served their tea, Elena inquired about reserving one of the larger family baths for herself.

In addition to traditional Japanese communal bathing, most *ryokan* had two types of baths for private use, the *kashikiri* for single private bathing and the *kazukoburo* for family bathing. Elena was interested in the *kazukoburo* even though she would be using it alone. The *nakai-san* informed her there would not be a problem, and Elena made the reservation for an hour away.

"Are you turning in early again, Elena?" Alexander asked as he raised his cup of *sake* to his lips.

They had all changed into their *yukata*, and he seemed exceptionally comfortable in the robes. In these surroundings, he looked timeless. He wore his *haori* loose over his shoulders like a cloak, without using the sleeves. It was a deep navy blue, like the wings of the butterfly Elena had seen that morning, and it made the blue of his eyes look much brighter. His long blonde hair he pulled to the side into a loose braid with stray strands framing his angular face. His effort was flawless, just like the way the *haori* opened across his chest to reveal the white and blue *yukata* beneath.

Alexander noticed her watching him and smiled. Elena prayed she wasn't blushing and quickly busied herself with one of the sweets.

"I'm afraid so, Alexander. I have to be up early for a meeting tomorrow." It was the first time in three days Elena had thought about it. Elena reached for her cup of *sake* and took a sip.

"Oh yeah, I'd forgotten. Cataline told me we wouldn't be going to see the *torii* gates until the afternoon. Are we still on for Fushimi Shrine then?" He sounded genuinely hopeful. Fushimi Shrine was where the avenue of *torii* gates was located.

"Of course we're still going," Cataline interjected, pouring Elena a little more *sake*. Alexander continued to watch her.

"She's right," Elena reassured him, "We're definitely going. You can't come to Kyoto without seeing those gates, and you're going back to Okinawa the day after tomorrow, right?"

"Yes," he confirmed with a smile. "Any plans for the evening tomorrow? I'd like to invite you guys to see the Miyako Odori with me. It's the yearly dance *geisha* put on in Kyoto during the spring. They say it's spectacular. The last show is around 4:50 in the afternoon."

"I think we can make that," Elena said, turning toward Cataline. "We should be done with our meeting by noon, I would assume. What do you think?"

Of course, Cataline was going to do what she could to accommodate Alexander—either for Elena's sake or for her own. Elena made a mental note to ask her later how far her exploits might have gotten her. Alexander certainly was one hell of a story to tell.

"We can meet at Fushimi after the meeting and try to make it back for the last show," Cataline replied. "Do you leave early on Tuesday, Alexander? We can always try to make it to the earliest show."

"I do, but I'll see what I can do if it gets to that." Alexander made sure all of their *sake* cups were full and then raised his. "To unexpected encounters."

They all raised their cups to his and then downed the *sake*.

BY THE TIME an hour passed, they were all a little tipsy. Elena had eaten more sweets than the rest of them, which made things worse. Plus, she was smaller than them also. Alexander and Cataline were statuesque, Elena not so much; she was petite, and that was the best thing she could say about it.

Elena excused herself, to much protestation from the peanut gallery, and then was led by their newest hostess to the family bath. It took Elena a little longer to communicate with this hostess than their last one because she didn't seem to have as good a mastery over her English, but Elena did manage to confirm, before arriving at the bath, that her regular hostess would continue to take care of them for the remainder of their stay. It wasn't that Elena minded the small language barrier, but she had already become accustomed to their usual hostess.

As Elena suspected, the family bath turned out to be much nicer than the single bath. It was a large rectangular pool made of wood that sunk into the floor. It had to be at least 16 feet long by 8 feet wide. Only a raised wooden border kept the water from spilling onto the stone floor. The bath was at the end of a large room against the back wall, which was made of glass sliding doors and opened out into a private garden. It was exactly what Elena needed to push away the creeping worry over tomorrow's meeting.

Elena removed her robes in the changing room, which was the first section she stepped into when entering the bath. It was separated by a partial wall from the main bathing area. Afterward, she stepped into the bathing area and washed herself off at one of the wooden stools, using the showerhead and bucket. Before entering the bath, she took a moment to admire the view of the garden. It was small but breathtaking against the foreground of the bath, as if it had been designed to specifically compliment the bathing experience. It had all the elements of the main inner garden, from the stone lantern to the gravel paths. There was moss, sculpted trees, and a blooming magnolia in one of the corners. The two middle sliding doors were open, bringing the garden into the bath.

Elena stepped into the warm water and instantly her worries faded away. For the moment, for this one instant, everything was perfect. The room was silent but for the sound of water and the soft chime of a garden bell. Elena rested against the front edge of the bath so that she could enjoy the view of the garden. It was like a painting had come to life around her, and the serenity she felt was overwhelming. It was incredible how a culture could revere nature so much that it was integrated, celebrated, in every aspect of their lives. Elena hadn't realized just how empty her life had been since her parents' death, and since leaving Japan, until now.

Elena was so wrapped up in her own thoughts that she didn't hear the other person in the room until they were walking across the stone floor toward the bathing area. The sound of their slippers roused Elena from her thoughts, and she turned around in the bath to find a man standing, half naked, in the room. Elena scrambled for the small towel she had brought with her into the bath.

It was Alexander. He quickly turned away, to allow Elena some modesty.

"Ele, I'm so sorry! I asked for a bath and she brought me here. That new hostess must think we're married or something."

"Married. Are you insane?" Elena felt a little calmer now because his back was toward her. He had a towel wrapped around his hips, thank god, but Elena could plainly see her initial assessment was spot on—the man was fit. Actually, fit was an understatement. He was nothing but lean muscle, not a hint of fat in sight. Through the dim light in the room,

Elena could see the sinewed shape of his back, perfectly defined, each muscle in sharp relief against skin as white as alabaster. All that masculinity was countered by the long blonde hair still bound in a loose braid.

"I'm not insane. You did ask for a family bath, didn't you? She probably thought you meant for us."

"For us? That can't be right." Elena whispered it, and he didn't respond. No wonder the woman had seemed so open to the idea. She wasn't their usual hostess, and there had been a few things lost in translation. "Well this is embarrassing."

"What did you think happened? Did you think I snuck in here or something?" he asked, feigning offense.

"No. I just... I don't know what I thought. I was lost in the scene and then suddenly there you were."

"I made a heck of a lot of noise changing, and I swear I didn't see a thing," Alexander assured her; Elena had been up to her neck in water. "It is a beautiful garden, though, so I can see how you got lost."

"It definitely beats the view in the private bath." Elena looked around her, trying to figure out where she put her towel. "It's a good thing you were wearing your towel. The gods know I never do. I leave everything in the changing room," which was exactly where her towel was.

All of her life, Elena had been awkward with men. Case in point, her most recent rendezvous with her boss' son. And yet here she was, naked in a bath, having a casual conversation with one of the most attractive men she had ever met. Cataline was having more of an influence on her than she realized.

"You believe in more than one god?" Alexander asked.

"What are you talking about?"

"You said '*the gods know*'. So I was curious, do you believe in more than one god?"

That was an extremely odd question to ask, particularly in such an awkward situation. Elena didn't know what to say.

"Do you mind if I join you? I'll keep the towel on, I promise."

That was also unexpected.

"Do you usually ask women you barely know to take baths with you?" Elena finally responded.

"No, not really. If you're asking whether I did with Cataline last night, the answer would also be no. It would just be a pity not to be able to experience this bath. We only have it reserved for another forty-five minutes at most, and, since I don't count as a family, the opportunity probably won't present itself again. There are *ryokan* and *onsen* in Japan that allow mixed bathing. People just wrap towels around themselves to soak. So, what do you say?"

Elena couldn't believe how completely nonchalant he sounded about it, and the fact that she was actually considering it. Two days from now, she'd never see this man again. Might as well enjoy the view while she could. She would draw the line at anything physical, but she didn't see the harm in bathing in the same pool with towels wrapped around themselves.

"Alright," Elena agreed. "I need to grab a towel and you need to wash before stepping in."

Elena didn't even have to give him instructions. The moment she said it, Alexander went back into the changing room while she stepped out of the bath to grab a towel. She let him know once she was back in the bath with the towel wrapped around her. Now she understood why some of the bath towels were thinner than the others; the thin ones were for use in the water. Once she was back in the bath, she turned toward the garden so that he could wash and rinse himself off in private. He didn't say another word until he was finally in the bath.

True to his word, he had a towel wrapped around his waist. "So, do you believe in more than one god?" he asked again.

They were both sitting facing the garden, about three feet apart.

"No one's ever asked me that question before." Elena turned toward him. He was smiling his usual smile, and this time it spread to his eyes. He really was a beautiful man, but Elena couldn't help comparing him to Ms. Callas's son. They were polar opposites, one warm like the summer sun and the other cool like a winter breeze. Truth was, she only had butterflies in her stomach with the cold one. That figured. "I guess my answer is yes, I do believe in more than one god, if I believe in anything at all."

Alexander watched her, weighing her answer. She had qualified it, and he wasn't sure if she did for the sake of simply doing so or because she perhaps didn't really believe in anything at all. "I believe in more than one," he finally said, "I've been in this country too long not to. I had my thoughts on it before, but living here solidified it. There are simply too many forces in nature for there to be only one god."

Elena noticed his tone had grown sharper and his expression somber. This was obviously something he felt strongly about.

"I know from personal experience just how much this country can affect your life. Leaving here when I was a child changed everything for me." Elena didn't realize she had revealed so much until his expression changed again. Suddenly, she had his undivided attention. For the first time since she met him, she felt tense.

"You lived here as a child?" Alexander inched closer.

"I did, but I'd rather not talk about it. It's still very painful for me. This is the first time I've been back since then." Why Elena was saying that much was beyond her. Even though she was tense, he still had a way of making her feel comfortable. There was genuine concern in his eyes.

"It has something to do with your meeting tomorrow, doesn't it?" Alexander's voice was soft as a whisper when he asked the question.

"Yes. Hopefully, I'll get the meeting over with quickly so we can all enjoy a visit to the *torii* gates. I'm guessing I'm going to need a little serenity by the end of the meeting." Elena hated that her voice was shaking. All of her anxiety about why she was in Japan came rushing back.

Alexander inched closer, and she didn't stop him. He finally came to rest shoulder-to-shoulder with her. He reached out and touched her hand, lacing his fingers with hers. They remained silent, looking out into the garden just a few feet away. Elena felt the sting of tears and she closed her eyes. Alexander turned toward her and pressed his lips to the corner of her mouth. They were so warm. Elena didn't dare turn toward him or open her eyes.

"Don't cry, Ele. Everything will be fine tomorrow," he whispered against her cheek. He kissed a tear away, and then slowly pulled back. "Thanks for letting me enjoy the view. Sleep well, and watch out for those butterflies."

Elena didn't open her eyes until she heard him putting his robes back on in the changing room. From the corner of her eye, she caught movement in the garden. When she looked through the open glass sliding doors, she saw a butterfly near the stone lantern. Its body was glacial blue and bled out to white through its wings, ending in black eyelets along the edges.

"Alexander?"

Elena called out to him, but she was already alone in the bath.

CHAPTER SIX

"I THINK I'M GOING CRAZY," Elena whispered to Cataline once they got into the private car the inn arranged for them the next morning.

Elena handed the driver the piece of paper with the address for the bank written in Japanese. Their *nakai-san* had been kind enough to assist with the written translation.

"I'd say," Cataline agreed. "Letting strange men into your bath. You're definitely going crazy."

Elena had told Cataline about the night before as they waited at the inn for the private car to arrive. "No, I meant the butterflies. Alexander is harmless. He was a perfect gentlemen, just like he was with you last night."

The night before, Elena returned from the bath to find Cataline already asleep. Alexander had put her to bed on his way to the bath. The *sake* had rushed to Cataline's head when she got up from the table, and Alexander was kind enough to help her to her room. He didn't leave Cataline's side until he was certain she was safe in bed.

The car began to move, and Elena watched as the scenery changed lazily across the window behind Cataline.

"He's a perfect gentleman… and romantic. He's definitely moved ahead in my scoreboard." Cataline smiled to herself, and then began to dig through her purse. "That other boy is a little too guarded, don't you think? I know a mysterious man is always attractive, but now he just seems a little smug in hindsight." She was talking about Ms. Callas's son.

"Don't you think that's a little unfair, Cataline? Not everyone can be naturally charming." Although, when she thought about it, Elena felt like Ms. Callas's son had been charming, charming and witty. If there was something she appreciated in a man, it was a sharp wit.

"Shit..." Cataline hissed as the car came to a stop. "We're already here?" With a pout worthy of a French actress, she put her pack of cigarettes back into her purse.

Both of them looked around. They hadn't been in the car for more than five minutes. They had gone down two streets, at the most. Even so, their surroundings were decidedly more modern.

The driver got out of the car and came to Cataline's door. He helped Cataline out first, and then Elena. When Elena tried to pay him, he refused. He would not accept a tip either. He pointed to a Western-style red brick building in front of them, and said he would wait for them to conclude their business. Elena and Cataline both bowed, and then turned around to face the building.

"The Museum of Kyoto? This can't be right." Elena stared at the sign in front of the building. They were standing in front of the entrance to the Annex building of the museum.

"Stay here." Cataline said, turned around and walked back toward the waiting car.

While Cataline went to talk to their driver about the address, Elena studied the building. Maybe they were missing something. It was a massive neoclassical structure of red brick and grey stone. It looked like many museum buildings Elena had seen in the United States and all over Western Europe. Two large red flags flanked the main entrance.

"He says this is the address written on the piece of paper," Cataline declared, as she took her place next to Elena again. The frustration was obvious in her voice. She handed Elena the piece of paper with the address. "Do you want to check with someone else?"

"Might as well," Elena said, resigned. This was not the way she wanted to start her morning.

She looked at her watch. They had ten minutes before the meeting was set to start. She decided it would be best to ask someone in the museum, so they made their way up the building's steps to the main door.

They stepped into an impressive main hall with beautifully ornate wooden features. This had definitely been a bank at some point. The hall was a large open room with stone walls painted in white, and neoclassical designs throughout. All the windows were framed in wood. The ceiling was stunning, with an elaborate design made of the same chestnut-colored wood as the window frames. Large diamond-shaped recesses were the centerpiece of the ceiling, inlaid in what looked to Elena like marble in warm shades of beige and green. There were two rows of windows in the hall, the upper ones belonging to a second story carved out by a wooden balustrade that overlooked the hall. The back wall had offices abutting the balustrade.

On the main floor to the left was an ornate wooden divide made up of a row of individually arched open-aired windows, built over a marble base almost three feet high, where Elena imagined each of the bank tellers would have stood to conduct business when the building had functioned as a bank. To their right Elena saw what she thought was a security guard standing close to the entrance. It was this man she approached regarding the address on her piece of paper.

"*Konnichiwa. Eigo o hanasemass-ka?*" Good morning. Do you speak English?

"*Hai.*" Yes. He responded in a clipped tone.

"Would you mind telling me if I have the correct address?" Elena tried to be as courteous as she could in her approach, handing him the piece of paper with a short bow of her head.

The man read the writing on the piece of paper and nodded. "*Hai.*"

"I was supposed to meet someone at a bank and I was given this address," Elena continued. Cataline came to stand beside her.

"Building here," the man motioned to the floor at his feet, "Kyoto branch of Bank of Japan... long, long ago. Museum now."

Elena and Cataline exchanged a look.

Elena looked down at her watch again. It was four minutes to ten. They would be late. She figured she might as well go for broke. "Is there a man who works here by the name of Inoue-san?"

Instantly, the guard's eyes widened. He looked between Elena and Cataline, obviously skeptical.

"You have meeting with Inoue-san?" he asked brusquely.

Elena could have almost kissed the man. She didn't think in a thousand years that they had the right place. "Yes. If you don't mind, could you let him know Elena Vicens is here? We're a little late for our meeting."

The man gave a curt nod and quickly disappeared.

"Well, this is certainly interesting," Elena whispered to Cataline as they waited for the guard to come back.

"You can say that again," Cataline replied with a huff. "You would think Mr. Inoue would have remembered to mention that the meeting was taking place at a museum that used to be the bank. And here I thought this wouldn't take all day." Cataline was edgy, and it was probably because she hadn't managed to have a cigarette all morning.

"Maybe we'll get lucky and the deposit boxes are nearby," Elena responded.

"Doubt it. Everything here in Japan is riddled in decorum and tradition. That's synonymous with slow."

The guard returned just as Cataline said it. He gave her a disapproving stare, and then turned his attention to Elena. "Follow me, please."

The guard led them through the hall toward the back of the building. They entered an open-sided covered walkway that led to an outside building. In front of the outside building, to the right of the walkway, was a wooden deck with cafe tables. The guard led them past the tables to the left of the outside building, where there was a set of cement steps against the side of the structure. The steps led downward. The guard began to walk down the steps without looking back.

Elena and Cataline stared at each other on the landing, reluctant to follow the guard.

"Excuse me," Elena called out after him, looking again at the scene of the deck and cafe, now in front of them and to their left. Everything seemed normal. The area was full of museum visitors, and no one seemed to be paying them any attention.

"Follow me, yes?" The guard's voice drifted up from the staircase below.

"What's it going to be, hon?" Cataline asked Elena, an irritated expression on her face. "We came this far. I don't see the point in worrying about it now."

Elena sighed. She looked down the staircase. There were small lights along the way, but the guard was past the point where Elena could see him. "Damn it," she hissed and then began her descent down the stairs.

The guard was waiting for them on the first landing. He smiled, bowed and motioned for them to continue following him. Another small set of steps led them to an underground walkway. Elena imagined they were beneath the open-aired walkway above. They were heading back in the direction of the main building, but underground. Cataline came up beside Elena and took her hand.

After a few minutes, the corridor ended in an ornate wooden divide identical to the one in the hall upstairs. This one, however, was a much smaller version spanning the width of the corridor. It was made up of five individually arched windows above a marble base. At the end of the divide, on the right-hand side, was a door made of glass where the last window should have been. Elena studied the door, but couldn't see any handle or hinges. As she looked closer, she saw it came directly out of the wall on the right.

The guard stood at the window to the left of the door, speaking to someone on the opposite end of the divide. Between them, seamlessly incorporated into the design of the divide, was a sheet of glass. The same was true with the other windows. On the other side of the glass was the remaining area of the corridor that worked as a small office, and then a set of massive wooden doors on the back wall. The doors were reinforced with metal and adorned in a coffered design with wooden latticework on the top panels.

Elena and Cataline stood silent, several feet away, waiting. After another minute of fervent whispers, the guard walked back toward them.

"Inoue-san here in few minutes. You wait." He bowed deeply and then continued on his way back up the corridor.

"What on earth do you think is going on?" Cataline whispered to Elena.

She was being uncharacteristically cautious, and Elena was thankful for it.

"I've no idea. I can't imagine mom going through all this trouble." Elena had been anxious since the night before, but now her anxiety turned to panic. Something about this seemed completely far-fetched.

The glass door opened suddenly, and Elena looked up to find a man dressed in a black *kimono* stepping over the threshold. He had long, salt and pepper hair down to the middle of his back, which he wore in a low ponytail at the nape of his neck. As he approached, Elena studied him further. He wore a white inner robe that peeked out from behind the collar of his *kimono*. His *obi*, or *kimono* sash, was of the same color. Most striking of all was the emerald green *haori* he wore over his shoulders. Like Alexander the evening before, he did not use the coat's sleeves. The front panels of the *haori* on each side had the design of a white heron in partial flight woven into the fabric. The design carried into the lower edges of the *haori's* sleeves.

The man came to stand about two feet away from Elena, and bowed.

"*Konnichiwa, Vicens-san. Hajimemashite. Watashi wa Inoue Takeo desu. Dōzo yoroshiku.*" Good morning, Ms. Vicens. How do you do? I am Inoue Takeo. Pleased to meet you.

The rhythm of his voice was just as Elena remembered it, and his expression matched it perfectly—restrained but warm.

Elena bowed in return.

"Good morning, Inoue-san. It's a pleasure to finally meet you. I'm sorry we're late. We got a little lost, to say the least." Elena smiled and then gestured toward Cataline. "This is my traveling companion, Cataline Ferrá."

Cataline bowed, and so did Mr. Inoue. Introductions were always a lengthy affair in Japan. After the initial pleasantries, Mr. Inoue led them through the glass door and across the small office to the wooden doors on the back wall. They were even more impressive up close.

"Please allow me to apologize again, Vicens-san, for not being more clear regarding our meeting place," Mr. Inoue said in a soft voice. "Sometimes it is difficult for me to articulate everything in English. I hope it was not too much of an inconvenience."

"No, not at all. It was an unexpected adventure." Elena smiled warmly, watching as Mr. Inoue took hold of the massive metal ring to open the door.

"The men from the Abe Firm, the firm your mother named as her agents, should arrive shortly," he said as he opened the door. "I've done as much as I can to make this as quick and painless as possible. Please follow me."

The door was slow to open, and at first Elena had to strain to see inside. They stepped into a large cavernous room, roughly the same size as the hall upstairs. In fact, Elena was certain this was directly beneath the hall. The room was lit by antique light fixtures that dropped from various large diamond shapes on the ornate ceiling, their design identical to the ones in the hall above. There were no windows in the room, and the walls rose two stories high.

Every inch of wall up to three feet below the ceiling was covered in wooden drawers. It looked like a room made entirely out of an apothecary or medicine chest. Rows upon rows of wooden drawers, each one about twelve inches wide by twelve inches high, spread out along the length of each wall creating an intricate but seamless grid. The wooden drawers were the same chestnut color as the ceiling above, and the grid itself a darker shade. Each drawer had its own metal handle, and beneath it a keyhole.

The first five feet of floor in the room, and the wall behind them with the entrance door, were lined in stone, after which the floor then sunk into the ground about two feet, where the grid of drawers began. A set of small steps allowed access to the sunken area, which was covered in wooden floorboards the same dark color as the wood of the grid.

Elena had never seen anything like it in her life. It was extraordinary, and all she and Cataline could do was stare at their surroundings in stunned silence.

Mr. Inoue allowed them to absorb their surroundings in relative peace. He quietly made his way to the center of the sunken floor. Four large wooden tables stood spread out at equal distances, one near each corner. Each table had two wooden *andon*, Japanese lamps made of rice paper stretched over a wooden frame. They were in the shape of a vertical box placed on an ornate wooden stand. Each was very delicate, and Elena guessed they had to be at least one hundred years old. Oil provided the fuel for the lamp, which effused a warm, flickering glow.

"Vicens-san, if you please." Mr. Inoue's voice carried over the silence. He motioned them toward one of the tables, which had several documents laid out carefully on its surface.

Cataline took hold of Elena's hand, and they slowly made their way across the room. She leaned closely against Elena as they walked. "This doesn't exactly seem very state of the art, does it?" Cataline whispered in her ear, and Elena elbowed her very lightly.

They took their seats at the table, as Mr. Inoue gestured to the various documents.

"Please feel free to look at the documentation. Once the gentlemen arrive, they will ask for proof of your identity and when they are satisfied they will provide you with the key. Once you have the key, I will show you the drawer and step outside." He explained the process very slowly, so that he was certain she understood.

"Inoue-san, I do not mean to offend, but what exactly is this room? I had imagined a very different kind of deposit box. Not to mention the location is very surprising." Elena tried to phrase her question as least offensive as possible.

"That is a very reasonable question," Mr. Inoue assured her, and then took the seat directly across from hers on the table. He made sure to address both she and Cataline as he spoke. "This is the original depository of the bank. This building was built in the early 20th century as the Kyoto branch of our bank. Even though the main building now houses a museum, the bank continues to use this depository for its most... important clients."

"Important?" Cataline interjected.

"*Hai.*" While short, his response was not meant to be abrupt. It was simply a statement of the fact.

Elena looked around, trying to reconcile his statement with what she was seeing. The room was extraordinarily beautiful, but it seemed a bit antiquated for today's security standards.

"I assure you, everything in this room is quite safe." Mr. Inoue seemed to instinctively guess Elena's observation. "Your mother was quite convinced of it when she leased her box."

His words came as a surprise, and it took Elena a moment to articulate her thoughts. Cataline reached out and took her hand.

"You knew my mother, Inoue-san?" Elena asked him politely.

"*Hai.* I helped her select the box myself. You look a lot like her."

Elena was stunned to silence. She had never heard those words from anyone other than Cataline. She wanted to respond, but words failed her. She felt the sting of tears in her eyes, but blinked them away.

"I assure you, Vicens-san," Mr. Inoue continued, "the fact that your inheritance is still safe within these walls after more than nineteen years is not only a testament to our distinguished reputation, but also to your mother's choice in entrusting us with something so precious. This room was built for specifically this purpose. Each drawer protects something precious, something priceless to each owner. It is not a room accessible or even known to the general public. I assure you that it is safer here than in any vault in any bank in Japan today."

He could have said "in the world," but he didn't have to. There was something in his demeanor when he spoke that told Elena this man did not speak in jest. In fact, she was almost certain there was a point she was missing; a fact or variable she wasn't privy to.

"Thank you, Inoue-san," Elena finally responded.

They were silent for another few minutes, as Elena took the time to look through the documents on the table. There were only a few, mostly the rental documents signed by her mother, but she still managed to get a paper cut. It was shallow, so she just sucked on it to make the bleeding stop. Mr. Inoue was kind enough to offer a piece of cloth, but Elena declined it. It wasn't necessary.

Within the documents, Elena saw a rental agreement, the proof of insurance previously discussed, and a typewritten document with detailed instructions regarding the handling of the contents of Isabella's box in the event of her death. All documents bared Isabella's signature. None of them declared in any form the exact nature of the contents of her box, but Elena saw very clearly the value Isabella ascribed to it in the proof of insurance. Seeing the value in paper was unnerving.

As Elena was finishing her review of the documents, the doors to the room opened with a weighted groan. Two men dressed in suits stepped into the room. They were identical twins, and looked like something out of one of Elena's anime series. They were young, at least a good four years younger than Elena. They were as distinctly modern as Mr. Inoue was traditional. They had medium-length hair, cropped and razor-cut to perfection. One had black hair, and the other silver. They walked with long, deliberate steps toward the table.

Mr. Inoue immediately stood from his seat and intercepted them. A heated conversation, made entirely in whispers, followed. Elena couldn't understand what they were saying, but she could tell from Mr. Inoue's manner that he was not pleased. After several minutes, the fervent whispers stopped and the twins stepped around Mr. Inoue.

Elena met their gazes as they approached. They were very fine featured, and had a playful demeanor. Where Mr. Inoue was reserved, they were markedly effusive. Their bow, at arriving at the table, was much more casual than what Elena had become accustomed to. The silver-haired one held a wooden box in his hands. Without a word, they took the two remaining seats at the table, and left Mr. Inoue standing behind them.

"I'm Akemi," the silver-haired one said with a smile.

"And I'm Rinji," concluded the black-haired one.

Akemi set the wooden box on the center of the table. He rested his left hand over it as he spoke, his long spidery fingers moving absently over the surface. Through his fingers, Elena noticed a white piece of paper with *kanji*, Japanese writing, written on it in black ink. It was placed over the seam in the front where the box closed.

"Identification please," Akemi requested, and Rinji extended an opened hand across the table.

Elena looked up at Mr. Inoue, who gave a short nod to indicate his approval. Then she reached into her purse and retrieved her passport and two pieces of paper. She placed them all in Rinji's open hand.

"*Arigatō*," they both said at the same time, and then began to look over the documents.

As requested, Elena brought copies of her passport and birth certificate for them to keep.

Each twin looked up to scrutinize her in staggered intervals. The synchronized effect was comical, and Elena had to feign a cough and cover her mouth to hide her grin. After a few minutes, they seemed satisfied.

"Okay, you pass inspection," teased Akemi, and lifted his hand from the box.

Rinji slipped the copies inside his blazer, and handed Elena her passport in return.

"That's it?" Cataline asked, a cynical edge to her voice.

Elena was asking herself the same question. The whole affair seemed too easy.

"Don't worry. The box won't open if it's not the right owner," Akemi said playfully and winked.

Elena and Cataline exchanged a skeptical glance. Mr. Inoue seemed resigned.

Finally, Elena reached for the box. She pulled it toward her with her left hand. It was a plain wooden box, made of the same or similar wood as the drawers lining the walls of the room. It had no clasp or hasp holding it shut. It sealed flush, and only the paper seal secured it.

Elena ran her fingers along the seam. She looked between the three men, surprised that they were staring at her hands so intently. She felt Cataline's hand brush her shoulder, and then she broke the seal. All of the excitement must have gotten to her head, because Elena could have sworn a draft swept around them the minute she did.

Elena didn't draw the moment out any longer than necessary. With her right hand holding the box firm, she opened the lid with her left. Inside, was a key. It wasn't particularly ornate. It was an old metal key about three inches long, nothing exceptional about it.

It was a little anti-climactic, Elena thought.

The twins were already getting up. The dark-haired one, Rinji, was having another firmly whispered conversation with Mr. Inoue.

The silver-haired one, Akemi, turned his attention to Elena. "Great doing business with you, Ms. Vicens. Hope to do it again soon. Bye-bye." He winked, waved and then turned on his heel. Elena wasn't sure how he managed not to smack into the table or his chair, his movements were so disjointed. Akemi caught his twin brother's hand by the wrist. They both nodded simultaneously to Mr. Inoue in mid sentence and then saw themselves out.

"I'm so sorry about that, Vicens-san," Mr. Inoue said in an apologetic tone. "I had been sure the Abe Firm would have sent someone a little older than the twins."

"You don't need to apologize for them, Mr. Inoue. Please don't worry yourself over it." Elena offered the man a warm smile, hoping it would appease his distress.

"*Arigatō*, Vicens-san. Now if you would, please follow me."

Elena followed him to the room's back wall. He approached it from the center of the room. When he was less than five feet away from it, he turned right. He walked in a ninety-degree angle almost to the end of the wall. Seven columns of drawers before the end, he stopped.

Elena realized there were no numbers on the drawers. There were no identifying marks at all.

"Inoue-san, how do you know which box it is?"

"I have them memorized."

The logistics of that was staggering. Elena took the man's measure again, searching for that variable she was missing in his eyes.

"How on earth do you identify it in the rental agreement then?" A detail only a lawyer would concern herself with.

"There is a corresponding seal on the back of each drawer," Mr. Inoue offered with a smile. "We keep a single written legend of the grid safely guarded on the premises." Mr. Inoue turned his attention to the floor a moment, and then bowed softly. "Please wait here," he whispered.

He turned toward the grid of drawers on the right-hand wall. He made his way across the floor to the last column of drawers on the left side of the right wall. He removed a key from the folds of his *kimono* and brought it to the drawer slightly above his eye level. He placed the key in the keyhole and unlocked the drawer. When he pulled on the handle, the drawer didn't slide out. Instead, the drawer's facade, and that of the one beneath it, opened out as a single door, like a wooden locker. Behind it was some kind of panel. Mr. Inoue pressed something on the panel. Immediately, Elena heard the sound of some kind of mechanism. It sounded more like the rustle of leaves than the cold sound of modern technology. From the right wall, several feet above where Mr. Inoue was standing, a single slab of wood, approximately two feet in width, began to extend outward.

"Hydraulics," Mr. Inoue explained as he returned to Elena's side.

Elena took a step toward the grid of drawers on the right wall. The piece of wood continued to extend slowly out of the grid on the right towards Elena, moving on a horizontal plane. It moved flush along the face of the grid of drawers on the back wall, creating a shelf along a row of drawers. Some kind of rail on that particular row of drawers had to be holding the shelf firm, but it wasn't visible to the naked eye.

Elena came to stand a few feet away from the source of the moving wood on the right wall. From there, she could see the wood extending forward was actually the bottom piece of the grid for the first two drawers from the left, sixteenth row up from the ground. This created a floating shelf for the sixteenth row of the grid on the back wall. The piece of wood continued moving along the face of the back wall until it came to a slow stop at the middle of the grid.

Mr. Inoue, who stood about five feet away from the grid on the back wall, pressed his foot down on a wooden floorboard in line with the seventh column of drawers from the right. Elena would have missed the gesture if she hadn't caught the movement of his *kimono* from the corner of her eye. The board, which was about six inches wide by three feet long, popped up from the floor. Mr. Inoue leaned forward, wrapped his hands around the risen floorboard and pulled out a wooden ladder from beneath the floor. The top lip of the ladder was the floorboard. He eased the ladder upward until it reached the height of the floating shelf. The ladder was the exact height of the shelf. With careful precision, Mr. Inoue maneuvered the ladder to the open end of the shelf, to his left, where it hooked into a groove Elena couldn't see. Mr. Inoue then rolled the ladder from the center of the grid to the seventh column from the right. He then turned to face Elena.

"Your key please," Mr. Inoue requested.

Elena stared at him, speechless. There were so many things she wanted to ask, was curious about, but she didn't know where to start. How did he reach the drawers above the sixteenth row, for instance, if he only had that one ladder? Were there other ladders of various heights? What about the floating shelf that had extended? Elena imagined there had to be others throughout the room, but she couldn't imagine how the mechanism actually worked. Were they staggered at intervals in each wall? If so, what were the intervals? And if he needed to reach the drawers on the side walls, where did those floating shelves extend from? All of these questions would have to wait.

Behind Mr. Inoue, Cataline rose from the table with the wooden box in her hands. She met Elena's gaze. The gravity of her expression sobered Elena's curiosity. Elena took a step forward, and met Cataline at Mr. Inoue's side. Cataline offered him the wooden box, but he wouldn't take it.

"It must come from you," he whispered to Elena. She was too dazed to question it. If she had been reminded of anything during this trip, it was the Japanese preoccupation with ritual.

Elena took the box from Cataline's hand and retrieved the key. She then placed it in Mr. Inoue's open hand. With a slight nod, he turned around and began to climb the ladder. He reached the shelf on the sixteenth row. Instead of opening the seventh drawer from the right on that particular row, he reached up to the next row, the seventeenth from the bottom up, and placed the key in the seventh drawer from the right. Mr. Inoue then began to make his way back down the ladder without anything in his hands. Elena just stared at the drawer with its inserted key.

Back wall, seventh drawer from the right, seventeenth row up from the bottom. This was what they had flown halfway across the world for.

"I hope you are not afraid of heights," Mr. Inoue whispered to Elena with a smile when he reached the bottom step. "I will take my leave now. Please knock on the door when you are ready to come out." With a gentle bow, he made his way out of the room.

The doors closed, sealing them in silence. Elena and Cataline just stared at each other, suddenly taken aback by the moment.

Cataline was kind enough to break the silence first. "No point in hesitating, sweetie. March yourself up that ladder and get that box. The quicker we get this over with, the sooner you can go to the shrine with Alexander."

"What?" Elena's voice sounded hoarse in the deafening silence. "Me? What happened to all of us going?"

"A bath happened." Cataline stepped closer, and took Elena's hand in hers. "He likes you Ele, and you should enjoy his company while you can. I saw those gates with your mother decades ago. I don't mind not seeing them today so that you can spend some much deserved alone time with a gorgeous guy. Now get your butt up that ladder."

Elena didn't know what to say. Instead, she pulled Cataline closer and into a tight hug. She wrapped her arms around Cataline's neck and held on to her for dear life. "I love you," she whispered into Cataline's ear.

"I love you too, sweetie," Cataline cooed, her hands smoothing down the length of Elena's back.

Elena buried her face against Cataline's throat. "Thanks for coming with me... for taking care of me my whole life." She struggled against the desire to cry.

"You know you don't need to thank me. I'm happy I can be here for this. Now go on, get on that ladder." Cataline pulled away gently, and caught Elena's face in her hands. She kissed both of Elena's cheeks, then turned her around and urged her forward.

Elena hesitated for a second. She called up the memory of her mother's face and when she finally had it clear in her mind, she stepped forward.

The ladder was surprisingly sturdy. Elena made her way carefully up each step. She reached the floating shelf and reached up to turn the key. To Elena's surprise, it gave easily. The drawer popped out a few inches over the grid. She took it in both her hands and gently pulled until it was free completely.

Elena set the drawer down on the floating shelf. She held onto the ladder and studied the drawer carefully. It was two feet long and closed at the top like a box. The drawer's lid closed flush with a seal placed vertically along the side seam. The seal was similar to the one she broke to retrieve her key, white paper with *kanji* written on it. This *kanji*, however, was written in crimson ink.

Elena breathed deeply and took the drawer in her hands. Slowly, she made her way back down the ladder. Cataline moved to the foot of the ladder and took the drawer in her hands as Elena climbed off. Then they both silently made their way to the table, where Cataline set down the drawer.

"I wonder how you open it," Cataline murmured.

"I have no clue. I guess I have to break the seal, like I did with the other one."

They both took their seats on the table, facing the entrance door. Elena brushed her fingers along the seal. She pulled the drawer closer to her, and then broke the seal with her nail.

"What is that?" Cataline whispered, looking around. "That's the second time I feel a draft in here."

Elena felt it too, but she didn't want to acknowledge it. She needed to focus on the drawer. Everything else she would think about later, when they were back at the inn.

She closed her eyes. The sound of her heartbeat was deafening. She was so nervous her hands were shaking. Elena turned the front of the drawer toward her and looked at the key. While on the ladder, she had turned the key clockwise, but it had stopped a quarter of the way to three o'clock. That's when the drawer popped outward. If she pushed the key further now, perhaps the lid would open. Elena didn't hesitate. She reached for the key and turned it. Again, it gave easily. This time it turned the full ninety degrees. Elena heard the sound of some kind of mechanism inside of the box. When she touched the lid again, it was loose. Elena felt around for a groove to lift the lid. It was on the back panel of the drawer. In a few seconds, the lid was off.

Inside, the drawer was as plain as it was on the outside, with the exception of a *kamon* emblem carved into the back panel. The *kamon* was in the shape of a roundel or disc encircling a symbol. In Japan, *kamon* were used as emblems to identify a family or clan. Elena imagined this was the identifying mark Mr. Inoue had referred to. Because of the

contents of the drawer, she couldn't decipher the symbol of this particular *kamon*.

Elena removed the contents. It was some kind of package
wrapped in silk crepe. There was something familiar about the fabric, but
she couldn't place it. There was too much going on in her head. Everything culminated in this moment, and the weight of it was overwhelming.
She needed to focus her thoughts on one thing at a time, so she decided
to focus on the *kamon* first. Instead of unwrapping the package, Elena
reached for an *andon* lamp. She grabbed the one closest to her and pulled
it toward the drawer.

"What are you doing, Ele?" Cataline whispered, looking around
self-consciously, like she had just spoken out loud in the middle of
Sunday mass.

"Taking my time and doing this my way." Elena offered her a
smile. She lifted the lamp by its handle, to get better light. "I want to
savor this, so might as well take it slow."

Cataline didn't respond. She just inched closer to Elena's
shoulder.

The light of the lamp illuminated the inside of the drawer and
brought the *kamon* into relief. It was the abstract figure of a butterfly.
Elena was certain the *kamon* had been carved centuries ago, and yet the
symbol looked almost modern in its design, curiously Art Deco. A
perching swallowtail butterfly was carved masterfully into the wood, its
forewings beautifully accented with curving lines and eyelets at the tips.
Its hindwings stretched out gracefully into the characteristic forked
extensions. Even its antennae and proboscis were represented with
delicate care.

"Another butterfly," came Cataline's hushed voice.

Elena couldn't form words. What were the percentages that her
mother had randomly picked a drawer with the *kamon* of a butterfly?
Elena didn't believe in random occurrences. Everything in life had a
purpose. She might not understand what that purpose was, but she was
certain there was one. It was not a notion as cliché as fate or destiny; it
was more the idea that life was an intricate web of connections people
couldn't see. Behind the scenes was a troupe of stagehands guiding the
production in the direction it needed to go. How one got from point A to
point B wasn't the issue, as long as the journey was made.

Elena set the *andon* lamp back down on the table. She couldn't
understand the significance of the butterfly, so she kept silent on the
subject. She reached for the package of wrapped silk and slowly began to
unfurl the fabric. As she did, strings of memory began to weave them-

selves together in her mind. The fabric was familiar—its weight, its delicate texture. Elena sobbed when the length of it was freed completely. It was her mother's *kimono*. Elena clutched it to her chest, shutting her eyes tightly as the emotion overtook her.

The *kimono* still smelled like Isabella, a delicate floral scent of hydrangea and gardenias. Elena recalled vividly in her mind the morning her mother had received the *kimono* as a gift. They had been playing in the garden when someone had arrived at the door. Because Elena's father was mostly always at work, he tried to make up for his absence with gifts. It was a game they played, as if he were still wooing her mother. That day, the gift had been a *kimono*. It wasn't an overtly formal one, but it lacked nothing in beauty and elegance. The inner robe was ivory hued, the outer a delicate crepe silk in a radiant midnight blue. Along the bottom hem of the front and back of the *kimono* was a woven and stenciled design. On the right side, butterflies in flight rose from an unseen horizon and reached across the bottom edge of the *kimono's* long sleeve. On the left, cascading branches of weeping *sakura* danced in the wind.

"There is no such thing as coincidence," Elena cried softly, her eyes wide as she lifted her gaze to Cataline.

Slowly, Cataline reached for her, her fingers warm as they pressed gently against Elena's wrist. "That is not the only treasure in that drawer, Elena." Cataline's voice was as gentle as a spring breeze. Slowly, she guided Elena's attention to the item her mother's *kimono* had been protecting, which had somehow ended up on the table.

The item was a beautiful dark wooden box with inlaid wood details. It had brass hinges, corners and hasp, and a beautiful gold motif painted on the surface of the lid. The left side of the lid showed three leopards at play among a cluster of bamboo trees, and the right side the branches of a blooming *sakura* against a backdrop of a three-pooled waterfall blanketed in snow. Perched between the blossoms on one of the branches was a butterfly, on the ground beneath them a giant heron.

Elena opened the box to find a necklace inside protected by a lining of black silk.

The necklace was magnificent. It was a circlet made of large emerald stones encased in a bright metal, like platinum or white gold but seemingly more delicate in quality. Any substantial metal surface was carved with figures that looked distinctly Greek. The circlet ended in two serpent heads at each end, like a torc. Where a torc would be open-ended, this necklace held an eagle in mid-flight, its wings positioned as if it were cutting through the air. It sat upright, enclosed by the open jaws of the two serpents. Each of the wings were divided into rows resembling long feathers, each one inlaid interchangeably in moonstone, lapis lazuli, green chrysoprase and red carnelian.

"Holy shit." Elena wasn't the kind of woman to curse too often, but it seemed appropriate at this moment in time. She stared at the necklace, reached for it and then stopped herself halfway there.

"Why are you stopping, Ele?" Cataline was obviously excited. Her voice was shaking, and her fingers bit into Elena's shoulder as she leaned even closer. "Go ahead and take it out. My god, it looks like a crown jewel."

"I... you take it out, Cataline. I'm too scared to even touch it."

Cataline was silent for a long moment, weighing something in her mind, and then nodded slowly. She straightened herself up on the chair and reached across Elena to the box. Elena watched in quiet amazement as Cataline slipped her long, delicate fingers beneath the necklace and gently pulled it out.

They gave a collective sigh as Cataline brought it closer.

"Turn around Ele."

"Why?"

"Why else, silly? To put it on you."

"Can I... do that?"

"Elena, it's your necklace. You can do with it whatever you want."

"You've never seen this necklace before, Cataline?"

"No. Your mother never showed it to me. It must have been one of your father's gifts. Although I have no clue how on earth he came across something this exquisite."

Elena turned to the left in her chair and faced the side wall of drawers, her back toward Cataline. She lifted her hair with her hands and held as much of it as she could against the crown of her head. The metal felt cold against Elena's skin as Cataline brought the circlet around her neck.

Once Cataline fastened the necklace in place, Elena brushed her fingers against the emeralds that sat against her collarbone. She looked down at the serpents and the eagle. Cataline was right, the necklace looked like some kind of crown jewel fit for royalty. It was unlike anything Elena had ever seen her mother wear.

"There is no way I'm taking this back to the inn." Always practical, Elena's mind was already ten steps ahead of them.

"I hadn't even considered that," Cataline confessed. "In all honesty, I thought this was going to be some kind of bond or financial certificate. Definitely not this."

Elena was quiet for a long time. While she considered a plan of action, Cataline preoccupied herself with admiring Isabella's necklace. Finally, after several minutes, Elena stood up.

"Can you help me take it off? I'll go knock on that door while you put it back in its box."

Cataline did as Elena instructed. She pushed herself out of the chair and stood behind Elena. She removed the necklace and gingerly walked back toward the table. Elena moved across the room and knocked twice on the door, and then she returned to the table. Cataline was just closing the lid of the box when Mr. Inoue stepped back into the room and bowed.

"May I be of some assistance or are you ready to take your leave?" he asked. He didn't say a thing about the necklace.

"Mr. Inoue, is there any way the necklace can remain in your vault?"

"I am sure that can be arranged, Vicens-san. Of course, a new contract must be entered into so that the deposit box and its contents are properly in your name."

It was as Elena suspected. For a monthly fee, she could sign her own contract and have the necklace remain safe.

"You won't be taking it back to the States?" Cataline asked.

Elena shook her head. "I can't. I didn't come prepared for this. What if something happens to it on our way back? I'd rather it stay here, where it's been safe for almost two decades."

"Don't you think perhaps it'll be better in a bank closer to home?" Cataline pressed further. Mr. Inoue did not join in their discussion.

"Honestly, no. Not for now, at least," Elena whispered. "I need to figure this out, research what the best options are, but for now this vault is our best solution. Something tells me that in the end, even after all my research, this is still going to be the best bet."

Cataline nodded and didn't say another word. Mr. Inoue then broke his silence.

"If I may be so bold, Vicens-san, your mother's necklace will be in no safer hands than ours. If it will appease your concerns, our bank is currently in the process of opening a second vault of the same nature as this one in New York City. It will be run by a handpicked staff that I will select myself. It should be ready within the year. I would be happy to transfer the drawer myself."

Elena and Cataline exchanged a look. Again, Elena felt like she was missing some of the facts here. Even so, Mr. Inoue's news offered the perfect solution. "That would be terrific. What documents do I need to sign?"

They were not many. In less than a half hour, Mr. Inoue had a rental agreement prepared in English for Elena to sign. She looked over the documents, not surprised when she ended up with another paper cut, this one more vicious then the last. In Elena's line of work, paper cuts were a daily hazard. This time, Elena accepted the piece of clean cloth Mr. Inoue retrieved from his *kimono*. She wrapped the cloth around the cut and put pressure on it for a few minutes, until it stopped bleeding.

All that was left now was to sign the documents. On his way out to retrieve a pen, Mr. Inoue took the soiled cloth with him to discard. Several minutes later he returned with a black lacquered tray in his hands. In the tray were an inkpot, a fine-tipped bamboo brush and a new seal with *kanji* written in crimson ink. Elena signed the documents, and Mr. Inoue instructed her on how to replace the seal once the necklace and its box were placed back into the drawer. Elena decided to keep her mother's *kimono*. She returned the drawer to its proper place on the grid, and then watched in awe as the ladder and floating shelf were returned to their respective hiding places. The key to the drawer Elena kept for herself.

"I don't know how to thank you, Mr. Inoue," Elena said to him with a courteous bow. Cataline was standing beside her, Isabella's *kimono* in her arms.

"No need to thank me, Vicens-san," Mr. Inoue said as he returned her bow. "I was happy to fulfill your mother's last request, and I look forward now to working with you. I should be able to get a new value on the necklace soon and provide you with a new insurance policy. The Abe Firm has been kind enough to provide me with a prior appraisal of the necklace. It should all be completed within the month. The finances I will work out directly with the bank that manages your Trust." Mr. Inoue reached into his *kimono* and retrieved a small business card. He handed it to Elena. "Abe Akemi asked me to give this to you, in the event you need anything further."

The business card, which provided only an email address, also included the following:

ABE NO AKEMI
For all of your onmyōdō needs.

Elena found it curious, but there was only so much novelty she could take in one day. She slipped the card into her purse, and then they all said their goodbyes.

Several minutes later, Elena and Cataline were once again standing on the sidewalk outside of the entrance to the Museum of Kyoto's Annex. The world below them disappeared into the realm of memory. If it weren't for the *kimono* in Cataline's hands, it would be as if none of it had happened.

Elena looked down at her watch. It was 1:15 in the afternoon. They had been in the vault beneath the museum for three hours. Their private car was still waiting for them on the side of the street.

"Are you sure you don't want to come, Cataline?" Elena asked, immensely happy to be back on the surface.

"Nope," she answered with a wry smile. "I'll have the driver drop me back off at the inn and I'll enjoy the baths while you go visit Prince Charming at the *torii* gates. I told you we'd make it in time."

They had made plans the night before to meet Alexander at Fushimi Shrine at 2 p.m. Elena had just enough time to make it.

"I'll take Isabella's *kimono* with me and put it with your things," Cataline said as they took their seats in the back of the car. She held the folded *kimono* in her lap.

The driver asked them politely how their business had gone, and then requested his instructions. He was to drop off Cataline at the inn first, and then drive Elena to the shrine.

As the car pulled away from the museum, Elena lowered her gaze to the *kimono* on Cataline's lap. Cataline had folded it in such a way that the collar on the back of the *kimono* was showing. Centered directly below the collar, where the family crest was often placed, was a white hand-painted *kamon*—a replica of the butterfly crest Elena had seen carved on the inside of her mother's deposit box.

CHAPTER SEVEN

Elena arrived at Fushimi Inari Shrine three minutes past 2 o'clock.

Alexander was waiting for her at the entrance, leaning against a vermilion-colored pillar that was part of a giant *torii* gate marking the entrance to the shrine.

Torii were an archetypal symbol of Japan and a type of gate mostly associated with Shinto shrines. Shinto was the native religion of Japan.

Typically painted vermilion and black, they denoted the entrance into sacred ground. As the visitor moved deeper into the shrine grounds, he or she might encounter other *torii* along the path representing the various levels of sanctity within the shrine.

Elena had always been fascinated with *torii*. They were a visceral reminder of the spirit world. Visibly representative of a portal, consisting of two vertical posts laid several feet apart with a lintel laid across the top horizontally, the ends of the lintel protruding over the posts, they marked for the mortal viewer the existence of the divine, more so than the largess of churches, temples, or physical shrines.

Fushimi Shrine was dedicated to Inari, the Japanese *kami* of rice and industry. *Kami* were deities, spirits and natural forces worshipped in the Shinto religion.

This particular shrine, made up of a main shrine complex at the foot of Mount Inari and several sub-shrines within the mountain itself, was famous for its avenue of *torii* gates. The avenue consisted of thousands of *torii* gates donated as offerings to Inari by individuals and companies, and was known as Senbon Torii—"one thousand *torii*". The gates lined a network of trails leading from the main shrine complex to the sub-shrines within the forests of Mount Inari. Also located in the heart of the mountain was the complex's inner shrine, which housed the *kami.*

"Glad to see you made it," Alexander said to Elena with a playful smile, pushing himself off the gate. He looked like a walking J Crew add, dressed in gray slacks, a light teal and gray plaid button-down shirt and a cotton shawl-collar sweater in navy blue. His hair he wore in the usual loose braid, hanging over his shoulder. "I was beginning to think you were going to stand me up."

"I thought about it," Elena quipped, letting him know with a smile that she was just kidding. Then she quietly began to look around.

To reach the main shrine complex from the street, they had to walk up a large stone-paved pathway lined with relatively modern buildings. Along the path were two giant *torii* gates, one near the foot of the pathway—where they stood now—and another two-thirds of the way up. Behind the second giant *torii* was the Romon Gate, the official entrance to the shrine.

"You look very pretty today," Alexander said as he came to stand beside Elena. Then with a mischievous smile he added, "You were secretly hoping your meeting would take all day, weren't you?"

"Am I that obvious?" Elena teased, casually looking herself over. After his first comment, she couldn't really help it. She was still dressed in the same thing she wore to the bank that morning—an emerald green vintage dress with a sweetheart neckline, black straps and a thin belt around the waist. She wore a black cardigan with it, and black flats. Perhaps too dressed up for the occasion, but then she saw a group of three teenaged girls walking up the pathway wearing *kimono.*

As they walked past, the three girls admired Alexander from a distance. He gave them a dramatic low bow, and the girls burst into a fit of giggles.

"I think it goes without saying that you look pretty handsome yourself," Elena told him with a grin. It was her way of thanking him for the unexpected compliment.

They followed the teenaged girls up the stone pathway toward the Romon Gate, passing under the second giant *torii* and stopping at the foot of a set of stone steps that led up to the Gate. There, amid an open-aired pavilion, was a purification font where visitors were expected to cleanse their hands and mouth before entering the shrine grounds.

"I hope you weren't waiting long," Elena said to Alexander as she watched him take one of the many bamboo ladles laid out for them to use. He dipped it into the water and then spilled its contents over his left hand. He did the same with his right. Finally, he poured water into his cupped hand and rinsed his mouth.

"I like these kinds of rituals," he whispered softly when he was finished, stepping out of the way so that Elena could perform the purification rite. "And no, I wasn't waiting long. You were right on time. Where's Cataline?"

Elena finished the purification ritual before responding. "She wasn't feeling well. Our business this morning was a little more emotional than expected. I hope you don't mind that it's just me."

"All due respect to Cataline, but I was hoping it would be just you." He watched her as he said it, his gaze the same color as the sky.

Elena felt the heat rise to her cheeks immediately and she looked away, placing the bamboo ladle back in its place. "She had an inkling you felt that way."

"You don't mind, do you? I'm not going to sit here and pretend you don't... interest me."

Elena looked up at him, surprised at his choice of words. They began walking up the steps toward the Romon Gate. The distance wasn't very far.

"How exactly do I interest you?" she asked.

"You're a mystery to me. You say only what's necessary for the conversation to move forward. You are full of conversation, yet very seldom is it anything to do with you. I've spent three days in your company, and I virtually don't know a thing about you."

They were standing at the foot of the Romon Gate. It was a beautiful two-story, white and red painted wooden structure with green accents and gabled roof dating back to the late 16th century. Flanking the gate were two large guardian statues of foxes. The fox, *kitsune* in Japanese, was said to be the sacred messenger of Inari. Because of that, shrines to Inari were dotted with fox statues portrayed with one of four items in their mouths: a key to a rice granary, a jewel, a scroll or a sheaf of rice. These particular ones held a key and a jewel in their maws.

"Alexander... I..." Elena was going to tell him that she didn't know how to respond to that, but he stopped her.

"You don't have to say anything, Ele. Just take it for what it is."

That was the second time he told her that. The first had been at Ryoan-ji Temple, about the butterflies no one else had seen. "You know, the last time you said that to me was about the butterflies at the temple," she told him, "and in the twenty-four hours since all I keep seeing are butterflies."

"Really?" He said it half-heartedly; preoccupied with trying to figure out which way they should go. They could go through the gate or around the left side. When he made up his mind a few seconds later, he took Elena's hand and led her through the Romon Gate.

Inside the gate was a giant wreath of miscanthus, a type of grass that grew in long sheaths. The wreath took up the width of the gate, and visitors had to step across it to enter the main shrine complex.

Alexander took Elena's hand and helped her across. "It's probably that since I brought your attention to it, you're seeing them everywhere," he said, returning to their conversation. "After all, it *is* spring. Butterflies like spring."

Elena thought about it. He was probably right, but that didn't explain why her mother's things were overflowing with the symbol. The drawer, the *kimono*, and the box had all contained images of butterflies, the drawer and the *kimono* the same crest.

"You're probably right." She finally agreed as they approached the *nai-haiden* across from the Romon Gate. "I'm letting my imagination get the best of me."

The *nai-haiden* was the hall of worship in the main complex at Fushimi Shrine. It was there that Elena and Alexander made their coin offering, or *saisen*. They pulled on the bell rope, tossed their coin into the offering box, clapped three times to summon the *kami* and then made a silent prayer.

Next they viewed the *honden* from the outside, since visitors were not allowed within. The *honden* was the most sacred building at a Shinto shrine. The bamboo shades of the *honden* in this instance were drawn up, allowing Elena and Alexander to see inside. Two Shinto priests were worshipping. They wore white upper robes with black stitch-work along the bottom hem of their long sleeves, lower robes in an icy blue shade, and a black hat. Each one held a small wooden plank in their hands. A third priest read a sutra scroll out loud. Elena found the chanting very soothing.

Afterward, Alexander wanted to go strait to Senbon Torii, the avenue of *torii* gates, but Elena convinced him they should finish exploring the main part of the shrine complex first, before heading into the mountain.

One of the most interesting things they saw in the main complex was a small shrine with *senbazuru*, offerings made of a thousand origami cranes garlanded together and hung in rows upon rows forming a veritable sea of myriad-colored paper cranes. *Senbazuru* literally meant "a thousand origami cranes", and it was believed that a person who made a thousand paper cranes would have their wish granted by a crane. In this particular shrine, they were wishing for success in studies.

Another curious thing they saw was a fence of wishes. It was made up of various wooden posts lined up about four feet apart with wire hung between them. There were seven rows of wires between each post, and each wire was covered in paper ties. Visitors wrote their wish to Inari on a piece of paper and tied it to one of the wires with a knot. Alexander and Elena purchased slivers of paper at a stand across from the fence, wrote down a wish, and tied it to a wire. Elena's wish was to see Ms. Callas's son again, so she could finally ask him his name.

"So what did you wish for?" Alexander asked on their way to the entrance to the mountain paths.

They were walking toward a giant *torii* gateway that marked the route to the Senbon Torii. Stone stairs led the way from the giant *torii* to the path's entrance.

"I can't tell you that! I'm pretty sure the *kami* won't grant my wish if I do."

"This isn't a shooting star, Ele," he insisted, nudging her with his shoulder. "I'm pretty sure *kami* aren't as petty as stars."

"Why do you think stars are petty?" Elena figured she might as well play along.

"They only shine at night, right? Don't you think that's a bit selfish?" Alexander gave her a knowing smile, and then inched closer. "So, are you going to tell me what you wished for or what?"

"Nope, I'm not taking any chances."

"Have it your way. I'll tell you mine, though, since I'm a live-on-the-edge type of guy," he declared with a wink. "That you'll let me kiss you by the end of the night."

Elena turned as bright red as the tunnel of *torii* gates they were now approaching, and Alexander just gave her a satisfied grin. Apparently, gorgeous men had no need for subtlety.

The path into the mountains began as a colonnade of large *torii* gates that were sizable and spread reasonably far apart, giving the impression of a large hall flanked by massive red columns. Interspersed within the vermilion and black wooden gates were stone *torii*. The pathway at this point was relatively smooth and on a flat surface.

According to Alexander's travel guide, which he had been carrying tucked into his back pocket the entire time, a full hike of the paths would take up to three hours, and they would see the complex's inner shrine and its various sub-shrines along the way. The terrain would begin flat and even at first, but would then become a little steeper as they moved further into the mountain. The particular path they were on at the moment would lead them first to the inner shrine and would then split into a circular route around the summit of the mountain. Elena and Alexander decided simply to begin the hike, and see how far they could get. If they got too tired along the way, they would just turn back.

They were not alone on the pathways into the mountain. Tourists, locals and priests walked quietly along the path, enjoying the stoic beauty around them. After some time, they arrived at a spot where the avenue of *torii* became two smaller corridors running parallel to each other and leading deeper into the mountain to the inner shrine; this was long before the mountain path split into its circular route. The break into two parallel corridors was guarded by two fox statues, after which the *torii* became smaller and spaced closer together, creating the feel of a tight tunnel. Elena chose the right corridor, and Alexander didn't complain; after all, they both led to the same place.

They soon reached the inner shrine area, known as Kumataka-sha, which adjoined a beautiful lake. It had various sub-shrines, places of worship and food stalls. One sub-shrine had an altar with fox statues and candles. Another, wishing plaques called *ema* in the shape of a fox head where visitors drew-in the face of the fox, wrote a wish on the back and then hung them in the shrine. There was an altar with offerings of miniature *torii* gates in different sizes, and another held the *omokaruishi*, "heavy light rock"—a large round stone lifted by the visitor, who's wish would be granted if when he or she lifted the stone it felt light.

Since they weren't tired yet, Elena and Alexander decided to continue along the paths. From Kumataka-sha the path of *torii* led to the halfway point on the mountain, which afforded some stunning views of Kyoto. Somewhere along the way, Elena and Alexander stopped at a cafe for *kitsune udon*, a noodle dish topped with sweetened deep-fried tofu. Fried tofu was said to be a favorite food of foxes.

At the halfway point, the path split into its circular route. The three famous peaks of Mount Inari were located along the path to the right, and various other sub-shrines were on the path to the left. In each of the three peaks of Mount Inari was said to be enshrined a different god. Elena and Alexander decided to take the route to the left, which would bring them through the various sub-shrines to arrive at the highest peak, Ichi-no-mine, first. The path would then take them through the second peak, Ni-no-mine, and the third, San-no-mine, before looping back around to the halfway point.

The route they chose wound itself up through the mountain, steep at times, and at others turned into steps, taking them through various sub-shrines, one of which Elena found particularly beautiful. It looked like an ancient cemetery nestled into the mountainside, but was in fact made up of stone monuments called *otsuka*, erected by worshippers for Inari and bearing the name of a manifestation of the god; it was said that there were ten thousand of these stone monuments clustered throughout the mountainside. They also came across a sub-shrine with a fountain in the shape of a fox, and several others with stone lanterns and offerings of various-sized *torii* gates.

The stairway up to the highest peak was steep, and it was here that Elena began to feel tired. At this point, though, it didn't make any sense to turn around. Once they got to the highest peak, the path would become easier since it was downhill from there. The shrines at the three peaks were on a larger scale than the others they had seen, and the path between them was more often stairs than not. Elena was thankful by the time they got back to the half-way point that would lead them back to the inner shrine, and then to the main shrine complex below.

The descent was definitely easier, and the view slightly different now since they could see the black writing carved along the length of the back of the posts of each *torii* gate; the front view had been clear of carvings other than a *kanji* where the lintel met each post. The light around them had started to fade.

Elena looked down at her watch. It was almost 5:30 in the afternoon. It seemed a little early for it to be getting dark, but they were deep inside a mountain and the forest around them was dense.

The tunnel of gates was illuminated by small metal lanterns hung at intervals from the top lintel of the gates. They were spaced just right to give visibility but not detract from the scene. The soft glow of the lanterns interplayed beautifully with the vermilion wood, making the path seem even more ethereal than before.

Elena stopped for a breather, calling out for Alexander who was a few feet ahead.

"Are you ok?" he asked as he came to stand next to her. His voice was heavier, but other than that he didn't look winded at all.

"You could hike here for the next five hours, couldn't you?" she asked him between breaths.

"I could, but if this is getting to be too much for you, Ele, we can pause here for a while. We're not in a hurry."

Elena nodded. She just needed a few minutes to rest. "Just give me a sec," she whispered, and leaned against the post of a *torii*. Her gaze fixed on the back of one of the gates. "What do you think they say?" she asked Alexander, studying the line of black markings against the red paint.

"I think it's the name of the donors, and probably the dates or something. Let me check." He pulled his travel guide out of his back pocket and in a matter of minutes confirmed it.

"It feels like there were *more* than a thousand of these gates out here," Elena murmured as she eased herself down along the post to the ground, referring to the formal name given to the gates. She rested her back against the base of the *torii* and sat with her knees together, tucking them to one side so that she could pull the skirt of her dress over her knees.

It felt like it had gotten much darker in the past few minutes.

"I think you're probably right," Alexander answered as he took a seat opposite her on the ground. He leaned against his own post, and quietly looked around. On the forest floor behind him were offerings. Elena had seen them dotted along the way, small dolls in the shape of white foxes or a round head painted in red and with a bearded face.

There was no one else on the path but them.

Alexander was quiet. His braid had become undone, and his long blonde hair fell past his shoulders. In the fading light, he looked like he had the night before—timeless. He realized she was watching him and raised his gaze to hers.

"What did you use to do before you came to Japan?" Elena asked him. The question was so random it even surprised *her*; it had come out of nowhere. Normally, she steered clear of these kinds of subjects, but she was feeling uncommonly comfortable. The scene around them was just too serene to feel anything other than that.

"Not until you tell me more about you," Alexander replied. The mischievous grin that spread on his lips was priceless.

Elena sighed. She hated talking about her past. She wasn't sure if it was because she was reserved or because it was still too painful. Either way, it was something she was always reluctant to discuss. However, she *had* been the one to bring up the subject. She would feel slightly guilty if she didn't open up, even a little.

"Come on, Ele, tell me something... anything," he pleaded before she could say a word.

"*Anything*?" The opening was too good to ignore. "Well, I just saw a butterfly over your right shoulder," and she had. It had just been for an instant, like a shadow, but its shape had been distinct. "Told you, I'm seeing them everywhere."

Alexander stayed quiet. In fact, he went completely still. He looked around himself, up and down the path, but he obviously didn't see anything. It had already disappeared.

"Maybe you're not seeing things," he finally said, his tone a little harder than usual.

"What do you mean?"

"Well, this is an ancient shrine and a very sacred mountain. Like I said at Ryoan-ji, maybe you're seeing between the veil."

"Do you really believe that?"

"Don't you?"

Elena thought about it, and deep down she did believe it. Like Cataline would say, there were definitely things beyond the mists. But thinking about them here, in an avenue made of a thousand portal gates one after the other, gave Elena the willies.

"Can we talk about something else?" she whispered, rubbing her arms with her hands. Suddenly, the air felt colder to her.

"Of course we can. We can change the subject back to *you*."

Well, Elena could say one thing about Alexander—he wasn't easily deterred.

"What do you want to know?"

"When we were in the baths, you mentioned you'd lived in Japan before."

Elena nodded. "I was born here. I lived in Tokyo until I was seven."

"What happened when you were seven?"

"My parents died."

Alexander's face smoothed. She could see it through the glow of a lantern. He watched her quietly, and then pulled himself up to his feet.

"Come here," he said when he was standing in the middle of the path.

Elena hesitated, but then she stood up. She took a few steps closer to him, unsure of where this was going. Then he reached for her, taking her wrist in his hand. Gently, he kissed the inside of her wrist and then pulled her against him, wrapping his arms around her.

The gesture was so unexpected; Elena couldn't help but be moved by it. She couldn't remember the last time someone had held her like this. The first thought in her mind was that Alexander's embrace was warm. His body, though, was as firm as she had imagined it would be. There was nothing soft or yielding about him. He held her so tightly she felt she might break.

Alexander pressed his cheek to hers. "How did they die?" he whispered, his voice breaking.

Why did he sound so hurt?

"Alexander?" Elena pulled herself back, enough so that she could look up into his eyes. There was emotion there; more emotion than she had seen in the three days she had spent with him. There was so much of it that she couldn't figure out what it was. Was the emotion for her, for her loss?

"I don't know the details, exactly," she finally told him.

It had been some kind of freak car accident in the outskirts of Kyoto, or so the authorities had said. Cataline had sought the details after her arrival in Japan, but received very little information. She pushed the investigation for years but came up empty handed, blocked by red tape at every which turn.

Alexander didn't respond immediately. He watched her quietly, searching her gaze, then bowed his head and without saying a word pressed his mouth to hers.

The gesture was so unsettling that Elena froze. His hands smoothed up her back and, as he brought his fingers to her cheeks, he deepened the kiss. He was gentle with her, but Elena could feel an edge to it; there was a hint of desperation, his mouth almost bruising. Even so, she felt herself giving in to him.

When it was over, he didn't let her go. He held her firmly in his arms, his lips brushing hers.

"Do you want me to tell you how they died?"

He said it as lovingly as if he had just confessed his devotion to her.

Elena tensed. His mouth was still on hers. She couldn't move. He was holding her so tight she could hardly breathe. She had closed her eyes during their kiss, and now couldn't bring herself to open them. She didn't want to look at his face. She didn't want to see his eyes.

"Elena, are you listening?"

Again, his tone was gentle.

He loosened his hold on her for an instant, and then caught her by the throat with one hand. The pain was agonizing. It forced her eyes open, and Elena saw a cold fire in his eyes.

"Do you want me to tell you how your parents died? Yes or no? It's a very simple question." The venom finally bled into his tone.

Tears burned Elena's eyes from the pain. Every breath she took was excruciating. His fingers bit into her throat, and she struggled to stay conscious. Her hands instinctively rose to his, clawing at his fingers, trying to free herself.

Then he let her go.

Elena fell on her knees. She doubled over, gasping for air. When she looked up, he was standing over her. She didn't even have a second to collect her thoughts.

"Come on, Elena. Join the game. I've waited for so long." He purred the words into her ear.

"Get away from me!" she tried to scream, but her voice was broken. She struggled to get to her feet, but he kicked her in the gut. It knocked the wind out of her, and for a second all Elena could see was black. When her vision cleared, she was coughing violently on the ground. He was several feet away. Elena scrambled to her feet and then ran.

Because of the tears, she could hardly see where she was going. One minute the path ahead was empty and dark, the next Alexander appeared in front of her out of nowhere. Elena put all of her weight into turning, but he caught her by the arm. He was so strong that he dislocated her shoulder.

Elena howled in pain, screaming as he drug her back against him. "Let go of me, Alexander! What the hell is wrong with you? Let me go!"

Alexander clamped a hand over her mouth. He held her against him by her hair, wrapping it around his wrist and forcing her head back. Her back was flat against his abdomen. The position made the pain in her shoulder a thousand times worse. Elena struggled to get free, but it was impossible. Between his grip and how much her shoulder hurt, Elena could hardly move at all. Worst of all, he was enjoying this; she could feel his arousal against the small of her back.

"I knew you'd be a fighter," he moaned into her ear, his voice soft as velvet. "I like it when your kind fights. For centuries, the Heirs were so fucking boring. They never fought back. They cried and begged like women in their time tended to do. They sucked the joy right out of the hunt. That's why I loved your mother so much. She gave me a hell of a fight."

He took his hand away from her mouth and caught her waist, pulling her hard against him. The pain in her shoulder turned sharp and Elena almost blacked out.

"What the fuck are you talking about?" Elena hissed. Nothing he was saying made any sense. "Let go of me, Alexander. Are you fucking insane?"

"That's it," he sighed, the sound low and heated, "that's what I want. Fight me, Ele. Scream at me. Claw at me."

He moved his hand from her waist to her breast. Elena felt the damp press of his tongue against her ear. She screamed.

"Gods, you're just like her," he laughed against her throat.

Elena was terrified. She had never been so afraid in her life. Everything was happening in slow motion. It was like a nightmare, but no matter how much she kept telling herself to wake up, nothing happened. The nightmare only got worse.

With his weight, Alexander pushed her toward the right side of the path and pressed her up against the post of a *torii*. He put his weight on her dislocated shoulder and she screamed, the pain cutting off her ability to fight back. Releasing her hair, he caught her by the throat, his grip like a vice, and held her firm. With his other hand, he began to undo his pants; he was pressed up against her so closely that she could follow the movement of his hand.

Elena screamed.

She couldn't believe this was happening to her; and yet there he was, pressing his left hand down the side of her thigh. He caught the skirt of her dress, and started pulling up the folds. His nails clawed into her thighs.

"Alexander stop! Please stop! Why are you doing this to me?" Elena pled between sobs, struggling as best she could to get away.

"Because I have to," he said, sounding dejected for the first time. "Because it's the way it's been for thousands of years." For a moment, he stopped his advance. He rested his weight against her back, and pressed his cheek to the back of her shoulder. The respite was only momentary. In a matter of seconds, he was back to a cheerful tone. "But somewhere along the way I learned to make it fun, Ele. I learned to get something out of it. Don't worry. I won't kill you right away. I like the thrill of the hunt. Isabella ran from me for seven years before I finally killed her. Best seven years in a very, very long time. Life can be so boring for my kind."

His kind? Elena didn't have a clue what the hell he was talking about. Nothing Alexander was saying made any sense. He was claiming to have killed Elena's mother, but he couldn't have been more than ten years old at the time. And he kept talking about heirs, thousands of years of heirs. This was madness.

"Alexander, you have the wrong person. Please stop this. Please don't do this to me." Elena tried one last time to reason with him.

"Nice try, Ele, but I know I have the right girl. You smell just like your mother." Alexander forced her head to one side. He kissed the back of her neck and lingered there, breathing in her scent. "Plus, I confirmed it in the bath. You have the mark."

Alexander stilled against her, and Elena knew the worst was about to come. She felt him shift his weight behind her. He caught the hem of her dress.

Then he stopped.

A sound broke the silence behind them, but Elena couldn't place it at all. Then a familiar voice followed.

"Step away from her," the voice said, apparently to Alexander.

"A little late, aren't you?" Alexander hissed in response.

"Your sister kept me preoccupied, but I handled it."

Elena couldn't make heads or tails out of their exchange, but noticed that Alexander tensed at the mention of his sister.

Several minutes passed—it felt like a lifetime to Elena—and then Alexander put a little space between them. He kept her facing the *torii* with the weight of his arm.

"Maybe you were being played, Snowflake," Alexander growled to their mystery companion.

"I doubt you two are that creative. Thousands of years, and you still go for the same approach. Zip your pants up, and back away from her completely."

"They're button-fly, pretty boy. It's going to take me a second," the hatred in Alexander's voice was palpable, "but you wouldn't know because I don't think you've ever put on a pair of jeans in your miserably long life."

Alexander removed his arm from Elena's back and slowly stepped away. From the rhythm of his step, Elena could tell he did so very gingerly. Elena straightened up and took a moment to compose herself. She smoothed the skirt of her dress before turning around.

It took her a minute to process what she was seeing.

Elena was facing the path back down the mountain. Ahead of her and to her right was Alexander. In the darkness, his skin seemed to glow with an internal light. His golden hair fell down to his waist, dazzling in the soft glow of the lanterns. He turned his gaze to hers momentarily, and Elena saw that his eyes were a brilliant, incandescent cobalt blue. As Alexander shifted his weight, she saw that he had some kind of weapon at his throat.

Elena stepped closer unconsciously, so she could get a better idea of what was going on.

"Elena, for the love of the gods, please stay back." The voice came from the man holding the weapon. Elena raised her gaze to the man's face and recognized him immediately. It was the face from her dreams.

He had glacial blue hair and red eyes. He was tall and very slender. His skin was as pale as snow, so pale she could almost see a shimmer of blue beneath the surface. Everything about him was icy, hence the derogatory nickname. His features were fine and sharp, his cheekbones pronounced. He was uncharacteristically beautiful for a guy, and he was dressed in yet another stunning suit.

It was Ms. Callas's son, and he was holding the blade of a scythe to Alexander's throat.

Even though Elena had never seen a scythe in person before, she knew this one was not an ordinary scythe. The weapon, including its body and grips, was made entirely of one piece of metal, a bright-colored metal that gleamed like starlight. In fact, Elena was certain that she could see the faint glow of thousands of stars beneath its surface. A long piece of white fabric was wrapped carefully around and between each grip, the only protection between the metal and the weapon bearer. Its blade was sharp on all sides.

"Would someone please tell me what the fuck is going on here?" Elena demanded in a broken voice. Her sanity was about to break. She looked between Ms. Callas's son and Alexander, confused. Instinctively, she took a step back.

"Yes, Snowflake, why don't you tell her?" Alexander said in a mocking tone, even though the blade was still at his throat.

Ms. Callas's son, who had been focusing his attention on Alexander, now turned his attention to Elena. Elena met his gaze openly, trying to reconcile this version of him with the one she knew. Overall he looked the same with the exception of blue hair and red eyes—and the intimidation factor. He looked positively lethal, and his form seemed to pulsate with the same frantic energy as Alexander's. In the back of her mind, Elena recognized that she should be afraid of him. She knew everything about this scene was wrong, including him, and her survival instinct told her to run from both of them, but she couldn't shake the sense of safety she felt now that he was here.

"Elena," Ms. Callas's son whispered her name in a stern but gentle manner. "I'm kind of in the middle of something. I'll tell you all about what's going on when you are safe. Please walk toward me, if you don't mind."

Alexander smiled and looked toward Elena as she began to move. "Don't worry, Ele," he said, "he'll tell you everything you need to know.

He's had to tell the same story to all of the Heirs. He has it well rehearsed."

Ms. Callas's son pressed the blade further into Alexander's throat, making him croak the last words.

"Fuck you, Alexander," Elena hissed.

"I tried to, Ele, but you wouldn't let me." The feigned hurt in Alexander's voice was flawless.

For the first time in her life, Elena felt a murderous rage. She didn't give into it, though. Instead, she decided to concentrate on something more productive—getting to safety.

Elena took her time walking, wary of them both. Technically, Ms. Callas's son was the best of both evils. Her mind kept telling her she shouldn't be listening to either of them, especially after the day's unexpected turns, but her instincts told her Ms. Callas's son was the safest bet, even more so than running.

After a few seconds, she was standing safely behind Ms. Callas's son. It was incredible how effortlessly he held the scythe. From this close, it looked very heavy.

"One thing before we go any further," Elena said casually to Ms. Callas's son. Her mind was wondering a million things. *Who are you? What are you? Why are you holding a scythe? What the hell are you doing in Japan? How did you find me? Why are you always in a suit? What's up with the hair and eyes?* Instead, Elena asked him his name.

Inari had granted her wish.

"You can call me Eiry," he responded. Through the lantern light, Elena could see the signature smirk at the corners of his mouth.

"I hate to break up your little reunion," interjected Alexander in a snide tone, "but one of you might want to get back to the inn before Cataline dies. My sister already has a head start."

CHAPTER EIGHT

THE FLIGHT down the mountain was perilous. Even with Alexander's self-serving generosity—he had imperiously declared he would graciously give them a head start—Elena found herself struggling to keep up. In a matter of minutes, her world had been turned upside down.

They pushed through the dark paths of the mountain as quickly as Elena's condition would allow. The times when her body failed her, Eiry was there, his movements too fast for Elena even to register. Whenever she would stumble or slip, he caught her before she touched the ground. When Elena could no longer move, he swept her up in his arms and pressed on, moving infinitely faster than before.

Elena was too shocked to do much of anything but press her face into his chest and cry. Her mind struggled to reconcile what had just happened. Alexander had tried to kill her. Alexander's sister was on her way to kill Cataline. Alexander had murdered her parents. Eiry was the man in her dreams, the man she had dreamt of most of her life. Everything Elena had ever believed in was a lie.

Somewhere along the way, they stopped moving.

"Are you cold?" he whispered softly into her ear.

Elena hadn't realized she was shivering. Now that she considered it, she registered how cold his embrace was. It bled through the fine wool of his blazer. The press of his hand against her back was ice, and his breath bit into her neck when he spoke. She was chilled to the bone.

"Yes," Elena finally managed to breathe, pressing herself closer to his chest in spite of the cold.

"I'm sorry for it. It can't be helped." His tone was calm, and it helped Elena keep some semblance of sanity.

Eiry shifted her weight in his arms effortlessly. Then Elena felt him reach into his pocket. In a few seconds, she realized he had taken out his phone. She could hear the ringing tone through the silence. In less than three rings, someone answered.

"I need you at the inn," he said to the person on the phone.

Elena heard a short response, but she couldn't tell what it was or the gender of the person speaking.

"Bryce, I don't need your lip," Eiry hissed into the phone. "Get to the inn. The woman is in danger, and you very well know I can't leave Elena alone. If you see Eos, take the kill." Then he hung up.

The last words made Elena feel nauseous.

In a matter of seconds, they were on the run again. Elena couldn't tell the scope of their progress. Even though he was on foot, it felt as if they were moving faster than a car. Surprisingly, Elena felt comfortable with the exception of the cold. She hardly felt any pain at all because of the way Eiry held her, carefully taking into account her condition, and the cold numbed any residual pain.

Elena felt him tense several minutes before they arrived, but he didn't say a word.

When she opened her eyes again, they were in the inner garden of the inn. It was dead silent, but for the trickle of water from the bamboo fountain. Slowly, Eiry untangled her from his arms and set her on the ground.

Elena looked around briefly to get a hold of her bearings, and then began to move toward her room. Eiry quickly moved to block her way. At the gesture, Elena's carefully held composure broke, and she began to cry.

"Please move," she begged him between quiet sobs. "*Please.*"

He stepped closer, quietly wrapping his arms around her trembling form. "I'm sorry," he breathed into her hair, "but she's gone."

In that single moment, Elena's world collapsed. She felt her heart sink and then shatter into a thousand pieces, the force of the implosion contained within her skin. The pressure was excruciating. Elena lost sight of everything but the pain she felt inside, which burned like venom and left in its wake nothing but complete devastation. Every organ in her body constricted, and Elena struggled to breathe. She wanted to protest, to deny Eiry's words, but her throat was dry and any sound she made came out a strangled cry.

Cataline couldn't be dead.

Elena looked up into Eiry's face, searching for an answer to the anguish she felt inside. He was as stoic as ever, any emotion buried deep beneath his icy features.

Slowly, he pressed his fingers beneath her chin and lifted her gaze. Cold fingers brushed the tears from her cheeks. "Elena, we must go. Helios will be here any minute." His manner was so gentle it made Elena's pain even more pronounced.

"Helios?" The name came as a broken sob. Elena had no idea who he was referring to.

"The one you call Alexander. He will get here any minute now, and he will do everything in his power to hurt you. I have to get you out of here."

At the thought of Alexander, Elena tensed. "Is Cataline still inside?" she quietly asked Eiry. She tried to look past his shoulder, but it was impossible. He was too tall.

"Yes, she is. My sister is taking care of her. We will go inside so you can say your goodbyes. Grab what you must, and then we fly."

Elena only nodded. Slowly, Eiry stepped out of her way.

The few short steps to the *engawa*, the wooden veranda bordering the garden outside of her room, were heavy from the weight of her grief. Without thinking, Elena removed her shoes at the stone step and carried them in her hand as she stepped inside.

The *futons* were laid out and Cataline's body was prostrate on one of them. She looked as if she were asleep, as if any minute now she would simply wake up. A broken sob escaped Elena's lips, and she covered her mouth with her hand.

As Elena raised her gaze, she caught movement in the corner of the room. Through the soft glow of the lamp, Elena saw the outline of a body. A cold fear came over her, and she took a step back.

Eiry quickly came up behind her. "It's my sister," he said, "no need to fear."

Elena swallowed hard. It took all of her strength to steady the beating of her heart.

"She was already gone," said the woman as she stepped out of the shadows. "Eos was standing over her when I arrived. The moment she saw me, she disappeared."

Like Eiry, the woman was naturally tall. She was made even taller by the six-inch pumps she was wearing. They didn't make a sound as she stepped across the delicate mats that lined the floor of the room. Elena wanted to tell her she shouldn't walk on the mats with those shoes, but figured it was best not to speak to her at all; she was even more imposing than her brother.

The woman had snowy skin and a mane of fiery red hair that spilled down her back in sculpted waves. Her cat-like eyes glowed like burnished gold in the dark. She had perfect bone structure, eyebrows to kill for, and a surprisingly delicate face. She wore skinny jeans and an asymmetrical shirt that fell off one shoulder.

This was Bryce, the person Eiry had spoken to on the phone, and she was studying Elena with an almost animalistic intensity.

"So this is the girl," Bryce purred in a semi-hostile tone, walking carefully around Elena and sniffing the air around her with a half smile.

"Bry, stop being a pain in the ass," Eiry said to her. "Can you keep a lookout outside while she collects her things? I need to get her out of here as soon as possible."

Bryce looked up at her brother, an irritated expression on her face. "You got me out of bed to be your little guard?" she growled.

Elena tried not to stare. This was what the woman looked like when she got out of bed?

"For once in your life, Bryce," Eiry hissed, "could you please not be difficult? Shut up and go be a lookout."

"You shut up, Snowflake."

"Goddamn it, Keres, if you don't go outside in the next second, I'm calling Mama and you can tell her how we all managed to die because you're being a selfish little bitch." Eiry's tone was uncharacteristically angry.

The woman stilled. Elena wasn't sure if it was the use of the new name or the mention of their mother—who happened to be the scariest woman Elena had ever met—either way, Bryce's demeanor changed. Her golden gaze moved between Eiry and Elena, and her perfect face smoothed.

"Fine," Bryce barked, "but do you mind telling me how the fuck she got the necklace in the first place? I thought those goddamn *onmyōji* couldn't be breached."

Elena froze. Immediately, she recalled the vault of ancient drawers. "I got a letter in the mail," she whispered, her eyes meeting Bryce's. A chill ran down her spine.

The woman laughed. She turned her gaze to her brother, the indignation clearly etched onto her features. "Did she just fucking say she got a letter in the mail? Are you fucking serious?"

"Bryce, we'll deal with the specifics later. All that matters now is getting Elena to safety."

"And what's your genius plan?" Bryce snapped.

Elena just watched them banter, too confused to say a word.

"Once Elena has her things, I will take her to the Hyakki Yakō. I'll need you to take Cataline's body with you," Eiry replied.

Bryce grinned, the kind of smile that made your blood run cold.

"Why is she taking Cataline?" Elena interjected, her voice shaking from the sheer insanity of the entire situation.

"Elena, we can't leave Cataline's body here. Bryce will take it with her," Eiry responded.

"It was a violent death, so technically it's my purview anyway," Bryce said nonchalantly.

"Violent death?" Elena asked, horrified. Nothing about Cataline's body suggested violence, but Elena had a feeling there was a lot she didn't know. "You know what, I don't want to know. Where are you taking her body?"

"Hades, you idiot. Where else?" Bryce snapped.

"Hades?" Elena looked between the siblings, almost at the end of her wits. One more little push and she would lose it. "Yeah, right. Hold on, let me go get a coin for you so she can pay the ferryman," Elena added, sarcastically.

"No need," Bryce replied cheerfully. "Employees don't have to pay the fare."

"Elena," came Eiry's voice, calm and controlled. He dismissed his sister with a wave of his hand and stepped closer to Elena.

Elena put her hand up to stop him. "Please don't Elena me," she begged, the tears bright in her eyes again. "Would someone please tell me what the hell is going on?"

Eiry drew himself up to his full height, his crimson gaze ghostly fires in the dark.

"I feel Helios approaching," Bryce warned.

"Elena, we don't have time. I have to get you to safety. Be satisfied with this—imagine for one moment that every major pantheon of gods believed in throughout the history of mankind existed, and are still in existence today. For eons, these pantheons have schemed to obtain or keep control in an ageless war. You currently find yourself smack in the middle of that war. Now I need you to grab your things, only the essentials, and say your goodbyes to Cataline so that I can make sure you don't die tonight."

An hour later, Elena sat at the foot of a long raised walkway made of wood, its surface lacquered to a lustrous shine. The walkway, a *hanamichi* or "flower path", ran, left of center, from the back of the hall to a large stage at its far end, cutting through the length of the main floor. Elena sat on her knees where the walkway met the stage, Eiry at her side. He had brought her to the last place Elena had expected to be, an old *Kabuki* theatre.

The spaces to the left and right of the *hanamichi*—smaller on the left than the right, and set lower into the ground than the walkway—were lined in *tatami* and curiously gridded with wooden planks that divided the space into open squares, forming box seats. Raised platforms, also lined in *tatami*, formed viewing balconies that bordered the left and right perimeter of the two-story hall on each floor. Paper lanterns dotted a coffered ceiling and garlanded the spaces between the balconies' wooden columns, bathing the hall in an otherworldly light. Beyond the balconies on the ground floor, Elena could see screens made of *shōji*, which separated the hall from the corridors that surrounded it. On their way into the hall, Elena had noticed several rain shutters lined the outermost walls of the corridors, some of which were propped open to let in the night air.

Facing Elena and Eiry, at the head of the stage, was a raised dais framed by a large curtain that spanned the length of the stage's back wall. Of black silk and embroidered with clusters of red spider lilies woven in crimson and argent thread, the curtain provided an eerie backdrop to the company on the stage. A solitary man sat on the raised dais, dressed in a black *kimono* lined in white, with black *hakama*—loose trousers worn over the bottom half of his *kimono*. His *obi* was also white, and his *haori*, or *kimono* jacket, an icy pale green. He had a mane of jet-black hair that fell just past his shoulder blades. His eyes were steel-gray, and structured wisps of chin-length hair swept over his right eye framing an angular face. He was an extremely handsome man and looked only a few years older than Eiry, his seeming youth jarringly juxtaposed by the unmistakable age in his gaze.

In front of the dais, along the sides of the stage, were seated a conclave of creatures unlike any Elena had ever seen, beings that made it impossible for her to dismiss Eiry's assertions of the existence of the supernatural and the divine; they were the Hyakki Yakō, the Night Parade of One Hundred Demons, which according to Japanese folklore would take to the streets every year during summer nights—a story familiar to even the youngest of Japanese children. This nightly parade was made up of demons, spirits and monsters known as *yōkai*, and their leader was one called Nurarihyon. Eiry sought to hide Elena among them and for this purpose had brought her here, to a long-forgotten theatre in the mountains outside of Kyoto.

The man currently sitting on the dais was none other than Nurarihyon, however, he didn't look anything like the stories and images Elena remembered as a child; stories which spoke of an old man with a gourd-shaped head, wearing monk's robes, who snuck into people's homes while they were away to drink their tea. Elena had always found it ironic that the infamous leader of the Night Parade of One Hundred Demons would be such a seemingly gentle creature. In contrast, the real Nurarihyon looked resolute and formidable, far from gentle, as did his retinue of generals, the creatures seated along the sides of the stage.

Elena and Eiry had arrived only moments before. After saying a heart-breaking goodbye to Cataline, Elena had gathered her things and Eiry had brought her here, telling her what he could as they were led from the main entrance of the theatre to the performance hall. They were somewhere in the outskirts of Kyoto, safe within a compound where the Hyakki Yakō lived, which had been enchanted centuries before to keep them hidden from human view. The compound consisted of the main theatre, made of wood and finished in white clay walls with traditional gabled roof. A garden connected the main building to a cluster of smaller buildings that provided the necessary living quarters. Elena and Eiry had arrived at the theatre's entrance in the same fashion they had arrived at the inn, with Elena gathered in Eiry's arms. The commotion was instant, with the household staff hastening to welcome their unexpected guests. A set of attendants took Elena's things while a woman led them to the performance hall.

That woman now sat closest to Nurarihyon's right. She wore an ornate midnight blue *kimono* with a heron stitched in silver thread. There were various layers of *kimono* underneath. Her *obi*, much wider than the men's, was made of black woven silk with gilded butterflies against a backdrop of white and golden flowers. The butterflies' wings were woven in jade, indigo and coral thread. The cord that held the *obi* together, the *obijime*, was of the same icy pale green as Nurarihyon's *haori*. Her hair fell down her back in downy waves; the strands light as feathers and in variegated shades of pale brown and white. The hair that framed her beautiful face was steel-gray. Her eyes were an intense golden hue, and her skin glowed with a faint luminescence. Eiry had called her Aosaginohi, the luminescent heron.

Opposite Aosaginohi, to the left of Nurarihyon, was a man called Shōjō, a sea sprite. He had been the first to greet them at the door of the hall. He had long hair the color of saffron. It was gathered into a ponytail at the base of his neck and fell past his waist. His bangs framed his face in various layers, the longest halfway past his cheekbones. The color of his eyes matched his hair. His skin was pale, and he had an almost feminine quality to his face. He wore a deep red *kimono* and white *hakama*. His *kimono* was lined in white, and open to reveal a sinewy torso. In his right hand, he held an earthen container filled with *sake*.

The remainder of the retinue had equally intriguing characteristics. Next to Aosaginohi was a man with caramel colored skin and white hair. He had hawklike eyes, pointed ears, nails like claws and a sharp nose. He wore light gray robes and a steel-blue cloak lined on the inside with white feathers barred with thin sable-colored bands that looked to Elena very similar to those of a Peregrine Falcon. Elena was certain he had to be a Tengu, a bird-like demon.

Yuki Onna, the snow spirit, was easy to recognize. She was seated next to Shōjō, dressed in a pure white *kimono*. The inside lining was black. Her *obi* was black with white *sakura* blossoms. She had scarlet lips and long black hair. When she spoke to the boy sitting beside her, her breath materialized in the air.

The boy, called Enkō, had emerald green hair, silver eyes, and webbed hands and feet. His skin was reptilian, made up of iridescent scales that reminded Elena of pearls. This kind of *yōkai* was known as a Kappa. Usually, Kappa were thought to be only roughly humanoid, but Elena was certain this boy had to be a Kappa because of the indentation on the crown of his head. It held water, and the stories said that if it spilled he would be unable to move. Only a Kappa had this characteristic.

Opposite Enkō, seated next to the Tengu, was Hinoenma, the Japanese version of a succubus. She was dressed in a barely held together crimson *kimono* made of light silk. A golden *obi* was the only thing keeping her from completely exposing herself.

Also in attendance was a cat *yōkai* in the form of a young boy known as Gotokuneko. He was seated next to Hinoenma. Out of all the *yōkai* present, he looked the most modern—at least in hairstyle. He had medium-length hair the color of burnished copper. It was razor cut and textured to frame his face and shoulders, his bangs swept to the side. Cat ears sprouted from his head. His eyes, also copper toned, were slit like cat-eyes. He wore a white and navy blue *yukata*. He sat with his legs crossed, two ghostly fires hovering above his knees.

Futakuchi-onna, the two-mouthed woman, was seated next to Enkō. She was a young woman with chestnut-colored hair who looked completely normal except for the second mouth in the back of her head, hidden by her hair. Every once in a while, her hair would move and Elena would see the strands take the shape of serpents. It was said women who did not eat turned into this type of *yōkai*. The second mouth would grow and demand food. Her hair would then become serpents that stole from the woman's food to feed her second mouth. Her second mouth could become quite spiteful.

Next to her was a man with a floating head called Rokurobei. It was said that he suffered from a supernatural illness that caused his head to float away from his body at night. In spite of this affliction, he was actually a very attractive man. Of medium-build and olive skin, he wore his hair up in a long ponytail to display his missing neck. He was dressed in a casual amber-colored *kimono* worn loosely enough to display the dark green under-kimono beneath.

The final *yōkai* in the room was a monk called Aobōzu. He sat across the stage from Rokurobei; closest to where Elena and Eiry sat. He had one eye in the center of his forehead, and green skin. He wore a traditional *kasa*, a mushroom-shaped hat made of woven straw, and monk's robes.

The moment Elena and Eiry were ushered into the performance hall, the room broke into fevered whispers. All eyes moved back and forth between them, some of the conversations growing heated. Elena was thankful she couldn't pick up half of what was being said, since they spoke in a very rapid-paced Japanese.

After several minutes, Nurarihyon raised his hand for silence. His steely gaze fixed on Eiry, who sat kneeling beside Elena.

"Once again, Shinigami, your family asks for our protection." Nurarihyon's voice was calm, but in it Elena recognized the unyielding quality of steel.

"That is correct, Nurarihyon-sama," Eiry responded in a cool and even tone, using the honorific reserved for a person of higher rank or someone greatly admired. "We would not impose on you again if it were not dire. We will owe you a great debt of gratitude."

"Indeed you will, Shinigami-sama," Nurarihyon replied, his acknowledgement of the honorific an important development. "Am I to understand the *onmyōji* have failed again?"

"Yes. I am not yet sure precisely how it occurred, but the necklace was put in her possession," Eiry responded.

"This child, then, is the new Heir?" Nurarihyon inquired.

"Yes," Eiry replied. "If you require proof I will gladly provide it."

"No, that will not be necessary. Your word will suffice." Nurarihyon held Eiry's gaze a moment longer. Satisfied, he turned his scrutiny to Elena.

All Elena could think of doing was bowing prostrate on the floor where she knelt. She held the pose for at least one minute. It was excruciating because of the pain in her shoulder, but she bit back the cry that threatened to come. When she eased herself back up, she saw a smile on Nurarihyon's face.

"I am glad to see your early years in Japan had a lasting impression," he said gently, the smile now reaching his eyes. "Even in pain you show the proper decorum. Tell me child, do you also ask for our protection?"

Elena nodded, averting her gaze. She was fascinated and terrified, all at the same time. It was overwhelming, and the day was beginning to take its toll.

"Very well," said the leader of the Hyakki Yakō. "Where the *onmyōji* failed, we will offer you protection—the same protection we offered your mother, for as long as you remain in Japan."

Again, Elena bowed deeply.

"Aosaginohi will escort you to your room now," concluded Nurarihyon, and they were soon ushered out of the hall.

THEIR ROOM WAS large and spacious, with the same elements as the room Elena had shared with Cataline at the inn. It was located in one of the compound's smaller buildings, its *engawa* opening out onto the large central garden. From the open *shōji* screens, Elena could see a small pond with an elegant bridge, the scene underscored by the soft song of evening cicadas. Two *futons* had been laid out for them in the center of the room.

Eiry had begun to move his *futon* away from Elena's, presumably because they had been placed closer than was appropriate, but Elena quickly asked him to stop.

"As close as you can get, please." Elena spoke softly, trying to maintain her composure while looking up at him. He looked concerned, and Elena was thankful for it. The last thing she wanted to see was the stoic indifference he reserved for everyone else.

Without a word, he placed the *futon* back down beside hers. He watched her quietly, his eyes lingering over the shoulder she had injured.

"I need to fix that for you," he said.

"You need to tell me what's going on," she countered, her voice heavy with sleep.

"Elena, it's late. You're hurt. I would like to heal you, get you cleaned up and put you to sleep. We can deal with this in the morning. We won't be running tomorrow, so we'll have all day."

"All of those things can wait," Elena insisted. "I need to understand what's happening. How is it possible *yōkai* exist? You know what, back that up, what you said earlier doesn't make sense. How can every major pantheon in the history of mankind exist?"

"It's the same answer to both of your questions, Elena. If I answer, do you promise to let me heal you and then go to sleep?"

Elena watched him, pouting as the stoicism began to bleed back into his expression. "I promise."

He held her gaze in silence for a moment longer and then nodded, apparently satisfied with her response. "If enough humans believe in something," he began to say, "that something will come into existence." He inched closer to her, and gently brushed her hair away from her cheek. "Human will, when strong enough, can shape the divine and alter the spirit world," he explained in a whisper, and then added, "It was an unexpected side effect of your creation."

Eiry brought his fingers to her neck and Elena flinched. The pain quickly pulled her mind away from the question she was about to ask. She opened her mouth to complain when she felt an intense cold where Eiry had placed his fingers. It immediately numbed the pain.

"You have bruises everywhere," he whispered, his red eyes now a deep crimson hue, so dark they almost looked black. "Whatever questions you have, let's leave them for tomorrow. We need to get you healed up."

Elena wanted to protest, but she couldn't bring herself to do so. He was being so gentle with her, and she had promised to do as he asked once he answered her question.

Eiry moved his hand from her throat to her injured shoulder. Again, the cold numbed her pain. This time, though, Elena felt it take root. It wove into the muscle and sinew beneath her skin, slowly pulling her shoulder back together without a single ounce of pain.

"Are you all healers?" she breathed, leaning against him as the ice began to recede.

"No, but my mother is. Some of us inherited her gift. I can't heal extensive damage, but this I can handle. Now come on, no more questions. We need to get you cleaned up and in bed."

While most of the Hyakki Yakō enjoyed the compound's communal bathhouse, Eiry and Elena had been provided a room in one of the few buildings with the luxury of a private bath. Eiry escorted her to the small narrow room at the end of the hall, and then waited for her outside the door. He left the *fusuma* cracked, as Elena requested. He would keep part of his body across the open space so she could see he was always there.

Elena bathed as quickly as she could. She didn't realize how badly she was bruised until she saw herself in the lamplight. The warm water was incredibly soothing, relaxing the terrible soreness she felt in every bone.

The day had been too traumatic to begin to process what had taken place. She knew tomorrow would be much worse. She would have to wake up and face the fact she had lost Cataline. The loss would be excruciating. For now, it was only the numbness of knowing that nothing would ever be the same.

Once Elena was done with her bath, she slipped into the robes Aosaginohi had provided her. The walk back to the room was silent.

"Do you mind if I change?" Eiry asked quietly as they made their way into the room.

"You're going to leave me alone?" Panic made Elena's voice tremble.

"No, of course not. I can do it here. The most you'll see, if you're lucky, is a very pale chest." He offered her a smile, and Elena found it made her feel quite a lot better.

"I'll turn around if you need me to," she whispered to him. "You seem like the modest type."

"Not if you don't mind it," he said, and began to unbutton his suit. "Do you mind holding this for me?"

He placed the blazer in her hands and then walked across the room to where a wooden stand sat against a corner. He removed his pants and placed them on the stand, followed by his shirt; to Elena's dismay, he was wearing boxer briefs. He grabbed his *yukata* from the chest next to the stand and slipped it on. Then he walked back to Elena and took the blazer from her hands. With a quiet panic, Elena noticed the front of his robe was open a little and she could see a smooth expanse of pale, sinewy skin.

Of course, he was fully aware of the effect he was having on her.

"Thanks," Eiry whispered to her with a hint of a grin ghosting his lips, and lingered for a moment before he moved back to the corner to place the blazer on the stand. He brought an *andon* lamp back with him.

He placed it next to the *futons* and motioned for Elena to sit down. "I'm just going to heal the visible bruises tonight," he explained in a quiet voice. "The rest we can worry about tomorrow if they become a bother. I could always ask one of the *yōkai* women to help if need be."

Elena nodded. She hesitated for only a moment and then opened the collar of her robe just enough to expose her shoulders, holding the front of it closed with her hand. Knowing Eiry's touch would be cold didn't keep her from tensing when she felt it. He healed the deeper bruises on her neck and shoulders first, then quietly moved on to those on her injured arm—pushing the sleeves of her robe up to get to those. The ones on her legs he healed up to her knees, making the experience as least exposing as possible. When it was over, Elena felt pleasantly numb.

Gently, Eiry helped her beneath the thick blanket of her *futon*; after such a terrible day, it felt like paradise. He blew out the lamp and slipped into the *futon* beside hers, inching closer when Elena asked. Thanks to the blankets, the cold from his body didn't bother her.

When Elena looked up at him, his demeanor had turned back to that of the human she had known—pale blonde hair and dazzling icy-blue eyes.

"Why the change?" she mumbled, her words already slurring from the exhaustion.

"I'm calm for the first time tonight," he explained and shifted onto his side, closer to her.

Elena put his response in the Rolodex so she could process it tomorrow. She was almost asleep when she remembered something. "Eiry," she whispered into the dark, "what does *shinigami* mean?" It was the term Nurarihyon had called him.

Eiry took so long to respond that Elena fell into a heavy sleep before he answered.

"Death deity."

CHAPTER NINE

Elena woke with a start.

She sat up slowly, struggling to shake off the shadows of a fitful sleep. Ghostly images wove into the fabric of the room around her, making it difficult for her to tell the difference between what was real and the imprint of a dream.

A cyclopean priest. A woman made of snow. A pale-haired bird-demon. A succubus. A reptilian child holding water on the crown of his head. A young girl with a second mouth at the nape of her neck. A handsome man with a floating head. A sea sprite. A cat. A night heron. All apparitions dancing before her eyes, a veritable waking dream of spectral effigies—intangible and insubstantial.

Afraid, Elena turned her focus to the physical, hoping it would anchor her to reality. The supple comfort of her *futon*. The texture of her blanket. The delicate weave of the *tatami*. The soft weight of the *yukata* over her skin. All of these things were palpable and real.

Slowly, the phantoms began to fade until Elena was left with the crippling weight of reality; a reality she was not yet ready to face.

Cataline was gone, and Elena was alone again. She would never again see Cataline's scarlet smile. She would never hear the soft melody of her laughter or feel the gentle warmth of her embrace. Reality became the nightmare, and dreaming its only escape. The weight of Cataline's loss consumed Elena, pulling her back into the darkness of dreams.

When Elena opened her eyes again, it was dusk. The room was bathed in twilight, its rose and amethyst hues making her surroundings seem less menacing than before. Shadows danced across the walls, abstract reflections of the garden outside.

The *shōji* doors that faced the garden were open. The *futon* beside hers had been gathered and put away. Elena immediately looked to the wooden stand in the corner of the room, and was surprised to find the suit still hanging there.

It hadn't all been a dream, after all.

"You're awake," someone whispered softly from behind her.

Elena turned to find Eiry pushing himself off of the back wall of the room and making his way toward her. To Elena's surprise, he was dressed in *kimono* and *hakama*, both black. He looked as comfortable in these clothes as he did in his expensive suits.

"How long have I been asleep?" she asked him.

"Most of the day. The sun is only just setting," he replied with a smile, and then knelt beside Elena on the floor and began to look her over carefully.

Elena blushed—a reaction she wasn't thrilled with—and then quickly looked away, focusing her attention on the weave of the *tatami* as Eiry inspected her former injuries.

"Does anything hurt still?" he asked gently, pressing his fingers to her jaw and easing her face to the side so he could inspect her throat.

"No, everything you healed feels normal."

"What about the things I did not heal?" he said, giving her a knowing look. "I'm not trying to make you uncomfortable, Elena, but I know I didn't heal everything. I can still smell blood."

Elena turned bright red. She had been about to tease him, ask him if he was part bloodhound, when she suddenly remembered; with all of the excitement, she hadn't really given it much thought. The only wound Eiry hadn't healed was the scratch marks on her thigh. She cleared her throat, and met Eiry's gaze. There was no point in being silly about it. "Alexander clawed my thigh by the hip."

"Is it infected?"

He was watching her so intently that Elena had to look away. If the next thing he said was that he could smell the infection, Elena would be mortified. "I don't know. It's festering a little, but with the robes it's not uncomfortable. It might be an issue when I change."

"You don't need to worry about changing. We are expected to wear *kimono* while on the grounds. You brought your mother's, right?" Eiry whispered the words as he inspected her shoulder.

"I did, yes." Elena busied herself with watching the garden outside while Eiry finished his inspection.

"If the wound becomes bothersome, let me know and I will ask Aosaginohi to heal it for you." Done, Eiry sat back, a soft smile settling over his features. "Your sleep was troubled," he added, as matter-of-fact as he would relate the weather.

Elena nodded, the color draining from her face.

Eiry didn't press. "You don't have to talk about it if you don't want to."

"No, it's just..." Elena hesitated. She wasn't sure how to explain it. "I think I woke up in the morning, but I was really disoriented. It could have all been a dream. At some point, I don't know if I was still dreaming or awake, I remembered everything. Cataline—" Elena's voice broke when she whispered the name. "It hurt too much. I just let myself drift." Elena's eyes burned with tears and she looked away, hating that he would see her cry. "Cataline was all that I had." The loss was overwhelming. Self-preservation was the only thing giving Elena the strength to wake up and face what was coming.

"I understand," Eiry replied gently. He didn't mention that he had held her through the worst of it, or that his sister had visited during the night. "I'm glad you found your way back, though. I know it's going to be very difficult, but we have a lot to discuss and time is of the essence."

A knock interrupted them. They turned in the direction of the sound, surprised to find Aosaginohi kneeling beside the open *shōji*.

"Forgive me for the intrusion," Aosaginohi whispered in a gentle tone. "Nurarihyon-sama asked me to attend to Elena-san. Shall I come at another time?"

Like the evening before, Aosaginohi was a vision of nobility and grace. The simple sight of her gave Elena pause, not out of fear but awe. Like Eiry, something about her seemed familiar and safe, although Elena couldn't begin to understand why.

"Can you come back in an hour, Aosaginohi-san?" Eiry's tone was kind, and he bowed his head in a sign of respect.

"*Hai*, Shinigami-sama. May I serve you both some tea? Then I shall return in an hour to assist her with bathing and dressing. Supper will be served in the dining hall in two hours. Several of us will meet after the meal." Aosaginohi bowed her head, the movement slow and graceful.

"Of course, Aosaginohi-san. Please come in," Eiry replied.

Elena was curious about the meeting that was mentioned, but she decided to wait until she and Eiry were alone again to ask about it. Instead, she watched quietly as Aosaginohi stood and made her way across the room, carrying a tray of green tea in her hands that Elena had not noticed until now.

"I hope you like sweets," Aosaginohi whispered to them both, kneeling down in front of them and placing the tray on the *tatami*. Slowly, she began to prepare their tea.

Elena tried to study the woman without being too obvious. It was difficult not to stare. Every time Aosaginohi moved her hands, her skin caught the fading rays of sunlight and shimmered like stars reflected on water. The darker it became in the room, the more luminous she seemed to become.

"I imagine this must be very confusing for you," Aosaginohi said to Elena, as she filled Elena's cup with tea. "You must have a lot of questions."

Aosaginohi's candor caught Elena by surprise. Panicked, Elena looked over at Eiry. When he didn't seem concerned, she responded. "I do have a lot of questions," she whispered, taking a bite out of a sweet rice cake. "I don't even know where to start, to be honest."

"The beginning is always best," Aosaginohi offered with a gentle smile. Then she excused herself, leaving Eiry and Elena to their prior conversation.

"Wow," Elena breathed when they were finally alone.

"What is it?" Eiry asked, and handed Elena another sweet.

"She's pretty amazing, don't you think? All the other ones were a little scary, but she feels different."

Eiry smiled. "She *is* different. She's much older than the rest of them, and she's a spirit *yōkai*, not a monster or a demon."

Elena considered that as she took another sip of her tea. The fact that they were discussing monsters and demons as a simple fact of life was unnerving. To consider this compound was home to such creatures was even more unsettling. What's more, they were protecting her. They had protected her mother.

Elena decided it was time to get some answers.

"So let's start with that," she whispered softly, watching Eiry take a sip of his cup of tea. He hadn't touched the sweets. "You said last night that *yōkai* exist because humans believe they do. Did I understand that right?"

That familiar smirk formed on the corners of Eiry's mouth. He sat up and lifted one knee, resting his elbow on it before answering. "Yes, *yōkai* are born of the thoughts and beliefs of humans, whether positive or negative." He paused for a moment and watched Elena quietly. Then he continued. "Since you like Aosaginohi so much, I will use her as an example. Thousands of years ago, enough humans worshipped the night heron as a benevolent spirit that it gave life to the woman you just saw. Deep-rooted beliefs in this country have given birth to things as extraordinary as monsters and demons, and as curiously simple as the *tsukumogami*—ordinary household items that become *yōkai* spirits after reaching their hundredth year of existence.

"The process also works in the opposite direction," he continued. "If the number of believers dwindles, the spirit, monster or demon dies. Japan is a country that still believes deeply in the spirit world, and so the number of supernatural beings here is much greater than anywhere else, and their history is rich. Just as humans have different cultures and societies, so do the supernatural."

Elena listened in quiet amazement, considering all the different implications of what he was saying. Did this mean Santa Clause was real? Bigfoot? Loch Ness? "What about vampires? Werewolves? If *yōkai* exist then technically so could they."

"Not necessarily," Eiry replied. "A big enough group of people has to truly believe in a being for it to come to life. How many people nowadays do you know who really believe in vampires or werewolves? It's all based on human belief. Vampires are tricky, since it depends on the culture. Some cultures today still believe in a being that thirsts for human blood. Japan, for instance, has a vampire *yōkai*."

"What about Santa Clause?" The question sounded just as ridiculous out loud as when she had first considered it, but Elena felt it was a valid point. She needed to understand the scope of what he was saying.

"Things like Santa Clause and the Tooth Fairy are bound by different rules because they are based on the imagination of children. Children's imagination changes their perception of the world, but not the world itself. The rules are also a little different for gods."

"Gods?" Elena paled. The weight of that one word was alarming. For some reason, it was harder to accept the existence of gods than it was to accept demons and monsters.

Eiry stilled and watched Elena quietly. For an instant, he seemed profoundly sad, the expression quickly replaced by the usual icy restraint. "Yes, gods," he finally replied. "I asked you to assume that all major pantheons exist. Pantheons are made up of gods, naturally. Gods hold sway over the spirit world and the divine. Your world is the middle-ground."

"Okay, so gods exist and they are higher in the totem pole than all the other supernatural beings we've previously discussed. Do I have that right?" Elena tried to keep the skepticism out of her voice. It wasn't that she didn't believe—she would be a fool to deny everything that she had seen in the last twenty-four hours—but talking about the existence of various pantheons of gods so casually felt insane.

"Yes, that's right, more or less."

"And how are the rules different for gods?" Elena heard the sound of footsteps approaching. She lifted her gaze to the open *shōji*. The saffron-haired sea sprite and the succubus from the night before walked past, having an animated conversation. From what Elena could hear, they were discussing the best *sake* makers to haunt.

Eiry never turned around to look at them. He kept his gaze on Elena's face the entire time. "Dwindling numbers of believers do not kill gods. It severely weakens them, but once gods come into existence they never flicker out. There are very few ways to kill a god. You can imagine the implications of so many different pantheons existing at the same time."

Once the sound of footsteps faded, Elena returned her attention to Eiry. His expression was somber, humorless enough to send a chill down Elena's spine. "Power struggles?" Elena guessed.

"An infinite number of them," Eiry replied. "I can't remember the last time there was peace."

"The different pantheons are fighting against each other to gain control?"

"If it were only so simple." Eiry's tone was flat. Exhaustion marred his features and his eyes grew distant. Elena could almost see the weight over his shoulders as he leaned forward against his raised knee. "It is not so much a fight between individual pantheons as it is a fight between the two major types of gods. Every pantheon is made up of two types of gods: chthonic gods and sky gods. Chthonic gods are deities of the earthly realm and the underworld. In the Greek pantheon they are ruled by the underworld gods of Tartarus—the Tartareans. Contrary to popular belief, the whole of the underworld is referred to as Tartarus, not Hades. Sky gods, on the other hand, are deities who dwell above the earthly realm—in the sky. In the Greek pantheon the sky gods are ruled by the Dodekatheon—or as you know them, the Olympians."

At the mention of the latter, Eiry's tone grew hard. Before he could continue, Elena raised her hand for him to stop. She needed to make sure she understood him correctly. "So this war you're involved in is between chthonic gods and sky gods across all pantheons? Isn't that kind of counter productive for the pantheon's self-preservation?

Wouldn't you want your entire pantheon to exist rather than just half of it?"

"That makes sense from a human perspective," Eiry explained, "but not from the god perspective. Modern religious faith is rooted in the dynamics between Good and Evil, the beings above the ground and the beings below—Heaven and Hell. Time changes the labels but the mechanics remain the same. In ancient times it was also about those above and below, but we labeled it in terms of Children of the Sun and Children of the Stars, Light above and Darkness below. Now Light and Darkness have turned into Good and Evil. Gods align based on these natures, irrespective of pantheons. The first major pantheon became divided giving birth to this war, and the other pantheons simply took a side as they came into existence. Are you familiar with the Greek creation myth?"

"Yes," answered Elena, quietly triumphant; at least she knew the answer to something. "The world began with Chaos. From Chaos were born a handful of elemental gods. From the Elementals were born all other gods."

"Precisely," Eiry said, his features brightening. "It is a story common amongst most mythologies. The elemental gods are the Protogenoi—the First Born. They were elemental beings, giving shape and form to the universe. All other gods were born from them. They owed no allegiance to a specific religion or pantheon, as humans did not yet exist and such order was not necessary for primordial gods. Such things did not occur until several generations of gods later, thousands of years after man was born and developed its first great civilizations.

"With the development of human civilizations came the expansion of divine history. In the beginning, the divine shaped the human world and accepted worship regardless of belief system. That, however, would later change as religion became more centralized and homologous with the rise of many great civilizations. One culture in particular, the Greeks, rose above all others before it to form an extraordinary civilization that would later become the foundation of the Western World, making their religion the most prominent theology of the time. It was then that human belief, on account of its sheer numbers and homogeneity, began to shape the world of the divine. Younger generations of gods who had risen to power began to be influenced by human mythology. They divided amongst themselves into the roles attributed to them by humans until the divine world mirrored that of human belief. Gods split between the ranks of their worship, the Dodekatheon and the Chthonic—Olympian versus Tartarean gods."

Here, Eiry paused his story. His face smoothed, and for an instant Elena was certain he had left her—his mind in some far reaching place she could never follow. When he began to speak again, his voice was heavier and richer than before.

"Because of the far-reaching influence of Greek civilization," Eiry continued, "the Greek pantheon has remained largely in control of the divine world, virtually unchanged through today. The Roman Empire took Greek religion for itself, changing only the names of the gods, and so the power of the Greek pantheon grew stronger as the Roman Empire took over the known world. The advent of Christianity only solidified the pantheon's hold through its amalgamation with the old religion, a move that not only preserved an Empire but also the providence of its gods. Christian theology has only increased the fervor of the war, adding the dimension of Good versus Evil."

Elena listened attentively, slowly absorbing what he was saying. It was a staggering revelation, and a thousand questions began to form in her mind. "How do the other pantheons come into play?"

"Greece, and later Rome, were not the only great civilizations to rise and fall in human history," Eiry explained as he absently traced his fingers along the edges of the *tatami*. "Throughout history there have been many other great civilizations. Their mythologies sprung to life out of the aether. We believe they are born out of the same primordial beings as our pantheon was born. The stronger the civilization, the stronger its pantheon. As their influence and power wanes, so does their pantheon. We have been the only ones that have managed to remain in power continuously."

"You said 'we'," Elena noted, studying him carefully. Eiry watched her through lowered lashes, his expression calm. The icy blue tone of his eyes was a bright contrast against the signature pallor of his skin and hair. "So, just for the record, you're part of the Greek pantheon?"

"Yes," came his response, short and to the point.

Elena nodded, trying to take the measure of exactly what that meant. He was a Greek god. That meant the scary redhead and Ms. Callas were also Greek gods. Most likely, his overtly friendly father was as well. It was alarming to consider, so Elena decided to put those facts aside for now. "So Greek, Roman and Christian all fall under the same umbrella? They aren't separate pantheons?" she asked.

"Yes, that's a good way to think of it." Eiry ran his hand through his pale hair, and then offered her a faint smile. "If one civilization transitions into another, it doesn't create a new pantheon. The changing ideology simply influences the existing one. The different Celtic pantheons and the Tuatha Dé Danann—the Fae—for instance, all fall under the same umbrella. The Japanese pantheon and *yōkai* as well."

"And all the other pantheons are involved in this war? Are there any neutral ones?"

"Yes, most other pantheons are involved. Chthonic beings, god or spirit, assist each other, and the same is true for sky gods. It is technically a Greek war, but every pantheon has something to win or lose because of it, and so they play the game as much as they can—it's the nature of gods. The Tuatha Dé Danann are neutral, however—they are both sky gods and chthonic." Eiry whispered the words as he pushed himself up to his feet. The light had faded entirely in the room. He lit the *andon* lamp and then took his seat across Elena once again before continuing. "You've forgotten the most important question of all."

"What's that?" Elena asked, intrigued. There were a thousand questions she wanted answered. She had started with the easiest ones, but there was nothing easy about what he said next.

"How do *you* fit in?"

OF ALL THE REVELATIONS of the evening, Eiry's final story was the most difficult to bear. In a solemn voice, he recounted for Elena the history of her blood—a tragic tale shaped by the indiscriminate nature of Fate and the cruelty of the gods. Elena was the Heir of the House of Thebes, an inheritance mired in misfortune and blood.

The House of Thebes were a noble bloodline, the legendary descendants of King Cadmus and Queen Harmonia of Thebes, whose history was deeply rooted in mythology. It was said that when Athena, goddess of wisdom, granted Cadmus the reign of Thebes, Zeus gave him Harmonia, goddess of harmony and concord, as his bride. Harmonia was the illegitimate child of Aphrodite, goddess of love, by her lover Ares, god of war. Bent on revenge for the illicit affair, Hephaestus, the god of metallurgy and volcanoes, husband to Aphrodite, crafted a cursed necklace that would bring disaster to anyone who wore it, and presented it to Harmonia as a gift on the day of her wedding.

The Necklace of Harmonia brought great misfortune to all who possessed it, and caused the ruin of the House of Thebes. Generation after generation, it was coveted by the women of the House for its priceless beauty. Fashioned out of emeralds inlaid in adamant, it took the shape of a serpent with a head at each end, an eagle rising between its open maws. First Cadmus and Harmonia fell, turned into serpents. Then

Semele, their daughter, who wore it on the day that she was tricked by Hera into asking Zeus to reveal his glory and was burned to death as a result, while carrying Dionysus in her womb. Several generations later, Jocasta, Queen of Thebes, killed herself after unknowingly marrying her son, Oedipus, who unknowingly murdered his father. Antigone, their daughter, hung herself after being sentenced to death by her uncle for burying her brother, who died in a civil war for the crown against his own twin—each one killing the other. And so it continued through the centuries until the bloodline was no more.

A generation before the tragic lives of Oedipus and Jocasta, it was prophesied by the Pythian Oracle that the Olympians would lose their war against Tartarus at the hands of a Daughter of the House of Thebes. With the use of the necklace, the Olympians formed a campaign that successfully destroyed the bloodline. They entreated Helios, titan god of the sun, with the destruction of the noble House. Centuries before, it had been Helios who discovered the affair between Ares and Aphrodite providing the catalyst for Hephaestus creating his cursed gift, the weapon they would now use to secure their success in the war.

For the next fifteen hundred years, Helios and his sister Eos, the titan goddess of dawn, ensured that the necklace fell into the hands of every female Heir by influencing the world around her. Only then could the gods directly intervene in the thread of her life, for beforehand her death was solely the purview of the Fates, the white-robed sisters called the Moirai. Only the Moirai could choose the manner and time of an Heir's passing, and the act of possession was seen as a direct manifestation of the Moirai's intent.

It was in this manner that after several centuries the House of Thebes fell to ruin, and the necklace faded out of existence. For over a thousand years, it was believed the bloodline had perished until another prophecy foretold of the existence of an Heir. A decade and four years later, Elena's mother was killed in the name of the ancient prophecy. That made Elena the only surviving Heir, and the hope of Tartarus.

The conclusion of the story brought with it a heavy silence. Elena sat still across from Eiry, lost for words. He watched her quietly, a mixture of exhaustion and defiance in his eyes. A thousand questions assaulted Elena's mind at once, each one more demanding than the other, but one was more pressing than the rest.

"How am I supposed to help you win a war?" Elena asked Eiry, so shaken that the words came out in a broken whisper. He hadn't mentioned on which side of the war he fought, but the fact that he had gone out of his way to save her could only mean one thing—Eiry was a chthonic god.

"Unfortunately, I don't know," he replied with a resigned sigh. Then he leaned forward and pressed his cold fingers to Elena's cheek, wiping away a tear Elena hadn't even realized she shed.

Elena was stuck somewhere between raw panic and immobilizing fear. She couldn't speak. She couldn't move. Life was unraveling at the seams. Her future was bleak. The past left virtually no room for a reasonable chance of survival. "How many Heirs have died?" she asked him, her tone cautious.

The question took Eiry by surprise. The familiar stoic expression broke, and for an instant Elena caught a glimpse of the depth of his frustration and disappointment. Pain hardened his eyes into a steely cobalt blue. Drive, desperation, and failure all lingered in his gaze, etching the lines of a terrible history into his beautiful face. When he finally replied, his voice was thin and brittle.

"My inheritance has been the survival of your line," he whispered, clearing his throat to wipe away the vestiges of emotion. "While your presence alone signifies my success, I do not consider myself to have been successful. Every Heir before you has died. Your mother was the thirty-seventh I was unable to protect." Here, his face grew hard. Defiance blossomed in his gaze. He watched her quietly, struggling with something Elena couldn't define. Then he added, "You are the first of any of them to ask me that question."

The mixture of pain and amusement in Eiry's voice produced a discordant melody mirroring the torment in his heart. In all probability, in spite of his valiant efforts, Elena would most likely die. There was no way to definitively know whether she was the one foretold. Their hope hinged solely on a possibility. Even so, he would bear the weight of the inevitable in the same stoic manner he had borne it before, etched indelibly into the infinite fabric of his immortal life.

Possibility, probability, and inevitability; thinking about it all made Elena feel numb. Thirty-seven Heirs, all of them dead. Soon she would be joining them. If by chance she managed to survive, not even Eiry could say what the scope of her role would be or how exactly she was to go about it. Elena didn't know the first thing about war, let alone a divine one. She wasn't good in a fight, and she didn't have any special skills. It was a catch-22 of epic proportions.

"So where do we go from here?" Elena asked, resigned. The knowledge would at least give her some semblance of control over her own destiny.

"Tartarus," Eiry replied, "to unseal the part of you that is divine."
Once again, the answer was more than Elena had bargained for.

FIFTEEN MINUTES LATER, Elena followed Aosaginohi in a daze as
the night heron led her through the cluster of buildings, weaving in and
out of *engawas* and covered walkways between buildings on their way to
the baths. After, they would dine with the rest of the Hyakki Yakō before
attending a smaller meeting where Elena and Eiry's escape to Tartarus
would be planned. The escape would take place tomorrow evening.

"Are you not feeling well, Elena-san?" asked Aosaginohi softly,
interrupting her train of thought. Aosaginohi fixed Elena with her golden
gaze, concern lining her usually worry-free expression.

"I'm sorry, Aosaginohi-san. I didn't mean to worry you. I was
just thinking about my discussion with Eiry."

Aosaginohi did not respond immediately. Instead, she took the
measure of Elena's words with the same quiet reservation she always
exhibited. Because of it, every word she spoke had substantially more
weight to it. "The burden of the past should not be borne by the both of
you alone," she whispered softly. "Perhaps I can help ease the load. A
warm bath is a wonderful place for heavy conversation."

Elena was touched by Aosaginohi's concern, and she made a
valid point about the bath—the warmth would ease the pace of Elena's
thoughts, and the water would lighten the burden in the same way it
lightened the weight of all things. Elena offered Aosaginohi a shy smile
and quietly continued to follow her through the grounds.

As they walked through a small portion of the central garden,
they observed Gotokuneko, the cat *yōkai* from the evening before, nestled
among the branches of a weeping *sakura*. He was lounging lazily along a
thick branch, shadow-boxing with a butterfly. This time, there were no
ghostly fires in sight.

After rounding a corner, they found themselves face-to-face with
Rokurobei, the handsome man with the floating head, walking along side
a tall man with blue skin and twin horns on his brow. They were on their
way to the dining hall. After exchanging bows, the blue-skinned man
introduced himself as Aoandon. Contrary to his outward appearance, he
was very soft spoken and his manner was gentle. He expressed to Elena a
great delight in knowing she had survived; an unexpected reaction, but
one Elena would hear repeatedly throughout her stay. Once they parted
ways, Aosaginohi explained to Elena that the man was the spirit of a blue
andon lamp.

In another garden altogether, nestled against the side of the communal baths, Aosaginohi pointed out the Jubokko tree. Jubokko were known to feed from human energy and were best avoided. At times, they even fed on human blood. It was said they were born by growing near battlefields where so much human blood was shed on the ground that it reached the tree's roots, giving it a taste for human blood.

Their journey ended in a more secluded area of the grounds, at a small building reached through a short stone path with sculpted trees on either side. Just outside the entrance was a stone basin for washing your hands and mouth. Like the main buildings, the single-roomed structure was made of wood with sand and clay walls. *Shōji* windows and doors lined the front of the building, which was surrounded by a small *engawa*.

The building's sole function was as a pre-bathing area. Here were the showerheads with their buckets and benches, chests to hold their clothes and various kinds of towels. The back wall, made of glass sliding doors, opened out onto an *engawa* that led to a secluded outdoor hot spring—a *rotenburo*. The bath was set into the landscape; a tranquil pool nestled between large rocks. Steam rose from its surface in a misty haze.

"We won't be bothered here," Aosaginohi assured Elena as she escorted her inside. They undressed quietly and rinsed their bodies before stepping into the outdoor bath.

They did not jump into conversation immediately. Instead, they both enjoyed the quiet comfort of the scene. The night was peaceful. The chill in the air made the warmth of the water exquisite. The silence between them framed a symphony of natural sounds, its melody as soothing as the bath itself.

Aosaginohi was the first to break the silence. "Isabella was just as confused as you are now when she first stumbled into our world," said the night heron.

Elena sat up and met Aosaginohi's golden gaze. "You knew my mother?"

"Yes, and for the first few years of your life I knew you," Aosaginohi replied in a lyrical tone.

"Forgive me, but I think I would remember you if I had known you."

Aosaginohi smiled. "I didn't look like this when you knew me," she explained in a gentle voice. Sadness settled in her eyes. "I was your mother's guardian when she visited Kyoto, and through the years we became close friends. Using my true shape in front of humans would have caused problems, so during the day I took on a human face."

Aosaginohi reached toward Elena. She brought her hand to the side of Elena's face and pressed her fingers gently to Elena's temple.

Instantly, Elena saw an image in her mind. She was at Ryoan-ji Temple as a child. She sat on the veranda looking out onto the Zen garden, listening to her mother speak with a friend—a woman dressed in a *kimono* with colors matching the blossoms of the cherry tree.

The image faded as Aosaginohi took her hand away. Elena held the woman's gaze, too shocked to speak. Aosaginohi had been their hostess in Kyoto all of those years; the woman Elena fondly remembered from her childhood but could never recall by name.

"Your mother's protector brought her here, the same way Shinigami-sama has brought you," Aosaginohi continued, as if the image she had just conjured in Elena's mind was as natural as breathing. For her, it most likely was.

"Aosaginohi-san, what does that mean—*shinigami*?" Elena remembered asking Eiry what the term meant, but she could not remember getting an answer.

"It is a term we use for all of his kind."

"I don't understand. What exactly is his kind?"

"He is a death dealer," Aosaginohi whispered, leaning back against the edge of the bath. "All the pantheons have them."

"What do you mean by a death dealer?" Elena was beginning to feel the first inklings of frustration. She had discussed the creation of the gods and her inheritance with Eiry, but had forgotten to ask the most basic thing—what kind of god he was, *who* he was.

Aosaginohi met Elena's gaze, weighing her words before speaking. Slowly, she lifted her hand out of the water and tucked loose strands of hair behind her ear. Most of it she had gathered on the crown of her head. "Elena-san, please forgive me, but that is not for me to say. I fear I have already said too much, assuming you had discussed this. There were more pressing things to discuss, so I can imagine now how it might not have come up. Allow me tell you what I can about your mother, and I will leave the nature of who Shinigami-sama is for him to divulge."

"That's fair." Elena offered Aosaginohi a conciliatory smile, hoping it would conceal her disappointment. "You mentioned my mother was brought here by her protector. Is there a particular reason why they chose Japan?"

"Yes," Aosaginohi replied. "Japan was the perfect place for your mother to hide on account of the large amount of chthonic beings. Japan is home to the largest contingency of them in the world. Here, sky gods could not identify Isabella by presence alone. There were, and still are, so many chthonic energies here that they could not isolate hers. More importantly, the Hyakki Yakō are skilled warriors, and we could offer protection in the event she was attacked. We were able to protect your mother for eight and one half years. No Heir had ever survived that long. Had we not been betrayed, I believe she would have survived even longer. Your mother was a very strong woman, and she was not afraid to put up a fight."

At the mention of her mother's struggle, Elena stilled. Tears lined her eyes, and this time she did not deny them. She focused instead on keeping her voice steady and her overall demeanor calm. She would not give in to the desperation she felt inside. "Aosaginohi-san, please tell me everything you know about my mother."

"Like you, she was not aware of her inheritance when she first arrived in Japan," Aosaginohi began, her golden gaze softening. She leaned back against the edge of the pool and gazed off into the distance, searching for the threads of the past in the darkness surrounding them. "Your mother and father arrived here a year and a half before your birth. At the time, she had no idea who she was or the lengths being taken for her survival. She was not yet in possession of the necklace, and direct influence was not allowed. No one could tell her what was happening; we could only influence the circumstances around her or risk punishment by the Moirai. It had been a few years since Tartarus had located her, and her protector was doing everything he could to ensure she was never found."

"Who was her protector?" Elena asked.

"Dionysus," Aosaginohi replied with a rueful sigh. "Being himself a descendant of the House of Thebes, he has always been your bloodline's champion."

"What about Eiry?" Elena hadn't met Dionysus. It was Eiry who was placing his life on the line for her.

"Shinigami-sama was the chosen warrior because of the nature of his element. Think of Shinigami-sama as the weapon for the cause. If anyone would be successful in preventing the death of Heirs, it would be he, but even he must abide by the Moirai's intent. Their law is divine. Breaking it, for any reason, brings with it a terrible punishment. It can be immediate or may take centuries to pass. Dionysus's punishment was immediate. Shinigami-sama's has yet to pass."

Aosaginohi's last words sent a chill down Elena's spine. The panic she felt was scalding hot, and it made her voice sound strangled.

Elena couldn't imagine functioning with something like that over her head. "Could he be killed as punishment?"

"Killed? No, Elena-san," whispered Aosaginohi. "Shinigami-sama is already dead. Why would they try to kill him?"

Obviously, something was lost in translation, Elena thought. Either Aosaginohi didn't understand her correctly or there was something very important Elena was missing, but either way Eiry couldn't be dead. He walked, talked, smiled, laughed, felt, hurt—things the dead could not do or feel.

"Forgive me," Aosaginohi said, realizing the effect of her words. "I forget that death can be terrifying for humans. For us, it is the nature of things. Those in the sky are of the sun—warm and alive. Those below are of the stars—made of darkness and ice. It is said the gods below are dead, but it is only a characteristic of their natural state of being. Gods cannot die, per se. They are immortal. If their bodies are destroyed, they are simply born anew, retaining all of their memory and former characteristics. There is only one sure weapon against a god, and it is Tartarus itself—the great Void from which the underworld derives its name. It is a deep abyss, which gravity is enough to imprison any god for all eternity. It is a pity the weapon is part of the fabric of the underworld, for this war would have been over millennia ago if Tartarus could wield the Void as easily as a sword.

"But I digress," Aosaginohi remarked with an apologetic smile. "Shinigami-sama would not be killed. The punishment of the Moirai is more costly than that. Dionysus, for instance, suffered great loss and was denied involvement in his greatest cause. He is bound to Tartarus and cannot interfere with the war on the surface in any way for the next five hundred years. It was an easy punishment to guess, since he is the type of god to wear his emotions on his sleeve. Shinigami-sama, however, is a mystery. No one knows what lies in his heart. His punishment may take much longer to come to pass, but rest assured it will come."

Elena did not enjoy hearing such things. The idea of Eiry's punishment made her ill at ease. She had seen enough to know he already suffered in silence. The weight of this war fell heavily on his shoulders. The loss of life he bore alone. "What were their crimes, Aosaginohi-san?" asked Elena, referring to Dionysus and Eiry.

Again, Aosaginohi weighed her response carefully before answering. "They interfered directly in the Heir's life before she had possession of the necklace," Aosaginohi said, her golden gaze fixed on Elena's. Something weighed heavily on the night heron's mind. Elena could see it clear as day in the depths of her golden eyes, but what it was exactly she could not decipher. It passed as quickly as it arrived, and then the night heron continued her story. "As I explained before, interfering directly in the Heir's life before possession of the necklace is against divine law. Before possession, gods are only allowed to indirectly influence the world around the Heir. Dionysus, for instance, made sure Isabella was safe in Japan without telling her why. She had no idea the reason for it or the lengths taken to keep her protected and out of Olympus' reach.

"Unfortunately, Olympus proved very cunning. Around the time your mother became pregnant with you, the sky gods of the Japanese pantheon learned of Isabella's presence in Japan and informed Olympus. Olympus then tricked her into taking possession of the necklace. After learning the truth, your mother's focus turned toward protecting you. Not even the Japanese pantheon knew of your existence. No one other than the Hyakki Yakō knew another Heir had been born. At your mother's insistence, certain precautions were taken for the sole purpose of ensuring you would never bare the weight of your inheritance.

"First, the necklace was placed in the hands of the *onmyōji*." Aosaginohi continued her explanation in a quiet and steady voice. "In the fringes of our war there have always been a small number of humans with knowledge of the divine. The strongest of these groups have done what they can throughout history to protect humans. Japan has the most successful of these groups—the *onmyōji*. They are practitioners of *onmyōdō*, an arcane tradition of divination and magic. They are specialists in protecting humans against supernatural evils with the use of familiars known as *shikigami*. They were once so revered that their influence reached the imperial courts of Japan.

"Initially, the Kamo clan were the premier practitioners of *onmyōdō*, but the practice was later split between two clans—the Kamo and the Abe. Today, both clans assist in neutralizing divine influence in the human world. Your mother turned to them for assistance. She gave the necklace to the Kamo family to place in their vault, and named the Abe clan as her agents regarding the contents of her deposit box. Both clans are outside of divine influence, and the Kamo vault is famous for being impenetrable by the divine. Once in the vault, the necklace should have never found its way out absent your mother removing it herself. It was the perfect way to prevent Olympus from ever gaining possession of the necklace again and using it against you.

"That precautionary measure, however, only took care of the necklace. Your mother needed to ensure that Olympus would never learn of your birth. For that, she turned to Dionysus. At her request, he removed all divinity from your blood so that your location could not be traced. This act violated divine law, as it constituted a direct influence in the thread of your life. By virtue of your blood, you were an Heir. By virtue of your age and your mother's survival, you had not come into possession of the necklace. By sealing your divinity, Dionysus knowingly influenced the thread of your life directly, and was punished for it."

Aosaginohi paused, giving Elena a chance to collect her thoughts. There were a thousand things she should have been concerning herself with. How had the Olympians learned of her existence? How had the Kamo vault been breached? How had both *onmyōji* clans been influenced by the divine? Why had Dionysus knowingly broken divine law for her sake? Instead, Elena was concerned with only one thing.

"How did Eiry break divine law?" Elena asked the night heron.

"By saving your life," Aosaginohi replied.

CHAPTER TEN

T HE DINING HALL hummed with the animated voices of the Hyakki Yakō—a cacophony of shrieks, shrills, cheers, whispers, laughter, and singing. The din was loud, but not unpleasant. It had the distinct feeling of a dining hall at school, except steeped in magic and the occult.

Contrary to what Elena had expected—and she couldn't say exactly what she had expected—the dining hall was not a separate building, but was in fact the performance hall repurposed for dining. The dais had been removed from the stage, and the stage's floor was now covered entirely in *tatami*. A low wooden table, large enough to fit eighteen and stained in a deep lustrous tone to match the wood of the hall, lined the stage, with eight silk seating cushions at each side and one at each end. The table was reserved for the leader of the *yōkai*, his generals and guests.

The rest of the Hyakki Yakō ate merrily in small groups within the grid of box seats on the main floor, concentrated around an *irori*—a hearth sunk into the floor—which had appeared where the central box seat had once been, its *tatami* now removed to reveal the hearth beneath. A large metal hook hung from the ceiling, suspended from a mechanism Elena could not see, and held a kettle made of iron over the hearth.

Every kind of *yōkai* imaginable was present in the hall, all boisterous and in high spirits. There were several ghosts singing loudly, a giant mountain man playing cards with a mischievous monk, a child-like snow spirit making shaved ice, and a man with eyes on his hands trying to play patty-cake with a spirit child carrying a block of tofu. In the back of the room sat a woman with a neck so long her head floated gingerly against the ceiling. A warrior made of earthenware drank *sake*, seemingly unaware that the liquid spilled out from between the seams of his makeshift suit of armor. A fiery ghost chased after a female rain spirit, the heat from his body evaporating the water stains she left behind.

In the opposite end of the hall from the woman with the tall neck sat a large creature with the head of a woman and the body of a snake; she had beautiful long black hair, snake-like eyes and fangs that fell past her chin protruding from her scarlet lips. Around the *irori* in the center of the space danced a dozen tiny tree spirits joined by Gotokuneko—the cat *yōkai* Elena had seen earlier in the garden—and a cat spirit in the form of a human girl. Gotokuneko danced with a shoot of bamboo in his mouth from which he breathed fire.

Also present was a man without a face, only a smooth expanse of blank skin where his face should be. He sat next to an old woman with a cloud of pestilence hovering over her skin, who demanded sweet *sake*. A jellyfish floated through the air over the heads of the Hyakki Yakō in the form of a fireball. A one-eyed paper umbrella monster with a long tongue and a single foot hopped onto a pillow next to the spirit of a straw sandal. They sat at a table with a paper lantern ghost, a gourd spirit, an *obi* that transformed into a snake, and the spirit of a *biwa*—a Japanese short-necked lute. A spirit monster made of smoke listened attentively to a celestial nymph playing a *shamisen*, a three-stringed wooden instrument.

Elena and Eiry were seated at one end of the large table on the stage; with Nurarihyon, Aosaginohi, Shōjō the saffron-haired sea sprite, Tarōbō the Tengu bird-demon, Yuki Onna the snow spirit, and Rokurobei the handsome man with the floating head. At the other end of the table sat Enkō the kappa, Aobōzu the cyclopean priest, Gotokuneko the cat *yōkai*—who had stopped dancing—Hinoenma the succubus, and Futakuchi-onna of the two mouths, as well as a Kirin and the four guardian spirits of Kyoto.

The Kirin, present now in humanoid form, was an auspicious mythical creature; a dragon shaped like a deer with a unicorn's horn believed to be a herald of prosperity. The four guardian spirits, also present in humanoid form, were Byakko the White Tiger of the West, Seiryū the Azure Dragon of the East, Suzaku the Vermilion Bird of the South, and Genbu the Black Tortoise of the North.

Elena quietly took note of all the different creatures in the room, fascinated by the sheer variety of them, until a familiar voice pulled her from her thoughts.

"Are you not feeling well?" Eiry asked Elena in a quiet whisper.

"I'm fine," she replied, distracted momentarily by Shōjō, who was attempting to refill her cup of *sake* with an impish smile. "I'm just processing," she assured Eiry.

Shōjō sat opposite Elena at the table, his saffron-colored gaze always vigilant even though he gave the impression of being drunk. He had a playful and fluid manner, and was very flirtatious by nature. Elena was certain his bottle of *sake* was magical, as it never seemed to dry up. Positioned near the center of the table, third from the left, Elena sat facing out toward the main floor of the hall, with Eiry to her right, who was followed by Aosaginohi. Nurarihyon, whose resolute and formidable demeanor, Elena now realized, was tempered by kindness and a wicked sense of humor, sat at the head of the table, flanked by Aosaginohi on one side and Tarōbō the bird demon on the other, whose intense and sober temperament was softened by a roguish wit. Yuki Onna the snow spirit, polite and watchful, sat to Tarōbō's right, followed by Shōjō and Rokurobei of the floating head, who had a kind but mischievous disposition.

Elena was so engrossed in absorbing everything she was seeing that she didn't realize she had been quiet for so long. There was really too much going on to process, but she was trying very hard to take it all in. She was trying to imagine her mother interacting with them all.

On the way back to her room from the hot spring, Aosaginohi had explained Isabella's relationship with the Hyakki Yakō. At first, they had seen her as a curious human, another one of the unfortunate Heirs they had heard so much about, but never before had an Heir come to live in Japan or request their protection. Never before had they seen one so close. They had expected many things, but not the kind, attentive woman they came to know; a woman who treated the Hyakki Yakō not only as equals, but also as an extended family. Nurahrihyon had been very fond of her, Aosaginohi confided, and also of Elena as a child.

Elena did not remember ever visiting the compound before, but Aosaginohi assured her that Isabella had always brought her when she visited; it was the reason why all of the *yōkai* present were so happy to know Elena survived unscathed until now.

"Will Akai Shinigami-sama be assisting us in the journey to Izumo?" asked Tarōbō the bird-demon, his tone even and his demeanor as stoic as Eiry's.

Shōjō snickered beside him, howling in laughter when Yuki Onna kicked him beneath the table. Tarōbō elbowed him hard, but the sea sprite simply laughed it off, leaning toward the bird-demon to refill his *sake* cup past overflowing. "Why do you ask Tarōbō-san?" Shōjō cooed. "You never pay any heed to me, and I'm also a redhead." He batted his lashes at the pale-haired bird-demon, taking another long drink from his bottle of *sake*. Tarōbō swung, but Shōjō ducked smoothly away causing Tarōbō to spill his own cup of *sake*.

"I ask because it is important to know who will be assisting us," Tarōbō growled.

Elena watched the interaction quietly, wondering who they were talking about. *Shinigami* was the term they had for Eiry's kind, which still remained a mystery to Elena because she hadn't had a chance to speak to Eiry alone. Shōjō's quip about redheads together with the use of *shinigami* made Elena suspect it was a reference to Eiry's sister.

"I am sorry, Tarōbō-san, but Bryce will not be joining us," Eiry confirmed in diplomatic tone.

"That's too bad," chimed in Nurarihyon with a wicked smile. "I quite enjoy your sister's treatment of him. She knows just how to handle a Tengu."

Tarōbō blushed enough for Elena to see it flush his dark caramel-colored skin. "What does *akai* mean?" Elena interrupted, their playful manner making her feel comfortable enough to ask the question.

Eiry fixed his icy blue gaze on hers, an amused look on his face. Everyone else at the table followed suit, except Tarōbō who snatched the *sake* bottle out of Shōjō's hand.

"*Akai* means red, Elena-san," said Yuki Onna. Her voice was as crisp and delicate as a snowflake. "Akai Shinigami is how we distinguish her from Shinigami-sama. She is the Red Shinigami."

"And Tarōbō-san has always taken a liking to her," added Rokurobei. "It is because he enjoys women as hot tempered as he is."

"She is strong and we need all the help we can get. That is the only reason I inquired," barked Tarōbō.

"Enough," chided Aosaginohi and the banter quieted down. "Let us leave strategy discussions for the meeting following our meal. Allow the poor child to enjoy her dinner in peace."

No one argued with Aosaginohi. Soon enough, they were all busy enjoying their meal. They were curious about her life after Japan and so Elena answered their questions, quickly falling into a comfortable conversation about New Orleans, her education, and what she did for a living. When she told them where she worked, all of the *yōkai* at the table exchanged knowing looks.

"Are you familiar with the firm?" Elena asked, surprised.

"Yes," Rokurobei answered.

Elena had gotten used to his floating head. She didn't know how, but it followed the movement of his body perfectly, making the image of him less disjointed than it could be.

"Everyone in the supernatural world is familiar with it," he explained. "It is run by Tartarus."

Eiry stirred next to Elena, but did not interject.

Elena grew still. She was beginning to really hate all of the surprises. She should have suspected something of the sort, since Eiry's mother had founded the firm. "My firm is run by the underworld?" she asked.

"Well, yes, technically, but that is not what I meant," Rukorobei replied. He didn't seem to realize Elena was uncomfortable, so she imagined she must be getting very good at hiding her surprise. "I was referring to the Protogenos Tartarus. They began the firm in New York several decades ago to assist the chthonic community. Their services are in heavy demand, as they facilitate dealings between the chthonic factions of the various pantheons."

Elena leaned forward against the table to steady her balance. This revelation was a little too much to digest at once. What the man was saying amounted to the fact that Elena had been working for a firm technically run by Hell. Of course, it wasn't the Christian Hell, but that didn't make it any easier to stomach. "Protogenos Tartarus," Elena repeated, a little dazed.

"He means the elemental god Tartarus," Eiry finally interjected, leaning closer to Elena. He wrapped his arm around her waist and Elena was thankful. The coolness of his skin, which she could feel through the fabric of his *kimono*, cleared the daze in her mind. His arm helped her keep her balance.

"It took form?" Elena asked beneath her breath, raising her gaze to meet Eiry's. "I thought you said Elementals didn't take form or order." She knew everyone was listening, but she said it as softly as she could, wanting this part of the conversation to be between them alone or as much as it could be under the circumstances.

"Initially, Elementals did not need to take humanoid form or be a part of the order that developed out of human theology," Eiry explained in a gentle tone, "but after several centuries of war within the pantheon some chose to take shape. Tartarus felt the need to do so because the war was being fought on their behalf. Chthonic gods are born of primordial Tartarus."

"You said '*their behalf*.'" It wasn't a question; it was a statement of fact. Elena knew the answer. There could only be one "their" at her place of employment; a job she had completely forgotten about until now.

Eiry leaned closer, concern lining his features. "Look at me," he whispered to her, and Elena did as he asked. "When Tartarus took shape, the element split into two."

"The twins," Elena thought out loud; Ms. Callas and her twin brother had founded Elena's firm.

"Yes, my mother and her twin," Eiry confirmed.

"I completely forgot I was supposed to be back in New Orleans," Elena mused. She began to calculate the dates. She was due back at work on Wednesday. The meeting with the bank was on Monday. That meant Cataline had been killed and Eiry had brought Elena here Monday night. How many days had she been at the compound? It felt like an eternity, but in reality it had only been less than twenty-four hours. That meant today was Tuesday, and Elena was due back at work tomorrow. She obviously wouldn't be making it back in time. "She's not going to fire me, is she?"

Eiry laughed. "No, Ele, she won't be firing you. She'll be waiting for us in Tartarus tomorrow night."

That should have made Elena feel better, but it didn't.

"The entrance to Yomi lies in Izumo Province, northwest of Kyoto," Tarōbō the bird-demon explained to Elena as they walked along the veranda facing the central garden. This close up, Elena could see he had amethyst-colored eyes, and his white hair was barred with thin bands of black—like the feathers of the underside of a Peregrine Falcon. He was very good-looking in a bad-boy sort of way, to the extent the term could apply to a several centuries old supernatural being wearing *kimono*.

Elena and Eiry had left the dining hall several minutes before, accompanied by Nurarihyon, his ten generals, the four guardian spirits of Kyoto, and the Kirin. The eighteen of them now moved quietly through the corridors and halls, making their way toward Nurarihyon's resi-dence—a small building toward the back of the compound. There, they would meet in his study to discuss the matter of Elena's flight to Tartarus. Yomi was the Japanese term for the underworld, and tomorrow evening Elena and Eiry would attempt to reach its entrance several hours away.

Nurarihyon's study was an intimate room lined in *tatami*. The walls were a mixture of earthen plaster and sliding doors. It featured a *tokonoma*, staggered shelving in smaller recesses along the walls and a built-in desk alcove lined in *shōji* to allow for light. It was simple and austere, typical of aristocratic and samurai households of the Edo Period.

After stepping inside, all eighteen of them took their seats on cushions placed carefully over the *tatami*-lined floor. Elena and Eiry were given a place of honor at Nurarihyon's side. The three of them sat facing the rest. Nurarihyon's ten generals sat toward the right, and the guardian spirits of Kyoto and the Kirin toward the left.

For the first few minutes the room was dead silent, the only sound the distinctive clack of a *shishi odoshi* heard from outside. *Shishi odoshi*, meaning "dear scarer", was a type of fountain once used to scare away animals but was now a common feature in gardens throughout Japan. Two shoots of bamboo were placed upright with a pivoting third balanced between. Water would pour into the pivoting shoot from a spout above, causing it to tip over once it was full. As the pivoting shoot fell back into its original position, it would make a distinctive clacking sound. It was this sound that scared away animals, and gave the fountain its peculiar name.

Elena lost herself in the rhythm of the fountain, the intervals between clacking sounds measured and precise. It calmed her nerves, which were beginning to get the best of her. Being in this room, in such close quarters with everyone, was intimidating. The *yōkai* alone were impressive, but the added presence of the guardian spirits and the Kirin made the gathering feel more intense.

Kyoto's four guardians and the Kirin were a striking display of contrasts. The Kirin was a celestial being of soft pale skin, hair spun of silver starlight, and eyes the color of smoky topaz. He was tall, slender, and of a quiet disposition. He wore many-layered robes of silk in varied tones of Tyrian purple, their delicate brocade weaved in white gold thread. Of all five, he appeared the most delicate and non-violent.

The White Tiger of the West, Byakko, was tall and powerfully built with a mane of dark raven hair, white eyes with blue irises, and milky skin with black markings. He wore a brilliant white *kimono* decorated with black plum-blossom crests at the collar and along its lengthy sleeves, white *sashinuki hakama*—a type of *hakama* that gathered at his ankles creating a ballooning effect—and a silver-thread *obi* that tied at the front with its ends loose and flowing to his ankles. Metal armor covered his torso. Of all five, he appeared the most noble and strong.

Seiryū the Azure Dragon of the East was equally impressive with opalescent scales for skin, hair and eyes of shimmering cyan, adamantine claw-like nails and sharp features. He was tall, sinewy and had a roguish smile. His hair fell past his waist and was gathered with a tie at the middle of his back. He wore a richly embroidered pearl and royal blue silk outer robe that reached mid-calf over silver *sashinuki hakama*. Of all five, he appeared the most cunning and shrewd.

The Vermilion Bird of the South, Suzaku, had golden skin, crimson hair, and eyes the color of fire agate. He was of medium build and height, and possessed a fiery temperament. He wore a silk *kimono* dyed a deep russet hue and matching *hakama*. The *kimono* had a white embroidered crest at each side of his chest bearing two crossing hawk feathers surrounded by a five-petaled circlet. Of all five, he appeared the most mischievous and ready for the hunt.

Genbu the Black Tortoise of the North was a large, brawny man with tawny skin and gruff features. He wore Ō-*Yoroi* armor, the armor of a high-ranking samurai that utilized iron plating covered in leather and lamellar segments of smaller plates laced together in parallel rows and covered in lacquer. The lacquer was the color of jade and the leather a rich umber hue. Of all five, he appeared the most vicious and fierce.

Of the eighteen gathered, Nurarihyon was the first to speak.

"All of you know what brings us here," he said in a steady voice, his rhythm slow and pronounced. His piercing silver gaze moved slowly over those gathered before him. "After nineteen years, Isabella's child returns to us in need of protection. She and Shinigama-sama must reach the entrance to Yomi without fail. We have many options, but none are easy or safe."

"You need not concern yourselves with your escape out of Kyoto," said Byakko the White Tiger in a gravelly voice. "My brothers and I will ensure no outside sky gods enter the city." He was referring to himself and the other three guardians.

A markedly more gentle voice followed. "And I will accompany you as far as I can, so long as there is no violence," said the Kirin to Elena directly. Everyone in the room lowered their gazes when he spoke.

Elena bowed her head to the Kirin, who did the same in return. Instantly, a hushed but fervent murmur spread through the room. Elena felt Eiry lean closer to her, the coolness of his skin signaling his approach.

"The Kirin cannot abide violence," he explained in a voice so low that only Elena could hear him. "That is why he may not be able to accompany us the entire way." Eiry paused and then leaned even closer, meeting Elena's gaze. "It is said a Kirin heralds the arrival of a wise and benevolent leader," he added with an equivocal grin, "and I have never seen one until today."

Nurarihyon raised his hand and the murmur in the room settled. Elena turned her attention back to the room; acutely aware of how close

Eiry was to her. She tried not to look openly at the Kirin, but it was difficult to ignore the weight of his quiet gaze.

"What are the concerns regarding the use of mirrors?" said a male voice from the back of the room, thankfully returning everyone's attention to the task at hand. The voice belonged to Rokurobei, whose floating head Elena could see through the faint glow of an *andon* lamp.

"They are not the best choice for a party as large as ours," Eiry replied. "We could be easily picked off during the crossing since only one may cross at a time."

"What about the sky?" interjected Tarōbō the bird-demon.

"You cannot protect her from the sky, Tengu," came a sharp female voice out of the shadows in the back of the room. "You should know that."

Elena strained to see who had spoken.

"I know the Tengu are stronger in the sky than your sky gods, Akai Shinigami-sama," growled Tarōbō.

"Sky gods control the sky, Tengu, no matter how good your clan of bird-demons might be. It is too big of a risk." Eiry's redheaded sister stepped out of the darkness in the back of the room. Dressed in a pink silk strapless mini dress and pumps made of silver python skin, Bryce made her way toward the front of the room, walking gingerly between the seated *yōkai*. An array of necklaces chimed rhythmically as she moved. She brushed her fingers irreverently against Tarōbō's shoulder as she passed him by. "Besides," she whispered to the bird-demon, "there is no way I'm getting on that floating whale skeleton of yours. The bones don't agree with my heels."

"No one has said anything about using the Bake-kujira," snapped Tarōbō in a bird-like cry. "The Hyakki Yakō only use it during the yearly parade."

Nurarihyon raised his hand again, this time begging his general's patience. "Welcome, Akai Shinigami-sama," the leader of the *yōkai* said to Bryce as she reached the front of the room. "We were not aware you would be joining us. We would have waited for you if we had known."

"Even I didn't know, Master Nura," sighed Bryce dramatically. She stepped between Nurarihyon and Eiry irreverently, making her way to the wall behind them. "Mother sent me to spy, to make sure we're all on the same page for tomorrow. Just pretend I'm not here," she added with a wink, and leaned back against the wall.

Eiry hissed something beneath his breath in a language Elena couldn't understand. It had weight to it, substance, and a lyrical tone. It was obviously archaic. Bryce responded with her own hiss, curt and full of venom. Elena had a feeling Eiry's words had been some kind of reproach.

"Are we in agreement then that the sky is not a viable option?" interjected Suzaku the Vermilion Bird. His fiery gaze fell on Bryce as he said it, a satisfied grin brightening his features.

It was Eiry who answered the question, exhibiting the diplomacy his sister lacked. "This is in no way a reflection or commentary on Tarōbō-san's clan, but I would prefer it if we keep our feet on the ground. Of course, whatever choice is made, the Tengu can provide air cover. It will surely be needed."

"What about modern ground transportation?" Gotokuneko the cat *yōkai* spoke for the first time. He sat with one knee raised, his elbow resting over it. "The rail system might be a viable option," he suggested. "The sky gods would not expect it, and the large quantity of humans would provide a buffer from open attack."

A soft murmur spread through the room again, at the first seemingly viable option.

"How long would that take?" asked Enkō the kappa, the water on the crown of his head reflecting the light of the few oil lamps in the room. It created a halo of refracted light around his emerald hair.

"Close to ten hours," replied Bryce, looking down at a cell phone in her hand. The glow from the screen bathed her red curls in a faint blue light, making her look almost human. She made a few adjustments to whatever she was looking at, and then added with a shrug, "a little over four if you drive."

"We're not driving," Eiry snapped.

"I didn't say you should drive," Bryce snarled in response, her top lip curling over her perfect teeth.

An uncomfortable silence followed. Elena turned to look at Eiry, who was locked in a silent staring contest with his sibling. Slowly, Elena reached toward him and placed her hand over his. At first, he didn't react but then after several seconds Eiry slowly turned his attention toward Elena. The extent of emotion she saw in his eyes was unexpected. Anger, annoyance, and shame all wove together into a slate blue hue. His lips parted as if he would speak, but then he turned his attention back to their audience, resignation clouding his gaze.

After several more minutes, a velvety voice broke the uncomfortable silence. "Can we not use the *torii*?" asked Hinoenma the succubus, as she brushed her long pale fingers suggestively across the dipping neckline of her crimson *kimono*. Everything about her was innuendo, from the dark wisps of floating locks against the pale column of her neck to the way her lips molded around the shape of every syllable. Every man in the room watched in rapt attention until someone cleared their throat and broke the effect.

"An excellent suggestion," said Nurarihyon in a clear voice. "There is a shrine dedicated to Izanami not far from the entrance to Yomi. However, there are no longer any such shrines in Kyoto to travel through."

Realizing Elena was unfamiliar with the subject, Shōjō interjected with an offer to tell the tale of Izanami-no-Mikoto, goddess of creation and death in Japan, and the *yōkai's* patron goddess. In a silken voice he spoke of Izanami and Izanagi, who were called into being by the first deities of Japan, who then entrusted them with creating the first land. To do so, Izanami and Izanagi went to the bridge between heaven and earth, and disturbed the sea below with a heavenly spear. The drops of water that fell from the spear created the first land, known as Onogoroshima. Afterward, Izanami and Izanagi made the island their home. There they were married, and from their union were born the eight islands of Japan and many other deities.

While giving birth to the incarnation of fire, Izanami was severely burned and died as a result. Izanagi, mourning deeply the loss of his wife, journeyed to Yomi in search of her. Upon finding her shrouded in shadow, he asked her to return with him to the land of the living but he was already too late, as Izanami had eaten of the food of the under-world and could never return. Upon her husband's insistence, however, Izanami agreed to speak with the god of the underworld to obtain permission to leave. In the meantime, she entreated her husband not to try to gaze upon her. Unable to resist, Izanagi removed a comb from his hair while his wife slept. He set it alight, and by the light of the comb beheld the decaying body of his wife ravaged by Death. Afraid, Izanagi ran, abandoning his wife. Enraged, Izanami chased after him, charging the Yomotsu-shikome—the foul women of Yomi—with the same task. Izanagi burst out of the entrance to Yomi, called Yomotsuhirasaka, and pushed a boulder over its mouth, preventing Izanami's pursuit. It was that very same entrance that Eiry and Elena now sought to reach.

"*Yōkai* can travel between the *torii* gates of shrines," Shōjō continued his explanation, "but only those dedicated to Izanami, as she is the goddess of death. Only she allows our passage without obstruction. To use the *torii* of a shrine dedicated to any other *kami* will require the blessing of the *kami* itself."

"Or the guardian of the shrine," came a voice from the left side of the room.

"Yes," agreed Shōjō, "or the guardian of the—" His words hung, half-spoken, in the air. He turned his saffron gaze toward the direction of the voice, a wide grin spreading over his lips. "Yes, Seiryū, Azure Dragon of the East and guardian of Kiyomizu-dera Temple, that's right."

"I thought Kiyomizu-dera was a Buddhist temple, not a shrine." Elena thought out loud, almost certain *torii* gates were associated with Shinto shrines and not Buddhist temples.

"That's right, Elena-san," replied Seiryū the Azure Dragon, his shimmering cyan gaze fixed on Elena's, "but Kiyomizu-dera's temple complex also has various Shinto shrines along with their accompanying *torii*." A sparkling smile touched the Azure Dragon's lips, and he tapped a single adamantine nail against the bottom one. "Each guardian of Kyoto has a temple dedicated to them. As I drink from the waterfall within the temple complex each night, Kiyomizu-dera has been dedicated to me," he explained, "and I will gladly grant you passage without obstruction."

THERE WAS DARKNESS in Elena's dream, darkness and shadow. The marble beneath her feet was cold and gray, but she could only see it after taking a step; the shadows would shift and a faint light would guide her forward. On and on it continued, through the cold and empty darkness. Each step she took resounded against the hollow emptiness, echoing loudly through the cavernous dark.

Finally, the faint light stopped. There were no other steps to take. Before her she saw the base of some kind of obstruction—whether it was a wall or something else, Elena couldn't tell. Then the faint light moved upward, illuminating steps made of the same gray marble as the floor. At the fourth step, Elena saw folds of fabric in a deep gunmetal shade. The folds shifted, revealing a sandaled foot. Startled, Elena cried out but there was no sound. Her voice was gone. The shadows shifted and began to fade, revealing the full measure of what stood before her.

A throne stood on a dais above the fourth step. It was made of tourmaline quartz, a clear smoky stone in variegated tones of gray shot through with prismatic needle-like crystals of black tourmaline. Sitting on the throne was a man Elena could only imagine was a god. He was Herculean, both in build and height. The throne was at least six and a half feet tall, and the back of it barely reached past his head. Behind his broad shoulders, Elena could see the shape of a great seal. Its circlet was familiar and although she couldn't see the full breadth of the image within it, Elena recognized the curve of its lines. They were the lines of the swallowtail butterfly Elena knew so well, inlaid in rainbow and black moonstones. The former, a colorless stone with a brilliant blue sheen, formed the body of its wings; the latter, a black stone with flashes of blue fire against clouds of dark blue-gray, the eyelets along their edges.

"I can give her back to you," said the god in a deep and rumbling voice. It reverberated in the marrow of her bones. He had short jet-black hair, a short-cropped black beard and midnight blue eyes. He was neither young nor old, and would be beautiful if not for the cruelty she could see in his eyes.

Elena didn't wait to see what he would say next. She turned around and fled, back through the shadows of the cavernous hall until she was swallowed by the darkness.

"Now is not the time, Elena," Eiry said firmly, his icy gaze leaving zero room for discussion.

But that little trick didn't work on Elena anymore. Not after everything that had happened. "Now is the *only* time, Eiry," Elena insisted, mimicking the seriousness of his tone. She cut off his escape, putting herself between him and the sliding door.

Eiry watched her, more amused than annoyed. "Elena, please move. We have to go. We don't have time for this."

In less than a half hour they would be leaving to begin their journey to Tartarus, and Elena still didn't know who Eiry was or why he had broken divine law to save her life. Elena had tried to talk to him about it the evening before, but Eiry had placated her with promises that they would speak of it today; yet their day had come and gone, and there had been no such conversation.

"We're going to make the time," she protested, "or I'm not going anywhere." Elena stood her ground. She knew it wasn't the smartest thing to challenge a god, but at this point she needed to assert some kind of control.

The amusement vanished from Eiry's gaze, leaving only annoyance. "Move," he commanded.

"I will not," Elena replied.

In less than a second, Eiry crossed the space between them and came to stand an inch away from Elena. The movement was so fast that she didn't actually register his stride, only his disappearance from one place and his reappearance in another. Elena flinched, but she didn't move. She swallowed a cry. Eiry caught her arm, but his hold was gentle.

He stood several inches taller than Elena. When she looked up, his face was so close to hers that she could feel his breath cold against her skin.

"Why do you keep insisting, Ele? Why does it matter so much?" Eiry's voice was strained, the look in his eyes unfamiliar. Was it fear Elena saw? Uncertainty?

It took all of Elena's strength not to step back. He was obviously trying to intimidate her, and it was working. Instead, she reached up to touch his cheek, but Eiry quickly pulled away. There was so much pain in him that she wished she could heal, so much turmoil under that icy skin. "It matters to me," she whispered. "I'm about to walk into the underworld with you—who knows where—and I don't even know who you really are! I need to know before we leave here. I don't want to die without knowing." Elena's voice broke, and the tears she had been holding back began to fall in silence.

"Elena," Eiry spoke her name softly. He brushed his fingers against her cheek, wiping away her tears.

As he studied her, Elena could see he was struggling with something. She wished she knew what it was.

"You won't die," he finally whispered.

He said it with so much conviction that every part of Elena wanted to believe him. "Don't say that," she begged, struggling to keep the fear out of her voice. "You can't promise me I won't die. We both know I'm probably not the one anyway. There's some long lost relative somewhere out there that's meant to do this. Not me."

"Stop," he growled softly, catching her face gently in his hands. The cold from his fingers bit into her skin, but Elena didn't mind it. "You can't go out there thinking like that. You can't give up, Ele. We've just started."

Elena stared at him, shaking her head. She reached for his wrists, trying to pull his hands away. It was like trying to move a column of stone—absolutely impossible. "I'm not giving up. I'm being realistic. Every other Heir has died before me, meaning they were not the one prophesied. Chances are I'm not either."

"You're the only one, Elena. You're Isabella's child. That is enough," he said, defiant.

"For you, Eiry, but not for me."

"Elena, for the love of the Moirai, stop this nonsense. We have to leave. I will get you safely to Tartarus. Trust me."

"I *do* trust you. You're the one who doesn't trust *me*." Elena searched his gaze, desperate for an answer. She needed to know who he was, to understand who she was doing this for.

Because that was the truth of it—Elena was going along with this whole thing for him; because of the pain he felt and the weight of every life before hers. She didn't want him to carry those burdens anymore. She didn't want to become a part of it.

"Please tell me who you are," she begged.

Eiry watched her quietly, finally resting his brow against hers. "Elena, you will not trust me if I do," he confessed, exhaustion making his voice heavy. "It is human nature to fear death. I can't have you fear me."

"I already know you're a death dealer, and I don't fear you." Elena said.

Eiry registered the term, and Elena immediately regretted using it. He obviously wasn't fond of it. "I saw the scythe, Eiry. Even a child could guess the connection. The term isn't important. Either way, I'm not afraid of you."

"You have no idea what you're saying," came his pained reply.

Slowly, he pulled her into his arms.

Elena stilled against him. His form was hard and cold as stone; like the dead. Even so, it didn't matter to her. "You're all I have left, Eiry," she confessed, exhausted of fighting over this. "I would like to know who you are."

"Very well," he said, his voice tight. Even though he had agreed to it, it was clear doing so was against his better judgment. "I am the thing all humans fear, Elena. It is not that I have something to do *with* death. Death is who I am; it is my element. When humans wax poetic about the cold hand of death, it is my hand they speak of," he whispered, slowly unraveling her from his arms. "It is my curse to collect what I have failed to protect," he added. His gaze moved frantically over her features, as he searched for words. "I have dedicated my existence to protecting your kind, but in the end I am also the weapon that kills them."

He caught her wrists, and a jolt of cold energy made Elena pull back.

Eiry smiled, sardonically. "Don't you see? It is my element that will snuff out your life."

A heavy silence followed. Elena moved to speak, but he silenced her with the gentle press of his fingers against her mouth.

"Do you know what the last thought in every Heir's mind has been at the time of her death?" he asked in an apathetic tone. "It has been fear—fear of Death, fear of me. Not of Helios, who has hunted them down incessantly and now struck the mortal blow, but fear of me—the one who tried in vain to protect them. The House of Thebes is not only my inheritance, Elena. It has become synonymous with Death because of every one of my failures. Your House even bares my mark."

"The butterfly crest," Elena guessed aloud.

Eiry began to walk away, but she caught his hand. In the back of her mind, Elena remembered that butterflies were an attribute of Thanatos, the Greek god of death. She remembered the times she had seen them during their trip, when no one else could. It had been him every time.

"I'm not afraid of you," she insisted, looking up into his eyes.

"You will be, Elena," he replied with a heavy sigh. "Even if it's not until that last minute. You will recognize my element in the act and you will fear me. Even Isabella did, if only for an instant. I have borne the imprint of their fear each time without protest, but yours I will not abide. I have to believe you are the one prophesied, if not I broke divine law in a vain hope."

"Why *did* you break it?" Elena whispered.

"I have asked myself that same question a thousand times, and I have yet to find the answer."

THE JOURNEY to Kiyomizu-dera Temple was uneventful. As the guardians had assured them the evening before, there wasn't a foreign god in sight over the skies of Kyoto that evening. Not that Elena had expected to see Helios or his sister swooping down from the sky like hawks. Truth be told, she didn't know what to expect. So Elena imagined it the only way she could—Helios as a boogieman waiting to lunge out at her from every corner.

The moment they stepped out of the main building of the compound, Elena looked up to the skies. She looked to the space above the central garden, to the tops of the earthen walls surrounding the compound, and to the sloping eaves of the various roofs. Her heart was in her throat and every nerve in her body was standing at attention, in spite of their repeated assurances that she would be safe.

The eighteen of them had set out just after dusk, traveling in the same fashion Elena had experienced before—with preternatural speed across the shadows and deepening darkness, Elena in Eiry's arms. Nightfall carried them along its fixed progression until they stood at the foot of the stone pathway that wound upwards through the hill to its summit at Kiyomizu-dera Temple.

They alighted on the path soundlessly, Eiry releasing Elena and setting her down gently at his side. In front of them on the path Elena saw Enkō the kappa, Yuki Onna the snow maiden, Rokurobei of the floating head, Gotokuneko the cat *yōkai*, and Hinoenma the succubus. Several feet ahead of them Byakko the White Tiger and Genbu the Black Tortoise emerged out of the shadows. One minute the space was empty and the next their bodies bled out of the darkness in the form of a shifting mist, taking shape before Elena's eyes. One by one, they all appeared in the same manner. Suzaku the Vermilion Bird took shape beside his brothers. Nurarihyon and his five remaining generals materialized several feet behind where Elena and Eiry stood. The Kirin alighted at Elena's open side. Their host for the evening, Seiryū the Azure Dragon, was nowhere in sight.

Elena and her guard made their way up the darkened path until they stood at the foot of a set of stone steps, at the crest of which sat a red and white two-storied wooden gate that marked the entrance to the temple. In the center of the gate, between its two massive posts, appeared Seiryū the Azure Dragon. Slowly, he raised both of his arms before him, and one by one the steps leading up to the gate became lit by ghostly fires, their bluish flames igniting magically along each side of every step, from the summit where the Azure Dragon stood down to the pathway where the rest of the party waited. Seiryū spoke the words of welcome and their effect reverberated through the hill in a phantom wave of energy, as if some kind of pent up pressure had suddenly been released. One by one, the eighteen entered through the threshold.

On the other side of the gate was another stone stairway that led upward toward the main temple. Seiryū led the party through the grounds of the complex until they reached a smaller stairway leading up to a collection of Shinto altars. In the center of this stairway stood a large stone *torii* gate designating the entrance into the sacred space beyond. Seiryū began his ascent while the others waited at the foot of the stairs.

A cool wind blew through the trees around them. The silence was profound. Energy stirred, becoming flux as the guardian came closer to the gate. Spectral energies took shape. Large and small, they rose out of every natural source. Tree spirits, rain spirits, mountain spirits, water spirits, wind spirits, animal spirits, and even ghosts, all converged to witness the Azure Dragon grant passage through Kiyomizu-dera's *torii* gate.

"Don't be afraid," Eiry whispered, taking Elena's hand. "There are only friends here."

Elena nodded, her gaze fixed on the glimmering figure of the Azure Dragon. He extended his hand and placed it in the center of the gate, suspended in the air as if it were pressed against a sheet of glass.

Elena held her breath as another, stronger, wave of phantom energy reverberated through the temple grounds. This time, it surged through every fiber of her being, leaving her breathless. When she looked back up, the space between the gate shimmered with an iridescent blue light.

"Five will travel through first," explained Eiry, as the Azure Dragon stepped away from the center of the gate. "Then you, the Kirin and I will cross together. Then the final six. The four guardians must remain behind."

Shōjō the sea sprite, Hinoenma the succubus, Aobōzu the cyclopean priest, Enkō the kappa, and Gotokuneko the cat *yōkai* were the first to step through. As they did so, the iridescent energy rippled like water. One by one, they stepped through the portal and disappeared.

It was now Elena, Eiry and the Kirin's turn. Without a single word between them, Eiry and the Kirin led Elena up the stairs. The Azure Dragon now stood before the left hand post of the gate. Elena met his sparkling gaze and instantly felt his energy wash over her, like the cleansing waters of a flowing stream. She gave herself over to it, allowing the current to carry her through.

"*Ogenki de.*" Keep well. Elena heard the words clear as day as she passed through the portal.

The cool feel of Eiry's hand holding hers kept Elena grounded as the world around her shifted. The ground fell away, and the temple complex shattered around her. Sound completely disappeared. Soon, all of Elena's senses vanished. In the space between the worlds, only the abstract existed. She had no body, no identity, no name. She was everything and nothing, all at the same time. The spirit world expanded around her infinitely, swallowing what came before and what was to come. The only thing it could not devour was the cold hand that held hers, anchoring Elena to who she had been and what she would become.

"Elena," called a familiar voice through the darkness.

It was faint, but Elena followed it, willing every part of her being to reach toward it. Little by little, every particle of who she had been wove itself together again until she could will herself to open her eyes.

She was on the ground, collapsed on her knees. Someone was helping her up. It had to be Eiry because she knew he had not let go of her hand. The cold bite of his touch was the only thing that had remained constant. Ahead of her, Elena could see the five who stepped through before her. They were on guard, searching through the dark; the guardians' protection did not extend this far.

"Elena, are you ok?" came the voice again.

She blinked, turning toward it. It was Eiry. He looked funny to Elena, crouching before her in his expensive suit, carrying her bags like some glorified bellhop. Elena laughed. She wasn't sure why it was so funny, but suddenly she couldn't stop laughing. She laughed so hard that she doubled over, her stomach cramping from the pain.

"Fuck," Eiry growled, and that only made Elena laughed harder. "Look at me, Ele. Focus on me," he begged, and she tried to listen, but it was impossible.

"It is not meant for a human to see the fabric," whispered a familiar female voice.

It was Aosaginohi, but Elena could not see her. Everything had suddenly gone black.

"She is not just human, and we had no choice," Eiry hissed in reply.

The anger was plain in his voice, and Elena wanted to beg him not to be short with Aosaginohi. She wanted to tell him this was not his fault; that the only thing that had guided her through was the touch of his hand. Without him, she would have been lost in the fabric between the worlds. How she knew that, Elena didn't know, but she was as sure of it as she was of the fact that she existed at all.

"What's happened?" asked another voice through Elena's laughter. It was the leader of the *yōkai*. The third party had crossed.

"The crossing," came Hinoenma's velvety voice.

"Keep watch," commanded Nurarihyon. "The guard falls on our shoulders now. Tarōbō, take to the skies! Hinoenma, Aobōzu, Enkō, Futakuchi-onna and Gotokuneko take the lead. Shōjō, Rokurobei, Yuki Onna and Aosaginohi with me."

The laughter was uncontrollable now. The pain began to draw tears. Elena's cries echoed through the laughter. Someone lifted her off the ground, and the cold press of his body assured Elena it was Eiry.

"Ele, damn it! Listen to me. Focus on me," he begged, his voice strained.

"Allow me," came the gentle voice of the Kirin. It was impossible to describe the weight of it or the quality of its substance.

The ice-cold arms that held her let go and Elena wanted to scream. The in-between was excruciating. The fear was immense. Then just as suddenly, it was gone. The laughter was gone. The pain vanished. The fear retreated until there was nothing left but a celestial light to follow out of the darkness, and that was precisely what Elena did. She allowed the light to enfold her, guiding her out of the madness that had torn her mind apart.

Elena blinked. She was lying on an earthen path a few feet ahead of a large wooden *torii*. Behind the *torii*, a steep stairway cut into the earth and led up to a shrine that was hardly visible through the trees. The Kirin held her up with an arm around her back and Elena could feel his energy course through her. It was unlike anything she had felt before. Something in the back of her neck burned, but not painfully. Eiry crouched in front of her, searching her gaze.

"Ele?" he whispered, visibly shaken.

Elena wanted to tell him she was fine, but she was having trouble finding her voice again. Her mind was a little muddled.

"She is safe," the Kirin assured him, slowly helping Elena up to her feet. "Give her a moment and she should be right as rain."

Eiry simply nodded.

"I'm fine," Elena finally whispered. The sound of her voice seemed oddly slow. It was also gravelly, as if she had just woken up. "I have a headache, but other than that I'm good."

"We need to go, Shinigami-sama," said Nurarihyon, stepping out from behind Eiry. He gave Elena a wink, and then turned his attention toward the sky.

Tarōbō the bird-demon swooped down from the sky, landing behind his Master.

"The skies are clear for now," he reported, "but the world is stirring. *Kami* across the area are waking and paying attention, which could only mean a foreign sky god. This province would not blink at Shinigami-sama's presence alone."

Tarōbō folded his giant wings behind him, and Elena noticed they settled into the familiar cloak of falcon wings she had noticed before.

"The entrance is only a few kilometers away. If we go through the mountains we will be better hidden. Izumo is the birthplace of our myths. There is too much energy converged here for Helios to locate us with precision," said Nurarihyon as he fell back behind Elena, Eiry and the Kirin.

They had begun to move down the dirt road, and Elena's guard took their various positions. Tarōbō the bird-demon flanked the guard, ready to take to the skies if Helios approached.

"If violence breaks, Elena-san," whispered the Kirin as Eiry quickly scooped her up into his arms, "I will not be able to remain, for violence causes me great discomfort."

A breeze stirred as he spoke, his silver hair catching the moonlight. He was a magnificent being, made of a purity Elena had never

before felt or seen. He was magical, like the rest, and yet entirely different—and Elena owed him her life.

"I am a Child of the Sun and a Child of the Stars," he said gently,
having guessed, or perhaps read, her thoughts. "I am bound to remain
neutral, unless my purpose in this world deems otherwise. You should
know that in your case, as of a moment ago, my purpose deems otherwise."

Elena did not have his eloquence of words nor could she actually
think of any that would appropriately express her gratitude. Just as she
settled on the simplest response, Eiry beat her to it.

"Thank you," he whispered to the Kirin, and Elena had a feeling
it had not been said on her behalf. And so with a shy smile she repeated
the words before the party began the second phase of their journey.

THE NIGHT CHILL was made worse in Eiry's arms, but Elena
didn't mind it. Compared to the sounds she heard around them as they
moved, Elena was certain she was better off in his arms. She didn't know
if she was becoming more sensitive to it or if the sheer number of it was
simply stronger in Izumo, but the spiritual energy here was a hundred
times more palpable than it had been in Kyoto. One might say it was
even more oppressive. It enveloped everything like a thick fog, making
the darkness come to life. Every shadow writhed. Every sound was bone
chilling. Elena felt eyes on them every step they took. Even in Eiry's arms,
she was terrified.

They traveled a good fifteen minutes without anything going
awry, and just as Elena was beginning to feel like they might make it to
Tartarus without a fight, all hell broke loose.

The Kirin was their only warning. Several seconds before the
clash, a voice resounded in her's and Eiry's mind. "Violence is upon you.
I must go. Keep her safe!" he cried, just before a loud crash knocked
Elena out of Eiry's arms.

Elena collided with the forest floor. The pain was excruciating.
She had claw marks on her right arm, and they burned like mad. It was
dark, but something glowed magnificently in front of her. The Kirin
stood ahead of her, the human shape of his form completely gone. He
was a majestic creature in the shape of a deer, his body glowing like
starlight. His mane shimmered like white fire, burning like the stars in
the night sky. In front of the Kirin stood Helios. With every step Helios
took, the Kirin's light grew fainter, Helios's violent intent affecting the
magnificent creature.

"Go! Please go!" Elena cried out to the Kirin, her gaze fixed on Helios.

And yet the Kirin stood his ground. He did not charge Helios, but he pulled himself up onto his hind legs, warning the god to stay back. Helios brandished a great gleaming sword in response, and again the Kirin's majesty dimmed. The shadows shifted and Elena watched as one drew itself up to its full height in front of Helios.

"Take her," said the shadow to the Kirin, in Eiry's voice.

"Take her where?" cooed Helios, laughing before he lunged at Eiry.

The sound of metal against metal filled the air, and, as Eiry pivoted, Elena could see the large scythe he held in his hands, blocking Helios's sword.

The moment their weapons clashed, the Kirin fell onto its front knees, almost as if he were bowing.

"No! Stop!" Elena cried, rushing forward.

Eiry turned and Helios caught his cheek with the tip of his blade. Silver ichor spilled from the wound and the Kirin fell to the ground. Elena threw herself onto the ground beside him, wrapping her arms around his neck.

"Where will he take her?" asked Helios in a mocking tone, taking a step away from Eiry, whose short blonde hair was now long and a brilliant glacial blue.

If Eiry were to turn his face, Elena knew she would see his eyes had turned crimson.

"Let's see," continued Helios, scratching the crown of his head with the tip of his gleaming blade. "Do you want the Kirin to take her to the entrance to Yomi? It's so close, isn't it? I can feel it. Eos is there already, waiting for a fight."

"Eos better be careful she doesn't fall in," Eiry replied, venom in his voice. "And you might want to feel a little closer. That bitch of a sister of yours is not alone. My money's on the redhead."

Helios grew still and then bristled angrily, no doubt having confirmed what he had just been told.

Around them, Elena heard sounds of a struggle. Helios had not come alone. If she searched through the darkness around her, she could pinpoint the battles in the dark. Those who were gods shimmered through the darkness with a preternatural light. There were not many, no more than four in total. That meant at least two *yōkai* per god.

Beside her, the Kirin shifted.

"I'll see you in a few," Eiry whispered to Elena in the dark.

Then suddenly, Elena was no longer on the ground. She was on the Kirin's back, holding onto his sparkling mane as he soared up into the sky. Elena chanced a look behind her shoulder and saw Tarōbō the bird-demon following behind.

"It will be over in just a minute," whispered the Kirin into her mind.

Elena leaned forward against his neck and buried her face into his mane. Being at this height was making her sick. Several minutes later they were on the ground in front of some kind of gate. Trees surrounded them. The gate was made of two standing stones with a rope strung between them. The rope, called a *shimenawa*, was made of twisted straw and indicated what lay beyond was sacred space.

Elena, the Kirin and Tarōbō stepped through the gate at once. They followed the dirt path into the shadows of the trees. There, within a small circle of dirt, were four standing stones—a small, a medium and two large. Starting from the left stood the medium, followed by a large stone and then the small. The large stone in the center was moved several feet back, leaving a gaping hole in the ground where the stone had once stood. A foot or two to the right of the smallest stone was another large one.

There, on top of the second large stone, sat Bryce with a satisfied grin.

"Took you all long enough," she hissed, her golden gaze moving between Elena, Tarōbō and the Kirin. She fixated on the latter longer than the rest. "How interesting," she said to herself, running a claw-like nail over her lower lip. Her hand was covered in gold ichor.

The Kirin instantly stepped back, the glow of his body dimming once again.

On the opposite side of the large stone where the goddess sat, Elena saw the body of a blonde-haired woman; her throat was torn asunder as if a great beast had bitten her.

"You don't have to stay here any longer," whispered Elena to the Kirin, running her fingers along his beautiful mane. "Thank you for everything."

"Interesting indeed," Bryce repeated, her tone heavy with bloodlust.

The Kirin pressed his muzzle into Elena's open hand. "*Ogenki de*," he whispered in her mind, and then he soundlessly pushed himself off the ground, soaring through the trees and into the sky.

"So you managed to get a Kirin to take sides?" asked Bryce in a silken voice, her golden gaze now on the bird-demon. "Nice to see you, *Tengu.*"

"Akai Shinigami-sama," said Tarōbō in response. His hawklike eyes fixed on the broken body of the goddess at her feet. "Is she dead?"

Bryce laughed, sucking the golden ichor off of one finger. "Silly Tengu," she purred, sucking the ichor off the next, "you know we don't die."

Tarōbō bristled, but he kept his eyes fixed on Bryce's hand, following attentively as she slipped a third finger between her lips. "You know what I meant, Akai."

"Oh no," Bryce protested, a pout forming on her perfect lips. "What happened to Akai-*sama*? Are you upset with me Tarōbō?"

"Leave him alone, Bryce," Eiry growled as he stepped out of the shadows. "And get the fuck off the boulder."

Eiry held the scythe in his hand, and he looked completely disheveled. His hair was still long and blue, and his eyes were a brilliant red. Through the collar of his suit Elena could see two large black markings, like tattoos, traveling up along the sides of his throat, one on each side; they stopped at the lines of his jaw. As he sat the bottom of his scythe on the ground, the sleeve of his blazer pulled back and Elena saw a similar black line stop at his wrist. From what she could tell, the lines started below the back of his jaw, one on each side, came down over his shoulders and then along his arms to his wrists.

Eiry caught her staring and Elena quickly looked away. "What happened to Alexander?" she asked, after several silent seconds passed by.

Eiry raised his crimson gaze to Elena's. He looked her over before answering. "You were not hurt?" he asked sounding relieved.

"Eiry, answer the question. You know full well I'm fine."

"Look at that!" exclaimed Bryce venomously, "the little Heir has spunk!"

"Are we seriously traveling with her?" Elena asked, just about fed up.

Bryce was off the stone in less than a second, and Eiry had to come between them.

"Keep your little Heir on a tight leash, Thanatos, or I'll muzzle her myself," Bryce howled. Her golden eyes began to turn lavender and her crimson hair white.

Eiry looked as if he was about to strike his own sister, but then Tarōbō eased in behind Bryce, quickly wrapping his arms around her and pulling her back. "Be still," he cooed to her, his hawklike, amethyst gaze on Elena from behind her shoulder. "You know you are being difficult. Now I think it is best if you focus on getting the Heir out of here. We cannot hold back Olympus forever."

Bryce bristled in the bird-demon's arms, her lavender gaze fixed on her brother. She seemed to weigh her options, the colors of her hair and eyes fluctuating in accordance with her mood. Then finally they settled on crimson and gold. "Fine," she said curtly. "What do you want to do with her?" she asked, motioning to the broken body of the goddess.

Eiry studied the broken figure on the ground, silent for several seconds before he replied. "The others are keeping Helios busy, but he will be here any minute. As much as I'd love to take her down with us, it was a huge headache last time."

"Last time? You've taken her down before?" Elena asked, surprised.

The goddess, even in her broken form, was quite beautiful. She was a female version of her brother, with long blonde hair and blue eyes. It was difficult to look at her beauty marred by such a bestial wound.

"He took her down after he was stupid enough to save your life," replied Bryce in a flippant tone.

Eiry's gaze lifted to his sister's and when he spoke his voice resounded through the woods. "Keres, be silent or I will make you silent."

The redheaded goddess stilled. There was anger in her gaze, but she kept her thoughts to herself. For his part, Tarōbō had not yet released her.

"It's time to go," Eiry announced. "I feel him coming closer." He looked ahead of them into the gloom.

Elena imagined he was trying to figure out how much time they had left.

His decision was quick. "Tarōbō, we're leaving the goddess here. Can you close the entrance after us?"

"Of course," the bird-demon replied. He pressed a gentle kiss to Bryce's throat and then stepped back. Nurarihyon had said that Bryce knew how to handle the bird-demon, but it seemed to be the other way around.

"Tell Nurarihyon-sama that I owe him a large debt of gratitude," Eiry said to Tarōbō as he made his way to the gaping hole on the ground. Bryce followed.

"Are you coming?" Eiry asked Elena, his lips curling into a smile. "The only way to go is down."

CHAPTER ELEVEN

"MAKE SURE YOU STEP directly behind me," came Eiry's voice through the dark.

The absence of light was so complete that Elena could not see him a foot in front of her. She knew where he stood only from memory, and the close proximity of his voice. Above, she had been able to tell how close he was by the cool press of the air around him, but in the darkness beneath the earth everything was cold.

"I can't see," Elena whispered, raising her hand in front of her. It was completely swallowed by the dark.

"Try opening your eyes," hissed Bryce, several feet ahead.

"Try being helpful for a change," Elena snapped in response, tired of being bullied.

Suddenly, there was movement in the dark. Elena heard the sounds distinctly—in the darkness, all other senses were heightened—the rustling of fabric, like the flutter of a thousand wings; the light tread of heels, like diamonds cutting through glass; a sharp sound cut through the gloom like an icy wind and ended in discordant strains of breathing. A light flickered to life in the darkness above them, pulsating and growing in size until it formed the shape of a luminous butterfly the size of Elena's open hand. Its light cut through the shadows and illuminated the immediate space around them.

The three of them were standing on a floating stairway that blended perfectly with the dark. It led downward from the mouth of the cave several feet above them, which Tarōbō the bird-demon had sealed with the stone only moments before. Eiry stood on the step below Elena, his pale fingers curled around the grips of his scythe, the blade of which he held less than a foot away from his sister's face. Bryce stood frozen two steps below her brother, anger distorting her features. The tension was palpable.

The goddess' golden gaze rose to meet Elena's, and a cruel smile touched her scarlet lips. Instinctively, Elena stepped back. She missed her footing and would have fallen had Eiry not caught her wrist as she stumbled. His movement was impossibly fast, and yet somehow he managed to keep the weapon at Bryce's neck. His crimson gaze held Elena's for several seconds and then he eased her back up gently, returning his gaze to his sister.

"Bryce go home," he said in a clipped tone, inching the blade away from his sister's throat. "I can't guide her to Tartarus and deal with your antics at the same time."

"*My* antics? She's the one testing my patience," growled Bryce, visibly wary of her brother's blade.

"Go home. Now." Eiry commanded, the weapon evaporating in the dark. It happened instantly—the stars within the metal shifted, collapsing the weapon on both sides, pulling inward and converging in his palm.

"Fine," came Bryce's venomous reply, and then she vanished in the dark.

Silence followed. Elena's body began to shake, the adrenaline finally kicking in—late. She felt lightheaded and would have sat down if she felt she could do so safely; she could hardly tell where one step of the stairway ended and another began, even with the help of the luminous butterfly.

Eiry turned to face Elena, still holding her wrist in his hand. "Are you okay?" he asked, a frustrated expression on his face for only a moment before it was replaced with the usual stoicism.

"Yes, I'm good," she answered, struggling to keep herself from shaking. It was impossibly cold, which was only making things worse.

Concern touched Eiry's expression. He quickly produced Elena's carryall from behind his back, holding it out between them. "Sorry about that," he whispered, an apology for both his sister and the unforgiving cold. "She can be a handful."

Elena hadn't really brought anything for the cold, so she took out two shirts and the cardigan she had worn with her dress on the day she visited the vault. "I hope you don't take this the wrong way, but what exactly is her problem?" Elena asked, carefully slipping on the extra clothing.

Eiry gave Elena a rueful smile. "She's never been very good at sharing," he explained. "It's nothing personal against you. She's like this with everyone."

Elena nodded. She wasn't really sure what that meant, but she decided now was not the time to get into that. There were more pressing things to worry about—like how they were going to climb down all of these stairs. From what little she could see, they were as smooth and transparent as glass, and wound endlessly deeper into the darkness. Elena couldn't tell what lay around or ahead of them. The faint echo of their voices told her they were in a cavernous space, but how large it was or how far down it went Elena did not know. She was certain of one thing— if any human managed to find their way here, they would not reach the bottom alive.

"Shall we continue on our way?" Eiry asked, interrupting Elena's train of thought. The luminous butterfly fluttered above his head, and by its light she watched as Eiry's hair and eyes returned to their usual color and the black markings disappeared from his skin.

"Sure," Elena replied, distracted by the metamorphosis. She recalled Bryce's hair and eyes had also changed. "Is that something all gods do?" she asked.

Eiry watched her quietly before providing an explanation. "It's our godhood. Most gods wear their godhoods on display at all times. Those of us who have lived on the surface, however, have become accustomed to masking it and only display it when roused in some way." He paused, but not long enough to allow Elena another question. "It's a long journey down, and it's not very safe for you. Do you mind if I carry you down?"

"How long exactly?" Elena asked, curious.

"On foot, it would take us half a day to reach the bottom. If you let me carry you we should be there in half an hour, at the most."

It wasn't the most comfortable way to travel, but it was a million times better than spending hours watching her step on the stairs. "What's at the bottom?" she asked, zipping up the carryall and placing it back in Eiry's hands. "And is there any way you could carry me piggy-back?"

Eiry laughed, the gesture softening his features. The tension and worry melted away, and he appeared more relaxed than Elena had seen him in the past two days.

"Piggy-back won't be a problem," he assured her, "and Izanami's garden is at the bottom. We must reach it to make our way to the Acheron."

Of course, he was referring to the River Acheron, the river of pain that souls had to cross to reach the Greek underworld. Elena should have expected it, but it was still bizarre to hear it spoken of as fact.

"Charon? Cerberus at the gates?" Elena asked, figuring it was better to get it all out in the open now. According to Greek mythology, Charon was the ferryman that carried the dead across the river to the entrance to the underworld, which was guarded by the three-headed dog Cerberus.

"Yes, all real, but you don't need to worry, Ele. I'll be with you the entire way. You are completely safe now. The sky gods cannot enter here to find you."

"Completely safe once I get off these stairs, you mean," Elena said only half in jest. It was a huge relief, though, to know she didn't have to worry about Alexander for now. It opened up her mind to worry about the myriad other things that awaited her—like seeing Ms. Callas, for instance.

"Yes," Eiry replied with a smile, bringing her back to the present. "Once I get you off of these stairs you'll be safe and sound."

THE DESCENT was much easier than anticipated. The temperature grew colder the further down they went, but other than that, the journey was comfortable, even with the added weight of Elena's carryall on her shoulders. The position gave her an excellent vantage point from which to fully experience Eiry's movements. It was incredible, actually, like being on a roller coaster but without any bumps or jolts. Eiry darted down the stairs at lightening speed, slowing down only when the air got too cold for Elena as they reached the bottom.

They reached Izanami's garden enveloped in darkness. Only when Elena's feet touched the ground did ghostly fires ignite before them and illuminate the way. Hundreds of them burst into white flames along a winding path. They rose at once into the looming darkness above them, converging to form a glowing sphere suspended in the cavernous space thousands of feet above—a phantom moon illuminating an eternal night. Elena and Eiry stood at the beginning of a stone path that led from the floating stairway, now faintly visible through refracted light, through a stroll garden of sculpted trees to a stunning palace set against a reflecting pond. Everything around them, including the graceful eaves of the palace, was enveloped in a blanket of powdered snow.

Elena looked around her in wonder, stunned to see such a beautiful place so deep beneath the earth's surface. "Is this what Tartarus is like?" she asked Eiry, following close behind him as he began to lead her through the path. Out of the shadows, the luminous butterfly reappeared and alighted on his shoulder. She glowed with an incandescent light, the eyelets now visible along the edges of her wings.

Eiry looked back at Elena over his shoulder and smiled. "Yes, and no," he whispered in response to her question about Tartarus, reaching out to take her hand. In the ghostly light, he was radiant. His skin glistened with the same shimmer as the snow around them, and his eyes shined with the same ethereal light as the phantom moon.

Above ground, Eiry was beautiful, but below he was unlike anything or anyone Elena had ever seen. For the first time since Elena had met him, he appeared truly happy.

"Tartarus," Eiry continued to explain as he led Elena further down the path, "is like this in that it is beneath the earth within a cavernous space. There is no sunlight, only starlight. Some spaces are darker than others, but the lightest it ever gets naturally is twilight. This part of the underworld in particular reflects Izanami's personality."

Elena nodded, silently taking in the meaning of his words and the quiet beauty of their surroundings as they continued down the winding path lined in trees, some of which were bare and others clothed in foliage. Every aspect of the garden was carefully arranged to fit the season—from the different types of trees with their varying outlines defined by the snow to the graceful curve of the snow-covered moss lining the edges of water and stone.

"Every pantheon has its own death deity," Eiry finished his explanation as he led Elena over a wooden bridge, "and each one presides over its own entrance to the underworld. They are all connected to Tartarus."

The palace rose up before them, an elegant structure with dark wooden details, platinum-plated fixtures and intricate gabled roofs. It was a collection of three staggered buildings with sliding *shōji* and *fusuma* doors connected by open-sided walkways. The buildings lined the northeastern edge of the pond with a walkway extending out over the water on the western most side, leading to a moon-viewing pavilion built on a small island within the pond.

Two white robed attendants waited for them at the entrance of the palace.

At Eiry's approach, each attendant bowed low and whispered their greeting in tandem. "Welcome, Shinigami-sama. Please follow us," they said, not once lifting their gazes to meet Eiry's. Then they stood up in unison and with bowed heads led Eiry and Elena in silence through the veranda and gabled walkways, along richly decorated rooms—each one with coffered ceilings, gilded screens, and elaborately painted doors—to the moon-viewing pavilion that extended over the water.

Inside the pavilion, beside a standing mirror framed in platinum filigree, stood a woman in exquisite robes spun of vermilion, pearl, gold and silver thread. She wore a brilliant white silk *kimono* and vermilion *hakama* beneath flowing and staggered layers of multiple outer-robes. The innermost robe matched the vermilion thread of her *hakama* and was followed by five robes in pearly white. The seventh robe was made of gilded thread, and was covered by an eighth and final outer-robe of a deep red maple silk with floating chrysanthemums stitched in white and silver thread, outlined in gold. The various colors were visible in staggered layers at her sleeves and along the collars of her robes; robes which fell past her feet and flowed in layers behind her. The woman's long black hair fell down her back and almost to her ankles. Her delicate features were hidden behind a gilded veil.

She was Izanami-no-Mikoto, the Japanese goddess of creation and death.

The two attendants stepped inside the pavilion and bowed low before their mistress. They spoke in whispers, which Elena could not hear. Once their exchange was complete, each one took their place at their mistress' side, prostrate and silent on the floor beside her feet.

"Thanatos-sama," whispered Izanami-no-Mikoto to Eiry with a bow of her head. Her voice was as ethereal as the song of a nightingale.

It was the first time Elena had ever heard someone from the Japanese pantheon use Eiry's proper name.

Eiry stepped across the *tatami* floor and came to stand before her. Elena caught a glimpse of a smile before he dropped to one knee.

"Izanami-sama," he whispered in the gentlest tone. He did not stand until she begged him to do so. The attendants then quickly took their leave—stepping backwards, facing Izanami and Eiry the entire time, and bowing repeatedly as they left.

Eiry stood silent beside the goddess until the three of them were completely alone. Then he turned his gaze to Elena and smiled. "Ele," he whispered in a playful tone, "this is Izanami-no-Mikoto, my godmother."

IT WAS ODD to say the least, to watch in quiet wonder as godson and godmother visited quietly with each other, speaking of the same things their human counterparts would—which made perfect sense if one considered the literal origins of the title. The goddess Izanami inquired about Eiry's family and well-being, greatly interested in the events of the past several weeks. They spoke of things Elena could not begin to understand and so her mind drifted, taking the opportunity to process all that had happened until this point.

She was at the entrance to the underworld, seated on *tatami* mats being served tea by the Japanese goddess of death. Actually, Eiry was being served tea. Elena was not. From now on, until the time she left the underworld, Elena could not eat. If she did, she would be bound to the underworld forever, unable to fulfill the prophecy. Eiry had assured her their visit would be brief, only long enough to unseal the divinity within Elena's blood. Without doing so, Elena would not stand a chance against the sky gods. As usual, Eiry was scant on the details, and Elena was too afraid to ask. She was anxious about what awaited for her in Tartarus. If all the gods were like Bryce, it was bound to be a very difficult experience.

The only thing that alleviated Elena's anxiety was the fact that Eiry would be with her the entire time; that, and a thought taking root in the back of her mind—a hope fueled by a dream that by going to the underworld Elena might be able to find Cataline and get her back. If there were any chance Elena could save Cataline, she would take it.

Eiry touched her hand and Elena jumped, startled.

"Are you ready to leave?" he asked gently. "I didn't mean to startle you."

Izanami knelt quietly at Eiry's side, her visage still hidden behind her veil. Elena recalled the myth speaking of her appearance as terrifying, but through the gossamer fabric of her veil Elena only saw the graceful lines of a beautiful face.

"I'm ready," Elena said, taking Eiry's offered hand. He helped her to her feet after assisting Izanami.

Elena looked around her. The water surrounding the pavilion was still, reflecting the light of the phantom moon like a mirror. The view of the snow-covered garden beyond was sublime.

"Once a year," Izanami whispered as she took her place beside the filigree-framed mirror, "the stone that seals the entrance above is removed and the moon is reflected against the water."

"We hold a festival then," added Eiry, a winsome smile on his handsome face. "The Greek and Japanese chthonic pantheons celebrate it together. Even the *yōkai* descend. Izanami is my mother's greatest ally and friend, and on that day we honor our alliance." Eiry came to stand before the mirror. He extended a hand and the luminous butterfly fluttered from his shoulder to the palm of his hand. Eiry's eyes met Elena's through their reflection in the mirror. "In a few seconds she'll come to rest over your heart, Ele. Don't be afraid. It's just part of the process."

"What process?" Elena grew completely still as the butterfly fluttered gracefully through the air and landed on her cardigan, over her heart. She held her breath and watched, as it flapped its wings twice, the movement slow and drawn out.

Eiry turned around, his icy gaze resting on the butterfly momentarily before rising to meet Elena's. "She needs contact with you for us to travel through the mirror," he explained.

"We're going through the mirror?" Elena felt two things at once—panic that she would be affected the same way she was when she traveled through the *torii* gate, and a cold, tingling sensation where the butterfly sat over her heart. Seconds later, the butterfly took flight again, this time landing on the surface of the mirror. At its touch, the surface rippled like water.

Elena's anxiety must have been obvious because Eiry quickly tried to reassure her. "There's nothing to worry about," he said as he extended his hand once again for the butterfly. "Traveling through mirrors is less complicated. *Torii* travel is fueled by the divine and involves crossing through the fabric between the worlds. Mirror travel, on the other hand, is fueled by magic—a human art. These mirrors, one of which resides at every entrance, were built to accommodate human souls. It'll be fine, like stepping through a curtain of mist."

Elena trusted Eiry implicitly, but she still couldn't help feeling a little nervous. The memory of her last experience wasn't exactly pleasant, and the Kirin was not here to help her through it.

"Do not fear, child," said Izanami in her lyrical tone. "It is perfectly safe. I am sorry our meeting was so brief, but it was indeed a pleasure to meet you, Elena of the House of Thebes."

The woman's words were unexpected, and the warmth behind them a surprise. "Thank you," Elena whispered, uncertain of what else she should say. Then Eiry offered her his hand.

"There's one more thing," Eiry whispered.

"Isn't there always?" Elena replied, taking his offered hand. She took her place beside him, facing the mirror.

"It will be crowded on the other side," he said before stepping through the mirror. "Make sure not to let go of my hand."

EIRY WAS RIGHT, on both accounts. Walking through the mirror felt like stepping through a thick fog, completely painless. They stepped out onto a small outcrop of rock on the other side, below them a black sand shore teeming with people. Twilight clung to the shore, held at bay by a darkness that floated like mist over the water. Elena couldn't tell whether it was a river or subterranean lake, nor could she see anything on the opposite side. A single boat made of pale birch wood broke through the darkness, heading toward the shore.

Thousands of bodies crowded the shoreline, their cries a cacophony of staccato rhythms that rose through the cavernous space. Trying to listen was a maddening effort. They spoke in every language of the world, their words beginning in their native tongue and ending in a universal language that Elena could somehow understand. The effect was dizzying.

Eiry squeezed Elena's hand. "Remember not to let go," he whispered. "We have to make our way through the crowd to the boat. I'll move as fast as I can, but there are too many souls for me to move as quickly as I usually do."

The thousands of bodies below weren't bodies at all—they were souls. Now that she was beginning to get used to the sights and sounds, Elena could see their images were insubstantial, denser than a shade but lighter than a physical body.

"And Ele," Eiry added in a gentle tone, "make sure to keep moving."

"Why do I have to keep moving?" she asked as they began to move down a small path cut into the rock beside them. It wasn't smooth, and Elena wasn't the best climber.

"You're alive—sharper and more physical than they are. Sooner or later they'll be able to tell. You'll be perfectly safe with me here, but it'll be easier if you know what we're walking into, just in case. Being in that mass of souls can be overwhelming."

"Is this where all souls come once we die?"

"Yes," was his answer—unpleasant but true. "Everyone has to pay the ferryman. Those who cannot pay wander the shores for an allotted time. As you can imagine, the types of payments have ranged over the centuries. Most make it across, but the wait can be long. You have the Christian concept of Purgatory to thank for that."

Elena followed Eiry down the path, pressing close to him once they stepped into the crowd. It was like Bourbon Street on the last weekend of Mardi Gras, but a thousand times worse. The sound was deafening. Souls cried out, pushing and shoving to try to get further ahead. The mass of souls became a sea, its movement unified, moving forward in waves only to be pushed back. Everyone was struggling to reach the same area, a point ahead where the sea of souls was funneled into a labyrinthine section leading to the shore. From their vantage point above, Elena had been unable to tell what exactly formed the winding sections, but it had reminded Elena of the winding lines at an amusement park. A smaller, linear corridor ran along the left side of the area, empty, without a single soul in sight.

As they moved forward through the crowd, Elena spent most of her time dodging hands that grabbed and pulled at her trying to get ahead. Eiry held her hand with an iron grip, guiding her through.

"Is there any other way?" Elena called out.

Eiry slapped a hand away as it grabbed at his arm, pushing a little further before answering. Elena couldn't see his expression, but his tone was filled with frustration.

"Unfortunately, no. I never have to travel this way. Gods simply appear wherever they want, but I can't do that with you. Like the *torii*, your human body and mind will not be able to withstand it. Once we get your divinity unsealed, we can begin to ease you into it, but for now this is our only option. As you can imagine, underworld gods do not fly. We can jump and glide great distances, but it's virtually impossible with this crowd. I have to be careful not to damage the souls."

Elena could hardly hear his explanation through the din. Half-way through, she heard his voice in her mind, the way she had heard the Kirin's. For the first quarter of the way through the crowd, none of the souls paid them any more attention than they did the others. That changed once they reached the middle. Those closest to them became much more aggressive, physically attacking Elena and Eiry in their desperation.

Eiry pulled Elena against him, wrapping his arms around her back to shield her from the pressing crowd. "The deeper in we get," he explained, "the longer the souls have been waiting. The daze of death has lifted, and desperation to reach the shore kicks in. They recognize life in you and their desire for it momentarily eclipses everything else. Stay close. I'm aiming for the left."

Elena looked toward the shore, but she couldn't see a thing past the throng of heads and shoulders. Someone pulled her hair and she cried out, dodging a hand as someone else tried to grab her. Eiry raised his hand to strike and then stopped himself, cursing.

"What'll happen if you hit them?" Elena asked, pushing back with all of her weight as someone pushed into her from the side.

Eiry stopped moving, positioning himself around her so that he took most of the hits. They swayed with the crowd, and Elena held onto him.

"They'll shatter and will be lost, no longer part of the fabric," he finally answered, his gaze fixed on something above them.

Elena looked up, but she couldn't see a thing. Just black.

"Climb on my back," Eiry commanded, and Elena didn't have to think about it twice.

It was a struggle to put her carryall on her own back with the tight press of the crowd, but she managed it. Someone grabbed onto it and began to pull Elena from behind, but Eiry grabbed their hand and with an animalistic growl pushed the soul away. Then he vaulted up into the air, Elena clinging to his back.

Eiry clawed into a ceiling Elena had not been able to see from the ground. The sound of his nails digging into the rock sounded like metal. Elena buried her face against the nape of his neck. She closed her eyes and breathed in deeply, trying not to get sick. It felt like her stomach was in her throat. Eiry used his weight and their momentum to launch himself toward the left, landing in front of the linear corridor that ran adjacent to the labyrinthine line.

They were standing a few feet away from where the crowd began to funnel, in an empty space leading into the adjacent corridor. The teeming crowd, seemingly unobstructed, did not cross over to where they stood. Like the First Class line at the airport, this line stood empty while the other was full to the brim.

"Ele, it's okay now. You can let go," Eiry whispered as Elena held onto his neck for dear life. He gently unwound her arms and let her down.

From this close up, Elena could see the winding corridor's walls were made with smooth, black stone that reached ten feet high. As Elena studied the crowd, someone from the main waiting area tried to cross over into the empty space in which they stood, but he didn't make it far. He was physically impeded, as if he ran into an invisible wall.

"What's going on?" Elena asked Eiry, watching as further down the crowd a few other souls tried the same thing only to find themselves against the same invisible wall.

"Only those who are called can use this corridor. It leads up to the front of the line," Eiry replied.

"Like a Fast Pass at Disney World?"

Eiry turned toward Elena, a slightly confused look on his face. "What's a Fast Pass? I've never been to Disney World."

That shouldn't have come as a surprise. "They have them at the line to each ride. You go up to a machine and it prints out a pass, giving you a time when to come back to the ride. When that time comes, usually a few hours later, you take the line on the left and walk right up to the front."

Eiry didn't reply immediately. Elena imagined the concept was as alien to him as all of this was to Elena.

"I wonder if that's what Charon had in mind," he finally said, contemplating it further before continuing. "Charon implemented this program a few centuries ago. It predates your example, but it works very much in the same way. Charon got tired of souls swarming the shore. As time passed and theologies changed, the crowds became much larger and the rules more complicated. Souls were staying longer on shore. He had the corridors built to control the crowd.

"Those who are destined for Elysium from birth—the descendants of gods—use the empty line on the left. They are drawn to it inherently. Everyone else must wait in the main line. Those who reach the pier through the main line without payment must return to the back of the line and serve an allotted time on shore. Once their wait period is over, their name is called and they may use the line on the left instead of having to fight their way to the front of the main line once again."

If Elena recalled correctly, the Greek underworld was divided into various parts: Erebus—where the souls passed immediately after death and waited to be ferried across the river to the gates of the underworld; the Domos Aidaou—the House of Hades where souls were judged and sorted into their afterlives; the Elysian Fields—home of the virtuous and the initiates of the ancient Mysteries; the Elysian Islands—where Heroes and descendants of the gods dwelt; the Asphodel Fields—a ghostly meadow where neutral souls resided; and Tartarus—the great void, an abyss used as the prison of the gods. There were also satellites to the realm, such as the abode of the Fates and the cave of the Oneiroi—the land of dreams.

As Elena thought back to what she had learned in school and university, a name was called. There was a commotion in the crowd. The sounds of wailing grew louder, and an altercation erupted near the middle of the mass. Several minutes later a woman dressed in a Georgian era gown, the once-fine silk and lace now faded and worn, pushed herself out of the crowd and through the barrier. Eiry and Elena watched her in silence as she slowly made her way past them and down the corridor on the left.

"She's been waiting here since the late 18th century?" Elena asked in shocked disbelief.

"She obviously didn't have payment or she lived a particularly wicked life."

"You can't be serious."

"Dead serious, Ele. Look through the crowd."

And she did, safe enough from this distance to finally be able to do so. The souls, attired in what Elena could only assume was their burial clothes, spanned various historical periods from the middle ages all the way through modern times. It looked a lot like the Bourbon Street crowd on Halloween.

"That's a hell of a backlog," she said, overwhelmed.

Eiry laughed softly, looking quietly over the crowd. "Not really. Charon's a stickler for productivity. It moves pretty smoothly. Now, if you'd follow me, there's a boat we need to catch."

Elena followed Eiry through the empty corridor. Now that she could see the walls up close, she saw they were made of a type of black stone with silver markings.

"It's called snowflake obsidian," Eiry informed her as she stopped to take a closer look. "Charon's little inside joke at my expense. He has to entertain himself somehow."

It took Elena a moment to understand, then she remembered Alexander's nickname for Eiry—*Snowflake*. Bryce had also used it, and not in a loving way. "I don't—" she began to say, as they continued along the path, but then stopped.

She had intended to say she didn't quite get the nickname, but then it hit her. If Elena didn't dislike Alexander so much, she would have to admit it was actually quite funny. Eiry's nature was lethal—literally— as were his abilities, and yet his godhood manifested as ice; as pretty as a snowflake, with snowy skin, hair the color of glacial water and eyes as bright as winterberries.

Watching him now, leaning against the obsidian wall with an unamused expression on his face, and seeing it all in context, Elena found the effect almost hysterical.

"Let's move it along," he said to her brusquely, pulled himself off the wall, and continued to lead them down the corridor, effectively ending the discussion before it began.

After several minutes of walking, they reached the head of the line. They stood on a small dark wooden pier, Charon and his boat moored alongside it. The woman in the Victorian garb was already on the boat. The pier was empty, the same type of invisible barrier holding the crowd back within the corridors. Eiry grabbed hold of Elena's hand and stepped out onto the pier, leading her toward the boat.

The ferryman appeared confounded that two souls had somehow crossed his barrier, but as Eiry and Elena approached he realized his mistake and quickly stepped off the boat, making his way toward them in a hurried pace.

Unlike the majority of his descriptions, Charon the ferryman was neither old nor grizzled. He was tall, of medium build and appeared to be no older than fifty. He had short salt-pepper hair and a cropped beard. His eyes were a bluish-gray, and his smile was incredibly kind. He reminded Elena of a Greek philosopher. He wore typical Greek robes made of dark gray wool fastened at the shoulders with brooches and a belt around the waist, over which he draped a heavier cloth of indigo blue that hung from his back over his left shoulder, the opposite end carried under his right arm and across his body to hold over his left arm. The cloak-like cloth reached below his knees.

"Master, why on earth have you come through the front of the house?" Charon inquired of Eiry in a respectful tone, worry lining his kind face. "Illyria will not be pleased."

"We have a guest, Charon," Eiry replied warmly, motioning toward Elena.

Charon looked Elena over with a keen gaze, worry quickly giving way to confusion. "She's human, Sir," he said softly.

"Hardly her fault, Charon," Eiry quipped. Elena elbowed him, and Charon's confusion quickly changed to distress. Eiry laughed, raising his hand. "Don't be alarmed, Charon. Mother knows. Plus, I've brought you something." With a bright smile, Eiry reached into his pocket to retrieve the item. It was a coin, and he flicked it expertly for Charon to catch.

Charon's face lit up once he caught the coin, and took a moment to inspect it. "Phoenician, Sir?" he asked in quiet awe, obviously touched by the gesture.

"Indeed it is," Eiry confirmed. "For your collection."

Charon took a moment to compose himself, slipped the coin into the folds of his robes and then stepped aside, motioning them toward the boat. "You are too kind, Master Thanatos. I have a few souls to drop off at the gates and then I will take you to the side entrance. Perhaps Illyria will not notice you going in through the side."

Eiry stepped onto the boat with relative ease, extending his hand for Elena. "Thank you, old friend," he said to Charon with a short nod.

"Who's Illyria?" Elena whispered to Eiry as he helped her onto the boat. There were no more than fifteen souls on the boat with them. Elena and Eiry sat alone on the back row, watching quietly as Charon expertly maneuvered the boat off the pier with a long wooden pole.

"Illyria is my mother's lady-in-waiting, so to speak," Eiry replied once they were on their way across the waters, the black shores of Erebus fading away into the mists behind them. "She's in charge of the royal household, and she's a royal pain in the ass." Eiry was facing toward Elena as he spoke, his glowing gaze the only light in the darkness.

THE SIDE ENTRANCE TO EIRA, the royal city of Tartarus, began at the mouth of an underground tunnel running west of the region of Hades, which included the gates, the Asphodel Meadows, all of Elysium and the Domos Aidaou itself. The tunnel was at least fourteen feet high and ten feet in diameter. It was hewn out of a dark stone. The air was cold and damp. The tunnel was dark, but for a faint glow of light Elena could see deep within the tunnel. Its proximity was misguiding, and it took much longer to reach than Elena expected. Eiry and Elena walked quietly side by side, the luminous butterfly fluttering silently in front of them, once again guiding their way.

"What should I expect when we reach Eira?" Elena asked, cursing softly as she stumbled on the uneven floor.

Eiry inched closer and took her hand in his. "Take it easy with the walking, Ele. We have all the time in the world, and I'll try to minimize the exposure as much as I can when we get to the city. I'm hoping to sneak you in unnoticed and then call on my mother. That way you have time to get acclimated before they call the inevitable meeting. You'll need to meet with the Moirai and a few others."

Elena froze where she stood, Eiry stopping patiently beside her. "The Moirai? You mean the Fates? I have to meet with the Fates?" Elena had met a lot of divine beings already, but she wasn't sure she could handle meeting the Fates. That was just insane. Elena's heart began to race just thinking about it, images of ghostly figures dancing in her head.

"Ele, relax. It's just my family. Don't let the titles freak you out." Eiry whispered the words, slowly easing Elena forward. "Ele, come on. Look at me, breathe, and then look around. You're missing the best part."

Elena hadn't realized they had reached the part of the tunnel with light. They must have been at least two miles in. A large portion of the wall to their right was cut out to form a type of lookout. It was twilight on the other side of the wall, and the difference in darkness was so stark that the twilight looked almost like daylight in the darkness that surrounded them.

As Elena stepped forward, guided gently by Eiry's hand, she looked out through the opening and was immediately floored by the view.

The opening overlooked the vast region of Hades, which sat within a massive underground lake, cavernous walls rising infinitely at each side and behind it. The space was so immense that Elena could not see the ceiling of the cavernous space above. From their vantage point, high on the western wall of the lake, she could see the entire breadth of it. Five landmasses rose out of the dark waters of the lake and formed concentric circles, channels of water in between each one, the fifth mass serving as the axis. Vertical channels cut through the eastern, western and northern cardinal points of the four outer circles leading into the central landmass, which housed the Domos Aidaou. The southern cardinal point consisted of land bridges connecting each circle, leading souls from the Southern Gate—the entrance to Hades—through each island to the Domos Aidaou, where each soul would be judged and sorted accordingly.

The outer island held the large Southern Gate, and served only the purpose of a perimeter. The same darkness that had hovered over the River Acheron clung to the waters and channels between the islands, making it impossible for those on each island to see the opposite shore, giving the viewer the sense of being on a solitary island. Only through the main road leading from the Southern Gate could all islands be observed properly.

The second island housed the Asphodel Fields, where neutral souls resided—souls who had been neither virtuous nor evil in life. It was a land devoid of any true color, covered entirely in a meadow of asphodels, the food of the dead. They were a type of pale plant with a tuft of narrow leaves at the base and an elongated stem ending in a cluster of white flowers. The Fields extended the full length of the island, forming the recurrent background of a ghostly life even more dire and imperfect than the one above. Before crossing into Asphodel, the souls drank from the River Lethe, losing their proper Selves so they could go about the mundane tasks of living in the space between lifetimes.

The third island housed the Elysian Fields, home to virtuous souls and those who were initiates of the ancient Mysteries. Handsome whitewashed villas lined the endless circular shore, forming a community nestled within narrow stone-paved streets lined in poplar trees and overflowing with fragrant and brightly colored flowers. The isle knew a perpetual spring, with shaded groves and sparkling fountains. Its inhabitants lived a pleasant life of leisure.

The fourth island, closest to the Domos Aidaou in the center, was known as the Elysian Islands. Unlike the outer three islands, it was not made up of a single mass of land but was a collection of smaller islands linked by stone bridges and narrow canals, very similar to the city of Venice. Although it was this island that was most commonly referred to as Elysium, the term technically comprised both the Elysian Fields and the Elysian Islands. It was on the Elysian Islands where Heroes and the descendants of the gods dwelt after death, a peaceful and happy afterlife lived amid interconnected buildings reminiscent of the Palace of Knossos in Crete. Each tiny island housed a collection of villas and buildings forming palaces of interconnected and labyrinthine rooms with hanging gardens and central courtyards. It was a utopian society exclusively for those descended from divine blood, where myriad Kings and Heroes feasted in honor of their former glories amid endless generations of their own bloodlines.

The fifth and central island housed the palace of Hades, the Domos Aidaou, a colossal structure made of cold gray stone. The palace stood as a citadel rising out of a large hill that took up almost the entire diameter of the circular island. The hill was made up of the same dark stone as the tunnel Elena and Eiry were currently standing in, its surface craggy and uneven. A massive stone wall surrounded the circumference of the hill with only a single gate allowing entry. This gate stood perfectly aligned with the Southern Gate on the outermost island. Behind the gate was a concentrated city of gray stone buildings skirting the area below the citadel, winding its way along the craggy rocks to the entrance of the palace above.

The city and palace were a mixture of Classical and Ottoman architecture, their elements perfectly balanced to form a unique blend of vast inner spaces with domed roofs and sculpted arches, colonnades and peristyle capped in decorated friezes, ornate balconies carved in stone, graceful courtyards built around fountains, and a masterful use of articulated light and shadow creating a delicate and stoic harmony. It was a stunning view, diminished by a monochromatic and haunting land-scape. Gray mists rolled across it like a gossamer shroud, leaving the viewer with a deep sense of melancholy and loss.

Eiry and Elena watched the scene from their perch high against the western wall, quiet for several moments. Then Eiry, leaning closer to Elena, asked in a gentle tone, "What do you think?"

"I've never seen anything like it," Elena replied, once again taking her time to study each concentric circle.

Every landscape was completely different than the one before or after it. This was the fabled Hades, no longer a thing of myth or legend; no longer abstract. The implications were staggering. For starters, there was no turning back. This was real. If Elena had held a glimmer of hope in her heart that this was all a dream fueled by an overactive imagination, that hope was now crushed. Reality had begun to shift in Japan, culminating in a very sharp and awful truth. Everything she knew before fell to dust, her history now completely re-written. What the future held, only the Fates could say.

"This is only the realm of the dead," Eiry said, interrupting Elena's thoughts. "Ironically, I'm not particularly fond of it. Eira is entirely different, rich in color and as beautiful and delicate as a snow flower."

Eiry sounded so alive when he spoke of his home that it made Elena acutely aware of how much she missed hers, and the regret she felt that Cataline would no longer be a part of it. "What does '*Eira*' mean?" she asked, her voice slightly shaken. "It sounds a lot like your name."

"It means *snow* in Welsh, and it is my namesake."

"Why Welsh?"

"Why not?" Eiry said with a grin, and reached for Elena's hand. "Ready to keep going? Eira is just around the corner."

Of course, he never answered the question.

CHAPTER TWELVE

STEPPING OUT OF THE DARKNESS of the tunnel into the royal city of Eira was like walking through the mists into another world. Like Hades, the city was situated within an enormous cavernous space, but all similarities ended there. Just as Eiry had described it, the city rose out the ground beneath it like the first sparkling blossom in the fading winter snow. Here, the winter of death was past its zenith. Rather than an ending, it was the beginning of a life renewed—fragile and yet extraordinarily resilient.

Eiry and Elena stepped out of the tunnel into a grove of pale birch trees, their thin trunks gleaming like silver in the twilight and their branches clothed in delicate leaves. A brilliant green moss blanketed the ground around them, covered in a light sprinkling of snow. A small dirt path wove its way through the trees, which grew so closely together that Elena could not see the city beyond. All was silent, but for the distant sound of water.

They took the path before them, both silent as they made their way through the trees. Soon, they were walking along a stream of running water, small at first but growing wider and stronger—into a river, the further they moved along. Several minutes later, Elena heard the sound of a waterfall. The path bent before they reached it, leading them away from the river and out of the trees into a stone pathway that led downward along a hill until reaching a beautiful stone bridge with two archways at its base.

"The view gets much better from here," Eiry said as he led Elena onto the bridge.

They were standing above the city of Eira, the waterfall cascading behind them, passing beneath the bridge and spilling into the city below. The rushing water cut through stone and earth forming several pools at different heights, the city rising out of the landscape around it—a collection of ornate wooden structures built over foundations of stone. Everything was covered in a light dusting of snow.

"It's the River Lethe," Eiry explained with a smile, his gaze turning to meet Elena's. He was happy to be home, and the emotion brightened his features. He almost looked carefree. "It's waters grant oblivion, and it is from this river that all souls must drink to forget their former lives. Contrary to popular belief, it, not the Styx, is the most sacred of the five rivers in the underworld, which is why the royal city is built around it."

"It's beautiful," Elena said as she studied the scene below them.

They were close enough to the city now that she could see the buildings were made of the same pale wood as the trees that surrounded it. All living spaces were open to the elements, the buildings' outer walls a collection of interconnecting wooden archways capped with latticework carved into a delicate filigree. Within the archways, like tiny jewels, hung delicate spheres made of glass. They were filled with an iridescent gas-like substance that was continuously in flux, each one in a specific tone of rich blue, deep green or brilliant red.

Elena followed Eiry to the opposite end of the bridge, where the stone pathway led along the cascading river through the center of the city. As they walked, something caught Elena's eye. Three floating lights flickered into existence in the misty air above the river, directly to her right. They looked like fireflies, but their light, instead of a soft yellow glow, matched the tone of the glass jewels that decorated the city's facade. As Elena looked down the winding path at the approaching city, she realized the air was filled with them, tiny lights flickering in and out of existence in a silent and ethereal dance.

"What are they?" Elena asked Eiry as one flickered into life in front of her, a brilliant pale blue. It floated up to eye level and for an instant Elena swore she heard the sound of tiny wind chimes whispering in the wind. Then just as quickly as the light had appeared, it faded away.

"They are weir lights," Eiry replied. "They are my mother's eyes and ears, made from the energy that created Tartarus."

"Now try that again, in English," Elena teased, watching as three more weir lights flickered into existence above Eiry's shoulder, dancing close to his ear. He bent closer to them, cupping his hand an inch beneath them, as if to hear. Then after several seconds of this type of interaction, they shined brightly and blinked out of existence.

Eiry offered Elena a smile before he reached for her hand. "They are sentient energy," he explained as he continued to lead her down the pathway into the city. "They are beings made of starlight. They love to play around, but they always have their eyes and ears open. They know everything that happens in Tartarus. There is a type of weir light that can take humanoid form, and *they* are the servants of the royal household."

They turned a corner as Eiry finished his explanation, the path ending in a courtyard lined in open archways. Up close, the architecture was even more stunning; intricate and delicate in ways no human hand could have fashioned. The buildings rose out of the ground sculpted by nature itself, as if the wood had taken shape of its own accord to design the otherwise unnatural formations. Unwittingly, Elena felt completely out of place, inadequate in comparison to her surroundings.

"Are you sure me coming here was a good idea?" Elena whispered to Eiry, rooted where she stood. Weir lights flickered in and out in the halls surrounding the circular courtyard, their glow frantic. Elena wasn't sure how she knew, but she was certain they were there because of her.

Eiry stopped moving and turned to watch her. "Of course I'm sure," he said softly. "I know the place can be a little intimidating, but please don't worry so much. You're among friends." He squeezed her hand, his icy gaze holding hers intensely.

For Eiry, Elena put on a brave face and they continued onward.

The circular courtyard was the northern most part of the city. It was built over one of the cascading river's many pools—the first one below the stone bridge Eiry and Elena had just passed. Its floor was made of flat stone that rose naturally out of the center of the pool of water like an island. Stepping-stones led into or out of the courtyard at the cardinal points. Eiry and Elena had entered through the northern path and now stood at its center, facing south. It was here that the city split into its distinctive linear geography of interconnected structures that followed both sides of the cascading river; the buildings clustered around the pools between waterfalls, multi-level halls, bridges and platforms of open archways connecting the staggered spaces in between.

The eastern and western paths of stepping-stones in and out of the circular courtyard led to two halls of open archways, each one leading to the respective buildings and structures following the river on either side. The southern path led to a semicircular veranda of open archways that connected the eastern and western halls, and overlooked a cascade of water as the river flowed from the pool beneath the veranda, and continued its path through the center of the city and the valley below. Eiry and Elena stood on the veranda for several minutes taking in the view, and then took the eastern hall into the buildings.

As they walked, Elena took the opportunity to study the scenery around her. The rooms and living spaces were lavish, decorated in beautiful wood furnishings as ornate as the buildings and hallways themselves. Tapestries lined the few bare walls. Ornate woodcarvings were everywhere the eye could see, along columns and lining the archways. Beautiful statues of carved wood and stone stood as silent sentinels along the way. Here and there, Elena noticed objects typical of Ms. Callas—rare artifacts from various different cultures throughout human history. Modern amenities were somehow seamlessly integrated into the decor.

The halls and common living spaces had a unified theme, while the rooms, which all faced the river and were open to view, represented the specific tastes of its inhabitants. Elena saw a room entirely done in modern decor, with sleek surfaces and a neutral palette. There was a distinct focus on angular shapes, and the only color was in the modern abstract paintings decorating the walls. The room was full of expensive electronics. Another room was decorated in different tones of white, a perfect blend of contemporary and traditional styles. The walls were blush with ornate paneling, the furniture sleek and modern in tones of soft gray, and the decorations were done in crystal, silver, lavender and pale pink. Another room appeared to be a large library with dark wooden paneling and bookcases along most of its walls, sets of brown leather couches laid out in clusters around the center of the room.

Details flooded in and out of Elena's mind, as Eiry led her around a corner into another hallway, which led down three large steps through another courtyard to a building below. They were on a floor level near the middle of the cascading river. Here, Eiry led Elena through an archway into a room.

Like every room Elena had seen along the way, this room's outer walls faced the river and were made up of the same beautiful archways capped in latticework that formed the unique architecture of the city. The moment she and Eiry stepped inside, the spaces between the archways turned opaque, with thin, variegated, petal-like membranes providing the missing privacy. The membranes were a snowy white and their veins a bright glacial blue.

Stunned, Elena walked toward them, curious as to how they might feel. Up close, they reminded her of the gossamer petals of a bougainvillea flower. Of course, they were much sturdier to the touch. Slowly, Elena began to take in her surroundings while Eiry quietly watched.

The room was distinctly masculine, decorated in rich, warm woods and leather. It reminded Elena of a Victorian-style study, its walls lined in cases filled with every style of book from large velum tomes to small, delicate manuscripts. Books and papers were strewn about the room in varying piles, a living map of the inhabitant's topics of interest. Curious artifacts were scattered around the room, between the myriad books and manuscripts—a telescope of polished brass, an antique globe map of the constellations, a working clock made up of its exposed gears, a Victorian typewriter and gramophone, complete with a small wooden antique bar in the far corner of the room.

Eiry led Elena to a sitting area in the center of the room and set down her carryall on a leather sofa. "These are my apartments," he said with a smile. "This is the front room. Behind us are my dressing rooms, a study, my bedroom and the bathroom. I need to go see my mother. In the meantime, a bath has been drawn for you. Feel free to take a well-deserved nap afterward or just take a look around the rooms. Don't leave them until I get back, though. I don't want you to get lost."

Elena was a little lost for words. Being here was overwhelming, and the idea of suddenly being in his rooms alone didn't help ease that feeling. In fact, it made it worse. She felt the first inklings of panic, but Elena braced herself against it. She was safe here, amongst friends. That's all she needed to know. Before leaving, Eiry gave her a quick tour around the rooms, each one as beautiful and richly decorated as the one before it. Once they reached the bathroom, he showed her where the towels and toiletries were, and then took his leave.

The bathroom was anachronistic, out of place with the other rooms. It was a modern Roman-style bath with a large circular pool sunk into the center of the room serving as the bathtub. The floor and bath were made of one continuous piece of travertine in a fawn and sandy hue. The counters lining the walls were chocolate brown wood with modern fixtures. There was a large shower carved into the opposite wall, the stone from the floor and central bath continuing into the shower. The room was sizeable enough to boast a small sitting area nestled beneath a set of archway windows overlooking the twilit valley below.

Elena's carryall sat on a small table where Eiry had left it for her. She took out what she needed, undressed, rinsed in the shower and then stepped into the bath. In a matter of minutes, she drifted into a deep sleep.

Once again, Elena dreamt of darkness. It faded to reveal the outline of the tourmaline throne. Sitting on it once more was the colossal god. Behind him, the shape of the great seal. "I can give her back to you," said the god in the same deep and rumbling voice as before. He watched her with his midnight blue eyes, a satisfied smile curling upward at the edges of his mouth. He leaned forward and extended a large hand, its shadow enveloping Elena. His laughter was the last thing she heard as the dream faded into darkness.

Elena woke with a start, completely disoriented. It took her a moment to remember where she was, her mind quickly rushing through the stages of her journey to Tartarus. Everything was silent, but for the sound of the river in the background. Elena stepped out of the bath and took her time drying off. She reached into her carryall, retrieving Cataline's silk robe. It took all of Elena's strength not to break down crying. Instead, she brought the silk to her face and inhaled Cataline's scent. The colossal god's voice echoed in the back of Elena's mind. She slipped on the robe, and resolved not to think of the dream any further.

Elena let her hair dry naturally and busied herself with putting on some makeup. When she was done, she collected her things and put them away in her carryall, which she decided to leave in the bathroom. Then she slowly made her way to the front room, studying the various rooms in between.

The study was the central room of the apartment, and was accessible from every other room. It had a beautiful desk, a pair of large comfortable reading chairs, a leather chaise and a piano. The dressing rooms were outfitted elegantly with a closet system complete with recess lighting and a three paneled dressing mirror. Suiting accoutrements lined every wall, in varying textures and designs. Eiry's bedroom featured an impossibly large bed as its focal point and nothing else.

When Elena reached the front room, she wasn't alone.

"Did you have a nice bath?" a velvety voice called out from the corner of the room.

"What kind of question is that?" chided a second voice, much kinder in tone than the first.

Elena turned around, startled. She screamed, but with the wave of a hand by the second speaker the sound was swallowed by the shadows.

"What was wrong with my question?" replied the first voice, which belonged to a man with long black hair to his waist, and bright blue deep-set eyes. He had an oblong-shaped face, a little longer than wide, with a strong but gently rounded jawline, small nose and lips that were thin on top but fuller on the bottom. He wore tight black slacks and a light gray turtleneck. "She was in the bath, wasn't she?"

"Yes, but that's not the first thing you say to a girl when you meet her," said the second voice in a far gentler tone. The voice belonged to a man with chin-length loose curls the color of honey and golden-green eyes. He had an oblong-shaped face slightly more oval than the other man's and a somewhat more tapered jawline, a Greek nose and a thin bow-shaped mouth. He wore designer jeans, an emerald green shirt and a gray scarf. Chains hung across the front right pocket of his jeans.

Both were young, appearing no older than Eiry or Elena. Like Eiry, they were both pale and breathtakingly beautiful. They continued their conversation as if Elena wasn't even there.

"I usually don't say anything at all to humans," countered the raven-haired one, "so as far as I'm concerned she's lucky I'm even talking to her at all."

"Galen," said the fair-haired one in a more serious tone. "Be nice."

"*You* be nice," responded the raven-haired one, shaking his head. "You're the one who wanted to meet her. I don't give a damn that Snowflake finally brought home a girl."

They stared at each other in silence for a few minutes, and then both turned their attention to Elena at exactly the same time. The fair-haired one had a warm smile on his face, the other a scowl.

"Hello, my name is Gavin," whispered the fair-haired one to Elena. "Tall, dark and gloomy over here is Galen, my evil twin." He elbowed his brother, who looked completely bored. "I hope we didn't startle you."

Elena shook her head. She didn't know what to say, but figured her name was a good place to start. "I'm Elena," she said, reaching for a throw on one of the couches closest to her. She wrapped it around her waist to give her some modesty, and kept her distance. She never moved from where she stood, which was thankfully across the room from the twins.

"We know who you are," growled Galen, the one with the raven hair. He had the same sunny disposition as Bryce.

"Don't mind him," Gavin told Elena with a resigned sigh. "Of the two of us, I got the looks and the charm. He got all the bad attitude."

"We'll see how far good looks and charm get you, Gav, the next time you try to get in my fucking pants," Galen replied.

"Fine by me, Galen. Maybe Eiry will share and I won't go without."

By rules that Elena didn't yet know or understand, that last comment somehow crossed the line. The raven-haired one pounced on his brother, the movement so quick that Elena didn't realize what was happening until Galen had Gavin pinned down on the couch, his long, slender fingers wrapped around Gavin's throat. "Say that again, Gav, and I'll fucking kill you."

"You promise?" replied Gavin in a raspy voice. Galen tightened his hold on Gavin's neck, extracting a soft, strangled moan. Gavin then raised his hips to press up against Galen, the gesture entirely too intimate.

"Excuse me," interjected Elena, completely confused and way past overwhelmed. She took a seat in a sitting area away from theirs. The two brothers turned their heads toward Elena at exactly the same time, their bodies still tangled indecently.

"What's wrong, Elena? Never seen two grown men play?" purred Galen.

Elena was too shocked to answer.

"I think she might be deaf, Gavin, or maybe she's just plain slow," Galen said to Gavin, who was struggling to get out from under his weight.

"You're being rude again, Galen. Now lemme up. We can play later." Gavin insisted until his brother acquiesced. The two had a silent exchange, and then they resumed their former sitting positions on the couch, mimicking each other's movements perfectly.

The effect was unnerving, and it made Elena think of the Siamese cats in *Lady and the Tramp*.

"Sorry about that, Elena," Gavin said, and offered her an apologetic smile. "Galen doesn't play well with others," a comment that prompted a grunt from Galen, but nothing more.

"Are you two really twins?" Elena asked, throwing decorum to the wind. That seemed to be the name of the game here.

"Yes," came Gavin's reply.

"And the two of you are... involved?" Elena chose the word carefully, as not to offend.

"Of course we are. All god twins are," Galen snapped. "See, Gavin, I told you she was slow. I didn't know Eiry liked them slow. Hell, I didn't know Eiry liked them at all."

"I'm not slow," Elena said to Galen in her defense, refusing to look away when the god held her gaze. She ignored the comments about Eiry. "That's just not acceptable in the human world, that's all."

"Well, in our world it's normal," Galen said, visibly annoyed. "And with twins, it's the rule."

Elena figured it was best to end the conversation there. She needed to take things in stride or she would go insane. Incestuous relationships between gods happened to be at the bottom of her list of priorities. "Was there something I could do for you, gentlemen? I was waiting for Eiry to get back."

"Actually, that's why we're here," Gavin said with a smile. "Mama sent us to come get you. The meeting is taking place now, so you might want to change."

"I CAN'T WEAR THIS," Elena said, staring at her reflection in the mirror.

Gavin, the fair-haired twin, stood beside her, a satisfied smile on his face. Galen, the raven-haired twin, stood beside the mirror, staring at Elena with a raised brow.

"Well, at least she cleans up well," murmured Galen.

In the few minutes Elena had spent in the pleasure of their company, she had learned it was best to simply ignore Galen's commentaries. They were never positive, and seldom constructive.

"She looks stunning," Gavin said with a smile, watching Elena through the mirror. He moved behind her, making a small adjustment at the waist. Then he met her gaze through the reflection and winked.

Elena tried her best not to blush, but she failed miserably. She didn't recognize herself in the mirror. She knew she was the woman wearing the dress, but she couldn't reconcile the image.

When the twins had informed her that the meeting would take place, Elena had quickly changed into a pair of jeans and a nice blouse. If the matching grimaces her outfit had earned her were ambiguous, the resounding complaints afterward had been very clear. Elena was to meet a gathering of gods, in particular the higher echelons of the Tartarean pantheon. If that wasn't enough to require a certain kind of decorum, the fact that the Moirai would be present did.

If she would not present herself before the Queen of England in jeans and a shirt, Gavin had said, she certainly would not do so before a pantheon of gods.

Elena had been unable to argue against that. It made sense, even if Eiry hadn't brought it up before. When Elena had quietly mentioned that fact to the twins, Galen had curtly reminded her that Eiry had been a little too busy trying to get her to Tartarus to worry about such things.

After that little exchange, Elena decided it was best to accept the advice and just be thankful for it. Of course, none of her clothing was deemed appropriate. Imagine her surprise when the twins announced they had 'just the thing' for the occasion.

On the short walk from Eiry's rooms to the twins'—the modern one with all of the expensive electronics Elena had seen earlier—Elena had imagined a slew of awkward possibilities, from the Princess Leia slave costume in *Return of the Jedi* to some Grecian getup that would leave very little to the imagination. What was actually presented to her was completely unexpected.

"I look like I'm in a beauty pageant," Elena said, concentrating on breathing. The dress was so tight that she could hardly breath. It was a floor-length sheath dress made of sparkling sequins. It had a built in corset and tailored draping. The fit was a little tighter than a glove. The color, a shifting spectrum of burnt amber hues, made her skin look as white as snow and the green of her eyes sparkle like emeralds.

Galen glowered at Elena, apparently unimpressed with her fashion commentary. "I doubt pageant girls have the money to own Armani Privé Couture," he growled, turning his attention to his twin. "I hope you realize you're wasting a perfectly good gown, Gavin."

"Stop being so grumpy, Galen," Gavin replied, his tone warm in spite of the obvious chide, "I think it's just right." He smiled brightly, smoothing the fabric over Elena's hips.

Elena blushed even brighter than before. Gavin was as handsy as Eiry was proper. "Is everyone there really going to be wearing this sort of thing?" she asked, still not convinced. She tried to move away, but Gavin held her in place. "And why is it you two just happen to have a dress like this available?"

Gavin feigned offense, his expression and manner perfectly exaggerated. "We're gods, Elena," he whispered close to her ear, smoothing her long hair behind her shoulders. "Everyone will be in their regalia, and the last thing you want to do is look like a country bumpkin." At the mention of the last word, Galen snorted; even a gesture so ludicrous sounded pretty from the mouth of a god. "Plus, Eiry will be there," Gavin said with a mischievous grin.

"And?" Elena protested, her fingers fussing with the fabric on the bodice of the dress. She felt like she was five years old, playing dress up. "Eiry's seen me at my worst these past few days."

"And now he can see you at your best." Gavin caught Elena's hand and gently pulled it away from the dress, offering her a dashing smile through the mirror. Like the others, he was striking—unnaturally so—but there was something incredibly warm about him, an easy quality that none of the other gods possessed. His twin bother was the polar opposite. The only thing they seemed to have in common was the mischievous glint in their eyes. "And to ease your suspicions, pretty Elena," Gavin continued, moving to stand beside his twin. "Galen and I dabble in a bit of business in the human world. Fashion is just one of the industries we deal in."

"You're in fashion?" It was impossible to keep the skepticism out of her voice.

"Yes, quite a few of us are. We need day jobs," Gavin replied in a matter-of-fact tone. "Being a god can get pretty boring. We were made for worship, so what better industry than fashion and modeling? You're telling me you've never seen Bryce's face before?"

The question took Elena by surprise. She was pretty sure she'd never laid eyes on Bryce until the night they met in Kyoto. "No, I'd never seen her before, but I don't follow fashion that much."

"That's obvious," Galen said in a cutting tone. He scrutinized Elena with his sharp blue gaze, idly weaving several strands of his long black hair into a braid over his shoulder. From the look of disappointment that followed, it was clear he didn't find anything to his liking. "This is boring me, Gavin," he declared, turning on his heel. "I'm going to go change."

Gavin watched in silence as his brother disappeared into the other rooms. Then he turned toward Elena, looking her over one last time. "You look great," he said with a smile. "It's absolutely perfect."

"Perfect for what?"

"Never mind about that, Ele. You'll find we're an odd little bunch. It's best just to go with it. Just so you know, this is the most fun we've had in decades. And now, it's time for you to go."

"Me? Go alone?"

"Of course not. If you went alone, then Bryce might snatch you up and no one would find you. We'd be in a bit of a pickle then, wouldn't we?"

Elena paled. Gavin smiled. "Relax," he said gently. "I'm just teasing. Remember one thing while you're here, Elena. You're the key to us winning a very long and tiresome war. No one here would ever harm you. My brother and I were supposed to escort you, but this little detour cost us some time, so I'll need you to head out first while Galen and I change. I'll have a weir servant take you."

Just as he said it, a weir light flickered to life beside Elena. She watched, stunned, as the green floating light took human shape. It was a man with long green hair and matching green eyes. He wore flowing robes of silver and green. His skin was luminously pale. He reminded Elena of an elf—tall, lithe and completely expressionless.

The WEIR SERVANT did not speak a word as he led Elena through the halls, and she was too busy worrying about tripping over her dress to be concerned about it. After several minutes, they reached their destination.

In the southern most region of the city of Eira, the Lethe cascaded down a final waterfall, spilling into a medium-sized lake before bending westward, carving its way through the earth to another region of Tartarus. Out of the center of this lake rose an island large enough to hold a great hall. Its walls were made up of giant birch trees whose canopies rose and bent naturally to form tall vaulted arches with bright green leaves and garlands of jewel-toned glass hanging from their branches. The ground was paved in a familiar colorless stone with a brilliant blue sheen, its surface so thin it looked like a layer of ice over the ground. The roots of the trees grew from beneath it, the brilliant green moss still visible underneath. The hall housed the thrones of the King and Queen of Tartarus, made of birch wood that rose naturally out of a raised dais at the end of the hall, intricately carved, inlaid with bright metal and stones of pale blue starlight.

As Elena was led over a stone bridge onto the island, she could hear the murmur of fervent voices from within. The voices stopped the moment Elena stepped into the hall. Eight different gods were gathered at a large table in the center of the room enjoying an evening meal. All of them were familiar faces except for two. Not a single one of them was dressed in regalia, which meant Elena was not only misinformed but also grossly over dressed.

"That's my dress!" cried out a familiar voice, followed by a soft chorus of laughter in the opposite end of the table. Bryce launched herself from her seat, her golden gaze ablaze as she stalked toward Elena.

In an instant, Eiry appeared at Elena's side.

"What the fuck is she doing wearing my dress?" growled Bryce, the twins, Gavin and Galen, quickly appearing at her side.

"I think it looks better on her," purred Gavin, his golden-green eyes fixed on Elena. He winked, catching Bryce's right arm. Galen took hold of Bryce's left with much less enthusiasm. "What do you think, Eiry?"

"I think you may be right," Eiry replied, protectively wrapping an arm around Elena's waist. "You do look very beautiful," he whispered quietly into Elena's ear. "And don't mind the twins. They live to torture Bryce."

"I look like a fool," Elena said in the same quiet tone.

Bryce lunged at her again, and Eiry easily pulled Elena aside. "No, you don't, Ele. The color suits you," Eiry assured her with a smile.

"No, she had it right the first time," hissed Bryce in a venomous tone. "A monkey in a silk dress." Bryce stared at Elena, white slowly bleeding into her red hair. "I want my fucking dress back."

"Bryce, that's enough," said a silken voice from behind them. Lucian, Ms. Callas's husband, stood from his chair and made his way toward them. The second Bryce heard his voice, she stilled. Gavin and Galen released her, identical smirks on their lips. Lucian, his pitch-black gaze on Elena the entire time, took Bryce into his arms. "You have a million such dresses," he cooed to her, his fingers smoothing her hair. "Now settle down. You're making a fool of yourself for no good reason."

Elena remained silent, trying not to stare. Lucian was watching her with the same hungry look he had given her at the firm's benefit. This time, it was even more uncomfortable since he was dressed in tight leather pants and nothing else. The pants hugged right below his hips, his perfect body on display for them all to see—particularly the upper half covered entirely in tattoos. The dark color of his eyes was matched by his hair, which fell loosely to his shoulders, and a trimmed goatee.

"Glad to see you made it safely," Lucian said to Elena. With a light slap to Bryce's ass, he sent her back to the table, followed by the twins. "Please don't take offense," he whispered, returning his attention to Elena. "The twins jump at any chance to kill the boredom, and Bryce is a very easy target. The twins are mine, Phobos and Deimos, which makes them your kin."

"I'm sorry, my kin?" Elena looked toward the table. Gavin was waving at her, a bright smile on his lips. He held a pennant in his free hand with blue letters on a white background. It read "House of Thebes", as if it were some kind of college sports team. Galen was trying to snatch the pennant out of his hand.

"I'm Ares, the god of war," Lucian replied with a grin, smoothing his hand over his stomach.

Elena blushed, realizing the man had a nipple ring.

"The one with the pennant is Phobos, the other Deimos," Lucian continued. "Fear and Dread, my sons, originally with Aphrodite, who also bore me Harmonia, the founder of your House. My sister Enyo, goddess of war, is also your kin."

At the mention of the latter, a tall, beautiful and remarkably exotic looking woman with caramel colored skin, nubile lips, long sable hair and sparkling golden eyes stood up and took the pennant from Gavin's hand, smacking both twins across the head before taking her seat once again.

"Why don't you let me introduce you properly to everyone, while we wait for our final guest?" Lucian added.

"Who's the final guest?" Elena asked without really considering whether it was rude or not.

"Dionysus," Lucian said with a seductive smile, as he hooked his arm around Elena's and led her toward the table. Eiry followed quietly behind.

At the head of the table sat a man Elena had only seen before in photographs, but never met. He was Ms. Callas's twin brother, Livius; the co-founder of the firm Elena was employed by. As Elena sat down toward the other end of the table, Lucian introduced Ms. Callas as Chione and Livius as Tartaros. Together, they made up the primordial god known as Tartarus.

Contrary to popular mythology, Eiry explained in a quiet whisper as he helped Elena into a seat, Tartarus had taken shape as two independent beings, a male and a female, each embodying different aspects of the primordial element. Ms. Callas embodied the death and icy aspects of Tartarus—delicate and ethereal in beauty, terrible and unyielding in strength. Livius embodied the darkness and absolute power of the Abyss—infinite, terrifying and impossible to resist.

Both had long inky black hair, snowy skin and gray-green eyes that settled more often on emerald. If Elena had found Ms. Callas intimidating before, it was nothing compared to how she appeared now—radiant and terribly beautiful. Livius was the embodiment of masculine power. Muscular and broad shouldered, he was as striking as his sister. Where her features were delicate, his were dramatic and defined. He had a rectangular face, strong jaw with a slight cleft on his chin, an aristocratic nose, high cheekbones and a gaze that pulled you in and never let you go.

"Hello, Elena," Ms. Callas said from across the table, a glass of wine in her hand. The tone of her voice was as severe as it had always been. She was seated to her twin's right, her husband now sitting beside her. "Glad to see you made it here alive."

It took Elena a second to find her voice. All eyes were on her, except for Eiry who was staring at his mother. He reached for Elena's hand under the table, and squeezed it lightly.

"Thanks," Elena replied in a shaky voice. "Thanks for having me." That sounded incredibly stupid, but what else was she supposed to say? *Thanks for not firing me? Why have you been such a bitch to me all of these years?*

Ms. Callas narrowed her eyes, as if she could read Elena's mind. Elena quickly dropped her gaze, looking at the empty plate before her.

"It's not me you should be thanking," Ms. Callas said, taking a sip from her glass of wine. "You owe your thanks to Eiry and Dionysus."

Elena had no idea how to respond, so she stayed quiet. It was obvious this woman didn't like her, even if Elena was some kind of prophesied weapon.

"How was Japan?" Ms. Callas pressed, the rest of the table conspicuously quiet. Elena remained so as well, which only spurred Ms. Callas's ire. "You do realize that if you would've shared with me the nature of your trip when I asked, *none* of this would have happened? That necklace would have stayed where it was."

And Cataline would still be alive; Elena took the thought to its logical conclusion. Ms. Callas's words stung, so much so that she had to blink back the tears. The guilt Elena felt was excruciating.

Bryce and Galen snickered. Gavin shook his head. Eiry kicked his sister under the table, who hissed in response.

"Mother, that's not a very fair assessment," Eiry said to Ms. Callas, whose expression was as icy and stoic as his.

"Perhaps you're right," she finally conceded, reaching to take a bite out of the meat on her plate.

The gesture made Elena hyper-aware of the elaborate spread on the table. The food smelled incredible, and Elena was starving. It was torture, and she was certain Ms. Callas was aware of it.

"Forgive me, Elena," Ms. Callas added, the apathy in her tone belying her words. "I'm sure you can understand the stress surrounding this entire situation."

Of course she could understand it, Elena thought to herself. She had lived through it, after all. It was *her* life in danger, not theirs.

"Before I forget, Elena," Lucian cut in with a smile, expertly changing the direction of the conversation. "Allow me to introduce you to Hecate." He pointed to the woman sitting to Livius' right, across the table from Ms. Callas.

The woman had long chestnut colored hair and gray eyes. She appeared to be the same age as Ms. Callas, Livius and Lucian—somewhere between thirty-five and forty. She wore a floral print silk dress in tones of gray, blush and lavender. A hound slept soundly at her feet. Lucian explained that she was the goddess who presided over the border between the mortal and spirit worlds, and it had been with her blessing that Elena was safely brought across the border into the underworld.

"Thank you," Elena said shyly to the goddess, unsure of what else to say.

"Your journey was an arduous one," replied Hecate in a soft voice, her manner markedly gentle compared to the others present. "I, for one, am glad to see Dionysus's efforts have finally paid off."

"Have they?" asked a familiar voice.

Deep and rumbling, it belonged to the Herculean god Elena had seen twice in her dreams. She almost fell off of her seat from shock when he appeared and took the empty seat beside Hecate. He kept his midnight blue gaze on Elena, a ghost of a smile on his lips.

"So this is the Heir of the House of Thebes?" he asked, as he reached for a bottle of wine to serve himself.

Was this Dionysus, Elena wondered? It couldn't be, but that had been the only guest missing. Dionysus was fabled to be an extremely beautiful and sensuous youth, aspects which this older god did not embody, in the least. Elena's question was quickly answered.

"What are you doing here, Hades?" Eiry asked in a clipped tone. "I don't recall inviting you."

"And I don't recall needing to be invited," Hades replied. "Nonetheless, the girl wants me here. Isn't that right, Elena of the House of Thebes?"

All eyes turned toward Elena.

"What is he talking about, Ele?" Eiry asked gently.

"I... I don't know," Elena replied, because in truth, she didn't know. She had only seen him in dreams. Dreams weren't real.

"She has something to ask of me," Hades insisted.

"Enough, Hades," Eiry hissed, slamming his fist down hard on the table.

"Eiry," Ms. Callas warned.

"Mother, this has nothing to do with him."

It was obvious there was no love lost between Eiry and Hades. Everyone in the room but Elena seemed to know why.

"As long as I am ruler of the Aidou, Thanatos," growled Hades in reply, "it has everything to do with me." Hades dismissed Eiry with a wave of his hand, turning his attention to Elena. "Go on, child. Ask away. I wouldn't have come all of this way for nothing. You've been having dreams, have you not?"

Panic settled in the pit of Elena's stomach.

Eiry watched her, a pained expression in his eyes. "Is he telling the truth, Ele?"

"You fucking fool," Bryce interjected before Elena could answer, her golden gaze intent on Eiry. She had been the only one to notice the emotion break through her brother's eyes. "You have feelings for her, don't you?"

"Shut up, Bryce," Eiry hissed. "Stay out of this."

Hades watched the interaction, amused. He reached for a pomegranate and began to open it carefully, his pale fingers quickly stained in red.

"We're Death, Eiry!" she howled. "We're not supposed to feel. You don't feel a shred for Hypnos, but now you feel for *her*? She's a goddamn human. She's worm food, and lest you forget, she's as good as dead!"

"I said, shut up, Keres," Eiry growled as he pushed himself up from his seat. "Don't you fucking dare bring Hypnos into this." His scythe appeared out of nowhere.

Elena was too shocked to say a word. She was shaking, both Bryce's outburst and Hades's insistence taking her completely by surprise. Shock was quickly becoming panic.

Suddenly, the temperature dropped in the room. It became so cold Elena was now shaking for a different reason. When she breathed, her breath materialized in front of her.

"That's enough!" commanded Ms. Callas.

Elena involuntarily looked up at the woman. Her usually green eyes were now a bright silver. Livius caught his twin's wrist, as if to ground her. The entire table went silent, except for the twins who were suddenly suffering from the giggles.

"Bryce, sit down. Eiry, put away the weapon," Ms. Callas said in a voice that left zero room for argument. Her silver gaze then fixed on Elena. "I would like Elena to respond to Hades."

Elena felt like she was at work all over again. Ms. Callas's tone sent an icy chill down her spine. She wished she knew what was going on between Eiry and Hades. Eiry looked upset at the mention of the dreams, hurt that she had not confided in him. "I've had two dreams," Elena finally said, her eyes turning to Eiry. "I thought they were just dreams, so I didn't say anything."

"Dreams are never just dreams," Eiry said gently. He then turned his gaze to Hades, who was quietly eating pomegranate seeds. Elena could see Eiry was going out of his way to control his anger.

Gavin and Galen were whispering fervently at the opposite end of the table, betting on who would win if a fight broke out between Eiry and Hades. Their focus turned momentarily to Eiry and Bryce, but they dismissed the idea almost instantly—they both agreed that Bryce would beat Eiry, hands down.

Enyo, the goddess of war, punched Galen in the arm. Then she turned her attention to Hades. "Get to the point," she said to him, annoyed.

"My point is that she has a question to ask me," Hades replied, unconcerned.

"About Cataline?" Elena finally spoke up. She wasn't sure what he was getting at.

Hades smiled a Cheshire grin. "Now we're getting somewhere," he purred.

In the dreams, Hades had told Elena he could give Cataline back to her. "Can you give her back to me?" Elena asked the god.

"I can do whatever I please with the spirits of the dead," Hades replied smugly. "The question is whether I want to."

"Stop toying with her," Eiry warned him.

"You of all people, Thanatos," Hades said his name in a venomous tone, "should know I am capable of this. All I ask is for a little something in return. Get me the Helm of Darkness, and I'll release the woman. The Keres brought me her body untouched. The soul is not yet sorted. It can easily be done."

"Are you mad?" Eiry said, looking over the others at the table, who remained silent. "She won't make it a day on the surface."

"Isn't that what this little meeting is about, Thanatos?" Hades asked, tapping his fingers on the table and leaving smudges of red pomegranate juice in his wake.

"I'll go with her," Gavin chimed in, excitement in his voice.

"The hell you will," replied his twin.

Elena felt dizzy. This seemed too good to be true. "What's the Helm of Darkness?" she asked.

"Ele, forget it," Eiry whispered, shaking his head. "It's a fool's errand. He lost it to one of the Fae during our last conclave. He was stupid enough to try to outwit a Fae."

Hades waved off Eiry's jab, his focus turning to Elena. "The Helm was a treasure given to me by the Cyclopes during the war against the Titans," he said in a patronizing voice. "To win, my brother Zeus allied himself with the three Cyclopes and received three treasures in return—his thunderbolt and lightning, Poseidon's trident and my Helm, which grants invisibility. Armed with these weapons, we were able to defeat the Titans. Do they not teach these things in your universities?" Of course, he didn't give Elena a chance to respond. He quickly shifted his attention to Eiry, a mocking smile on his lips. "I think it's a fair offer, Thanatos, if she truly desires this. I was simply honoring a request, that's all. She will have to return to the surface soon, and by then her divinity should be unsealed. She will face the same hardships whether she is in New Orleans or in Ireland at the Fae Court. Are you saying you can't protect her?"

"That's not what I'm saying at all," Eiry replied, restraint in his voice.

"Can I give you an answer later?" Elena asked Hades, determined to put an end to the discussion. She would talk to Eiry about it later.

"Of course," Hades replied.

"Glad that's over with," came a voice from the shadows, soft as velvet and rich as honey. Everyone turned toward it. A figure was making its way across the floor to the table. "You're in my seat," said the voice to Hades.

"Dionysus," was Hades's only reply. Reluctantly, he stood. "Come see me when you have made your choice," he said to Elena before taking his leave.

The room fell silent, the retreating steps of Hades the only sound. Dionysus took his place at the table. As he moved, Elena thought something about him was familiar, but she couldn't put her finger on what. Finally, the patron god of the House of Thebes turned his attention to Elena.

In a single breath, time stilled. Elena knew his face, intimately. She knew everything about it, from the curve of his cheekbones to the line of his jaw, the exotic shape of his eyes to the graceful slope of his nose. It was a face she had burned into her mind, a face that even now looked exactly the same as when Elena had last seen it, almost twenty years before.

The face belonged to her father.

CHAPTER THIRTEEN

E LENA COULDN'T TAKE her eyes off of her father.

For the next hour, as the gods finished their meal, all Elena could do was watch him in quiet wonder. Those moments when their eyes would meet, she would quickly look away. She felt afraid and yet completely elated. Confusion mingled with awe, leaving her in a quiet daze, observant but guarded.

The moment did not evolve into the reunion one would expect. There were no open declarations of love, no soliloquies that spoke of loss culminating in salvation, nor was Elena received with the warmth and abandon she remembered from her youth. Instead, her father was reserved. He took his seat beside Hecate, made his apologies for being late and joined in the meal, regarding Elena with a quiet restraint. The anguish she saw in his eyes the few times their gazes met, was the only thing that kept Elena quietly patient as dinner progressed to its inevitable conclusion.

To Elena's surprise, she was allowed drink. A wine glass was placed before her and filled with an iridescent amber liquid. When no one explained what it was, Elena leaned toward Eiry and asked.

It was her father who answered.

"It is ambrosia, the drink of the gods," Dionysus spoke in a soft voice.

The table was silent. All godly eyes were on them.

"It will sustain you without the need for any other food."

Dionysus paused, and watched his daughter quietly. He offered her a charming smile, but Elena could see the sorrow in his eyes. She could see there was so much he wanted to say, but he remained cautious. Elena could not begin to imagine why he would need to do so in front of his kin, but she decided it was best to mimic his restraint and worry about the reasons why later.

"Is it safe to drink?" she asked.

Eiry stirred beside her. Several seconds later, Elena felt the cool press of his fingers on her hand. Like Dionysus, he remained silent.

Everyone else had moved closer to the edges of their chairs, listening attentively while pretending to be otherwise engaged. The twins, however, did not employ such subterfuge. They whispered fervently to each other at their end of the table, their voices loud enough for everyone to hear, a play-by-play commentary on the scene.

In the voice of a radio broadcaster, Gavin remarked on the meaning of such a momentous occasion for Elena, a human girl who only weeks before had been living a seemingly ordinary life and who now found herself thrust into the world of the divine, finding out only moments before that her dead father was not only alive but also happened to be a flamboyant god with a penchant for wine, debauchery and excess, and, who rumor would have it, enjoyed wearing women's lingerie.

Galen gave his own account, remarking on Dionysus's presently forced restraint and the probable inner monologue that waxed poetic on how much Elena looked like Isabella.

The two then entered into an exaggerated dialogue with Galen playing the part of Dionysus and Gavin that of Isabella, in a rendition of what the twins guessed would be the subject of their next encounter.

Elena was too shocked to be offended. Ares reprimanded the twins lightly, as he struggled to hide his grin. Bryce giggled openly. Ms. Callas and Livius made no reaction at all. Enyo kicked the chair out from under Galen, putting an end to the sordid display. Dionysus and Eiry ignored the twins' antics entirely, continuing the conversation as if there had been no interruption at all.

"It is safe to drink," Dionysus whispered in response to Elena's earlier question, as Galen returned to his seat. "Ambrosia is not of the underworld, and so partaking of it while you are here will not bind you to Tartarus."

Elena hesitated for a moment, her eyes on her father's, and then brought the glass to her lips, drinking as the gods resumed their meal. The bevarage was exquisite, like a delicate dessert wine made with notes of honey, red currants and overly ripened grapes. It was served chilled, and Elena found that a few sips of it were enough to make her feel completely full. Any weariness or fatigue she felt from her journey disappeared entirely.

Toward the end of the feast, at Ms. Callas's request, Eiry told the story of their journey. Those things he could not account for, Elena filled in.

The older gods were particularly interested in her visit to the Kamo Vault.

"Do you believe the *onmyōji* are siding with the sky gods?" Livius asked Eiry, his expression troubled. He reached for his glass of ambrosia, exchanging a look with Ares and his twin.

"No, I don't think that's the case." Eiry leaned forward in his chair, his manner suddenly very professional, as if he were giving an official report. "I received word from Nurarihyon, who has spoken to both clans, the Kamo and the Abe, and it appears both were breached in the same manner—by use of falsified documentation."

"Are you saying that the two oldest clans of *aequus* in existence were tricked by a fake paper trail?" Galen scoffed, leaning back in his chair, unimpressed with Eiry's assessment. "They must take us for fools. If any of us stepped into that underground corridor right now, we would be rendered as useless as any human, and yet with all of that power they can't tell when documents are fake? You've got to be fucking kidding me."

"You should know better than most, *Galen*, that technology makes lazy fools even of gods," Eiry replied.

"What the fuck is that supposed to mean?" Galen snarled, itching for a fight. He moved to stand, but Gavin caught his arm and slowly eased him back into his chair.

Eiry continued, unaffected. "It means that we are all archaic beings dealing with a modern world. Something is bound to fall through the cracks during the transition."

"Well, isn't that poetic?" Galen snapped, earning him another smack from the war goddess Enyo, the sound of metal bracelets echoing in its wake.

"Stop hitting me!" he hissed at her.

All the goddess had to do was get up from her chair for Galen to quickly settle down.

"Keep it up, Deimos," she warned, a sinister smile brightening her face, "and I'm asking your daddy to let us spar in the training halls. I have a new axe I've been dying to try out."

Enyo cooed the last words softly to her nephew, the sound ending in a steady hum, and then she carefully resumed her seat. The interaction was almost comical. Enyo looked more like a Brazilian supermodel than Xena Warrior Princess, and yet the lethal quality of her nature was palpable, like the razor edge of a finely tempered blade.

"Knock it off, you two," Lucian chided, scratching his goatee, "let your brother finish."

With a resigned sigh, Eiry continued his report.

"As I was *trying* to explain, for almost twenty years the box remained sealed and forgotten, while the Abe modernized and the Kamo struggled to remain relevant. Helios bid his time and exploited the holes in their system. As you all know, *aequus* function within the confines of the human world and are bound by their laws. The Kamo Vault may cater to the divine and supernatural worlds, but they operate as an actual bank. There are rules and regulations they must follow, and Helios used that to his advantage.

"Deposit boxes function on the concept of anonymity. The Kamo were not aware of the nature of the contents of the box. They were simply the repository and were instructed to contact the Abe in the event of Isabella's death. The Abe were supposed to be the second level of protection, they were supposed to ensure ownership did not transfer to Elena."

"What is an *aequus*?" Elena interrupted, completely lost by the conversation.

"It means impartial," Dionysus interjected before Eiry could reply. "It is the title we give to all human neutrals."

"How are they neutral if they were helping our side?" she asked, an assumption on her part.

"We mean neutral in that they neutralize the power of the gods, with the explicit intent of protecting human life," Dionysus explained. "They are impartial to the result of the war. They do not care who wins. They do what they must to balance the odds so that the least amount of human lives are lost. There are those of the divine who are also impartial to the outcome of the war, like the Moirai and the Fae, but we do not use the term to describe them."

Elena nodded, a little confused but satisfied with the response. Eiry continued his report, as if the interruption had never happened.

"Everything seems to have gone according to plan until three years ago. Payments for the deposit box ceased. To address the issue, Mr. Inoue of the Kamo reviewed their records and found documentation indicating that ownership of the box was due to transfer to Isabella's heir at that time. He contacted the Abe, who searched their computer records and found the same documentation providing for the transfer to Isabella's heir. It took the Abe three years to locate Elena, but they ultimately did and that is how she came into possession of the necklace."

Eiry paused, to see if anyone had questions up to that point, and when no one did he continued. "Neither clan had reason to believe the information in their systems was fabricated. The heads of the clans, who had handled the transaction at the time of Isabella's death, were deceased, and no one existed who would question the legitimacy of the documentation. The records for both clans were somehow altered completely, but we do not know how."

"What about the third level of protection?" Dionysus asked in a strained voice. "Elena could not take possession of the contents without signing in blood."

For several moments Dionysus remained silent, and then he reached for his glass of wine and took a long drink. "The fact that Elena knew nothing of the necklace or our world should have made it impossible for the *onmyōji* to obtain her blood without divulging our existence or their magic. It is strictly forbidden for them to do either, and it is doubtful a human in today's world would agree to sign documents in their own blood."

"While it is forbidden for them to divulge the information, Evius," Eiry attempted to explain, his tone deferential, "nothing stops them from obtaining the necessary blood in more clever ways. Elena is not the first blind beneficiary to walk into their halls."

Dionysus held Eiry's gaze, but he remained silent. His fingers wrapped around the glass of wine he held in his hands and although he struggled to remain controlled, the anger slowly bled into his beautiful face. "It's unacceptable," he hissed sharply, and slammed the glass of wine down on the table. The stem shattered in his hands. "She gave her life to ensure this would not happen! Isabella gave her *life*," he roared, "and you are telling me nothing stopped the *onmyōji* from being clever? Nothing stopped them from weaseling the blood out of our child?"

"Evius, I..." Eiry faltered, completely taken by surprise. His expression was stricken. Beneath the table, his hands balled into fists.

"Papa, that's enough," Elena said without thinking, an unexpected edge to her voice.

Dionysus lifted his gaze to meet Elena's. Tears streamed across his cheeks and for a moment he appeared completely lost. Then he exhaled sharply.

"Forgive me," he whispered to her in a broken voice before resuming his seat, placing his hand on Eiry's shoulder as he did so.

"Forgive me, old friend," he offered Eiry before he fell into an uncomfortable silence.

Servants were called to clean up the spilt wine, and Eiry poured Dionysus another glass. Dinner resumed as if nothing had happened.

The mention of blood stirred something in the back of Elena's mind, but she was reticent to speak of it. The last thing she wanted to do was to cause Eiry or her father any more grief.

In spite of her effort, Eiry noticed.

"What is it, Ele?" he asked her gently. He was sitting beside her again, his expression filled with concern. He saw her hesitate and he took her hands, focusing her attention on him alone. "You can tell me anything, Ele. You know that."

Her gaze lifted momentarily to her father, then she whispered, "I think I know what happened with the blood."

"Go on, Elena," Dionysus urged her in a quiet voice.

Elena lifted her gaze to her father's. In it, she saw regret. Behind the regret, she saw devastation. While he was happy she was here and alive, he was horrified that Isabella's sacrifice had been in vain and that their struggles had been insufficient to ensure Elena's safety. The fact that Elena was here meant her life was at stake, threatened by the same thing that had taken Isabella's life. Elena could see the depths of it written in her father's eyes. Like Eiry, her father held the loss of each Heir etched into his soul, but none so deeply as the loss of Elena's mother.

As Eiry and Dionysus both looked at her, a quiet expectation in their gazes, Elena was struck by how young her father looked. He appeared the same age as Eiry, which meant he looked only a few years older than her. It was an unnerving realization.

"Is it possible for the *onmyōji* to have gotten my blood from a tissue?" Elena finally asked.

Eiry narrowed his gaze, contemplating his answer before giving it. "I would assume so. They usually need a reasonable amount of blood, since they have to execute the documents and then replace the seal once the account is transferred to the new name, but I would assume they've developed spells to work with less, if need be. Why do you ask?"

"Because when I was handling all of the paperwork, I got a pretty bad paper cut. I didn't really think anything of it because I get those all of the time. Work hazard." Elena met Ms. Callas's gaze and was not surprised to find that she kept a blank expression; Elena was certain she'd never seen the woman smile a day in her life. "Mr. Inoue offered me a tissue, and once I had it under control he offered to throw it away. The ink came after that."

Dionysus nodded, and Eiry mimicked the gesture without realizing it.

"They must have found a way to use the blood from the tissue," Eiry concluded. Just as he said so, a servant entered the hall.

Elven-featured, with pale blue hair and eyes, the servant made her way quietly toward the table, her emerald and silver robes rustling lightly against the floor. She came to stand beside Dionysus and produced a sealed letter from within the folds of her robes.

Dionysus smiled when he recognized the seal. He broke it gently, and read the letter.

"Please inform Aisa we will be there shortly," he whispered to the servant, who nodded and silently walked away. Dionysus then dropped the letter, which burst into white flames before reaching the floor.

"Should we not discuss our strategy for Elena's protection before you take your leave?" Ms. Callas asked Dionysus, smiling as her twin brother leaned toward her and pressed a less than chaste kiss to the corner of her mouth.

Lucian threw a grape into Livius's lap.

Their interaction was distracting, to say the least.

"I am certain Thanatos can provide the necessary protection, Chione," Dionysus replied, and slowly pushed himself up from his chair, "but with the three of you, the twins and the Keres also living in New Orleans, it should not be an issue."

"Have you ruled out Japan?" Ms. Callas asked, diplomatically.

Dionysus narrowed his gaze, and reached for his glass of wine. "I'm taking this with me for the trip," he said nonchalantly, before offering a reply, "and no, I have not ruled out Japan, but for now let us assume Elena will return to New Orleans. If she decides to take a detour through Ireland, I would like the Keres to accompany them."

"Don't you think the twins might be better suited to handle the Fae?" Lucian asked, pulling Bryce into his arms and babying her before she could consider being offended.

"Yes, Ares, they would, but the Keres would be most effective against Helios and Eos, and they concern me far more than the Fae." Pausing briefly to take a drink from his glass of wine, Dionysus seemed to extend the silence simply for the sake of effect. "I will consult with Aisa and let you know. Sending four gods, and a demigod, to the Fae might not be well received."

Dionysus motioned to Eiry, who stood, taking Elena's hand and pulling her up with him.

"Thank you for dinner," the god of wine declared to his hosts, offered a dramatic bow, his shoulder-length hair almost touching the ground, and then turned to take his leave.

As she was quietly led out of the hall, Elena asked, "Where are we going?"

"To the Temple of the Moirai," replied her father with a smile, "to hear them sing."

ELENA WAS TOO NERVOUS to speak as Dionysus and Eiry led her through labyrinthine tunnels carved out of stone, on their way to see the Moirai. Instead, Elena enjoyed the rare opportunity to simply observe. Her father and Eiry had quickly fallen into a quiet conversation of what had happened and what was to come, their exchange giving Elena a glimpse of an intimate partnership that reached far deeper than family or friend.

It was odd for Elena to see her father in this light, to observe with an adult mind a man she could only remember through the eyes of a child. Every memory Elena had of him focused entirely on his face, and the warmth of being wrapped in his arms. Those two things obscured all other factors. Elena could not recall his preference for clothing or his exact height. She could not recall his manner of walking or the full outline of his form. Everything she remembered of her father was from the vantage point of being held in his arms; his surprisingly strong embrace, the sharpness of his profile, and his scent—a mixture of honey and what Elena now realized was wine.

The details she hadn't noticed as a child now superimposed themselves over the image in her memory. Her father had an easy walk, preferred modern clothing—a pair of old broken-in jeans, a fitted plain white shirt and a scarf made of a light and textured fabric hanging loosely from around his neck—had waves of thick black hair that fell to his shoulders, warm olive skin and eyes even darker than his hair. Tall and lean, his mannerisms, while fluid, were distinctly masculine. He looked exotic; the kind of person you knew by sight was of a diverse ethnicity, although you couldn't pinpoint a specific one. His facial features exuded that ethnicity, perfect in every way and breathtakingly beautiful.

Other than the color of his hair, Elena had not inherited a single one of her father's features. Standing side by side, they could pass for perfect strangers.

These thoughts occupied Elena's mind for the duration of their short journey through the tunnels to the Temple of the Moirai, thankfully keeping the panic at bay. If Elena stopped to consider where they were headed, she wouldn't be able to take another step.

The Moirai were responsible for the fate of humans and gods alike, governing over both worlds. It was by their law that Dionysus had been bound to the underworld for the past two decades, and it would be by their law that Eiry would ultimately be punished for saving Elena's life when she was a child.

As had been true of all other such forays into the underworld, their journey ended in a cavernous space, this one illuminated by the fragile glow of a slow approaching dawn. It was much smaller in size than Eira or Hades. They stood at the bottom of a large chasm deep within the earth, circular in shape. Its diameter was no more than two acres wide. Walls of hewn rock surrounded them on all sides, rising steeply to a height the eye could not see.

All around them, gentle streams of water trickled downward along the walls and into five distinct pools carved into the ground and lining the circumference of the space. They framed a mound of earth and stone that rose to fifty feet at its highest point, and formed the foundations of an ancient circular temple.

"All five rivers of the underworld find their way here," Eiry explained to Elena in a quiet whisper, as the three of them took the measure of their surroundings. "The Acheron, the Lethe, the Styx, the Cocytus and the Phlegethon—each one spills down these walls into their respective pool."

"How do you know which river is which?" Elena asked.

It was her father who answered, as he reached gently to take her hand. "Only the Moirai know for sure," he said, leading her onto a small path lined in stone, worn by the passage of time. Eiry followed in silence. "It is said that when you approach the pools, you should see the nature of each river within their depths. The water that does not reflect light is the Acheron. If the depths glimmer with the light of stars it is the Lethe. You will see fire in the Phlegethon and ice clinging to the surface of the Cocytus, which is also identifiable by the wailing of the dead when the water stirs. And last, but not least, is the Styx, which is known for its murky and tenebrous depths."

The ground around them, along the pools and across the rising mound, was covered in patches of moss and bright blue flowers. Everything was covered in a thin layer of mist, like morning dew. The small path lined in stone cut through the mound and led up to the temple, which was made almost entirely of aged white stone. Three steps formed the foundation, leading up to the main floor of the temple. Two rows of columns divided the space within. An outer row of twenty-six columns lined the outermost edge, creating a peristyle around an inner circle of fourteen columns that formed the central chamber. There was neither a roof nor walls. Each row of columns was capped with an architrave topped by carved friezes, which, according to Eiry, depicted the birth of the gods.

Dionysus led the way through the path to the temple, their steps the only sound besides the constant trickle of water along the walls. The entrance steps led them onto a floor paved with alternating black and white stone slabs, forming a continuous pattern throughout the first peristyle. From where they stood, Elena could see through the second row of columns into the central chamber. The pattern of stone on the floor shifted to form what her father explained was a map of the ancient Greek constellations, in the center of the chamber.

Three white-robed figures stood in the center of the map, each one identical in appearance except for the color of their hair; tall, voluptuous women with bronze skin and opalescent eyes. Although their likeness appeared no more than four decades old, their eyes bore the weight of their terrible knowledge. They moved as if of one mind, the gossamer folds of their robes dancing across their skin like smoke.

"You have come," whispered the Fate with long, white hair.

"And he has brought Thanatos," purred another with hair a deep Stygian-black.

"And let us not forget the Heir," sang the third, whose hair was a deep sanguine red.

Their three identical gazes moved over them, scrutinizing each of them with an eerie synchronicity. Instinctively, Elena stepped closer to her father.

"Aisa," Dionysus said to the white-haired Fate with unexpected warmth in the tone of his voice. "This is Elena, mine and Isabella's daughter."

"She is lovely, Evius," replied the Fate with a ghost of a smile. "I see my Eiry has done well, bringing her to us unharmed."

Eiry bowed his head and stepped forward, offering the Fate a roguish smile. "I did my best, Aisa."

"As you always do," said the white-haired Fate, as she stepped closer to Eiry. Her movements were fluid, but disjointed. She extended her hand, brushing her fingers to Eiry's cheek.

Instantly, his godhood bristled. His skin shined with the light of the stars, and his eyes burned like glowing embers. His hair turned a brilliant glacial blue. Elena had to avert her gaze. As the Fate pulled away, his godhood dimmed and slowly returned to normal.

"Are you happy, Evius?" asked the Stygian-haired Fate, drawing her and her sisters' attention to Dionysus.

"To have your child beside you once again," added the sanguine-haired Fate.

"Indeed I am," Dionysus responded, his gaze meeting Elena's with the warmth and adoration she remembered as a child.

Elena blinked. The desire to cry was suddenly overwhelming. The Moirai stepped closer and Elena stilled, finding it difficult to keep her mind clear. The Fates moved and something inside of Elena moved with them. It was unnerving, and she instinctively reached for Eiry's hand.

"She clings to you both for safety," cooed the white-haired Fate named Aisa, her voice like the gentle murmur of water along a stream. "She is quite lovely, and clever. Strong willed, like her mother. It will serve her well."

The mention of Isabella roused an agonizing curiosity in Elena, but she could not bring herself to speak. She was having trouble bringing order to her thoughts, let alone to her words.

"Will you sing for her?" Dionysus asked the Moirai. His hold tightened on Elena's hand, but otherwise he remained completely still.

The Moirai's movements calmed and they turned their threefold gaze onto Elena. "Is this your wish, child?" they asked in unison.

Elena was petrified. She had not discussed this with her father or Eiry, and she had no idea what it meant for the Fates to sing. She looked between the two men, and saw the same determined look in their eyes.

Without another thought, she answered briskly, "Yes," trusting them both implicitly.

"Very well," the three replied, identical smiles playing across their features. Two stepped back while the third, the sanguine-haired Fate, lowered herself onto a tripod seat that conjured itself out of the shadows.

"I am Lachesis," said the sanguine-haired Fate to Elena in an ageless voice, her tone steady and measured. "I am the Allotter, she who measures the thread of life. I sing of things that once were."

Her sisters stood still as sentinels behind her seat. Each one placed a hand on Lachesis's shoulder, and immediately the light of their eyes extinguished. The ancient goddess parted her lips, and the world around them grew still and silent. The trickle of water along the walls slowed to a stop, and was brought back to life solely by the breath of her voice—ethereal and haunting. Its pace waxed and waned until it matched the rhythm of her Delphic melody, *this* her singular accompaniment.

LACHESIS SANG FIRST of the deathless gods, the Protogenoi or First Born, who shaped the universe seeking neither kingdom nor throne and from whom all other gods descend.

In the beginning, five elements took shape out of the Nothing by will alone: mighty Chaos, the infinite space; inevitable Ananke, the force of destiny; plentiful Gaia, the earth; tenebrous Tartarus, the underworld; and lustful Eros, procreation and sexual desire, fairest of the deathless gods. These elements then gave birth to a second generation of Protogenoi gods. Of Gaia were born Pontus 'the sea', Uranus 'the sky', and Ourea 'the mountains'. Ananke begat the Moirai; Clotho, Lachesis and Atropos. To Chaos were born Erebos, the darkness, and Nyx, the night, who together begat Aether, the bright upper air of the gods, and Hemera, the day.

Lachesis then sang of the Titans—the second race of gods—descendants of Gaia and Uranus. Unhappy with his offspring, Uranus imprisoned them in Tartarus, causing great pain to Gaia, who forged a sickle for her sons to use against their father. Unyielding Cronus, wielder of time, their youngest son and most ambitious, castrated Uranus and established himself above all others gods. From the sea-foam created when the castrated genitals were cast into the sea was born Aphrodite, goddess of love and beauty. From the blood spilt were born the Gigantes, Cyclopes and avenging Furies, who were instantly cast down to Tartarus.

Third was sung the legacy of the First Prophecy, which predicted the fall of Cronus by his own son. To avoid this fate, Cronus devoured all of his children by his sister, the Titan Rhea, but he was deceived when he attempted to devour the youngest of his sons, Zeus. Rhea hid Zeus on the island of Crete, and to Cronus fed a stone wrapped in the robes of a newborn child. Once grown, Zeus secured the release of his siblings and waged a successful war against the Titans, deposing his father and establishing himself as king of the gods. Of the First Prophecy were born the Olympian gods, also called Dodekatheon, the third and final race of gods.

Next Lachesis sang of a Second Prophecy, one that predicted the birth of a son by Zeus more powerful than he, and who would eventually overthrow him. Here, the Moirai's song began to deviate from the mythology Elena had known. She sang of a prophecy that divined a son of Zeus by Semele, daughter of the goddess Harmonia and King Cadmus of Thebes, who would overthrow Zeus, his father, and bring about the fourth race of the gods. At the time the Second Prophecy was made, Semele was pregnant with Zeus's son, Dionysus. Zeus then entreated his wife, Hera, to assist him in avoiding his fate.

Zeus and Hera devised a scheme whereby Hera would befriend Semele in the guise of an old crone, and trick Semele into questioning the identity of her lover, the father of her unborn son. Semele, by Hera's advice, would ask Zeus to grant her a blessing, who then would swear by the River Styx to do as she asked—an oath that would bind him to grant her any request. Semele would then ask the mighty Zeus to reveal himself in all his godly splendor. Forced by his oath to abide by her request, Zeus would have no choice but to reveal his godhood, which no mortal could withstand. Semele and their unborn son would be consumed in flames, and the Second Prophecy would hold no power. Their scheme was almost successful.

The heart of an unborn Dionysus survived the flames, untouched. The Moirai intervened, beseeching Persephone, wife of Hades, to swallow the heart and carry Dionysus as her own child, to be raised in the underworld to adulthood so that he might fulfill the prophecy and bring about the fourth generation of gods. Dionysus grew to adulthood, but the prophecy remained unfulfilled. Then came the influence of human belief on the gods, who divided themselves into the roles attributed to them by humans and split themselves between the ranks of their worship—Olympian and Chthonic. This fueled the weight of the Second Prophecy, pitting Zeus's Olympians against Dionysus's foster family, the Tartarean gods, setting the stage for the Great War that now consumed the world of the divine.

Then a Third Prophecy came to pass. A low-ranking sky god, seeking to know the outcome of the Great War, sought counsel with the Pythia, Apollo's Oracle, who, after the sky god inquired whether Olympus would be victorious, responded, "The ambition of the Dodekatheon will fail at the hands of a Daughter of the House of Thebes." Thus began the hunt of Heirs by Olympus that ultimately led to the demise of the House of Thebes. Elena was intimately familiar with this part of the Moirai's song. After several centuries of the Hunt, the House of Thebes fell to ruin and the necklace faded out of existence. But the story did not end there.

Lachesis's haunting voice faded to silence, leaving Elena feeling inexplicably bereft. Hearing the story of her father, twice born, of the treachery of Zeus and the systematic murder of her father's family— Elena's own family—was numbing. She lowered her gaze and found that both, Eiry and her father held her hands, and neither one of them moved. Elena raised her gaze to her father, and found standing beside her a stone-faced god. He squeezed her hand, but otherwise remained inanimate.

When Elena returned her attention to the Moirai, their positions had changed. Sitting before her, on the tripod seat, was the Stygian-haired Fate. Lachesis and the white-haired Fate stood behind her. They had yet to place their hands on their sister's shoulders. Elena realized the sound of water had ceased. Again, the world around them was silent and still.

"I am Clotho," said the Stygian-haired Fate to Elena in a hushed and rasping voice, like the whisper of falling leaves. "I am the Spinner, she who spins the thread of life. I sing of things that are." She paused, shifted her gaze to Dionysus and then added, "Give or take a few generations." She offered Elena an unexpected smile, which looked strange and unsettling on her ageless face.

Lachesis and Aisa placed a hand on their sister's shoulder, and again the light of their eyes extinguished. Clotho then parted her lips and began to sing, breathing life back into the water around them to match the rhythm of her melody.

CLOTHO BEGAN HER SONG with the coming of a Fourth Prophecy. For over a thousand years, the gods believed the House of Thebes had perished, until another prophecy foretold of the existence of an Heir. A millennium had passed since the eradication of the House, and Olympus had not succeeded in winning the endless war. Once again, a sky god sought the counsel of the Pythian Oracle. Having been asked the same question as before, the Pythia responded, "The ambition of the Dodekatheon will fail at the hands of an Heir of the House of Thebes." Olympus's attempt to avoid their fate had resulted in a change to the prophecy. No longer did it speak of a *Daughter*, but now spoke in terms of an *Heir*.

The Moirai's song then reached into the distant past, weaving it with the present. Stygian-haired Clotho sang of an unknown bloodline of the House of Thebes that survived undetected for one thousand years through Ismene, daughter of Oedipus and Jocasta of Thebes. Once believed to be the last Heir of the great House, Ismene gave birth to a female child in secret before taking her own life. Aware of the ruin the necklace had brought to her noble House, Ismene gave the child to a servant, to be reared away from the eyes of the gods. Her child, blind to the truth of her royal blood and hidden from knowledge, gave new life to the ancient bloodline, which continued through the centuries, unnoticed, to the present day.

The Fourth Prophecy gave birth to a renewed war, after a one thousand-year-old impasse. Sky gods and chthonic gods alike threw their full might behind a single purpose, to locate the surviving Heir. The Dodekatheon searched for both, the Heir and the location of the necklace, while Dionysus focused his strength on the Heir alone—a search he had begun with Ares several decades before, unconvinced of the demise of their bloodline. Three years after the Fourth Prophecy, Dionysus and Ares succeeded where the sky gods did not. While their divinity in the bloodline had thinned through the passage of time, they recognized their godhoods in the blood of a seventeen-year-old girl named Isabella. Like Thanatos did with Elena, Dionysus installed himself in the periphery of Isabella's life, under the guise of a human identity.

By then, chthonic gods had assimilated themselves into the human world on account of Tartarus's business facilitating the dealings between the different chthonic factions. Learning of the identity of the new Heir, Tartarus installed their business in New Orleans, where they could assist Dionysus in protecting the Heir without arousing the suspicion of the Olympians. They were successful for two and a half years, until the sky gods learned of Isabella's identity. She and Dionysus had fallen in love by then. They married, and Dionysus devised a plan to hide among the Hyakki Yakō of Japan.

Clotho then wove the epic tale of Dionysus and Isabella's flight to Japan, which would prove essential for their survival. On account of the large amount of chthonic energy in Japan, sky gods would be unable to identify him or Isabella by presence alone. More importantly, the Hyakki Yakō were skilled warriors and could offer the protection Dionysus could not once he lost his divinity, a consequence of his choice to marry a human; little by little, his divinity would fade until he was as weak and vulnerable as any mortal.

The sky gods had not located the necklace, which gave the Tartareans a much-needed reprieve. For a year and a half, Dionysus and his Heir lived in relative peace, protected within the Hyakki Yakō, Isabella completely unaware of the forces at play around her. Then the necklace was found, and the war began anew. The Japanese sky gods betrayed Isabella's presence to the Olympians, and by Helios's cunning came she into possession of her inheritance. Learning that Dionysus would shower his wife with gifts, Helios devised a ruse to place the necklace in the hands of the Heir under the guise of one such gift.

Even so, Dionysus and Isabella survived for another seven years, fighting alongside the Hyakki Yakō and keeping the birth of their daughter, Elena, hidden from the eyes of the gods. To protect their child, the necklace was placed in the hands of the *aequus*, locked away from the reach of the divine. At the request of his wife, Dionysus would later break divine law to seal the divinity within his child, in an attempt to keep her connection to the gods forever hidden.

The Moirai's song ended with details of Isabella's death and the fall of Dionysus. After seven years of successfully thwarting Helios's attacks, the Hyakki Yakō were overwhelmed in a surprise attack with the assistance of the Japanese sky gods. The Hyakki Yakō held long enough for Isabella and Dionysus to escape into the woods with the assistance of the Head of the Kamo clan. Isabella gave Elena to the *onmyōji*, and then she and Dionysus engaged Helios to buy them time. First, Dionysus fell, and later Isabella. As the *onmyōji* carried Elena through the woods with the help of his familiars, Eos, sister of Helios, came across their path and learned of Elena's existence.

The Head of the Kamo was defeated at the edge of a cliff bordering the sea. Consumed with bloodlust, Eos took Elena and cast her into the churning waves with the wish to end the bloodline. Thanatos and Ares appeared on the cliff a moment before, in time for Ares to subdue Eos while Thanatos dove into the waters to save Elena's life; thereby hindering Eos's success and assuming for himself the 'will' that belonged to the Moirai alone. After placing an unconscious Elena in Ares's care, Thanatos drug Eos through the depths of the ocean into Tartarus, where he forced her to drink of the River Lethe before cutting her down with his scythe.

In those last crucial moments, the song and the accompanying flow of water reached a fevered crescendo. Elena followed their pace until the absence of sound floored her. The ground fell from beneath her feet, and Elena started. She opened her eyes, not sure of when she had closed them. Her father and Eiry were studying her with mirrored expressions of worry across their faces. Elena shifted her attention to Clotho, who had already removed herself from the tripod seat, which was now occupied by Aisa, the white-haired Fate.

"I did not speak of your journey, for I assume you need not hear me recite those things of which you have personal knowledge," Clotho said to Elena in a melodic voice, as she placed her right hand on Aisa's left shoulder.

It took Elena a great deal of control not to quickly respond with a *"Yes Ma'am"*. Instead, she nodded, and nervously tucked her hair behind her ear.

Aisa cleared her throat.

"I am Atropos the Unturning," said Aisa of the White Hair to Elena in a honeyed voice, "she who cuts the thread of life after choosing the manner of death. I sing of things that are to be." She studied Elena with a probing gaze, her demeanor more foreboding than that of her sisters. She motioned Elena forward with a wave of her adamantine nails before saying, "I require a lock of your hair."

Eiry and Dionysus slowly let go of Elena's hands, the latter urging her forward. Elena swallowed her fear and did as she was told, taking three steps to stand before Atropos. With a graceful wave of her hand, the white-haired Fate bid Elena kneel. Once she obeyed, Atropos sheared several strands of Elena's hair with a quick swipe of her sharp nails. She then held the strands cupped in her hands, and murmured a few words beneath her breath. The strands rose and spun together, suspended in the air above Atropos's delicate hands. The woven strands then caught fire, and disappeared in a pale white flame.

Elena, having pulled herself to her feet only seconds before, stood motionless before the Fate.

Clotho and Lachesis placed a hand on their sister's shoulder, and again the light of their eyes extinguished. Atropos then parted her lips and began to sing, breathing life into a melody through water. She sang with the power of Ananke, the primordial force of destiny, in her voice.

> *Where one was sought, two will surface;*
> *Only one will endure alive.*
> *Resignation will prove its purpose,*
> *Good Counsel will deprive.*
> *By an act of love, another compelled.*
> *The House of Thebes will bear no more.*

"ARE YOU RESOLVED TO DIE, Daughter of the House of Thebes?" asked Atropos in a soft but hollow voice. Her fingers, cold as ice, traced across Elena's shoulders.

They stood alone in a chamber beneath the floor of the circular temple, within the earthen mound that formed its foundation. Above them, Eiry and Elena's father waited for their return, in the company of

Clotho and Lachesis. Some time had passed since the white-haired Moirai sang of Elena's future.

"If I must, then I shall," was Elena's honest answer. Atropos's fingers curled over Elena's shoulders, sending a chill down her spine. "I am resigned to do what I must. I do not take lightly my mother's sacrifice."

Elena looked around her. Sparsely decorated, the chamber held three chests, an altar and a small sitting area with klismos chairs and three Greek klines. The klismos were a type of ancient Greek chair with tapering, outcurved legs and a concave backrest. The klines were tall reclining couches with a backrest at one end, and an accompanying footstool for stepping onto it.

"And what of your father's sacrifice?" asked the Moira.

Elena stood motionless, her gaze falling to Atropos's fingers on her shoulder. The Moira tapped a single adamantine nail against Elena's skin before she smoothed her hands down Elena's arms. The contact was paralyzing. Every nerve in Elena's body was screaming. The hairs on the back of her neck rose slowly. Static charged the air between them and Elena's breath caught, as she felt Atropos's fingers settle on the clasp of her gown and slowly undo the zipper. Elena crossed her arms over her chest to hold up the gown, since she was not wearing a bra.

"I don't take his sacrifice lightly either," Elena answered, a light tremor in her voice.

Atropos slowly wrapped her arms around Elena from behind. She then gently took a hold of Elena's wrists and eased her arms open. The gown fell soundlessly to the ground. Elena startled. The Moira placed her cold hands on Elena's hips and pushed her underwear downward.

"And Thanatos, what of his sacrifice?" asked Atropos as she eased her way around Elena, coming to stand before her. "You are aware he has broken our laws for the sake of saving your life?"

"Yes," Elena whispered, unable to meet the Moira's gaze for more than a few seconds. "His sacrifice weighs heavily on my heart."

Atropos smiled. "Are you in love with him?"

The question took Elena by surprise. She raised her eyes to meet Atropos's, lost for words. So little time had passed since the day she ran into Eiry in the conference room, and yet it felt like a lifetime ago. She was not the same person she had been on the day they met. Her world had forever been altered. The only constant in Elena's life was gone, and Eiry had, to some degree, stepped into that person's role. Elena felt more for him than she had for anyone other than Cataline and her parents, but she didn't know if it was love or simply circumstance. "I'm afraid I can't answer that question. I have no idea."

Atropos's smile faded. "Do you think it possible he is in love with you?" Her ageless features slowly settled into a pensive expression.

Elena immediately recalled Aosaginohi's words. The Night Heron had spoken of Eiry's suspended punishment, and the reason behind it. Her father's punishment had come swiftly, as the Moirai knew well what lay in Dionysus's heart. Eiry's heart, however, was a mystery—even to the Fates.

"I find that doubtful," Elena answered. "He has shown no such inclination."

If the Moira was dissatisfied with Elena's response, she did not give any indication of it. Instead, she offered Elena another enigmatic smile, and then stepped away into the shadows of the chamber. She returned carrying a folded bundle of white gossamer fabric.

"Raise you arms," she commanded in a gentle tone, waiting patiently for Elena to do as she asked. "Things in our world are much more ritualized than in the human world, and somewhat more somatic."

Elena raised her arms. "What does that mean, exactly?" she asked, never having heard the term 'somatic' before.

Atropos unfolded the bundle of fabric and slipped it over Elena's head. It floated delicately over her skin, hugging every curve. "You will understand once the ritual is over," the Moira assured Elena.

This was all in preparation for the ritual to unseal Elena's divinity.

"What will the ritual consist of?" Elena asked.

Atropos took hold of her hand and led her across the chamber. "It requires two steps. First, I must remove the seal. Second, Dionysus must breathe his divinity back into your body." They reached a door and Atropos opened it gently, leading Elena into another chamber.

Much smaller in size, it held a single artifact—the Moirai's loom. Made of wood, the vertical loom stood on two uprights with a beam across the top from which nine weighted warps hung vertically, and a second horizontal beam two feet below it crossed the warps to create the necessary elements for weaving. A distaff of unspun adamant fibers sat on a klismos chair beside the loom, another of unspun copper in a basket at its feet. A third held fibers of unspun gold and rested on a stool in front of the loom. The completed fabric within the loom was woven out of all three fibers.

Without a word, Atropos led Elena through the chamber to a set of stairs near the opposite wall that led upward to the main floor of the Moirai's temple.

Dionysus waited in the central chamber. His modern clothes had been removed, replaced with a tunic of light fabric draped across his hips. His upper body, anointed with oils, was left bare. His shoulder-length hair now spilled past down his back in thick, flowing waves. He wore a wreath of ivy on his brow.

Elena followed Atropos into the central chamber. She tried to meet her father's eyes, but she felt inexplicably self-conscious. Seeing him like this, less as a father and more as a god, was overwhelming. To look directly into his eyes gave her vertigo, and so Elena looked to Eiry instead.

Eiry stood silent behind Dionysus, his modern appearance sharply juxtaposed by the now predominant classical elements. He wore a stoic expression, keeping his thoughts to himself. Elena desperately wanted to know what he was thinking.

"You look stunning," Dionysus said to Elena, gently taking her by the hand.

Atropos moved to join her sisters, who stood together beside a column bordering the chamber.

"You look like a god," Elena whispered to her father, feeling uncomfortably timid.

Dionysus smiled. "Your mother said the same thing to me the first time she saw me dressed in this fashion." He spoke softly, leading Elena out of the chamber, through the main peristyle and down the steps of the temple toward the winding path.

Eiry and the Moirai followed in silence. The trickle of water along the walls had resumed its original cadence.

"It's unnerving," Elena confessed, so nervous now that she spoke simply for the sake of talking. They had walked the full length of the path down the earthen mound, and were making their way toward one of the five pools of water. "Where are we going?" she asked her father, her voice slightly shrill from her nerves.

"The ritual must take place in the Styx," he replied softly, leading Elena up to its edge.

The pool cut into the earth, edged in stone. The surface of the water was smooth as glass, even in those places where it met the steady stream. The water itself was opaque, a cloud of dark matter churning within. Elena's nerves quickly turned to fear.

"Don't be afraid," Dionysus whispered beside her.

Clotho and Lachesis took their place at opposite ends of the pool. Atropos crossed the ground beside Elena and Dionysus, and without saying a word stepped into the dismal waters. Eiry remained several feet behind them, observant but silent. Elena met his gaze, searching for the courage she desperately lacked. Instead of the usual restraint, she found a reassuring expression.

"You're safe, Ele. I promise," he whispered in her mind.

"Elena," Atropos said, commanding Elena's attention. "Come forward, and step into the pool."

Before doing so, Elena met her father's eyes. Again she felt vertigo, but fought past it. A ghost of a smile touched her father's lips, and then he let her go. Elena then did as Atropos instructed.

The water was neither warm or cold, and much denser than Elena expected. It molded to her form, hugging her hips once she reached the center. Atropos stood beside her. Without preamble, she began to sing. Her voice rose much deeper and richer than before, her words so ancient that even Tartarus's power, the force that transformed all languages spoken in the underworld into a universal one, could not assist Elena in understanding them.

The Moira's words breathed life into everything around them— the pace of the streams, the brightness of the moss and flowers, the starlight beneath their godly eyes and skin. Even Elena was affected, her body straining against the might of Atropos's spell. Her skin seemed to grow brighter, her hair thicker and more abundant. Her nails glistened in the darkness, and every fiber of Elena's being strummed with the rhythm of the Moira's song.

Soon, the water of the Styx began to stir. The cloud of Stygian darkness came to life, clinging to Elena's skin. From her feet, it crawled up her legs, slithering across her skin like a serpent. Elena cried out, startled as it moved between her inner thighs and continued upward, contracting tightly around her hips and abdomen. No matter how much she wanted to look down, Elena couldn't. Atropos held her gaze, her words commanding the water higher until it made its way to Elena's throat. Suddenly, it was cold as ice. It branched at the line of her jaw, a web of dark capillaries smoothing across her cheeks. She felt them at the corners of her eyes and instinctively shut them. As Atropos's words began to fade, the Stygian water seeped into Elena's skin. She felt it soak into every part of her, its path cold as venom, until she could no longer feel the difference between it and herself.

Atropos had completed her song.

Elena opened her eyes. Her father stood before her, the bottom half of his body submerged. He appeared the same, and yet he felt completely different. She did not recognize the presence in his eyes. When he touched her, Elena felt a sharp sting of energy, which only worsened as he wrapped his arms around her waist. She struggled for an instant, and he begged her to be still. He held her tightly against him, a single hand smoothing up the side of her body to the nape of her neck. Elena could no longer feel the bite of his energy; she had grown numb. Dionysus looked down into her face and inched closer until his mouth brushed intimately against hers. Elena wanted to object, but she couldn't find the words.

"Do not be alarmed," he breathed against her lips, holding her face in both of his hands.

Something damp spilled onto Elena's cheek, and when he kissed her she tasted his tears. Instantly, Elena felt something hot pour down her throat, then it burned cold. Neither heavy or light, in a state between liquid and gas, it moved through her body until it filled every inch of space beneath her skin.

Dionysus did not release her until the substance fused with her completely.

CHAPTER FOURTEEN

WHEN ELENA OPENED HER EYES, she was lying in bed. She sat up and looked around her. The bed, which was impossibly large, was the only thing in the room. Elena was alone in Eiry's bedroom. She sat back, cradled comfortably by an array of pillows set against the headboard. Her body felt sore, and she stretched beneath the sheets. They felt wonderful against her skin. Someone had dressed her in a nightgown, a matching robe laid out thoughtfully against the foot of the bed.

"How are you feeling?" asked a familiar voice.

Elena looked up to find Eiry standing by the door. He had removed his blazer, and stood in his shirt and tie, his slacks perfectly ironed. Slowly, her recollection of the ritual began to surface.

"I'm a little sore," she finally admitted. She also felt different in a way she couldn't put into words. Everything was just a little sharper, as if every one of her five senses had been fine-tuned.

Eiry gave her a short nod and then stepped into the room. He undid his tie as he walked. "Aisa said it would take a few days before you would no longer feel the difference," he said, as he took a seat beside her on the bed. He watched Elena quietly, concern softening his features.

No matter how familiar Eiry was to her now, Elena still found him absurdly beautiful. The thought brought back the memory of a conversation.

"She asked me about you," Elena whispered to him, as he quietly looked her over. He checked her for a fever, and his cold hand felt wonderful against her skin. Until that moment, Elena hadn't realized how hot she felt.

"You have a bit of a fever. Aisa said it was a natural reaction. You should be back to normal by tomorrow morning." Eiry slipped the tie from his neck and set it down on the bed beside him. "And who asked you about me?"

"Atropos." Elena reached for his tie, smoothing her fingers along the textured fabric. The sensation felt much more tactile than Elena anticipated, as if her skin was hypersensitive. "I couldn't help but feel like she was digging."

Eiry stilled, his gaze on Elena's fingers. "Digging for what?"

"For something to punish you with." Elena didn't know how she knew, but she was sure of it. "She asked how you felt about me."

Eiry instantly lifted his gaze to hers, his eyes betraying his bewilderment. Her response had taken him completely by surprise. "What did you tell her?"

"I told her you had shown no inclinations of any kind." Elena held Eiry's gaze, as he slipped the tie from her hands.

Eiry nodded, and leaned forward. He brought his forehead close to Elena's and pressed his lips to her brow; they were so cold they sent a chill down Elena's spine. He thanked her in whisper, and then eased himself off the bed.

"You should get some rest," he told her.

"Don't leave yet." Elena leaned back against the pillows, turning onto her side so that she could face him. "Where will you sleep?"

"I planned on keeping an eye on you most of the night. I'll rest on one of the sofas in the front room if I get tired," he replied in a matter-of-fact tone.

"The bed's big enough for the both of us, you know." Elena patted the space next to her, but Eiry hesitated. "You've slept next to me for days, Eiry. I would feel a lot more comfortable if you stayed with me now."

He considered it in his usual way, quiet and thoughtful. Then he nodded.

"It'll be nice to finally see you in something other than a suit or a *kimono*," Elena joked, enjoying the opportunity to tease him; it was so much easier than thinking. If she stopped long enough to think, Elena would get lost in everything that had happened, but she didn't want to obsess about the past. She wanted simply to consider the future, and what needed to be done.

"Where's my father?" Elena asked Eiry, suddenly very aware of his absence. Her thoughts returned to the ritual, and she paled. "Did he kiss me?"

"It was necessary," Eiry replied, quick to defend her father's actions. "He had to breathe his divinity back into you. That's how it is always done, even during apotheosis. "

"Apotheosis? As in deification?" The concept took Elena by surprise.

"Yes. The instances are rare in our history, and they require the blessing of the Moirai, but it has been done and the process requires the same kind of ritual. The god must breathe their divinity into the chosen vessel."

Elena laughed, the gesture making her chest feel strained. Vessel was such a ridiculous word for someone being deified, as if that person had been empty the entire time—vacant until they were made a god. Actually, it was kind of insulting, but Elena decided not to share the thought. If she had learned anything these past few days, it was that the mind of a god worked very differently than the mind of a human.

Eiry watched her curiously, knowing something was going on in her head but not sure about it. As would be expected, he didn't pry. Instead, he began to unbutton his shirt. "Evius and I brought you back here after the ritual," he said, responding to Elena's earlier question. "You collapsed in his arms toward the end of the ritual. We brought you back here and put you in bed. He stayed with you for a few hours, but then he was summoned by my mother and Livius."

Elena remembered the kiss and immediately shut her eyes, as if that would get rid of the realization that it had stirred something inside of her. Even now, she felt it, mingled with her attraction to Eiry. When she opened her eyes, Eiry was watching her with interest. Elena instantly felt the heat rise to her cheeks. She looked away, careful not to stare as he undressed.

"What are you thinking about?" he asked her, with that familiar ghost of a grin. He ran his hand through his short blonde hair and then un-tucked his shirt. He removed it, revealing an undershirt that hugged him perfectly. He then placed his shirt over the edge of the bed, along with the tie he had taken from Elena. He also removed his watch and belt, placing those at the foot of the bed as well.

Elena watched him quietly, distracted. It took her a second to remember what they had been talking about. "I was thinking about the ritual," she finally said, answering his question. "It was just weird, that's all." Elena looked away as Eiry dropped onto the bed beside her.

"It's bothering you isn't it, what happened with Evius?" He searched her face as he said it; his fingers gently brushing against Elena's cheek and guiding her gaze back toward him.

The gesture made her stomach tighten and her pulse quicken. She was wondering if Eiry could pick up on such things, when he smiled.

"Don't beat yourself up over it," he said to her softly, keeping his observations to himself. "Our rituals are all like that, physical in some way. Plus, your father happens to be the god of the flesh. He's very hedonistic… and handsy. And to a god, there aren't a lot of boundaries, family or otherwise. Your mother was the only person who could make him sensible."

His words made Elena feel a little better about it, but they didn't alleviate her uneasiness completely. "I'm sorry, Eiry. It's just been a lot to take in. Everything is so different."

Elena had worshipped her father as a child. The loss of him had devastated her. Getting him back was more than Elena had ever dared to dream, and yet the reality of him was disconcerting. Who he was didn't exactly match the memories of who he had been. On the one hand, doting father and loving husband. On the other, decadent god. The father Elena knew was there, but the god in him was so much more predominant. He felt familiar and strange, all at the same time, and it left her feeling utterly confused. It was so much to process in so little time, a seemingly recurring theme in Elena's life since she came into possession of her inheritance.

Eiry smoothed his fingers against the line of her jaw, and quietly searched Elena's gaze. He was infinitely patient with her. He inched closer, and for a second Elena swore he was going to kiss her, but then he quickly pulled away.

"I know it's been a lot, but you're not alone in this, Ele," he whispered, taking her hand and squeezing it gently. "I'll be next to you every step of the way, and so will your father." He waited until Elena nodded, let go of her hand, and then pushed himself off the bed. "I'm going to step out for a second to change and I'll be right back."

He was absent only for a minute, taking his shirt, tie, watch and belt with him. When Eiry stepped back into the room, he carried a blanket in his hands and wore only pajama bottoms, his upper body completely exposed. Of course, he was perfect. His stomach was a smooth expanse of pale skin, lean and sharply cut. Without another word, he slipped into bed with Elena. He wrapped the blanket around her and then pulled her against him. Elena could feel the cold from his skin seep through the blanket, but it wasn't uncomfortable.

"You should be good by tomorrow," he whispered to her, rubbing her arms over the blanket. "The changes will be gradual, but you're technically a full fledged demigod now. My cold shouldn't bother you much after a while."

The term took Elena by surprise. Even after everything that had taken place, she hadn't realized what it really meant. She was a demigod; her mother was a human, her father a god. The thought of it was staggering. "Does that mean I'll have powers, like Hercules and Perseus?" she asked.

"Yes, that's exactly what it means," Eiry replied, his cheek resting against her temple, "but I personally think you're much better looking."

"Thanks." Elena smiled, but then grew quiet. Being a demigod was not something she had counted on. She had counted on fighting tooth and nail, for Eiry's sake more than her own—to save him the pain of losing another Heir—but she hadn't really thought she would stand a chance. If she was lucky, she would survive as long as her mother did. This revelation, however, added a glimmer of hope; demigods were famous for fighting against the might of the divine.

"There's something I've been meaning to ask you about," Elena finally said to Eiry, her mind knee-deep in the mythology she had studied earlier in life.

"Ask away," Eiry said, growing still.

"Remember when we met, when I told you I studied the Classics in college?"

Eiry shifted against Elena. He moved gently, positioning himself so he could look at her. "Yes," he whispered, "and I told you Greek art called to me. It was an inside joke."

Elena nodded, watching him quietly. She had his full attention, and that was something she really liked about him. He was completely different than the other gods she had met, different than the rest of his family. "At dinner, I noticed something. I don't remember every detail of the genealogy of the Greek gods, but I remember Thanatos was said to be the son of Nyx, the goddess of night, not Chione. I've never heard of a goddess named Chione."

Eiry gave Elena a knowing smile. "Actually, human mythology claims Chione was the goddess of snow, which is technically correct, but they also claim she was a nymph, the daughter of Boreas, god of the north-wind, and Oreithyia, a mountain nymph. That part is obviously inaccurate."

Eiry's tone took on a more academic air, very similar to how he had given his report of their journey to Livius and his mother. He was very comfortable in this role, and Elena enjoyed watching him assume it.

"The genealogy passed down in human mythology tends to be inaccurate either because it is inaccurate in origin or because it has changed as a result of our war. My mother is a good example of this," Eiry continued to explain. "In the beginning of human worship, Tartarus had not taken humanoid form; it remained an element, abstract and infinite. Around the time Greece became a patriarchal society, humans naturally thought of Tartarus as a male element. When Tartarus willed itself into taking form, however, it split into two beings.

"By that time, the covenants of human worship were already established and the female aspect of the element hardly made its way into religious culture, which was not an issue since the worship of Tartarus benefited both aspects alike. In those few instances where her identity did make its way into the culture, my mother was accounted for as a goddess of snow, never linked to what she truly was. Because of this, human theology erroneously attributes some of her children to Nyx, the only powerful underworld elemental goddess they had to choose from. All of the children Greek mythology claims Nyx begat on her own are actually my mother and Livius's children. That, of course, includes me."

"Livius? Her twin?" Elena sat up, looking back at Eiry from over her shoulder. She was a little shocked, even with the prior warning from Gavin and Galen.

"Yes, with her twin," Eiry said with a shrug. "That's a rule in our world. God twins are made for each other. They cannot exist without the other. They cannot even be physically separated for long periods of time. There are very few exceptions to that rule."

"Then why did you tell me Lucian was your father?" Elena asked.

"That's a little more complicated." The blanket had fallen off Elena's shoulder and Eiry pulled it back up, gently, his fingers lingering for a few seconds before he dove into an explanation. "Gods are deathless by nature. While their physical forms can be destroyed in battle, their elements cannot. The element survives to be reborn again into a new body. That, along with the advent of this war, has created a bit of a problem. In some cases, the original parent is from the opposing pantheon, and the Moirai must then choose a new parent.

"That was the case with Gavin and Galen. Although chthonic gods by nature, their original parents were Ares and Aphrodite, who were both Olympians. When the House of Thebes, the direct decedents of Ares and Aphrodite, was targeted, Ares defected to Tartarus. Phobos and Deimos are some of our strongest fighters, but they once fell in battle and could not be reborn to Aphrodite for obvious reasons. In that case, the Moirai chose a new mother. Their choice was easy, since Lucian and my mother had been bound to each other for decades already. So my mother carried the twins, and in their second incarnation has raised them as her own. It wasn't much of a stretch, since she had always been a mother figure to them. Aphrodite hardly ever visited Tartarus before the Great War, and her relationship with Phobos and Deimos was always strained."

"It is the same for me and Lucian," Eiry continued, without giving Elena a chance to interrupt. "I have been reborn once. At the time, Livius was technically unavailable. The Moirai chose Ares to be my father, and he has raised me as his son ever since. We have lived many decades as such in the human world."

"Wait a minute," Elena cut in before he could prevent her from doing so. "Didn't you say god twins can't be separated from each other for long? How was Livius unavailable?"

"I also said there have been rare exceptions. It's too complicated to get into right now, Ele. This is hardly the Greek pantheon of ancient times. Our dynamic is very complicated, and there's no reason to worry about it now. We have other things to focus on. I promise you, when this is all over, we'll talk about it *ad nauseum*. You'll be bored out of your mind," he assured her with a playful grin.

"When this is over? You sound like you think we'll come out of this alive," she said, trying not to sound dismissive.

"That's exactly what I think."

"How can you be sure?"

"Call it a hunch," he whispered and then shifted in bed, until he was lying on his back and she was lying against him, her head resting against his chest and his arm wrapped around her.

If she listened carefully, Elena could hear a heartbeat, but it was very faint. A beat every two minutes, at best. When he spoke, the sound vanished completely.

"Get some rest, Ele. I honestly don't know why I feel that way, except that I do. Even the Kirin was moved to take a side. If that is not a good omen, I don't know what is. For now, let's just take it day by day. Today is over, and tomorrow will be a very busy day."

"What's tomorrow?"

"Tomorrow we go to Elysium to visit your mother," he answered, his voice already thick with sleep, "and then to the Domos Aidaou where Hades awaits your response."

A FEW HOURS before Elena woke, two gods sparred over a game of chess. The black pieces on the board belonged to Hades Eubuleus, he of good counsel, the white to Thanatos Paean, he who delivers men from the pains and sorrows of life.

"Why must you always question my intentions?" Hades asked Thanatos in a deep and rumbling voice, a hint of offense inflected in his tone. He ran a large hand across his beard, and pondered his next move. After several moments, he lifted his gaze and fixed his dark eyes on the god sitting across from him—one who had a gift for winning; in simple games at least, Hades thought to himself, in everything else Thanatos was most unfortunate. The thought made Hades smile. "I simply want to help the Heir regain her friend. It was unfortunate that you were unable to reach the woman in time to save her," Hades added defiantly. "You know I am bound by rules, Thanatos, and so the Heir must offer something in exchange if I am to help her. You and the Keres would accompany her, so it would be a simple task."

Death narrowed his crimson gaze and watched quietly as Hades finally moved his chess piece on the board. "Are you not also called Clymenus, the Notorious?" he asked in an apathetic tone, moving his own chess piece immediately. "You will forgive my reservations, Lord Hades, but your reputation for notoriety precedes you. This is the first time you show any such interest in an Heir." Death met Hades's hateful stare with a cold but calm indifference.

"Do not patronize me, Thanatos," growled Hades in reply. "That is an unfortunate epithet. You, better than anyone, should know humans give terrible names to chthonic deities. To them, we are terrible creatures, things to be feared. You would be wise to remember that." Hades reached for the chessboard and then stopped midway, changing his mind for the dozenth time. Frustrated, he ran a hand through his hair.

Death watched him quietly, a ghost of smile touching his features. "I was not aware you counted yourself chthonic, Lord Hades. Here I thought you were no more than an exiled Olympian biding his time." A touch of sarcasm colored Death's voice, sharp and as biting as the edge of a blade.

Hades narrowed his eyes, visibly provoked by the accusation. Several seconds before, he had picked up a piece from the board, which he now squeezed in his hand until his knuckles turned white and the ire left his expression. "Was your purpose in visiting me to abuse, Thanatos?

I have much more pressing things to do than to banter with an infantile god." Hades placed his piece back on the board and made his move.

"I was not aware that sorting human souls was such a pressing matter. Even a monkey with a crown could do it," Death countered in an unaffected tone, never slowing the pace of his game. He quickly made his move, and then leaned back against his chair with the same indifferent expression. "And, if memory serves me right, I am older than you."

"Funny how Chione preferred you be the monkey with the crown," Hades crowed, rushing into his next move.

"You should be thanking me for refusing her." Death shrugged, and moved another piece on the chessboard. "Check," he whispered with a satisfied smile.

Hades snarled, and slammed his fist down on the table. The board shook, but the pieces remained unchanged. "Why should I be thankful?" he asked, hastily making another move.

"If I had not, Hades, what function would you play? What would you be Lord and Master of, exactly?" Death asked, not a hint of mockery in his voice, his eyes trained on the board. "You could no longer be called Aidoneus, the Ruler of Many, for you would no longer rule over a single soul, nor could you by that same token be called Polydegmon, Receiver of Many. Plouton, the Rich One, would no longer apply since in losing your rule you would lose the realm and the precious minerals that come from it. What, then, would you be? What is a god without a purpose? Would you fade until you were insubstantial, like one of your shades, or would you give yourself to the Void? When I consider it, I cannot even recall what your purview was before you drew our lot, other than elder brother to Zeus." As he said the last words, Death made his move on the board.

The White Queen was positioned directly in front of the Black King. The White King protected its Queen. "Checkmate," whispered Death, and the empty halls of the Domos Aidaou shook with its Master's anger.

ELENA WOKE TO SILENCE and an empty bed. She quickly sat up and surveyed the room around her. It was dark, and a fire burned in the hearth on the opposite side of the room. She could not tell if it was morning or evening. The windows in the room were obscured by the petal-thin membranes that passed for curtains in this world, making it impossible for her to see outside. Of course, nothing in the room gave away the hour. There was no clock or electronic device that might have the time. The watch Eiry had taken off the evening before was nowhere to be seen.

Elena hesitated for a moment and then crawled out of bed. A robe had been left for her once again at the foot of the bed, and she put it on before walking barefoot to the nearest window. She stared at the petal-like membrane, confounded. She had no idea how to make it work. There was no evidence of any mechanism or switch. Open Sesame, Elena thought to herself with a nervous laugh, but of course that didn't work. Just as she reached to touch the variegated surface, an unfamiliar voice called out from behind, startling her.

"They do not respond to touch, girl," said the female voice in a stern and unobliging tone. "In fact, it would be best if you did not touch them at all."

Elena turned to find a tall and slender figure standing at the door. Like the other servants, her eyes matched the color of her hair—white and pale as moonlight—and she wore green and silver robes. She had delicate features, accented by a straight and pointed nose, deep-set eyes and an overtly severe expression. She reminded Elena of a governess, and the woman carried herself with the same kind of gravity; sharp of tongue, she made no attempts to hide her disapproval.

"I'm sorry," Elena said automatically, reacting unconsciously to the woman's harsh demeanor. "I had no idea what time it was, so I wanted to take a look outside."

"Time does not pass here as it does above. In Eira it is always twilight. The gods need no instruments to tell the passage of time. You will just have to do without knowing," replied the woman as she casually stepped into the room. She carried a silver tray in her hands, a folded piece of paper and a glass of ambrosia its only contents. "I am Illyria," she said to Elena. "Lord Thanatos has asked me to deliver this message, and Lord Dionysus bids you to drink."

Illyria did not wait for a response. She walked to the foot of the bed in silence and placed the tray on a folding table that Elena was certain had not been there moments before. Once her task was complete, Illyria took her leave without uttering another word, and it took a second for Elena to recover. In a matter of moments, that woman had sucked the magic out of the entire room. Elena was beginning to think that being ornery was a requirement here in Tartarus. Eiry and her father were the only ones who made Elena feel welcome, and the young twins in their own insane way; Lucian had also been kind.

Thinking of Eiry brought Elena back to the present, to the folded message on the tray. She quickly made her way to the foot of the bed and reached for the piece of paper. It was a note written in a steady and elegant hand, sealed with the now-familiar butterfly crest. Bearing Eiry's signature, it explained the cause for his absence—he had business to attend to before escorting Elena to Elysium, where she would be reunited with her mother.

Elena had forgotten that tiny detail. It had fluttered to the surface of her mind when she woke, a fragment of a thought, but she had dismissed it as the product of a dream. She had never imagined, in a million years, that she would see her mother again. The reality of it now was as terrifying as it was exhilarating. Her recent experience with her father had left her somewhat apprehensive of miraculous reunions.

As Elena considered these things, her eyes fell on the glass of ambrosia on the tray. It's contents glowed with a warm amber light, and just looking at it made Elena feel better—stronger. Perhaps that's why her father had sent it. Without giving it another thought, Elena drank the contents of the glass and crawled back into bed with Eiry's note still in her hands.

The effect, once again, was instant. Elena's anxiety melted away, replaced by an overwhelming sense of elation. It crawled its way into every recess of her being, finally leaving her with a pleasant sense of satisfaction. Lying in bed felt almost like she was floating. Elena closed her eyes, clutched Eiry's note in her hand, and gave herself over to it. Slowly, the elegant lines of Eiry's writing surfaced in the back of her mind. She traced the script with her subconscious, until her mind completely emptied.

Elena heard someone call out her name and she started, sitting up in bed to find the room empty. The note had fallen from her hands. She had no idea how much time had passed. She must have been dreaming. Her heart beat furiously, and she focused on calming herself down. She leaned back against the pillows and closed her eyes. Something was taking shape in the back of her mind. Elena couldn't tell if she was remembering something that actually happened earlier that morning or what took place in a dream.

Elena remembered someone calling her name. She had tried to open her eyes, but she was too far-gone. He called her name again, and the cold press of his fingers against her cheek followed the sound. Elena tried to open her eyes again, but her lids felt as heavy as lead. *Ele, wake up.* This time, he whispered it in her ear, pulling her closer. He pressed his lips to her temple and breathed in deeply, his thumb smoothing across the line of her jaw. *I have to leave for a minute, and I don't want you to be afraid when you wake up alone.*

Elena managed to open her eyes enough to see the faint outline of his face. He was leaning over her, his habitually groomed bangs now hanging loosely over his eyes. His usually icy gaze was a deep slate blue. Elena tried to focus harder. He smiled, and Elena was lost in the curve of his perfect lips. For the first time, she noticed he had a small beauty mark below the inner corner of his left eye, near the center of the bridge of his nose. Elena breathed his name, but it was the only thing she managed to say. She was too tired. She could already feel herself slipping again.

Her eyes closed, and she felt him shift his weight. He gave a half-suppressed laugh, and his cold breath brushed against her cheek. *I'll leave you a note*, he whispered, then everything stilled. If it weren't for the fact that she could still feel the chill, Elena would have thought he'd disappeared. Just as she began to drift, he pressed his mouth to hers in a kiss.

"Who do you think she's dreaming about?" Gavin whispered to Galen, who was leaning over to pick up the folded note from the ground. They were both standing next to Eiry's bed, peering down at Elena.

"This idiot, probably," Galen said with a shrug, and handed his twin the note. He looked back down at the sleeping girl, still completely unimpressed.

An impish smile curled the corners of Gavin's mouth as he read the note. "Awww. That's cute, don't you think?" he asked, and slipped the note into his pocket.

Galen made a face, pretending to gag. "I guess, if you like humans and sickeningly sweet moments... puppy dogs and kitty cats, and all that shit," he replied in his perpetually acerbic tone. "I think it's nauseating."

Gavin pinched him, hard. When Galen glared back and was about to protest, Gavin shut him up with a finger to his lips, and then quickly replaced it with his mouth.

Of course, that got Galen's attention. He wrapped an arm around Gavin's waist and dragged him closer, catching his throat with his hand, his nails biting softly into his brother's skin. "You shouldn't tease in front of the human," Galen growled softly, and bit Gavin's lip before pulling away.

"What do you think would happen if I did?" Gavin asked, glassy-eyed. He touched his lips absently.

Galen followed the movement of Gavin's fingers and replied in a heavy voice, "I'd have to bend you over that bed, and she would likely wake up... screaming her pretty little head off. Snowflake would be very upset."

Gavin stared at Galen, wide-eyed, his pout almost heartbreaking. "Do you think it's worth it?" he asked in an affected tone.

"I don't know. It depends. How badly do you want to go on this little trip?" Galen caught Gavin's wrist and pulled him close, pressing him back against the side of the bed. He grabbed the waist of Gavin's pants with his other hand and began to undo them. "I say fuck Snowflake," Galen whispered in his twin's ear.

Gavin watched as Galen's hand slipped into his pants. His breath caught, and he leaned his forehead against Galen's shoulder. "But I really want to go on this trip," he complained with a dramatic sigh. "I like her, Galen. She's fun."

Galen turned his gaze to the girl and shrugged. Then he quietly withdrew his hand.

"You're impossible," Gavin said to his twin, and then hopped onto the bed.

It was so large, the girl didn't feel a thing, and so Gavin tiptoed his way toward her. He winked at Galen and then eased himself down beside her. Human or not, she was really quite beautiful. He sent the thought to Galen, and then leaned closer. Galen came around from the opposite side, and they both peered down at her. Gavin reached to touch her but stopped himself, lifting his eyes slowly to meet Galen's gaze. A thought crossed between them, the two exchanged a wicked smile, and just as Gavin leaned forward, all hell broke loose.

Eiry caught Gavin by the collar of his shirt and slammed him against the wall.

Elena woke with a start. She opened her eyes to see Galen staring down at her, his long black hair brushing against her cheek. Instinctively, Elena screamed and then lashed out, catching him on the throat with her nails. She pressed herself back against the headboard, somehow scrambling to her feet, extending her arm to keep Galen at bay while she tried to get her bearings. Galen smirked, and Elena felt the urge to slap him. She hesitated for a second, and then turned her gaze to her left, where Eiry stood holding Gavin against the wall. His nails had extended into sharp daggers made of the same material as his scythe—a bright-colored metal that gleamed like starlight—and Eiry held them against his brother's throat.

"What the hell are you two doing in here?" Eiry growled. His eyes locked with Gavin's. "And why the fuck are your pants undone?"

"I wanted to talk to her," Gavin said softly, his fingers smoothing against Eiry's dagger-like nails, "but she was really deep in sleep, so we were going to try to wake her up."

"With your pants undone?" Eiry hissed.

"Get off of him, Snowflake," Galen called out, an edge to his voice.

It sent a chill down Elena's spine and she turned to study him, narrowing her gaze. Galen held it, an amused smile on his lips, then touched his fingers to the scratches on his throat and blew Elena a kiss.

"You're right, Gav," he called out to his brother, "she *is* fun." The scratches on his throat slowly disappeared.

"I told you!" Gavin said with a triumphant smile and then returned his gaze to Eiry, the amusement slowly draining from his features. "The pants were Galen and I being lecherous, as always. You know we'd never hurt her, Eiry."

"This isn't funny, you two. She has enough shit to deal with." Eiry retracted his nails and smacked Gavin across the head, adding, "you're a jackass," before sitting down on the edge of the bed. "And try giving her some space," he snapped at Galen, then reached for Elena, his manner markedly more gentle. "Are you okay?"

"I'm fine," Elena whispered—other than the fact that these idiots had virtually given her a heart attack. Elena sat back down on the bed, and pulled her robe tighter around her. She could feel Galen's eyes on her and she shrugged, moving closer to Eiry. While the ambush had frayed her nerves, Elena's mind was on something else entirely. Had she been dreaming of the past or of a dream? Elena didn't even remember falling asleep.

"What did you want to talk to her about, Gavin? I'm on a bit of a time schedule," Eiry said, running a hand through his hair; he seemed more anxious than usual.

Gavin sat down on the foot of the bed, and Galen followed suit. Their movements were identical. "Well, that's actually why we're here *now*," Gavin explained. He looked at Elena and offered her an apologetic smile. "I'm sorry we scared you, but I wanted to get to you before the two of you left. You've seen the Fates already, so we assumed you would be leaving today..."

"We're leaving tomorrow," Eiry interrupted.

That was news to Elena. She watched Eiry quietly, and then finally turned her attention to Gavin. "I'm sorry I screamed," she offered, but she sure as hell wasn't going to apologize for scratching Galen.

Gavin smiled, almost beaming. Galen rolled his eyes, and Gavin smacked his twin on the arm before he continued speaking. "We want to accompany you to the Fae, if you decide to go."

"Correction, *he* wants to accompany you," Galen qualified his brother's statement.

Gavin shook his head, and gave an exasperated sigh. "Regardless, I came to ask if you'd let us go with you to the Fae."

Elena was completely surprised by his request, and apparently so was Eiry. He watched his two siblings, his eyes narrowed, as if by staring alone he would will the truth out of them.

"Why the interest?" Elena asked, hoping she didn't sound too rude.

Gavin didn't seem offended, in the least. "You'll need us," he said proudly. "Bryce is great in a fight, but she can't handle the Fae. Above all things, the Fae cherish games. They're experts at the art of manipulation, and it's very difficult to navigate their world if you're not the kind of person who knows how to play their games. Galen and I happen to be experts at it. You'll want us around." Gavin smiled brightly. "Galen won't admit it, but we like you, Elena. We want to help you retrieve the Helm."

Galen shrugged, but he didn't deny it.

Elena didn't know how Eiry felt about it, but for her part she was shocked. Eiry and her father were the only two people who had expressed any desire in assisting her, even though she was technically suffering through all of this to ultimately give Tartarus the win in their never-ending war. Where the Hyakki Yakō had been warm and inviting, the Tartareans, in general, were difficult.

"Sure, if Eiry's okay with it," she finally answered, offering Gavin a conciliatory smile.

Eiry's only response was a nod, and then he kicked them both out of the room unceremoniously. On his way out, Gavin danced around his twin, excessively enthusiastic about the entire thing, while Galen was distinctively indifferent by comparison.

"Sorry about that," Eiry was quick to apologize as he made his way back towards the bed.

"No worries." Elena offered him a smile, and quickly crawled out of bed. The stone floor should have been cold to the touch, but felt normal against her bare feet. "I'm sorry I was still in bed," she whispered as they met in the center of the room. "I'll go take a quick shower and get ready." Without thinking about it, she gave him a kiss on the cheek.

Eiry stilled, but caught Elena's hand before she could walk away. He searched her gaze, and Elena felt the blood rush to her cheeks. She lowered her eyes, but seconds later he was guiding her attention back to him with the gentlest touch of his fingers. Elena's stomach tightened.

"Are you sure you're okay?" he asked her, his voice soft and his tone gentle.

"I am. I just had some crazy dreams last night, and this morning," she offered, hoping that would be enough to alleviate his concern, but then immediately regretted it.

She shouldn't have mentioned her dreams, especially when she didn't want to consider her most recent one—assuming it was a dream at all. While not overtly explicit, the intimacy of it made Elena feel self-conscious. She had begun to develop an attachment to Eiry and was too afraid to entertain the idea—the hope—that he might feel the same.

Eiry studied her carefully and his features smoothed. Elena panicked. She tried to make an exit to the bathroom, but it didn't work. He cornered her in less than a second.

"Ele, don't run from me," Eiry whispered, the plea more in his eyes than on his lips. He had her cornered against the wall, a hand at each of her sides. "If you're having any more dreams about Hades, you have to let me know."

"Oh, gods no, that's not it at all," Elena said in a single breath, relieved that his suspicion had fallen on Hades as the subject—she had forgotten that her dreams had been a sore subject for him recently.

Her relief did not go unnoticed. Eiry inched closer and narrowed his eyes. Then he arched a brow, the expression as unnerving as it was unexpected. He was so close to her that Elena could see all of the details she had seen in her dream, including the small beauty mark below the inner corner of his left eye.

"If you're having dreams about any gods, I need to know," he admonished her quietly, searching her face for the answers she was refusing to give, "because we'll have to see Morpheus before we leave."

"Morpheus? As in the god of dreams?" Elena's voice was shrill. She tried to ease her way out of her current position but it was impossible; and Eiry watched her, thoroughly amused. Her dream had technically been about a god, but Elena was certain his concerns didn't extend to dreams she had of him. "Eiry, it's not like that."

"Ele, I'm serious. This is important."

"I'm serious too, Eiry. It was nothing."

"You said they were crazy."

"Yes, I did, but I didn't mean like that. Don't you think you're being a little silly about this?"

"Silly? Ele, the dreams you were having about Hades were no laughing matter." Eiry stared at her, his face smoothing.

"Come on, don't be upset with me," she pleaded with him. "I know it was serious. I would tell you if it were about any other god."

"So you admit you've been dreaming about a god?"

"Yes. Fuck!" she hissed and pushed at him again, to no avail. "I had a dream about you. There, I said it. Are you happy? Do you want me to tell you about those too?"

Eiry stilled, the surprise on his face priceless. If the moment weren't so mortifying, Elena would be feeling mighty triumphant right about now.

"Me?" he repeated in a whisper, searching Elena's face.

Elena's cheeks felt hot and she knew she was beet red. She just wanted to crawl under a rock somewhere, but instead decided to go for broke. "Did you kiss me this morning when I was half asleep? That's what I dreamed about, except I couldn't tell if it really happened or if it was a dream."

Eiry didn't answer. He stayed completely quiet, his eyes boring into hers. It made Elena livid that after all of that he didn't even have the decency to answer her. She pushed at him with everything she had and to her surprise he gave. That single gesture was infinitely more hurtful than the silence. Elena felt the tears sting her eyes and it took all of her control to deny them. She turned toward the door, but Eiry caught her wrist. He pulled her back against the wall, and suddenly his mouth was on hers, hard and almost bruising.

"It wasn't a dream," he moaned into her mouth, his fingers biting into the nape of her neck as he pulled her even closer, deepening the kiss.

He was careful with her, but for now the gentleness was gone. Whatever he couldn't say, he poured into this single moment. It left Elena breathless, literally pushing her off axis. She lost any sense of self, her body automatically giving into his and responding with equal need.

When the kiss ended, Eiry didn't pull away. His mouth rested against hers and he cupped her cheek, his hands trembling. "I didn't mean to hesitate," he whispered against her mouth. "I'm not good at this sort of thing, and I was just a little surprised that you called me out on it. I hope I made up for it."

It took a second for Elena to find her words. Her mind was racing a mile a minute, and she was hardly catching up with the moment.

He had kissed her. Even now, it was his weight she felt against her, his lips that smiled against her own. When Elena looked into his eyes they were red, and streaks of pale blue had bled into his hair, which was far from perfectly groomed—a casualty of the moment.

"You made up for it," she breathed, instantly covering her mouth with her fingers when she heard how shaky her voice was.

Eiry smiled and gently removed her hand. He studied her quietly, his thumb tracing the swell of her lips before he pulled her into his arms, holding her gently against him by the back of the neck. "As much as I hate to be so abrupt," he whispered, kissing her forehead, "you need to go get ready. Now we're really late."

Elena was surprised to find the bedroom empty when she returned from the bathroom. Concerned, she stepped out of the bedroom and back into the study, searching for Eiry. The room was empty, but from its center Elena had a clear view into the front room and could see the wall of open arches illuminated by the soft glow of a weir lamp—a glass container with half a dozen weir lights of the same color floating inside. Elena stepped quietly into the front room and called out for Eiry, who responded from somewhere to her right.

Elena followed the sound of his voice out into a courtyard located off the front room. It faced the Lethe, and Eiry was standing against the stone railing that lined the courtyard on the river's side— creating a small balcony overlooking the cascading river. Trees and flowering plants bordered all other sides of the courtyard, the flowers unlike any Elena had ever seen. Delicate and crystalline in appearance, they seemed to glow with a faint internal light in pale hues of arctic white, lilac and glacial blue.

"I'm ready when you are," Elena said softly, joining him at the railing.

He was fiddling with something in his hand. Elena lowered her gaze and was surprised to see the object he held was a black chess piece. He noticed her watching, winked, and slipped the wooden piece into his pocket. Elena followed the movement, admiring the suit Eiry had selected for the occasion; an ensemble of unlikely hues that somehow worked perfectly—dark plum and gray blue wool sports jacket, dark indigo slacks, navy blue on white patterned shirt, black textured tie and a purple and white print silk pocket square.

"I always feel a little under-dressed next to you," Elena mused out loud, looking at her own attire—skinny jeans, a red cashmere sweater and ballet flats. She wore her long thick hair in a side braid, Cataline's vintage earrings and her mother's opal ring. She wasn't really sure what she should wear to visit her mother, but this was the best she could manage without going to the twins, which she refused to do.

"That's silly, Elena. You look great." Eiry watched her quietly, his eyes a calm icy blue again, identical to some of the flowers that surrounded them. "How did you sleep? I'm sorry I forgot to ask you earlier, but the twins kind of knocked me off course."

"Very deeply. First time in days I wasn't afraid." Elena hadn't really thought about it until he asked, but it was the best night's sleep she'd gotten since Cataline's passing. "How did your business go?"

"Very well," he said with a roguish smile, not expounding any more than that. "Are you ready to go?"

"As ready as I'll ever be," Elena replied. She didn't push him about his business. "I'm a little nervous, which I'm sure will turn to panic the closer we get to Elysium. I'll try to work on that along the way."

"Well, I hate to be the bearer of bad news, but the journey won't be as long as before. We're so late, we can't walk it."

The way he said it made Elena worry. "How exactly are we going to get there, then?" she asked, trying to mentally brace herself; it seemed like every step they took was a mental and physical roller coaster ride.

"God travel." Eiry said it as if those two simple words explained everything. "Now that your divinity has been unsealed, it's safe for you to travel the way gods travel. We have to start somewhere, and this is the perfect time to start."

"Is it going to be like traveling through the *torii* gates?" Elena asked, apprehensive about the entire thing, and for good reason. She was not fond of her memory of passing through the gate.

"In a sense, but you won't have to worry about losing your mind. It'll have its physical toll at first, but that should only be temporary."

Elena narrowed her eyes. His response was suspiciously ambiguous. "What do you mean by physical toll?"

"Nothing serious," he insisted. "You're head might hurt a little, and you may get dizzy and a little nauseous at first. After a few times you should be right as rain. You'll be able to do it without experiencing any side effects. You just have to make sure to always hold onto me."

"What happens if I don't hold onto you? What if I trip and lose my grip right as it's happening?" Elena was slowly reaching panic mode, and they weren't even on their way yet.

"We'll get separated, and end up a distance apart."

That response was suspiciously concise. "How much of a distance? Are we talking different countries here? Different states?"

"Not unless we happened to be traveling to a place close to an official border or something," he said, swallowing a laugh.

"Not funny, Eiry, you know this freaks me out."

"It'll be fine, Ele. If we were to get separated, it would only be by a few miles at most, worst case scenario. I could locate you in seconds. Easiest thing to do is just not let go."

Elena watched him, still a little reticent. Coming out of the other side of the *torii* gate had been a harrowing experience, so it was only natural that these kinds of things made her jumpy. Eiry extended his hand, giving her time to consider everything before accepting. After a split second of hesitation, Elena took his hand.

GOD TRAVEL was not unlike traveling through the *torii* gate—the world shifted and her spatial perception shattered—but Elena's mind remained intact. Elena was able to watch as the world around her became fragmented, each piece quickly fading into darkness until they were suspended in time, held aloft by an umbral fabric woven in threads of adamant, gold and copper. If Elena turned her gaze just a fraction of an inch, the fabric disappeared completely. It formed the foundation from which the world around them rebuilt itself, one fragment at a time, until they were standing on solid ground.

"How do you feel?" Eiry asked gently, letting go of Elena's hand so he could lift her chin and look her over. "Any worse for wear?"

For a moment, Elena could not find her words. She was completely disoriented. It felt like she had just crawled out of the rabbit hole. As Eiry had predicted, she was dizzy, a little nauseous and had a pounding headache.

"I think I'll survive," she whispered to him, her voice unsteady. "The vertigo really sucks." Elena took a tentative step forward, and the world around her began to spin. She shrank back against Eiry, and closed her eyes tight. "Maybe I need a second. It kind of sneaks up on you, doesn't it?"

Eiry laughed softly, affably, his chest rising and falling rhythmically as Elena clung to him. "Take all the time you need," he said gently, wrapping his arm around her waist and holding her firmly.

Elena concentrated on her breathing, taking deep and steady breaths until she didn't feel lightheaded anymore. Then she opened her eyes and took her bearings. They were standing on the causeway of land bridges that led from the Southern Gate of Hades, through Asphodel and Elysium, to the Domos Aidaou; a trajectory all souls traveled on their way to be judged and sorted. In particular, she and Eiry stood on the bridge that connected the Elysian Fields to the Elysian Islands. Behind them, Elena could see as far as the Southern Gate, the causeway of land bridges passing through two concentric circles—the Elysian Fields and the Asphodel Fields—before reaching the Gate. Ahead of them, the causeway led through the Elysian Islands, where Isabella's soul resided, to the Domos Aidaou—the House of Hades.

Beneath the bridge where they stood, dark water flowed. At first glance, it did not appear to reflect light, it's depths as deep and bottomless as an abyss. But after several moments, the darkness stirred. Beyond its obsidian surface, Elena could see the glimmer of stars and stellar flares of red fire burning through the darkness. Frozen clusters of water and gas swam across the current like astral fish with streaming tails of icy dust, and blooms of russet-colored nebulae drifted through the depths like jellyfish. Dizzy, Elena looked away.

Several feet ahead of them, the bridge sloped downward to join the causeway through the Elysian Islands to the Domos Aidaou. From where they stood, Elena could see the vast collection of islands, linked by stone bridges and narrow canals, which made up the Isles of the Blessed. Somewhere within those islands, Isabella lived out her afterlife amongst the Heroes and descendants of the gods. Each island contained its palaces of interconnected villas and labyrinthine rooms with hanging gardens and central courtyards to pass eternity away.

Amidst the mostly Greek architecture, there were islands representing different cultures—an opulent Persian palace complex made up of lavishly decorated halls, corridors, and terraces, accented by massively tall colonnades and extravagant reliefs; a Japanese castle town of the Tokugawa Shogunate, its structures painted a brilliant white and crowned with indigo-colored tiles; a Norse Mead-Hall complex of hewn wood trimmed in bronze; an extravagant Chinese imperial palace with yellow tiled eaves; a Celtic oppidum—a large fortified hill-top settlement of roundhouses—with crannóg dotting the island's shore, roundhouses built on wooden platforms that extended over the lake; and an Indian palace made of exquisitely carved wood with a three-story high pillared-hall as its centerpiece.

Also visible were islands serving purely communal functions. One was dedicated entirely to the theatrical arts, with a large amphitheater facing an elaborate stage; others to temples, gymnasia, fountain houses, baths, agora—ancient Greek commercial centers—and large halls of state.

"Do they have some form of government?" Elena asked Eiry, surprised by her own question. Of everything she was processing, that detail was by far the least remarkable.

"In a way," he replied, equivocal as ever.

After asking if she felt well enough to walk, he began to lead her down the sloping bridge. "Elysium's inhabitants interact more as tribes than an actual governing body," Eiry explained. "Each island you see belongs to a particular bloodline descended from the gods, called a House—the House of Thebes is one such example. Descendants live among their bloodline, within the island belonging to their House. Each House has its own head. The rare times communal decisions must be made, the heads of each House meet in the halls of state.

"Elysium reflects the desires of its inhabitants, and the gods have very little to do with the shape of their afterlife. Since most modern souls who attain this afterlife belong to an ancient House, the shape of Elysium has remained mostly ancient and Greek. Those Houses that descend from a different pantheon shape their households as they see fit, which is why you see different cultures sprinkled throughout."

At the foot of the bridge, they stepped off of the causeway and onto a narrow street. Immediately, the scenery changed. Twilight gave way to a warm mid-summer sun and a clear blue sky, the shoreline bordered a cerulean sea, and Tartarus itself disappeared. Elena could see no sign of the causeway or the concentric circles beyond.

"Whoa," Elena exclaimed, taken aback by the changing landscape. Again, she felt disoriented. "A warning would have been nice," she chided Eiry, who had begun to walk down the narrow street. Elena quickly caught up with him. "Is there a reason for the change in view?"

Eiry slowed his stride, the faint impression of a smirk softening his icy features. "Sorry about that," he said with a pleasant rhythm to his voice. "It's hard for me to anticipate such things. I have no idea what it's like to be human."

With a wink, he reached for her hand and continued to lead her through the narrow street, which cut inward, never in a straight line, crossing over bridges and canals, through various courtyards, and onto the other islands.

"The reason for the change is that no human's idea of paradise includes a sunless eternity on a pitch-black beach," he continued. "Elysium mirrors the human ideal of paradise. It also serves to ensure that souls do not wander outside of Elysium. The change in view is an illusion, and only gods can see through it to find their way out."

"About the pitch-black beach," Elena said, as they passed a fountain house where several souls gathered to collect water with clay amphorae. "What exactly is that lake made out of? At first, all I saw was black, and then I started to see things... things I don't even really know how to describe."

"What you saw were the five rivers of the underworld converged into a single body of water," Eiry replied, leading them through a bend in the street. "All the elements your father told you about when we visited the Moirai come together and form a whole—a contained cosmos. Asphodel, Elysium, and Hades all rose out of its depths."

The street ended at a bridge and Eiry led Elena across, onto the neighboring island, his words carried softly by the wind as they resumed a steady pace. They continued in the same fashion, walking hand-in-hand, speaking quietly, through shaded paths, across temple sites and busy markets.

They walked, for the most part, unnoticed. The majority of souls they came across wore some form of Classical Greek attire, but the numbers shifted as they neared an island belonging to a House of a different pantheon. As had been the case in the shores of Erebus, all the souls they came across spoke in their native tongue, which the magic of Tartarus reshaped into a universal language everyone could understand.

Finally, they reached an island with a distinctly Greek complex of staggered villas and terraces arranged irregularly in a step-like formation over various, seemingly incongruent, levels. As they climbed the steps and crossed the main gate, the lines of flat roofs cut across the horizon in uneven planes, interrupted by open spaces, as the first large courtyard came into view. The walls of the buildings surrounding the courtyard were painted in saturated pigments, their outside facades bordered by porticoes, the supporting columns of which were made of red-painted cypress wood. Unlike Classical Greek columns, these were typical of Minoan architecture—thinner at the base with round capitals.

On the opposite end of the courtyard stood two wooden columns bordering a porch that led to the megaron, or great hall. Eiry and Elena crossed the porch in silence. They walked through a narrow corridor—its ceiling open to serve as a natural lightwell—to an anteroom with walls lined in painted spirals and figure eight shields. The anteroom was separated from the great hall by a set of square piers framing massive double doors that folded back into shallow recesses.

Elena had read countless accounts of the megaron of fabled Grecian palaces, but nothing prepared her for the magnitude of what she saw. A large, circular open hearth was the central feature of the vast hall. Surrounded by four massive wooden columns, it vented through an oculus in the roof. Also made of wood, the roof was supported by beams and tiled throughout with ceramic and terracotta tiles. The use of color was almost dizzying. Varying shades of blue, red, yellow and white provided the palette. There was hardly a surface free of color. Even the border of the risen hearth was stained in a geometrical design of white on light blue. Vibrant frescoes lined the walls, depicting Minoan bull-leaping, lions, and white-winged griffins. The floor was made of large stone slabs selected for their natural grain and positioned to form an almost subconscious geometrical design.

An alabaster throne was built into the right wall. In it sat Elena's father, dressed irreverently in a pair of broken-in jeans and a vintage 70's button-up shirt. He wore a leather cuff on one hand with beaded bracelets, and several necklaces around his neck. The contrast between ancient architecture and contemporary god was almost comical. Beside him, on a curved wooden stool, sat a woman with long raven hair and pale skin. She had striking green eyes and a warm smile. In contrast to Dionysus's casual appearance, she wore a long one-shouldered dress made of draping black silk, held together by a stunning gold brooch over her right shoulder; modern but of obvious Greek design. Appearing only a few years older than Elena, the two of them were almost identical.

Eiry stepped forward, but Elena found she couldn't move. Isabella's gaze held hers, and Elena was transfixed; she hardly registered Eiry's soft words of encouragement or her father's quick steps across the hall.

"One foot in front of the other," Dionysus whispered cheerfully in Elena's ear. He put his hand on the small of her back, Eiry mirroring the gesture, and they both guided Elena forward.

Isabella stood, and Elena's knees faltered. If it hadn't been for her father and Eiry, she would have tripped and made an idiot of herself.

What the hell was wrong with her? How many times had she dreamed of her mother since her death? How many times had Elena wished to see her again, to speak to her, to ask for her advice? So many times, they were innumerable. Since she was seven years old, Elena had dreamed of being with her family again, and here they were, but every coherent thought failed her. For the first time since this journey had started, her mind had reached its limit. Seeing her mother made the rational human side of her register just how impossible all of this really was. Any minute now Elena would wake up alone in her bed, haunted by the cruelty of a dream that made such a reunion possible.

But Elena didn't wake up. Isabella crossed the space between them with the same delicate grace Elena remembered. A smile brightened her beautiful face, and without a word she gently took Elena into her arms. The shock of the contact left Elena reeling. She clung to her mother in a desperate attempt to anchor herself to the dream. Harrowing sobs echoed through the silent hall, and only distantly did Elena realize they were her own. Everything about Isabella was the same as the final memory Elena had of her, from the delicate floral scent of hydrangea and gardenias, to the light rain-like quality of her laughter and the satin-smooth feel of her touch. The only notable difference was the cool temperature of Isabella's skin—the indelible mark of death. It should have given Elena pause, but her fondness for Eiry cut through her human instinct like a knife.

How long Elena wept in her mother's arms, she couldn't venture to say except that she wept until her voice grew hoarse and her throat raw. All the while, Isabella held her, soothing her until the moment had passed—just as she had when Elena was a child and woke from a night-mare, or was frightened because she'd seen a monster near her room.

Now that Elena thought about it, those monsters had probably been real, and for some unknown reason the thought calmed her. She saw Aosaginohi's face in her mind, and the gentle wisdom of the Night Heron's eyes. She recalled in detail the sound of Aosaginohi's voice and the admiration with which she had spoken of Isabella. These memories gave Elena the strength she needed to regain her composure.

"I met Aosaginohi," Elena whispered in her mother's ear, as she pulled away to look at her properly. It pained her to see her mother's cheeks streaked with tears. "I'm sorry, Mama," Elena murmured apolo-getically. "I didn't mean to make you cry."

Elena hated that she let her emotions get the best of her, but her mother didn't seem to mind. Isabella smiled, took Elena's hands in hers and held them tightly.

"They're happy tears, Elena," Isabella assured her lovingly. "You cannot imagine how happy this makes me."

Her voice was as soft and melodic as Elena remembered. Letting go of one of Elena's hands, Isabella cupped her cheek, her expression filled with so much adoration that it made Elena want to cry all over again. It hurt like mad to miss her.

"Your father has told me of your journey. I am sorry to hear of Cataline's loss, but for now I have room only for gratitude that you are alive and safe, that you are here with me and your father, and that you have grown to become more than we could have possibly wished for."

Elena blushed under the weight of Isabella's words, feeling the heat rush to her cheeks almost instantly. Her mother laughed softly. The mention of her father reminded Elena that they were not alone in the hall. She looked around her and found Dionysus and Eiry sitting on the throne and stool behind them, carrying on a quiet conversation. Elena and Isabella had somehow found their way to the floor.

Elena's gaze caught Eiry's, and for a moment she felt something twist in the pit of her stomach. Her world was in this room. Everything she lived for was right here, except for Cataline. Elena found herself wishing she would never leave, which in its most basic sense was a death wish. The only way she could have this moment forever was if she died. Soon, they would leave Tartarus, and she would never see her parents again; she would surface to fend for her life. Suddenly, the idea of death was not so paralyzing. If this was to be her afterlife, she would welcome it with open arms.

As Elena considered these things, Isabella continued speaking. Behind them, Eiry watched Elena with a curious expression on his face. Elena decided it was best to ignore it, hoping he hadn't picked up on the dark nature of her thoughts.

"I am happy to hear you had a chance to meet Aosaginohi again," Isabella said to Elena. "She was very fond of you when you were a child, as was Master Nurarihyon. How was your time with the Hyakki Yakō? Your father tells me a Kirin appeared."

"They were amazing," Elena said excitedly, and quickly recited for her mother everything that happened from the time she and Eiry arrived at the *yōkai* compound to the moment they descended into Yomi.

All the while, Isabella listened in rapt attention. She grew pensive at times, and Elena made a point of making her narrative more animated during those moments. Without meaning to do so, Elena fell into an almost euphoric rhythm as the story continued through its natural progression, detailing for her mother the creatures that stood out the most in her memory.

"The Kirin protected me. You should have seen him in his true form, Mama. He was dazzling," Elena emphasized the last word, the image of the majestic creature bright and brilliantly vivid in her mind. After a brief pause, Elena continued, an easy smile brightening her expression. "The four guardians of Kyoto were very intimidating. One of them was particularly handsome—I think it was the White Tiger—and the Azure Dragon had scales that shimmered like opals. Aosaginohi was beautiful and very kind, and her words gave me strength. Then there was Tarōbō the bird-demon—did you know he and Bryce have a thing?"

Elena distinctly heard Eiry snicker, and the sound pushed away any remaining shadows from her thoughts. Recounting for her mother everything that had happened made Elena realize just how extraordinary her journey had been. Yes, it had been terrifying, filled with loss and pain, but it had also been filled with joy, not just from being reunited with her father and her mother but from all the people she had met along the way—all those who had put themselves in harms way to help her; Eiry, the Hyakki Yakō, the guardians, the Kirin, even the red-headed banshee Eiry had for a sister. Elena wasn't alone and once she managed to get Cataline back, all of it would have been worth it.

As Elena continued her story through to the events that had brought her to their current reunion, Dionysus and Eiry joined them on the floor; Eiry interjecting where he could, her father doing the same when his part in the journey finally came around—albeit in a much less subdued manner than Eiry. The conversation developed easily, and it continued as such when they were led to Isabella's apartments to enjoy a mid-day meal.

After concluding the story of her journey—which included Cataline's death, Elena's desire to save her and Hades's offer to return her soul in exchange for the Helm—Elena's parents wanted to hear about her life and so she told them as much as she could, starting from her first day in school when she moved to New Orleans with Cataline through her time in college and law school. Elena told them about her first kiss, her first heartbreak, and anecdotes of Cataline's colorful love life. She told them about her first year working at Ms. Callas's firm, and her first impression of Eiry. She even told them about Cataline's impression of him, the three of them laughing merrily at Eiry's mortified expression.

Before Elena knew it, the sun was past its zenith. They had retired from the courtyard, where they had enjoyed their mid-day meal, to a breezy anteroom in Isabella's apartments. Lounging on reclining couches, they enjoyed the luxury of their surroundings. Elena sat with her mother, who re-braided her hair as she had so frequently done when Elena was a child. Dionysus, whom Isabella only referred to as Evius, sat on his own couch, strumming a guitar that he conjured out of thin air. Eiry sat quietly beside them, listening and watching, smiling every time he met Elena's gaze. It was a perfect afternoon, and Elena quickly forgot that this was an afterlife and that her mother was technically dead. She forgot what came before and did not concern herself with what would come after; such was the power of Elysium.

Sometime later, when the walls around them burned with the light of the setting sun, Isabella excused herself and asked Elena to join her. Eiry and Dionysus continued their conversation, while Isabella led Elena to her room, which was separated from the anteroom by the same pier and door partitions Elena had seen before. The partitions formed a wall of wooden doors that could be pushed back and tucked away, joining the anteroom to her mother's private chambers, creating a larger space. There were three sets of doors in total, held up by two square-shaped stone piers in between.

Isabella's bedroom was ample in size with white washed walls bordered in a pale blue and white wave-like spiral motif, outlined in burnt sienna. Frescoes depicting marine life adorned parts of the wall. Dolphins danced across a white background above the threshold to her mother's bathroom. The room was large enough to fit a bed, a small seating area with two Greek chairs and a reclining couch, three chests, a table, and several large terracotta vases. Fresh-picked white hydrangeas sat in small glass vases on various surfaces of the room.

Like the anteroom before it, the outside wall of the bedroom faced a portico that bordered the villa, and contained the same pier and door partitions that could be tucked away to open the room to the elements. Currently, the wall was open to a view of the sea. It was breathtaking, and Elena moved quietly toward the seating area facing the sea.

"Do you miss modern technology at all?" Elena asked her mother, as she looked out at the endless horizon. Even though she knew it was an illusion—that beyond the shores lay a less peaceful reality— Elena could not help but be moved by the serenity of the view.

Elena's question stemmed from the fact that she had not seen a single modern convenience during her visit. While this appeared to be a tranquil existence, it was hard to imagine a modern soul spending an eternity in the ancient past.

"No, not really," Isabella said from behind Elena.

As Elena had taken her seat, Isabella had moved to a wooden chest that sat against the back wall. Elena could hear her rummaging through its contents as she spoke.

"The only thing I missed at first was you and your father."

Elena heard the chest close and several seconds later Isabella appeared at Elena's side, holding a package folded in indigo-dyed fabric. Isabella took a seat beside Elena, placed the package on her lap, and continued the conversation.

"There aren't that many modern souls here. The gods no longer proliferate the way they once did, which has diminished the number of descendants greatly, and there are certain rules regarding who can enter that have diminished that number further—you must have a certain amount of divine blood, for instance, which keeps out distant descendants, or, if your divinity is too thin, you must have given birth to a demigod. That is how *I* was allowed in."

Isabella offered Elena a smile that was at odds with the hint of melancholy Elena could pick up in her words. The melancholy, however, quickly disappeared. Like Elena, Isabella was not the kind of woman to wear her emotions on her sleeve.

"To answer your question more directly, we can request whatever amenities we like," Isabella continued, "but most of those things are useless in this world. Everyone lives like royalty, with servants performing the tasks of modern amenities. The library has computers for those souls who know how to use them and want to keep track of the human world, or you can request one for your personal rooms if you prefer. I have no idea how they work in this world, but they do. We travel by way of mirrors between Houses. If we don't want to use mirrors, there are palanquins we can use. The servants can also create any kind of clothing you might desire or obtain any modern item.

"Most souls, though, conform to the ancient way of life. For me, that was simple. Being alone was the hardest part in the beginning. Your father was ill for a very long time while the Moirai restored his divinity, and I waited without really knowing if they would allow him to visit. You see, the gods usually have very little to do with Elysium past sorting. I was told your father would most likely never come to me—his mother and grandmother rest here, and even they seldom had the pleasure of his company.

"Those were very dark times for me, even in this paradise. It can be difficult for souls to accept death. There are those who never cross over, who remain chained to the world below, but I was here, alone, victim of a curse that had very little to do with me. There was a lot of anger, and for a long time I was so blinded by it that I failed to realize I was not the only one. This House is home to a great majority of Heirs, and each one has suffered loss because of that necklace—Harmonia herself lives within these walls. Once I was able to accept my fate, things became easier here. I am not alone, Elena. Our entire line, our history, is within these walls.

"At some point after that, your father was given leave to come here. He visits often, always with some anecdote he's heard of you. This is the first time Thanatos has accompanied him."

Isabella said the last words with a knowing smile, and Elena felt the heat rise to her cheeks almost immediately. She had turned away from the view of the sea halfway through her mother's story, and she found refuge in it now, as she processed everything her mother was saying.

This life was so different from the idea Elena had of an afterlife. Pain, suffering, anger; those were not things she associated with life after death for people who had lived a good and honorable life. It was supposed to be peaceful. Those who had passed were supposed to be sitting on a cloud somewhere in the endless sky, looking down happily on the people they loved—at least that's how popular culture would have it. Elena had never truly believed in the Christian ideal of heaven, but she definitely believed in some kind of peaceful afterlife, where the dead watched over the living and they were free from their mortal coil. Wasn't that the common thread?

Reality, however, was just a little different. Yes, there was an afterlife, but it was far from perfect. Neutral souls, neither exceptionally good nor exceptionally bad in life, had their memories and identities erased and lived a mundane afterlife in the Asphodel Fields, waiting for the time when they would be reborn. Only the virtuous, the initiates, and the descendants of the gods were free of being reborn; they kept their identities, but that could be a burden for those who had died before their time or with any consuming regret.

If that reality was not difficult enough to accept, there was the inescapable fact that in this beautiful place lived every soul Eiry had been unable to save. Here lived Harmonia, daughter of Ares and Aphrodite, grandmother to Dionysus and great-grandmother to Elena. Here too lived Harmonia's daughter, Semele, Dionysus's mortal mother and Elena's grandmother. Queen Jocasta and King Oedipus, their daughters Antigone and Ismene. Did their twin sons, Eteocles and Polynices, who murdered each other in battle, also live within these walls? What of Jocasta's brother, Creon, also of the House, who passed the law refusing burial to Polynices and sentenced his niece, Antigone, to death for breaking that law? So much pain and loss in a House plagued by the curse of a Pythian Prophecy.

Within these walls smoldered the embers of a ruined bloodline, and a living testament to Eiry's own cursed inheritance. Only now did

Elena consider how difficult this journey to Elysium must have been for Eiry, and she was thankful they had not run into any other Heirs.

"I'm afraid to fail," Elena confessed to her mother, sighing heavily. That was the truth of the matter. Elena wasn't afraid to die, she was afraid to fail and cause Eiry any more pain. She was afraid of failing before she could save Cataline. "Generations of loss for what, Mama? I'm supposed to fulfill a prophecy that I don't even know how to begin to fulfill. Hell, I don't even know if I'm the prophesied Heir. All of you struggled under that ideal and you lost your lives for it, for what?"

Isabella leaned forward and cupped Elena's cheek with her hand. There were so many conflicting emotions in her eyes—sorrow, regret, unerring love, and fierce pride. It made Elena want to cry.

"I did not struggle for the prophecy, Elena," Isabella said as she affectionately smoothed the hair away from Elena's eyes. "I fought for you. I fought for your father. I did not fail, and you are living proof of that. You must find your own role within the prophecy, your own truth. Once you find that, you must follow that path wherever it leads you. Do not let them define your purpose, Elena. No matter what gods you meet and the wisdom they share, only the Moirai truly know where our paths lead. Even Thanatos is bound by that truth—he is as much a servant to the Fates as we are. He has no control over the time and manner of death. He is an element forged by their hands. No one, not even your father, can change their will."

Isabella's words brought back the images of Elena's time with the Moirai, and she trembled at the thought of them—indelible creatures, beautiful and horrifying.

"When they sang for me," Elena whispered to her mother, as if saying it out loud would provoke their ire, "they told me about the past. They sang about Papa and his love for you, about your journeys. Atropos sang of my future, and I have no idea what her words meant. It was like a giant riddle, except for the first two lines. '*Where one was sought, two will surface; only one will endure alive.*' That message was pretty clear. Another Heir will surface, Mama, and one of us won't survive. One of us is meant to die. That is the will of the Moirai."

It was the first time Elena had acknowledged that to herself, let alone out loud. Everyone present that day had heard Atropos's song, and yet no one had broached the subject at all. Now, in the midst of her own desperation, Elena laid her worries bare for her mother, selfishly hoping to somehow alleviate her worst fears. Isabella accepted the burden with the same quiet and infinitely calm composure she had displayed throughout their visit.

"They always sing in riddles, Elena, because destiny can take various forms. Even the Moirai answer to another—their mother Ananke guides their words and actions. Prophecies work in the same way. They did not say one would die—they said only one would endure alive. In the world of the divine there are many different ways to endure, and being alive is a matter of degrees." Isabella paused, and then gently took Elena's hands in hers, her expression unexpectedly defiant. "Try not to give stock to any of it. Your fate is your fate. What is important is how you live in spite of it. In a world of gods and monsters, life can feel like an exercise in futility, but it isn't, Elena. Find your own truth and the rest of it be damned. That is the only thing that kept me alive for so long—it is the only thing that gave me the strength to see my destiny through. Whether you end up in Elysium soon or many years from now does not matter. It is out of your control. Focus only on what you *can* control. Hades has made you an offer. Have you decided to accept it?"

Elena was surprised to hear the fortitude in her mother's voice, a keen edge to her usually warm disposition. It gave Aosaginohi's words about her mother much more weight, and made that image of Isabella more substantial. This had been the woman who fought against Alexander for years and survived; this was the kind of woman Elena needed to become.

"Yes, I've decided to accept his offer. I couldn't live with myself knowing I could have saved her, especially since she died on my account."

"Are you willing to accept the consequences of that choice?" Isabella asked, the softness in her voice gone. "Will you be satisfied even if you die in the attempt? Will you be satisfied if you fail in saving her? Make sure this is part of your truth, Elena. I loved Cataline very much, and it pains me to know that she has passed because of her involvement with our family, but this attempt will only be worth the fight if it is part of the role you have chosen to play. Any step you take from now on must be considered in that same fashion—in preparation for fulfilling your truth, the role you choose for yourself within the prophecy."

"Like *bushidō*," Elena whispered, a half smile touching her lips when she considered the similarities. *Bushidō* was the code of the samurai, and its most basic principle was to die a good death with one's honor intact—everything a samurai did in his life was in preparation for that death. Thinking of her future journey in those terms would make Elena's choices much easier.

"Precisely," Isabella said, and then the two of them fell silent.

They looked out onto the horizon, each considering the weight of her own thoughts. Isabella smoothed her fingers along the indigo-colored fabric covering the package on her lap, drawing Elena's attention to it.

"This is for you," Isabella said in an affected tone, placing the package in Elena's hand. "We come to this life only with those items on our person at the time our death rites are performed. Wrapped within this fabric is my white funeral *kimono*. I would like you to have it. The only other thing I carried with me were six coins, which are part of Charon's collection now. Thanatos picked them himself for the journey."

"Do you remember dying?" Elena asked, her voice breaking. The idea that Eiry led her mother to Elysium was comforting.

"No, it is the one thing even those in Elysium forget. I remember everything up until that moment. Then the next thing I recall is Izanami's Garden."

"You traveled through Yomi?"

"Of course," Isabella replied. "I died in Japan. When I first opened my eyes as a shade, Thanatos was carrying me in his arms through her garden. It was there that he told me what had happened—even though I knew the moment I opened my eyes that I was dead. It was a comfort not to be alone, even if my companion was Death itself. Thanatos has always been implacable and understandably reticent, but I came to count him as a friend. I believe you have as well."

Elena blushed, and didn't know exactly how to answer that.

"More than a friend, then?" Isabella pressed, leaning closer so she could look at Elena's face.

"I don't know, Mama. These aren't exactly simple circumstances."

"Neither were mine, and I fell head over heels for Evius."

"Yes, but that was long before you knew the truth about him being a god. Eiry and I, we're a little different."

"I don't think so," Isabella said with a knowing smile, the kind of smiles mothers always give their daughters. "Why are you fighting, Elena?"

The question took Elena by surprise. Even though she knew the answer immediately, she couldn't voice it. Other than to get Cataline back, Elena was fighting because Eiry needed her to survive. He dreaded being faced with her fear when his element finally took her, and Elena wanted to save him the pain of another failure as long as she could, long after saving Cataline.

Isabella did not press Elena for an answer. Instead, she offered Elena another piece of the puzzle. "Thanatos has watched you all of your life because Evius and I could not. It seems even an element as immutable and unfeeling as Death can change. He has always been cold and indiscriminate, detached because his element required it. Death does not have the luxury of kindness, and yet his role as your guardian has changed him. That one variable could alter the game entirely."

"It is time for us to leave," said a voice from the threshold, interrupting their conversation.

Dionysus stood by the door, watching them with interest, a smile curving the edges of his lips. He stepped across the room and came to stand behind Isabella, offering her his hand. Once she took it, he swept her up into his arms and kissed her deeply, the gesture so intimate Elena had to look away.

"You should listen to your mother," Dionysus advised Elena once he and Isabella broke their kiss, never quite unwrapping from each other's arms. "She's the shrewdest woman I have ever met."

"I'M SORRY you had to come with me," Elena said to Eiry as they walked the gray marble steps up to the Domos Aidaou. They had arrived here in the same manner they had arrived in Elysium, and Elena walked carefully now, trying to shake the side effects of their method of travel. They were lessened since their first attempt, but not by much.

"There's nothing to be sorry about," Eiry said to her softly, reaching for her hand as they climbed the last step.

A massive wooden door stood before them. Behind them, the steep path all souls had to climb to reach the top of the citadel. It wound its way to the summit, a pale serpent against the black jagged earth beneath. The House of Hades was a dreadful structure made of cold gray stone. It stood at the crest of a massive crag of black stone. Their juxtaposition was jarring. A colorless city rose out of the dark earth, its buildings skirting the crag like specters clinging to the last vestiges of life. An enormous wall surrounded the circumference of the city with a single gate allowing entry.

"Yes, there is," Elena insisted, bracing herself against Eiry as a harsh wind ravaged the summit. It felt spiteful, and Elena had the distinct impression it was a response to their presence at the door. "You could have run into one of the Heirs. I didn't realize most of them lived within those walls. Mama told me it was your first visit to the House, and I can completely understand why. So, I just wanted to say thank you, and I'm sorry if it caused you any kind of stress."

Eiry watched her, his expression smoothing. As always, he considered his words, and his answer gave away very little. The only time Eiry seemed to open up were those few instances when they were completely alone, which now that Elena thought about it—considering everything she had observed about gods—was probably a smart move.

"Thank you for the concern, but there was no stress involved. I promise," he added the last part when he saw Elena give him a skeptical look. "I was happy to see you all together again." With that, he ended the conversation.

The sound of creaking startled Elena, and she turned around to find the massive doors being pulled open. They swung inward, an attendant peering out at them from the shadows.

"Welcome, Lord Thanatos. The Master is expecting you," said the attendant in a serpentine voice, each word prolonged and flowing into the next with hardly a break between them, ending in a slithering hiss.

His appearance was as unsettling as his voice. Like the servants in Eira, he was lithe and tall, with an angular face and pale skin; his demeanor, however, was markedly more menacing. He had long black hair, blood-red eyes, a cruel smile set against a waxen face, and short black claws for nails. He wore dark gray robes, and a set of large bronze keys hung from his belt.

"Thank you, Aiakos," Eiry said to the attendant, and pulled Elena through the threshold. "Please accept our apologies for being a little late. Our prior engagement went on longer than expected."

This was the first Elena heard of this. When she looked over at Eiry, he offered her a sly grin and shrugged, resuming a sober expression the moment Aiakos turned to look at him.

"The Master only has a few moments to spare," Aiakos explained curtly. "We will be resuming the sorting shortly."

"This should only take a few minutes," Eiry assured the man.

Without a word, Aiakos turned and took his place in front of them. It was presumed that they should follow, as he began to lead the way. They were in a corridor lined by massive stone columns to their left, the space beyond the columns shrouded in shadow, and a wall of stone to their right. The ceiling rose in vaulted arches, gray mists clinging to the highest points, trapped by the merciless stone. Torches of white fire hung at intervals on the wall to their right, providing sufficient light for them to see the way. Halfway through the corridor, Aiakos turned left and led them through a break in the columns.

The moment they stepped into the space beyond the columns, the shadows parted. Two great fires of white flame rose out of massive stone basins at the end of the hall, flanking a monumental throne sitting above a foundation of four tall steps made of gray marble. This was the scene from Elena's dreams, of the tourmaline throne with the butterfly crest. The white flames illuminated the clear smoky stone, causing the needle-like crystals of black tourmaline beneath its surface to shine like burnished metal.

The butterfly crest lay hidden behind Hades's hulking form. As in her dreams, and the single time Elena had been in his company, he appeared the epitome of a Greek god. Strong and powerfully built, he made Elena think of a Spartan. His body was cloaked in dark robes, but even through them she could see the cut of the man beneath. He was a terrible figure, but not on account of a ghastly appearance. On the contrary, he was ruggedly handsome with jet-black hair and beard—both cropped short—and midnight blue eyes. It was the cruelty in his eyes that gave the proper warning.

"How kind of you to finally grace us with your presence," Hades said in a biting tone. He reached beside him to pet a small tawny screech owl that sat on a wooden perch beside his throne. He produced a mouse out of the shadows and fed it to his pet.

"Our timing could not be helped," Eiry replied, offering neither explanation nor apology.

Elena stood stark still next to Eiry, trying not to stare at the god.

"Yes, of course it couldn't. I trust you had a pleasant time frolicking through Elysium. Must be nice not to be bogged down by responsibility." Hades pet his owl one last time and then descended from his throne.

The surface of the butterfly crest gleamed with the light of the fires once it was no longer obscured. Blue flashes of light danced across the surface of the colorless stones of its wings and within the dark blue-gray stones that formed the eyelets.

"If you prefer, we can trade places," Eiry said flatly, his attention on the lines of the swallowtail butterfly carved into the throne. "I'll sort souls and you can worry about killing them and guiding them here. Of course, you'll also have to find time to protect the Heir, and you can't use Rhadamanthys, Minos and Aiakos to assist you."

"Unyielding as ever," Hades replied with a shrug, his eyes moving to Elena. He offered her a smile and extended his hand. "Don't mind him, dear. He's just upset that he said no to the job before, and now he's stuck with the difficult tasks."

"I was born as Death, Lord Hades, a job I cannot shirk. I would have been stuck with both jobs, and you would have been unemployed."

Eiry's tone was openly hostile, something Elena had only seen before directed at Alexander.

When Elena hesitated to take Hades's hand, he slid closer to her and hooked his arm with hers. He then led her away from the throne and through a peristyle corridor opposite the one they had arrived through.

"Keep up, Lord Thanatos," Hades called out to Eiry in his booming voice, and led Elena through a labyrinth of domed halls and vaulted corridors that opened in and out of each other by the seemingly infinite use of colonnades and sculpted arches.

Finally, they arrived at a garden courtyard where several pomegranate trees grew. Water features that grew out of the natural stone acted as irrigation canals, creating a quadrilateral design that joined in the center of the courtyard in a fountain made of alabaster, in the form of a large basin supported on the backs of twelve hounds.

Hades led Elena through the garden to a wall of carved stone columns and sculpted arches that held up the roof of the courtyard and formed its farthest border; smooth walls of stone belonging to adjacent rooms flanked the left and right sides of the courtyard.

Standing beneath one of the arches, on the ledge beside the colossal god, Elena looked out to see the vast region of Hades. They faced the direction of the Southern Gate, which was clearly visible from this height, as were the islands in between. As Elena had seen from the tunnel on her journey into Eira, grey mists rolled across the landscape souring the view. She looked down to find they stood on a precipice. Startled, she shrunk back against a column.

"What the hell are you doing, Hades?" Eiry growled, as he stalked across the garden toward them.

"What's the problem, Thanatos? I wanted to show her the view. Plus, this is where I prefer to make my deals. The Styx waters this garden," Hades said in an irritated tone, stepping away from Elena and off of the ledge. He extended his hand, helping her do the same. "This is my wife's garden," he explained to her in a whisper, before turning his attention back to Eiry. "If all you are going to do during this visit is whine, Thanatos, then perhaps you should leave."

Eiry reached Elena's side before she took another step. He eased her away from Hades, his upper lip curling over his teeth in a snarl when

Hades attempted to step closer. Elena was at a loss for the hostility between them.

"It's fine, Eiry. I'm fine," she whispered to him, trying to prevent an altercation. "It is a stunning view, Lord Hades," she said to placate the other god. All Elena wanted was to make this deal and get out of here. She repeated the last thought in her mind, hoping Eiry would pick up on it the way he always seemed to do.

Eiry watched her quietly. After several minutes, he grew still, his expression finally smoothing to its usual indifference. "Enough sight-seeing," he said sharply to Hades, and led Elena around the god to the fountain in the center of the courtyard. "Let's just get this over with."

Hades followed close behind. "You have the patience of a five-year-old," he said to Eiry as he came to stand beside them, a satisfied expression on his face.

"And you are as trustworthy as a fox," Eiry snapped back.

"Enough, boys," commanded a female voice from the entrance to the courtyard, her tone leaving zero room for argument. Then in a silken voice, she added, "You are distressing our guest," obviously referring to Elena.

The three of them looked up at the same time. Eiry smiled, while Hades grimaced.

The voice belonged to a woman with long auburn hair, warm golden skin, and eyes the color of sapphires. Voluptuous and statuesque, she was as exotic looking as Hades was imposing. Her features were a mixture of Middle Eastern and Mediterranean, the highlight of which were her Byzantine eyes. She was dressed in modern clothing; tight black leather pants, a blush-colored blouse and white blazer. She had the same taste as Elena in heels, the sight of the red soles making Elena smile in spite of everything. It was incredibly foolish of her to find comfort in something so trivial, but the sight of them was exhilarating under the circumstances.

"Persephone," Eiry said with a grin, the first to respond to her appearance. "Has spring come and gone already?"

The goddess of spring smiled, her azure gaze resting on Elena, who shifted nervously beside Eiry. This was the wife of Hades, famed queen of the underworld, whom Hades had kidnapped and tricked into eating pomegranate seeds, thereby forcing her to remain in the Land of the Dead. To appease her mother, Zeus, her father, gave Persephone leave to return to Olympus for two-thirds of the year. It was through this myth the ancient Greeks explained the changing of the seasons, winter being the third of the year Persephone spent in the underworld.

It had been spring when Elena journeyed into the underworld, which meant that Persephone was currently living with the Olympian gods. The thought made Elena tense instantly, and she couldn't help but wonder to which side this goddess owed her allegiance.

"My love, you're home early," Hades said in an overly affectionate tone, dripping with sarcasm.

Persephone stared at her husband, a sardonic smile spreading across her lips. "It's only temporary, *dear husband*," she said tersely, her attention quickly returning to Eiry and Elena. "Olympus is up at arms about a certain Heir, and you could imagine my curiosity when I learned it was Evius's child. I couldn't help but come to see for myself. She is my grandchild, after all."

"Oh, for the love of the Moirai," growled Hades impatiently.

"Is there a problem, *husband*?" Persephone snapped back.

"No, only that he's not your son," said Hades. "If you would pay half as much attention to our daughters as you do Dionysus, these halls would be much more pleasant... and quiet."

The last comment seemed odd to Elena, since the halls she had seen were as silent as a tomb.

"Forgive me, *husband*," Persephone replied, mockingly. "I was not aware my purpose in life was to make your life more pleasant and as for our daughters, they receive enough attention from you. I am as much Evius's mother as Semele was, and I raised him. It is only natural for me to be curious. I've heard about the child constantly for twenty years. It is nice to finally put a face to the name, and what a lovely face it is." With a warm smile and the ire bleeding out of her voice, Persephone turned her sapphire gaze from her husband to Elena.

Elena stood silent, inexplicably timid in the goddess' presence and a little lost in the conversation. The Moirai had sung of her father's birth, and so she was able to follow Persephone's connection to him. Persephone had been given his heart after Zeus's treachery, and had ingested it in order to give birth to him. She had also raised him in the underworld, protecting him from his father's wrath. And so it seemed Persephone was adept at keeping secrets from Olympus; even though she was the daughter of Zeus, apparently abhorred her abducting husband, and resided twice as along among the sky gods than she did in Tartarus. In a sense, she was both sky god and chthonic. Elena wondered if such deities were neutral among the gods. She made a mental note to ask Eiry about it later. For his part, he did not seem suspicious of her at all.

Persephone moved toward them, skirting around the alabaster basin, her fingers brushing the surface of the water before she came to stand behind Eiry. "Hello," she said cheerfully to Elena, settling her hand on Eiry's shoulder. "Lovely indeed," she whispered into Eiry's ear, ignoring her husband for the moment, who happened to be seething silently opposite them. "I overheard you were about to broker a deal. I'd be happy to be a witness."

"We don't need another witness," Hades growled impatiently.

"I beg to differ, *dear husband*," Persephone replied with a smile.

"Um, hello," Elena said shyly, responding to Persephone's earlier salutation.

Eiry wore a grin from ear-to-ear. "I agree with Persephone. Another witness would be a good thing, unless you have something to hide, Hades."

"Oh, be quiet, Thanatos," Hades barked, rolling his eyes. "Lets us be done with this then," he said and reached for Elena's hand.

Elena tensed, looking at Eiry for guidance. He quietly whispered that she would be okay, and allowed Hades to guide her closer to the basin. When Elena peered down at the glassy surface of the water, she saw within it the same blooms of russet-colored nebulae she had seen before. They drifted through the water, never disturbing the surface. Hades interlaced his fingers with hers—her hand appearing minuscule next to his—and dipped their joined hands beneath the surface of the water. Elena jumped, startled at how cold the water was. She bit down a cry when she felt one of the jellyfish-like creatures brush against her hand.

"I, Hades Eubuleus, do swear by the Styx to release the soul of one Cataline Ferrá, daughter of Joan and Katherine Ferrá, in exchange for the Aidos Kyneê, to be returned to me by the hand of Elena of the House of Thebes, daughter of Evius. This contract is contingent on the Aidos Kyneê remaining in her possession once obtained, never to be delivered into the hands of or used by another immortal or supernatural creature, until the time the item is delivered to me. Do you accept my offer, Elena of the House of Thebes?"

"Do not answer yet," Persephone intervened, slowly making her way toward her husband. "Your end of the bargain is a little abstract, don't you think? You agree to release the soul, but in what condition?"

"The girl is an attorney who works for Chione, Persephone. I am certain she knows how to strike a bargain," Hades said curtly, visibly cross with her. "Stop interfering."

Persephone dismissed her husband's command with a wave of her hand, her sapphire gaze fixing on Elena once again. "Perhaps you would like to set your own terms, love?"

Elena was thankful for the goddess' interference. With everything that had happened in the past two weeks, the last thing Elena was doing was thinking like a lawyer. Persephone was correct in that Hades's proposition agreed to free Cataline's soul, but it didn't explain in what condition. For all Elena knew, there were a million ways a soul might be released; he might release her into an animal or another person's body, for instance. The thought was terrifying, and Elena wanted to make sure her intent was clear.

In the interim of their exchange, Eiry had come to stand at Elena's side. He took her free hand in his and squeezed it lightly, giving her the quiet support she needed to go forward with this madness. Elena couldn't be afraid anymore. She had resolved to save Cataline at any cost. From now on, she needed to be as formidable and unyielding as her mother.

"Where is Cataline's body?" Elena asked Hades.

Hades narrowed his eyes, his hand clenching into a fist. If he had been seething before, now he was smoldering. The anger made a tempest of his dark blue eyes. "Here," he said between clenched teeth, his gaze intent on Elena. "She is in a pretty glass coffin, like Snow White waiting for a kiss from Prince Charming. I am in possession of her soul. She has not been sorted yet. If you'd like, I can tell you the temperature at which I'm preserving the body."

"That won't be necessary, Lord Hades," Elena said defiantly. "I am satisfied. However, just to be clear, I do have my own terms. Cataline's soul must be returned to her body, and she must be restored to life in the condition that she was immediately preceding any involvement with the supernatural or divine. I want her exactly the way she was on the morning we visited the Kamo Vault. I would like you to place her in Thanatos's care once that is complete. If you agree to my terms, Lord Hades, then we have ourselves a deal."

To Elena's surprise, Hades smiled.

"It is agreed," he said, and let go of Elena's hand.

CHAPTER FIFTEEN

"WERE YOU PLANNING ON LEAVING without saying good-bye?" Sleep asked his twin as he appeared by the door to the room. "Never mind you never said hello." There was no judgment or accusation in his voice, merely an observation. Only his twin knew the truth that lay dormant in his heart.

Death, who was preparing for his departure, stilled, his instantly crimson gaze rising to meet his twin's. "I was told you were asleep, and it is not my policy to wake you." Once said, he returned his attention to his preparations.

"No one else in this existence but you, Thanatos, knows the exact moment of my waking, and yet here I find you. I must confess I am hurt." Sleep stepped into the room and quietly made his way toward his twin. They were identical except for a reversal in the color of their hair and eyes.

Death did not pause at his brother's approach. He met his gaze briefly, and then continued gathering his things. A carryall lay open on the bed, a majority of its contents removed; the things Death gathered he placed gently inside. "I doubt you're hurt, Hypnos. You're just cranky from oversleeping."

Sleep eased himself down on the bed beside the carryall, a ghost of a smile touching his lips. He watched quietly as items disappeared into the bowels of the bag—a carved wooden box, a dagger made of starlight metal, and two vials. One of the vials contained a thick red substance, the other an amber liquid that glowed faintly in the dark. Hypnos tensed at the sight of the last vial. "You're a horrible twin," he said sharply, a scowl replacing his smile.

"That can't be helped," Death replied as he moved away from the bed once again, collecting several more items to place in the bag. He was fully aware of his brother's watchful gaze, and it would be a lie to say it did not affect him. Even without looking at him, Death could feel Sleep's pain through their connection. It was something he had become accustomed to, the disappointment in his twin's heart.

Having Death for a twin was a terrible cruelty of Fate. Twins survived through their connection alone; nothing else sustained them. They were either made of the same element or ones so complimentary that they could not survive without the other. Hypnos and Thanatos, however, were a necessary exception to the rule. To have a twin in Death was to share an unyielding and apathetic soul. Sleep survived Death's apathy only by virtue of his nature; endless intervals of sleep regenerated a bond that in any other instance would have been destroyed entirely, dispersing their elements into the Void—a god's true death.

"I'm sorry. I didn't mean it," Sleep offered in a broken whisper, reaching to catch Death's wrist as he withdrew his hand from the bag. They stared at each other quietly, the regret mirrored in each other's gazes.

Death lowered his crimson gaze to their hands; Death's arm was clothed in its perpetual suit and Sleep's in the soft folds of a silk crepe robe. They were so different—one as indulgent and capricious as the other was unyielding and severe—and yet at the basest level they were exactly alike. "You meant it, and I deserved it," Death remarked in a dejected tone. He slipped his hand away from his twin's and looked up at him through a fringe of glacial blue lashes. "I should be the one perpetually apologizing to you."

Sleep didn't contradict him. Instead, he leaned forward and pressed his lips to his twin's brow, his knuckles brushing the line of Death's jaw. "I want to meet her," Sleep whispered, as his fingers slipped to the nape of his twin's neck.

"I can't let you, Hypnos. Not now," Death replied, stilling when he felt Sleep's mouth brush against his. His lips tasted of poppies, and for a moment Death felt their slight effect—his limbs relaxed, his mind became clouded and his body yielded when Sleep pulled him close.

"I would never harm her," Sleep assured his twin, holding Death tightly in his arms. A desperate need to protect what was his—to protect his twin—coursed through Sleep's body, and he buried his face in Death's throat. "She's healing something in you. I just want to meet the one responsible."

"Hypnos..." Death murmured his twin's name, his hands smoothing the crimson strands of Sleep's hair, which spilled down the length of Sleep's back like blood-spun silk. "Give me time," he begged softly. "After this madness is over and we've settled her properly on the surface, I'll come wake you."

AN HOUR LATER, Eiry made his way out of the shadows and onto a semicircular veranda overlooking the city. Elena stood alone by the railing, looking out into the darkness.

"How was your time with Evius?" he asked her quietly, taking his place beside her. The cascade of water murmured rhythmically beneath them, as the Lethe continued its path through the center of the city and the valley below.

They were on the northern most courtyard, where Elena had experienced her first real view of Eira only days before. It felt like an eternity ago that Eiry had led her quietly through the stepping-stones onto the circular courtyard that floated over the water, the large waterfall looming in the twilight behind them. It was in this courtyard that the city split into its distinct paths along the sides of the river, the semicircular veranda of open archways connecting both halves along the southern side of the courtyard.

"It was good," Elena whispered, her eyes on the outline of the staggered buildings before them. Somehow, Elena had begun to feel comfortable here, safe. The thought of leaving Tartarus left her feeling empty, and nervous. It was odd to consider she had gained so much in the underworld, and she felt a desperate reluctance to leave it behind. Again, she considered that death might not be such a terrible thing after all; everything she cherished was here. As long as she restored Cataline's life, she would have no regrets.

"What are you thinking about, Ele? You keep getting this look on your face, and I can't read into it at all." Eiry fixed his icy gaze on hers, concern lining his features.

Elena couldn't help but smile. She was grateful he couldn't read her, grateful that her thoughts couldn't disappoint him. His entire purpose was to protect her, to save her life, and here she was considering how sweet death could be. It left Elena feeling conflicted, and with a heavy heart.

"It's nothing important," Elena said softly.

"Are we there yet?" asked a disembodied voice from the darkness behind them, followed by a stifled laugh. With a hollow pop, Gavin appeared behind Elena.

"You're an idiot," growled another voice from the shadows, the sound of metal bangles and the click of heels signaling Bryce's approach.

"We haven't even left yet, so shut up," Eiry said sharply, pinching the upper part of his nose with his fingers.

Galen appeared beside Elena without a sound, the brush of his long hair against her upper arm making her jump.

Quiet time was officially over, Elena thought to herself and groaned, which earned her a stern look from three sets of eyes. Eiry smiled. They had been waiting for Bryce and the twins to arrive and, of course, they were late. Elena inched away from Galen, and suddenly found herself face to face with a grinning Gavin.

"How did you get Eiry to carry your bag?" Gavin asked in a playful tone, his grin widening even further. It was unnerving. He bowed his head slightly and tucked a honey-colored curl behind his ear, his golden-green gaze intent on Elena. "I've been trying for ages and he always says no."

Galen and Bryce snickered. Eiry rolled his eyes.

"Just ignore them," Eiry reminded Elena, and then took hold of her hand, "they're idiots." He had given her the same advice at least three times before they left his rooms.

"Why does she even need a bag?" Galen asked in an irritated tone.

"Because she's human, you half-wit," Eiry replied, "and the journey will last more than a day. Not to mention we have no idea what will happen on the way there, and you know better than I do that she can't just appear before the Fae Court in torn jeans and a t-shirt. She is the Heir, and they will know instantly. She must act the part."

Eiry had explained all of this to Elena earlier, but that didn't make it any easier to hear again. Elena's anxiety kicked in just as quickly as it had the first time she heard the explanation. Immediately, she began to twist the opal ring she was wearing—an item that had turned into a personal talisman. It had belonged to her mother, and every time Elena touched it now she saw her mother's face, clear as day, and remembered her resolve.

"I was just asking," Galen snapped, "you don't have to be a dick about it."

As Eiry and Galen bickered about the bag, Gavin snuck up beside Elena and took her other hand. "I call dibs on Elena," he declared excitedly, offering her a wink when she met his gaze.

Instantly, the bickering stopped. Eiry and Galen turned around, unamused, their contrasting blue gazes alight as they stared at Gavin. Bryce stood behind them with a wry smile.

"Why not?" Gavin asked with a pout.

"Because you'll get distracted by glittery things and sell her out for a bauble," Bryce remarked before the boys could respond. She stepped between Eiry and Galen, the chime of her bangles filling the silence—the bell that tolled for the dead. "Not that I would care." Bryce's scarlet smile deepened, and Elena unconsciously took a step back.

"Bryce, knock it off," Eiry and Galen warned simultaneously.

Bryce shrugged.

Gavin tightened his grip on Elena's hand before reluctantly letting go. He looked almost crushed. "That only happened once," he protested, "and I didn't sell you out. For the millionth time, I'm sorry I got distracted and we lost."

"What are you talking about?" Elena asked, completely confused.

"Something that happened during the Games almost five-hundred years ago," Galen said with a resigned sigh. "Bryce is still sore about it. Just ignore her. That's what we all do."

"Fuck you, Galen," Bryce hissed.

"Been there. Done that. Didn't enjoy it," Galen said flatly. He waited for her reply, and when it didn't come he returned his attention to Elena with a satisfied smile. "Any more questions?" he asked with an arched brow, taking a step closer to her.

Elena stood her ground. "What do you mean by Games?" she asked him, avoiding Bryce's stare.

"Every five-hundred years the pantheons come together under a temporary cease-fire and participate in various tournaments. Alliances are re-established and confirmed in public. Since outright battles have become less frequent in modern times, because of the lack of available space where humans won't be affected, the Games have become even more popular—the highlight of a cold war."

Galen spoke softly, inching closer to Elena with each word. Eiry watched him attentively. He stopped less than a foot away from her, a sardonic smile touching his features as he pushed a curtain of black hair behind his shoulder.

"During the last Games, Hades lost the Helm you're about to retrieve, and Bryce lost at her particular event." Behind him, Bryce hissed. Galen ignored her entirely. "Speaking of games," he said, turning his attention to Eiry, "what exactly is the game plan for this little mission?"

Elena studied Galen closely before lifting her gaze to Eiry. Like Eiry, Galen was gorgeous—Elena hadn't seen an ugly god yet—but in a very cold and forbidding way, a beautiful demon. As if he had read her thoughts, the corners of Galen's mouth curled into a ghost of a smile. Eiry crossed the space between them, gave Galen a look, and took his place at Elena's side before going into the game plan.

"The mists only appear at twilight so either way you look at it Helios will have the advantage since we'll have to travel during the day." Eiry spoke quietly, his eyes trained on the city below. Weir lights flickered in and out of existence like twinkling stars, and the city itself was eerily silent. "It'll take most of the day to reach the dolmen. God travel will take twice as long as in a car, since we'll have to travel in shorter spurts for Elena to keep up, but it will be safer because it'll be harder for Helios to track our movements.

"Of course, we'll have to avoid moving in a straight line. I've timed it so that by the time we make it to the surface it'll be early morning. Surprise will be our only advantage. Helios will have no way of anticipating where we will appear, and he won't be able to locate us until we reach a stop and he can pinpoint our presence. To avoid detection, we can't stay between stops for long. Helios will most likely guess our destination, but that won't do him any good since the area has been declared neutral by the Fae." After a brief pause, Eiry turned his attention to Bryce. "Did you make the calls?"

"Yes," Bryce replied, her tone short. She was studying her manicure.

A silent exchange passed between the four gods. Elena could feel it, like the rustle of leaves in the background. Then one by one their forms faded into the shadows until Eiry and Elena were the only ones left standing on the veranda.

"Don't let go," Eiry whispered to Elena as he took her hand, and then the city of Eira vanished before her eyes.

When the world righted itself, Elena found herself on a familiar outcrop of rock. Galen was passing through a mirror, Gavin standing close behind. Bryce was filing one of her nails. Behind them, a cacophony of souls rose sharply in the background, the sound dissonant at first as the myriad of languages transformed and melded together into a universal sound. Elena had just enough time to look behind her to see the shape of Charon's boat emerging from the darkness before Eiry pulled her through the mirror.

Elena stepped out on the other side of the mirror and instantly shielded her eyes. There was light all around her, brilliant at first and then gradually settling into a warm radiance that clung to the cool air like mist. Slowly, she opened her eyes, squinting until the light no longer bothered her.

She was standing on a carpet of downy moss and grass, its emerald hue brighter and richer than any she had ever seen before. In front of her stood Bryce and the twins, Eiry a silent sentinel at her side. The light came from above them. Elena looked up to find they stood under a bower of branches that spread as far as the eye could see, the limbs and leaves emitting a shimmering glow. The branches belonged to a giant tree whose golden trunk was at least two hundred feet wide, its height seemingly infinite, and its multitude of leaves an iridescent silver-green. The tree stood at the center of an island barely larger than the tree itself. Several massive stones dotted the remaining landscape, each one lying on its side and carved with circle and spiral motifs. The water surrounding the island was a sparkling blue, and anything beyond a foot off its shores was shrouded in a thick white mist that fell across the horizon like a curtain of clouds, so dense Elena could not see past it.

"Welcome," came a steady voice from behind them.

Elena and the four gods turned at once to face the mirror they had just stepped through.

Lying beside the mirror was a large megalithic stone carved with a repeating triskele motif of three interlocked spirals. Sitting on the stone was an impossibly tall, lean man with long silver-blue hair, the front strands of which were held back from his elegant face by a platinum coronet, exposing his pointed ears. He wore an ankle-length tunic held in place at his waist with the use of a woven belt fashioned out of gold and silver thread. The cloth was made of a fine ash-blue fabric with silver needlework at the neckline, wrists and hem in a distinctly Celtic design. A cobalt-blue cloak was draped loosely across his chest, fastened at the shoulder with a metal brooch in the shape of a torc.

The man leapt lithely off of his perch and landed soundlessly on the grass. As he moved, his cloak shifted color from blue to green, and then to silver, settling back to its original shade once he reached his guests.

"You are expected, Daughter of the House of Thebes," said the man, fixing his silver gaze on Elena. His smile was almost predatory. "I am Manannán mac Lir of the Tuatha Dé Danann, keeper of the gateway between our worlds."

Elena didn't have a chance to answer. Impatient as always, Bryce chimed in.

"Enough showboating, Manannán," she said in an unfriendly tone. "We just need to get across the sea."

"And if you wish for my assistance, Keres, then you know the price," Manannán replied sharply, never looking away from Elena. His smile never faltered. "Of course, you can try to sail through the mists on your own. If we're lucky, you'll get lost, and then our lives would be all the more pleasurable in your absence."

Baited, Bryce stepped forward with an unearthly growl. Eiry raised his hand and with a single word stopped her advance. From the corner of her eyes Elena could see the goddess' nails had extended into claws—like they had on the night of their flight to Yomi, when Bryce wounded Eos at the entrance to the underworld. For his part, Manannán ignored Bryce entirely. His attention remained on Elena, and his gaze kept her rooted to the ground. Every instinct she had screamed for her to look away, but for some reason she was incapable of doing so.

Once Bryce was in check, Eiry slowly lowered his arm and took Elena's hand in his. His touch, cold as ice, broke through the spell of Manannán's gaze and Elena took a step back.

"I have brought your tribute," Eiry said to Manannán in an icy tone, returning the conversation to its proper course.

Manannán's smile deepened. "You seem very protective of this one," he remarked, amused. "Áine will be most pleased." He regarded Elena a moment longer and then gently bowed his head, turning his silver gaze on Eiry. "I do hope your tribute is more gracious than your sister's manners."

"Up yours, Fairie," Bryce hissed, and instantly the twins were at her side.

"Don't mind her," Gavin said to Manannán with a smile, hooking his arm with Bryce's on her right side.

"It's that time of the month again," added Galen unceremoniously, hooking his arm with Bryce's on her left side.

They both pulled the redheaded goddess back, Galen clamping his free hand over her mouth while she struggled in their arms. Manannán dismissed them with a wave of his hand, as if he were used to Bryce's antics.

"Where are we?" Elena wondered out loud.

Everyone turned to look at her. Manannán seemed pleased.

"Emhain Abhlach," he answered, as if that name should say it all, but it didn't mean a thing to Elena.

Elena knew enough about Celtic mythology to know that the Tuatha Dé Danann were the people of the goddess Danu, a divine race of ancient Ireland who were ultimately driven underground by the Milesians, the human ancestors of the modern Irish. Thereafter, they dwelled underground in the Sídhe, the hills or earthen mounds common in the Irish landscape. Throughout history, the Sídhe became synonymous with faerie mounds and the Thuatha Dé with the modern concept of fairies or elves. They were said to be greatly skilled in art, poetry and magic, and were reputed for being fickle creatures that greatly disliked humans. That was the extent of Elena's knowledge.

"Forgive my ignorance, but what is Emhain Abhlach?" Elena asked Manannán in a quiet tone.

"It's like the Irish concept of Elysium," Galen interjected before Manannán could say a word. He had left Bryce in the care of his twin and was making his back toward them.

The silver-eyed god looked up at Galen and gave an exasperated sigh. "The response is not so simple," he said in a reproachful tone. "This is why we do not waste our time with your little war. Far be it for the Greeks to concern themselves with the details of any other race but their own."

Galen was about to counter, no doubt in his usual acerbic way, when Gavin appeared beside him and whispered for him to leave it alone. Eiry followed with a look that ended the matter, and Gavin led his reluctant twin back to Bryce's side. With a shrug Eiry dropped to the ground, produced Elena's carryall and began to search through it. Manannán returned his attention to Elena with a satisfied grin.

"Emhain Abhlach is one of two realms that make up the Otherworld in Irish mythology," Manannán explained to Elena in a gentle voice, his silver gaze brightening. "It is my home—the Plain of Apples. It has been known by many other names, such as the Blessed Isles of the Western Sea, the ever-popular Tír na nÓg—"The Land of the Young"—and the fabled Avalon. It is a realm inhabited by gods—some, not all—and reached only by a select few mortals. Here, sickness does not exist, nor does the cold hand of death reach us." With the last phrase Manannán gave Eiry a poignant glance, then continued.

"It is a realm of eternal youth and beauty, where all the pleasures of life are celebrated. Food, drink and music are in infinite supply. One day here could be hundreds of years in the human world. All the same is true in the underground kingdoms of the Sídhe mounds, the second realm of the Otherworld. While it is true that some souls may journey to Emhain Abhlach, it must be by my invitation. In our mythos humans are reincarnated, and we have no true land of the dead. This is why it is incorrect to compare Emhain Abhlach to the Greek Elysium."

The silver-eyed god finished his explanation and regarded Elena quietly. He was obviously waiting for some kind of response, but Elena didn't even know where to begin. Her mind had gotten stuck at the mention of Avalon, a place that had fed her imagination since she was a child. The thought that she was standing on the mythical island of Arthurian legend brought a nervous giggle. Self-consciously, Elena looked up at the giant tree and wondered if it was an apple tree. From what she could see, it wasn't bearing any fruit.

"Are there other islands?" Elena asked shyly, trying to appease Manannán's continued stare. She found it improbable that Avalon was simply one island with a giant tree and a single inhabitant. Shouldn't there be a temple or a palace? Where were his chosen gods and humans?

Manannán mac Lir smiled. "Yes, there are other islands," he replied, his gaze lifting momentarily to Eiry, who had removed a small wooden box and a folded package from Elena's carryall. "They are hidden within the mists. Only I can navigate between them. You must pass the mists in order to reach the path that leads to the surface."

"Are we underground?" From her surroundings, Elena could not tell. They could be on an island in the center of a lake, for all she knew, which would make sense if the stories about Avalon were true.

Eiry interrupted their conversation with an apologetic smile. "Yes, this realm is underground, as are all the kingdoms of the Sídhe mounds. The Tuatha Dé Danann's retreat into the underworld made them chthonic, while their origins are in the heavens. This is why they are neutral in our war. It is why we must offer tribute in exchange for safe passage."

Manannán watched Eiry as he spoke, nodding once to show his agreement. Eiry then took the wooden box and folded package in his hands and slowly approached Manannán. With a short bow of his head, he presented the items to the silver-eyed god, once again returning their conversation to the task at hand.

"The folded package contains a cloak woven by Atropos herself as tribute on behalf of the entire pantheon," Eiry said in his serious voice. "The wooden box is a personal tribute from Dionysus, a bottle of his rarest vintage in exchange for his daughter's safe passage."

The moment Eiry presented the gifts everyone fell silent. It was obvious from their reaction that these were not your average tribute. The cloak alone was a gift of the highest honor, woven by the hand of a Fate. The addition of the second gift, however, bore the greatest weight, and was a brilliant tactical move. To a Tuatha Dé Danann, for whom the pleasures of food, drink and music were unparalleled, a rare vintage prepared by the god of wine himself was a singular and precious gift; a personal request that could not be easily ignored.

And yet Manannán mac Lir appeared most taken aback by the revelation of Elena's parentage. He studied her with much more scrutiny than before, his interest irrevocably peaked.

"A child of Dionysus," Manannán remarked, more to himself than to any of them in particular. His face smoothed, and a faint light entered his gaze.

When his eyes met Elena's she quickly looked away. He accepted the proffered tributes without a word, his long fingers smoothing over the lid of the wooden box. He opened it carefully and looked down at the contents, a smile touching his lips.

"Áine will be most pleased indeed," he whispered, slowly lowering the lid, satisfied. Then he lifted his gaze to Eiry and gave a curt nod. "We accept your tribute."

To reach their destination, they would pass through the mists to a distant shore where they would follow a pathway that would lead out of Emhain Abhlach, like the stairs from Izanami's garden, to the surface above. Manannán mac Lir led Elena and her four companions to a wooden ship moored to the shore on the opposite side of the giant tree. It was shaped out of a single piece of dark gray wood, its profile graceful, long and narrow. It had a shallow hull with edges carved in knot-work, and a symmetrical bow and stern, the former of which was shaped into the head of a sea serpent. As they stepped onto the ship, Elena counted thirteen benches built into the hull. Manannán mac Lir took his place on the bow of the ship, Bryce and the twins sat in the center, Eiry and Elena toward the stern.

Elena looked around the ship for oars but found none, nor could she find any evidence of fittings to be used for rowing. Just as she wondered how the ship would be steered, it began to move of its own accord. Manannán stood at the bow, silent and still, his silver gaze fixed on the horizon. As the ship pulled away from shore, Eiry, leaning closer so he could whisper, explained to Elena that Manannán steered the ship by thought alone. He was the Irish god of the sea. It was through his wisdom that the Tuatha Dé Danann divided into kingdoms beneath the mounds—with one High King to rule over them—and through him found protection from humans within the mists.

As Eiry spoke, Elena watched in quiet amazement as the ship moved steadily through the mists, the clouds parting only enough to give the necessary clearance. At times, the sharp edges of rocks would peek through the dense fog only to be swallowed up seconds later; rocks large enough to capsize the ship if they were to accidentally come too close. The margin of error was small, and Elena quickly understood Manannán's earlier warning—none but he could sail through the mists unscathed.

Eiry had finished his story and everything around them grew silent, but for the soft sound of the parting waves as the ship continued along its hidden path. Every so often, Elena heard the faint sound of music or laughter floating across the water from a distance, but never saw their source through the mists. Never once did she see the shores of another island or the soaring outline of Manannán's palatial home. The only visible thing had been the image of the colossal tree behind them, which had risen high above the mists at first, shimmering like burnished metal, but soon faded into obscurity.

Just as their journey began to feel long, the ship lurched as it came ashore, the sound of groaning wood and shifting sand shattering the silence. One by one, Bryce and the twins leapt out of the boat and onto the shore. Eiry helped Elena up and across the ship to the bow, where he cleared the side in a graceful vault and then reached back up to assist Elena.

Before she could move, a hand settled on her left shoulder and Elena turned to find herself staring into Manannán's silver gaze.

"Safe journey, Child of Dionysus," he said gently, bowing his head so he could place a kiss on her brow.

Elena froze. She wasn't sure what she should say or do, so she simply closed her eyes and bowed her head, accepting the god's warm gesture. "Thank you," she replied in a shaky voice, "for safe passage and your blessing." Suddenly, she felt the weight of his fingers in her hair. Startled, Elena opened her eyes. Manannán was smiling, his silver eyes locked with hers.

"Remember one thing when you visit my wife," he said to her softly, commanding her attention as he eased her back into Eiry's reach. "We cannot easily ignore ingenuity and resolve. Do not waver."

He stepped away, and Eiry quickly pulled Elena off of the ship.

The moment her feet touched shore the light around them vanished, replaced by total darkness. Elena heard the twins and Bryce speaking in whispers a few feet away, and felt Eiry's cold form against her own, but she couldn't physically see any of them. The ship, the shore and Manannán mac Lir were also lost to the darkness. As she heard the sound of a ship pull away from shore, a light flickered into life and Eiry's luminous butterfly took shape above them.

"We're in the mouth of a tunnel that leads up to the surface," Eiry explained to Elena, his voice echoing against the walls. "It's too dark and cramped to use god travel accurately, so I'm going to carry you, okay?"

"Okay," Elena replied, and gasped when Eiry suddenly pulled her up into his arms.

The twins made kissing noises in the background, and Eiry warned them with a growl that rumbled faintly against Elena's side. As always, the position in his arms was surprisingly comfortable. She rested her temple against his chest, and soon they were moving; the rush of air and the change in Eiry's breathing the only evidence of movement.

Elena let her mind drift. She thought of Manannán's advice, and the overall nature of their encounter. Would all the Fae be like him? Was he singular among them or a good representation of the personalities that Elena would have to face? She couldn't help but wonder what kind of woman Manannán would take for his wife, and whether that boded well for them. Elena's thoughts then drifted backward, unconsciously following the continuum of her journey until this point.

She thought of her deal with Hades and instantly saw herself in that courtyard again. She saw the god's wife, Persephone, who had raised Elena's father and protected him. Elena then thought of her mother and the brief hours she had spent in her company, the sound of her father playing the guitar, and their quiet laughter. Elena thought of the journey into Elysium, and the hours preceding it, culminating in Eiry's confession in the form of a kiss. The thought made Elena's stomach twist into knots, and she realized, disappointingly, that he had never brought it up again, but perhaps it was for the best. Elena didn't want to be used against him as punishment, and a fight for her life wasn't exactly a conducive environment for romance; her mother and father had been an exception to the rule.

Elena didn't realize she had drifted into sleep until Eiry quietly roused her, whispering her name gently into her ear. When she came to, she could hear the twins giggling and Bryce's now-familiar growl. Their surroundings were as pitch black as before. Eiry gently placed Elena back on her feet. The luminous butterfly appeared above them and fluttered a few feet ahead, illuminating an earthen wall. Apparently, they had hit a dead end. Eiry took the few steps necessary to reach the wall. Beneath the glow of the luminous butterfly, he looked very much the ethereal creature he was. He pressed his hand against the wall, spoke words in the ancient tongue Elena could not understand, and seconds later the wall rippled like water and then vanished entirely.

The butterfly floated through the threshold, illuminating the way. Immediately ahead of them was a stone slab with a large basin stone sitting on top of it. They were standing at the end of a small recessed chamber lined in stone. The luminous butterfly reached the end of the recess and suddenly floated upward, illuminating a large circular central chamber. Its walls were lined in standing stones, and as Elena crept around the basin stone and ducked into the central chamber, she realized she recognized where she was.

The central chamber had a high, corbelled ceiling made of jutting stone slabs, and three recessed chambers—each with a stone basin. The recesses were positioned like the head and arms of a cross, and Elena stood facing the central recess. She turned around and, as she suspected, found herself facing a passage of standing stones that led from the outside into the central chamber. She could only see a foot or two into the passage, but she was sure of what it was. They were standing in the heart of a passage tomb, and Elena had been here before.

"Are we inside Newgrange?" Elena asked, turning to look at each one of her companions.

Eiry had just stepped out of the recess they had entered through. "Keep it down just a little, Ele," he whispered softly. "We don't want to wake the neighbors."

Elena hadn't realized she had spoken loudly. "What neighbors?" she whispered, peeking at the recess they had stepped through. The back wall had materialized once again.

"We're in Newgrange," Eiry confirmed in a low voice, and moved behind Elena. "The recess we came through leads to the under-world, but the other two lead to Sídhe kingdoms. We don't want to rouse the other Fae. They're used to more traffic than the other Sídhe because of the daily tours, but it's just better to move on quickly. It's not good to be in here outside of tour hours."

The luminous butterfly was already hovering by the entrance passageway with Bryce and the twins standing beneath it, waiting. With a nod from Eiry, they began to file out one by one.

Elena had been to Newgrange only once before, on a trip to Ireland she had taken with Cataline. Of all the places they had visited—

and they had taken a car through most of the country—Newgrange had
been the one place that had stuck with Elena the most.

One of the most popular tourist sites in Ireland, Newgrange was
a five thousand year old megalithic burial mound that stretched two
hundred and fifty feet across and forty feet high. Its facade was covered
part way with a wall of white quartz stone, and a passage of standing
stones led sixty feet into the central chamber. On the Winter Solstice, the
rising sun would align with the passage and illuminate the inside of the
tomb.

When Elena had visited the tomb, around ten tourists were taken
into the tomb at one time and the Solstice was simulated with the use of
electric lights. Even as a simulation, the experience had been transfor-
mational. The actual event could only be witnessed through a lottery.

"If I'm alive next Winter Solstice, I want to see the sunrise from
inside," she whispered to Eiry as he led her through the shadowy passageway that led out of the tomb.

"It's a deal," he replied with a smile, and helped her clear the
capstone over the entrance, gently guiding her out into the chill morning
air.

A light morning rain welcomed them, as the dawn broke un-
evenly through an overcast sky. Thunder rumbled steadily in the distance. Elena pulled her coat tighter around her and rubbed her arms. It
was cold and wet, and the pregnant clouds hung heavily across the
horizon.

Elena and Eiry stood at the entrance to the tomb, quietly taking
in their surroundings. A circle of standing stones, laid horizontally on
their sides, skirted the perimeter of the mound, unbroken across the
entryway, which was built further back into the facade of white quartz,
creating a space of several feet between the standing stones and the
entrance to the tomb. A pair of wooden stairs were built on each side of
the entrance to allow access to the tomb over the circle of standing
stones.

At the top of the stairs, looking down at them, stood two familiar
faces, Tarōbō the bird-demon and the Kirin.

"Elena-san," Tarōbō whispered in greeting. He offered her a
roguish smile as he bowed, his hawklike gaze peering out at her from
behind a fringe of white hair that danced across his face in the breeze.
Unlike most of his Japanese comrades, he wore his hair short, styled in
such a way that it fell to his chin in textured layers, weightless and soft as
feathers. He was dressed in a light gray *kimono* with a white sash holding
his *katana* in place. His *haori* was steel blue with pied feathers painted

along the bottom hem and edges of his sleeves. In this setting, he looked like a flesh and blood version of an anime character.

Behind him, the Kirin, dressed in his robes of Tyrian purple, bowed his head, a serene expression on his noble features.

Elena was ecstatic to see them. She rushed toward them, bowing deeply to both. "What on earth are you two doing here?" she asked excitedly. "How is Aosaginohi-san? Nurarihyon-sama? The guardians? The Hyakki Yakō?" It felt like an eternity had passed since Elena had been under their protection, and she had not expected to see any of them again. The fact that Tarōbō and the Kirin were standing in front of her now was almost too good to be true.

Undoubtedly surprised by the unexpected onslaught of questions, Tarōbō blinked and then quickly recovered with a deep laugh, the sound warm and heartening in the cold and dreary morning. He had met Elena halfway down the wooden stairs. "Shinigami-sama asked for my help escorting you once again," he said softly, "and I could not rightfully decline his request. We have all been worried about you since you left, Elena-san." Suddenly, Tarōbō pulled her into a hug, the gesture completely unexpected.

His embrace was warm, and Elena felt as if she were enveloped in a soft blanket of feathers. When she looked up into the bird-demon's eyes, they were a deep violet hue.

"Plus," Tarōbō whispered into Elena's ear, "Akai-sama is here, and I have always wanted to visit Ireland."

Behind them, Bryce hissed. Elena and Tarōbō laughed softly. Then he released her, as Eiry made his way up the stairs.

"When I arrived," Tarōbō concluded his explanation with a smile, "Kirin-sama was already here."

The twins, who stood the farthest away from everyone, suddenly burst into fervent whispers. From the little bit of it Elena could hear, they were discussing the meaning of the Kirin's appearance. They didn't seem to care that everyone could hear them. Gavin was using the opportunity to convince Galen that he had been correct in surmising that Elena was special, while Galen kept telling him it could simply be that this particular Kirin had gone mad—perhaps a sprite had bitten him and he had contracted some kind of disease. The two were arguing their points quite adamantly.

"Will you two shut up?" Eiry hissed at them, succeeding in only getting the twins to lower the volume a little.

Bryce was conspicuously silent. Elena had a feeling it had to do with Tarōbō's presence. The red-haired goddess kept her golden gaze fixed intensely on the bird-demon.

"Thank you for coming," Eiry said to their new companions, offering them a short bow. "I am surprised but humbled to see Kirin-sama here."

The Kirin smiled gracefully, the gesture brightening his dignified features. "My purpose in this world has once again deemed I not remain neutral," he explained in his infinitely gentle voice. Even in Ireland the wind stirred when he spoke, his silver mane dancing softly in the breeze.

"Then I thank you, Kirin-sama," Elena replied, "from the bottom of my heart."

"Please call me Kiyoshi," said the Kirin. "It is my proper name."

The second he said it everyone went quiet, including the twins. From the looks she was getting, and the content expression on the Kirin's face, Elena could only presume this was a rare honor. She bowed deeply, stumbling through her words.

"Thank you, Kiyoshi-sama."

The Kirin crossed the small space between them. When he stood on the step above hers, he bowed his head, touching his forehead to hers. Instantly, Elena felt a cold, tingling sensation in the nape of her neck. When Elena looked up into his face, his topaz-colored eyes sparkled. On the center of his brow, the shape of a five-petaled flower appeared, its surface prismatic and shimmering like ice.

"You are most welcome, Elena-san," said the Kirin, and pulled away.

An awkward silence followed. A strong wind blew and Elena stepped closer to Eiry, who was much taller and could block the wind, which was cold and biting.

"Have there been any signs of Helios or the other sky gods while you waited?" Eiry asked Tarōbō and the Kirin, who shook their heads in response.

"It has been relatively quiet, Shinigami-sama," said Tarōbō. "As you instructed, we remained within the circle of stones," he added, referring to the circle of standing stones skirting the mound, "and so our presence should not have been felt. I can only assume Helios will notice once we step out of the circle."

"That's correct," Eiry confirmed. "Everything within the circle is part of the Fae world, and our presence blends perfectly with that of the Fae. It is a different matter entirely once we step outside of it. Is everyone clear on the path we'll be taking?" Eiry waited until everyone nodded, and then continued. "If anything happens and you fall behind, go straight to the dolmen—it is neutral ground and Helios will be unable to make a move. If he tracks us before hand, engage him any way you can. The moment you see Elena and I leave, disengage and wait at the dolmen. I assume you will be traveling with Elena and I, Kirin-sama?"

"*Hai*," the Kirin replied, taking his place at Elena's side and reaching for her hand.

Eiry did the same. "Are you ready?" he asked Elena with a warm smile.

Elena nodded. The twins, Tarōbō and Bryce stepped closer. The world around them grew silent, and then one by one they disappeared.

THE SEVEN OF THEM alighted on a hill, a field with grazing sheep spread out before them. Elena felt the ground beneath her feet before she saw anything, the world taking a moment longer to shape itself before her eyes. She didn't feel nauseous as she had before, and the dizziness was very faint. Her head ached like mad, though, and unlike before a dull pain began to throb in her stomach. Elena realized it was hunger. She hadn't eaten a proper meal since her last evening in Japan.

In just a few seconds, Elena was doubled over in pain.

"Ele, are you okay? Can you hear me? Ele?" Eiry said from her right.

"What the hell is wrong with her now?" came Bryce's venomous voice.

"Bryce," Tarōbō chided from a few feet away.

Elena could hear the sound of his sandals against the dry grass beneath their feet, as he approached.

"What happened to '*Akai-sama*', bird-demon?" Bryce growled, the jingle of her metal bangles echoing in the wind.

Elena was on her knees now, and the pain was intense; a terrible burning pain at the top of her ribcage. The Kirin was kneeling beside her.

"I'm fine. I need food," Elena said between gritted teeth. "I'm famished."

"Bryce, go keep watch with the twins and stop being a pain in the ass," Eiry barked, the sound of the twins' laughter rising in the background. "Tarōbō, did you bring what I requested?"

"*Hai*," replied the bird-demon, kneeling down in front of Elena. "Take a seat, Elena-san," he whispered gently.

Elena did as Tarōbō asked, and the Kirin remained kneeling beside her.

"Aosaginohi made these for you," Tarōbō whispered with a smile, producing a small package from within his *haori*. It was wrapped in bamboo leaves. He set it gingerly on the ground and unwrapped it, revealing three large *onigiri*—rice balls. "One is filled with pickled plum, another with salted salmon, and the last is plain rice."

At the sight of them, Elena almost cried. With a quick nod, she reached for the first rice ball. In less than a minute, she had devoured them all.

Eiry, who had been keeping watch along with his siblings, returned and took a seat at Elena's side. "I don't feel Helios at all, and we've been here long enough for him to notice." He spoke quietly, as he produced the carryall and began to search through it. He pulled out a vial of what appeared to be ambrosia and offered it to Elena. "Just a sip."

"Did you know about this?" Elena asked him, bringing the vial to her lips. The ambrosia was warm, and it instantly made Elena feel refreshed and strong. Every nerve and muscle in her body tingled from the effect. "That I would feel this hungry, I mean?" She looked ahead of her, past Tarōbō's shoulder to the open field. The twins and Bryce were standing about fifty yards away, waiting for something to happen.

Eiry nodded. "I had an inkling, which is why I had Bryce ask Tarōbō to bring some food. I couldn't prepare for it in Tartarus because any food from there other than ambrosia would bind you to the realm. I had a feeling not eating for a few days would have its effects once we hit the surface."

Elena was about to complain, but he brought his fingers to her lips before she could say anything.

"Don't be upset with me," Eiry said gently. "I would have told you if I would have been sure, but I didn't want to worry you needlessly. It's not often that a human is allowed into Tartarus, so it's a learn-as-we-go process. Now we know for next time."

"Not that I'm complaining or anything," Elena replied, bowing her head to Tarōbō, who was looking at her curiously from his perch directly in front of her, "but next time we're doing this in Ireland, let's fit in an Irish breakfast with some Guinness. If I might die in the process, I may as well eat something I don't get to have often and I really enjoy."

"What is a Guinness?" Tarōbō asked.

Eiry and Elena burst out laughing.

Bryce appeared behind the bird-demon and smacked the back of his head. "It's a famous Irish beer, you idiot."

"It's a love tap," Tarōbō assured Eiry, Elena and the Kirin, before catching Bryce's wrist and pulling her down onto the ground beside him.

She was hissing and clawing as usual, but she stilled the moment the bird-demon caught her chin with his hand.

"You need to be more patient, *Akai-sama*," he said to her sharply, his hawklike gaze narrowing as he stared at her, his fingers slipping into her blood-red curls, "or I will no longer play along."

"Look at that," Galen remarked to Gavin as they returned to the group, "Bryce has a master. How the hell did you manage it, Tarōbō?"

"She's just like any other wild animal, Galen-sama," Tarōbō replied with a wicked smile, releasing Bryce. "A little love, a little handling... and bribery."

Tarōbō and the twins laughed. Bryce hissed and pushed herself off the ground, clawing Tarōbō's arm as she did so. She was about to say something venomous, when the Kirin cleared his throat.

The Kirin's eyes were on Tarōbō's arm. He held his sleeve up to his face, covering his mouth and nose until the bird-demon's wound healed entirely. "I think perhaps it is best if we continue on, yes?" he said gently, his ever-vigilant gaze on Bryce.

Surprisingly, the redheaded goddess lowered her gaze and didn't say another word. In a matter of seconds, everyone took their places at the top of the hill, and one by one they disappeared.

THEIR JOURNEY was tiring at first, mainly on account of the frequent stops. For the first few hours, they could only travel small distances, but as the morning wore on Elena began to feel accustomed to their method of travel. They would continue with the same distance until Elena felt no side effects, and then the process would begin all over again. By midday, they were moving much faster, and the increase in distances became easier to handle.

A positive note about their journey was the scenery. Every stop was different, but always somewhere remote where the chances were less that a human would see them. They often found themselves within shaded groves or thick woods, along the shores of a babbling brook or one of the many lakes the country was famous for. Once, they appeared in the middle of a field of blooming heather at the foot of a large craggy hill with the ruins of a medieval castle at its summit. Another they alighted within the ruin itself, but this time it was the ruin of ancient monastery deep within the mountains.

The ever-changing scenery held the majesty Ireland was famous for, each scene intensified by the presence of Elena's party. Wherever they landed, the nature around them reacted to the presence of foreign gods—colors became saturated, winds stirred, wildlife surfaced, and at times mist began to settle over the ground. When the mists moved in an otherworldly fashion, Elena's party was careful not to make contact with them; the last thing they needed was to get lost in the mists and end up in the wrong Sídhe.

Not once did they feel the presence of a sky god.

The sun was below the horizon by the time they reached their destination. The soft glow of twilight bathed their surroundings in pallid shades of amber, amethyst and rose. The sky was still heavy with clouds, and the fractured light broke through in splintered patches. They stood in a hollow between hills, the landscape made up almost entirely of gray limestone. Soil was sparse and there was hardly any vegetation except for moss and lichen, which grew between the crisscrossing cracks and crevices that formed the massive limestone pavements.

A dolmen stood ahead of them, dignified and ancient, protected by the rolling hills of the barren landscape surrounding it. It was a single-chambered portal tomb consisting of a large, thin, tabular capstone supported by two upright stones at least six feet in height, which were flanked by two smaller standing stones used as walls and an end stone creating a chamber within a low cairn. It was a spectacular sight, and the seven of them began their silent approach, careful as they moved across the uneven terrain.

As they neared the dolmen, a heavy mist began to crest over the hills, rolling sluggishly across the landscape. It pooled at the edges of the hollow, slowly making its way toward the dolmen. No one seemed concerned, and Eiry quietly explained to Elena that there was no need to avoid it.

They continued silently across the limestone pavement. The wind stirred and carried with it the sound of a footfall, faint but distinct. Before Elena knew what was happening, the gods around her fell into formation. Eiry and the Kirin flanked Elena at each side while the others formed a line of defense ahead of them. A familiar laughter filled the heavy silence.

Alexander stepped out from behind the dolmen, cutting an imposing figure against the darkening sky. His long hair, restrained in its usual braid, glowed like burnished gold in the light of the setting sun. His bright eyes, which burned like blue flames through the rising darkness, came to rest on Elena.

"You're late," he said with a menacing smile, as the mists converged on the ground beneath them.

CHAPTER SIXTEEN

FEAR; it trickled down Elena's spine, cold as venom. Alexander's gaze held her rooted to the ground. The deepening of his smile sent another shock of it across her body, making her tense. The adrenaline didn't kick in.

Would the rest of her life feel like this?

"Yes," Alexander said in response, as if he had picked the thought right out of Elena's mind.

Eiry turned his head a fraction of an inch, glancing at Elena from the corner of his eye.

Alexander's smile deepened even further.

"Get out of my head," Elena hissed at the sky god, the first hints of anger burning in the pit of her stomach.

The Kirin took a step closer to Elena, and she felt the soft press of his consciousness brush hers. Instantly, she felt calm.

Alexander stifled a laugh. "Don't worry, Ele. I'm not in your head. I just happen to know you that well. You're just like Isabella, and I spent many years becoming intimately familiar with your mother's expressions. I can still see them clearly in my mind."

"Shut up!" Elena stared defiantly at the sky god, the mention of her mother fueling her anger. Unconsciously, she began to twist the opal ring she wore around her finger.

The gesture did not go unnoticed. Alexander's gaze dropped to Elena's hand, and the glee that touched his features was almost euphoric. For a moment, he appeared lost in his thoughts. He traced his fingers along the length of his braid, his gaze fixed on the opal ring. Then, suddenly, he was gone.

He reappeared an inch away from Tarōbō, who instantly reached for his *katana*. Elena heard the first delicate notes of the sword's song as Tarōbō edged its guard away from the scabbard with his thumb, and took a defensive stance.

Eiry quickly appeared at Tarōbō's side. "No blood can be shed here," he said softly to his friend, his gaze intent on Alexander.

"An eternity of servitude would be well worth his death," Tarōbō crowed. Elena wondered what he meant.

"Not when he would not die, my friend," Eiry reminded the bird-demon.

"He's the worst kind of weed," Gavin added, off-handedly.

Tarōbō did not back down until Bryce called out his name, the closest to a plea the goddess would utter.

Alexander appeared immensely amused. "Perhaps if you didn't concern yourself with everyone's safety, Thanatos," he remarked, "you might actually be able to save an Heir for once."

"That's quite witty, Helios. Did you come up with that all on your own?" Eiry replied.

Elena was growing impatient. They were at the entrance to the Sídhe they had been searching for, and here they were wasting time with Alexander.

"What exactly do you want, Alexander?" Elena asked. "We're in the middle of something."

"I just wanted to see you, Ele, just in case you never come back," he replied in a dejected tone, a hint of melancholy bleeding into his handsome features. He seemed to lose himself in his thoughts again, but quickly recovered. "I'll miss you, you see," he cooed to her softly, an edge to his voice. "It would be a pity if you never came out of the mists. I was hoping we'd get to play for a few more years. I'm craving a little excitement in my life."

"Then why don't you join them, sky god?" asked an unfamiliar voice. "There is much excitement in the Daoine Sídhe."

The voice echoed from within the dolmen. Seconds later, a tall, graceful figure emerged from within. Golden-skinned and dark featured, he wore close-fitting trousers the color of charcoal, a short jacket in a lighter shade and armor made of what looked like scales shaped out of lapis lazuli. The scales were linked together with platinum and belted at the waist with the same metal inlaid with moonstone.

From behind him a second soldier emerged wearing the same armor, this one fair-skinned and with copper-spun hair.

"The High Queen extends her welcome to you as well, Helios of Olympus," said the dark-haired soldier to Alexander.

"Please give my thanks to your Queen, but I must decline," Alexander replied curtly.

The dark-haired soldier smiled; a savage, and yet graceful, smile. "If that is the case then you should leave," he said plainly.

Alexander glared at the soldier. His brilliant blue gaze burned through the darkness as he considered his position. Finally, he shrugged. With a dismissive wave to the soldier, he turned his attention to Elena.

"I'll be waiting for your return with bated breath," he said to her gently, bowed dramatically, and then vanished into the night.

A heavy silence fell over them, as Elena's party turned their attention to the two soldiers.

"Queen Áine bids you and your party welcome, Elena of the House of Thebes." The dark-haired soldier addressed Elena in a formal tone. His eyes locked with hers and Elena's breath caught. His gaze was the color of a ripe plum—a dark reddish-purple—and held an unwavering sense of power, instantly rooting her to the ground. "If you will follow me, please," he added with a haughty expression, and turned to face the dolmen. Without another word, he stepped inside.

They were obviously expected to follow. The twins stepped through first, followed by Bryce, then Eiry, the Kirin and Elena. Tarōbō would be last.

One by one, Elena's party stepped through the portal tomb in silence, the copper-haired soldier completing their guard from behind.

STEPPING THROUGH the portal tomb was a somewhat different experience. The dolmen's entrance was six feet in height, and the ceiling tapered as they stepped further into the tomb. From the outside, it looked as if they would have to crouch to reach the end of the tomb's shallow chamber, but once they stepped inside the dimensions changed entirely.

It was as if they had stepped through the door into a stairwell leading downward, the stairs narrow and cut steeply out of the earth. The passage was completely dark. If it were not for the fact that the Kirin stood immediately behind her and his skin glowed like starlight in the darkness, Elena would have been unable to see where she walked. Even so, the path was treacherous.

Deeper into the tomb, the air around them grew thick. Elena hesitated but Eiry quietly led her by the hand, pulling her closer to him as the passage widened. Looking down, through the faint glow of the Kirin's light, Elena saw a thick fog begin to gather at their feet. Soon, it was so dense that Elena could hardly see Eiry's hand in hers, and in seconds it swallowed the Kirin's light. The only thing that kept Elena from screaming was the feel of Eiry's ice-cold grip.

Just as quickly, they stepped out of the fog. The transition was physically jarring. Elena's skin was slick with dew. Her clothes clung to her body, and her hair to the nape of her neck. Sound returned before sight. Elena heard the distant roar of the ocean crashing against a shore. She felt a biting wind, and when her sight cleared she saw they were standing at the edge of a massive cliff.

A deep-rooted fear settled over her. Being so close to the edge triggered a memory Elena had only ever recalled in dreams. Clotho's song had revealed the truth, but Elena had never fully remembered it until now. She remembered the same lashing wind, savage against her skin, the bloodlust in Eos's face when she attacked, and the memory of falling weightless into the cold, dark and churning sea. Someone had shielded her from the shattering surface of the waves, the ice-cold grip that Elena remembered in her dreams; the same hands that held her now and pulled her gently away from the edge of the cliff.

Elena opened her eyes. Eiry stood before her, concern lining his face. He studied her quietly, and Elena could feel he knew her thoughts; there was a hint of alarm in his gaze that Elena had seldom seen.

"I'll always catch you," he whispered only for her to hear, and pulled her gently into his arms.

Suddenly, it didn't matter that they weren't alone; that two Fae soldiers watched them with open curiosity. Eiry didn't let go until Elena's heart settled back into its normal rhythm. All eyes were on them when they pulled away from each other, and Elena made sure to avoid the watchful gaze of their escort. Instead, she took a moment to take in their surroundings.

They were standing beneath a clear and starry sky. If it were not for the biting wind, the temperature would have been pleasant. They were near the edge of the cliff, looking out onto a stunning coastline. Elena recognized it instantly. They were facing the Cliffs of Moher, "the cliffs of the ruin", one of Ireland's most impressive sights. At their highest point, they rose out of the sea at a height of at least seven hundred feet. They consisted mainly of beds of shale and sandstone, the different strata of rock and earth visible along the entire face of the cliffs.

Elena had been here before with Cataline, and she knew they were standing at the apex of a small dip in the coastline between the main view of the cliffs and the underground visitor centre, which was built into the hillside looking south over the cliffs. In this realm, however, there was no such modern centre. A structure was built into the hillside, but it was far more whimsical than the human counterpart. It was shaped out of the earth and stone, and consisted of multi-tiered, arcaded galleries cut into the cliff-face.

The architecture reminded Elena of the Spanish Alhambra, with its whitewash and clay color-scheme, horseshoe and Mocárabe arches held up by thin round columns, and decorative arabesques; and yet it was something altogether unique. The Mocárabe—filigree-like ornamental carvings of vertical prisms resembling honeycombs and shaped into stalactite-like formation—for instance, was carved in an intricate array of Celtic knot-work and cut through the stone completely so that the rays of the rising sun could pass through. In those few instances where the stone was not carved through entirely, the ornamental work was carved out until it reached a layer of gemstone—in most instances lapis lazuli or carnelian.

More impressive still was the fact that these staggered galleries opened out to the cliff-face without the use of a single protective railing; they were open balconies bordered by the use of arches alone. There were no visible connections between the galleries on the outside, and so Elena could only assume they were connected from the inside. Armored soldiers weaved in and out of the galleries; all wearing the same scaled armor as the two who escorted Elena and her party.

"Welcome to the Daoine Sídhe, the capital kingdom of our people," said the dark-haired soldier, turning to face them. "It is the seat of the High Queen. The structure to your right houses the army and the Queen's Guard. It is off limits. Please remember this throughout your stay."

The soldier watched them quietly. Once he was satisfied that everyone understood, he waved them toward the cliff's edge, to the top landing of a stairway carved into the cliffside. Silently, he led them down the stairs to a large open pavement. The wind was vicious and Elena held on to Eiry, who shielded her as best he could.

When they reached the pavement, nine giant birds were positioned in a line, all of them with harnesses. A harsh cry echoed around them. Elena searched for the source, but realized too late that the sound had come from one of her companions.

"What is the meaning of this?" Tarōbō demanded, his hawklike gaze intent on the dark-haired soldier. The copper-haired soldier remained as silent as a tomb, but ever vigilant.

Bryce was at Tarōbō's side in an instant, her hand over the hilt of his sword.

The dark-haired soldier smiled, a cruel and beautiful smile that sent a chill down Elena's spine. "Transportation," he replied, indifferently.

"Transportation? They are bird-deities," Tarōbō cawed. His body shook with anger, and Elena could see his hair slowly begin to turn to feathers.

"We use slaves in any way we see fit, bird-demon," said the soldier with an apathetic shrug. "This is the only way to enter the palace. There is no route from the surface."

Tarōbō's outrage was palpable, and understandably so. Elena was too shocked to say a word. Bryce began to whisper fervently to the bird-demon in Japanese, trying to soothe his anger. Eiry and the Kirin remained silent sentinels at Elena's side. Surprisingly, it was the twins who stepped forward.

"This will do, Creidhne," Galen said sharply to the dark-haired soldier, obviously familiar with the man.

"I am sure that a Faerie Prince such as yourself can understand the shock of this revelation," added Gavin with a forced deference. "Stories of Fae custom reach far and wide, but seeing it firsthand is always disconcerting."

Creidhne stared at the twins, his features smoothing. He nodded, and then turned his attention to his copper-haired companion. "Assist the girl, Irél."

It was a command, and the copper-haired soldier began to make his way toward Elena, as Creidhne leapt onto the back of the first bird-deity positioned on the pavement, a pied brown Steppe Eagle.

Eiry stopped Irél's approach by placing himself between the copper-haired soldier and Elena. "Thank you for your assistance, Irél, but it will not be necessary," he said to the soldier with an apologetic nod. "I can assist her myself."

The copper-haired soldier seemed unsure for a moment, but then he shrugged and made his way to the last bird-deity on the line.

"Allow me, Elena-san," whispered the Kirin to Elena, his hand gently settling on her shoulder. "I would rather you ride with me."

"Kiyoshi-sama, are you certain?" she asked, turning to meet his topaz gaze. Instant relief settled over her. The last thing Elena wanted to do was travel on a bird-deity who was forced into such a humiliating servitude. Elena was uncertain how such deities came to be slaves to the Fae, but she was sure whatever the case was she would not approve of it.

"I would not have it any other way," the Kirin assured Elena, and then shifted into his mythical form.

Majestic and noble, he stood before her, a dragon in the shape of a deer, his mane shimmering like white fire and his scales glowing like silver starlight in the evening sky. He was truly a magnificent creature.

Beside them, Bryce had managed to calm Tarōbō. He was now in his demon form, a giant Peregrine Falcon, and Bryce was perched on his back. Elena couldn't help but wonder if Boudicca, the famed warrior queen, had looked as fierce to the Romans on her steed, her mass of flaming red hair an omen of the blood she would shed.

The Kirin bent to his knees in front of Elena. The warm press of his muzzle against her hand roused her from her thoughts. With Eiry's help, she carefully climbed onto his back. All the while, Creidhne watched her, his scrutiny disarming.

Elena began to feel self-conscious. Eiry had explained to her before that being in Faerie—what the Tartareans called the Faerie realms—would be like walking on a tightrope over a windy cliff with the Fae controlling the wind. They wouldn't throw you off deliberately, but they would test your balance for the sake of entertainment; if you fell, it was because you were weak.

"Never mind him," Eiry whispered quietly into Elena's ear once she was steady on the Kirin's back. With the howling wind and the distance between everyone, no one could hear him. "He's never before seen a Kirin. Until this moment, he had no idea who or what the Kirin was. All he has heard are myths, and such things are of great interest to the Fae. He will not show it outwardly but he is surprised, and it is near impossible to surprise the Fae. Remember this, because you are about to gain the same reaction from the Fae Court."

Eiry's words made Elena tense. Were they about to appear before the entire Court? If Elena had felt that being in Tartarus was nerve-racking on account of the difficult nature of most Tartarean gods, being in Faerie would be much worse. These people made slaves out of other gods, and they would not hesitate for a second to make Elena fall. At the thought, Elena lifted her gaze to meet Creidhne's. If she was going to appear before the Fae Court, she needed to find her resolve now. She would not waver, beginning with this man, whom Gavin had called a Faerie Prince.

Creidhne held her gaze. He seemed amused, and Elena swore she saw a faint smile ghost across his lips. The twins had told her that amusing the Fae was the key to navigating their world. If that was true, perhaps she was succeeding.

Without any warning or signal, Creidhne suddenly took flight. The twins followed behind him, their bird-deities—dark gray crimson-eyed Sparrowhawks—diving into the air and cutting through the violent wind with their powerful wings. They were stunning creatures, their undersides light gray and barred with thick black bands. They reminded Elena of a darker version of Tarōbō, and she wondered what their humanoid form might look like and what pantheon they belonged to.

The Kirin took a step forward and Elena leaned into his neck, holding tightly onto his lustrous mane. She prayed she wasn't hurting him. Suddenly, they vaulted into the sky, weightless. The horizon shifted and Elena was instantly dizzy. The wind was brutal, and she clung to the Kirin's neck, thankful when she felt his warm energy wash over her. His voice echoed softly in her mind, calming her. Elena didn't dare open her eyes.

THEY LANDED SOUNDLESSLY. The Kirin assured her they had made it safely, and only then did Elena open her eyes. They were at the mouth of a great hall. Immediately behind them was the open edge of the cliff-face, bordered by an arcade of giant ornate arches; one step past the arcade and the person would plummet to their death. Elena could hear the roar of the sea below them, much closer than before. If she looked out of the opening, she could see the spot they had just taken off from on the cliffside directly opposite of them; they had traveled from the cliffs on the north side of the dip in the coastline to those on the south.

The capital kingdom of the Daoine Sídhe was built deep inside the landscape of the Cliffs of Moher, its halls and palaces open to the sea. It was as if nature itself had hollowed out the beds of rock to form the vast network of rooms, and then water and the passage of time were manipulated seamlessly through magic to finish guiding the stone into its extraordinary formations. They stood in a large rectangular hall of polished alabaster. Giant rounded columns sprouted out of the floor like trees and lined each side of the hall, framing a smooth causeway of stone. The columns were joined to the ceiling by capitals carved into spectacular arches of honeycombed Celtic knot-work. In the center of the causeway, rectangular pools were cut into the stone, each one placed vertically after the other and dividing the hall in half. Multi-colored water lilies and lotus flowers danced on the surface of the water.

The pools stopped at the end of the hall where a dais was carved out of the stone within a portico of ornamented arches identical to the arcade at the entrance. The entire back wall of the portico was carved in an ornate arabesque of Celtic design, the alabaster carved through until lapis lazuli and carnelian surfaced from behind the stone, providing a colorful backdrop; lapis lazuli on the outside borders of the wall, and carnelian closer to the center framing the great throne. The alabaster throne grew out of the floor in the center of the dais and was carved in the same intricate manner as the rest of the hall, its backrest etched through completely into filigree made of stone.

The hall was magnificent, particularly when viewed as a whole. It was smooth bare stone up to the column capitals where the stone suddenly erupted into a spectacularly delicate design spanning a breadth of at least seven feet until touching the smooth ceiling. The pools of water in the center of the hall added a soft, delicate touch to the lower half of the room. Lighting was achieved with the use of mirrors strategically placed in the hall.

No less magnificent than the hall itself were the people gathered in the room. Mostly silver, raven or copper-haired, they were all possessed of an arresting beauty. Even from this distance they appeared statuesque and unmistakably ethereal. The men wore tunics of fine fabric and the women flowing gowns of gossamer silk that danced across their skin like mist and smoke. They appeared to have an affinity for jewelry, but only a few wore coronets of the style worn by Manannán mac Lir.

Chief among them was the Faerie Queen Áine who sat gracefully in her throne of filigreed alabaster, a vision in an emerald gown—the saturated hue a sharp contrast against her radiant skin. A platinum coronet beset with jewels rested on her crown of copper-spun hair, which spilled down her back in fluid waves. She was speaking with a raven-haired woman and a golden-haired man at her side, but raised her hand for silence when she noticed the arrival of her guests. The man was the only person in the room with hair the color of the sun.

Creidhne dismounted, and Elena's party followed suit.

The Faerie Host had fallen silent, and a murmur erupted as the Kirin slowly bent to his knees so that Elena could dismount. The murmur reached a fevered pitch when he returned to his humanoid form and bowed his head to Elena, who then bowed even deeper in return.

Creidhne watched with an unreadable expression. Once everyone was assembled, he nodded and turned to lead the way toward the Host.

Behind them, the copper-haired soldier led the now riderless bird-deities back into the air.

Elena and her party remained silent as they were led down the right side of the hall to the dais where the Faerie Queen waited. Elena knew they were a motley crew of companions, but never before was it as poignant as it was now—in sharp contrast to the seemingly more patrician Faerie Host. By the time they reached the dais and bowed before the Faerie Queen, a lump had formed in the back of Elena's throat.

"Welcome Elena of the House of Thebes," said the Faerie Queen to Elena as she gracefully eased herself out of her throne. "I am Áine, wife of Manannán mac Lir, and High Queen of the Tuatha Dé Danann."

Elena met the Queen's gaze. Green and hard as malachite, striated with slivers of copper, it rooted Elena to the ground; like Manannán and Creidhne's before her. Elena could sense the danger in her blood, but the spell threaded in the Queen's gaze wouldn't allow her to look away, pulling her in in-spite of herself. This was the Fae's defense against humans, Elena realized with a startled shock.

The High Queen of the Tuatha Dé Danann was an exceptional beauty possessed of an equally exceptional strength.

It took Elena a long moment to find her voice. All the while the room hummed with a restless silence. It was true that Elena was human, but she was also half god. The deified blood of Dionysus flowed through her veins, and it was that strength that Elena reached for now to weather through this.

"I thank you for your hospitality and your words of welcome, Your Majesty," Elena said in a strained voice while trying to emulate the Queen's imposing gaze, countering the spell the Faerie had woven only moments before.

The Queen's features smoothed and she narrowed her eyes, taking Elena's measure. "You are joined by four familiar faces and two which I have never seen before," remarked the Queen, her gaze falling on each one. "Four Greek gods, a Japanese bird-demon, and a fabled Kirin. You are by far the most interesting human I have ever met."

Elena had no idea how to reply and so she simply bowed her head, hoping it would be enough. Thankfully, Eiry stepped forward; the sound of his shoes echoed lightly through the silent hall.

"On behalf of Tartarus, we are grateful for your hospitality. As you are aware, we seek to retrieve an item, and we are grateful that you have so graciously allowed us the opportunity to make the attempt." Eiry spoke eloquently, his tone formal.

"You might want to save your gratitude until you have heard the terms, Lord Thanatos," the Queen replied. There was no malice in her voice, but a steadfast resignation. "As you know, I am bound by rules as much as you are. Before we speak of such things, however, are you in the position to prove the girl is truly the Heir?"

Elena tensed. Eiry had never discussed with her the possibility of having to prove her lineage, and Elena couldn't begin to guess how that would be done.

Now that she thought about it, when Elena had first appeared before the Hyakki Yakō, Nurarihyon had mentioned the requirement of some proof but had ultimately been satisfied with Eiry's word. Elena had a feeling that in this instance Eiry's word would not suffice.

"Of course, Your Highness," Eiry answered the Queen, "she bears the mark."

This was the first Elena had heard of any mark. She wanted to ask him what the hell they were talking about, but this was definitely not the time to snap at him for concealing important information.

Eiry turned toward her and Elena felt the first inklings of panic. His quiet gaze begged silently for her trust.

"Ele, I need you to turn around," he said gently, once he reached her side.

Elena swallowed hard and tried to remain calm. She did as Eiry asked, turning slowly so that her back faced the Queen. A moment passed and she felt Eiry's fingers in her hair. He gathered the mass of it in one hand and pulled it over her shoulder, exposing the back of her neck. Elena flinched when his cold fingers unexpectedly brushed the nape of her neck, followed by a tingling sensation.

A murmur moved through the Host.

Had they seen a mark, Elena wondered? If so, what on earth did it look like, and why had Eiry never told her about it?

"Thank you," the Queen said. From the sound of her voice, Elena couldn't tell if she was pleased or not.

Eiry let go of Elena's hair and whispered, "Every Heir bears my mark," only for her to hear. "A butterfly," he clarified in the same private whisper, as he took Elena's hand and slowly turned her back around.

"Now that the preliminaries are over with," declared the Queen, "let us discuss your purpose."

Elena fell back in line with the rest of her party.

"Before we do that, Majesty," Eiry interjected with an apologetic bow, "I would like to present our tribute."

"None is required, Lord Thanatos," the Queen replied, but was obviously intrigued; her eyes sparkled and her lips were curling into a smile. "This is a *dúshlán*. No tribute is necessary."

"While that is true," Eiry countered gently, "granting safe passage and an audience to the Heir is no small endeavor. For that reason, we offer tribute as a show of our good faith."

The Queen's smile broadened, and she appeared genuinely pleased. "Very well, then," she said to Eiry. "You may proceed."

Eiry nodded and quickly produced two items; when, exactly, he had taken them out of Elena's carryall was a mystery. Both items were boxes, one carved of stone and the other of metal. Eiry presented the Queen with the box carved of stone and said, "Tartarus offers as tribute the light of the stars to brighten your halls."

The Host suddenly erupted into a fevered pitch, those gathered pressing closer to the center of the hall to get a better look as the Queen stared at the box placed in her hands, stunned into silence. She hesitated for only a moment, and then slowly opened the lid. From inside, she drew out a glorious necklace wrought of adamant and beset with opals. In the center of the necklace was a beautiful teardrop made of glass, a multitude of white weir lights dancing inside of it.

At the sight of the necklace, the Host fell silent.

If the twins and Bryce were surprised by the offering, they did not give their emotions away. They stood silent and expressionless before the Host, as if they had known all along what the tribute would be.

Tarōbō and the Kirin also observed in silence, concealing any possible interest.

Elena was the only one of their group who looked directly at the offering. It called to mind her inheritance, which made her instantly uneasy.

Eiry watched the Queen with a ghost of a smile on his features. "They are everlasting," he assured her in a silken voice, his manner slightly more fluid. "May they follow you always and bathe you in their light."

Without waiting for the Queen's acceptance, Eiry proffered the second box, the one carved out of metal. In the same silken voice, which carried perfectly through the hall, he announced the nature of the second tribute. "This is a personal tribute from Lord Dionysus, a bottle of his rarest vintage for the risks you have taken in entertaining his daughter's request."

A cacophony of voices erupted in the hall, the tone much louder and more aggressive than before.

The Queen's shock was visible. She stilled in her throne, her eyes narrowing as she focused her gaze on Eiry. "His daughter?" she asked, unconvinced.

"Yes, Highness," Eiry replied.

The Queen placed the necklace back in its box and accepted the second offering. Instead of opening it, however, she shifted her attention to Elena and examined her with an unapologetic scrutiny. If what she was searching for was Dionysus in Elena's features, the Queen would be sorely disappointed, as Elena took after Isabella. If, instead, she searched for some kind of distinctive quality that would mark Elena a demigod, she would find none, as there was nothing overtly extraordinary to find.

Confounded, the Queen looked between Elena and Eiry. To question their word would be a serious breach of decorum, particularly in light of the tribute she now held in her hands. The Queen opened the metal box and examined its contents. After several silent moments, she chose to consider the vintage itself proof sufficient.

"We accept your tribute," the Queen declared for all to hear. "Let us now discuss your purpose."

"Of course, Highness," Eiry said softly, and stepped away from the dais.

"It is my understanding you wish the opportunity to retrieve the Aidos Kyneê, Hades's Helm of Darkness," the Queen remarked, and then turned her attention to Elena. "Is that correct, Elena Dionysia?"

"Yes, Your Majesty," Elena quickly replied, averting her gaze and bowing her head. Her voice resounded against the stone walls, making her feel self-conscious.

The Queen nodded, pleased. The Host had fallen silent once again and she looked over her subjects slowly, her long, graceful fingers smoothing over the boxes on her lap. A glass sphere appeared suspended in the air beside her and she placed the tributes inside, her hand passing through the glass as if through water. Once inside, the stone and metal boxes hung motionless in the center of the sphere.

Returning her attention to Elena, the Queen continued their conversation. "Hades lost the item you seek in a game of *fidchell*. Our law allows you the opportunity to attempt to win it back. You will only be able to do so by succeeding where Hades failed. Do you follow my meaning, child?"

"Yes, Majesty," Elena answered, her voice unsteady. She had no idea what *fidchell* was, but she was not going to admit that in a hall full of

Faeries. Hopefully, someone would fill her in later. "In order to win back the Helm, I must defeat someone at *fidchell*."

"Precisely," said the Queen. "You must play against the person who defeated Lord Hades. In accordance with our laws, you will have a full day and night to learn the game. We will provide you with our most skilled player as tutor, although it seems you already have two proficient players in your party." The Queen turned her gaze to the twins, who bowed dramatically in response. With a satisfied smile, she returned her gaze to Elena. "If you win, the Helm is yours. If you lose, you will remain forever in the Daoine Sídhe."

At the Queen's last words, Elena almost choked. It took all of her ability to keep the shock from showing on her face. Elena chanced a glance at Eiry. He had turned his attention away from the Queen and was looking at Elena with a blank expression. It was clear, at least to her, that he had not seen this one coming. His surprise, however, quickly gave way to anger; Eiry was not the kind of man to be blindsided, or to take it lightly.

The hall fell into an uncomfortable silence. Beside them, Gavin cleared his throat. At the sound, Eiry's features smoothed and he returned his attention to the Queen.

"Majesty, while we understand tradition, these terms are impossible for us to meet. She is the Heir. If she were to lose, these terms would affect the war, and your neutrality."

The pleasure drained from the Queen's expression. "Forgive me, Lord Thanatos," she said in a measured tone, "but I warned you the terms might not be to your liking. While I recognize what our terms would mean, I, like you, am bound by rules. Of course we do not wish to take a stance that would be interpreted as partisan, but you have come to us with a request and we would like more than anything to oblige you. In order for us to do so, however, certain rules apply.

"If this were taking place during the Games, as was the case with Hades, or in any realm outside of the Sídhe, the stakes would be different. However, we are within a Sídhe and our laws are binding. As this is a *dúshlán*, a challenge, you have all been invited here with the freedom of leaving openly, which is already an exception to our law. Normally, once a human or foreign god wanders into the Sídhe, they can only return to the surface by winning a game of *fidchell*. In the case of a *dúshlán* made by an outsider, the challenger is exempted from that particular requirement so that he or she may enter and leave the Sídhe freely if it is decided our terms are too steep.

"As such, your party is free to leave now if the Heir decides she cannot agree to our terms. She will have visited the Daoine Sídhe freely, which is a rare gift indeed. On the other hand, she may choose to agree to our terms. If she does, she risks remaining in the Daoine Sídhe. The choice is hers and so absolves us of any partisanship in this war, as would the fact we offered Helios of Olympus the same invitation as we did you—although he declined. The best that I can do, Lord Thanatos, is promise you that if the Heir loses, she will not be treated as a slave within these walls."

The Queen ended her explanation and watched Eiry quietly, her interested gaze betraying a rueful expression. They were, undoubtedly, engaging in a careful game of politics. Elena felt sick to her stomach.

Eiry offered the Queen a sardonic smile. "The semblance of partisanship, Majesty, depends entirely on those judging the situation from the outside," he replied, treading carefully; if anyone was adept at this game, it was he. "I would prefer to avoid the situation altogether, for the sake of all parties concerned. I am sure you would agree that it is as imperative for the Dananns to remain neutral, as it is for Tartarus that the Heir safely returns. Is there not the possibility of a mutually beneficial exception? I am sure that in your long and illustrious history some exceptions have been made."

The Queen leaned forward in her throne, her gaze intent on Eiry, her expression unreadable. "What exactly do you propose, Lord Thanatos?"

"An Act of Substitution."

Again, the Host burst into fervent whispers.

The Queen smiled deeply, and she raised her hand for silence. "If any tradition among the divine could be said to be universal, Lord Thanatos, it would be that of Substitution. However, an agreement to such would depend entirely on the quality of the thing being offered in exchange."

"I will offer myself in her stead," Eiry replied in a very business-like tone. "If she loses, I will take her place and remain within the Daoine Sídhe."

Elena felt a sharp pain in her chest, and a dry sob caught in her throat. For a moment, she didn't know what was happening. It took several seconds for her to process what Eiry had just said. When his meaning finally hit her, she couldn't breathe. The panic was paralyzing. She couldn't let Eiry sacrifice himself for her; she wouldn't. This was her decision. This was something *she* needed to do. If she lost, being stuck here was a proper punishment for her failure. Cataline had died because of her, and it was only fitting that she lose her freedom if she failed at trying to get Cataline back.

Seconds passed, and the Queen did not speak. If Elena was going to say something, it needed to be now. It was a strain to breathe deeply, but she forced herself so that her voice would steady.

"I can't agree to that," she said before the Queen could accept Eiry's offer.

Elena wasn't looking at him, but she could see he had turned to look at her. When their eyes finally met, he wore a stricken expression on his face, and seeing it was excruciating for Elena. She wanted desperately to explain her reasoning to him, but this wasn't the place to argue the point.

"Nor can I," added the Queen before Eiry could say another word. "As much as I enjoy your company, Lord Thanatos, and would welcome you gladly, the thing being offered must be of equal or greater value than the thing it is meant to replace. In this instance, an Heir of the House of Thebes is a rare specimen indeed—only two have surfaced in more than a millennia. The thing to be substituted must, therefore, also be possessed of a similar rare quality. Death deities, however, are hardly rare among the pantheons. I can think of five who count as such in your pantheon alone."

The comment would have angered any god—such as the Keres, whose unearthly growl broke through the tension—but Eiry's infamous stoicism held. With a caustic smile, he bowed mockingly to the Queen.

"Your presumption, Majesty, is flawed," he said sharply, the edge in his voice the only warning of his displeasure. "Even among the whole of the divine there is always the first of a kind from whom all others descend."

"Even so, Lord Thanatos," the Queen replied, unconcerned, "I decline your offer."

Her hard gaze held a challenge, and the air around them was suddenly charged. It made the hair on Elena's arms stand on edge. Bryce and the twins stepped closer to their brother. The blonde-haired Fae took his place beside the Queen.

Before things could escalate further, the Kirin stepped forward and a heady calm stole over the hall. "Would I be more to your liking, *Heika*?" he said in a clear voice. *Heika* was the Japanese honorific for "Your Majesty", but the Kirin said it in such a way that it was almost patronizing. His topaz gaze, now intent on the Queen, fiercely commanded her attention.

The hall instantly fell silent, as if a gust of wind had stolen their voices all at once. All eyes were on the Kirin, including the Queen's. If she was displeased with his tone or expression, her displeasure was far outweighed by the quality of his offer; a Kirin was as rare a being as existed in the world.

"Can a fabled Kirin agree to such a thing?" the Queen asked in a far gentler tone than she had last used with Eiry.

The Kirin did not mirror her gentleness. On the contrary, his reply was unexpectedly sharp. "A Kirin may do as it pleases."

"Is that so?" replied the Queen, piqued. "Isn't your kind famed for being neutral?"

"An old wives tale, I'm afraid," said the Kirin with an equivocal smile. "Like the beings born of the stone beneath your feet, *Heika*, Kirin are beings born outside of any pantheon," he explained, the indignation now clear in his voice. "Our sole purpose is to maintain the balance in nature when disturbed by the divine. We are few in number and act only when our purpose is revealed. Until that time—and it may take innumerable centuries—we simply observe. Our perceived lack of interest is the source of the inaccuracy. I assure you, we are far from neutral. I am not bound by the yoke that binds you, and so I may do as I please. My pleasure, now, is to take the Heir's place in the event she fails at the task you place before her."

Although the Queen was unsure what to make of the Kirin's words, she was far too ambitious not to be taken in by the idea of owning him; for that was the purpose of their law, to own those who were unfortunate enough to fall within their grasp. It was a display of great power to own that which should not be, and her desire for the Kirin was plainly written on her features.

"I accept your offer," she declared with a triumphant smile. "Speak your intent out loud, Kirin, so that it is binding."

Elena felt a cold panic at the Queen's acceptance of his offer, one she could not accept—not in a million years. "I cannot agree to this," she interjected once again, repeating herself when her words went unheard. "This is my desire, and my failure will be mine alone to atone for."

All eyes turned to Elena, the Host due to her impudence and those of her party out of concern. The twins were infinitely amused. Galen watched her with a sordid, almost hungry curiosity, while Gavin hung on his arm and whispered conspicuously in his ear.

The Queen reluctantly tore her attention away from the Kirin, annoyed by Elena's interruption. "You have a most commendable sense of honor, Elena Dionysia," she said in a condescending tone. "However,

Lord Thanatos is most wise in his suggestion of an alternative solution to our little quandary. Above all, the Tuatha Dé Dannan must remain neutral. As the Kirin has so astutely pointed out, we are not as free to act as he. His offer provides us with the perfect solution to prevent any fallout."

Elena wasn't listening to the woman anymore, Queen of a divine race or not. She'd had enough of the pomp and charade, and their visit had only just begun. The Fae Court was exhausting. Elena made her way to the Kirin without responding to the Queen.

Taking his hand in hers, she spoke only for him to hear. "Kiyoshi-sama, please do not agree to this. If I lose, you will be stuck here forever because of me. I can't accept that."

The Kirin smiled warmly at Elena's words, and the contempt he had for the Queen disappeared from his gaze. He was breathtaking, and the idea of him being lost to the world because of a mistake she made was unbearable. Elena felt tears sting her eyes, but the Kirin quickly soothed her.

"Allow me this honor, Elena-san," he whispered, touching his forehead to hers. "Your destiny is my purpose. If you were to lose, I will have fulfilled my purpose by taking your place." He saw she would protest and did not allow her to do so. He begged for her silence with a gentle press of his fingers to her lips, before he returned his attention to the Queen.

"If the Heir loses," the Kirin declared his intent for all to hear, "you may rescind my exempted freedom in her stead."

And so it came to be that the Kirin would remain should Elena fail.

ELENA WAS RELIEVED once they were finally led out of the hall by Creidhne, the dark-haired soldier with the plum-colored eyes. As Elena had suspected, the galleries and halls of the Daoine Sídhe were connected from within. This was achieved with a network of atriums and stairwells carved out of alabaster stone and trimmed in heavily decorated archways—at times the columns carved in relief out of a wall of solid stone and at others standing alone as if hewn by nature itself. The way was lit by the alternate use of mirrors and braziers, the natural light scarcely able to make it deeper than a hundred feet past the open galleries facing the cliffside.

As they were led through the dimly lit halls to their rooms, they came across several creatures that were not Tuatha Dé. What looked like a Naiad scurried across the corridor carrying a large amphora in her arms. A faun bowed as they passed a large hall. A Norse demigod grunted past, covered in soot and holding a hammer; Elena could sense his godhood and guessed his identity from his attire. An Egyptian goddess wearing a finely braided wig and live snakes curled around her forearms carried linens in a basket to be washed. A human girl tended an inner garden.

"Who are they?" Elena asked Eiry quietly, startled when Creidhne replied.

Though silent and seemingly withdrawn, Creidhne was keenly observant. "Slaves, Elena Dionysia," he said in a dispassionate voice, turning to watch her from over his shoulder. "Those who have not won their freedom in accordance with our laws."

Elena loathed his apparent ambivalence. "Do all Sídhe kingdoms practice this custom?" she asked him, ignoring Eiry's quiet glances her way.

Creidhne stopped mid stride. They had stepped out of a corridor into a large stairwell. "The great majority of the Sídhe kingdoms practice the custom. It has become an indication of a kingdom's wealth. Our Queen is an avid collector."

"Collector?" Elena asked, incredulous. "You say it as if she were collecting stamps."

Creidhne glared at Elena, his plum-colored gaze unsympathetic. "Humans are always such sentimental creatures," he remarked, irritated.

A cough interrupted Creidhne's reproach, and Gavin stared at the soldier from behind Elena's shoulder. "And your kind are humorless bores," he said flatly.

Creidhne stared at Gavin, his expression as somber as ever. "Better humorless than base," he replied and turned on his heel, the gesture meant to be dismissive.

Gavin kissed Elena on the cheek, and with a grin fell back into place beside Galen.

They were standing at the head of a deep stairwell, flanked at all sides by a square peristyle of honeycombed arches. The walls behind the peristyle were of smooth alabaster bordered at the top with a lattice of carved knot-work in a darker hue; those to their left and right held massive double doors framed by the same type of knot-work as the lattice, and the one opposite them continued the corridor. Bronze braziers sat nestled into the four corners of the walls surrounding the space.

A Greek sky goddess stood motionless by the door to their left. Elena couldn't be certain how she knew what the woman was; something inside of her just knew, recognizing the danger instantly. This was obviously the Queen's idea of a joke.

Tall, dark skinned, and blue eyed, with deep ginger hair, the goddess stood at the threshold, a warm smile on her features as they approached. "Lord Creidhne," she whispered, and bowed her head when the dark-haired soldier stood before her. She did not lift her gaze again until he gave her leave to do so.

Quietly, the sky goddess waved them through the door on the left, the entrance to their room—a massive pointed-arch door made of carved translucent gemstone set within a large frame of floor-to-ceiling knot-work hewn from a darker alabaster than the smooth walls. Inlaid within the lattice at the top edge of the wall was a continuous sequence of horseshoe-arched windows.

Before entering the room, Elena noticed that the door on the right wall of the peristyle—the one opposite theirs—was identical to their doorway with the exception of the gemstone used for the arched door; theirs was made of iridescent fire agate while the opposite one was made of a clouded green jade.

Elena and her party were led into an atrium-styled room capped by a domed canopy of honeycombed stonework held up by a base of filigree arches and columns. Blue, red, green and yellow stones formed a multitude of colored designs within the stone filigree. Light and air filtered into the room from the open wall facing the cliffside, opposite the entrance. Reclining couches lined the space, which was set deeper into the floor, and were draped in luxurious cushions and fabrics. In the center was a basin fountain made of the same alabaster as the floor.

The opulence was overwhelming, and Elena found herself transfixed. Nor was she the only one, as Tarōbō and the Kirin studied their surroundings with a quiet hesitance. Eiry's attention was on their escort and the sky goddess. Bryce stepped down into the space and dropped onto a couch. The twins made their way across the room to a small table with a crystal liquor decanter and were already pouring themselves drinks.

Creidhne cleared his throat. "This is the pavilion that joins your rooms," he declared, going through the motions at a hurried pace. "There are five rooms in total. You will find a door at each corner of this pavilion. The fifth room is above." Creidhne pointed to the canopy above them, bringing their attention to a space above the first layer of honey-combed carvings that served as the base-frame of the dome. A lattice of wooden knot-work containing several trellised openings lined the space, which held up the heavily decorated dome.

"Melia will ensure the ladder is properly placed for access," Creidhne continued. "She will be your personal attendant during your stay. The feast will begin in a few hours. Please remember to dress accordingly. If you get lost within the halls make sure to remember the color of your door. Each apartment's main door is made of a different stone. It is of great assistance after an evening of merrymaking. The tutor will arrive here first thing tomorrow morning to assist the Heir. Now if you will excuse me, I must take my leave." With a curt bow, Creidhne exited the room.

The sky goddess, Melia, who had been standing aside as everyone took in their surroundings, quietly stepped into the center of the room and bowed before Eiry, who stood beside the basin fountain. "Lord Thanatos," she whispered in a deferential tone, "it has been many, many centuries. So long ago I cannot remember."

To Elena's surprise, Eiry offered the sky goddess a smile, and cordially returned her bow. "It is good to see you, Melia," he said gently. "It has been over three thousand years. The feuds have become war in your absence."

Melia looked stricken, but only for an instant. The shock was quickly replaced by a carefully practiced smile. "That long?" she asked timidly. "Time here passes very differently than on the surface or in Olympus."

"I am truly very sorry," Eiry said in return, while everyone listened silently. Even the twins looked up from their drinks. "Your sisters have not given up on your freedom. Each time, they approach Áine during the Games on your behalf. Even Zeus has made a personal inquiry."

At the mention of her sisters, the goddess' eyes glazed with tears, but she did not allow them to fall. Instead, she reached for Eiry's hands, her own trembling, and kissed his knuckles. "Thank you," she whispered, her voice affected. "It is the first real news of them I have received since arriving here. I had lost hope long ago. No matter how many times I ask, the Queen will not allow me to attend the Games. And as you can see, I have not succeeded at *fidchell*."

At the mention of the game, Elena paled. She felt dizzy and quickly took a seat, thankful when the Kirin sat down beside her. Her gratitude was short lived once she looked into his noble face and remembered with a gut-wrenching guilt that he would bear the brunt of her failure, which was now certain. If this sky goddess had been prisoner here for three thousand years and in that time had not succeeded in winning a game of *fidchell*, what chance in hell could Elena possibly have?

"Forgive me, have I said something wrong?" Melia asked, her voice shrill with panic.

Galen choked on his drink trying to suppress a laugh. "Not at all, Melia," he said in an acerbic tone, raising his glass of amber liquor. "You've only reminded the little demigod of how horribly she will lose. That's all."

"Lord Deimos, I do not understand what you mean," Melia replied, wide-eyed as she looked to Galen, who rolled his eyes in response.

Gavin smacked Galen's arm. "Never mind him, Melia," he said, sweetly. "He's upset I forced him to come along on this little trip."

Eiry gave an exasperated sigh, as he pinched the top of his nose between his fingers. He mumbled something to himself, shook his head, and then moved toward the small table to prepare himself a drink. "You've done nothing wrong, Melia," Eiry assured her. "Elena is here to reclaim the Helm of Darkness."

At the mention of the Helm, Melia paled and a trickle of fear bled through the blue of her gaze. It was obvious she was not comfortable with the mention of Hades or his Helm. "It's here? How?"

Bryce, who was draped over her couch like a large feline, shifted her position to face them, her movement accompanied by the rain-like chime of her bangles. "He lost it to Áine at the last Games," she said with a grin, staring at them over the back of her couch.

"To Áine?" Elena and Melia cried out simultaneously, both equally panicked.

Just when Elena had thought things couldn't get any worse, now she had to win at *fidchell* against the Queen. It was like a bad joke. "When the hell did any of you plan on telling me? And if anyone says it's on a need-to-know-basis, I swear by the gods I'll strangle you."

"Are you swearing by me, Ele? I'm a god!" Gavin asked excitedly.

"No, Gav, you're a twat," snapped Bryce.

"Right back at you, bitch," Gavin hissed, Galen growling behind him.

"Shut up!" Elena and Eiry yelled at the same time. "The three of you can be so draining," Elena added, completely aware of the wounded look Gavin was giving her.

Melia, Tarōbō and the Kirin watched in shocked silence. Bryce rolled her eyes and sunk back down into the couch. The twins took their glasses and moved to stand by the open wall, looking out at the ocean.

Melia decided to take her leave, and assured them she would return in time for the feast.

"I'm sorry, Ele," Eiry said once the sky goddess was gone, and came to stand behind her. He offered her a drink, which she downed without hesitation. "I wasn't sure what form this little test would take, because of how capricious Áine can be," he explained, staring at the empty glass with an arched brow. "I didn't want to worry you needlessly, and we haven't exactly been alone until now, since finding out."

Elena looked up at him, feeling the need to be petulant but deciding it wasn't worth the aggravation. In the end, it didn't matter when he told her about it, because she would have gone through with it anyway. Worst of all, knowing didn't change the fact that it would be impossible for Elena to win against Áine and the Kirin would be stuck in this realm forever because of it. The thought shattered Elena's resolve, and the tears began to fall in earnest.

"Fucking great, now she's crying. I'm out of here," Bryce growled. She pulled herself off the couch and ducked out into one of the rooms.

"I'm sorry," Elena apologized through a quiet sob, before Eiry squeezed into the couch next to her and pulled her into his arms.

Galen made for the room closest to the open wall, but Gavin caught his arm and held him in place.

Tarōbō sat down on the couch opposite Elena, Eiry and the Kirin. "Maybe I should go check on Akai-sama," he said softly.

"I would let her be for now, Tarōbō," Gavin warned from his perch by the open wall. "Unless, of course, you like getting clawed."

Crestfallen, Tarōbō excused himself. He vaulted into the air and landed gracefully on one of the canopy's trellised openings before disappearing into the fifth room—the perfect choice for a bird-demon.

Eiry held Elena quietly, trying to calm her. He smoothed his hand through her hair and down her back, offering her his glass of liquor when that didn't work.

Elena took the drink and downed it as well. "I don't want Kiyoshi-sama to be stuck here because of me," she admitted, struggling to get her emotions under control.

"He won't be stuck here, Ele. Relax, okay?" Eiry whispered and gently kissed her temple, tucking a tangle of her hair behind her ear.

"Eiry's right," Gavin chimed in, as he and Galen made their way back to the center of the room. "Galen and I are awesome at *fidchell*. We'll have you trained in no time. Right Galen?"

Galen replied with a grunt, and downed the rest of his drink.

"Elena, I will not be bound to this realm, I promise you," said the Kirin. His energy permeated the room and Elena's sobbing settled. He leaned closer and kissed the crown of her head. "I am an auspicious being, a herald of great things," he whispered, "...and I am in your pocket. I have faith that you will not lose."

Gavin whooped and did a little cheer to make Elena smile. Once she did, he kissed her cheek, and then he and his twin left for one of the rooms.

"Wait, I still don't know what *fidchell* is," Elena suddenly remembered, looking up at Eiry. Concern lined his eyes, and Elena felt awful for making him worry.

"If I tell you, will you promise to come rest with me for a little while before we all have to go to the feast?"

"*Hai*," Elena said, teasing him—hoping the gesture would lighten her mood.

The Kirin laughed softly.

Eiry gave in with a resigned sigh. "It's an ancient board game. Similar in style to chess, but with different rules and pieces. The blonde gentleman from earlier, Lugh mac Ethnenn, invented it."

Elena pictured the golden-haired man from before, standing at the Queen's side. He hadn't appeared menacing but, by the same token, he hadn't appeared amiable either. "Do you think he'll be my tutor?"

"I don't believe so," Eiry said softly, and pulled Elena off the couch. "Rumor has it the best *fidchell* player of the Tuatha Dé Danann is a woman."

ELENA DREAMT OF DRAGONS.

The beautiful beasts soared through the skies, their scales sparkling in the sun like gemstones. Some looked like the Western notion of the mythical creatures, and others like the giant serpents of Eastern lore. Elena soared among them, perched on the back of the Kirin, his radiant mane dancing in the wind like blazing white flames. She was fearless, even as the Kirin dove through the clouds toward the horizon, flanked by columns of fire, the roar of dragon's breath coursing through her.

She could feel it even after waking, the sound of dragon's breath a soft, fading melody.

Eiry was asleep beside her, and Elena crawled out of bed as quietly as she could. Shadows danced across the room scattered by the glow of a brazier, as she made her way toward the wall of open archways that looked out onto a sea of stars. The sound of the crashing waves filtered upward from below, filling the silence, but did not drown out the resonance of breathing.

A light caught Elena's attention from the corner of her eye. She turned and looked through the door of her room to see shards of light flickering against the gemstones on the walls of the pavilion. Sitting quietly on a couch looking out at the horizon was the Kirin, fragments of refracted light dancing around him like multi-colored fireflies. A small brazier was lit against the wall, behind him.

At the sound of her approach, he turned to meet Elena's gaze, his topaz-colored eyes giving off a faint light. His smile was dazzling, but Elena could see it was strained.

"Kiyoshi-sama, you look troubled," Elena whispered as she took a seat beside him. "I hope it is not because of my foolishness."

Slivers of light danced off the surface of the fountain, and for a moment they were both distracted. The Kirin grew unnaturally still beside her. Elena couldn't be sure how much time passed before he roused himself from his thoughts. With a graceful shake of his head—his hair shimmering like spun starlight—he rested his hand over hers.

"Never because of you, Elena-san," he assured her in his gentle voice, his gaze finally settling on hers. "Can you hear them?" he asked after a brief pause.

Elena watched the reflection of colors dance against his silver hair. "Hear what?"

The Kirin tilted his head and touched his fingers to the back of his ear. "Their breathing," he said in a whisper, his gaze shifting back to the horizon, "I've heard it since we arrived."

An image from Elena's dream flashed through her mind—a white dragon—and again she heard the sound of breathing. "I thought it was my dream," she confessed, oddly calm.

"You dreamt of dragons?" the Kirin asked. A gentle breeze stirred his hair and disturbed the fragments of light reflected on it, like ripples in water.

Elena nodded. "How did you guess?"

"It seems we shared the same dream," he said with a rueful smile. He watched her for several seconds before returning his gaze to the sky. "I share a lineage with dragons," he explained, "a kind of kinship. Kirin are chimerical in nature, but of all mythical beasts we are closest to the dragon. This is why it is difficult for me to hear them now and know I cannot speak with them."

"The sound we're hearing, is it really dragons breathing?" Elena followed his line of sight to some infinite point in the skyline.

"*Hai*," the Kirin replied.

"Why can't you speak with them?"

"Because they are not free to speak."

Again, there was a brief pause. In the room above them, someone stirred.

"There were many breeds of dragons once," the Kirin continued, "but almost all are now extinct, hunted for the wealth in their hides. Most dragons are born of dragonstone, Elena-san, a rare and precious stone. An egg will sprout from it like a giant jewel and give birth to a beast with scales of the same stone. This city—the great palace of the Daoine Sídhe—is built on what was once breeding ground for a tribe of Western dragons. The red, white and blue stones you see along the walls are a prime example."

His eyes drifted momentarily to a colorful design along one of the columns; the brazier's light reflected mainly against the lapis lazuli and carnelian-like stones. "They are a sign of wealth and power. Dragon-stone is harder and stronger than any other substance, moreso than any metal or stone. I am sure you can imagine its value in a war between gods."

The Kirin's voice drifted, the crackling brazier the only sound for several long seconds before he took a deep breath and continued his story. "More than a thousand years ago, fearing extinction, the dragon tribe born of these cliffs accepted the protection of the Sídhe. The Tuatha Dé Danann have grown rich on account of the arrangement. Whether it is a mutual arrangement is anyone's guess, but no one can deny that the Dananns's unique position within divine politics is due in great part to their control over dragons. It has also ensured Áine's continued election as High Queen."

Elena was at a loss for words. She was trying to process the information as quickly as she could, and, as always, the Kirin was infinitely patient with her. There were so many things she wanted to ask him. What, in truth, was a Kirin? How were they born? Where? How long had he been alive? Why was her destiny his purpose? Like Kirin, what other mythical creatures were born outside of pantheons? How many dragon tribes had there once been? Were Eastern dragons also born of stones? How many dragons could he hear, at this very moment, within the city? Elena's mind was racing a mile a minute. When it stopped, it settled on an unexpected image—the dark-haired soldier with the plum-colored eyes.

"The armor our soldier escort was wearing," Elena remembered, "it was made of scales of blue stone. Were they dragon scales?"

The Kirin nodded and lowered his gaze. "I cannot say whether they harm the dragons they have sworn to protect. Dragons shed their scales, and they can also be harvested from the dead. One scale would be large enough to fashion from it an entire suit of armor. My concern lies in that no one has had any contact with this tribe of dragons for over a thousand years, and, as the dark-haired soldier noted earlier, Áine is an avid collector of rare things. She is a wicked creature, Elena-san, and she vexes me."

"And thanks to me," Elena said in a dejected tone, "she might now be able to add you to her collection of rare things."

A roguish smile curved the Kirin's lips. He lifted his gaze to Elena's, topaz burning through a fringe of silver lashes. "You will not lose, Elena," he said in a tone matching his shrewd expression. He leaned forward, and a curtain of silver hair brushed Elena's shoulder as he whispered into her ear. "However, if you were to somehow lose, the Queen would find that coveting a Kirin is beyond her reach. I am far more cunning than she."

His words stirred a memory in Elena's mind.

Isabella painted in a garden, Elena at her side. Plum blossoms fell around them like blushing snow. Elena was riveted by the dragon-like creature that took shape on the canvas in the form of a deer with an ox's tail, its hide white with scales of pearly blue and its body alight with flames. After drawing its *kanji*, Isabella spoke its name—Kirin—a benevolent creature that would not feast on flesh, could walk on water and when it stepped on grass did not bruise the blades or tread on any living thing. Peaceful by nature, a Kirin would become fierce to protect the virtuous or punish the vile.

CHAPTER SEVENTEEN

FEASTS IN THE DAOINE SÍDHE were a spectacle unlike anything Elena had ever seen, and in the past two weeks Elena had seen many things.

The Feast was held in a sprawling hall with ceilings that rose higher than thirty feet, a colonnade of tree-like columns shooting up from the ground at all sides to form a canopy of honeycombed leaves stretching into a continuous bower above them. Curtains of silk spilled out of the spaces between stone branches, holding aloft acrobats that danced through the air above them.

Three impossibly large tables were arranged along the sides and end of the hall, nestled beneath the bower of stone. The center was left open for entertainment, the background of which was an open wall facing the cliffside. The roaring sound of waves rose through the air and into the brazier-lit hall in a subconsciously affecting melody.

Food was plentiful, and the libations never-ending. The Faerie Host and their guests dined on gilded plates, an endless parade of culinary delights eclipsed only by itself, each plate more extravagant and succulent than the last, culminating in a breathtaking array of exquisite desserts.

The evening's entertainment began with the song of a bard who sang of the history of the Tuatha Dé Danann, the fifth race to invade the island of Eriu, who fought and won two divine wars before being forced underground by the will of man.

Cairpre mac Oghma, bard and satirist of the Danann tribe, took his seat before the Host, clothed in unassuming robes and an unadorned harp held between his knees. Neither thickset nor slender, with ageless black eyes, long black hair, and possessed of hands so large they were more suited for warfare than the delicate strumming of his instrument, Cairpre mac Oghma was the physical antithesis of the voice that he possessed.

Weaving a delicate but striking melody, he sang of his people, who, after arriving in dark clouds and landing on the mountains of the Conmaicne Rein causing a darkness that lasted three days and three nights, conquered the island from the Fir Bolg—a divine tribe. In the First Battle of Magh Tuireadh, brave Nuada, king of the Dananns and son of Echtach, led his people to victory at the cost of his arm. No longer "unblemished", a requirement to being king, Nuada was forced to give up his kingship to half-Fomorian Bres, who later became a tyrant to his mother's people. To restore Nuada to rule, physician Dian Cécht, with the help of the artificer Creidhne, fashioned Nuada an arm out of silver, making him whole once more.

Deposed Bres, unhappy with his lot, complained to Balor, king of the Fomorians, a race of divine titans, and so came about the Second Battle of Magh Tuireadh. There fell Nuada, now called Airgetlám—"of the silver hand"—to Fomorian Balor's poisonous eye, but was there avenged by Lugh, Balor's own grandson and champion of the Dananns, who with a sling-stone drove Balor's poisonous eye out of the back his head, wreaking havoc on the Fomorian army that stood behind him.

For two centuries, the Dananns ruled Eriu in peace, until the arrival of the Milesians, sons of Míl Espáine, who invaded Eriu to avenge the death of Milesian Íth by Eriu's three kings. After a truce of three days, whereby the Milesian ships retreated beyond the ninth wave, the Dananns concocted a storm to drive the invaders away, but Amergin, poet of the Milesians, calmed the sea with his verse and made it possible for the sons of Míl to land and defeat the Dananns at Tailtiu. When called to divide the land between the two tribes, quick-witted Amergin allotted the land above ground to his people and the underground to the Tuatha Dé. And so it came to be that Manannán mac Lir led his people into the Sídhe.

A presentation by the Trí Dé Dána followed the bard's song. Identical, with golden skin and eyes the color of ripe plums, the three sibling gods of craftsmanship—Goibniu, Creidhne and Luchtaine— differed only in the color of their hair. Goibniu, god of smithcraft and brewing, was silver-haired; Creidhne, Elena's former escort, artificer and god of bronzecraft, black; and Luchtaine, wheelwright and god of woodcraft, red. Seeing them together, Elena was instantly reminded of the Moirai, on account of their number and peculiar coloring.

The Trí Dé Dána presented to Queen Áine an impenetrable shield crafted of gold and bronze, and to the Court a barrel of Goibniu's ale, which was said to grant the drinker invincibility. A demonstration in weaponry followed, by golden-haired Lugh, warrior champion of the Dananns, god of light and the harvest—and apparently not as deceased as the stories told.

Succeeding Lugh's display was a recital performed by the harper Cas Corach, his delicate melody weaving seamlessly into the rhythm of the raging sea, calming its fury and infusing it with a delicate majesty.

Then stood Macha before the Host, wife of Nuada, goddess of sovereignty and one of three morrígna—goddesses of war—who conducted an exhibition in falconry. Dressed in a gown the color of ripe apricots with stenciled knot-work in varying shades of green, she hardly fit the description expected of one of the raven women that instigates war. With a saffron-colored veil laid delicately over the crown of her head, she wore her light-brown hair woven in two intricate braids, one resting over each shoulder. Her exhibition, which included a demonstration with a small bird-deity, was followed by that of her sister Nemain.

The spirit embodying the frenzied havoc of war, silver-haired Nemain, goddess of strife and panic, demonstrated her skill with a longbow. She shot from the center of the hall to a moving target fastened to the side of bird-deities that dove in and out of view from the open wall facing the cliffside. If that alone wasn't difficult or alarming enough, it was late evening and the only light in the hall was the light of braziers. Even so, Nemain did not miss her mark, the bird-deities emerging unscathed each time. Bryce spent the whole of the presentation restraining Tarōbō.

Last to appear before the Host was the Dadga, god of magic, time and protector of the crop, whose living oak harp, called Uaithne, held sway over the seasons, restoring them to their proper order. Uaithne played three types of music—that of sorrow, joy and dreaming. And on this night the Dagda wove a song of dreaming using a melody to call forth the spring.

A hush fell over the Host, as stone gave way to living things. The floor beneath them turned to earth and grass, the columns around them into the trunks of ancient trees, and the intricate lines of the honeycombed arches above them into a living bower of branches and leaves. The sea calmed, the cold dampness of stone disappeared, and the light scent of flowers grew thick. The Dagda's song cast its spell until they dined within a perfect kind of dream.

Somewhere in the middle of the evening, Elena was asked to recite her story, and she found herself standing in the center of the room, addressing the Faerie Host. It was a harrowing experience, on account of the quality of presentations that had taken place before hers, but, to Elena's surprise, her story was accepted with an unreserved enthusiasm. She began her recitation alone, as she had her journey, but was soon joined by Eiry and the twins when she arrived at their roles in the tale.

Once the dinner service was complete, the Host splintered off into smaller groups, which dispersed through the hall after the tables were cleared away and replaced with clusters of reclining couches. Some entertained themselves with music and dancing, some with poetry or a small number of games, and others with simple and pleasant conversation. All the while, Goibniu's ale made it's way through the crowd, easing everyone into the Dagda's dream.

Throughout the course of the festivities, Elena met other Dananns, who were not as calculating and forbidding as their Queen. Nuada, the first Danann king, for instance, not surprisingly a strikingly handsome figure with hazel eyes and moon-spun hair, was amiable and quite the talker. The Dagda was also kind, but he had a filthy sense of humor and the mind of an ancient god, which meant he knew nothing of personal boundaries. Ogma, the Dagda's brother, on the other hand, was the opposite; the god of writing and knowledge, and champion of the Dananns before Lugh, he was polite, erudite and held a quiet dignity that belied a warrior's ferocity.

Elena enjoyed most the company of silver-haired Goibniu, god of smithcraft and brewing, and sable-haired Airmed, herbalist and goddess of healing. Unlike his brother Creidhne, Goibniu had a cheerful and friendly disposition. With his silver hair, plum-colored eyes, and refined features, he had the bearing of a king but was unexpectedly humble. The Dananns's version of a god of wine, he made an interesting counterpoint to Elena's father.

Equally kind was Airmed, daughter of Dian Cécht. Soft spoken with a sweet and gentle disposition, she was the opposite of Queen Áine but was no less astute. There was a quiet strength about her that reminded Elena of Aosaginohi. The Kirin and Tarōbō must have felt the same because their persistent wariness lessened on her account, and they joined more frequently in the conversation.

And so the evening passed, until the spell of the Dagda's song subsided.

THE NEXT MORNING, Elena woke to the sound of silverware striking plates and the chiming of glasses. A muddle of voices rose through the din. Galen was asking Gavin to pass the marmalade. Gavin was reading out several options—boysenberry, currant or fig—and at the same time going on about the black pudding. Bryce was complaining that her coffee wasn't warm enough. Tarōbō was asking, in a quiet and deferential tone, whether they might have miso soup, a staple of Japanese breakfast. The Kirin asked for a glass of water.

Elena sat up in bed to a splitting headache. It was pounding, and the morning light from the open wall wasn't making the pain any easier.

"Morning," a familiar voice called out from the doorway.

Elena looked up to see Eiry peeking in through the door. He smiled at her and stepped inside, a glass of water in his hand.

"Did you sleep alright?" he asked her, as he set the glass down on the table beside the bed.

"I feel hungover," Elena confessed with a sour expression. She didn't remember drinking much at all, but her mind was mush, her head was heavy, and her body was responding much too slow. At least she didn't feel nauseous. "What time is it?" she asked him, trying to remember when they got back from the feast.

Eiry sat down next to her. He had a small paper packet in his hand, no larger than two inches wide, and set it down on the table next to the bed. "The sun rose about two hours ago," he said gently, as Melia appeared at the door.

The goddess bowed, begged Elena's pardon for the intrusion, and then stepped inside. She was holding a tray in her hands with a small cup of steaming water. Eiry took the cup from the tray and set it down on the table, next to the small paper packet and the glass of water that were already there. Melia then took her leave.

"Sit up for me, a little straighter," Eiry said to Elena, and carefully tore open the top of the paper packet. He dropped its contents into a metal infuser, which he then dropped into the steaming cup.

Instantly, the room smelled of herbs—fennel, chamomile, peppermint, honey, and another scent Elena couldn't quite place.

Elena sat up straighter. "What is it?" she asked him, watching him take note of his watch.

"Something Airmed sent with Melia. She said it would help with the effects of the Dagda's spell."

"Is that why I feel like this? I was wondering what it could be, since I hardly drank."

"The music of the Sídhe is enough to enchant any human, particularly the songs of dreaming." Eiry noted his watch again, and then removed the metal infuser from the cup. "Such a prolonged exposure to it the first time, even for a demigod, has its effects."

"And you planned on telling me when, exactly?" Elena took the cup he offered and brought it close to her face with both hands. She breathed in deeply, and instantly her mind felt clearer. She looked up at Eiry from behind the rim of the cup, her brow arched; she was getting really tired of finding out about things after the fact.

Eiry smiled. "Drink it up," he told her, and crossed his arms over his chest. "And telling you now was the plan from the start," he added in a matter-of-fact way. "It was going to happen no matter what, so why worry you over it when you have a million other things to worry about? You couldn't refuse the invitation, nor could you rightfully request that they not sing. Even if I had mentioned it, we'd be exactly where we are now. So I filter for your benefit."

Elena wanted to complain, especially since it sounded so parental—it reeked of "I know what's best for you"—but Elena decided it would be better to let him win this little battle. He was putting a lot on the line to keep her safe, to bring her here at the risk of her life for a purpose that had nothing to do with her inheritance, and so the least she could do was let him have his little victories.

With a shrug, Elena brought the cup to her lips. The infusion was a little bitter, but in a matter of seconds she felt much better.

Eiry watched her the whole time, his hand outstretched to receive the cup once she was finished. "Drink it down with this," he said to her afterward, handing her the glass of water he'd brought with him into the room. "When you're done, come have breakfast. Your tutor will be here soon." With that, he cleared the table and made his way out of the room, leaving Elena to change.

Ten minutes later, Elena was having breakfast with the rest of the group, their lively conversation making it impossible for her to dwell on what was to come. Gavin had stuffed forks at the end of two small bread rolls and was making them dance, like Charlie Chaplin in *The Gold Rush*. Galen was throwing fresh currants at the rolls to see if he could dodge them, which Gavin did perfectly, and Bryce proclaimed them cheaters since they were twins and could obviously read each other's minds.

"Can't all gods read minds?" Elena interjected, not surprised when Bryce glared at her. Elena took another bite of her scrambled eggs, unconcerned.

"Yes, technically, but twins are different, little miss know-it-all," Bryce snapped back, taking a drink of her coffee. She looked almost human, sitting back in her chair with a white coffee cup in her hand and a half eaten plate in front of her. "Gods can read human minds if they want but not each other's minds. Twins, however, are of one mind and they can never fully block each other out. They don't need to communicate at all—they know what the other is thinking, feeling or doing at all times, some even at great distances although the majority can't function well when they are apart. I bet you Hyp— Ouch, Eiry! Fuck off!" Bryce growled at her brother after something he did made her jump and strike the table hard with her knees, which interrupted Gavin's bread roll dance.

Annoyed, the twins turned to stare at their two siblings, who were already locked in their own silent stare-down contest. Elena had no idea what was going on. Tarōbō and the Kirin remained conspicuously silent, their attention on their food. Bryce threw her napkin at Eiry and was reaching for her glass of water, when a knock was heard at the door.

Everyone froze.

Bryce's fingers hovered over the rim of her glass for a few seconds before she withdrew her hand. Eiry relaxed his stance. Slowly, the Kirin eased himself out of his chair.

"I will see who it is," he said softly, as Bryce returned to her seat.

Breakfast resumed, the vibe much more subdued than before. Everyone's attention was on the door, even though not a single person was looking directly at it. An exchange could be heard, but it was impossible for Elena to make out the words.

Seconds later, the Kirin returned to the table. "Your tutor is here, Elena-san," he said with a hint of a smile in his voice, and stepped aside to reveal sable-haired Airmed, daughter of Dian Cécht, standing behind him.

"FIDCHELL IS A GAME of gods and kings," were the first words Airmed said to Elena.

They sat at a table facing each other, a wooden board between them, its edges and corners decorated with knot-work inlaid in bronze. The four-sided board consisted of nine straight rows divided into nine squares each, rendering a total of eighty-one squares in all. Twenty-five game pieces were arranged on the board—sixteen made of silver, eight of bronze and one of gold.

The arrangement of the pieces was completely unfamiliar to Elena. The single golden piece was placed in the center of the board with the eight bronze pieces surrounding it in the shape of a cross—two above it and two below it to form a vertical row, with two at each side to form the horizontal row. The silver pieces were placed along the four edges of the board, one in each of the four corners and the other twelve flanking the arms and ends of the cross—three on each side, leaving two open squares between them and the corner pieces.

"At its core is the abstract pursuit of wisdom," Airmed began to explain, "be it personal or divine, for that is how Lugh Ildánach envisioned it, but, as with all things crafted by the gods, it soon assumed an element of the prophetic. It was by a game of *fidchell* that Midir, the Dagda's son, won back fair Étaín, and that a battle between King Arthur and Owein son of Urien, was decided."

Elena listened quietly, her eyes trained on the board. She was nervous, but was trying desperately not to show it. The game had been set up in the center of the canopied pavilion, the couches surrounding them filled with Elena's escort, who insisted on observing. The twins sat closest to them, ready to 'assist' in her lessons.

"There are several variants of the game," Airmed continued, her tone calming. "This is the first variant, where one player's goal is to pursue while the other's is to escape. The second variant of the game is more akin to warfare, where the goal is to conquer and destroy your enemy. Today, I must teach you both variants of the game and determine which one you are most suited for. During the *dúshlán*, you, as the challenger, will choose the variant of *fidchell* to be played."

"Is there a variant Queen Áine is less suited for?" asked Gavin.

"I'm afraid not, Lord Phobos," Airmed replied, meeting Gavin's gaze momentarily before returning her attention to Elena. "But that is not to say she does not have weaknesses," she added, offering Elena an encouraging smile. "It is important to know your opponent. The Queen plays always to demonstrate her prowess. She will never take pity on an opponent, and she will always take the opportunity to strike. But champions do not win battles relying on might alone."

At her words, Elena's heart began to race; Airmed's candor gave her hope. The Queen had agreed to provide Elena a tutor but that agreement did not require the person to be kind to her, let alone to give her valuable information. Encouraged, Elena nodded to Airmed, sat up straight, and asked her to proceed.

And so Elena's lessons in *fidchell* began.

"This is the king," Airmed explained, as she touched the golden piece in the center of the board. "He is protected by a guard of eight bronze soldiers. The sixteen silver pieces along the edges of the board are the opposing forces closing in on them—they are the attackers, and their aim is to pursue and capture the king. The bronze pieces, the defenders, aim to protect the king and help him escape through the corners of the board.

"In order for the attackers to win, they must capture the king by surrounding him on all four sides. If the king evades them and escapes through a corner of the board, he wins. Only one piece may move at a time, in any direction, but only in a straight line—never diagonally—and as far as the player chooses so long as the path is unblocked by an opposing piece. To capture an opponent's piece, called a move of banishment, the opponent's piece must be flanked on two sides. Banishing must be active, not passive—meaning, a piece may move through two opposing pieces without being banished. However, it can only do so as part of its path—if it stops between two opposing pieces, it is automatically banished. Attackers cannot move through the center space, the king's throne. However, if the king is on a space immediately next to his throne, he may be captured if surrounded on three sides."

Elena listened carefully, studying the board as Airmed spoke. There were several things that stood out to her. The side attacking the king would most likely move the corner pieces last, since the king could only escape through the corners. Second, the side defending the king should attempt to move their pieces in a way to keep the king protected on at least one side at all times. The rules sounded easy enough, but Elena had a feeling that playing the game would be much easier said than done.

Within two minutes of the start of the first game, Elena had lost. It happened so quickly that she didn't really understand what had taken place. It was like a whirlwind, Elena's pieces banishing one after another, while Airmed's attackers closed in on the king. In the blink of an eye, the king was captured.

"Just relax a little, Ele," Gavin said as he pulled a chair with him across the floor and came to sit beside Elena, turning the chair around so he could sit facing the backrest, his arms folded over the top, his golden-green gaze fixed on the board with a smile.

Galen did the same, bringing his seat to Elena's opposite side and sitting down almost daintily, crossing his left leg over his right before weaving his long black hair into a braid. His light blue gaze settled on

Airmed. "Again," he said to the goddess of healing, and so continued the first few hours of Elena's tutelage.

They proved to be the most difficult hours, with Elena losing again and again, while the twins tried to explain to her the strategy behind Airmed's moves. Bryce became frustrated within the first hour, and left the pavilion for her room. Sometime in the middle of the day, Elena looked up and saw her with Tarōbō, lying beside him and looking down on the game from a trellised opening between the canopy and dome above them. The Kirin and Eiry remained in the pavilion the entire day, the Kirin observing quietly from the same seat while Eiry sometimes paced around the room. Melia brought lunch sometime in the early afternoon, but Elena hardly ate anything.

As the hours passed by, and with the help of the twins, a few patterns began to emerge. Getting the king to an empty row or column, for instance, was the best option for the defenders to win. If Elena could manage to place the king on an unobstructed row or column along the edges of the board that had both end corners open, she would win, since Airmed would only be able to block her path to one of the corners, her turn limited to the movement of only one piece. Those kinds of openings, however, were rare. Elena saw it only a few times, and every time her king was boxed in near his throne and she couldn't move him to the edges of the board.

Flanking the king with at least two defenders proved to be a reasonable defense strategy, but it was much more effective if Elena left a space between the defenders and the king, since any attacker who landed between them was automatically banished. She focused on this tactic for a while before she stumbled onto the happy discovery, while she was playing against Galen, that four defenders worked even better. If she flanked the king with a defender on each side and spaces in between, it created a kind of shield. However, the tactic had two major weaknesses.

The first was the shape of the shield. Protecting the king in this manner created a cross-shaped shield around the king, with the king as the center of the cross and a defender at each end, with spaces in between. This shield, however, was still open to attack if Elena moved the king into any of the four open spaces between him and his four defenders, since the space around the cross was still accessible to attackers. If she moved the king into the open space to his left, for instance, attackers could be placed above and below him, along the arm of the cross, to capture the king. This meant the shield was only effective if the king remained stationary.

Keeping the king stationary within the shield revealed the second weakness of this tactic. It only worked as long as the remaining four defenders on the board, the ones not used to create the shield, remained active. If the remaining four defenders were banished, Elena's only choices were to move the king within the shield, where he could be captured, or break the shield and risk the capture of the king. Either scenario proved fatal in games against all three of Elena's tutors.

Even so, Elena didn't give up on the concept of the shield. She was certain there had to be some kind of way to expand it to protect the king from all sides, and allow him the freedom to move within the shield without risk of capture if Elena ran out of pieces to move. Sometime in the late afternoon, Elena found her answer while she was playing against Gavin.

Instead of making a shield in the shape of a cross, she could use four defenders to form a box around the king, making sure she left an open space between every piece. This box-shield was impregnable and the king could move freely within it, creating a stalemate. The box could be expanded to include eight defenders, but that was virtually impossible to create since it required the use of every defender on the board.

Elena was so excited by her discovery that she actually cried out when she realized it, slamming her fists on the table and almost falling out of her chair.

To Elena's surprise, Galen caught her. "About fucking time," he grunted, as Gavin grinned at Elena over the board.

"If you knew, why didn't you just tell me?" Elena snapped back at him, crossing her arms over her chest.

A smile ghosted over Galen's lips, as he watched her through the corner of his eye. "Because if I just gave these things away, Elena, you would never really learn the strategy behind the game. You would just parrot, and you'd lose in a heartbeat. Last time I checked, you didn't want that."

Elena hated to admit he was right. Instead, she glared at him and then after a second nudged his arm and whispered a "thank you" before returning her attention to the board.

"The likelihood of forming the box-shield without the attacker intervening is very small," Airmed cautioned Elena, "almost near impossible because the attacker will always be striving to restrict your movements by boxing the defenders in. Have you noticed any patterns in the offense's strategy?"

Elena had. "I've noticed the attacker tends to go for a diagonal pattern to box in the defenders. It looks like it's the easiest pattern to achieve from the outset because of their starting position. The defenders start from an already cloistered position. If the attackers close in on them and restrict their movements, the king will never break free and escape."

"That's right," Galen interjected, running his fingers along his braid, his eyes on Elena instead of the board. "And with a diagonal pattern, the attacker can surround the defender with a diamond-shaped wall and continue to close in on you, banishing defenders until reaching the king. This can even be done without moving a single attacker from the four corners of the board."

"All this time I've been playing as a defender. Shouldn't I practice playing as an attacker?"

"If you choose this variation of the game," Airmed replied, "you will automatically play as the defender. That is why I've focused this part of your lessons on defending. And as you've seen for yourself, defending is also a good way to learn about the attacker's strategy. I think this is a good point to begin instruction on the second variant of the game."

The twins agreed, and everyone watched quietly as Airmed began to set up the game, having switched seats with Gavin, who had resumed his perch beside Elena. Eiry had stopped pacing minutes before and pulled up a chair behind Airmed, his eyes on Elena.

"You need to eat, Ele," he said gently, looking down at his watch as if that would give him the correct time.

"Shinigami-sama is right, Elena-san," the Kirin said as he moved closer, switching seats to the couch closest to the table.

Elena sat back in her chair, taking the moment to relax for the first time in hours. The late afternoon sun spilled into the room through the open wall, the sea below much calmer than it had been the day before. The water in the basin fountain was as still as a mirror, even though it flowed in a thin and steady stream over the edges of the basin, along its sides into a circular channel at its base.

"I'll eat when Melia comes with dinner," Elena assured the two of them before returning her attention to the board.

The arrangement for the second variation of *fidchell* was completely different from the first. Both sides had equal number of pieces, with nine silver pieces placed on Elena's end of the board, on the first three rows, and nine bronze pieces placed in the same fashion on Airmed's side of the board. Both sides had king pieces, rather than just one.

On the row closest to Elena, there were four silver pieces—one on the first, fourth, sixth and ninth spaces counting from left to the right, with a king piece made of blue dragonstone on the fifth space. On the second row there were three silver pieces—one on the second, fifth and eight spaces. On the third row there were two silver pieces—one on the first and ninth spaces. The arrangement on Airmed's end of the board mirrored Elena's, with her king piece made of red dragonstone. Together, the pieces formed three triangles on opposite ends of the board, with a center triangle protecting the king and a triangle on each side facing inward.

"The object of this variation is to conquer and destroy your enemy," Airmed explained. "Where the first variant is like a siege, think of this as warfare, with two opposing sides made up of nine warriors each, and their king, on an open battlefield. Like before, warriors and their king can move in any direction so long as it is a straight line and their path is not obstructed. Banishing works in the same way, by surrounding the enemy on two sides, including the kings. The first side to lose its king loses the battle."

Airmed's explanation made the game seem easy enough—Elena no longer had to be concerned with the corners of the board, the number of warriors were now even and the starting positions were equally balanced—but that proved to be deceiving. Having to capture the enemy king while protecting her own was difficult and fractured her focus. Before, to move to the corners of the board, she needed to protect her king and could rally all of his defenders around him. Now, she had to divide her numbers, some to protect her king and others to actively pursue the enemy's.

Actively pursuing the enemy king also made it doubly hard to manage a shield, the peculiar starting positions making the box-shield much harder to achieve than before. The same was also true for the diagonal attack approach from the first variant of the game. Elena had a little more success forming the cross-shield, but she faced the same problems as before; the king had to remain stationary, and when her other warriors were banished then her only option was to break the shield and risk the capture of her king.

All of the patterns Elena had relied on before were no longer reliable, and by the time dinner was brought in, Elena felt fairly certain she was better at the first variant of the game than the second. After dinner, another hour was spent on the second variant of the game before Airmed announced that Elena's strengths were better suited to the first variant. By this time, Tarōbō and Bryce had rejoined them, and everyone had crowded around to watch Elena play the last few hours of the evening. A dessert cart had been brought in after dinner, and Bryce had already devoured half of the cart. Tarōbō had produced some tea and was preparing it with the Kirin's help.

As they enjoyed dessert and Tarōbō's tea, Elena played against the twins and Airmed continuously, and even twice with Eiry, before Airmed finally announced they had reached the end of her lessons, sometime before the witching hour had passed.

"I have taught you all that I can. May the morrow bring you what you seek, Elena Dionysia," Airmed said to Elena as she prepared to take her leave. "Remember not to rely on might alone," she added and then, with a warm smile and a graceful bow of her head, sable-haired Airmed took her leave.

THE ANXIETY didn't really kick in until Elena was alone in the bath. Like everything else in this realm, it was ultra luxurious—a large hexagon cut into the floor in the center of the room, which was also hexagonal in shape and carved entirely out of alabaster dragonstone with arcades of honeycombed arches and columns carved in relief out of walls of solid stone. Elena sat near the edge of the bath, looking up at the domed roof, her mind drifting. The panic was uncoiling, deep inside of her, like a waking snake; it made her breathing shallow and her eyes sting with tears, but Elena blinked them back, trying not to let her fear get the best of her.

Even though the Kirin had promised her that the Queen's spells could not bind him to this realm, Elena was still very much afraid about the consequences of losing tomorrow's challenge. There was always the chance the Kirin was mistaken, compounded by the fact that Elena would not be able to save Cataline if she didn't recover the Helm. Neither outcome was an option, and yet Elena couldn't escape the reality that she had no chance of winning at *fidchell* against the Queen. Like any game meant to measure skill in strategy and tactics, *fidchell* was not something Elena could hope to conquer in a day.

Closing her eyes, Elena eased down into the bath until she was below the surface of the water. Instantly, every sound became muffled, and every thought faded until the only thing that existed was the steady beating of her heart. Several seconds later, Elena heard a second sound, stronger than her heart but just as pleasant; a deep, steady rumble that reverberated through the water, echoing against the melody of her heart until it matched it. Only then did Elena recognize it as a dragon's breathing. An image flashed through her mind, so vivid it startled her— the white dragon from her dream, his scales gleaming in the sunlight, his eyes carved of red stone. Elena pushed herself to the surface of the water, struggling to breathe as she reached for the edge of the bath.

Eiry was standing there, still decked in an impeccable suit and tie. The first thing Elena saw was his dark shoes, and then his watch as he reached for her hand.

"Elena, are you okay?" he asked her, his eyes wide with worry. "For a second, I couldn't feel you anymore."

"What?" Elena didn't understand what he was saying. She was struggling to catch her breath and wrap her mind around what she had just seen.

Eiry was looking down at her, and Elena suddenly remembered where she was. She would have been doubly mortified if Melia hadn't put herbs and some kind of honeyed milk into her bath, which allowed her some semblance of modesty, not that Elena would have minded if he just pulled her out of the water right then and there and kissed her the way he had before, but of course that didn't happen.

"I didn't feel you," Eiry repeated, suddenly remembering himself and averting his gaze to give her some privacy. "I got worried. I called your name out, and when you didn't answer, I came inside."

Elena smiled, in spite of herself. It made her happy that he was always worried about her. It was incredibly selfish of her to feel that way, but she couldn't help it. "I'm fine. My head was running a mile a minute so I slipped underwater for a second to see if it would stop. It makes the world stop spinning. What do you mean, you didn't feel me anymore?"

Once he was certain she was fine, Eiry stepped away from the bath and took a seat on a couch against the wall, which sat between two columns and beneath an ornate arch.

"I can feel your presence," he said in a whisper. "I always have, ever since the day you were born. I can technically do it with any human, since being Death connects me to the thread of every life, but with you it's always been constant. It was the same with your mother. This is the second time in my life I haven't been able to feel you. The first was when you entered the Kamo Vault."

Elena nodded, her attention caught by something he said. Was there a connection between what had just happened and the Kamo Vault? The Kamo clan were neutrals, *aequus* who neutralized the power of the gods with the explicit intent to protect humans. Dragons were not *aequus*, since they were not human, but they seemed to be the divine equivalent of them. If Elena had understood the Kirin correctly, any divine being born outside of a pantheon served this purpose; to maintain the balance in nature disturbed by the divine. It seemed to Elena that their purpose in neutralizing the reach of the gods mirrored that of the *aequus*. In fact, this shared purpose was so strong that it interfered, in some fashion, with Eiry's connection to her; it was strong enough to interfere with Death's reach. More importantly, if dragons were divine creatures that neutralized the influence of the gods for the purpose of restoring balance, how had Queen Áine managed to keep them? And by that same token, would she able to do the same to the Kirin? Were the Kirin so different from dragons?

"What are you thinking?" Eiry asked Elena, interrupting her thoughts. He had leaned forward in his seat, his elbows resting on his knees, and was watching her intently, wringing his hands in front of his chest.

Elena had been so lost in her thoughts that she hadn't realized minutes had passed in complete silence. "I'm working through something," she told him, half of her still lost in her thoughts. She knew the connection she had just made was important, but she had no idea how, and perhaps it didn't really matter. "We'll talk about it when I get out of the bath, yes?"

Eiry narrowed his eyes, doubtful. His features smoothed and he continued to watch her, struggling with some inner conflict that he would never share. Then he pushed himself to his feet and with a silent nod stepped out of the bathroom, leaving Elena to her thoughts.

ELENA'S SLEEP WAS TROUBLED. She dreamt of *yōkai* and Kirin, of the four guardians of Kyoto and Aosaginohi's quiet voice. The dream then shifted into fragmented images, eerie and undefined. Nurarihyon hosting a party for the Hyakki Yakō in the Kamo Vault. Mr. Inoue and the Abe twins—the three dressed in the traditional robes of the *onmyōdō*—competing in a drinking contest against Shōjō the red-haired sea sprite, Byakko the White Tiger and a woman made of smoke. Alexander sitting on top of a grid of drawers, Elena at his side—wearing her mother's white funeral *kimono* and the Necklace of Harmonia around her neck.

Later, she dreamt of a giant game of *fidchell* where the pieces were gods. On one side were the Dananns, on the other dragons in humanoid form. Elena was among them, standing on the same space as a man with long white hair and crimson eyes; the king piece among a sea of dragon warriors born of stone. Elena was linked to each one the way Eiry was linked to her, her life connected to their thread. Each move of banishment was a physical blow; a wound to Elena's soul, chipping away at her strength as each warrior fell before her. Elena woke with a cry when the dragon-king fell before her eyes.

The room was silent. Even the ocean was still. The dawn was beginning to break, and the darkness in the room was receding. Someone touched the small of her back and Elena flinched, turning to find Eiry studying her, concerned. Lately, it felt as if all Elena did was put him in a constant state of concern.

"I'm sorry," she whispered to him, lowering her gaze. She held her hands in front of her, and Eiry reached for one silently, lacing his fingers with hers. His hand was ice-cold, but the difference in temperature was no longer striking, and didn't feel as extreme.

"Sorry for what?" Eiry asked her gently, reaching for the glass of water on the side table while still holding her hand. He handed it to Elena quietly.

Elena accepted it with an uneasy smile, momentarily distracted by how close Eiry's body was to hers; she had fallen asleep in Eiry's arms again, like she had every night from the moment he saved her on Mount Inari. Every moment with him was intimate, and yet painfully chaste and controlled. Whatever was between them, if anything at all, was buried by the weight of their journey and the future ahead; how Elena's parents had found the strength to bear the weight of both was beyond her.

"For always making you worry," Elena told him, as a knock was heard at the door.

Eiry was out of bed in an instant. Elena watched the silhouette of his back as he reached for a robe, and then made his way to the door. After a brief exchange, and giving Elena enough time slip out of bed and into a robe, he opened the door for the Kirin to come in.

"Forgive my intrusion at such an early hour," said the Kirin to the both of them with a gentle bow of his head, and then made his way to a seating area in the corner of the room.

Elena followed him quietly, taking a seat at his side. With a courteous bow, Eiry excused himself and disappeared into the bathroom.

"There's nothing to forgive, Kiyoshi-sama," Elena assured the Kirin, wishing she had something to offer him, some tea, but there was nothing. "I was already up."

The Kirin watched her, his topaz gaze unreadable. Elena had a feeling he might know of her dream, but, if he did, he did not say. After several quiet seconds, his expression smoothed. He reached into his robes and retrieved something, placing it gently in Elena's hands.

"This is for you," he said quietly, and offered Elena an enigmatic smile. "Please keep it with you always."

The Kirin removed his hand to reveal a necklace of cabochon topaz and hand-carved *ojime* beads of yellow jade. The topaz was identical to the color of his eyes, and the yellow jade indistinguishable from the golden glow of his gaze when roused. The beads were strung interchangeably, eight of each, by the use of a thin woven chain of starlight metal. At the bottom of the thread, where two topaz cabochon met, a metal ring connected the necklace to a *netsuke*, or toggle, by the use of a ninth *ojime* bead that hung vertically from the main body of the necklace. The *netsuke* was made of a pearlescent silvery stone carved into the shape of a peony flower beginning to bloom.

The gesture, and his gift, was so beautiful that Elena was at a complete loss for words. She held the necklace in the palm of her hands, unsure of herself. "This is too much, Kiyoshi-sama," she whispered, raising her gaze to meet his.

"This is how it should be, Elena-san," the Kirin replied, placing his hands over hers, holding the necklace between them. "It is a show of trust among my kind. Our paths have been woven together. Once a Kirin's purpose is revealed, his life and being are devoted to it entirely. In the future, if there are places you go that I cannot reach, this will bind us together. The chain is woven out of my hair, and the *netsuke* out of one of my scales. It was fashioned with an ancient spell that will keep us connected even when apart. My life and being are yours, Elena-san."

Elena shook her head. Tears stung her eyes. She was staring at the Kirin, her hands trembling. This was too much. It was hard enough Eiry was devoting everything he had to her. "I am not worthy of such a gift, Kiyoshi-sama. Who am I for you to devote yourself to? I'm just a human girl trying my hardest to stay alive long enough to save a friend."

The Kirin, infinitely patient, gave Elena a knowing smile. "It is precisely for that reason, Elena-san. You cannot see it now, but you are different from the ones who came before you. Whether you believe it or not, you are an integral part of a much-needed change that is to come. It is my job to see you through it."

With those words, the Kirin took the necklace out of Elena's hands and placed it over her head. The *netsuke* rested just below the center of her collar. The moment it touched her skin, Elena felt the Kirin's warm energy wash over her. She felt the same way she did when she rode on his back, connected and safe.

"Wear it always," the Kirin said in gentle plea, and with a kiss to her brow he made his way out of the room before Elena could say another word.

THE TIME FOR THE *DÚSHLÁN* had finally come, and Elena and her escort found themselves being led through the halls by Creidhne, the dark-haired soldier and Danann artificer. He led them deep into the heart of the palace, to halls that were older and seemingly more esoteric than the ones before. No less whimsical, they reflected a much older race, a race of beings still closely tied to an ancient mysticism worshipped in earthen halls and temples befit of arcane rites.

The path led them deeper into the earth, closer and closer to the ocean, which now echoed through the halls steadily, reverberating against carefully hewn stone. Where everything above them had been polished and faceted to create an opulence worthy of the gods, here the dragonstone was left in its raw form, carved and decorated beautifully but less ornately than before. Here, the true soul of the Danann was not only felt, but seen.

Creidhne led them silently, through barely illuminated halls in spite of the constant use of braziers; it was as if the darkness here took a life of its own, so far away from the reach of the rising sun. The deeper they went, the stronger the darkness became. With the loss of visibility came the enhancement of sound. Soon, the roar of the ocean swallowed every sound. Through it, Elena recognized the steady rhythm of a dragon's breathing, faint at first but growing louder as they continued deeper into the halls. If anyone else heard it, they didn't mention it out loud. Only through the necklace did Elena feel the Kirin's recognition of it, and the erratic imprint of his response.

Seconds later, they found themselves standing before a massive set of doors, identical to the ones leading into their room but twice as large and made entirely of white stone, one hundred times whiter than the alabaster dragonstone. Two braziers stood before it, one at each side, their light reflecting against the surface of the doors and illuminating the hall.

As Elena and her party approached the doors, they opened of their own accord, revealing a large cavernous room hollowed out of raw alabaster dragonstone. A large subterranean lake took up the majority of the space, surrounded by walls decorated with a colonnade of arches and columns carved in relief against solid stone. Its surface was mirror-like and reached the base of the columns. The space itself had the feel of a natural grotto selected as a temple for worship.

Along the right side of the lake was a narrow causeway of hewn stone that led to a raised pavilion, which extended from the right side of the room partly over the water. A portico supported by ornate arches created three open walls and a roof for the pavilion and its section of tiered seating, which grew out of the solid wall on the right.

Creidhne led Elena and her party up the causeway to the pavilion, where Queen Áine and the Faerie Host waited. A small table with two lavishly carved chairs was set up in the center of the pavilion. To their left, closest to the water, was a raised dais with three empty chairs. To the right was the wall of tiered seating, which held a throne of hewn stone in the center, against the back wall, where the Queen currently sat surrounded by her Faerie Host.

As they reached the pavilion, Queen Áine stood, followed by Nuada Airgetlám, his wife Macha, and Manannán mac Lir—who winked at Elena as she met his gaze. His presence was a complete surprise, and Elena wasn't sure if it would be a blessing or a curse. The four of them made their way to the floor of the pavilion, where Queen Áine took her place beside the central table and the other three Dananns made their way to the raised dais with three empty chairs.

"Welcome," said the Queen to her guests, as Creidhne led Elena's party to six empty seats on the bottom tier, leaving Elena behind to take her place before the Queen.

As before, Queen Áine was a vision, this time in a gown of amber silk. She wore the necklace Tartarus had presented to her as tribute, the weir lights dancing merrily within its glass tear. Her hair was a tumble of copper locks that cascaded over her shoulders elegantly.

The other Dananns present were dressed just as spectacularly, the judges as beguiling as their Queen. Macha, the goddess of sovereignty, wore a rich gown the color of red currants that complimented the paleness of her skin and golden undertones of her hair. Silver-haired Nuada wore a dignified tunic of sapphire blue, and Manannán mac Lir the ash-blue tunic Elena had seen before with his color-changing cloak of green, silver and blue.

Next to them, Elena had never felt so human.

"Have you chosen the variant of the game you will play, Child of Dionysus?" asked Manannán mac Lir, addressing Elena.

With a steady intake of breath, Elena answered, "The siege, My Lord."

"Excellent choice," replied the god of the sea and motioned for his brethren to take their seats on the dais; Macha the middle and her husband the one to her right.

Then Manannán mac Lir turned toward the lake, which none but the audience was facing. With a wave of his hand, a mist began to take shape over the surface of the water. Little by little it grew, reaching the pavilion and spilling onto it in a single fluid motion, until finally it carpeted the whole of the cavernous room. Then with another gesture of his hands, jointly downward and then breaking open to each side, the mist parted.

Now sitting on the table, between Elena and the Queen, was a *fidchell* board carved of white dragonstone, its edges, corners, and rows inlaid in bronze. The Queen's attackers were fashioned of red dragonstone, and Elena's defenders of blue. The single king-piece was carved of the same white dragonstone as the board.

Immediately behind Manannán mac Lir, as the mists parted over the lake's surface, a life-size version of the board appeared. Eighty-one interlocking basalt columns rose out of the lake to form the board, like a miniature version of the Giant's Causeway. Twenty-five beings, some of which Elena recognized, stood on the basalt board. Sixteen of them were dressed in red, eight in blue and one in black—the starless shade eclipsed by the pale color of the being's skin and hair. All of them were divine creatures the Dananns held as slaves.

Elena froze as the black-clad king turned to meet her gaze. White-haired and crimson-eyed, it was the dragon-king she had seen in her dream.

CHAPTER EIGHTEEN

EVERYTHING SLOWED when Elena met those crimson eyes, so similar to Eiry's in color and yet completely different.

The crimson-eyed dragon-king stood motionless in the center of the board, a magnificent creature with hair the same color as his pure white skin, the long strands burnished silk against black-scaled armor belted at the waist with a crimson sash. In him, the difference between god and mythical beast was clear.

Like the Kirin, he was an enlightened being, but seemingly more primitive and fierce. He was a force of nature somehow contained within a human form that was much too fragile to accommodate him. Even now, Elena could see the hum of energy pushing outward from the inside of his skin, constantly seeking release.

Looking across the length of the basalt board, Elena was reminded of her dream. She had been connected to every dragon on the board, and had felt their pain when each was overcome. The last to fall had been the dragon-king. While the faces were different now, the gist of it was the same.

A cold anger settled in the pit of Elena's stomach. It was faint at first, but was quickly fed by a burning heat in the center of her chest, where the blooming *netsuke* rested against her skin. It was then that Elena realized her anger was not just her own.

At that moment, the Kirin's consciousness brushed gently against hers and molded itself around Elena's until her body could accommodate them both. At first, Elena's skin felt too tight, as he settled into the cramped spaces beneath her skin. Then just as quickly, everything snapped into place.

"What is the meaning of the second board?" Elena asked Queen Áine, surprised at the disapproving tone in her voice. She had been wondering about it, but hadn't considered asking. The Kirin, however, wanted an answer, now.

It was an odd sensation, to share her consciousness with another being. If Elena had considered it possible, she would have thought it would happen with Eiry first; Eiry who was staring at her now, intently, knowing something was off. Elena was seldom this curt.

The question took the Queen by surprise. She narrowed her eyes and took Elena's measure once again. Her lips settled into a thin line, as her fingers traced the spine of her chair. Then, with a forced smile, she settled into her seat, the causeway of stone and lakeshore visible behind her.

"Certain challenges call for a more elaborate display of the game," the Queen said to Elena in an expertly controlled voice. "When King Arthur played against Owein son of Urien, their game was reflected in the battle that raged between their forces. Consider the basalt board our battleground."

Elena's features smoothed, mimicking the Kirin's mood, who sat still as the dead in his seat, expressionless. Neither of them trusted the Queen, and the presence of the basalt board made Elena uncomfortable. "How accurately will our game be reflected upon the basalt board, Your Majesty?"

"You need not concern yourself with such things, Elena Dionysia. Gods cannot die, and I was careful not to place humans on the board," the Queen said magnanimously.

"Even gods can experience pain," Elena replied, her voice strained. The Kirin's consciousness bristled inside of her. A flash of anger clouded her gaze for an instant, before his energy settled once more. From the corner of her eye, Elena saw Eiry shift in his seat.

The Queen's smile deepened, but Elena saw the suspicion in her gaze. She couldn't reconcile Elena's current manner with the girl she had met before; but, being a mercurial creature herself, she expected everyone else's personalities to be as erratic as hers.

"Yes, that is true, but pain is fleeting," replied the Queen at last, her tone guarded. "They are simply providing entertainment for the Host, and they are happy to do it. It is their duty as slaves."

"I was not aware the dragon-king was a slave," Elena said sharply, holding the Queen's gaze, the Kirin's anger making her bold.

Instantly, the Queen's expression became hostile. The transformation was jarring, her beauty twisting into something terrible and cruel. "Know your place, *human*," she growled, hissing the last word venomously.

The blooming *netsuke* burned against Elena's skin, as the Kirin's consciousness blazed white-hot in Elena's mind. From the corner of her eye, Elena saw Eiry stand, the twins quickly grabbing his wrists and pulling him back down into his chair. Tarōbō looked wary, and his hand was already at the hilt of his *katana*. Bryce's expression was blank. The Kirin was staring at the Queen with open hostility.

Elena turned her gaze toward them, begging them silently to stand down.

Manannán mac Lir cleared his throat. "I assure you, Child of Dionysus, that the dragon-king is on the board of his own volition."

Elena turned her face partly to the right and chanced a look at the board, past the heads of the three judges. Her gaze met the dragon-king's, who nodded almost imperceptibly, his face as expressionless as before.

There was obviously more to this *dúshlán* than met the eye, and Elena got the distinct feeling she was in over her head again. Ever since she held her mother's necklace in her hand, all that she had been doing was treading water. This situation was no exception.

"Now, if you are ready to proceed, the first move goes to the attacker." With a wave of his hand, Manannán mac Lir brought everyone's attention to the board, and the tournament began.

THE QUEEN'S OPENING MOVE was to begin a diagonal formation from the side of the board. With her delicate fingers, she picked up a red gaming piece to Elena's left and moved it into position. The move was reflected on the basalt board immediately, with the corresponding god—the missing cat from the Chinese zodiac, according to the Kirin—taking a step forward to the appropriate basalt column. The room held its collective breath, a shower of applause erupting around them once the god-slave was in position.

It took all of Elena's control not to roll her eyes. If this was going to be a trend, it would get old quickly. Elena closed her eyes and breathed in deeply, concentrating on the warmth of the blooming *netsuke* against her skin, hidden beneath the fabric of her dress. Its warmth radiated through her chest and ribs, calming the tension in her body. When she opened her eyes, she was much more focused than before, never mind the incredulous look she was getting from the Queen. Elena took her time, considering all of her options before settling on an opening move of her own. The longer she took, the more impatient the Queen seemed to become, which only made Elena want to move slower.

The pace of the game continued in the same fashion for an hour without the banishment of any pieces, with the Queen making her moves decisively while Elena took her time at every turn. If Elena stopped to think about it, the lack of banishments was a miracle. Rather than get overly excited about her streak of luck, though, she decided her time was best spent focusing on the game; while the Queen didn't seem to break a sweat, it was taking all of Elena's concentration to keep her defenders on the board and the dragon-king intact.

Elena was in the midst of trying to inch the dragon-king away from the center of the board, when the Queen managed to flank one of his guards.

Seeing the banishment play out on the basalt board, once the Queen had removed the corresponding blue piece from the game board, was appalling. The Norse demigod Elena had seen the day before stepped into the space behind the dragon-king's guard, a shape shifting seal-woman known as a Selkie. Brandishing a giant axe, he raised it over his head and brought it down in a distinctly mechanical movement, as if a force far more powerful than his will compelled him. He struck the Selkie across the back, who then crumbled beneath the weight of his attack, her piercing cry echoing through the cavernous room. Then, with a blank expression on his face, he dragged her to the edge of the basalt board and threw her into the lake.

Elena's blood ran cold. The display was barbaric, made worse by the look of despair Elena saw in the face of the demigod as he returned to his proper place upon the board. There was no blood or ichor spilt on the mystical battleground, but the violence of the display was enough to make Elena feel sick. It was like the Roman Colosseum, but without the gladiators having any control over their own movements; their survival depended solely on the abilities of a capricious Queen and a human girl.

Disgusted, Elena turned her gaze away from the basalt board and returned her attention to the Queen, who was holding the blue game piece in her hands.

"Do not fret, Elena Dionysia," said the Queen with delight in her voice, "the Selkie is not dead. The waters of the lake are healing waters."

"I did not agree to this," Elena hissed between clenched teeth. She felt nauseous, and was finding it difficult to keep herself under control with the Kirin's anger fueling her own. How could creatures so strikingly beautiful on the outside be so savage within?

"You are welcome to forfeit anytime, and leave the Kirin in my care," the Queen said sweetly, and placed the banished game piece on her side of the table.

Anger stirred inside of Elena once again, but she focused her energy on staying calm. Forfeiting was not an option, and the Queen was keenly aware of that fact. She was toying with Elena, and Elena refused to give the bitch any satisfaction. She might be at the mercy of the gods once again, but Elena would be damned if she was going to let this woman get the best of her.

The Queen smiled, and motioned for Elena to make her next move.

Within ten minutes, the Queen had banished a second defender, this time a Hindu Asura with blue skin and dark purple hair. Asura were power seeking divine beings of the Hindu pantheon, generally associated with negative qualities. The Queen's attacker, a German Ondine—a female water spirit—with her thick blonde hair woven into a long fish-tail braid, caused an arm made of churning water to rise from the lake and close over the Asura's body, who then struggled for several minutes within the column of water until his body grew limp. The same watery hand then plucked the Asura's form off the basalt board and pulled him beneath the surface of the lake.

The Queen, and most of the Host, watched the spectacle entranced, enjoying the violent display of godly powers. The fact that they took so much pleasure in such a gruesome exhibition made Elena furious, so she decided to rob the Queen of her entertainment as much as she possible could.

With a focused effort, Elena began to maneuver the dragon-king toward the corners of the board, determined not to lose another guard. It was a difficult task, and her moves took twice the time as they did before, but with the help of the Kirin, whose energy kept her calm and encouraged, Elena managed to push another two hours without incident.

The strain on her was excruciating and Elena began to feel drained, fast. Soon, the tension between her and the Queen was palpable, weighing much more heavily on Elena than the goddess. By the fifth hour of play, Elena's mind was jelly and she was on the verge of physical collapse, the Kirin's energy the only thing keeping her seated on her chair. Manannán mac Lir paused the tournament for the afternoon meal, but Elena chose not to join them. Instead, she begged Eiry to take her to their room. The Kirin's consciousness had withdrawn from hers by then, and she fell fast asleep by the time Eiry helped her into bed, too tired to dream.

EIRY WOKE HER GENTLY a half an hour later, a steaming cup of Airmed's medicine waiting for her. The vial of ambrosia sat beside it on the table next to the bed. Airmed's medicine would clear Elena's mind, and the ambrosia restore her physical strength. Eiry looked Elena over as she quietly sipped Airmed's infusion.

"You're doing great, Ele," he whispered, as he leaned closer to brush her hair away from her face. He pressed the back of his hand to her forehead and smiled. "Your fever's gone."

Airmed's infusion was slightly more bitter than usual, but Elena drained the cup without complaint. She would do whatever it took to feel better, because at the rate she was going she wouldn't last another second against the Queen. "What's going on with me anyway?" Elena asked Eiry, the fog already clearing from her mind. She placed the empty cup on the table and reached for the ambrosia. After taking a measured dose, she lay back down and stretched against the pillows behind her.

Eiry put away the vial of ambrosia and quickly returned to the bed, sitting down gently beside Elena. "*Fidchell* is a difficult game," he began to explain, his eyes on hers. "It is more like a test of wills. Playing takes a mental and physical toll on the players. There are gods here who have tried to win their freedom for thousands of years, and have been unable to stand against the Queen the way you are now. The concentration required to do what you have been doing, avoiding her assaults and protecting your defenders, it has a huge effect on your human body."

"Like when I used to concentrate for hours studying for an exam in school," Elena mused, studying his handsome features. "An hour of that was more tiring than an hour playing sports, not that I ever played sports." Elena felt a little lightheaded, and the look Eiry was giving her made her giggle.

"Do you feel all right? You sound a little drunk," he said playfully, and watched her with an amused look on his face. "You're drunk on ambrosia," he observed, and tried to hide the grin.

"Maybe."

"Well, that's not good. I'll ask Melia to bring you some food. I should have known better than let you drink these things on an empty stomach."

"Can I kiss you?"

"What?"

Eiry watched her, his icy gaze narrowed. "Ele," he began to say, but Elena didn't let him finish.

Without thinking it over too much, she pressed her mouth to his. His lips were hard at first, like ice, but then softened, molding to hers. He wrapped his arms around her and pulled her close. Their kiss deepened. His fingers bit into her arms and back, her own clawing at the multiple pieces of clothing he always wore. She managed to get his blazer half off and undo his tie, his own hands fumbling with the buttons of her dress, when he suddenly stopped himself.

"This isn't the time," he whispered against Elena's mouth, his voice gravelly. His hands wrapped around her arms and he held her still, his chest pressing against hers as he breathed.

"Fuck the timing, Eiry," Elena hissed, uncharacteristically aggressive. Frustrated, she pushed and shoved at him, annoyed when he stayed as rooted as a mountain. Worst of all, he just watched her, completely amused. Finally, he caught her wrists with one hand and held her still, his grip like a vice.

"Ele, in just a few minutes, we need to get you fed and back in that hall. This isn't the time. I can't be a distraction for you—I *won't* be." His voice was gentle. He rested his forehead against hers, and sighed into her mouth. He let go of her wrists and gently cupped her cheeks, placing a single kiss on her forehead before pulling away. "Come on, princess. You have a Queen to beat."

THE TOURNAMENT RESUMED the moment Eiry walked Elena back into the cavernous room, the last to arrive.

The moment Elena sat down in her chair, the *netsuke* burned against her skin and the Kirin's consciousness joined with hers. The Queen resumed the game aggressively. Elena struggled to keep her defenders one step ahead. An hour or so after resuming the game, Elena saw an opening that the Queen missed, Elena's first opportunity to banish an attacker.

Elena reached to move her game piece into position, but suddenly hesitated. Her fingers hovered over the piece before she withdrew her hand. She turned her gaze away from the game and looked toward the basalt board. If she made her move, one of the god-slaves on that board would be forced to cut down another. It didn't matter to Elena whose side the god was on; either way, she refused to participate in the grotesque spectacle that the Queen enjoyed so much.

"Why do you hesitate?" asked the Queen, unamused. "It is a logical move. I made a mistake, and you should benefit from it."

"Why should I play by your rules?" Elena replied, annoyed.

"Because it is the only way to win," the Queen said with a satisfied smile. She shifted her weight in her chair, and twirled several strands of her copper hair around her fingers.

Elena didn't answer her. Instead, she dropped her gaze to the board between them and studied it carefully. The object of the game was for her to get the dragon-king to the corners of the board. To do that, she didn't need to banish attackers; she just needed to evade them. It would be much more difficult to play in this manner, but there was no reason for her to be a part of the Queen's sadistic little ritual.

Elena moved a different defender, to the Queen's annoyance, and managed to do it again at least four more times in the next three hours. The Queen, becoming careless in her frustration, would scoff and balk each time, confounded that Elena refused to banish her attackers while somehow managing to keep the defenders from her reach. Elena ignored the Queen, and tried to use the woman's increasing anger to her advantage.

Even so, the game did not get any easier. Elena would come close to a corner only to find her path blocked and have to retreat, all the while struggling to keep her defenders close to the dragon-king. Still, she managed to stay one step ahead of the Queen. It wouldn't be enough to win, but it was enough to stay in the game for the time being.

The pace of the game slowed during the late afternoon and into the evening meal, when again the tournament was paused briefly. This time, Elena joined everyone for the meal. She excused herself early, and had Eiry take her back to their rooms for another dose of ambrosia. When they returned to the hall, Bryce and Galen had excused themselves to go rest in their rooms. Tarōbō, the Kirin and Gavin were sitting in the audience when the game resumed.

Soon, Elena and the Queen fell into the same cat and mouse pattern as before, with the Queen aggressively pursuing the dragon-king while Elena somehow successfully kept her attackers at bay. At some point, frustrated with the pace of the game, the Queen suggested Elena's approach was cowardly, but Elena decided it was best to ignore the jab and answered by blocking another one of the Queen's attackers.

Two hours after the evening meal, Bryce and Galen just having returned to the hall, the Queen managed to maneuver her attackers so that she could close in on the dragon-king from all sides, effectively cutting off the chase Elena had managed to keep up for hours. Now, the only option left for Elena, other than to actively begin to target attackers, was to successfully form a box-shield around the dragon-king, and with very little time. Soon, the Queen's attackers would be in the position to begin to pick defenders off one by one, after closing the noose around them.

Elena panicked and lost a third defender, a bird-deity, leaving Elena with only five. Seeing the bird-deity's banishment was particularly difficult, especially at the hands of a Dökkálfr—a Norse Dark Elf—who used a grotesque looking sword to cut through the center of the bird-deity's stomach before kicking him into the lake. He didn't seem at all perturbed by the actions he was compelled to take.

The Queen once again watched the brutal display with glee, impressed by the fruits of her own prowess. Elena wondered how many centuries it had taken for her to become like this. Áine was the Irish goddess of love, summer, and wealth. At some point in time, her personality must have mirrored those elements. Elena wondered what had twisted her into this. The Danann's mistrust of humans was understandable enough, considering it was the human Milesians who drove them underground like animals, but what could be responsible for this? Was it centuries of power struggles or was this simply the nature of the gods? Was it the same thing that had twisted Helios, god of the sun, into the sadistic monster that Elena had come to know?

A fit of rage erupted inside of Elena—anger that had been turning to fury slowly, without Elena ever realizing it. She was tired of being helpless, tired of living for the entertainment of gods. Her vision faltered, and something inside of her slid into place. White-hot, like the Kirin's anger, Elena felt it wash over her, then burn cold, filling every inch of her being and fusing with her completely.

Elena had felt something similar to this before, in the Stygian waters during Atropos's ritual. This was the weight of her godhood, her father's blood boiling inside of her, surfacing after a decade and a half of being sealed away. Elena felt it in every fiber of her being, and she knew she had changed; she didn't need to see the bewilderment on the Queen's face or hear the rumbling whispers in the crowd to know it.

Elena looked down at the board between her and the Queen, and it was as if she were looking at it for the first time. She saw patterns written in the stone, sealed in bronze. The paths became clear to her, humming with energy in a way that Elena could physically see. When she raised her gaze to look at the Queen, the woman appeared somehow diminished, less bright.

Suddenly, Elena realized that Airmed had given her the key. The Queen's weakness was her conceit, a woman who played for the sake of displaying her prowess. If given the opportunity to do so, the Queen would never pass it up.

Elena had five defenders left on the board. Four would be needed for the shield. That left her one to bait the Queen. The path was clear in front of her. All she had to do was sacrifice a single defender. Presented with the opportunity to banish a defender, the Queen would be unable to pass it up, and would be too blinded by her own self-worth to notice the weakness in her attack. The Queen had been out for blood from the beginning, and Elena's refusal to play by the rules had made her desperate for it. If Elena distracted the Queen with the scent of blood, the woman would miss what was happening with the other pieces around her. If Elena arranged the remaining pieces correctly, the sacrifice of her defender would set up the move needed for Elena to complete the shield.

Having made her choice, Elena began the play.

She would have to lure the Queen into the necessary position, which would take several moves but was not impossible. Ultimately, the Queen was not the kind of woman to end the game quickly and rob the audience of their entertainment. She would take down each defender viciously, leaving the capture of the dragon-king for last.

The Queen responded as predicted, too quick and eager for her own good, and the time came for the clinch much sooner than Elena had expected.

To her surprise, Elena felt herself hesitate. She didn't like the idea of sacrificing a defender, of being the reason another god-slave was cut down. The Queen, on the other hand, was already savoring another banishment, her green eyes gleaming with anticipation.

Elena prolonged the move and turned her gaze toward the judges, who sat patiently in their chairs observing the proceedings. Elena realized for the first time that not one of them had turned around throughout the tournament to witness a single one of the demonstrations on the basalt board.

Behind them, the dragon-king turned his attention to Elena, his crimson eyes cutting through the shadows of the hall, bright as embers. His consciousness touched hers, and Elena gasped. It was not warm, like the Kirin's, nor was it as cold as Eiry's touch; it was cool and textured, reptilian, as it asserted itself over her own.

"Sacrifice the defender," said a voice in Elena's mind, ancient and remarkably visceral. Against the beating of her own heart, Elena felt the familiar rhythm of his breathing. An image of him as a white dragon flashed before her eyes. Elena's fingers closed over the defender, and the dragon-king moved her hand of his own will.

Immediately, the Queen flanked the defender and banished him. On the basalt board, a woman dressed in scarlet robes with long ginger hair and ice-gray eyes began to move. She was a Japanese *kitsune*—a fox spirit—and she cut down Elena's defender, an Assyrian lightning deity, with the use of one of her many tails.

Without hesitating, the dragon-king moved Elena's fourth defender into its proper place, completing the box-shield around him.

The last thing Elena saw before she collapsed, as the dragon-king withdrew from her consciousness, was the shape of the defender on the basalt board taking his place beside the king.

When Elena opened her eyes, she was alone in bed.

The sun had risen and its warmth filled the room. Everything was quiet and still, except for the steady murmur of the ocean below.

Elena closed her eyes.

She breathed in deeply and allowed the breath to fill her lungs. She could taste the afternoon sun on the tip of her tongue, and savor the whisper of salt in the air.

For the first time in days, Elena felt relieved. A hint of anxiety bordered the edges of her consciousness, but for now Elena didn't concern herself with it. While she had no idea what had taken place after she collapsed, Elena knew one thing for sure—she had managed to stalemate the game.

As Elena lay in bed, allowing her mind to drift, she heard the soft murmur of voices coming from the pavilion between the rooms, indecipherable but distinctly cheerful. Curious, Elena eased herself out of bed and headed straight for the door.

The voices quickly became clearer.

"I'll agree Draig was impressive," said an apathetic voice, "but that's as far as I'm going."

"Ignore him. He was even more impressed with Elena," teased a second voice, "especially when Evius' blood surfaced."

"I was not!" Growled the first.

The sound of scuffling followed. A glass shattered on the ground. A fit of giggles drifted through the threshold, followed by a gnashing snarl.

"Enough," warned a third voice, sharply.

"I think it's safe to say we were all impressed with Elena," interjected a fourth voice, calm and gentle in its manner.

"Not Áine," cawed a fourth, and everyone laughed.

A sharp slap broke through the laughter.

"For the millionth time, Gavin, don't touch it," hissed the third voice, and Gavin yelped.

Elena reached the door and stepped through it.

All six of her companions were seated together in a cluster of couches near the open wall, a gleaming metal helm resting on the ornate coffee table between them.

Gavin was rubbing his hand with a sour expression on his face, ignoring the broken glass near his feet. Galen was threatening Eiry never to lay a finger on his twin again, while serving himself another drink. Bryce was staring at the helm, unnaturally quiet. Tarōbō and the Kirin observed the scene, unconcerned.

The moment Elena stepped into view, everyone froze and Galen reluctantly settled back into his seat. Elena's attention, however, was on the helm.

Corinthian in style, which covered the entire head and had stylized slits for the eyes and mouth, the helm was forged out of a single piece of black hematite. A crest of black horsehair ran from the front to the back of the cap. The front of the visor projected past the jaw to protect the neck. Asphodel fronds adorned the bottom corners of the projections and a curved neckpiece at the nape of the neck. A tight band of carved spirals ran along the inner edges of the projections, closest to the mouth, and continued upward, around the exaggerated slits for the eyes, meeting in a pointed dip at the top of the nose-guard. An identical band lined the edges of the cap. An ornate metal ridge fastened the crest to the cap, the front of which was capped by the head of a hound with an open maw, baring its fangs.

"Is that what I think it is?" Elena asked in a whisper. Already her body felt numb.

For a few moments, no answer came, and then suddenly everyone started talking at the same time, their voices clashing violently in Elena's mind.

She dropped onto the couch next to the Kirin, who placed his warm hand over hers. Elena's mind cleared, and the voices slowed to a decipherable pace. The blooming *netsuke* burned softly against her skin.

Gavin was going on about her divinity; how it had taken everyone by surprise, even the Queen. Galen spoke of a man called Draig who assisted Elena when she collapsed, and defended her against the angry

Queen. Eiry was discussing her successful stalemate and the panel's decision to grant her the Helm of Darkness, in addition to the Kirin's freedom.

Elena let them talk over each other. Soon, the three of them realized no one was listening and settled into an uncomfortable silence, with Eiry glaring at the twins.

"One at a time, please," Elena said to them, and rubbed her temple.

The three of them looked at each other, and Eiry finally conceded that Gavin should be the first to speak.

"It all happened very quickly," Gavin began, clearing his throat dramatically and shifting in his seat. He leaned forward, his golden-green gaze fixed intently on Elena. "The Queen must have said something to you, upset you in some way, because your divinity surfaced."

Elena recalled getting upset, but at the moment she couldn't remember what she had gotten upset about. She also recalled it had stirred something inside of her, the same thing that had stirred during Atropos's ritual to unseal her divinity. "What do you mean my divinity surfaced?"

Gavin smiled. He ran his hand through his amber curls, and then reached for a drink resting on the coffee table. "Demigods are what they are because of divine blood. Emotions stir that divinity. While in most instances demigods look like any other human, there are moments when their divinity physically manifests itself. It was very common in the old days, when the bloodlines weren't diluted and demigods were really half and half. I hadn't seen it in a really long time, though."

"How long?" Elena asked.

Gavin's smile deepened. "Probably like a millennia and a half?" He ventured a guess, turning to his twin for confirmation.

"A little more than that," Galen said with a shrug, his deep-blue eyes on Elena.

"And you're saying my dad's blood manifested during the game?" Elena asked Gavin.

"Towards the end of it," Gavin replied. "It was the turning point in the match. You took her completely by surprise. I doubt the Queen had ever seen a demigod manifest, let alone Evius's child. Your father's divinity has a huge effect on the Fae."

"How so?"

"He's the god of revelry, and the Fae have become a people of revelry during their time beneath the mounds. They revere his element, and are affected by it more strongly than others. You became her equal when you manifested, at the very least. It threw her off."

"What did it look like?" Elena asked, curious. She wondered if she changed the way Eiry and Bryce did.

Gavin grinned. "Your presence became stronger. Most humans don't have a very strong presence. Demigods tend to shine a little brighter, but with the diluted bloodlines it's not strong enough to rouse the attention of the gods without some kind of close contact. The demigods of old, though, could be seen from Olympus, their divinity shined so brightly—like a reflection of metal that catches your eye from miles away.

"That's what it was like when your divinity manifested. You became bright, and there were certain physical changes. Your father's characteristics surfaced. Your skin became darker, more golden, like his. Your hair grew out like his does, in a tumble of waves that look and writhe like living vines. I couldn't see your eyes, but I'm sure they changed—that's always a given."

Gavin caught her hand, and Elena gasped as an image flashed through her mind. She was seeing Gavin's memory of it; seeing herself go through the change. It was completely unnerving. The woman she saw looked like her, but Elena didn't truly see herself in the reflection. She looked like one of the many divine beings Elena had met or seen these past couple of weeks—completely otherworldly.

"Is that really me?"

"It was pretty impressive," Gavin said excitedly, offering Elena a wink as he pulled his hand away.

"Not as impressive as what happened next," interjected Galen. He crossed one leg over another, and took a drink from the glass of amber liquid he held in his hand. "You baited the Queen and formed the shield. She did not take her loss well. Draig intervened."

"Who is Draig?"

"The dragon-king," Galen replied.

The room fell into a heavy silence. Elena saw the crimson-eyed king in her mind, his ancient face fierce and defiant. His long white hair blazed hot against black-scaled armor, the sash at his waist matching the color of his eyes.

Try as she might, Elena could not recall the dragon-king coming to her rescue. She remembered the weight of his consciousness over hers, more obtrusive than the Kirin's but non-threatening. She recalled the timbre of his voice, and the feel of taking a back seat when he made the final two moves in the game. Elena's memories ended with the final defender taking his place next to the king.

"What happened exactly?" she asked, not addressing anyone in particular.

"You collapsed," said Eiry in an even tone, his gaze lifting from the Helm, "right after you made your last move."

"The Queen was just staring at the board," added Gavin cheerfully, and took another sip of his drink.

"Then she snapped," said Bryce, speaking for the first time.

Everyone turned to watch her. The red-haired goddess lifted her golden gaze to Elena's and arched a perfectly sculpted brow. A smirk ghosted over her lips. Then she produced a nail file from somewhere in her clothing and turned her attention to filing her nails—the usual Bryce dismissal.

Galen picked up where his sister left off. "The Queen lunged at you, which is most unusual. The Fae are famed for their decorum, Áine more than most. We knew she would be upset if she lost, but we never imagined she would act on it. Then again, we couldn't have imagined what was really at stake here."

"What do you mean?" Elena asked. "What more could have been at stake?"

"Draig's freedom."

It was the Kirin who spoke, his voice a whisper in the gentle breeze that suddenly stirred around them. Elena could feel the weight of his gaze, and she turned to look at him. He was smiling.

Elena was completely confused. She couldn't begin to understand how the dragon's freedom had anything to do with her. She chanced a look at Eiry, who nodded, confirming what Galen and the Kirin had said. Elena felt the first inklings of fear, as the twins turned in tandem to look at her.

"There has to be some kind of mistake. Not that I'm not happy for him or his clan if they are free now, but that has nothing to do with me." Elena's voice was trembling. A cold panic settled in the pit of her stomach. The last thing Elena needed was to upset another group of gods. The Fae's position in the system of pantheons was directly related to their control over dragons. If what everyone said was true and Elena *was* responsible for freeing the dragons, then the Fae might lose their political advantage because of Elena and that couldn't be good.

"No mistake," the Kirin said to Elena, his gentle tone begging for her to relax. "Draig explained the situation after he brought you here. His agreement with the Queen more than a thousand years ago was predicated on her accepting a challenge that would be brought by an Heir sometime in the future. She was to accept the challenge and win. If she lost, the dragons would no longer submit to her. The Queen accepted his terms, never believing she would be defeated by a human."

"We wondered why the Queen had accepted the *dúshlán* in the first place," Eiry admitted, "since they seldom accept such challenges from humans. I could have never imagined she was bound to do so by a thousand-year-old contract with a dragon. The stalemate ensured she couldn't win. Of course, Áine could not accept that. When she attacked you, Draig and Manannán interfered."

Elena listened carefully as they explained, too shocked to say anything at all. She was caught between gratitude that the dragon-king was free and fear that she had made another set of enemies in the process; enemies as lethal as the sky gods that already hunted her. Ironically, no one else seemed to share her concern. In fact, everyone but Elena was very pleased; Bryce's indifference was par for the course.

"You should have seen him, Ele," Gavin added, overly excited, gesturing wildly with his hands. "Draig leapt from the basalt board and landed in front of you with a roar that shook the stone around us. Even the basalt board cracked, and he was only in human form! Manannán restrained the Queen, and shielded her from the dragon-king. Once she was taken away from the hall, the panel of judges convened. Draig escorted you here, where we were told to wait while the panel reached a decision. He was also the one who delivered the Helm once the panel made its ruling an hour ago."

"How long has it been since the tournament?" Elena looked toward the open wall on her right. The sun had definitely crested, its amber glow filtering softly into the room and making everything seem blushed. It had to be sometime in the mid-afternoon. Elena couldn't tell if it was the same day as the tournament. "And why would they give me the Helm after costing them the dragons?"

"Ele, relax," Eiry said to her softly.

Concern lined the corners of his perfectly shaped mouth, and Elena suddenly remembered she had kissed him. The heat rose quickly to her cheeks and Elena looked away, busying herself with a pattern of gemstones on the wall. Eiry didn't skip a beat.

"It's only been a few hours. We have to wait until twilight to leave," he continued to explain. "As for the panel, your refusal to give into the nature of the game impressed them. There is a story among their kind, of a man who once refused to strike his opponent's attackers but could not, in good conscience, throw the game. Instead, he played an entire day evading his opponent, without capturing attackers and still preventing the capture of his men. Lugh declared the feet champion-like, and it seems your tournament reminded them of that. The Fae can be sentimental creatures when it comes to their past. As for the dragon clan, it falls on Áine's shoulders, not yours."

Bryce snorted at his last words, and Eiry kicked her in the shin. Her nails turned to claws, but Tarōbō caught her wrist before she could lash out at her brother, risking his own hide. Elena had intended to ask more questions, but in a matter of seconds the four Greek gods were sparring again, Tarōbō attempting to keep the peace between them.

Elena closed her eyes. A lot had happened, and she needed time to process it. She pushed the sound of the bickering gods aside, and focused instead on the steady rhythm of the ocean below them. A cool breeze entered the pavilion. The Kirin's consciousness brushed against Elena's, and the *netsuke* opened the connection between them. The Kirin was happy, genuinely happy, for Elena's triumph and Draig's freedom.

Soon, any concern Elena felt about the Dananns was gone, eclipsed by the awareness of her triumph. She had done it. Somehow, she had won. The feeling was overwhelming. Elena's heart was beating a mile a minute, completely elated at the fact that the Helm sat on a coffee table two feet away from her, and with it Cataline would soon be free.

THE RETURN TO THE SURFACE occurred in the same manner as their descent, escorted by Creidhne to the opposite cliff where they entered a passage shrouded in mist that would lead them to the stone dolmen on the other side.

Sable-haired Airmed came to see them off, accompanied by Draig, the crimson-eyed dragon-king. He and the Kirin greeted each other warmly, their foreheads touching. Elena saw the five-petaled flower glisten on the Kirin's brow. A similar marking glowed in the center notch of the dragon-king's clavicle, the symbol some kind of rune. The two engaged in a brief exchange, their language completely indecipherable.

Airmed came to stand beside Elena. "Well met, Elena Dionysia," she said with a smile.

They were in the mouth of the great hall where Elena and her party had first appeared before the Faerie Host.

"You must be the only Danann in this kingdom to think so," Elena said to Airmed, surprised by her own candor. She held the Helm gingerly in her hands, still surprised by how heavy it was. Elena was not looking forward to wearing it.

"If you stayed longer, you would find that was not the case," Airmed assured Elena in the same gentle manner as always. "Nuada sends you his regards and his wishes for a safe journey, as does Goibniu." Airmed looked to Creidhne when she mentioned his brother.

Creidhne did not react in any way. He remained silent and aloof until the bird-deities arrived from the opposite cliff, at which time he busied himself with the preparations.

"Please give them my thanks for their kindness," Elena said to Airmed, distracted momentarily by the shifting of wings and the sound of talons against stone.

Airmed nodded.

The Kirin and the dragon-king had finished their conversation and were making their way toward Elena. Like the Kirin, the dragon-king did not show deference to another, but to Elena he offered a bow of his head. The smile he offered her was as fierce as his presence, and Elena did everything she could not to flinch. To tell the truth, he was terrifying, a formidable beast in human form. Like before, his skin hummed with the power contained within him, and it made Elena feel a little jumpy. His energy was completely different from the Kirin's.

"You need not fear me," the dragon-king said, his smile turning into a grin. He had a rasping voice that sounded like rolling thunder. "Thank you for your tenacity. While I had foreseen your arrival, every-thing else was up to you. I owe you my freedom, Heir. I will not soon forget it."

Elena was shaking; she couldn't help it. The dragon's energy was simply too much. He felt like the brewing of a storm—like air charged with electricity as thick, heavy clouds converge in a churning sea sus-pended in the sky. Elena bowed to the dragon-king, and forced herself to hold his crimson gaze. "Thank you for protecting me," Elena whispered, her voice far from steady.

Again, the dragon-king smiled. He stepped closer to Elena and she tensed, pressing her lips into a thin line as he touched his forehead to hers. Instantly, Elena felt the weight and texture of his consciousness. The rune below his throat appeared once again. An icy sensation settled at the nape of Elena's neck, and she was certain Eiry's mark was showing. The dragon-king's voice echoed in her mind.

"If you should ever call on me, I will not deny you."

Elena nodded, unsure of how to reply. She stammered through a thank you, aware of Eiry's watchful gaze.

Beside them, Airmed was saying her goodbyes to the others. Melia had appeared with a letter for her sister, which she gave to Eiry before bidding everyone farewell. Galen was entertaining himself with braiding his hair, undoing it every time to start the process over again. Gavin had been staring at the dragon-king quietly the entire time.

"Fucking fangirl," growled Bryce, shattering the rare moment of tranquility, bristling when Tarōbō chastised her for it.

Gavin flipped her off.

The dragon-king held Elena's gaze for a moment longer and then stepped away with a smile, resuming his place at Airmed's side.

Creidhne barked that it was time to go, and the Kirin and Tarōbō shifted into their original forms.

Elena was happy to climb onto the Kirin's back. Immediately, she saw the image of the white dragon from her dream, but when she looked at the dragon-king he was speaking softly to Airmed, seemingly un-involved in Elena's vision. It shouldn't have surprised her when he swooped past them on their way to the opposite cliff, his giant scales shining like opals in the twilight sky, the thunderous boom of his roar heralding their departure.

Elena buried her face in the Kirin's mane for the remainder of their short flight, thankful when they alighted on the pavement at the foot of the barracks. They all turned to see the dragon-king soar high into the sky before diving back down toward the cliffs, surrounded by a column of fire that snaked around his form and turned his scales afire. Elena rushed to the edge of the cliff just in time to see him dive into the ocean, a blazing white shadow beneath the darkening waves.

"Why is he going back, Kiyoshi-sama?" Elena asked the Kirin, wondering why the dragon-king would return to the cliffs even though he and his clan had been freed.

"The cliffs are his birthplace," replied the Kirin in a hushed whisper, once he had returned to his humanoid form. By then, everyone had dismounted and he had no time to explain further; Creidhne was already climbing up the steps carved into the cliffside, barking for them all to follow.

Eiry took his place at Elena's side. "Remember, you're going with Bryce," he said to her softly, helping her up the last step.

Elena nodded, deciding it was best not to object again. Bryce had objected enough for the both of them, and Elena had been trying her best not to think about it. They had gone over the game plan several times before leaving the pavilion. Elena had hoped that the plan would change, but it hadn't.

Unlike before, they would not be traveling in a group. The more spread apart they were, the harder it would be for Alexander to keep up with any one of them. Elena was to travel with Bryce the entire way back to Tartarus. Elena had insisted she would be safer with Eiry, but everyone agreed that would be too expected. Alexander would never consider the possibility that they would place the Heir in Bryce's care, and of all the god-siblings Bryce was the most vicious in battle. Elena was to wear the Helm at all times, as it would hide her presence completely—physically and spiritually. No one would be able to detect her, not even Bryce, so it would be important for Elena not to let go of her. When they reached Newgrange, she and Bryce were not to wait for anyone to arrive; Bryce was to take her immediately into Tartarus, and the rest would follow.

As Elena and her escort crowded together in front of the barracks, mists began to rise from the edges of the cliff, defying gravity at Creidhne's command. Thick as clouds, they gathered at their feet, rising to form a wall around Elena's party until they stood at the mouth of a passage made of mists. The second they stepped into it, the walls collapsed. The mists converged, and a heavy darkness settled around them. Elena couldn't see. She felt the icy hold of Eiry's hand, and the warmth of the Kirin behind her. Soon, the Kirin's skin began to glow, revealing the earthen passage from before—steep, and its walls tight. One by one, they climbed the steps to the tomb's single chamber, and then out into the night.

Elena put on the Helm before exiting the dolmen. A cold sensation moved through her, and she instantly felt claustrophobic. She could feel her own breath, damp and tepid against the sides of her mouth. It was a little difficult to see at first, but soon the darkness began to recede. The shadows within the tomb's chamber shifted and wove together, crowding around her and enveloping her entire form. At first, it felt like a cloak had been placed over her shoulders, but soon the fabric of shadows pulled tighter, molding itself to Elena's form. She could hardly feel the cold when she stepped out into the night. She knew the evening was cold from the breath that crystallized in the air around everyone as they breathed, but Elena's breath couldn't be seen.

Slowly, Elena made her way toward Bryce.

As they had suspected, Alexander was waiting for them at the dolmen, and this time he was not alone.

Fully healed, Eos stood beside her brother, the two a brilliant spectacle of burning light; the last vestiges of day before the night swallowed the rays of the dying sun. It was a war fought twice a day, with a different victor at dawn.

The moment Eos saw Bryce she left her brother's side and appeared before the Keres, baring her teeth. Bryce clicked her tongue, and grinned. Elena stepped in behind her.

"Did I leave a scar?" Bryce goaded Eos.

The goddess of dawn bristled. She had been holding her hands behind her, and now brought them forward to reveal a short sword whose blade gleamed like fire. It reminded Elena of the dagger Eiry had given her earlier to use for protection, which now lay hidden at her back. Instinctively, Elena stepped back.

Tarōbō took his place beside Bryce, and quickly eased the hilt of his *katana* away from its scabbard. For the second time, Elena heard the short-lived cry of the blade's song.

"Do not interfere, bird-demon!" Growled Eos, her celestial features twisted with hatred; she had worn the same expression when she threw Elena off the cliff as a child.

The sight of it now made Elena's blood run cold.

Bryce laughed. "Don't concern yourself with her, Tarōbō. I'll have her on her knees again in seconds. She is not worth your blade."

Eos hissed and stepped closer to Bryce, but Alexander stopped her. "Now, now, leave that for when the hunt begins," he said with a sinister smile, his gaze on Creidhne, who stood beside the dolmen's entrance. "We wouldn't want to shed blood on neutral ground, would we?"

"Oh, please do. It would prove most entertaining," said Creidhne, mirroring Alexander's smile.

Alexander ignored him. "Where is Elena?" he asked, his tone demanding, as if he had all the right in the world to know. "Have you hidden her from me already?" He crossed his arms over his chest and peered into the shadows around them. His blue gaze burned through the darkness, the bloodlust in his eyes at odds with his prep-school appearance.

"She decided a lifetime of servitude in Faerie was far less painful than listening to the sound of your obnoxious voice for the rest of her life," Gavin said, irritated.

"You know she needn't worry about that, Phobos," Alexander said in a wistful tone. "Her life won't be very long at all. Just a few years of continued torture to make it all worth my while." For a moment he grew silent and then a joyful smile transformed his features, as the energy around him hummed at the thoughts he was entertaining. "I keep holding out for one of these Heirs to get Stockholm syndrome. Dionysus and Thanatos shouldn't be the only ones having fun."

"You never get tired of listening to the sound of your own voice, do you, Helios?" Eiry asked coldly.

Elena turned to look at him, and through the moonlight saw hints of glacial blue bleeding through his hair.

"And you never get tired of playing James Bond in those ridiculous suits," Alexander snapped back. "Tell me, Thanatos, is it the suits that do it for her? I can definitely rock a suit, if that's what she prefers."

Eiry's hair turned blue completely and Elena saw the glint of his scythe begin to form, but the Kirin quickly interfered, placing a hand over Eiry's shoulder to calm him.

"Know this, Helios of Olympus," the Kirin said to Alexander, his voice filled with the promise of violence, "you will never again lay a hand on your prey." Like the dragon-king, a savage energy radiated from to the surface of the Kirin's skin, which now glowed with the radiance of starlight.

The Kirin's display cut through Alexander's bravado. The sun god stilled and his manner sobered. He held the Kirin's gaze as long as he could, and then quickly returned his attention to Eiry. "The whole of the divine world knows the Heir has recovered the Helm and singlehandedly freed the dragons. I know she's here because I can smell her fear, Helm of Hades or not." He purred the words, flicking his tongue to taste the air. "Protective ponies aside, I will have her as I have had all the others. You can be sure of that."

"Would it be too much to ask you to take this elsewhere?" Creidhne interrupted, unamused. "I would rather stick my eyes with hot needles than listen to the lot of you any longer."

"That can be arranged, Faerie," Alexander hissed, and took a step closer.

"Try it, sky god, and I will own you," Creidhne replied with a menacing smile.

Eos stepped between them. "Let's just get this over with," she growled, her gaze fixed on Bryce.

The red-haired goddess blew her a kiss. "Make sure you keep up, Eos. I don't want to get bored waiting for you," and with a wink, the Keres turned her attention to her brother.

At Eiry's signal, one by one Elena's party disappeared into the night, Bryce and Elena the last ones to move.

So began their flight back to Tartarus.

CHAPTER NINETEEN

HOLDING ON TO BRYCE'S HAND wasn't difficult on those first few stops.

Appearing in the ruins of a medieval priory was simple enough. The distance between it and the dolmen must have been reasonable because Elena felt fine as the world rearranged itself within the nave of the church, facing the chancel. Moss and lichen grew between the stones of the nave and chancel walls, and Elena looked around quietly, enjoying the serene atmosphere. Above them, the roof was missing and the nighttime sky hovered close. Scattered stars twinkled from behind tufts of diaphanous clouds.

It was a picture perfect scene that ended almost instantly, the hollow echo of Bryce's bangles the only sound as the world shifted again.

This time, they appeared in the banquet hall of a weathered medieval castle, an equally weathered hearth to their left. Once again, moss and lichen clung to decaying walls. They stood in the center of the room, facing a wooden table with two chairs positioned at the end of the hall, beneath the shelter of a gothic arch. A tapestry hung from the wall behind it, and broken moonlight filtered in through a gothic window to its left. The floor beneath them was made of wood, and Elena tapped her foot on it subconsciously, testing its sturdiness.

Without any warning, the world slid apart once again.

The distance must have been longer this time because Elena felt the first pangs of a headache, and it took a second for her surroundings to stop spinning.

"Bryce, that one hurt," Elena whispered, as the world around her finally focused.

She was on her knees in a cemetery facing a low wall made of stones, a ruined abbey rising up behind it. A large round tower stood to its right and was in surprisingly better condition than the abbey itself. As Elena stared at it, using it to maintain her balance, she realized the masonry work on the tower was of much better quality than the main building.

"Stop complaining," Bryce hissed, and took a tentative step forward.

"Ouch! You fucking stepped on me," Elena howled and turned to glare at Bryce, who had quickly backed away.

Elena was suddenly thankful the goddess couldn't see her.

For the second time, Bryce had the look of a warrior queen, never mind the modern attire. She stood tall, a blazing counterpoint to the anachronistic landscape around them. Her blood-red curls spilled over bare shoulders and framed a perfect face with golden eyes lined in kohl and cupid's bow lips stained the same color as her hair. In Bryce's case, the adage was true—makeup was a woman's war paint.

Bryce's gaze was fixed on the lake to the left of the abbey. A ghost of a grin touched her lips, and then she shrugged. "It's not my fault you have to wear the Helm or that you couldn't hack the distance," she said sarcastically, then added in a softer tone, "I felt Eos closing in, so I had no choice but to move us further out."

Elena wanted to match wits with her, to at least say something witty, but Bryce's last sentence took the wind out of Elena's sails. It was hard to be upset with someone who was keeping you safe, even if she came in the form of an eternally sardonic goddess of death.

"You could have warned me," Elena said softly, following Bryce's gaze to the lake. It was really beautiful here, and quiet. "Why exactly do you hate me so much?" The question came out of nowhere, and Elena didn't realize she had asked it out loud until she felt Bryce staring at her. With a resigned sigh, Elena pulled herself to her feet.

"I don't hate you. Humans just annoy me. In fact, this whole existence annoys me. Grab my hand. We need to go."

Bryce's answer took Elena by surprise. Her candor was unexpected, and Elena couldn't help the sense of relief she felt. Bryce was one of those people you simply couldn't please, no matter the lengths you went to do so. Knowing that made it a little easier to deal with her, even if she was a completely unreasonable person—who in their right mind went into battle wearing runway perfect clothing and impossibly high heels? If someone took a picture of Bryce at exactly this moment, they could use it for any advertising campaign and consider the thing a success; it was almost ridiculous.

Then again, this entire scenario was ridiculous.

The thought made Elena giggle. Bryce turned toward the sound, a perplexed look on her face. Elena began to move toward her, but stopped short when the goddess suddenly growled.

"She's coming. Stay back and don't say a fucking word," Bryce hissed, just as Eos appeared a foot away from her.

The goddess of dawn stood resplendent against the evening sky, a breeze stirring the light in her hair, and her lips curled into a menacing sneer. "You know, Keres, it seems to me I have been the one left wanting. For all of your boasting, all you have done since the hunt began is run. Why is that?"

"It's your perfume," Bryce said in a deadpan tone. "It's horrible."

Eos narrowed her eyes, and her fingers twitched against the hilt of her short sword. "You are a vile and lewd creature, you realize this, yes?"

"No more vile and lewd than you and your precious brother." Bryce said the words softly, a smile curling at the edges of her lips. She raised her right hand and stretched out her fingers, which slowly turned into claws beneath the faint light of the moon.

Elena watched Eos closely, waiting for the moment when the woman would lunge. Even though she knew what she was waiting for, the movement still came as a surprise. Eos shifted her weight, and Elena heard Bryce's heel carve through the ground as she stepped back, bracing her weight on her back foot.

Elena caught Bryce's hand just as Eos rushed forward. As Bryce dove into the assault, Elena felt her body lurch toward Eos. Then all movement slowed. The glint of the blade caught Elena's eye, as Eos bore her weight down on Bryce, who only had one free hand to defend herself with. Rather than catch the hand with the blade, Bryce used the attack as leverage, driving her hand into Eos's throat as the blade cut through Bryce's abdomen.

The world shifted as Eos's cry echoed through the dark.

BRYCE AND ELENA LANDED ROUGHLY, and the ground beneath them swayed. Elena opened her eyes, and she couldn't stop the scream that formed in her throat. It echoed around them, a bloodcurdling cry, before Elena managed to clamp her hand over her mouth, steadying herself with the other.

They were on a suspension bridge high above a craggy coastline, the sea raging beneath. The wind whipped violently around them, and Elena could feel the biting cold even through the shadow-fabric that enveloped her skin. The bridge swayed and wobbled mercilessly in the wind, making Elena's dizziness much worse. Bryce was sprawled beside her; her abdomen cut open, silver ichor spilling onto the planks beneath them.

"This isn't where…" Bryce began to say but then started to cough violently, silver ichor bubbling out of her mouth. She struggled to speak, her words drowning. "I didn't… aim here… fucking bitch."

Elena tried to wipe the ichor away from Bryce's mouth with her sleeve. The bridge swayed in the bitter wind and Bryce cried softly, her hands searching for her wound. Elena took hold of them, and begged her to be still. Slowly, she pressed her own hand to the gaping wound, as if that would stop the bleeding; at the very least, it seemed to calm Bryce. "Tell me what's going on. I can't help unless I understand," Elena whispered to her gently, studying their surroundings at the same time.

The bridge joined the coast to a small island. They had appeared closer to the coast, prostrate against the double-planked walkway that formed the path of the bridge. Made up of wooden planks wired together, it was laid over pieces of wood that ran across the width of the bridge, from beginning to end. A mesh of rope ran beneath the walkway, and attached to the roped sides of the bridge. The walkway was smaller than the width of the bridge, and if Elena reached past its edge she would touch the rope mesh beneath.

Elena looked up. At each end of the bridge were stone walkways that followed along the edges of the coast. A continuous railing made of pale wood kept onlookers away from the edge.

Bryce hadn't answered Elena's question. Elena looked back down at her and could see the goddess was moving her lips, but the wind was too loud to hear anything. Elena leaned forward, closer to Bryce's face, but even then she couldn't understand a thing she was saying.

Elena removed her hand from Bryce's wound. Somehow, it had gotten bigger. Bryce had lost so much ichor now that it spilled over the planked walkway and onto the rope mesh beneath. Elena began to panic. She had no idea what was going on. Remembering she was carrying the vial of ambrosia in her jeans, Elena quickly pulled it out, tilted Bryce's head back and poured the glowing amber liquid into her mouth. Elena took the last drop for herself, and then threw the empty vial over the side of the bridge; she didn't hear the sound of it reach the bottom.

After a few seconds, there was hardly any change in Bryce. Elena knew she needed to get them to the other side of the bridge, fast. It was only a matter of minutes before they would be tracked, and it would be much safer for them on firm ground. The drop of ambrosia had given Elena strength, and she hoped it would be enough to pull Bryce across the bridge onto the pathway at the opposite end, which climbed a steep stairway before evening out along the coastline.

Elena managed to drag Bryce halfway up the steps before her strength left her completely. They were safer now than they had been moments before, but the pathway was still open to attack. There was nothing to hide behind on the stairway. If Elena could get Bryce to the top of the stairs, she could prop her up behind a stone archway that had been built at the mouth of the stairs leading down to the bridge.

Elena hooked her arms under Bryce's shoulders and began to pull her up one step at a time, careful not to slip.

Bryce stirred as they reached the top.

"You're destroying my back," the goddess said sarcastically, her speech slurred.

Elena stopped moving and peered down at Bryce's face. The goddess' eyes kept fluttering open and close, her gold irises shining through the darkness. She looked much better than she had moments before, but nowhere near healed.

"Bryce, I have to get you up these steps," Elena explained, turning her head to look behind her shoulder. Just three more steps.

"You fed me ambrosia?" she asked, and grimaced as Elena began to pull her up the steps again.

"I did. Don't talk. Let me get you up the stairs and we can talk then."

It took a heck of a lot more effort than Elena thought she had in her, but she finally got Bryce to the top of the stairs. Getting her through the narrow opening of the archway, which she could only assume had been built that way to force a single-file line onto the bridge, was another struggle all together. How a sky god hadn't appeared yet was beyond Elena.

Once she got Bryce propped up against the inside of the archway, Elena inspected her wound. Ichor was still spilling out, but it was much less than before and the wound had become smaller. Elena felt the weight of Bryce's gaze, and looked up to find herself face-to-face with the goddess.

"You didn't have to go through all of this trouble," Bryce said softly, wiping the ichor away from her mouth.

"What the hell are you talking about? Of course I did," Elena said defensively.

Bryce started when Elena spoke. "Shit, I didn't realize you were so close. I still can't see you." She blinked several times, her golden irises expanding and contracting as she tried to focus on the space in front of her.

With all of the commotion, Elena had completely forgotten about the Helm. She took it off quickly and set it down beside them. She was instantly assaulted by the cold. The icy winds cut through her skin and into her bones, making Elena tremble violently. The sound of her teeth chattering echoed painfully in her head.

"Put it back on," Bryce growled.

"I can't. I'm going to put it on you while I try to call for help."

"You haven't called yet?"

"In case you hadn't noticed, I've been a little busy getting you off a suspension bridge."

Bryce parted her lips to speak, but then stopped herself. She stared at Elena and her expression softened unexpectedly. "Thank you," Bryce whispered, her tone still a little brusque, but Elena didn't mind.

"You're welcome. Now put this thing on." Elena reached for the Helm, but Bryce caught her hand.

"Elena, I can't do that. Eiry will kill me."

"I'll fucking kill you myself if you don't take it," Elena warned her, her tone dead serious. "Plus, you'll be dead in a minute if we don't hide you. You can hardly move."

"It'll take her a little bit to get here," Bryce barked through a strangled laugh.

"What do you mean?" Elena asked, and sat down in front of her.

Bryce leaned her head back against the stone. "It'll take her a few minutes to heal, and a bit longer than that to find us. I moved us as far north as I could without risking your life. Plus, the Hind's blood in my system will make it a little hard for her to hone in on my presence. I bet that dumb bitch didn't think of that when she stabbed me."

"Hind's blood?" Elena repeated to herself, her eyes wide with panic. Eiry had told her about Hind's blood when he handed her the dagger for protection before they left the pavilion earlier that afternoon; he had anointed the blade with it, one of a few known substances powerful enough to affect gods. It was a kind of poison that could incapacitate a god almost instantly. Its use was infrequent on account of its rarity, since only the blood of a golden-horned hind was poison to the gods.

Only five golden-horned hind, known as the Elaphoi Khrysokeroi, existed in the world, and all five of them were sacred to Artemis, the Greek goddess of the hunt. Four drew her chariot, and the fifth was left to roam freely through the world. Although Artemis was a sky god, she did not allow the four creatures in her possession to be drained of their blood. That left only one hind from which to draw the poison, and it had not been seen in almost two thousand years.

"Bryce, how the hell do we reverse it?" Elena asked, reaching to shake the goddess gently, who looked like she was on the verge of passing out.

Bryce blinked and for an instant her eyes flashed, as if she didn't recognize Elena. Then just as suddenly, she remembered herself. "Sorry," she breathed, hissing as she pressed her hand against her wound. "I have to get to Tartarus to reverse it. Only Atropos can, if the amount wasn't too much."

"What'll happen if she can't reverse it?"

"I'll die," Bryce said with a shrug. Realizing Elena was freaking out, Bryce tried to calm her. "I'm already dead, Elena. I'll just shed this body and be reborn. It's a pain in the ass, but it won't be the first time. Stop worrying about me and call out to Eiry. Just be vigilant because there's a chance Helios will be able to pick up on it."

Elena tensed at Bryce's words. She breathed in deeply, and without warning slipped the Helm over Bryce's head. Instantly, the goddess vanished.

"What the fuck, Elena? I told you not to!" Bryce hissed.

She must have been reaching to remove the Helm because Elena could see ripples tearing through the image of the empty space in front of her. Quickly, Elena reached for the spot where she saw the faint outline of the Helm, and held it down on Bryce's head.

"Bryce, stop protesting. You're hurt and you can't move. I can, and I have a dagger with Hind's blood on it to use if anything comes our way. You're Eiry's sister, and I can't let anything happen to you."

"Why do you always have to protect everyone?" Bryce growled, trying to fend Elena off, to no avail; she was too weak. "You go to Faerie to save a human's life when all humans are bound to die. That's an exercise in futility if I've ever heard one, completely pointless. Then, while in Faerie, you refuse to banish any of the Queen's attackers, which you needed to do to win mind you, because you didn't like that her slaves were being hurt in the process. That was plain stupid. Now, you want me to wear this damned thing out of some goddamned honorable notion that you should protect me, when I would never do the same for you if I were in your shoes. Notice a pattern?"

Bryce stilled and Elena sat back on her heels, her eyes on the now empty space in front of her, where Bryce's eyes should be. "I know you like to be a hardass, but you're here with me right now. You got me all this way, and you're still trying to protect me. You say you wouldn't, but you've already done the same thing for me."

There was silence for several minutes, and then Elena heard Bryce's disembodied voice.

"Stupid humans."

The way she said it was almost endearing. With a nod, Elena pulled herself to her feet. She felt for the knife hidden flush against the small of her back and slowly retrieved it.

"I'm going to call for the Kirin. There's no risk of alerting the sky gods with that," Elena told Bryce, and reached for the blooming *netsuke* that lay flat against the top of her chest. There was hardly any warmth to it. Elena closed her eyes and began to concentrate, trying to open her connection to the Kirin.

Just as she did, Eos appeared behind Elena. She felt the ripple of energy just before her arrival, and Elena managed to turn around in time to brandish her dagger.

Surprised, Eos started, but just as quickly began to laugh, the sound a melody that parted the shadows. "Little Heir, what will you do, stab me with it?" she asked Elena, and stifled another laugh.

Elena took a step back and pulled her hand away from the *netsuke*. She held the dagger with both hands and braced herself for an attack.

Again, Eos laughed. "Where is the Keres?" she asked sweetly, the tone completely unnatural; she might look like a celestial being, but there was nothing saintly about her. "I know she's around here somewhere. I can see the glint of her ichor on the bridge, leading to the stairs."

Elena hadn't thought about that. She had been too busy worrying about getting Bryce to safety to concern herself with a possible trail of ichor left behind. "Why worry about the Keres when I'm right here?" Elena hissed at the goddess, and slowly began to move back down the stairs, trying to get Eos away from Bryce.

The goddess of dawn watched Elena, hesitant for only a moment. Then she slowly began to follow, stopping at the top of the stairs. "Do you think I can't see through you, *human*?" Eos snarled, her nails biting into the metal railing that lined the stairs. "How fitting that we should meet on a cliff once again, don't you think? The irony of it is quite lovely."

"This time I'm old enough to put up a fight, you savage bitch," Elena hissed at her, and inched further back along the path, almost at the bridge.

Eos lunged for her, and the now-familiar rage settled over Elena as she took her first step onto the bridge. Everything around her instantly came into focus. She must have physically changed, because Eos stopped her advance at the foot of the stairs and watched her warily.

"Come on!" Elena goaded her, shifting the dagger to one hand. She held it expertly, as if she had trained to fight with daggers her entirely life. Elena touched the *netsuke* at her chest, and it blazed hot. In a matter of seconds, she felt the brush of the Kirin's consciousness against hers.

"Are you safe?" Elena heard the Kirin ask in her mind.

She had no idea how to answer, but decided it would be wise to try it as a thought. "I am. Bryce isn't. She's down from Hind's blood. I hid her with the Helm. Eos is here, and I'm sure she'll be attacking soon." Elena sent the thought to him, focusing it on the warmth of the *netsuke* against her skin.

Eos took a step closer, forcing Elena to take another step back. The bridge swayed violently beneath her and Elena reached for the side, struggling to keep her balance. Eos smiled, and bared her fangs like a beast. The familiar bloodlust settled over her features, and twisted them in a rage-filled fever.

Elena heard the Kirin's voice echo in her mind a second time.

"Eos must not have told her brother about you because he is still here," said the Kirin. "He has been engaged with Thanatos this entire time, convinced that you must be here because I joined him. You must get out of there now, Elena!"

"I'm a little trapped on a suspension bridge right now," Elena sent back to him, her eyes on Eos the entire time, "and Bryce cannot god travel."

The goddess moved and Elena's eyes immediately focused on the way the woman distributed her weight. Eos lunged and Elena saw it slowly, anticipating exactly where she would land. Rather than run away, Elena rushed toward the goddess, taking the woman by surprise. She swung her dagger just as Eos reached her, stabbing the goddess in the shoulder before leaping over her to the opposite side.

Eos howled in pain, but Elena was already rushing up the stairs. She wasn't sure what had come over her but, whatever it was, she was thankful for it.

The Kirin's voice echoed in Elena's mind a third time. "We'll be there in a minute. Helios has just learned of your location. Just hold on one minute longer."

Behind her, Elena heard the sound of Eos's movement. From it, she knew, somehow, that the woman would be coming at her from the right. "Be ready!" Elena screamed to Bryce, and vaulted over the rest of the stairs just as Eos lunged at her. The goddess' claws dug into Elena's ankle, but it wasn't enough to stop her. Elena heard the goddess stagger in pain, and the sound of the dagger strike stone as Eos missed her mark.

"I'm getting us out of here," Elena sent to the Kirin, and dove towards Bryce. In a spurt of madness, Elena wrapped her arms around the space where Bryce's body should have been, and with all of her being thought of Tartarus, and prayed to her father for help.

THE WORLD BECAME BLACK and pressed against Elena from every side like a giant vice. Even so, she held on to Bryce, as something pulled them forward. Every muscle in Elena's body screamed in pain, and she felt like her head might explode. Her cries were silent, and her bones ground together as they were crushed against a hard surface. The entire time, Bryce remained still in Elena's arms.

The sound of metal struck stone and Elena opened her eyes to find herself in a familiar place. She was lying in the garden courtyard where Persephone's trees grew, sprawled on the ground by the alabaster basin fountain. Elena looked up to find herself looking into the eyes of one of the twelve stone-carved hounds that held up the basin stone.

Quickly, Elena crawled to her knees. She felt a violent wave of nausea, but pushed through it, ignoring the vicious pounding in her head. Slowly, she began to look around. Bryce was several feet away, the Helm lying on the stone pavement between them. Elena crawled toward her, unaware they were being watched.

"We're home, Bryce. I don't know how, but we made it home," Elena whispered to her, smoothing a damp curl away from the goddess' face. She pulled Bryce against her and began to look over her wound. It wasn't any smaller, but the ichor had finally stopped.

Bryce opened her eyes and immediately began to struggle, unaware of where she was. Elena caught her hands as gently as she could, and repeated herself softly. After several seconds, Bryce stilled in Elena's arms.

"How did we get here?" she asked, her voice broken. "Eos?"

"You don't need to talk," Elena said to her gently, palpating the wound. Bryce hissed and Elena pulled her hand back, humming softly to try to calm her. "We're safe. That's all that matters. I don't know how I managed to get past Eos or how I got us home, but it doesn't matter."

Someone cleared their throat, interrupting them.

"Home, what an interesting choice of words," said a deep and rumbling voice from the portico of arches that held up the roof of the courtyard.

Elena looked toward the sound of the voice. Hades, dressed in his usual dark robes, stood beneath an arch, his midnight blue eyes fixed on Elena and Bryce. He had a black hound at his side and Elena started, as the hound growled menacingly, it jowls exposed.

"Lord Hades, there is your Helm. Please help me with Bryce," Elena said to him, pointing to the Helm quickly before returning her full attention to Bryce, who was groaning and writhing in pain.

The moment Elena spoke, the hound barked ferociously and Elena stilled, her eyes on the colossal god, who watched her with an unconcerned expression on his face.

"Now, now, Kelainos, settle down," Hades cooed to his hound. "She is not a soul... not yet." Hades smoothed his hand between the hound's ears, and the beast settled. He touched two fingers to its brow and then slowly began to make his way across the courtyard to Elena.

A sinking feeling took hold of Elena. Hades had ignored her request for Bryce, and his manner was alarming. "Lord Hades, please," she implored him, "Bryce is hurt."

Hades clenched his jaw and broke his stride only briefly. He looked to Bryce momentarily, before returning his gaze to Elena. "How is it you are here?" he asked her, once again ignoring Elena's request.

"Lord Hades, she will die!"

"It would serve her right," he growled, his ire etched into his features. "I will ask you again, how is it that you are here?"

"I don't know! It just happened!" Elena snapped, tensing as the hound growled behind its master. She couldn't understand Hades's hostility, but that was precisely how he was acting now, openly hostile.

Hades held his hand out and the hound once again stilled. Its predatory gaze remained fixed on Elena. "That is not what I meant," Hades said in a measured tone, his patience wearing thin. "How is it you recovered the Helm?"

He was now less than three feet away from them and Elena pulled Bryce closer to her, protectively. "A stalemate," she replied, cautiously.

The colossal god laughed. The sound made the stone beneath them tremble.

"Cut the shit, Hades. I'm hurt," Bryce spat out unexpectedly. "I need to get to Atropos."

Elena looked down to see the goddess staring at Hades, her golden eyes bloodshot with a sheen of silver instead of red. She coughed and ichor spilled from her mouth. Elena begged her to stop speaking.

"Do you think I am concerned with your well-being, Keres? You should be intimately associated with dying. Just give in, you will be reborn quickly enough." Hades said the words cruelly. He snapped his fingers and the hound barreled through the courtyard, tearing through Elena to clamp its maw over Bryce's throat.

Elena screamed, the sound of tearing flesh making her feel sick. Bryce moaned, her anguish a visceral thing, like the ichor that poured out in streams of silver from between the beast's savage teeth.

Without thinking, Elena threw herself at the hound and stuck her hand into its mouth. Its teeth cut into Elena's skin, making her cry out in pain, but she continued to shove her arm even further. Once it was in up to her elbow, Elena twisted it, the skin of her arm tearing as she shoved it deep into the hound's throat. Finally, the thing let go of Bryce, snapping at Elena's face as it pulled away. At the same time it did so, Elena kicked it as hard as she could, just barely eluding its snapping jaws. The hound lunged for her again, but Hades barked an order and it drew back to stand still at his side.

"You are an interesting human," Hades said to Elena in a rueful tone, "pitying gods who would not pity you."

Bryce was coughing violently in Elena's arms, and ichor was now spilling from the gash in her throat. Elena was so angry she could hardly feel her own wounds. "What is wrong with you?" Elena hissed at the god, throwing decorum and caution to the wind. "She is one of your kind. Why would you add to her suffering? And even if she wasn't, there is honor even in war. Champions honor their enemies. This is madness."

"That is where you are wrong," Hades said, impatiently.

He drew in a steady breath, exhaled sharply, and then ordered his hound to stay before taking the few short strides to Elena's side. His sandal brushed against her hand and she flinched, quickly pulling it away.

"I am not Tartarean," he told her, stone-faced. "She is nothing to me."

Elena narrowed her eyes. She didn't have time for this. The poison was slowly consuming Bryce. She had delivered the Helm, and they could worry about Cataline in a few hours, once Bryce was safe. "If you won't help, I will do it myself," Elena said, and began to position her arms under Bryce's shoulders.

Hades placed his hand on the crown of Elena's head, impeding her movements. "Unfortunately," he said, as he ran his fingers through Elena's hair, "I can't let you do that." Then he wrapped her hair around his wrist and snapped her head back, dragging Elena away from Bryce, kicking and screaming.

"You have the Helm! What more could you want? Let me go!" Elena reached up as Hades pulled her, and dug her nails into his hand. Like Eiry, his skin was stone, and all the effort did was tear Elena's nails apart. "Let go! My father will come for me!"

Hades drug Elena through the ground, across the garden toward the entrance to the courtyard. "I am certain your father will come, but you will be dead by then," he said with a smile. Then he pulled Elena up by the hair until her feet hovered over the ground. He caught her throat with his other hand and slammed her hard against the back wall of the courtyard, next to the entrance. "By the time he or Thanatos break through the barriers I have placed, it will be too late."

"We had a deal! I brought you the Helm! Why are you doing this?" Elena forced the words out, as the colossal god slowly began to crush her throat. The image of him began to waver before her eyes. The pain she felt was excruciating.

"Because you were not supposed to survive that little trip, and in exchange I would be welcomed back in Olympus. That was the promise I made my brothers, but, since you somehow managed the impossible, it now falls on me to complete the task."

Hades spat the words in Elena's face, his mouth so close to hers it was almost too intimate. He ran his tongue along Elena's lips and she screamed, struggling in his arms.

"I wouldn't squirm if I were you," he warned her. "You'll end up snapping your own neck. I *am* going to kill you, but it's going to be slow. I like to savor my kills."

"Fuck you!"

Elena bit the god's lip and wouldn't let go until she felt it tear. The slap that came was well worth it. Hades braced himself and pulled Elena away from the wall, slamming her back down harder. Elena heard the sickening crack of her skull when the back of her head hit the wall. Her vision began to falter, but she clearly saw the wound on his lip begin to heal.

"Humans are such delicate creatures," Hades whispered into the shell of Elena's ear. He took Elena's arm and pulled sharply, dislocating her shoulder.

Elena screamed, feeling the sensation for the second time in her life—both times at the hands of gods. "What about our oath?" Elena asked between heavy breaths. The tears had started to spill now, and there was no way she could stop them.

"What about it?" the god asked, pleased with himself. "You did not meet your end of the bargain."

Elena felt a surge of rage move through her again, but it wasn't enough to give her any more strength; she had arrived here with her father's blood already manifested. The rage she felt now was simply that, rage, fueled by a single thought—she wanted to kill this god.

"The Helm is right behind you. I met my end," she hissed defiantly. "By the Styx, you are bound to yours."

"Do not lecture me on Stygian oaths, *human*," Hades barked, and squeezed his hold on her throat even tighter.

Again, Elena tried to claw at his hands, but it was impossible.

"If you recall correctly, our oath was contingent on the Helm remaining in your possession once obtained, never to be delivered into the hands of or used by another immortal or supernatural creature, until the time you delivered it to me. You did not meet either requirement. You placed the Helm in the Keres' possession and allowed her to use it before arriving here. I owe you nothing."

Elena stared at the god defiantly, but she felt her spirit break. Those had been the terms of their agreement and in her desperation to protect Bryce, Elena had forgotten all about it. "She was dying," Elena protested, as the tears spilled down her cheeks. "She is dying now. There are exceptions to every rule."

Hades smiled, a terribly beautiful smile. He cupped her cheek with his large hand and smoothed his thumb across Elena's lips. "A contract is a contract, child. You should know that."

"There must be some kind of way. I was saving one of your gods!" Elena cried softly, her will almost completely gone.

"Again, she is not one of mine. This existence was not my choice." Hades sighed, and drew close enough to breathe-in Elena's breath. "I was born above. I have never been accepted here. Chione herself offered my position to your precious Thanatos. Had he wanted it, where would that leave me? This is my chance at redemption and I am taking it."

"Please release Cataline before you do. I'm begging you."

"Why should I? You did not meet your end of the bargain."

"I will give you anything you want."

"There is nothing you can give that I desire."

"You desire my life."

Hades stilled. His midnight blue eyes fixed on Elena and slowly he loosened his hold on her throat. "What do you propose?"

"An Act of Substitution," she whispered. "My life for hers. I will have made the choice, and no one need know of any of this. I simply didn't meet my end of the bargain and brokered another deal, that is all."

"Do you even know what that means?" Hades growled, and shook Elena violently. "Do not toy with me, *girl*," he warned.

Elena coughed, struggling to breathe. "I saw the Kirin do so in the Daoine Sídhe. I know what it means."

Hades stilled against her and loosened his hold on her throat even further. His eyes narrowed and he watched her quietly, taking her measure. "What of the Keres? How will you ensure she will not speak?"

"She is dying. She will not remember any of this if she survives on account of the poison's fever. If she dies, does it not take years for gods to remember things once they are reborn? I doubt this would be important enough to remember quickly, if at all. And even if they did learn of it, what would they do, Hades, send you back to Olympus?" Elena was grasping at straws, hoping his hubris would be his weakness, as had been the case with the Queen.

Hades watched her quietly, considering her words and weighing his options. Finally, he nodded. "Speak your intent out loud so that it is binding."

"By the Styx, I offer my life in substitution for Cataline's," Elena said without a second thought.

Hades let go of her throat and stepped aside. "It is done then," he said, a satisfied smile on his lips. He looked up toward the roof of the infinitely cavernous space, as if he could speak to the heavens.

In the center of the garden courtyard, the sound of churning water could be heard. From the depths of the basin fountain rose the shape of a woman carved out of the river Styx. The Stygian waters rippled and writhed for several minutes, and then finally stilled. As they receded, Cataline's body was revealed.

"You now have twenty-four hours to live," Hades said to Elena, his expression transformed by the long-awaited rapture of his success.

Elena didn't reply. There was no need to. The only thing she was concerned with now was Cataline, whose body hovered vertically over the fountain, her toes almost touching the mirror-like surface. Her eyes were closed, as if she were sleeping.

It was done. In twenty-four hours, Cataline would be alive and Elena had no regrets.

MINUTES PASSED and Elena slowly made her way across the courtyard, back to Bryce's side. Her entire body was in pain, but it didn't matter. The relief she felt eclipsed all things—pain, anger, and even the promise of death. To her surprise, Elena found that she could smile. For the first time since she had begun her journey, all worry was gone. She touched the surface of the water in the basin fountain as she passed by and looked up at Cataline fondly, before dropping to her knees at Bryce's side.

The hound growled, but Elena didn't pay it any attention nor did she concern herself with her wounds. Already she could feel the magic in her father's blood begin to heal her; Eiry would have to re-break her shoulder to set it correctly. What was important at this moment was Bryce. Her breathing was shallow, and Elena prayed someone would arrive soon. "Did you lift the barriers?" Elena called out to Hades, fully aware he was still in the courtyard, watching her.

"Yes, they have been removed," replied the colossal god. He scratched his beard and then added aloud, more to himself than Elena, "You are indeed a most interesting human."

Seconds later, the sound of running echoed through the halls of the Domos Aidaou, as Eiry and Elena's father made their way into the courtyard.

"What is the meaning of this? Why did you block our path, Hades?" Dionysus demanded, his dark gaze taking in the scene. He seemed rich and textured against the monochromatic landscape of the courtyard, very similar to Bryce's saturated hues—Bryce who now lay dying in Elena's arms.

Eiry stood beside Dionysus, his clothes disheveled and a tear across the front of his blazer, but otherwise completely unscathed. His icy gaze was fixed on Elena, and she could see the relief in his eyes that she was alive.

"I need help, Papa," Elena called out to her father, who had stopped in the center of the courtyard, Eiry at his side. The two gods stood frozen before Cataline's form, their faces drained of any emotion. For the longest time, they just stood there, staring at the sleeping form— Elena refused to think of her as a corpse.

"Papa," Elena said again, and the two gods turned to look at her.

"What have you done?" Eiry asked her, his eyes stained crimson. His hair began to bleed a glacial blue, and it was Dionysus who caught his hand and begged for him to calm his anger.

"As is quite clear, she has entered into an Act of Substitution," Hades replied when Elena hesitated, his tone smug, "but you already knew that, did you not, Thanatos? Do you not feel every deathly bargain when it is struck?" With a pleased expression, Hades slowly began to make his way toward the fountain. "You must collect the debt in twenty-four hours."

An unearthly growl erupted from Eiry's throat, as his godhood exploded. His rage fueled the transformation until he stood before them in his true form. Long strands of glacial blue hair fell over his broad shoulders to the small of his back. Two small, slightly curved, pointed horns appeared at his brow. Black lines marked his skin, two thick bands peeking out through the collar of his suit, starting at the back of his jaw on each side. Like twin serpents, they traced a path downward, along the sides of his throat, seemingly over his shoulders and down his arms, peeking out again at the wrists as he brandished his metal scythe, ebony-nailed fingers wrapped around the grip.

"I don't need to do anything," Eiry growled as he lunged at Hades, his scythe cutting through the air in front of the colossal god, its blade cresting at Hades's neck. Eiry's crimson gaze held the god's, scathingly.

Hades laughed, his skin brushing against Eiry's blade as he did so, droplets of golden ichor staining its edge. "Oh, I think you do. Acts of Substitution are solely your purview, Thanatos."

"All debts are cancelled upon your death," Eiry replied, and pressed the blade of his scythe closer to the god's throat.

"Too bad that is not true," Hades said with a satisfied smile, running his fingers along the far edge of the blade.

"Stop it!" Elena cried out. "Bryce is dying!"

Eiry stilled. Rooted to the ground before Hades, his scythe motionless against the god's throat, he turned his head toward Elena. His crimson gaze cut through the darkness, and he let out a baleful cry as he beheld the broken body of his sister. Until now, he hadn't realized the urgent nature of her condition.

"Do not act yet," Dionysus commanded, and quickly made his way toward Elena.

She could see he was angry by the way his mouth was set, and there was a deep sadness in his eyes. For a minute, Elena hesitated—a remnant of her childhood whenever her father appeared upset. Then she roused herself, determined to save Bryce. "Papa, please help her," she begged him, as he knelt at her side.

Dionysus's features smoothed as he saw, up close, Elena's physical state. A flash of anger hardened his eyes and his godhood surfaced, a ripple beneath his skin. Tendrils of inky black hair grew long and writhed through the air with his anger. Elena took his hand, and he held it tightly. A feral hiss left his lips, and then he finally lowered his gaze to Bryce. He looked her over carefully, his fingers gently probing her wounds, and once again his eyes flashed with anger.

"Hind's blood and hound marks. Explain this, Hades, *all of it*," Dionysus growled, his eyes on his daughter, his voice heavy with indignation.

"There is nothing to explain," replied the colossal god, his voice choked when Eiry pressed the blade of his scythe even deeper into his throat. Hades coughed, but otherwise pretended not to notice Eiry at all. The only evidence of any displeasure were his robes, which shifted like shadows, his godhood constantly exposed.

"The Hind's blood was Eos," Elena quickly explained to her father. "I gave her all of the ambrosia I had."

Dionysus nodded, his expression grave. He kissed Elena's brow, and whispered softly, "That was very smart, Elena."

"Why was she not taken to Atropos immediately?" Eiry demanded from Hades, his gaze holding the god in his place.

"Can we please talk about that later?" Elena interrupted them, her voice breaking from desperation. She was at the end of her wits. "Someone needs to take Bryce away, right now!"

Dionysus took Elena's hands and squeezed them gently. He held her gaze, and she felt her anger slowly begin to melt away. A wave of thick black hair spilled over her father's eyes and he quickly tucked it away, the leather bands on his wrists catching Elena's eye. They reminded her of Bryce's metal bangles and suddenly she began to cry, the weight of everything crashing down on her all at once.

Slowly, Dionysus pulled his daughter into his lap, while Eiry kept Hades immobilized with the point of his scythe. "Elena, do you realize what you agreed to, what has transpired here?" her father asked her gently, whispering the words into her ear as he tried to soothe her. The pain of Elena's choice was evident in his voice.

Elena nodded. Of course she understood; it was something she had resolved to do, especially since her visit with Isabella. "Mama told me to find my own role within the prophecy, my own truth. She told me not to worry about fate, and focus on what I can control. She said her truth was my survival, and I realized then that mine was Cataline's." Elena was certain she had made the right choice, but it did not make the consequences of her choice any easier to stomach. She felt miserable for the pain she was causing her father, and the pain she knew her death would cause Eiry, but this had been a choice she needed to make.

"I can't control prophecies, Papa. I can't control that gods will hunt me every day of my life. I can, however, control the manner of my death and make sure that it has meaning. I will die on my terms, not Alexander's or anyone else's. As for the prophecy, my choice simply proves I was not the prophesied Heir. Atropos has foretold of another, and let her concern herself with that. I've been thinking about this for a very long time, Papa. The day I spent with you, Mama and Eiry in Elysium was the happiest day of my life. This is my home. Here, with you and Mama, with Eiry. A life in Elysium is better than any life I could have up there. Death is a small price to pay."

The moment Elena said it, the sound of blade cutting through flesh echoed through the courtyard. In a single movement, Eiry cut through muscle and bone, leaving only a sliver of skin so that Hades's head remained attached to his body, allowing it to hang forward into his cradled arms as the mighty god collapsed to his knees.

CHAPTER TWENTY

Hades's beheaded body was left where it fell, upright on its knees near the basin fountain, his dark robes stained in golden blood. His severed head remained embraced in his arms, resting gently on his lap; the only honor afforded him. His eyes were left open so he could witness his own disgrace, his hound the only one present to mourn him.

Since that moment, Eiry hadn't spoken a word.

They parted ways with Elena's father in the garden courtyard and walked through the empty halls of the Domos Aidaou, nothing but silence between them as they wandered aimlessly through the spectral palace. Eiry walked in a daze; scythe in hand, while the image of him, savage and unforgiving, echoed in Elena's mind. When he finally remembered himself, Eiry took hold of Elena's hand and transported them to his sitting room in Eira, but the silence remained the same.

Several hours passed. Elena bathed, Eiry healed her wounds and they received a report on Bryce's condition, all without a word passing between them. Every time Elena tried to speak, words would fail her. Her choice had driven them to this moment, and her lack of regret even in the face of Eiry's pain kept Elena silent. What could she possibly say in her defense, when her choice went against even the most basic human instinct? Would it matter that it made her free, that by doing so she had regained what little control she had over her own destiny?

Elena couldn't find the strength to begin the argument, and so the silence between them simply continued to grow.

Eiry had been pacing now for the better part of an hour, back and forth in front of his bed, while Elena sat at the foot of it, following his movements without saying a word. His crimson gaze would rise to meet hers repeatedly but then he would quickly look away, frustrated, shaking his head as if the act alone could undo the choice she had made.

Thinking a gesture might ease the tension between them, Elena reached for Eiry's hand but he quickly pulled it away, his crimson gaze ablaze. He stared at her with a mixture of fear and anger, his infamous stoicism completely gone.

"How could you do this?" he finally said; his voice fractured beneath the weight of their prior silence.

He stared at her, wide-eyed, and then took a step back—until he found himself pressed against the wall—putting several feet between them. He wore his godhood still, the black markings visible on his skin, more so now that he had removed his torn blazer. His tie lay discarded on the floor, covered in silver ichor. Similar stains marked his shirt and blotted his skin. His hair, long and icy blue, glistened with streaks of silver and gold, remnants of the day's fighting.

Elena didn't answer him immediately, too surprised by the bitterness in his tone. She held his gaze as she struggled to find the right words, caught off guard by the desperation she saw in his eyes. He was praying for her to say something that would end his suffering, but the truth was that anything Elena could say would only make things worse. In saving Cataline, she had inadvertently made Eiry's worst fear a reality. Worst yet, not only would he be forced to collect her soul, her death would now be at his hands and not Alexander's. She couldn't have known then that the Moirai's law would require him alone to collect her debt, but thinking like that was simply a way to placate her own guilt. The awful truth was that had Elena known then what she knew now, her choice would have still been the same.

Elena breathed in deeply, and tried to find the nerve to express her thoughts. He had asked her how she could have made the choice, and he deserved an honest answer. More than anyone, he deserved the truth. Elena closed her eyes and focused her mind on the air she drew into her lungs, and then, exhaling sharply, relaxed the tension in her body. All the while, Eiry watched her, waiting patiently for her reply, the hope for relief ablaze in his eyes.

With a resigned sigh, Elena shifted her weight on the bed, un-tucked her legs and let them hang over the edge of the mattress. Her feet had barely touched the ground when Eiry flinched. He watched Elena, his eyes wild, and pressed himself back against the wall, holding the back of his arms, his grip so hard that small bruises blossomed beneath the tips of his fingers; he looked like he was on the verge of breaking.

"Are you afraid of me?" Elena asked, beside herself; his reaction had thrown her frame of mind in a completely different direction.

Eiry lifted his gaze to hers, and Elena could see he was struggling with something. His expression was strained and his body tense—like the string of a bow pulled too tight, which might snap at any minute.

Slowly, he shook his head. "Of course not," he replied, so softly Elena could hardly hear him. "I'm afraid of myself."

"What the hell are you talking about?" she said, and slid off the bed. Her tone was much sharper than she had intended. The conversation was not going as planned.

Eiry raised his hand for Elena to stop.

"Don't," he warned her, his expression smoothing—the quiet before the storm.

"Don't what?"

"Don't come near me," he snapped, and then quickly looked away.

His words stung and Elena blinked back tears, the first time they had risen since she had made her pact with Hades. "Why would I stay away from you?" she demanded, visibly upset. She searched for his gaze, but he wouldn't look at her. When she took a step closer, he begged her again to stay away. "Eiry, talk to me," Elena begged him. "I don't understand."

"How could you understand?" he replied through a choked laugh. He began to pace again, this time running his hand roughly through his hair. "Reluctant Death, merciful Death," he murmured to himself. "I have grown weak. Death is not meant to feel."

"I'm sorry," Elena whispered, not sure of what else she could say.

Eiry stopped pacing and leaned back against the wall. He lifted his gaze to hers and, with a resigned sigh, slid down the wall to the ground.

"I don't want to hurt you," he confessed; desperation made his voice shrill. He had raised his knee and now rested his weight against it. He was coming undone. Reaching into his pant pocket, he retrieved a silver flask and brought it to his lips.

Elena had never seen this side of Eiry, and had no idea what she could say to soothe him.

"Eiry, please," she whispered and leaned back against the foot of the bed, maintaining their distance; at least doing so seemed to calm him.

"This was my choice. This is what I want. Don't think of it as hurting me."

"You're right, I won't be hurting you. It'll be much worse than that," he said bitterly, and took another drink from his flask. "In less than twenty-four hours, you will die by my hand, Elena. Do you realize this? *These two hands*," he seethed, and held his hands out in front of him. He stared at them, wild-eyed, his crimson gaze shining like embers through the pale fringe of his lashes.

"Yes, and it was my choice," Elena reminded him, her tone rougher than she meant it to be. "I would rather die by your hand than Alexander's."

"You have no idea what you're saying!" Eiry growled, and in less than a second was off the wall, his weight bearing down on Elena. His cold fingers wrapped around her throat and he forced her down against the side of the bed, his crimson gaze hard. "These hands will squeeze the life out of you," he hissed against her cheek. "The same hands that have fought to protect you, the same ones that have wanted nothing more than to touch you. You put on a brave face now, but you will fear me when that moment comes, Elena. You will loathe me, and you have forced me to bear it!"

Elena stilled beneath his weight, unafraid of his anger. "I could never fear you," she said to him, defiantly. "I feared not saving Cataline. I feared the Kirin being enslaved and Bryce dying on my account. You I do not fear, no matter how hard you try to scare me. I know who and what you are, Thanatos. I see you clearly, and I do not fear you."

At the mention of his true name, Eiry flinched. He pulled away enough to look into Elena's face. His hold loosened on her throat and he moved his hand upward, his fingers tracing gently along the lines of her jaw.

"I don't want to kill you," he breathed, "I can't bear the thought of it."

There was so much pain in his gaze that Elena's heart shattered at the sight of it. She hated that he suffered because of her.

"You are Death," Elena reminded him in a steady voice, and reached to still his hand against her face. "You have done this countless times before. You will do it again. I will choose the meaning of my own life, Eiry, and I have chosen this."

Something shifted in Eiry's gaze and he pressed a trembling hand over her mouth for silence. The anger drained from his eyes, leaving behind something as raw and primal as the power she had sensed in the Kirin and the dragon-king. It was the nature of his soul, his element—

cold, indiscriminate, unyielding, and yet devastatingly pure; the mechanism by which souls evolved. It called to something deep inside of Elena, and she felt herself yield to it naturally, her body stilling beneath his weight.

Gently, Eiry wrapped an arm around her waist and eased her body up against his, his fingers biting into her lower back as his mouth found hers. "Please don't hate me," he begged her, and kissed her with the same abandon he had the very first time.

He didn't stop her when she pulled the torn shirt off of his shoulders or when she smoothed her fingers against the tight skin behind the waist of his pants. His hand slipped beneath her jeans and Elena breathed his name out softly.

The sound of snickering interrupted them.

Elena and Eiry froze, the latter stealthily removing his hand from Elena's pants. Turning their faces toward the sound, they found Gavin and Galen all over each other in a corner of the room, near the bed, Gavin with his legs wrapped around Galen's hips.

"Oh, Eiry," Gavin cried out in an affected tone.

"Oh, Elena," mimicked Galen.

"You're so hot, but your fingers are sooooooo cold," added Gavin in a high-pitched voice.

"The better to touch you with, *my dear*," purred Galen, and then they both broke into a fit of laughter.

Eiry whispered an apology in Elena's ear and then reached over her head for a pillow, hurling it at the corner of the room.

The sound of a heavy crash startled Elena, and she twisted beneath Eiry's weight so she could get a better look. The pillow lay shattered on the floor in fragments of ice at the twins' feet, the space of wall between them marked by impressions of compressed ice. They wore identical expressions of feigned surprise, the moment made even more comical by the shirts they wore; Gavin a black t-shirt with bold white letters that read "Team Draig", and Galen another that read "Fuck Dragons".

Eiry didn't seem to appreciate the humor, or the interruption.

"What the fuck are you two doing in my room?" he snarled at them, his crimson eyes flashing with anger.

"Is it true?" Gavin asked, his tone suddenly serious.

Eiry narrowed his eyes. "Which part, exactly?" he asked, his body tense.

Galen looked down at Elena pointedly, and then lifted his eyes to meet Eiry's gaze. For an instant, he appeared upset. Then just as quickly, his features smoothed.

"Hades is dead," Galen remarked, his fingers tracing along the spine of his long braid as Gavin climbed off of him. Then he pushed himself off the wall and stepped closer to the bed, only stopping when Eiry growled at him in warning. "And *she* has chosen to die."

"Both are true," Elena confirmed, unconsciously pressing her hand to Eiry's chest when the muscles in his arms twitched.

The black markings on his skin caught the faint light in the room and a curtain of his hair fell forward over his shoulder, drawing Elena's attention. With a reluctant sigh, Eiry dipped his head down, pressed a kiss to Elena's brow, and then eased himself down on the mattress beside her.

"Why would you do that, Ele?" Gavin asked, a wounded expression on his face.

"Because she has a hero complex," snapped Galen, as he wrapped his arm around Gavin's waist and pulled him closer.

"I'm touched, Galen. I didn't know you paid attention," Elena replied, not surprised when he hissed at her. She smiled, in spite of his surly disposition. Somewhere along the way, she had grown attached to these two. "It was the only way to save Cataline once I used the Helm to save Bryce," Elena said, answering Gavin's question.

The twins looked at each other. Something passed between them and then they both returned their attention to Elena, their expressions identical.

"Thank you for doing what you did for Bryce," said Gavin.

"You were under no obligation to do so," added Galen, completing the thought.

Elena nodded. Eiry draped his arm over her waist, reminding her he was still there; as if he was so easy to forget. Again, the twins looked at Eiry with a disapproving look.

"Can we come visit you in Elysium?" Gavin asked quietly, his manner more shy than usual. "And for the record, I think it's bullshit you have to die."

Galen smacked Gavin's arm, and gave an exasperated sigh. "And also for the record, when he says 'we' he means just him."

"Yes, of course," Elena said, and laughed. It was refreshing to see Galen was as difficult as always. If her choice would have made him act differently, Elena might have lost it altogether. "And I mean yes about both things. Of course you can come visit me any time, Gavin, and of course you obviously only speak for yourself—Galen wouldn't be caught dead visiting me."

Galen narrowed his eyes but Gavin smiled broadly, his cheerful demeanor returning. He stepped closer to the bed and again Eiry growled, the gesture rumbling loudly in his chest, against Elena's back.

"Give it a rest, Eiry," Gavin complained, his golden-green gaze on Elena, begging her to intervene. "I just want to give her a kiss on the cheek."

Elena laughed. She convinced Eiry to back down, and he did so with an exaggerated sigh.

"Make it quick, and then you two monkeys get the fuck out of my room," Eiry growled to the twins, and shifted positions to lie down on his back, hands behind his head.

Gavin rolled his eyes and gingerly stepped closer to the bed. He gave Elena a hug, in addition to the kiss on the cheek. "One more thing," he said to her as he pulled away, "you two might want to make a run for it now if you don't want to spend the final hours of your human life in a meeting with my mother. We overheard her arguing with Evius a little while ago. She's über pissed."

Elena tensed but before she could ask for details Gavin and Galen vanished into the shadows, their laughter echoing behind them. She sighed heavily—always a little drained after dealing with those two—and then turned to face Eiry, who watched her quietly before drawing himself up and gently kissing her mouth.

"I'm going to kill them before they ever make it to Elysium," he whispered as he pulled away, his tone a little too serious.

"Does this at least mean you're in a better mood now?"

"I wouldn't go so far," he said, and then hugged her close. "I can't undo the choice you made, or the role that I must play in it. All that I can do right now is make sure that I don't ruin the time you have left, Elena."

"That's fair," she said softly, placated by the feel of him so close to her. He held her tightly and Elena relaxed against him, happy that the worst was over for now.

Eiry held her a moment longer and then gently pulled away. "So, where would you like to go, princess?" he asked, running a finger along the slope of her nose. "I'll take you anywhere you want."

There was only one place Elena wanted to be. "Are you familiar with the house where my parents and I used to live in Tokyo?"

"Yes, the one with the beautiful garden."

"Take me there."

Less than an hour later—thanks to Elena's newfound tolerance for god travel—Elena and Eiry found themselves standing at the front gate of her childhood home. Nestled in a residential part of Mitaka City in Western Tokyo, near Inokashira Park, the home was a traditional two-story *kominka* house restored to perfection and moved to its current location before Elena was born. A gabled roof tiled in blue-slate and white-plastered walls with warm wooden accents gave the house its traditional facade. A gabled wall of white plaster, built over a foundation of stone, surrounded the property, and kept the garden and first story hidden from view.

Elena stood silent facing the roofed gate, taking in the details that were different from what she remembered. A smaller wooden door had been added to the gateway, built into the wall to the right of the original wooden gate, as well as new lighting and a state of the art intercom and security system. The exterior of the property had been meticulously maintained, its walls freshly painted and the wooden accents flawlessly varnished.

"I think it's safe to assume someone lives here," Elena whispered to Eiry, running her fingers along the surface of the new door, admiring the wood's grain. "Can you tell if there's anyone inside?"

"Yes, there is," Eiry said as he leaned against the wall, an amused look on his face.

"What's so funny?" Elena asked with an arched brow, her arms crossed over her chest. "I doubt I can just knock on the door and introduce myself. All I really want to see is the garden. Do you think we can sneak in? It should be dark pretty soon."

They had arrived just as the sun was setting.

"That won't be necessary," Eiry said with a grin, "I know the owner," and with a playful wink, he pressed the intercom.

The electronic sound of a doorbell echoed from the speakers. A small screen flickered to life, revealing a middle-aged Japanese woman. She was incredibly beautiful, with rich black hair and skin as pale as snow. Her eyes were grayish-blue, and reminded Elena of river stones. The moment she saw Eiry, her face brightened.

"Shinigami-sama," the woman said in a gentle but surprised tone, and immediately bowed deeply in front of the camera. "I was not expecting you this evening, but I am most happy to see you. I will meet you at the front door."

The sound of a buzzer echoed in the twilight air, and Eiry pushed the smaller door open. Taking Elena's hand, he ducked inside.

The front garden was exactly as Elena remembered it, with added lighting to accent the colors and overall scene at night. A stone pathway led the way from the gate through the garden to the entrance to the house, the path lit by a stone lantern to their left. A beautiful pond was nestled within the sculpted plants and trees to the right of the path. A weeping cherry tree lined its shore at the farthest end, its branches nearly touching the water. Koi fish of every size and color glided gently beneath the surface of the pond. Elena heard the distinct clack of a bamboo fountain, and the chime of a small bell stirred in the wind. A stone basin filled with water stood near the entrance of the house, a bamboo ladle placed across it for guests to wash their hands.

The blue-eyed woman Elena had seen in the intercom stood at the entrance of the home, waiting for them patiently, two pairs of slippers in her hands. The stones immediately in front of the entrance were splashed with water, welcoming them.

Elena immediately felt at ease.

"Shinigami-sama," said the woman in greeting, bowing low once again.

Eiry and Elena returned the gesture, and then carefully went about removing their shoes. They left them at the entrance and put on the slippers, stepping quietly inside.

The interior of the house was as Elena remembered it. The entrance led into a large, open space with floors made of gleaming wood. Taking up the majority of the first floor, it served as the main living and dining area. Square wooden columns held up exposed beams that ran along the edges and corners of the space, and subtly marked off its divisions; to the left of the entrance the living space and to the right the dining room, the far portion of which was partitioned with *fusuma* and *shōji* doors into a separate room lined in *tatami*. The ceiling was high and open to the roof. *Shōji* doors lined the outside walls of the space.

The open floor plan formed the shape of an "L" around the *tatami*-lined room in the top right corner of the space. The *shōji* on the left, bordering the living space, opened out to the wooden *engawa*, the veranda that ran along the perimeter of the house, bordering the garden that surrounded the home at every side. Glass sliding doors framed in wood lined the *engawa*, and could be opened or shut depending on the weather or the occupant's mood. The *shōji* on the right, bordering the dining area, opened to a hall that led to two rooms on the right side of the house, which faced the *engawa* and the garden beyond.

When Elena had lived here as a child, the living space to the left had been furnished more traditionally than it was now. The current owner had chosen to divide it into two separate spaces by the use of large modern rugs. The space closest to the entrance, nearest the bottom corner of the "L", was an entertainment area with state of the art television and music equipment. The space was decorated with a surprisingly harmonious mixture of period appropriate pieces and contemporary furnishings, blending together the best aspects of modern and antique Japanese aesthetics.

The space farthest from the entrance, toward the top end of the "L", was a living area lined in modern couches and armchairs, and decorated with beautiful pieces of art—both modern and antique; a balanced mixture of Western and Eastern influences. The back wall, which divided the space from a kitchen facing the back of the house, was lined with built-in shelves forming three vertical bookcases nestled on top of a wall-wide bureau of drawers and cabinets also built into the wall. Books of every kind filled the shelves, stacked asymmetrically and accented with various pieces of art.

Put together, the living space was breathtaking, familiar to Elena and yet altogether new.

The partitioned room in the top right corner of the space was eight mats in size, with a small hearth built into the central mat. Four silk cushions were placed strategically around it. As Elena stepped closer, she saw a *tokonoma*—the formal alcove in every Japanese home—built into the far wall, displaying a scroll and a flower arrangement. An antique iron kettle and charcoal burner used in tea ceremonies was also on display. During Elena's childhood, the room had been used as a formal dining space, but it appeared the new owner used it as an in-house tearoom.

"I am sorry the house is not fully prepared for your arrival, Shinigami-sama," the Japanese woman said, as she led them deeper into the home. "Shall I prepare a guest room in addition to the master bedroom?"

"No need, Miyuki-san," Eiry replied with a smile, "the master bedroom will suffice."

"Have you dined already or would you like me to prepare you a meal?" the woman named Miyuki asked Eiry in a deferential tone, her manner elegant and refined. "The inside baths have not been drawn, but the outdoor bath is ready, as always, should you desire to bathe before the meal."

"A meal would be lovely," Eiry said, and thanked her with a gentle bow of his head. "You don't need to worry about the towels or *yukata*. I know where they are. I'll show my guest around first, and then we'll enjoy a bath while you prepare the meal. We can worry about the *futons* in the master bedroom later."

Elena watched their interaction in stunned silence.

Miyuki excused herself, but before she could leave Eiry called her name and asked her to wait. "Miyuki-san, before you leave I would like to introduce you to my guest."

"Shinigami-sama, I would never presume," replied the woman, and bowed her head. She was so elegant it made Elena's heart hurt. There was a grace about the woman that Elena knew she could never possess.

"Don't be silly Miyuki, you have met her before. It was just a very long time ago." With a wide smile, his eyes glinting with mischief, Eiry turned toward Elena. "Miyuki-san, this is Elena, Isabella-sama's daughter."

"*Hajimemashite. Dōzo yoroshiku.*" How do you do, and pleased to meet you, Elena said to Miyuki, bowing once again.

Miyuki stilled. Wide-eyed, and visibly shaken, she bowed deeply to Elena. "*Dōzo yoroshiku,*" Muyiki repeated the greeting. Then, in a very shy manner, she continued in English, "I am one of many Edo yōkai who cared deeply for you parents, and fought to protect your mother. It is a great honor, Elena-sama, to see you again. How I missed the resemblance between you and Isabella-sama is shameful, and I beg your pardon."

Elena instantly shook her head, wanting to ease Miyuki's concern. "There's no need to apologize, Miyuki-san. It's been many years, and Eiry's played a dirty little trick on the both of us. If anything, this is his fault." Elena smiled and Miyuki relaxed, to Elena's relief. "I'm very thankful for the help you and your kin provided my family, and I'm honored to be in your company again."

Miyuki bowed deeply, and Elena returned the gesture—a custom she always enjoyed; an expression of profound gratitude without the need for words. With a second bow to Eiry, Miyuki excused herself to prepare the evening meal.

Elena turned towards Eiry and found him watching her, a smug expression on his face. "How did you end up with this house?" Elena demanded, unable to keep the awe from the sound of her voice. She was so happy right now, she could almost cry. She would have never imagined, in a million years, that she would spend these final moments in her childhood home, which somehow now belonged to Eiry. "And since when does this place have an outside bath?"

"Since I made a few creative renovations," Eiry replied with a wink. Then he took Elena by the hand and began to lead her through the dining space toward the two rooms on the right side of the house.

The first room they came across was lined in *tatami*, partitioned by the use of *fusuma* on the inside walls and *shōji* on the outside walls, which opened out to the *engawa* and the garden on the right side of the house. As it had during her childhood, the room was being used as a kind of traditional study, with staggered shelving along the left-hand wall, which divided the room from the one adjacent to it, and a desk alcove built into the bottom right corner of the room, *shōji* windows lining that part of the space so the view could be opened to the garden. Elena had spent countless hours in this room as a child, her mother's favorite because of the particular view of the garden. Isabella would paint on the *engawa* or beneath the shade of the blooming plum tree outside, while Elena read books or played games on the *tatami* inside the room.

With a grin, Eiry pulled Elena further down the hall, toward the room adjacent to the study. During her childhood, it had been used as a type of storage room with wooden chests, sideboards, and various shelves. From where Elena stood now, she couldn't see what was inside the room, since its *fusuma* doors were slid shut.

"Your parents loved this house," Eiry explained as he led her toward their destination, "and when they died I promised your father I would purchase it so that it would always stay in the family. They couldn't leave it to you because they didn't want your connection to them revealed. Evius said he wouldn't mind if I made a few renovations, since I have such discerning tastes," he added proudly.

"Oh, yes, of course," Elena teased, and followed him happily into the second room once he pushed open the *fusuma* doors. When she stepped inside, Elena couldn't believe her eyes. She literally stopped dead in her tracks.

Instead of the room from her childhood, the space was lined in slate tile in varying tones of umber, green and gold—along the floor and halfway up the left wall, which held an open shower. To the right, antique iron bookcases filled the width of the fixed wall, its shelves of distressed wood filled with towels and toiletries shelved in staggered spaces between various industrial artifacts—a large wooden pulley threaded with rope, metal wheels, antique trays, small wooden chests, vintage bowls, old trunks, and wooden models.

The room was stunning, and Elena was properly floored. It was completely different from anything she could have imagined. It had the feel of a luxury *onsen*, the spa-like facilities built around hot springs in Japan.

"This is beautiful," Elena said, as Eiry slid shut the *fusuma* doors behind them. "Completely insane, but beautiful," she added. "What else have you done?"

After closing the inside doors to the room, Eiry stepped across the space to open the *shōji* doors that faced the garden.

"I renovated the indoor baths in the back of the house on the first floor, as well as the ones upstairs. The kitchen is completely renovated. There are still five bedrooms upstairs. The master still faces the front, but the space is a little bigger. It's still very traditional. The two back corner rooms are guestrooms, both modern, and I made the room between them an attached study. The room in the middle of the floor, between the master and the guestrooms in the back, I left the way it was."

Elena listened to him explain the changes, and she registered them for future reference, but her attention was fixed on the space outside the sliding doors of the *engawa*, revealed slowly as Eiry slid open the *shōji* doors.

Cradled by the elegant lines and graceful beauty of the garden, the open air bath had the look of a natural hot spring, nestled between sculpted pine, white-barked maple trees with deep purple leaves, shapely bushes of white peony and shrubs of flowering red camellia. It was reminiscent of the bath Elena had shared with Aosaginohi, sunk into the earth and made out of natural stone. The area was lit by the glow of a stone lantern, as well as a few strategically placed accent lights along the ground.

"I have a really odd question to ask you," Elena told Eiry, as he made his way back toward her across the room.

"Ask away," he said with a smile, obviously satisfied with Elena's reaction.

"Will you inherit the Domos Aidaou?"

Eiry stilled and watched Elena curiously. "Why do you ask?"

"Because if you do, then you could give mom and I a hall pass to come here once every couple of years, maybe."

"Look at you coming up with all the angles," he said to her softly, and reached to take her hand. There was pain in his voice, but he tried his best to keep it hidden. "I'm sure it'll piss someone off, but I'm game if you are. I'll be stuck running the hateful place anyway, so I might as well enjoy whatever small pleasures I can get from it. Now, if I could draw your attention to the present, I have a little favor to ask of you."

"Ask away," Elena said, mimicking the way he had said it only moments before.

With a roguish smile, Eiry leaned close. His ice-blue gaze reflected the scant light in the room, as shadows played across his features. Gently, his fingers barely touching Elena's skin, he pushed her hair back off of her shoulder, exposing the pale column of her throat. Slipping his fingers to the nape of her neck, he drew her closer, until his lips brushed against the shell of her ear. With a playful edge to his voice, he whispered, "Please undress."

IT WAS RARE the man who could match the gravitas of such a request, and yet in this instance it was the gravitas that paled in comparison to the man.

Elena stood motionless against Eiry's form, suddenly too nervous to respond. She felt butterflies in her stomach, and almost passed out because she forgot to breathe.

"Elena."

Eiry whispered her name softly, a cool murmur against her skin as he pulled himself back slowly, his cheek touching hers before his fingers traced the line of her jaw to her chin. He guided her gaze upward to meet his, which burned with a need Elena had never seen before.

"Please."

He pled with her, his voice as gentle as the touch of his hands, which now traveled down the length of her arms, leaving a tingling sensation in their wake—ice-cold pins and needles. Elena exhaled sharply and Eiry brushed his mouth against hers, not quite kissing her. She felt the cool whisper of his breath against her lips, and her stomach tightened. She felt lightheaded, and, for an instant, the uncontrollable urge to laugh—an involuntary reaction when she felt extremely nervous.

"Did you just ask me to take off my clothes?" Elena asked him, her hand against his chest, giving herself a little room to breathe.

For the first time since they met, not including the brief moment she had seen him in a *kimono*, Eiry wore something other than a suit. Before coming here, he had quickly changed into a pair of slacks and a navy blue v-neck sweater that hugged his body a little too perfectly. It was made of some kind of soft material, probably some cashmere blend, which Elena was happily distracted by. She didn't realize she was kneading her fingers into his chest until he dropped his gaze to her hand and grinned.

"You're welcome to join me in the bath with your clothes on, but I wouldn't recommend it," he teased, and caught her hand with his. "Plus, it wouldn't be any fun." With a wink, he pressed his thumb to the inside of her palm and began to massage it lightly.

"There was more to it than that," Elena insisted and tried to pull away, but Eiry held on to her hand, easily pulling her closer again.

His body felt cool and unnaturally hard against hers, far from human. In fact, Elena wasn't sure how anyone could mistake him for human at all. He was the very definition of otherworldly. He was too beautiful, too striking. His eyes shined with a preternatural light and his skin was as flawless as polished stone. When she had first met him, though, Elena's mind had not processed these things; it didn't have the proper language or programming to do so. Now that she did, Elena couldn't help but notice the stark differences between them.

"Yes, much more to it than that," Eiry whispered, "but I prefer not to rush, even if we have a very limited amount of time." His expression grew troubled, the way it had several times in the last hour whenever he spoke of the reality that awaited them at the end of the night. Remembering himself, he shook off his somber mood and playfully kissed Elena's brow. "I want to enjoy this moment with you. Now, undress so we can get into the bath."

Elena nodded, and slowly began to undress. To her surprise, Eiry turned around to give her some privacy. "Now you're just making fun of me," she said, annoyed. She undressed and placed her clothes on one of two teak benches placed vertically in the center of the room, which divided the shower from the wall of toiletries. As she did, Eiry made his way to a sitting area in the far end of the room, close to the *engawa* facing the garden.

"Never," he said in a serious tone, and eased into one of two lounge chairs woven out of a honey-colored rattan. The lines were clean and modern, with an understated elegance that matched the home's Japanese aesthetic.

Elena found something to tie her hair up in one of the vintage trays on the shelves of the opposite wall, and then took her time washing herself off in the shower before selecting a towel to take with her into the bath. She found a stack of thinner towels and wrapped one around herself, tucking the corner in tightly. Eiry never once turned around. He waited until he felt her standing at his side before he drew himself up from the chair.

"I'll only be a minute," he whispered to her, and motioned to the open-air bath before making his way to the showers.

Elena tiptoed across the *engawa* to the path of stone that led to the bath. Just as she stepped into it, she felt someone behind her.

"The water's great," she whispered and turned around, expecting to see Eiry. Instead, she was looking up at Alexander, who was staring down at her with a cold fury in his eyes.

"What have you done?" Alexander growled, his anger making his sky-blue eyes shine brightly in the darkness. He looked a mess, shirtless and with his long blonde hair loose. An angry wound was healing across his chest.

In a movement faster than Elena could follow, he backhanded her. The strength of his strike split her lip open and sent her staggering into the water. Blood gushed into her mouth and Elena screamed for Eiry, her hand instinctively covering her mouth. She took several steps back in the water, trying to put as much space between them as she could.

Ever since she'd made her pact with Hades, she hadn't spared Alexander a second thought. She hadn't even considered the possibility that he might still come after her.

"I put an end to this stupid little charade," Elena snapped at him. "Now you can go back to doing whatever it is you do when you're not hunting my kind."

Alexander bristled, making his way around the edge of the bath. "Hunting your kin is the only joy I know in life."

"Then you should get a day job," Eiry snarled as he appeared next to Alexander, his nails already extended into dagger-like claws. "What are you doing here, Alexander? You can't touch her. She belongs to me now."

"You did this!" Alexander howled, and turned his ire toward Eiry. "Her life belonged to *me*, Thanatos, like every other Heir's, like her mother before her. You had no right to let her throw it away!"

Alexander brandished his gleaming sword and rushed toward Eiry, who easily dodged him. Unable to stop his momentum, Alexander stumbled, clumsily stabbing the ground with the tip of his sword to maintain his balance. He turned around as quickly as he could, but Eiry was already at his back, nails at his throat.

The image was almost comical. A blue-haired man wearing only a towel around his waist pressed to the back of a shirtless, longhaired blonde who was spitting and cursing in spite of the four blade-like nails at his throat.

"Shinigami-sama," came the gentle voice of Miyuki from the shadows.

Elena turned to see her standing on the *engawa*, delicate and beautiful, dressed in a light blue *kimono* and white *obi*, her hair gathered gracefully at the nape of her neck. Her eyes were the only unusual thing about her, as they glowed with an otherworldly light. The air around her shimmered with energy, and a cool breeze swept over the garden. Flurries of snow began to gather around her.

Alexander stilled.

"You need not concern yourself, Miyuki-san," Eiry said to her, his nails inching closer to Alexander's throat. "Helios was just leaving."

"As you wish, Shinigami-sama. The meal is ready, whenever you are," Miyuki replied, and excused herself with a bow.

Eiry retracted his nails and shoved Helios away. "You're drunk. Go back to Olympus. There is nothing left for you here."

"You're pathetic," Alexander roared and whirled around to face Eiry, his sword clanging against the stone pathway beneath him as he walked. "You've never been able to save a single one of them from me, and now you've failed to even keep them safe against your own kind."

"Go home, Helios," Eiry warned him, the black markings slowly appearing along the lengths of his arms, traveling upward towards his shoulders and neck. "You should be rejoicing. Another Heir falls, and this time you didn't have to lift a fucking finger."

Alexander swung his sword, and missed Eiry by an inch. "I like lifting a finger, you impotent excuse for a god! I love to hear them scream. I love to feel their bodies break beneath mine. I should cut you down now and break her while she still has a pulse. I don't fancy them dead, like you and Dionysus."

Eiry moved so quickly that Elena didn't see it until he had Alexander by the throat and was driving the god down to his knees. The scythe appeared in his open hand and he held it aloft, ready to strike.

"Leave now, Helios," he growled, his face so close to Alexander's their lips were almost touching. "By the law of the Moirai, Elena's life belongs to me now. Only I may collect such a debt, and I take great pleasure in knowing she is the one Heir you never touched." Eiry spit the last words, his lips curling over his teeth in a snarl. "Hades will be given to the Void for his treachery. Make sure you inform Zeus and Poseidon of their brother's glorious fate," Eiry added in a menacing tone, then lifted his arm and readied himself to strike.

As the scythe swept downward toward Alexander's neck, the sky god vanished into the night.

THE SOUND OF EIRY'S SCYTHE striking stone was the only sound in the garden for several long seconds. Then, with a heavy sigh, Eiry pulled himself up to his full height and dislodged his weapon from the stone. He raised his arm and held the scythe out in front of him. A faint, slick sound echoed through the silence and then the weapon disappeared, folding into itself from the outside in.

When Eiry finally turned to face Elena, his expression was unreadable.

"Please don't let Alexander ruin the night," Elena said to him softly, as he dropped down at the edge of the bath and lowered himself into the water. Somehow, his towel had remained in place.

He didn't say a word but made his way to the far end of the bath where Elena was sitting. When he reached her side, he looked her over carefully, hissing when he saw the swell of her lip and the bruise that was forming. Elena felt the anger roll through his body, and for a moment his eyes turned a deep, vivid crimson. Then he drew in his breath and pressed his fingers to her lip, healing the wound. Afterward, he sat down beside her and leaned back against the edge of the bath.

"I'm sorry about that," he whispered, tilted his head back and closed his eyes. Slowly, the black markings along his neck began to disappear. "I had hoped we'd have a little more time to relax in the bath before dinner, but that idea just went down the drain."

Even though the markings faded from his shoulders, the tension remained; Elena could see it even in the faint glow of the lantern, the lines of taut sinew beneath his skin. "You don't need to apologize, Eiry," she assured him. "Let's just relax here a few minutes, and then we'll go in for dinner."

Eiry nodded, a gesture Elena saw through the corner of her eye, and then reached for her hand beneath the water, gently lacing his fingers with hers. Above the water, he remained motionless and his expression never changed.

After several moments of silence, the song of a cicada the only sound, Eiry spoke, so softly that Elena could hardly hear. "I hope you didn't take offense to what I said."

Elena had no clue what he was talking about, but the sadness in his voice resonated with her in a very visceral way, almost as if it had been carried by the water and seeped through every pore in her skin. "What are you talking about?" she asked him, turning so that she could look at him directly.

Opening his eyes, Eiry turned towards her and met her gaze. They were their usual icy blue again, and the black markings on his arms were completely gone. "What I said about taking pleasure in knowing that you're the only Heir he never touched. I don't want you to think I'm satisfied with this situation. I would rather you lived. A human life is so short as it is, ephemeral and brief. But if there's one silver lining I can find in all of this madness, Elena, it's that his violence has never touched you, and now it never will."

Elena leaned closer and placed a kiss on the corner of Eiry's mouth. "I'm not offended," she whispered to him, "I'm flattered. I'm happy to know that you care."

"It's much more than just caring, Elena," he replied, and held her still when she tried to move. "The Kirin cares for you. Tarōbō cares for you. The twins, and even Bryce, care for you. I'm a little more invested than that." Pulling her closer to him, so that her head came to rest under his chin, Eiry continued. "I've watched over you from the day you were born. You were given to me to protect, and I watched over you in this very house, even played with you when no one was watching. I delivered you to Cataline when you were orphaned, and watched you grow in her house. I watched over you all of your life from a distance." He paused briefly, sat up straight and eased Elena up gently so he could look directly into her eyes. "Never in my long existence have I been so attached to a single living creature, not even a sibling or parent. Death must not know love or have any attachments, Elena. He must remain unchanged and unmoved at all times, completely indiscriminate. That is my nature, and yet I am changed. I am moved. I am entirely devoted to you, irrevocably in love with you, and it kills me that I must take the one life I cherish most in this world."

Eiry grew silent, but his confession hung heavily in the air between them. Elena was speechless, her mind reeling from the reach of his words. They were unexpected, and she felt inadequate against their weight. Words and thoughts failed her. Elena had known for some time now that she was in love with Eiry. She couldn't pin point a time or a place, she couldn't recall a specific gesture or moment, but it had happened. Somewhere along the way, in the middle of the roller coaster that had become her life, Elena had fallen in love with him, but she had never dreamed that he might feel the same, let alone that his affection could run so deeply.

Suddenly, Eiry kissed her, hard. His need was bruising, and he held her so close Elena could hardly breathe. It was the kind of kiss where you bared your soul, pouring into it every hope and dream, even your fears, praying that they would somehow resonate with the other person. Elena relaxed into Eiry's arms and returned his kiss in earnest, pouring into it all of the things she felt.

After losing her parents, too afraid of experiencing the same kind of loss, Elena had shut her heart away, sealed it so deep inside of her that no one could ever reach it. She had experienced the world in this half-numbed state ever since, too guarded to feel anything deeply, good or bad. Meeting Eiry had been a shock to her system. Although their first encounter was brief, Elena felt his presence so sharply that her reaction was immediate. In a world shaded in gray, Eiry was bright and vibrant, like Cataline, demanding Elena's undivided attention. It had been out of her hands ever since.

"Did you really play with me when I was a kid?" Elena asked him in a breathy voice, pulling away just enough to look up into his eyes.

Eiry held on to her tightly, refusing to let her stray too far. "Of all the things I said," he whispered with a ghost of a smile, wrapping his arms around her waist, "you latched on to that part?"

"Well, I want to know, because I don't remember ever seeing your face before, and you have a pretty distinctive face," Elena insisted. She struggled playfully in his arms, resorting to splashing him with water when he refused to let her go. Of course, that didn't work, and Elena finally grew still in his arms.

With a sigh, Eiry leaned against the edge of the pool, pulling Elena with him. He loosened his hold around her waist and propped himself up on his elbow, against the ledge.

"Children are too close, temporally, to the cycle of birth and rebirth to recognize Death appropriately, even when it's in front of them," Eiry explained. "If you think back as hard as you can, you might recall memories where you'll see parts of me, but never my face. After your parents died, I kept my distance. Usually, humans have strong reactions to me. They don't actively recognize me but their bodies instinctively tell them to stay away, the whole fight or flight phenomenon. You're one of the few who've reacted positively. That was unexpected, just as meeting you was. We weren't ever supposed to cross paths physically, not unless the necklace surfaced, and bumping into you at the firm took me completely by surprise. That's why I was so rude."

"I was wondering about that," Elena admitted and laughed, remembering how angry he had made her the first time they'd met. Just the mere thought of him had made her furious for days. "About tonight," Elena added, abruptly putting the conversation back on track. There were a few things she needed to say before they went inside, and it was just about that time. "I didn't set out on this journey hoping to die and I definitely didn't think I'd fall in love, let alone with the Greek god of death, but here we are and both things are true. That means that someday, be it now or sixty years from now, you would have to take my life no matter how much you cherished it. My parentage makes that window more like now or ten years from now, if I'm lucky. I would rather go now, on my terms, than die a painful death later. The only thing you need to worry about is smuggling my cat Cicero into Elysium, alive. Can you do that?"

Perplexed, Eiry answered, "Yes," and then narrowed his eyes. His features smoothed and his expression grew serious. "Was there a declaration of love in there somewhere?" he asked in a humorless voice, "Because I didn't hear one."

Elena covered her mouth so he couldn't see her grin, and nodded; his somber expression was too cute for words, and Elena was certain cute was not an adjective Death was fond of. "Oh," Elena added, remembering something else, "one more thing. When the time comes tonight, don't tell me. Just do it. I'll trust you to kill me softly."

MIYUKI PREPARED a superb meal of mackerel cooked in miso, pickled cucumber and seaweed salad, miso soup with sesame and tofu, and a serving of steamed white rice. If Elena had given any consideration to the issue of her last meal, she could not have asked for anything better. There was an understated elegance to Japanese cuisine, a harmony of delicate flavors and textures presented with the utmost care, the choice of bowl or plate as important an element as any single ingredient. It was incredibly satisfying, even more so when paired with good company and pleasant conversation.

The three of them enjoyed their meal slowly, between anecdotes of Elena's childhood in Japan and substantial portions of sake. Miyuki spoke very fondly of Elena's parents—Isabella in particular—and Elena's insatiable curiosity as a child. She was genuinely happy to see Elena again, to know that she had survived and was doing well. Eiry and Elena didn't ruin the mood with the reality of their situation, and they all seemed to be of the same mind because Helios's impromptu visit never came to the conversation. When the meal and conversations were over, Elena and Eiry excused themselves for the evening.

Eiry led Elena up the stairs to the master bedroom in the front of the house, the room that had belonged to her parents. As he had promised, very little had changed other than a few adjustments to the size of the room and the renovation of the bathroom, which was Japanese in style and also very modern; *ofuro* bathtub, wooden bath stool and bucket, bathroom slippers, and *yukata* juxtaposed against modern lines, quartz surfaces, and textured tiled walls. Any of Eiry's personal belongings were kept hidden within drawers or chests. The only evidence he occupied the room at all was his suit on its wooden stand in the corner of the room and a few items on an alcove desk—his watch, his wallet and a vintage cigarette case made of tiger agate.

A modern light fixture in the shape of a paper lantern flooded the room with light, but Eiry opted for the dimmer lighting of an *andon* lamp. He lit it with a lighter he retrieved from a small wooden chest that sat on his desk, and then brought the lamp with him to the *futons* that had been placed side by side in the center of the room, covered with thick, downy quilts. Eiry dropped down onto one of the *futons*, placed the andon lamp on the floor behind him, and called for Elena with a gesture of his hand.

In the dim glow of the lamplight, his *yukata* loose above the waist, Eiry had an unearthly look about him. His eyes caught the light of the lamp and gleamed like stars in the darkness. A pale luminescence shined beneath the surface of his skin, and the luster of his hair glistened like moonlight. Next to him, Elena couldn't help but feel plain.

"I don't bite," Eiry teased her, and Elena shot him a look.

Slowly, so as not to seem overeager, Elena made her way to the *futon* next to his. They had been sleeping in the same bed now for the past few weeks, but this was the first time Elena remembered feeling so nervous. With a deep breath, she crawled into bed beside him. She reached for the quilt but Eiry stopped her, catching her wrist with his hand.

"No hiding," he breathed against Elena's ear, his chest so close to her back that she could feel the chill. Gently, he took hold of her other wrist and, with the weight of his gaze keeping her still, he eased Elena back against the *futon*.

Elena's heart beat furiously as Eiry inched closer, his icy gaze glowing behind strands of pale hair that partly covered his eyes. He settled on his side next to her, their bodies touching. The coolness of his skin escaped from beneath the silk of his robe, and a chill ran down Elena's spine.

Eiry smiled, a devastating smile that left her breathless as his fingers traced the collar of her robe. Following the lines of the silk to her waist, he untied the sash that held the robe together. He slipped his fingers beneath the inner collar, his cold touch making her breath catch, and then eased the folds of her robe open until Elena was completely exposed.

Holding her gaze, Eiry smoothed his hand down her side and Elena's hip shot upward, her back arching automatically from the cold. He swallowed her moan with a kiss and gently pulled her up against him, his arm cradling her waist. With his other hand, he slipped the robe from her shoulder and tugged at it gently until the entire thing dropped. His hand then slipped between her legs and Elena cried out into his mouth, as his fingers slowly began their work.

They had just started, and Elena was already drowning. The ice in his skin drew out her need almost instantly, every muscle in her body tingling from a thousand frozen pins and needles. As he continued his attentions between her thighs, his energy strummed each needle, sending a shot of cold electricity into every spot. Elena cried out softly, overwhelmed by the unexpected sensation. She had never felt anything like it in her life—a hundred waves crashing over her, one after the other, without relief until the last possible moment. It left her completely undone, and Elena clung to him as the last cold waves crashed over her body.

"Not fair," Elena whispered to him as she struggled to catch her breath, her body still spasming. Eiry laughed and the reverberations of it made her body clench sharply. Elena had to stifle a moan with her hand.

"Are you complaining?" Eiry breathed against her mouth and then slid his fingers to the nape of her neck, forcing her still. He watched her intently; his eyes filled with a heavy desire that tinged the blue of his irises a darker shade. Elena shook her head and Eiry kissed her deeply, easing her back down until she lay flat against the *futon*. He parted her legs with his hand and settled his hips between her thighs.

Elena reached for the sash of his robe and tugged it free. It fell open and she smoothed her hands up along his sharply cut chest, enjoying the pleasure that touched his features. She tucked her fingers beneath the robe at his shoulders and eased the fabric down his back, her nails digging into his sides when Eiry pressed his hips down hard against hers. He moaned into her mouth and kissed her hard, as the need tightened every muscle in his body. Elena could feel the tension beneath his skin, making his body tremble.

Grasping the back of her thigh, Eiry hooked her knee over his hips, searching for the angle he needed before he eased himself inside of her, a groan rumbling in his chest as the pleasure rolled through him. He caught her hips, bruises blooming where he touched, and took control of the rhythm; slow at first, drawn out to coax Elena's pleasure, the feel of him inside of her so cold it burned.

Elena lost herself against the cold press of his body and the bruising crush of his mouth, in the feel of his fractured breath against her skin and the bite of his nails across her hip. His need was overwhelming and Elena gave herself over to it, surrendering herself entirely.

It wasn't over for hours, their need urging them forward even when their bodies were spent. It was a desperate attempt to make up for lost time, a silent acknowledgement that it would never be like this again. This was a first and last time, a fleeting moment they could never get back and could never recreate. After tonight, a heart wouldn't beat in Elena's chest, her body would not be warm, and if such pleasures could be known by the dead Elena was certain it would not feel like this. Her mother possessed a physical body, but she was not human; what Elena had seen was a physical manifestation of Isabella's soul. What the physical limitations of that were, in a world where gods and monsters existed, was a mystery to Elena. She didn't know if she would ever have a moment like this again and it was already too late to inquire, and so Elena took from Eiry everything he could give; every kiss, every touch, every inch of skin that she could claim, until there was nothing left to give or take.

Elena didn't realize they had fallen asleep until she was woken up by the cool press of Eiry's body between her thighs. When she opened her eyes, he was looking down at her, his gaze searching hers, his expression calm. He smoothed his thumb along her mouth and kissed her, whispering her name against her lips.

His hair was mussed and Elena brushed it away from his eyes, smiling as she looked up into his face. He kissed her again, and this time it was deeper. His hands cradled her cheeks, and he eased his weight down against her. The cold energy from before poured into Elena's mouth. It spilled down her throat, settled in the pit of her stomach, and then split, branching out into streams of icy energy moving slowly through her body. Her muscles tingled and Elena cried softly into Eiry's mouth as a shot of pleasure moved through her, the ice making its way below her waist.

Elena wrapped her arms around Eiry's neck and deepened the kiss further, her body writhing against his as the sensation pushed through her. She yielded to it, and just as it crested Elena felt her father's blood rush to the surface of her skin. She saw herself reflected in Eiry's eyes, otherworldly and beautiful; rich black hair as dark as a starless night, hazel eyes that shimmered with variegated shades of gold, gray and green, and olive skin that glistened like gold against Eiry's snowy white.

They had stopped kissing and Eiry held her in his arms, their mouths still touching. His breath tingled against the inside of her lips, and when he kissed her again Elena realized she had gone numb. She couldn't feel anything below the waist anymore, and she could hardly hold her arms around Eiry's neck. He kissed her eyes, her cheeks, her throat, the tip of her nose, and then her lips, each kiss moist with his tears. Elena lost sensation in her arms and they dropped to her sides, as Eiry clutched her body tightly to his. Elena's breathing had grown shallow, and now she struggled to breathe.

"I'm not afraid," she managed to say, the spaces between each word drawn out so she could catch her breath. A tortured cry filled the silence in the room, and Eiry's entire body trembled. "Look at me," Elena begged him in staggered breaths. Her eyelids fluttered open and close, and her vision was beginning to blur. Everything felt pleasantly numb. She couldn't feel him holding her anymore, the lightness in her body making her feel like she was floating. When Eiry turned to look at her, thin streaks of silver streamed down his cheeks. "Promise to meet me on the other side?" she asked him, as he leaned as close as he could to hear her.

Eiry brought his lips to Elena's ear, and she knew it only because she could hear his breathing. Her sight was now gone and her heart was hardly beating. "Yes," Elena heard him promise, and then drifted into death as gently as if she had fallen asleep.

CHAPTER TWENTY-ONE

"I WAS TOLD YOU REFUSE YOUR DUTIES," Sleep said to his twin, as he made his way across the garden courtyard to where Death stood beneath a portico of archways that held up the roof. As he passed a pomegranate tree, he picked a fruit, pulling back the sleeve of his *kimono*. Fruit in hand, he continued on his way, moving with a soporific rhythm that could induce even the greatest deities to sleep.

Death, who was staring out at the vast region of Hades with an emptiness that nothing could fill, did not turn at the approach of his twin. In fact, he ignored the visit altogether, hoping in vain that Sleep would leave.

"Again, you wound me, Thanatos," Sleep whispered as he took his place beside his twin, and looked upon the landscape his brother was so preoccupied with. "All you ever do is wound me. The least you could do is veil your thoughts. That way, I won't be so repeatedly offended."

Death did not turn to face his twin but from the corner of his eye saw Sleep cut into the ripe pomegranate with an extended nail, his movements purposely drawn out. "What are you doing here, Hypnos?" he asked in an apathetic tone as he ran his fingers through his hair, frustrated. There was nothing more annoying to Death than his twin's languid manner.

Cerise-colored juice spilled down Hypnos's snow-white hand, and he caught the fluid with his tongue as it dripped past his wrist. "You promised to come for me when it was all over, and you did not. I awoke, and imagine my surprise when I am told you are now Lord of the Domos

Aidaou. I came to see you, and find Hecate on your throne. So naturally, I have come to find you."

"It is not over, Hypnos, and so I saw no reason in waking you," was Death's reply. Beside him, Hypnos stilled. A breeze stirred his blood-spun hair, which was tied loosely at the nape of his neck, strands of it left free to frame his delicate face. Death ignored him when he pressed closer, keeping his eyes fixed on the landscape ahead.

Hypnos, hooking his fingers on the loose sash of his *kimono*, leaned even closer to his twin and followed the line of his gaze. Not surprisingly, it led directly to the Elysian Islands. "Do you stare at it thinking if you stare long enough something might change?" he asked, unconcerned with its possible reception. "It is over, Thanatos. She is dead and gone. Thousands like her will come and go, but I am constant," he added, always careful to remind his twin.

"Get out of my sight!" Death roared and turned his crimson gaze on his brother, who watched him with the quiet patience of someone who shared the wretchedness of his soul. Sleep reached to touch his face, but Death caught his wrist and dug nails into the delicate flesh, a low, steady growl escaping him.

"Will you strike me?" asked Sleep with a derisive smile, and then shamelessly pressed himself closer to his twin, snaking his body around Death's grip so that they stood as close as lovers. "It is over. Accept it. Fulfill your duties as you always have, and the new ones you have acquired. You are Death, indomitable even against your better half!"

Death's grip faltered and for a moment he lost himself in the mirrored reflection of his twin's face, a much softer and less cruel version of his own. Slowly, he released Sleep's wrist and brushed the back of his trembling fingers against the line of his twin's jaw. "I cannot strike you," he said in a broken whisper, and then pulled his brother into his arms. Steeling himself, Death confessed his affliction. "I love her," he whispered, and readied himself for the struggle that would surely come.

Sleep stilled in Death's arms and the cry that escaped him was heart wrenching. His knees gave out and his body crumbled against the unyielding form of his twin. A cold rage consumed him. "You do not love her!" he howled in protest again and again, each time clawing and beating at Death's motionless form. "You do not love her. You cannot love her."

Sleep raged and Death remained unmoved. He took his twin's violence without word or protest. When Sleep's fury lost its vigor and the blood-haired god stilled, Death wrapped his arms tightly around Sleep's delicate form and lowered his lips to the shell of his brother's ear. "I promised her I would meet her on the other side," he whispered through clenched teeth, his tone biting, "but the Moirai took her the moment I arrived and will not allow me to sort her. And so, I refuse my duties. If I cannot sort her, I will sort no others. Let the shores of Erebus drown in a sea of souls, for all I care."

The easiest part about death was dying.

Elena had never expected that what would be waiting for her on the other side was pain. She had expected to wake up on the black shores of Erebus, Eiry at her side, and go on with her happy afterlife, but instead she regained awareness in total darkness; a cold, menacing darkness that pulled at every inch of her skin—if souls had skin. It spread her thin against the black horizon, every cell in her being destroyed, scattered and then transformed; the process repeating itself over and over again until it became unbearable, each time more painful than the last. Elena screamed for help, but no one would come, the menacing darkness her only companion. She couldn't say if she endured this for a couple of hours or a million years, but at some indecipherable moment in time the process stopped.

Through the darkness, Elena felt something cold as ice; a faint whisper of icy words lost behind the steady thrum of writhing darkness. The words converged in a thunderous stream and then shattered, splintering into small rivers of ice—thousands of them, each one breaking through the impenetrable darkness, weaving together into the semblance of a form. The rivers of ice became veins, forming a permanent web of adamantine filigree that grew brighter and stronger, carving a body out of the darkness; a body with skin as pale as snow, hair the color of mercury, eyes of silver-blue twilight, and lips a deep vermilion red.

The menacing darkness spoke her name and Elena opened her eyes, her spirit giving life to primordial flesh. All at once, a multitude of fractured impressions coursed through her consciousness, a river of infinite memories flooding her mind. Elena struggled against it, reaching with her newly shaped hands to tear the memories apart. They were horrifying, an endless parade of human recollection as far back as the farthest reaches of time; a composition of discarded images, the incongruous and dissonant history of humankind.

Suddenly, Elena was drowning. Memories, more intimate and visceral than the ones before, came rushing back; of a churning sea and waters so cold she could hardly breathe. The roar of crashing waves was deafening. Elena's eyes were wide open, but all she could see was the swirl of rushing water. She heard someone's voice and tried to latch on to it, but the flood of memories was too strong. They kept coming in waves, rushing over her like rapids, pulling her under and thrashing her against the rocks.

Someone or something caught her wrist, and Elena was suddenly anchored. Ice-cold arms wrapped around her waist and pulled her upward, out of the water. She gasped for air and her lungs burned as she coughed up water, her body convulsing painfully when she attempted to stand. She fell to her knees and felt the hard earth, cold beneath her hands. Sound was muffled and her vision blurred. Elena saw shards of colors. Brilliant, icy blues. Bright, vibrant reds. Pure, sparkling whites. And a rich, inky darkness that swallowed everything in its wake.

WHEN ELENA CAME TO, she was lying in bed. Eiry was fast asleep, doubled over on the edge of the bed from a chair he had positioned beside it. His head rested gingerly on his arms, and his face was partially obscured by his hair. He looked peaceful in his sleep, and Elena didn't have the heart to wake him.

Instead, she took stock of her surroundings. To Elena's surprise, they were not in Elysium; this was not the palatial home that housed her kin nor was the scent of the ocean carried in the wind. She was in Eiry's bed, in his rooms in Eira. Eternal twilight filtered in through the open-arched windows, bathing the room in shades of blue, violet and late evening rose.

Sleeping in an armchair in the corner of the room was the Kirin and Elena flinched, startled, as he opened his eyes, his sparkling topaz gaze fixed intently on Elena. He bowed his head ever so gently and then drew himself up from his chair, moving fluidly across the room to Elena's side. The blooming *netsuke* burned softly against her skin, and the Kirin's consciousness brushed hers in greeting.

Eiry stirred as the Kirin came to stand at his side.

He lifted his head, and smiled when his eyes met Elena's. For a moment he seemed hesitant, his gaze searching hers, before he reached for her wrist and pulled her into his arms.

"What's going on?" Elena whispered, and wrapped her arms around Eiry's neck.

She breathed in his scent, happy to see that her sense of touch was as strong as it had been before, maybe even stronger. In fact, there were details about Eiry's body that she could feel now that she had never felt before—the defined lines of the muscles in his arms, a tiny dip in his shoulder, the angle of the line of his jaw, and the gradual tapering of his torso. His body felt firmer than before, but the cold was now completely gone.

"Why are we in Eira and not in Elysium?" Elena asked, as she pulled away to look into Eiry's face.

Eiry drew back, his smile broadening. "There's been a change of plans."

"A change of plans?" Elena repeated, suspicious of the mischief in his gaze. "What did you do? Whatever it is, please tell me Cataline is alive."

"She's alive and well," called a familiar voice from the doorway and Elena looked up to see her father step into the room, followed closely behind by Atropos, the white-haired Fate.

The moment Atropos stepped into the room, the energy shifted around them, converging on her fey body as she walked, bending and shifting like light. Before, Elena had felt the reverberation of this phenomenon, but never physically seen it. It was as if she could see the flow of energy around them, emitted by everything in the room, animate and inanimate alike. Elena wondered what it could mean, if it was some kind of side effect of being dead.

Elena's father and the white-haired Fate came to stand at Elena's opposite side, while Eiry and the Kirin remained where they had been. Something passed between the four of them, a murmur Elena could hear but not understand, rousing a familiar sense of anxiety that Elena had hoped she would never feel again.

"What's going on? Am I dead?" Elena asked, her gaze shifting between the four of them.

"Very much so," answered the white-haired Fate in her timeless voice, her tone dry and brittle.

Dionysus shot her a look and then eased himself down onto the bed beside Elena. With a warm smile, he placed a kiss on her brow. "You did good," he whispered gently, and lifted her chin. "You met your end of the bargain."

"All debts have been paid," interjected Atropos, her opalescent gaze fixed on Elena from behind Dionysus's shoulder. "What was meant to be has come to pass. Thanatos has endured his punishment, and the curse that plagued your House has lost its teeth. A new chapter begins."

"Aisa," Dionysus begged the Moira gently, looking behind his shoulder at the Fate.

A hint of a smile touched Atropos's lips and she bowed her head to Dionysus, the gesture coy. The result was jarring, a human gesture mimicked to perfection by an immutable spirit as old as time, detailed but empty. It sent a chill down Elena's spine.

"Papa, I don't understand." Elena said to her father, a little overwhelmed by the presence of the Fate. She tried not to look at Atropos directly, focusing instead on Eiry, her father and the Kirin. "How long have I been dead? Why aren't I in Elysium with Mama? Eiry," Elena whispered his name, the panic slowly rising. He met her gaze quietly, his eyes filled with concern. "What punishment did you endure?"

"Killing you was my punishment," Eiry answered, the tension in his voice making it waver at the end. He avoided the Kirin's gaze, which Elena suddenly realized was fixed on him intently.

"Kiyoshi-sama," Elena whispered the Kirin's name, thankful when his gaze met hers and the displeasure was gone. "How are you in Eira?"

The Kirin exchanged a look with Atropos, nodded, and then retrieved a box from a small table that had been placed beside the bed. Elena recognized it immediately. It was a dark wooden box with inlaid wood details she had only seen once before. Its brass hinges and corners caught the late evening light, as the Kirin placed it in Elena's hands.

"Inoue-san entrusted me to deliver this item to you," the Kirin said softly, and pressed a kiss to Elena's brow. "He also asked me to convey his most heartfelt apologies for his clan's failures regarding your inheritance."

With trembling fingers, Elena traced the familiar details of the gold motif painted on the surface of the lid; three leopards at play among a cluster of bamboo trees, the branches of a blooming *sakura*, a three-pooled waterfall blanketed in snow, a butterfly perched between the blossoms, and a giant heron on the ground beneath the bower of blooms. Elena reached for the brass hasp but hesitated, her eyes rising to meet her father's.

What lay inside of the wooden box was the single item that had been the bane of her bloodline's existence, responsible for all of the death and pain her House had endured. It was a terrifying and awful thing, and Elena couldn't help the fear that began to trickle down her spine at the mere thought of it.

"Go on," Dionysus whispered, and reached to place his hand over Elena's.

Together, they opened the box. As had been the case the first time, the Necklace of Harmonia lay inside protected by a lining of black silk.

"It is yours now, to do as you will," said Atropos. "Its power can no longer hold sway over you."

Elena ran her fingers over the circlet of emeralds, before tracing the lines of the serpent heads at each end. "Why can't it hurt me anymore?" Elena asked, her gaze rising to meet Atropos's. The moment their eyes met Elena felt dizzy, and she almost dropped the box.

Eiry gently took it from her hands, giving Dionysus a poignant look before rising from the bed to return the box to the table.

"The Necklace of Harmonia cannot affect gods, only human descendants of the House of Thebes," Atropos replied casually, as if the answer was perfectly logical; and it would have been, if Elena were a god.

"What about ghosts? Does it affect ghosts?" Elena asked, getting a little frustrated with all of the cryptic answers. "Will someone please just tell me what's going on?"

The white-haired Moira shook her head. "Evius, I leave this to you," she said with a resigned sigh, and drew herself away from the bed. Halfway out of the room, she paused and her opalescent gaze fixed on Elena. "You should know that you are the first Heir to voluntarily choose to die. Your father will explain the rest," and with an enigmatic smile, Atropos took her leave.

Elena turned to look at her father. Eiry had returned to his place at her side, and the Kirin stood quietly behind him. Looking between the three of them, Elena sighed. "Someone spill it. Now."

"Do you know what apotheosis means, Elena?" Dionysus asked, while the other two stayed conspicuously silent.

Elena narrowed her eyes. "That's a joke, right?"

The three of them shook their heads, and Elena had to cover her mouth to stifle the strangled laugh that rushed up to her throat. A fit of laughter threatened, and she twitched as she tried to control it, choking back the sounds.

Dionysus, Eiry and the Kirin looked at each other, confused. Another silent conversation passed between them, and Elena reached for a pillow to throw; she'd had enough of all the whisperings and secret conversations. Her father took hold of her hands, and then Eiry began to speak.

"Elena, do you remember when we first met and I explained to you that initially Elementals didn't need to take humanoid form but later on some chose to do so because of the Great War?"

Held still by her father, Elena nodded. She had to breathe deeply several times to stop the giggles, but she finally calmed down enough to answer his question. "Yes, you said Tartarus felt the need to take shape because the war was being fought on their behalf."

"Exactly," Eiry replied with a relieved smile. "Three days ago, the River Lethe gave birth to its humanoid form. It's the first Elemental—the first Primordial—to take shape in a really long time. In fact, it's the first time a part of Tartarus takes human shape independent of Tartarus itself."

"Okay, I think I follow you," Elena whispered, the giggles completely gone.

"Remember, there's a big difference between Elementals and Olympian gods," said Elena's father. "Olympians reflect human order—gods of marriage, gods of hunting, gods of music, gods of metallurgy, and so on. They reflect the characteristics of a human society. Primordials are elemental gods, the first forces of nature that created this world. We call them the Protogenoi. Tartarus is one of them, and, as a part of Tartarus itself, so is the Lethe. The same would be true for any of the other four rivers or the Void itself, if they were to take shape. The fact that a part of Tartarus has taken shape independently is a huge development in this unending war."

Elena nodded, but it was more to make him stop speaking than an indication of understanding. Her head hurt, and as her father spoke Elena remembered her dream. She saw the menacing darkness and recalled in detail the pain, the torrent of unwanted memories, and the sense of drowning. Without realizing it, she had started shaking. In the back of her mind she saw rivers of ice become veins and form a body carved out of darkness. She saw snow weaved into skin and threads of mercury spun into hair. Silver-blue twilight was shaped into eyes, and blood into the likeness of lips. The menacing darkness had called out a name, commanding her to open her eyes, but the name had not been Elena's. It had been *Lethe*.

Eiry took Elena's hands in his and slowly pulled her into his arms. "Ele, calm down," he whispered into her ear, holding her tightly. "You're safe. There's nothing to be scared of. I pulled you out of the water myself."

"I'm a god?" Elena asked in disbelief and met her father's gaze over Eiry's shoulder. Even though he held her, she couldn't stop shaking. "I am the Lethe, the river of forgetfulness? Why?" She was too floored to come up with any questions more complex than that. She had steeled herself for death, prepared herself for a peaceful afterlife in Elysium, and yet, somehow, she had come out of this madness a god. That made the least sense of all.

"I know this is overwhelming, Elena," whispered her father, who snaked around Eiry to give her a kiss on the cheek, "but for whatever reason, Ananke chose you to be a god, and I, for one, am extremely happy it was you who Eiry pulled out of the river. You are now a deathless god. You were half that before, so it shouldn't be too much of a stretch," he teased her, his eyes belying the lighthearted nature of his words. "You're also a Tartarean god now, and you will have a role to play in this war. The prophecy is more applicable now than ever before. You are an Heir who cannot be killed, which changes everything. Enjoy these first few weeks of freedom because after that it's training, and gods only know what Livia has planned."

"What did my dad mean by training?" Elena asked Eiry as they stood at Cataline's front door in the early afternoon sun.

Several hours had passed since Elena had woken up to her newfound life, and after heckling Eiry for most of it he had finally obliged to let her see Cataline.

They had dressed for the occasion, Eiry in one of his dapper suits and Elena in a silk chiffon pleated dress in a pale lilac—the only conservative looking thing in Bryce's wardrobe. Eiry looked like a model right out of a magazine, and Cataline was sure to melt at the mere sight of him.

To Elena's relief, when she looked in the mirror to get ready for the visit, she found her old reflection staring back at her, with a few otherworldly improvements. When Elena shared her concern with Eiry, he explained that the woman she had seen take shape during her apotheosis was the true form of her godhood.

"All gods have powers," Eiry whispered, waiting patiently for Elena to knock on the door. "Gods train to hone those powers. We're not born good fighters. Lucian is the god of war, so he's in charge of the training halls where our legions train. He's the best at helping gods reach their full potential depending on their attributes. It'll be important for you to train so you can at least defend yourself, and to help your element awaken."

"My what?" Elena asked, completely confused.

She had no clue what he meant by her element awakening, and the idea of being taught how to fight by Lucian—in training halls, no less—was intimidating. She felt like she was in some kind of fantasy movie. Elena had accepted the apparent reality that she was a god, but that didn't mean she felt like one. In fact, she pretty much felt exactly like she did before, except that she had no pulse and had that same strange quality as the rest of them.

Eiry gave her a look and Elena sighed. "Will you be there during my training? Can't you train me instead of Lucian?"

"I'll be involved, but I won't be the only one. We train in groups. It's a lot of fun, you'll see. And don't be too intimidated. The Kirin asked for permission to visit Tartarus during your stays, and my mother has agreed. There will be plenty of familiar faces." With a warm smile, Eiry reached forward and knocked on the door, since Elena was hesitating. "And elemental gods control an element. You are the River Lethe, the river of forgetfulness, which grants oblivion. Through you all human souls are reborn, even some gods. Your powers will revolve around that element, but it'll take time for them to awaken fully."

Suddenly, Elena felt extremely nervous. Even worse, Eiry's answer had only raised more questions, and she couldn't ask them now because Cataline was already on her way to the door. Cataline had announced she was on her way over a clamor of noises—the sound of pans in the kitchen, the staccato of heels, the shuffle of papers, several things crashing to the floor, and the jingle of keys. She arrived at the door completely out of breath, a whirlwind of color and vibrant energy.

"Elena," Cataline stumbled over her name before she screamed exuberantly and threw herself into Elena's arms, not realizing she had another guest. When she finally registered Eiry's presence, Cataline leaned back and looked him over unreservedly, a pleased smile brightening her beautiful face. "My, my, aren't you handsome?" she said to Eiry with a wink, before returning her attention to Elena, never stopping to catch her breath. "Tell me *everything*," she whispered to Elena dramatically, and then ushered them both inside.

"I had no idea you were back from Japan already," Cataline declared, as she led them both through the parlor and kitchen to the patio at the back of the house. "What's your poison, handsome?" she asked Eiry, easing him into a chair and giving Elena a thumbs-up from behind his shoulder.

"Scotch, if you have it," Eiry replied with a smile. He seemed extremely amused.

"Oh, I have anything you need, honey," Cataline said suggestively, openly flirting. There wasn't a handsome man Cataline had met that she didn't flirt with. "Ele, you good with scotch or you want brandy? I brought back some great *sake* from the trip, if you prefer that."

Elena chanced a glance at Eiry, who pretended like he didn't notice her. Before her death, Elena had asked him to stage Cataline's return from Japan. Cataline was to have come back from the trip as scheduled—the time in between filled with fabricated memories of their final days spent touring in Kyoto—while Elena stayed a few extra weeks and died in a motorcycle accident while still in Japan. Although the last part had been altered on account of recent developments, the rest of the story had been put into place. Not only had Eiry staged things the way Elena had asked, he had gone so far as to elaborate on the details, such as a souvenir of fine *sake*.

"I would love an aged brandy, actually," Elena answered Cataline, still a little overwhelmed by everything. Elena realized for the first time that her sensory experience was different now; things were sharper and brighter, which made Cataline's effervescent energy almost dizzying.

With a flourish of her hand, Cataline disappeared into the house to get the drinks, swishing her hips the entire way like she was on a catwalk. The woman was a force of nature. Less than a week revived, and she was as vibrant and exuberant as ever.

Several minutes later, Cataline returned to the patio with the requested drinks and a scotch for herself. "So, you're Livia's son, aren't you?" she asked Eiry without skipping a beat, offering him a beguiling smile and then dropping down into the chair next to him, the jingle of her jewelry echoing her every move.

Dressed all in white—white pants, thin white cotton blouse buttoned to the precise point of accenting her ample breasts, and brown belt—the color scheme made Cataline's chestnut-colored hair, hazel eyes and light olive skin look even richer than usual. The amber highlights in her hair sparkled in the afternoon sun, as she leaned back in her chair and took out a cigarette, placing it in a vintage cigarette holder.

"Yes," Eiry answered Cataline with a smile, and retrieved an antique lighter from his pant pocket. "My name is Eiry," he said, introducing himself, and offered Cataline a light.

"I see you have an affinity for things from another era," Cataline remarked, her smile deepening. She leaned toward Eiry and brought the tip of her cigarette to the flame, her body language all too suggestive.

She was shameless, and the thought made Elena smile.

"You have a beautiful name," Cataline told Eiry, as she took the first hit off her cigarette, "although I'm surprised, since it doesn't sound very Greek or Latin. Everyone in your family seems to have a Greek or Latin name."

"It's Welsh, actually. My mother's way of rebelling against an old family custom," Eiry said charismatically. Once Cataline's cigarette was lit, he slipped his lighter back into his pocket. "And yes, I love old mechanical things—lighters, music boxes, clocks, gramophones, type-writers. Things like that."

Cataline studied Eiry openly, her manner the opposite of demure or reserved. With a fluid gesture, she took a sip from her drink. "So tell me," she said to Eiry, her tone suddenly serious. "How did you two finally get on the same page? Last time I saw Elena, she didn't even know your name. You were an enigma that we discussed for hours," Cataline declared, to Elena's mortification.

This was a ritual Cataline had engaged in since the moment Elena had first shown an interest in boys, so Elena should have been used to it by now.

"Really? For hours?" Eiry played along, his smile suggesting he was deeply satisfied by the revelation. He took a long sip from his drink, his gaze on Elena over the rim of his glass.

"Can you two please stop conspiring against me?" Elena asked sweetly, and downed her drink.

"Why whatever do you mean?" Cataline asked in a singsong voice. "I just want to know what's going on with you, Ele, that's all." Cataline leaned closer to Elena and scrutinized her with a raised brow. "In fact, you seem different somehow. You're glowing," Cataline mused, suspicion coloring her gaze. She looked between Elena and Eiry, and then her hazel eyes dropped to Elena's glass. "Oh, and darling, you shouldn't down brandy like that. You can't savor it properly that way."

"Let's not change the subject," Eiry interjected, urging Cataline on. "I want to know all about these endless discussions the two of you have had about me. But to answer your question, Cataline, we ended up being seated next to each other on the flight back from Japan yesterday. I invited Elena to dinner tonight, and she asked if we could stop here first. I'd heard so much about you on the flight back that I couldn't say no."

"I hope I can live up to all the hype," Cataline said with a grin, and raised her glass. She held her cigarette in the opposite hand and clicked a perfectly manicured nail against the holder, ashing the cigarette before bringing it back to her lips. "How incredible that the two of you should end up in Japan at the same time," she announced after setting her glass back down on the table. "It would make for an enchanting story, don't you think? Girl meets mysteriously handsome boy who eludes her until they meet halfway across the world. Do you believe in fate, Eiry

Callas?" she asked him, leaning forward in her chair and resting her chin on the back of her hand.

Eiry leaned closer to Cataline, and met her gaze straight on.

"I think I do," he whispered with a meaningful smile.

His icy gaze caught the fading light of the sun, and a cold sensation settled at the nape of Elena's neck; the telltale sign that Eiry's butterfly crest was showing.

<u>ABOUT EVA</u>

Author. Attorney. New Orleanian. Lover of Cherry Ring Pops. Confirmed Japanophile. Dreamer. Sometimes Obsessive. Blunt to a Fault. Wishful-Thinker. Tea and Anime Compulsive. Diehard.

In the beginning of 2011, Eva Vanrell took a blind leap of faith to pursue what she loved most. The result of that journey was her debut novel, *The Butterfly Crest*. She is currently working on Book Two of the series, so please stay tuned.

Eva currently lives in New Orleans with her husband, two cats and a Japanese maple.

Thank you for reading.

To receive exclusive updates on Eva's latest news,
sneak peeks and special promotions, please visit
Eva's website and sign up on
Eva's List today!

www.evavanrell.com

You can show your support for Eva by
following her on social media:

 @EvaVanrell
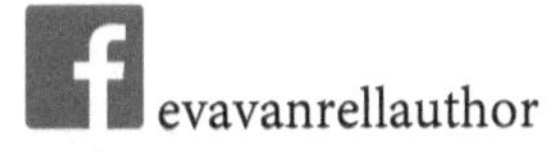 evavanrellauthor
 evavanrell

<u>**APPENDIX**</u>

A collection and reference of important characters and terms

Abe no Akemi – *Onmyōji* of the Abe clan; silver-haired twin bother of Abe no Rinji; human *aequus* (neutrals).

Abe no Rinji – *Onmyōji* of the Abe clan; black-haired twin brother of Abe no Akemi; human *aequus* (neutrals).

Acheron – River of Pain; one of five rivers in the Greek underworld; its waters do not reflect light.

Act of Substitution – a tradition universal among the divine races whereby one offers something of great value in substitution for another.

Aequus – 'Impartial'; name given to human neutrals, humans who can neutralize the power of the gods with the explicit intent of protecting human life; they balance the odds so that the least amount of human lives are lost in the war.

Aether – Greek Protogenos of the bright upper air; second-generation primordial god, born of Erebos (Darkness) and Nyx (Night).

Aikos – one of three judges of the dead in the Greek underworld; demi-god.

Áine – High Queen of the Tuatha Dé Danann (divine tribe of ancient Ireland); wife of Manannán mac Lir (god of the sea).

Airmed – herbalist and goddess of healing of the Tuatha Dé Danann (divine tribe of ancient Ireland); daughter of Dian Cécht (god of healing).

Aisa – another name for Atropos, one of three Greek Fates.

Akai – 'red' in Japanese.

Ambrosia – the drink of the Greek gods.

Amergin – poet of the Milesians (human tribe that invades Ireland); was called to divide Ireland between the Tuatha Dé Danann (divine tribe of ancient Ireland) and the Milesians, following the Dananns's defeat; allotted the land above ground to his people and the underground to the Dananns.

Ananke – Greek Protogenos of destiny; first-generation primordial god.

Andon – Japanese lamps made of rice paper stretched over a wooden frame.

Aoandon – Yōkai, spirit of a blue *andon* lamp; appears in the form of a man with blue skin and twin horns on his brow.

Aobōzu – Yōkai, a one-eyed monk with green skin; wears a traditional
  kasa (a mushroom-shaped hat made of woven straw).

Aosaginohi – Yōkai, the luminescent heron; spirit in the form of a
  woman with long mane of downy feathers, intense golden eyes,
  and skin that glows with a faint luminescence.

Aphrodite – Greek goddess of love and beauty; wife of Hephaestus (god
  of metallurgy and volcanoes) and lover to Ares (god of war);
  born from the sea-foam created when the castrated genitals of
  the Uranus (Sky) were cast into the sea; Olympian god.

Apollo – Greek god of music, prophecy and oracles, and healing; son of
  Zeus (King of the Olympian gods) and Leto (goddess of motherhood); twin brother to Artemis (goddess of the hunt); second
  generation Olympian god.

Ares – Greek god of war; Olympian god; defector.

Artemis – Greek goddess of the hunt, wilderness and wild animals;
  daughter of Zeus (King of the Olympian gods) and Leto (goddess
  of motherhood); twin sister to Apollo (god of music); second
  generation Olympian god.

Asphodel Fields – part of the Greek underworld; a ghostly meadow
  where neutral souls reside after death, waiting to be reincarnated.

Asura – power seeking divine beings of the Hindu pantheon, generally
  associated with negative qualities.

Athena – Greek goddess of wisdom; born from the head of Zeus (King of
  the Olympian gods), fully-grown and arrayed in arms; Olympian
  god.

Atropos – Greek Protogenos, one of three Fates (Moirai), the white-
  robed sisters; the 'Unturning', she who cuts the thread of life
  after choosing the manner of death; she sings of things that are to
  be; white-haired Fate, also known as 'Aisa of the White Hair';
  second-generation primordial god, born of Ananke (Destiny).

Bake-kujira – Yōkai, the skeleton of a whale that floats through the air.

Balor – King of the Fomorians (divine titans of ancient Ireland).

Biwa – Japanese short-necked lute.

Bres – half-Fomorian King of the Tuatha Dé Danann (divine tribe of
  ancient Ireland); a tyrant to the Dannan tribe; became King of
  the Dannans when Nuada was forced to give up his kingship due
  to the loss of his arm.

Byakko, White Tiger of the West – one of four guardian spirits of Kyoto;
  noble and strong; when he appears in human form, he takes the
  shape of a tall and powerfully built man, with a mane of dark
  raven hair, white eyes with blue irises, and milky skin with black
  markings.

Cairpre mac Oghma – bard and satirist of the Tuatha Dé Danann (divine tribe of ancient Ireland).

Cas Corach – harper of the Tuatha Dé Danann (divine tribe of ancient Ireland).

Cataline Ferrá – Isabella's best friend and Elena's caretaker since childhood.

Cave of the Oneiroi – satellite realm to the Greek underworld; cave where the Greek daimones (spirits) of dreams reside.

Ceo Sídhe – Fairie mists

Cerberos – three-headed hound that guards the entrance to the Greek underworld.

Chaos – Greek Protogenos of the infinite space between heaven and earth; first-generation primordial god.

Charon – Greek underworld daimon (spirit) and ferryman of the dead; son of Erebos (Darkness).

Children of the Stars – another name for chthonic gods, deities of the earthly realm and the underworld; exist across all pantheons.

Children of the Sun – another name for sky gods; deities who dwell above the earthly realm, in the sky; exist across all pantheons.

Chione – female aspect of Tartarus, the Greek Protogenos of the underworld; also called 'Tartara'; embodies the death and icy aspects of Tartarus – delicate and ethereal in beauty, terrible and unyielding in strength; mother to Thanatos (Death), Hypnos (Sleep) and the Keres (Violent Death); surrogate mother to Phobos (Fear) and Deimos (Dread); Tartarean Queen; first-generation primordial god.

Clotho – Greek Protogenos, one of three Fates (Moirai), the white-robed sisters; the 'Spinner', she who spins the thread of life; she sings of things that are; Stygian-haired Fate; second-generation primordial god, born of Ananke (Destiny).

Cocytus – River of Wailing; one of five rivers in the Greek underworld; ice clings to its surface.

Creidhne – artificer and god of bronzecraft of the Tuatha Dé Danann (divine tribe of ancient Ireland); one of the Trí Dé Dána (three sibling gods of craftmenship).

Cronus – Greek Titan god of time and the ages; son of Gaia (Earth) and Uranus (Sky).

Cthonic gods – deities of the earthly realm and the underworld; exist across all pantheons; also known as 'Children of the Stars'.

Cyclopes – Greek race of one-eyed giants; born of the blood spilt when Uranus (Sky) was castrated.

Dadga – god of magic, time and protector of the crop for the Tuatha Dé Danann (divine tribe of ancient Ireland); his living oak harp, called 'Uaithne', held sway over the seasons.

Daimyo – Japanese feudal lords.

Dango – a type of Japanese dumpling made of rice flour.

Daoine Sídhe – capital kingdom of the Tuatha Dé Danann (divine tribe of ancient Ireland); seat of the High Queen (Áine) and her people.

Deimos – Greek god of dread and terror; twin brother to Phobos (Fear); son of Ares (god of war), originally by Aphrodite (goddess of love and beauty) and later by Chione (female aspect of the Underworld); Tartarean god.

Demeter – Greek goddess of the harvest, grain, and fertility of the earth; daughter of Cronus (Titan god of time and the ages) and Rhea (Titan goddess and mother of the Olympians); Olympian god.

Dian Cécht – physician and god of healing of the Tuatha Dé Danann (divine tribe of ancient Ireland).

Dionysus – Greek god of wine and pleasure; also known as 'Evius'; patron god of the House of Thebes; Olympian and Tartarean god.

Dodekatheon – another name for the Olympian gods.

Dökkálfr – a Norse Dark Elf.

Domos Aidaou – 'House of Hades'; part of the Greek underworld where souls are judged and sorted into their afterlives.

Draig – Dragonking of the Western tribe of dragons.

Dúshlán – 'challenge' to the Tuatha Dé Danann (divine tribe of ancient Ireland).

Eira – royal city of the Greek underworld; where the Tartarean gods reside; 'snow' in Welsh.

Elaphoi Khrysokeroi – the five golden-horned hind sacred to Artemis (Greek goddess of the hunt); four drew her chariot, and the fifth was left to roam freely through the world.

Elemental(s) – primeval gods; gods that emerged at the beginning of time, from whom all other gods, and the universe, derive; synonym for 'Primordial'.

Elysian Fields – part of the Greek underworld; where the souls of the virtuous and the initiates of the ancient Mysteries go to spend their afterlife.

Elysian Islands – part of the Greek underworld; where the souls of Heroes and descendants of the gods dwell after death.

Emhain Abhlach – one of two realms that make up the Otherworld in Irish mythology; home to Manannán mac Lir (god of the sea); it has been known by many names: the 'Plain of Apples', the 'Blessed Isles of the Western Sea', Tír na nÓg – 'The Land of the Young', and 'Avalon'; a realm mostly inhabited by gods, where sickness and death do not exist.

Engawa – wooden veranda that runs outside the rooms in a traditional Japanese home/building and provides access to the inner garden or courtyard.

Enkō – Yōkai, water spirit with an indentation on the crown of his head that holds water; also known as a 'Kappa'; appears in the form of boy with emerald green hair, silver eyes, webbed hands and feet, and reptilian skin with iridescent scales.

Enyo – Greek goddess of war and destruction; daughter of Zeus (King of the Olympian gods) & Hera (goddess of women and marriage); Tartarean god.

Eos – Greek Titan goddess of the dawn; twin sister to Helios (Sun); second-generation Titan god.

Erebos – Greek Protogenos of darkness; his element gives shape to the darkness in the world, and that which encircles the underworld; second-generation primordial god, born of Chaos (Infinitude).

Erebus – place within the Greek underworld where souls pass immediately after death and wait to be ferried across the river to the gates of the underworld.

Erinyes – Greek goddesses of vengeance; born of the blood spilt when Uranus (Sky) was castrated; Tartarean gods.

Eriu – another name for Ireland.

Eros – Greek Protogenos of procreation and sexual desire; first-generation primordial god.

Evius – another name for Dionysus (Greek god of wine and pleasure).

Fae – another name for the Tuatha Dé Danann (divine tribe of ancient Ireland); short for 'Faerie'.

Fidchell – ancient board game of the Tuatha Dé Danann (divine tribe of ancient Ireland); similar in style to chess, but with different rules and pieces; invented by Lugh mac Ethnenn (god of light and the harvest).

Fir Bolg – a divine tribe of ancient Ireland; predecessors of the Tuatha Dé Danann (divine tribe of ancient Ireland).

Fomorians – a race of divine titans of ancient Ireland.

Fusuma – sliding doors made of wood and heavy paper, used to divide the interior of traditional Japanese houses/buildings.

Futakuchi-onna – Yōkai, a two-mouthed woman; seemingly normal in appearance but for a second mouth in the back of her head, hidden by her hair; it is said women who do not eat turn into this type of *yōkai*.

Futon – thick cushioned bedding of traditional Japan that is laid out on the floor.

Gaia – Greek Protogenos of the earth; first-generation primordial god.

Genbu, Black Tortoise of the North – one of four guardian spirits of Kyoto; fierce warrior; when he appears in human form, he takes the shape of a large, brawny man with tawny skin and gruff features, wearing Ō-Yoroi armor (the armor of a high-ranking samurai made with iron plating, leather and lacquer).

Geta – wooden Japanese sandals worn with *yukata* (informal cotton *kimono*).

Goibniu – god of smithcraft and brewing of the Tuatha Dé Danann (divine tribe of ancient Ireland); one of the Trí Dé Dána (three sibling gods of craftmenship); his ale grants the drinker invincibility.

Gotokuneko – Yōkai, a cat spirit; appears in the form of a young boy with copper hair and cat-like eyes, and cat ears sprouting from his head.

Hades – Greek god and ruler of the Domos Aidaou; god of the hidden wealth of the earth; brother to Zeus (King of the Olympian gods); Olympian god.

Hai – 'yes' in Japanese.

Hakama – loose trousers worn over the bottom half of a *kimono*.

Haori – a shorter robe, of hip or thigh length, used as a jacket over *kimono*.

Harmonia – Greek goddess of harmony and concord; daughter of Ares (god of war) and Aphrodite (goddess of love and beauty); Olympian god.

Hecate – Greek goddess of the crossroads, who presides over the border between the mortal and spirit worlds; also associated with magic, knowledge of herbs and poisonous plants, sorcery and witchcraft; Tartarean god.

Heika – Japanese honorific for 'Your Majesty'.

Helios – Greek Titan god of the sun; twin brother to Eos (Dawn); second generation Titan god.

Helm of Darkness – treasure given to Hades by the Cyclopes (one-eyed giants) during the war against the Titans; to win the war, Zeus (King of the Olympian gods) allied himself with the three Cyclopes and received three treasures in return—his thunderbolt and lightning, Poseidon's trident and the Helm; grants invisibility.

Hemera – Greek Protogenos of day; second-generation primordial god, born of Erebos (Darkness) and Nyx (Night).

Hephaestus – Greek god of metallurgy and volcanoes; husband to Aphrodite (goddess of love and beauty); Olympian god.

Hera – Greek goddess of women and marriage; wife of Zeus (King of the Olympian gods); Queen of Olympus.

Hermes – Greek god of roads, travel and boundaries, trade and athletics; herald and messenger of the gods; interceded between mortals and the gods; son of Zeus (King of the Olympian gods); Olympian god.

Hind's blood – a kind of poison that can incapacitate a god almost instantly; its use is infrequent on account of its rarity, as it is made from the blood of a golden-horned hind.

Hinoenma – Yōkai, a Japanese succubus; appears in the form of a woman dressed in a crimson *kimono*.

House of Thebes – noble bloodline in Greek mythology; the legendary descendants of King Cadmus and Queen Harmonia of Thebes (Greek goddess of harmony, who was given to a human king in marriage); bloodline cursed by the god Hephaestus (god of metallurgy and volcanoes).

Hyakki Yakō – Night Parade of One Hundred Demons, which according to Japanese folklore would take to the streets every year during summer nights.

Hypnos – Greek god of sleep; twin brother to Thanatos (Death); Tartarean god.

Illyria – servant in charge of the royal household in the city of Eira; weir light (sentient energy) that has taken human form.

Inoue Takeo – *Onmyōji* of the Kamo clan; keeper of the Kamo Vault; human *aequus* (neutral).

Inrō – traditional Japanese case for holding small objects while wearing a *kimono*; suspended by a cord from the sash of the *kimono*.

Irél – a soldier of the Tuatha Dé Danann (divine tribe of ancient Ireland).

Irori – traditional Japanese open hearth.

Isabella Vicens – Elena's mother; also an Heir to the House of Thebes.

Izanami-no-Mikoto – Japanese goddess of creation and death; patron goddess of *yōkai*.

Jubokko tree – Yōkai, tree that feeds from human energy and, at times, human blood; it is said they were born by growing near battle-fields where so much human blood was shed on the ground that it reached the trees' roots, giving them a liking for human blood.

Kabuki – a form of traditional Japanese drama with highly stylized song and dance; known for their use of elaborate make-up and costumes; now performed only by male actors.

Kaiseki – traditional multi-course Japanese dinner.

Kami – 'god' in Japanese; deities, spirits and natural forces worshipped in the Japanese Shinto religion.

Kamon – emblems used in Japan to identify a family or clan; Japanese family crest.

Kanji – Japanese system of writing using Chinese characters.

Kelainos – black hound belonging to Hades.

Keres – Greek goddess of violent death; Tartarean god.

Kimono – traditional Japanese garment; long robe with wide sleeves, tied with an *obi* (sash).

Kirin – auspicious, mythical creature; celestial being; a dragon shaped like a deer with a unicorn's horn believed to be a herald of prosperity; benevolent, does not feast on flesh, can walk on water and when it steps on grass does not bruise the blades or tread on any living thing; peaceful by nature, will become fierce to protect the virtuous or punish the vile; when he appears in human form, he takes the shape of a man of soft pale skin, hair spun of silver starlight, and eyes the color of smoky topaz; believed to be impartial to the outcome of the war.

Kitsune – Yōkai, Japanese fox spirit; may have as many as nine tails.

Kline – tall, reclining couches of ancient Greece.

Klismos – a type of ancient Greek chair with tapering, outcurved legs and a concave backrest.

Kominka – old house built in traditional Japanese style.

Lachesis – Greek Protogenos, one of three Fates (Moirai), the white-robed sisters; the 'Allotter', she who measures the thread of life; she sings of things that once were; sanguine-haired Fate; second-generation primordial god, born of Ananke (Destiny).

Lethe – River of Oblivion and Forgetfulness; one of five rivers in the Greek underworld; it is the river from which souls drink to forget the memories of their earthly lives; its depths glimmer with the light of stars.

Leto – Greek Titan, goddess of motherhood; second-generation Titan god.

Luchtaine – wheelwright and god of woodcraft of the Tuatha Dé Danann (divine tribe of ancient Ireland); one of the Trí Dé Dána (three sibling gods of craftmenship).

Lugh mac Ethnenn – warrior champion of the Tuatha Dé Danann
(divine tribe of ancient Ireland), god of light and the harvest; also
known as 'Lugh Ildánach'.

Macha – goddess of sovereignty of the Tuatha Dé Danann (divine tribe
of ancient Ireland), and one of three morrígna, goddesses of war;
wife of Nuada (first King of the Dananns) and sister to Nemain
(goddess of strife and panic).

Manannán mac Lir – one of the Tuatha Dé Danann (divine tribe of
ancient Ireland), god of the sea; through his wisdom the
Dananns divided into kingdoms beneath the mounds, with one
High King to rule over them, and found protection from humans
within the mists.

Matcha – fine-powdered Japanese green tea.

Melia – Greek Okeanid Nymph of the Ismenian spring and stream of
Thebes.

Milesians – sons of Míl Espáine; human tribe (Gaels from Iberia); in
myth, invaded Ireland to avenge the death of Milesian Íth by Ireland's three kings; defeated the Tuatha Dé Danann (divine tribe
of ancient Ireland), who then retreated beneath the ground.

Miyuki-san – Yōkai; yuki-onna (snow spirit); caretaker of Elena's
childhood home in Tokyo.

Mocárabe – filigree-like ornamental carvings of vertical prisms resembling honeycombs and shaped into stalactite-like formation.

Moira – singular form of 'Moirai' (Greek Fates).

Moirai – the Greek Fates; three white-robed sisters; singular 'Moira'.

Nakai – hostess that cares for guests at a traditional Japanese inn.

Nemain – goddess of strife and panic of the Tuatha Dé Danann (divine
tribe of ancient Ireland), and one of three morrígna, goddesses of
war; spirit embodying the frenzied havoc of war.

Netsuke – a carved ornament or toggle used in Japan to suspend articles
from the *obi* (sash) of a *kimono*.

Nuada – first King of the Tuatha Dé Danann (divine tribe of ancient
Ireland); led his people to victory against the Fir Bolg (also a
divine tribe of ancient Ireland), at the cost of his arm; also known
as 'Nuada Airgetlám', of the silver hand, due to the silver arm
crafted for him by Creidhne (artificer and god of bronzecraft)
and Dian Cécht (god of healing).

Nurarihyon – Yōkai, Leader of the Hyakki Yakō (Night Parade of One
Hundred Demons); resolute and formidable, with a wicked sense
of humor; reputed to be a spirit that sneaks into people's homes
while they are away to drink their tea; appears in the form of a
man with jet-black hair, steel-gray eyes, and an angular face.

Nyx – Greek Protogenos of night; second-generation primordial god, born of Chaos (Infinitude).

Ō-Yoroi – the armor of a high-ranking samurai that utilized iron plating covered in leather and lamellar segments of smaller plates laced together in parallel rows and covered in lacquer.

Obi – sash of a Japanese *kimono*.

Obijime – cord that holds the *obi* (sash) of a *kimono* together.

Ofuro – traditional Japanese soaking tub; originated as a short, steep-sided wooden bathtub.

Ogma – god of writing and knowledge of the Tuatha Dé Danann (divine tribe of ancient Ireland); champion of the Dananns before Lugh (god of light and the harvest); brother to Dagda (god of magic, time and protector of the crop).

Ojime – a type of bead used in Japan to fasten the cord that suspends an *inrō* (case) from the *obi* (sash) of a *kimono*.

Olympians – third race of Greek gods; reside on Mount Olympus.

Ondine – a female water spirit from German mythology.

Onmyōdō – arcane tradition of Japanese divination and magic, once so revered that their influence reached the imperial courts of Japan; the Kamo clan were the premier practitioners of *onmyōdō*, but the practice was later split between two clans, the Kamo and the Abe.

Onmyōji – practitioners of *onmyōdō*; specialize in protecting humans against supernatural evils with the use of familiars known as *shikigami*; human *aequus* (neutrals).

Onsen – Japanese hot springs; also used to describe the spa-like facilities and inns built around them.

Ourea – Greek Protogenos of the mountains; second-generation primordial god, born of Gaia (Earth).

Persephone – Greek goddess of spring; wife of Hades (ruler of the Domos Aidaou); surrogate mother to Dionysus (god of wine and pleasure); Olympian and Tartarean god.

Phlegethon – River of Fire; one of five rivers in the Greek underworld; fire burns from within its depths.

Phobos – Greek god of fear, flight and battlefield rout; twin brother to Deimos (Dread); son of Ares (god of war), originally by Aphrodite (goddess of love and beauty) and later by Chione (female aspect of the Underworld); shield piercer; Tartarean god.

Pontus – Greek Protogenos of the sea; second-generation primordial god, born of Gaia (Earth).

Poseidon – Greek god of the sea, brother to Zeus (King of the Olympian gods); Olympian god.

Primordial(s) – primeval gods; gods that emerged at the beginning of time, from whom all other gods, and the universe, derive; synonym for 'Elemental'.

Protogenoi – first race of Greek gods; means 'First-Born'; singular 'Protogenos'; elemental/primordial gods.

Pythian Oracle – prophetess in Greek mythology; also known as the 'Oracle of Delphi' and the 'Delphic Oracle'.

Ramma – wooden lintels above *fusuma* (sliding doors made of wood and heavy paper, used to divide the interior of traditional Japanese houses/buildings).

Rhea – Greek Titan queen of heaven, goddess of female fertility; mother of the Olympian gods.

Rokurobei – Yōkai, a man with a floating head; has a kind but mischievous disposition; it is said he suffers from a supernatural illness that causes his head to float away from his body at night.

Rōnin – lordless samurai in feudal Japan.

Rotenburo – Japanese outdoor hot spring.

Ryokan – traditional Japanese inn.

Sakura – 'cherry blossom' in Japanese.

Sashinuki hakama – a type of *hakama* (loose trousers worn over the bottom half of a *kimono*) that gathers at the ankles creating a ballooning effect.

Seiryū, Azure Dragon of the East – one of four guardian spirits of Kyoto; guardian of Kiyomizu-dera Temple; cunning and shrewd; when he appears in human form, he takes the shape of a long-haired, tall, sinewy man with opalescent scales for skin, hair and eyes of shimmering cyan, adamantine claw-like nails, sharp features and a roguish smile.

Selkie – shape shifting seal-woman.

Shamisen – a three-stringed Japanese musical instrument.

Shimenawa – lengths of twisted rice straw rope used for ritual purification in the Shinto religion, and/or to indicate a sacred space.

Shinigami – Japanese death spirit or deity.

Shinto – native religion of Japan.

Shishi odoshi – a type of bamboo fountain once used to scare away animals, but now a common feature in gardens throughout Japan; literally means 'deer scarer'.

Shogun – hereditary military governor in feudal Japan; they were the *de facto* rulers of Japan from 1192 to 1867.

Shōji – screens made of Japanese paper that allow light to filter through; used as windows and doors in traditional Japanese architecture.

Shōjō – Yōkai, sea sprite with a fondness for *sake*; appears in the form of man with hair and eyes the color of saffron; vigilant even though he gives the impression of being drunk; has a playful and fluid manner; very flirtatious by nature.

Sídhe – hills or earthen mounds common in the Irish landscape; faerie mounds; one of two realms that make up the Otherworld in Irish mythology; underground kingdoms where the Tuatha Dé Danann (divine tribe of ancient Ireland) reside – realms of eternal youth and beauty, where all the pleasures of life are celebrated, food, drink and music are in infinite supply, and one day could be hundreds of years in the human world.

Sky gods – deities who dwell above the earthly realm, in the sky; exist across all pantheons; also known as 'Children of the Sun'.

Soba – 'buckwheat' in Japanese; also the name for a type of noddle made from buckwheat flour.

Styx – River of Hatred; one of five rivers in the Greek underworld; binds the oaths of gods; its waters are murky and tenebrous.

Suzaku, Vermilion Bird of the South – one of four guardian spirits of Kyoto; mischievous and ready for the hunt; when he appears in human form, he takes the shape of a man of medium build and height, golden skin, crimson hair, and eyes the color of fire agate; possessed of a fiery temperament.

Tarōbō – Yōkai, bird-demon (Tengu); appears in the form of a man with caramel colored skin, white hair, hawklike amethyst-colored eyes, and a steel-blue cloak lined in the feathers of a Peregrine Falcon; has an intense and sober temperament, softened by a roguish wit.

Tartaros – male aspect of Tartarus, the Greek Protogenos of the underworld; embodies the darkness and absolute power of the Abyss – infinite, terrifying and impossible to resist; Tartarean King; first-generation primordial god.

Tartarus – Greek Protogenos of the underworld; took shape as a set of twins, one male (Tartaros) and one female (Chione/Tartara); first-generation primordial god; also the name used when referring to the whole of the Greek underworld as a realm; also used when referring specifically to the Great Void of the underworld, an abyss used as the prison of the gods.

Tatami – woven straw mats used as flooring in traditional Japanese rooms.

Tengu – Yōkai, bird-demon.

Thanatos – Greek god of death; twin brother to Hypnos (Sleep); Tartarean god.

Titans – second race of Greek gods, descendants of Gaia (Earth) and
 Uranus (Sky); immortals of incredible strength.

Tokonoma – a wooden-floored alcove used for displaying scrolls, flowers
 or ceramics in traditional Japanese rooms.

Torii – a type of Japanese gate mostly associated with Shinto shrines; they
 denote the entrance into sacred ground; shaped like a portal, they
 consist of two vertical posts laid several feet apart with a lintel
 laid across the top horizontally, the ends of the lintel protruding
 over the posts; typically painted vermilion and black.

Trí Dé Dána – the three sibling gods of craftmenship of the Tuatha Dé
 Danann (divine tribe of ancient Ireland); Creidhne (artificer and
 god of bronzecraft), Goibniu (god of smithcraft and brewing)
 and Luchtaine (wheelwright and god of woodcraft).

Tsukumogami – ordinary household items that become *yōkai* spirits
 after reaching their hundredth year of existence.

Tuatha Dé Danann – 'people of the goddess Danu', divine race of
 ancient Ireland; also known as 'Fae'; throughout history, have
 become synonymous with the modern concept of fairies or elves;
 neutral, impartial to the outcome of the war.

Udon – a type of thick noodle in Japanese cuisine, made of wheat flour.

Uranus – Greek Protogenos of the sky; second-generation primordial
 god, born of Gaia (Earth); castrated by his son, Cronus (Time).

Weir light(s) – sentient energy in Tartarus (the Greek underworld);
 beings made of starlight; the eyes and ears of the underworld;
 appear as floating lights that flicker in and out of existence; some
 can take human form.

Yōkai – demons, spirits and monsters in Japanese folklore; born of the
 thoughts and beliefs of humans, whether positive or negative.

Yomi – the Japanese underworld.

Yomotsu-shikome – the foul women of Yomi (the Japanese underworld).

Yomotsuhirasaka – entrance to Yomi (the Japanese underworld).

Yukata – an informal cotton *kimono* used during the summer; also used
 as garments after bathing.

Yuki Onna – Yōkai, a snow spirit; polite and watchful; appears in the
 form of a woman with scarlet lips, long black hair, white *kimono*,
 and inhumanly pale skin.

Zeus – Greek god of sky and weather; King of the Olympian gods.